CW01459930

THE EDUCATION OF SEBASTIAN & THE EDUCATION OF CAROLINE

The Education Series

JANE HARVEY-BERRICK

HB
HARVEY
BERRICK
PUBLISHING

ISBN 9780957496194
Harvey Berrick Publishing
www.janeharveyberrick.com

Cover design by Nicky Stott
Cover photographs by Shutterstock and Justin Bell QGM

Thanks for permission to EMI Music Publishing to reproduce lyrics from 'Martha's Harbour', All About Eve
Acknowledgement to 'How to Avoid Being Killed in a War Zone' by Rosie Garthwaite and 'One Dog at a Time: Saving the Strays of Helmand' by Pen Farthing
'High Flight', John Gillespie Magee, Jr. (1922—1941)

Created with Vellum

THE EDUCATION OF SEBASTIAN

The Education Series: Book 1

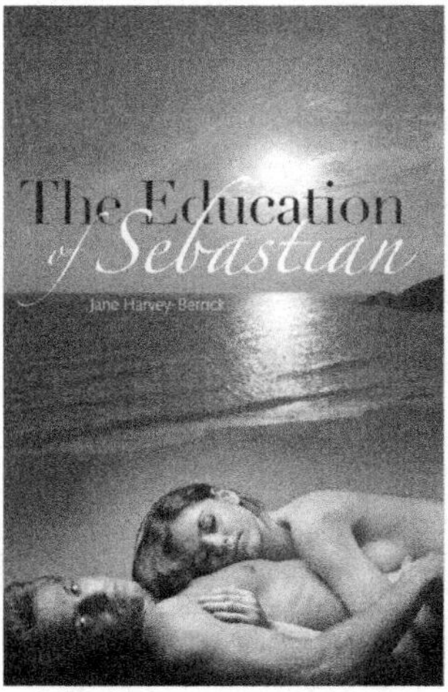

To Lisa Ashmore, for telling me to write this series
To Sheena Lumsden, for her humour and energy and loyalty
To Audrey Orielle, for loving Sebastian so much

Thank you.
JHB

PROLOGUE

I'VE OFTEN WONDERED WHY BRIDES-TO-BE SPEAK WITH SUCH EXCITEMENT OF their wedding day –*the best day of their lives*. Doesn't that imply that it's all downhill from then on?

My own wedding day was the culmination of the briefest of romances, if you could call it that. My husband was not a romantic man. He was not many things. Perhaps if he had been many, perhaps if he had been more, things might have turned out differently between us. Then again, perhaps it would have been exactly the same.

Despite what happened later, I can't bring myself to regret the events of that summer.

I think it was the uniform. My husband dazzled me in his US Navy whites and with his flashy sports car that was so low to the ground, it seemed to skim along the road like a pebble on a lake.

David was a medical officer in the US Navy, newly promoted to Lieutenant Commander and assigned as a flight surgeon. He was 11 years older than me. He seemed urbane and sophisticated and to a girl from nowhere who had seen nothing, he was every wish fulfilled.

My mother smelled a good catch and my dear, sweet father was talked over and down by the two women in his life who vied for his attention.

Competition with my mother was relatively new. She had always been rather ashamed of her plain, gawky daughter, who seemed to have no breeding and no wish for it, but at the age of 17, I blossomed, quite literally, growing breasts almost overnight, and attracting the attention of young men who had formerly cast their glassy-eyed looks at my elegant and glossy mother. Suddenly, I was interesting, the sexy one, and she loathed it. Of course, she couldn't and wouldn't admit to that, so we fought. My father hated it and would descend to the basement to listen to Puccini or Rossini, and wonder why his 'two best girls' were at each other's throats.

So when David came along to sweep me off my feet, my mother couldn't help a quick shove to speed the process and send me on my way.

She'd never thought of college as an option for me—consequently there was no college fund. She'd always told my father I wouldn't last a single semester: 'too weak', apparently. Besides, marriage was supposed to save me from all that tedious studying.

"He's too good for you, of course, Caroline," she said, "but we'll do the best we can." *Well, I'll do my best to make you attractive, although 'pretty' is too much to hope for.* "Oh, you look so much like your father."

My father was short and dark and very Italian. I inherited his bright hazel eyes, thick, uncooperative hair that rippled in waves down my back, his olive skin and quick, passionate temper. I also inherited certain hirsute qualities that meant I was waxing my legs from the age of 10 and my armpits from the age of 12. But for all that, I blessed the deity who made me, that I had inherited little from my mother except her slender build, and height.

I used to wonder why she and my father had ever married because she undoubtedly despised his immigrant Italian ancestry and flaunted her own WASPishness at every opportunity. Her hair was blonde and coiffed, her eyes blue and sharp, her complexion strawberries and cream.

It didn't surprise anyone, least of all me, when I jumped the moment I was pushed, and found myself a bride at the age of 19. The year was 1990.

What David saw in me is less easy to understand. A young wife with European aspirations perhaps, fluent in Italian and with an appreciation of wine that was unexpected and, later, unwelcome. I was different enough from the other Navy wives to mark him out for distinction, and myself for alienation and loneliness.

The other wives tried very hard to include me in their artificial social whirl—coffee mornings, lunch dates, baby-sitting, play dates for children I didn't have, and 'drinks with the girls'.

They weren't unkind, merely satisfied with their lives, happy at home and fulfilled with their roles in a way I could never be. I was too young, too myopic and too self-contained to see the pitfalls of my willful isolation. I went to their book club once, but when I found they preferred bestsellers and romances to the chilling wildness of Hemingway, or the maverick prose of Nabokov, I had nothing to say and we merely stared at each other with fragrant disdain.

There was one thing about me that pleased my husband—I was athletic. He taught me to sail a dinghy and later a yacht, I could shoot almost as well as the Corps' best marksman, I was fearless of heights and I could dive from the top diving board at the Base swimming pool.

Those were the only things he liked about me, and even that was limited to the first twenty months of our marriage. He hated the way I dressed, the way I spoke, what I spoke about and the things that interested me to speak about. In the end, the irony was that he wanted me to be more like the other wives, while relishing my alienness. It was confusing and wearying and I didn't know how to be myself. I think that during those early years I forgot how. So I wore the clothes he liked and kept my mouth shut ... a slow descent into silence.

By the time we realized that children weren't going to happen for us, well, for him, I had undergone a number of invasive and unpleasant examinations and, blaming each other, we had both lost interest in procreation, fortuitous happenstance, I suppose. Sex was desultory and uninspiring. I was uninspired. I was dull.

After two years of marriage, David was transferred to the Naval Medical Center in San Diego and he very much wished me to be friends with the wife of his new CO. Estelle was everything that I was not—poised, charming and perfect. She was also cold, controlling, and a snob. I loathed her. The feeling was mutual. But for the sake of appearance, we cultivated a chilly friendship. It was easy for her to fake, less so for me. I pitied her child, perhaps feeling some kinship with his loneliness. Sebastian was eight years old, I was 21.

He was cursed with sensitivity, and with his bitch of a mom and his monster of a dad, he was damned twice.

Between us there arose a sweet and gentle friendship. Sebastian got into the habit of dropping by after school to tell me about his day. I'd pour him an alcohol-free *limoncello* made from Sorrento lemons, when I could find them, syrup and soda. We talked about books that he'd read, and I would suggest stories he might enjoy—the stories I had read as a child that were far removed from the anodyne books his mother thought suitable. Together we worked our way through the casual brutality of the Brothers Grimm and easy psychopathy of Hans Christian Andersen, whose little mermaid felt the pain of knives slicing into her feet when she walked, and whose angelic voice was bargained away for love.

At about this time, my dear father came to stay. My mother, of course, was too busy—involved with her clubs, her Bridge, and her good deeds for everyone but her family. It was a relief to us all, although David was determined to remind us of, and lament her absence at every meal. *Such a fine woman.*

Sebastian and my father adored each other, and happily spent hours together making model airplanes and blowing them up with the powder extracted from fireworks. David disapproved, of course, so—from him—they hid most of their activities. It was their special time, innocent and childish, if typically destructive play.

One day, Sebastian entered my kitchen when we failed to hear his knock. 'Madame Butterfly' was playing at full volume and my father and I were wailing along to the wonderful lyrics of '*Un Bel Dì*'.

"What are you singing?"

"*Sto cantando in onore di Dio, giovanotto*," said my father.

Sebastian frowned and my father looked puzzled. "I don't understand what Papa Ven is saying."

"You're speaking in Italian, papa," I said, smiling. I turned to Sebastian. "He says he's singing to God."

"Ah, *cara! Italiano!* The language of Dante! The language of cooking! The language of love!"

Thereafter, every day of my father's visit, Sebastian learned a few more words of Italian, not all of them were entirely suitable for a child of his young years, but my father had a wicked streak in him. As it turned out, one that I inherited.

I was reasonably happy in San Diego. I became involved with the Base's magazine and helped out on open house days at the Base or the hospital. I had even put in an application to go to evening classes in journalism, one of the few individual forays I had ever made. It was at this time that David informed me he'd been assigned to Camp Lejeune in North Carolina, and that we were leaving. It was another sideways move for an officer who had failed to live up to his early promise. David chose to see it as a promotion, but then he would.

Within 48 hours, David had disappeared to the far side of the continent, and I had a week to watch the contents of our little home being packed into containers.

Sebastian came to see me every day, every day he cried.

And then, on a Tuesday in September, I was gone.

CHAPTER ONE

THE SUN WAS WARM ON MY SKIN, AND THE BOOK HAD BECOME HEAVY IN MY hands. I'd missed the California sun, it felt good to be back, even under these less than ideal circumstances.

I tossed the book aside, pushed my sunglasses up to my hair, and rested my head on my arms, soothed by the warmth of late morning.

I wasn't entirely sure I'd wanted to make this return journey with David. I had friends in North Carolina independent of Navy life, I had a job I enjoyed as an administrative assistant on a small but respectable local newspaper, and had finally gotten my English Lit degree after six years of night school.

But at the same time, I was feeling restless and ready for a change. Turning 30 had shifted my world view somewhat, and I was a little surprised to find myself still married. I felt ready to try something new ... or something old, as it turned out, because we were back in San Diego. It was a prized location and considered a step up from Camp Lejeune. In any event, David was happier, which made my life easier. We'd found a way to coexist that was not unpleasant. He wasn't always an unkind man, or so I told myself, and I wasn't a faithless wife, we were just fundamentally unsuited to each other. We'd grown apart.

At least I was enjoying the beach. Point Loma was seven miles from the hospital and patronized by nearly all the Base personnel, a finger of land that separated the ocean from San Diego Bay. The less popular part was at the north end of Adair Street, here, I thought, I was less likely to be disturbed.

Perhaps fate was watching, but I suppose the meeting would have happened sooner or later, if not that day.

"Hello, Mrs. Wilson."

I didn't recognize the light, tenor voice. I twisted around and cupped my hand over my eyes, squinting against the sudden brightness of the sun.

"Yes?"

Two men of about 20 were standing awkwardly a few feet away, and a third was leaning over me, dripping onto my beach towel.

"It's Sebastian."

"Who?"

His radiant smile faltered.

"Sebastian Hunter."

My mind unraveled. *Little Sebastian Hunter—all grown up.*

"Oh, my gosh, Sebastian! I ... I didn't recognize you. Wow!"

I rolled over and sat up.

"I heard you'd come back. I was hoping I'd see you," he said, smiling again.

The sweet, sad-eyed boy of eight had become a truly handsome young man. His light brown hair was long for the son of a Navy officer, curling nearly to his chin, and bleached to a dark gold by the California sun. He was slim, muscled like an athlete, with broad shoulders and narrow hips.

A bright blue surfboard was tucked under one arm and he wore deep red swim shorts that were heavy with seawater, pulled down to show a sliver of paler skin at his waist, highlighting the tan on the rest of his body. The thought passed through my mind, *He must have his pick of girls at school.*

"Look at you, Sebastian. So grown up. It's good to see you. How are you? How are your parents?"

His smile faltered.

"Oh, they're fine."

I didn't know what to say, it was so strange to see him again after all these years. With a stretch of the imagination, I could just see the child I had known in the young man before me.

"Well ... that's great. I'm sure I'll see you around the Base. Um ... do you guys need a ride back?"

I looked uncertainly toward his friends, unsure how I'd manage to load three full sized surfboards on top of my old Ford.

"No, we're good thanks. Ches has got a van." He nodded to one of the boys. "And we're going to catch some more waves. When I saw you, I just wanted to ... come say hi."

"Okay, well, good seeing you, Sebastian."

He smiled again, hovering tentatively. "I'll see you again, Mrs. Wilson?"

His voice held a question.

"Yes, I expect so. *Ciao*, Sebastian."

He beamed. "*Ciao*, Mrs. Wilson."

I watched him walk away, drops of seawater dewing on his muscled back. Good Heavens! Little Sebastian Hunter—and not so little. How old was he?

Seventeen? Eighteen? Certainly not twenty. I frowned, trying to do the math. He'd really grown into a fine young man. Amazing, considering his wretched parents.

Oh, God, I'd probably have to see the rancid Estelle and the monstrous father, Donald. The gloomy thought killed my good mood, and I scowled at the writhing, hissing ocean.

Sebastian and his friends strolled toward another group of surfers hovering on the shoreline. I could see they were laughing at him about something, I guessed it was to do with me. I shook my head—teenage boys ... they don't change.

I watched as they paddled out, a small flock of brightly plumed beach rats, disappearing abruptly behind the rising surf. I could just pick out a bright blue board weaving along the leading edge of a breaking wave. I gasped as the rushing water suddenly swallowed the boy, then relaxed when I saw his head break the surface, and he swam back to his board, paddling again toward the line-up.

For perhaps half an hour I continued to watch as they took turns racing across the hills of green water before being engulfed by the roiling froth, then paddling back to chase the next wave, over and over. It was pointless and beautiful and utterly mesmerizing.

Reluctantly, I checked my watch, time to head back to the Base. I was expecting a delivery of some more of our belongings. I couldn't be late, it wasn't worth the ensuing argument if all was not ship-shape before David returned from the hospital.

I slipped a yellow sundress over my bikini and headed back to the car. It was super-heated, of course, the air inside arid. I rolled down all the windows and drove back, singing along to Figaro's aria on my temperamental CD player.

When I pulled up, the delivery guy was pounding on my door, frustrated by the lack of response.

"Sorry! Sorry! I'm here now."

He glowered at me. I smiled pleasantly and offered him a cold beer.

"Well, ma'am, I wouldn't say no to a cold soda if you've got one."

He stood and poured it down his throat in one swallow, wiping sweat from his glowing face. Then he happily deposited two large crates in the garage and drove away.

I stared sourly at the boxes, wondering if my withering gaze would force them to unpack themselves. But no.

Three hours later, dirty and sweaty, and with aching muscles, I admitted defeat with one-and-a half crates still left to unpack. Tomorrow would have to do, although I knew it would mean a fight. But I just didn't have the energy.

At 6PM David drove up in his pride and joy—a newly purchased silver Camaro, vivid symbol of his promotion. He frowned at the unpacked crates, and

I waited for the dissection of my day—where had I been, what had I done, who had I seen. But instead he tapped his watch, a habitual gesture of irritation.

"We're due at the Vorstadts' in an hour, and you're not dressed."

"Who?"

"Captain Vorstadt has invited us for drinks."

"You didn't say."

"I put it on the calendar, Caroline. Didn't you check the schedule?"

No, sir. Sorry, sir.

"I thought you might have mentioned it, that's all, David."

"I want to leave at 1850. Wear the green cocktail dress."

I hated it when he ordered me around—which was most of the time, admittedly. But it was really grating on me.

"I'm tired, David. I've been unpacking crates for the last three hours—it's exhausting."

"Making life and death decisions all day is exhausting, Caroline. For once, could you just do something to support me? I don't ask for much, considering the lifestyle I give you."

I bit back the retort that sprang forward. What was the point? We'd been here before. I'd never won an argument with him yet. It was so damn tiring to even try.

"Fine. I'll go shower."

I dressed quickly, applied a little eyeliner, mascara and some clear lipstick: the minimum makeup I could get away with. David liked women 'to look like women'—that meant heels and make-up. Not really my look, inasmuch as I had one. He wore his favorite sports jacket and an open-necked shirt. He still looked handsome, I suppose.

"What did you do today?" he said, breaking the silence as we drove the short distance to the party.

"Before I spent three hours unpacking crates?"

"Just half a crate, I noticed."

Pedantic ass.

"I read a book at the beach. Before the crates were delivered. Oh, I bumped into Sebastian."

"Who?"

"The Hunters' boy. You know, from last time we were here."

He grunted, which could mean anything, but I suspect it meant he didn't remember. David wasn't good at remembering people, something of a handicap for a doctor. It gave the impression he was cold.

"Who's going to be there tonight?"

"I wasn't given the guest list, Caroline."

Jeez, I was only asking.

Mrs. Vorstadt met us at the door of her townhouse.

"David, how lovely. And you must be Caroline. I'm Donna."

Donna was a strong-looking, attractive woman in her fifties. She kissed me on the cheek. Her breath smelled of gin and tonic.

"Do come in."

The room was crowded and noisy, people spilling out into the large yard at the rear of the house. A barbecue was spitting away under an awning—men gathered in little groups drinking beer from bottles and laughing loudly, women huddled together sipping Manhattans, their high heels sinking into the recently watered turf. I was glad I'd worn flats, despite David's frown of disapproval.

I mentally prepared myself for an evening of tedium. But it was worse than that.

Donna furnished us with the mandatory beer for David and cocktail for me, then ushered us toward a couple who seemed vaguely familiar. When the blonde turned, I recognized her icy smile.

"I believe you know the Hunters from last time you were in San Diego."

"Caroline, dear," said Estelle in a cool voice. "And David, you haven't aged a day."

We air-kissed insincerely, the men shook hands and Donald wandered off to speak to some of the other officers.

"Hello, Estelle." I spoke mildly without inflection. "I saw your son today."

She stared at me in disbelief. "Sebastian?"

"Yes. At the beach. It was a nice surprise."

"He was at the beach?"

For God's sake, I'm not talking Serbo-Croat.

"Yes."

Her eyes narrowed, and I had the distinct impression that I'd somehow given away his secret.

"Sebastian!" Her clipped vowels carried across the yard, and several people turned around to stare.

I followed her eyes and saw him again, leaning against the deck, by himself. He was taller than I'd realized now that I was standing, too: as tall as his father, taller than David. This time Sebastian was more formally dressed in khaki chinos, a white shirt, sleeves rolled up his strong forearms, and a loose, black tie around his neck. He still looked more casual than the majority of the men.

"Mother?" he said, his eyes wary.

"Caroline said you were at the beach today."

He smiled suddenly and walked over to join us, his expression lightening as he saw me. "Hello, Mrs. Wilson. I said we'd meet again."

"You were right. How was the surf?"

"Great, thanks! We..."

"Sebastian!" interrupted Estelle in a low, furious voice. "You were supposed to be studying for your advanced placement tests. You need to pass these if you're going to be a semester ahead, for God's sake. You've got your college credits to think about. Do you want your Associate degree early or not?"

He shrugged nonchalantly in that infuriating way that most teenagers learn simply to annoy their parents, but I could see that he was anxious, too.

"I studied this afternoon," he replied softly. "There was a good swell this morning, Ches..."

"We'll talk later," she hissed. "Your father will want to hear about this."

She marched away, leaving an embarrassed silence behind her. Donna steered David away, and I was left with Sebastian.

"I'm so sorry about that—I wouldn't have said anything if I'd realized I was going to make trouble for you."

He shrugged again and smiled. "I'm always in trouble, so it doesn't make any difference."

"Oh, well then ... here's to trouble!" I raised my glass in an ironic toast.

Sebastian grinned at me, his eyes crinkling happily. I realized they were blue-green, the color of the ocean. I'd forgotten.

"Have you been surfing long? You looked pretty good."

"Did you see me?" he seemed delighted. "There were some really gnarly tubes."

"I have no idea what that means! But I did watch for quite a while, you looked very graceful."

He blushed suddenly and looked down.

"How's school?" I asked, changing the subject.

"Oh, okay. I graduate a week from Thursday..."

That would make him 18, I guessed.

"And then off to college in the fall?"

"Maybe. Dad wants me to enlist, but Mom wants me to get my degree first."

"What do you want?"

He looked surprised, as if no one had asked him that question. Then he smiled wickedly.

"I want to surf."

"Of course. The perfect career path—a beach bum. Perhaps we should drink to the endless summer."

He laughed, a carefree sound that had me grinning back at him.

"I could drink to one of your special *limoncellos*."

I must have looked puzzled because he clarified his comment immediately.

"You used to make them for me—alcohol-free!"

"Oh, yes. When you were a kid."

He frowned, as if something about what I said didn't please him, but he quickly threw off the thought.

"Do you go to the beach a lot?" he asked, his eyes surprisingly intense.

"I did in North Carolina, although I had a job, too. But we've only been back here a week, so today was my first chance. I still have a lot of unpacking to do."

I shuddered at the thought of those one-and-a-half crates in the garage.

"I could help you. Unpack, I mean. Carrying things."

"Oh, well, thank you. But I expect I'll manage, it's not that much really."

"I'd like to help. It's great having you back."

I was nonplussed by his offer and his comment, although part of me acknowledged it would be useful to have someone to do all the carrying. No, he had studying to do, it wouldn't be fair.

Over his shoulder, I saw Donald Hunter stalking toward us and a shiver ran through me: he looked furious.

My expression must have alerted Sebastian because he turned to see what had caught my attention.

"Your mother says you were at the beach again this morning," barked Sebastian's father, without preamble. He gripped Sebastian's arm, spinning him around to face his wrath.

Sebastian blanched. "Yes, but..."

"I fucking warned you what I'd do if you did that again when you should be studying."

I was utterly shocked that this foul man would speak to his son like that in front of me, a virtual stranger.

"Dad, I..."

"Quiet!" he snarled.

People were staring. And I was caught in a horrifying paralysis, unable to tear my eyes from this nasty little family drama.

"You can kiss your surfboard goodbye—and no more beach. No son of mine is going to waste his life being a beach bum."

Sebastian tugged his arm free and faced down his father.

"I studied in the afternoon, Dad. And I paid for that surfboard, I worked for it. It's mine. You can't touch it."

Donald's face turned an ugly puce, and I thought he was going to hit his son. At the last second he realized that people were staring.

"This isn't over," he hissed, then marched away.

Sebastian stared at the ground, humiliation and anger vying for dominance on his face.

I felt terribly guilty, this was all my fault.

"I'm so sorry, Sebastian," I whispered. "I had no idea..." My words trailed off lamely.

He shook his head. "He's just an asshole. I really hate him. I can't wait to leave home," he said, fiercely. "The sooner the better."

I didn't know what to say to that. I just nodded sympathetically. After all, hadn't I left as soon as I could to get away from my mother? I searched desperately for a change of topic, but my brain was unwilling to cooperate. Donna returned quickly, looking suitably irritated at Donald's outburst. *Such bad manners*, I could see the thought flickering across her face.

"Can I refresh your glass, Caroline?"

Without realizing it, I'd downed the cocktail already.

"Oh, yes, thank you."

"Sebastian, more soda?"

"No, thank you, Mrs. Vorstadt," he muttered, then left abruptly, his expression mortified.

Donna shook her head. "That poor boy. What he has to put up with."

"Is his father always like that?" I was still shocked.

Clearly the answer was 'yes' but Donna didn't want to commit herself to anything too definite—or damning.

"Oh, well, Donald is Donald. I'm sure you must remember."

I stared after Sebastian, recalling other instances of Donald's bullying from when his son was a boy. I was amazed Sebastian hadn't turned into a monster himself. He seemed just as gentle and sweet as when I'd known him all those years ago.

The rest of the evening passed with uninteresting small talk, as usual. I stayed away from Estelle and Donald, Sebastian seemed to have disappeared, and David and I ignored each other, as usual.

I was relieved when he decided it was the right time to return home.

CHAPTER TWO

The next morning the damn crates hadn't miraculously unpacked themselves. I was staring at them with antipathy when I heard a car pull up.

Donna Vorstadt stepped out of her new Chevy and waved when she saw me.

"Hello, Caroline, dear, I thought I'd just come and see how you're settling in. Goodness, I think you've got your work cut out there."

She smiled, commiserating, and I warmed to her a little more.

"Do you time for a cup of coffee, Donna?"

I didn't usually feel the need to socialize with the wives of my husband's fellow officers, but she seemed genuine, and I still knew how to follow some of the niceties of Base behavior.

"Sure, that would be great."

I realized too late that the breakfast dishes were still scattered across the counter. Oh well, I'd blown my chance of pretending I was perfect.

"Cream and sugar?"

"Just the cream. Do you have skim milk?"

I cleared a space, and we sat down to drink our coffees.

"So, how are you settling in? It's a pain moving, isn't it?"

"I don't mind the physical aspects of moving ... it's just ... I had a job I really liked back in North Carolina." *Oh, too personal.* "Mind you, those crates won't unpack themselves."

I sighed and she looked sympathetic.

"I have to run to the shops now, but I could come by this afternoon and help if you like."

Before I could reply, there was a knock at the front door. I hoped to hell it wasn't another wife come to help by drinking my coffee.

"Hi, Mrs. Wilson."

Smiling hugely, Sebastian stood there, dressed in torn jeans and a plain, white t-shirt.

"Oh, hello! It's nice to see you again, Sebastian. What can I do for you?"

"You said you had to unpack crates, I thought I could help."

I was taken aback by his offer.

"That's very sweet of you, Sebastian, but I don't think your parents would be happy if they knew you were here instead of studying."

"I'm taking a break," he said, his lovely smile slipping at the mention of his parents.

"I'm sure they won't object to Sebastian helping a neighbor," said Donna, appearing behind me. "That's very thoughtful of you, Sebastian," she continued, kindly.

Sebastian reddened when he saw her, and he looked down.

"Well, I could certainly use some help," I said, feeling flustered.

"Great!" said Sebastian, his smile returning. "I'll get started."

"Thank you," I muttered to his back.

Donna winked at me. "I think you have got admirer there," she whispered. "Thanks for the coffee. Call me if you need anything."

I watched her drive away, and then headed for the garage. Sebastian had already made inroads into the second half of crate number one.

"You really don't have to do this, you know," I said, shaking my head in bewilderment.

"I want to," he said simply.

I decided I'd let him help for half an hour, then kick him out and send him back to his parents before I caused any more trouble for him.

It was useful having him there—he heaved tables and chests and boxes full of who knows what, and before I knew it, two hours had flown by.

"Oh crap! It's nearly lunchtime." I said, looking at my watch, horrified.

"Do you have to be somewhere?" Sebastian asked, looking concerned.

"No, no, I'm worried about you. Your parents ... your studying."

He shrugged. "No sweat."

"Look, I'm not going to be responsible for you flunking out. I'll fix you some lunch and then you must go study. Deal?"

"Okay, deal!" he said happily.

He followed me into the house and I showed him where he could wash his hands. I was stretching up to get some of the tall glasses when I heard him come into the kitchen.

"I'll get those for you," he said.

His sudden proximity behind made me jump as if an electric shock had jolted through me. It was the strangest feeling, I suddenly felt almost nervous as he reached past my shoulder, lightly brushing against my back. I took a step away and turned to find him staring at me, a glass in each hand.

"Thank you," I said, awkwardly.

He didn't reply and I had to look away first. The intensity of his gaze made me feel uncomfortable—and in my own home, too, damn it! Yes, and annoyed. I took refuge, hunting through the refrigerator, trying to restore some equilibrium.

"I have soda or a lemon *pressé*," my voice was half swallowed by the fridge.

"I've never had a lemon *pressé*. What's that?"

"Oh well, just lemon juice and sparkling mineral water."

"I'll try that, please, Mrs. Wilson."

The tension left my body and I smiled at him.

"Sebastian, you can call me Caroline. Mrs. Wilson is so formal ... and it makes me feel ancient."

"Okay, Caroline," he grinned at me.

"Now, I can make you a chicken salad sub or ... tricolored salad."

"*Insalata tricolore, per favore*."

I turned to him in surprise.

"I've been learning Italian," he announced proudly. "A correspondence course. My high school only offered Spanish."

"Really? *Molto bene!*"

"And I've been listening to opera, too. I like Verdi."

"The fallen woman."

"Excuse me?" he gasped.

"*La Traviata*: I presume that's what you mean when you say you like Verdi. Or maybe *Aïda*? *Rigoletto*?"

He let his breath out in a gust. "Yeah, all of those."

"I thought teenage boys only listened to heavy rock music," I teased him.

He looked wounded and I regretted my comment. He was obviously trying to impress me.

"I'm glad you like opera, my father loved it."

"I remember. I remember you and him singing opera in your kitchen."

"Really, you remember that?"

He nodded, serious. "I remember everything."

I sighed. "That was a great visit when Papa came to stay."

Sebastian smiled. "Yeah, he was fun. We blew up a lot of things."

I rolled my eyes at the memory. "Yes, David wasn't very happy about it."

Why I mentioned David at that moment, I couldn't say.

Sebastian frowned. "How is your dad?"

And the painful memory lanced through me. My dear father, lying shrunken and in pain, tiny and helpless in a hospital bed, the morphine failing to tame the pain of cancer that devoured him whole.

"He passed away—two years ago."

I could barely speak the words, taken by surprise at the crushing force of the memory. I felt tears hot in my eyes. *Ridiculous, I scolded myself.*

"I'm sorry. I didn't know," Sebastian whispered.

He looked like he wanted to say something else, but now I was craving his absence. I heartily wished I hadn't offered him lunch.

"Thank you for your help this morning, Sebastian. It was really very thoughtful of you, but I'm going to have to insist that you go and do some studying as soon as we've eaten. I don't want to get you into any more trouble."

He pouted, suddenly looking his age. It made me want to laugh, but I truly didn't want to hurt his feelings. Especially not when he'd been so helpful. I changed the subject.

"Will you go surfing with your friends again soon?"

He sighed. "Maybe. I'll have to borrow a board."

"Oh, what happened to the blue one?"

"Dad trashed it—snapped it in half. Said I wasn't to waste any more time surfing."

He said the words casually, but I could hear the anger and hurt beneath them, and I remembered his father's threat at the barbecue.

"That's awful. And it's all my fault. I should never have said..."

He interrupted me, speaking softly. "It's not your fault that my father is a sadistic bastard, Caroline."

My hand fled to my mouth as he spoke, my eyes fixed on his.

"I'm so sorry." My words were whispered and faint.

He shrugged. "No big deal. I'm used to it."

"I must buy you a new board, Sebastian. That's all there is to it."

I tried to lighten the mood.

"Thanks, Caroline, but it's cool. I can always borrow one of Ches's. His dad surfs, too."

"Well, let me give you a ride home after we've eaten. It's the least I can do."

He grinned at me, and the tense moment had dissolved.

I sliced some mozzarella and tomatoes, diced the avocado, drizzled virgin olive oil, and ground some black pepper. I was irritated that I hadn't had time to buy any fresh basil to shred over it. It would have to do.

I found some bread I was going to use for bruschetta, and put a plate in the middle of the table. I imagined a teenage boy would eat a lot more than me.

He tucked in with gusto, swallowing everything in sight.

"Boy, you really can cook, Caroline."

I laughed at his enthusiasm. "This isn't cooking, Sebastian."

"Mom never cooks anything," he said, raising his eyebrows at me. "Dad thinks she does, but it's all store bought."

"Hmm ... well, anything you say or do can and will be held against you in a court of law."

He looked horrified. "Don't tell her I told you!"

"What's it worth?" I teased him.

"My ass!" he said, forcefully.

The expression on his face made me laugh out loud.

"Oh, Sebastian, you've left yourself open to blackmail now."

"You can blackmail me anytime, Caroline," he said huskily.

His eyes were suddenly intense, and I blinked at him in surprise.

"Time to go," I said blandly, and began to stack the dishes.

He stood and watched me uncertainly for a moment, then helped me clear the kitchen table.

"That insalata was good," he said, shyly.

"Thanks. Glad you liked it."

I looked at my watch, a not very subtle gesture. "I'll get my car keys."

I played the same CD that I'd listened to yesterday, but I didn't feel like singing now, the atmosphere in the car was uncomfortable again. I was having trouble keeping up with Sebastian's mood swings. It must be a nightmare living with a teenager, I reasoned, even one as seemingly mature as Sebastian. Or maybe it was just men in general—David's mood swings could almost be set by a metronome. The thought made me grimace.

"Can you drop me here?" Sebastian said suddenly.

"But we're not at your place yet?" I said, confused by the request.

He twisted his mouth in the semblance of a smile. "There'll be fewer questions this way," he said.

I felt guilty again—he'd spent the whole morning helping me when he should have been studying. And it was obvious his mother had no idea what he'd been doing. I hoped Donna didn't mention anything to her.

I pulled the car to the curb and waited for him to get out.

He sat for a moment, fiddling with his seatbelt.

"Will I see you again?" he said.

I frowned, puzzled by his odd question. "I expect so. Everyone bumps into everyone on the Base. Now, promise me you'll study this afternoon."

He forced a muted smile. "Okay, Caroline. See you later."

"Bye, Sebastian."

I drove away. I couldn't help glancing in the rear-view mirror—he was still watching.

Donna's words came back to me: *You've got an admirer there*.

Oh hell. Just what I didn't need—a teenager with a crush on me.

Irritated, I returned to my duties in the garage. By the time everything was put away and each assorted oddment had been found a home, I was bone weary. I was grateful to Sebastian—I would never have finished so soon without his help. I didn't have much experience of boys his age even when I *was* his age, but in my opinion he seemed different ... more mature than I would have expected. I wondered if he really did like opera, or whether that was just for my benefit.

God, what it must have been like growing up with those parents. Although Estelle was disturbingly like my own mother, at least I had one parent who'd loved me unconditionally.

I poured myself a glass of water, and took it to the yard to sit in the sun for a few moments of peace. I felt curiously adrift, as if the ties to my life were unraveling one by one. My mother, long absent by mutual choice, my father dead, my job gone, even David was AWOL in spirit.

And I was a shadow.

Oh, stop being so melodramatic.

I blamed my father: the Italian genes.

I needed to get out of the house, off the Base, and do something.

I threw myself in the shower, washing off the grime, and pulled on jeans and a t-shirt. That was deliberate—David hated seeing me in jeans, but today, right now, I wanted to feel like me—just for a few, precious hours.

I pulled out of the driveway and drove, too fast, down the road and past the hospital. From the corner of my eye, I recognized the figure walking away from me. I almost drove on, but something made me stop.

I leaned over and rolled down the passenger window.

"Hi. You need a ride somewhere?"

Sebastian's face lit up.

"Yeah, thanks."

He climbed in, folding his long legs into my compact Pinto, and grinned. I waited for him to give me directions, but he just leaned back in his seat and smiled.

"So, where can I take you?"

He shrugged. "Anywhere."

"Excuse me?"

"I just needed to get out of the house—you know, get some space. Mom is ... well, Mom."

"Oh, okay."

I felt awkward. I wouldn't have offered him a ride if I'd imagined he was just out for a walk.

"Did you finish your work?"

I really didn't want to be responsible for him neglecting his studies twice in one day.

"Yeah, I guess."

"Well, I was going to go downtown. You want to come?"

Part of me hoped he wouldn't, things were already awkward enough.

"Sure, that'd be great, Caroline."

There was a short pause while I thought of something to say. We'd chatted so easily this morning in the garage, but now I felt awkward. Maybe it was the memory of his intense gaze, the way his body had pressed against mine as he'd reached for the drinking glasses. I shook my head to clear it.

"How is the studying going?"

He shrugged, as if bored of that topic.

"Not a problem. On practice tests, I've scored high. It's all good."

"What AP classes are you doing?"

He glanced sideways at me. "Math, English Lit ... and Italian."

"Oh, well ... that's good."

I knew I ought to ask why those particular subjects—except I could guess, one of them at least.

"I want to do an Associate of Arts degree. It's only two years."

"So I understand," I said, briskly.

He looked like he wanted to say more, but instead turned to gaze out of the window.

"Why don't you put the radio on?" I said, hoping it would provide a suitable diversion.

"Okay," he said evenly.

It's ridiculous that this 18-year-old boy is more at ease than I am. Come on, Venzi, pull yourself together. Even after 11 years of marriage, there were times when Caroline Wilson was still Carolina, feisty daughter of the immigrant Marco Venzi.

The radio hissed and crackled until Sebastian found a reasonably clear signal—Blue Grass. His choice surprised me—from Verdi to this? It made me smile.

"You like Doc Watson?"

"I like all kinds of music."

I parked in a lot on Harbor Drive and we wandered up the hill to Little Italy, talking about music and food. I remembered this area from when I'd lived here before. There was a Mercarto every Saturday, and I looked forward to being able to buy Italian specialty oils and vegetables that weren't stocked in regular stores.

"Do you want to grab a coffee?" Sebastian said, sounding hopeful.

Mmm. Good Italian coffee. "Oh, a real espresso. Yes, that would be lovely."

Too much enthusiasm. Don't encourage him—no mixed signals.

But the day was too beautiful to be half-hearted, and I found myself delighted with all the pretty cafés, gelateria, and ristorantes.

We stopped at a tiny coffee shop just off India Street. The owner's wife came out to serve us and was ecstatic when I spoke to her in Italian. She kissed me on both cheeks and summoned the rest of her family to come out and meet me. Sebastian looked overwhelmed, then offered a few careful Italian phrases and was engulfed in the bosom of the family. I couldn't help laughing—their exuberance reminded me so much of my father.

They rattled out Italian like peanuts, with such speed and vigor, each talking over one another so that I struggled to catch everything they said. Sebastian probably only caught one word in fifty, but he sat there grinning, only wincing when the owner's mother, a little, round *nonna* of about eighty, grabbed him with both hands and kissed him repeatedly.

Then they all pulled up chairs and surrounded our small table, which soon overflowed with affection. Someone fetched half-a-dozen espresso cups and I sipped happily at the thick, bitter coffee. I was amused to see that Sebastian added several spoonfuls of sugar before he found the rich brew palatable.

Eventually some more patrons arrived and the family scattered, returning to their various roles of cook, cleaner, chef and bottle-washer.

"Whoa! That was something else," said Sebastian, as we were left to our own devices.

"Wonderful, wasn't it?"

"They kind of reminded me of your dad."

I sighed and leaned back in the uncomfortable chair.

"Yes, crazy—just like Papa."

"I'm sorry," he said softly, "I didn't mean to make you sad."

Then he laid his hand on mine and I felt his gentle touch. My eyes flew open in surprise and I jerked my hand away.

"I'm sorry," he said again, his cheeks heating.

"No, that was rude of me. I was just..."

Tension returned and to my horror, I found my hands were shaking. I fumbled in my wallet for some money and placed the bills on the table under an abandoned coffee cup.

"I have money," he said, awkwardly.

"No, it's fine. I've got it," I muttered. "I have to get back now."

Sebastian stood in silence, then followed me back onto the main street.

"*Aspetti, signor!*"

The coffee shop owner had followed us and was waving the notes I'd left on the table.

I stared, bewildered as he forced the bills into Sebastian's hand.

"No, please. You and your beautiful wife must come again. You are like family. Please!"

Refusing to keep the money, he kissed us both and trotted away smiling.

Sebastian's bemusement turned into a broad grin as he passed the money to me. "For you, *signora*. Beautiful wife, huh? Well, he was half right."

It was my turn to flush, but I tried to laugh it off. "Free coffee always tastes the best."

"Yeah! We should definitely do this again."

I couldn't return his puppyish enthusiasm, I simply smiled weakly.

"You know," he said thoughtfully, "I only got about one word in every sentence. I thought my Italian was better than that. Hell, I've been studying it for four years. Maybe you could teach me, I mean, just some Italian conversation practice. That would be awesome!"

My automatic response was a big NO, but I didn't get the chance.

"Hey, Seb. What's up?"

Sebastian's face froze.

"What do you want, Jack?"

"Who's your cute friend?"

A look of anger and deep dislike crossed Sebastian's face.

"Ah, come on, dude! I'm just saying."

I was pretty certain Jack was one of the surf rats that I'd seen with Sebastian the day before. He was slightly older than Sebastian and his friends, with dark hair and dark, feral eyes. I disliked him from the first sentence he spoke.

"Caroline Wilson," I said, hoping to defuse the sudden tension.

"Howdy, *Mrs.* Wilson," he said slyly, his eyes swiveling from my wedding rings to my cleavage.

We both looked at Sebastian, who seemed very ill at ease.

"Well, it was nice bumping into you again, Sebastian. Do you want a ride back to the Base or perhaps you'd prefer to stay with your *friend*."

I waited less than a second before I fixed an insincere smile to my face.

"See you around then. *Ciao*."

And I walked away.

I was furious with myself. Why had I pretended we'd just bumped into each other? It had all been perfectly innocent, so why lie?

And then I remembered the touch of his hand on mine and my ridiculous over-reaction.

Oh, this was not good, not good at all.

My temper was free-wheeling by the time I got back to the car. I was angry with Sebastian, with myself, with the loathsome Jack: stupid, pathetic little shit. He'd made me feel ... guilty, and I hadn't done anything. I was used to David making me feel guilty, but this was insufferable.

I wound down the windows before I got in, to let the heat escape, feeling some release of pent-up energy in the trivial task.

When I heard footsteps behind me, I didn't need to turn to see who it was.

"Caroline, I'm sorry, I..." his words trailed off.

"What? What!"

The words came out more forcefully than I'd meant. He stared at me, wounded. I badly wanted to kick something.

I took a deep breath, and reminded myself it wasn't his fault.

"Do you want a ride back?"

He nodded, still looking hurt.

I drove in a quiet rage. After a few minutes, I felt calm enough to risk a glance at Sebastian, he was gazing out of the window.

Eventually, he broke the heavy silence.

"I'm sorry about Jack and what he said." There was a brief pause, then he added, "The guy's an asshole."

I exhaled slowly, forcing some of the tension and irritation from my body in one long breath.

"Yes, he is, but don't worry about it."

He looked at me hopefully. "So, will you help me with my Italian? We could..."

"Sebastian, no. I don't think that would be a good idea."

"Why not?"

"It just isn't."

We sat mutely for several more minutes before he said softly, "I had fun today."

So did I.

But I didn't reply.

~

I dropped Sebastian off near his house and drove home, feeling irritated and petulant.

I stomped around, finding places for the final pieces of detritus from our marriage, items that didn't seem to fit were unceremoniously shoved into a closet in the guest room, metaphorically as well as literally.

Out of some guilty urge, I fixed David his favorite meal: lasagna and green salad, with a heavy dessert of apple pie and ice cream that he'd have to eat alone. I sat on the porch facing out into the yard and stared moodily at the yellowing grass. It needed watering, another chore. It was one of those days when I wished I'd taken up smoking years ago just to have something meaningful to do with my hands—and a purpose for being outside.

What was it about that boy? He really got under my skin. It had been simple when he was a child, and I'd enjoyed his uncomplicated company. Things had certainly changed. I'd enjoyed his company today, until Jack showed up. The thought was unwelcome.

When I heard David's Camaro outside, I pushed all thoughts of Sebastian Hunter from my mind.

"Mmm ... something smells good."

"Lasagna and apple pie."

David looked pleased. "It was the right decision coming out here again, Caroline."

If you say so.

"So what did you do with your day?"

"Puttered, mostly. Finished putting things away. I thought I might see if I could get some work—maybe writing. I'd like to use my degree. There's a cool, local newspaper, *City Beat* ... maybe I..."

"Good girl. Well done."

And that was the end of the conversation about me. Instead, I listened to a blow-by-blow description of his day at the hospital. Despite his snide comment about making life and death decisions while I played the little woman, most of his work was with orthopedic medicine.

After the meal, he leaned back in his chair and folded his hands over his stomach.

"I was talking to Donald Hunter today. Seems that son of his is running with a bad crowd."

"Sebastian? Is that likely? He seems such a nice boy."

David frowned. He didn't like having his story interrupted. I stood up quickly to clear the dishes—I didn't have the energy for either a fight or a lecture.

"He's spending all his time at the beach, surfing." He sneered the last word. "He's wearing his hair long, and Donald thinks he's probably smoking pot—he caught him with a lighter."

I hid a smile. Didn't most high-schoolers do things like that? It hardly seemed the crime of the century. But David's mantra was that rules were to be obeyed. I preferred my Papa's version: 'Rules are for the obedience of fools and the guidance of wise men'. A version which covered a multitude of small sins.

"He says he'll have to put his foot down."

"What does that mean?"

"He wants him to enlist—sooner rather than later. I think it's a good idea. A young man out of control—he needs some discipline. It made a man out of me."

I didn't want to start an argument so I stayed quiet, for a moment, seething inside, before I said, "Oh, I got the impression Estelle wanted him to go to college first."

David's frown deepened. "Well, Donald's the one paying the bills, so he's the one calling the shots."

And this was what it always came down to. I became even more determined to get some work—writing, if possible. I wouldn't mind serving in a shop or a bar, but David would never allow that. Pursuing my writing was acceptable, a suitable hobby for an officer's wife.

I loaded the dirty plates into the dishwasher and stacked the pans by the sink. I liked doing the dishes, it meant I could stay busy while David filled me in on more of the dull trivia that completed his day. I'd have washed the plates, too, except then he'd complain about me not using the household appliances properly.

I felt sorry for Sebastian. He'd seemed so happy and carefree as we'd wandered through Little Italy. It must be awful living with a controlling bastard like Donald Hunter—and Estelle, so cold and heartless. Well, I didn't have to guess how it felt to have a mother like that: I knew exactly.

Perhaps it would be a good thing if he enlisted, if only to get away from his damn parents.

I realized I was spending way too much time thinking about Sebastian, and I had enough concerns of my own. I resolved to get my résumé up-to-date, and to contact *City Beat* in the morning. And then I had an idea—it was something that might help Sebastian—and it would definitely wind up his father at the same time. Undoubtedly it would irritate David, too, that was practically a given.

Pleased with my idea, I finished up in the kitchen and hunted down my notepad. I wanted to sketch out my thoughts while they were still fresh in my mind.

I sat cross-legged on the bed and began to make some notes. I really needed internet access, but we hadn't yet got around to hooking up DSL. David expected me to take care of things like that, for once I was in agreement with him. In the meantime, I'd have to find a café with Wi-Fi, or head to the library.

"What are you doing?"

Sometimes I wondered if it would be simpler if I just gave David an itinerary of my day rather than answer his endless questions on how every hour had been spent, or was going to be spent.

"Just jotting down some notes, I had an idea for an article."

"You look tan, it suits you."

I looked up, recognizing the tone in David's voice: he wanted sex.

He took the notepad and pencil out of my hands and tossed them on the floor.

"Come here."

Dutifully, I stood up and went to him. He unzipped my dress and lifted it over my head, dropping it on top of my notepad.

I started to unbutton his shirt, but he brushed my hands away.

"Turn around."

I followed his instruction and he unhooked my bra, then briskly yanked my panties down.

"Lie on the bed. No, face down. You really have gotten some nice color today, I can see your tan lines."

I felt the bed shift as he lay down next to me.

"I've always liked you with a tan, Caroline."

He ran his hand down my spine and stroked my ass several times. I heard him undo his zipper and I rolled onto my side as he stroked himself, steadily encouraging his erection.

"Do you want me to do that?"

"Okay."

I carried on, watching his eyes close and his mouth slacken.

"Okay, that's enough."

Then he lay down on top of me, his weight forcing me into the bed, and entered me carefully. He thrust half a dozen times, shuddered, then stopped.

"Mmm!"

He lay back on the bed, smiling. I stared at the sheets. I'd have to wash those in the morning.

"What are your plans for tomorrow, Caroline?"

"I'm going to get my résumé together and then contact that newspaper I mentioned. Oh, and I'll call the telephone company to get DSL hooked up."

"Good idea. I'd like to throw a little party for the guys at the hospital—a week from this Saturday okay? About 7PM."

"Sure. Canapés and red wine?"

"Better get some beer, too. And that fancy *pressé* you like, for the wives. Maybe some of those little ... what do you call them ... cannelloni?"

"Oh, *cannoli siciliani?* Sure."

Damn it. It would take me all morning to make those.

"Great. Thanks, honey."

He heaved himself off the bed and strolled into the bathroom. I heard him pissing into the toilet bowl and, a moment later, running the faucet to brush his teeth. He flushed the toilet afterwards—that had always irritated me.

I knew from experience that I'd find his uniform tossed onto the floor. I pulled my nightgown out from under the pillow, picked up my dress and notepad, waiting for him to finish.

CHAPTER THREE

David was up and out early. Getting that promotion had made the world spin his way, for a while at least. I hoped the good mood would last. He was easier to live with when he wasn't mad at me all the time.

I wasn't keen on the idea of a party, but it was something that was expected. I looked forward to these little soirées with the enthusiasm of someone going for root canal.

I cleaned up the kitchen just in case anyone decided to drop in for coffee, then finished off the notes I'd started last night. I wasn't entirely happy with the necessity of asking Sebastian for his help, but I suspected he'd get a kick out of my idea for an article.

When I'd cornered the laptop and intimidated it into crawling into action, I updated my résumé. It certainly looked a lot better than last time I'd had to do this. Now I had solid experience under my belt, sort of, not as much perhaps as many women my age, but enough—I hoped. I also knew that the fact of my being a military wife garnered enough cachet to get me through the door. Civilians were always intrigued by the idea of a world within a world: nearby, but closed.

I called the phone company and they agreed that I'd be hooked up by Friday, and they were usually pretty good at attending to military folk. It made them feel patriotic.

Having ticked off all my chores but one, I was now faced with the tricky prospect of contacting Sebastian without raising his hopes—or getting him into more trouble with his parents. I had no idea how I was going to do that. But, unwittingly, Donna Vorstadt was kind enough to help me out.

The phone rang, loud and demanding.

"Hello?"

"Hi Caroline, it's Donna. I just thought I'd ask, if you're not too busy unpacking, some of the girls and I usually get together on a Monday afternoon and have coffee ... chew the fat. I was wondering if you'd like to join us? You'll know some of them: Penny Bishop, Estelle Hunter, Margarite Schiner."

"Oh, that's so kind of you, Donna, but I'm just up to my ears in jobs. I have to call the phone company to get DSL, David is on my case about that. And I have a thousand and one things to do. Did he mention we're having a few friends over for drinks a week from this Saturday? About 7PM. Maybe we could catch up then. And coffee another time—for sure."

She accepted my excuses with good humor and said she was looking forward to Saturday. We hung up on good terms after she gave me Estelle's number, obviously surprised by my request. Donna was easy company—I was beginning to feel she was a woman I could like.

Estelle, however, was something else altogether.

I started to dial her number and, to my surprise and chagrin, I felt a nervous knot in my stomach. *Oh, for crying out loud. You're a woman of 30!* I really didn't like having to ask her for help.

Irritated, I dialed the number.

"Hunter residence. May I help you?"

Sebastian's voice was cool and polite. I was so surprised, I couldn't speak immediately. I'd assumed he'd be at school.

"Hello?" he said again.

"Hi, Sebastian ... it's Caroline," I stuttered.

Over the phone I heard him take a sudden, sharp breath.

"Caroline, hi! How are you?"

"Good, thanks. I was expecting to reach your mother..."

"I had a free period—and I'm graduating on Thursday anyway," he reminded me.

"Oh, well, as luck would have it ... I wondered if you could help me—with an article I'm writing?"

"Sure, anything!"

I tried to ignore the obvious delight in his voice.

"Well, when we were talking at the barbecue the other day, you mentioned that your friend's dad surfed—I think you said his name was Ches? Well, I wondered if you could give me his number, I'd like to speak to him."

There was a short pause.

"You want to speak to Ches?"

He sounded hurt.

"Well, I really wanted to talk to Ches's dad," I said hurriedly. "I'm writing an article about Base personnel who go surfing. I thought it would make a great piece for *City Beat*."

"Oh, right." He sounded ridiculously relieved. "Sure, I can get you that. We were going to hang out at the beach this afternoon. There's a swell coming in off the Pacific that looks awesome. Mitch was going to ride with us. You want to come, too?"

"Mitch?"

"That's Ches's dad. He's a Staff Sergeant."

"Well, that would be great. What time were you going to go?"

"About 3:45PM. We could pick you up?"

"Um ... are you going to Point Loma again?"

"Maybe ... we were going to sort of drive around till we found the best break."

Oh, well...

"In that case, yes, I'd love a ride. Are you sure it'll be okay with Mitch and your friends?"

"Sure!"

He answered so quickly I couldn't help a small chuckle escaping. "Well, okay, but I'd feel happier if I could talk to Mitch first."

With some reluctance that had me smiling to myself, Sebastian gave me his friend's number and confirmed three times that he'd see me after school at 3:45PM.

I hung up, still smiling. Then I redialed for Sergeant Peters. A woman answered.

"Hi there, Peters' residence."

"Oh, good morning. My name is Caroline Wilson—I'm Commander David Wilson's wife. I was wondering if I could talk to Sergeant Peters."

"Oh. Good morning, Mrs. Wilson. This is Shirley Peters. I'm afraid Mitch isn't available at present. May I take a message?"

"Yes, thank you. This will probably sound a little odd, but I understand Mitch is taking the boys surfing this afternoon and I wondered if I could tag along."

She hesitated long enough to let me know that this sounded more than just a little odd. I rushed to fill in the blanks for her.

"It's just that I used to write some stories for the local paper back east," I said, exaggerating slightly, "and I hoped to try and do the same here—I thought an article on Base personnel who go surfing would be interesting. I was hoping your husband could give me some tips."

"Oh, I see. Well, I'm sure that Mitch will be just fine about that, Mrs. Wilson."

She still sounded surprised and I knew why—officers' wives didn't have much to do with the families of the enlisted ranks. A distinction that had always bothered me.

In the end, we agreed that Mitch would call me if there was a problem, otherwise I was to be ready to go at 3:45PM.

"Um, Mrs. Wilson, that van is pretty old, and the boys use it for all their surf stuff. It's got half the beach in there. Well, I wouldn't want you to ruin any of your clothes."

I was touched by her thoughtfulness.

"Thank you, Mrs. Peters. I'll wear an old beach dress then. Thank you so much."

After that, I felt full of energy, delighted with how the day was panning out. I drove over to the library, got online to check up on the local surf spots, and also to find out more about what kind of stories *City Beat* ran.

I just had time to stop by the Kwik Shop to stock up on groceries for supper and, as an afterthought, picked up a dozen focaccia rolls before running home to change into my old, yellow sundress and pick up my notebook.

I filled the rolls with pastrami, lettuce and tomatoes, and was finishing wrapping them up in kitchen paper and loading them into a cardboard box when I heard a horn honk outside. I grabbed my camera and notebook, swiped a bottle of *pressé* from the refrigerator and scooted out to meet my surf Svengalis.

Sebastian had already leapt out of the van, smiling hugely.

"Hi, Caroline!"

He looked so thrilled to see me, I didn't have the heart to be cool.

"Hello, Sebastian. Could you help me with this? I brought some sandwiches for you and your friends."

"Wow, thanks!"

He tucked the box under one arm and opened the passenger door. "This is Mitch, um, Staff Sergeant Peters."

Mitch Peters was a thick-set man of medium height with the trademark Marine buzz-cut. "Mrs. Wilson, pleased to meet you."

"Oh, call me Caroline, please. You're doing me the favor. I really appreciate you letting me crash your surf safari."

He smiled and his face immediately relaxed. "No problem, Caroline. It'll make these beach bums mind their manners. Right, boys?"

Then he introduced me to his son Ches, Sebastian's friend, whom I recognized from a few days back, Bill, Mitch's buddy, and another boy they called Fido, for some reason.

I sat in the front, sandwiched between Mitch and Bill, and the boys crowded into the back of the van among a motley collection of surfboards, body boards, wetsuits, and strange, shiny t-shirts that I was told were rash vests.

"To stop the wetsuits rubbing around the neck and under the arms when you're paddling out," explained Mitch. "We won't need them today—the water at this time of year is around 63°F."

I made a note of that and snapped a quick photo of the back of the van with all the boys pulling faces and flipping the bird.

"Caroline brought food," Sebastian announced happily.

They must have all been starving because the rolls evaporated like water in the desert, and the *pressé* was passed around between them. I was sure I could have brought twice as much food, and it would have disappeared the same way.

We drove across the spectacular Coronado Bridge, then headed south, stopping occasionally for a surf check.

Mitch explained that they were looking for a steady swell and offshore breeze to hold up the waves, the best conditions for producing long, workable rides.

In the end, Mitch pulled up at the side of the road near Cays Park and the boys spilled out of the back, their reckless enthusiasm catching. Mitch and Bill were somewhat more circumspect, but I couldn't tell whether that was because of their seniority, or because I was inhibiting them from the whole male-bonding ritual.

"Just forget I'm here," I added, somewhat helplessly. "I'll just watch and soak up the vibe."

"Yes, ma'am," said Bill, smiling at me, as he tugged off his t-shirt to reveal a barrel chest, thickly coated with reddish-brown hair.

Out of the corner of my eye, I saw Sebastian scowl at him, yanking off his own t-shirt. His skin was the same beautiful, golden color that I remembered, but I hadn't noticed before how well muscled he was. All those hours of surfing had left him with long, lithe muscles, and a marvelously toned body. In fact all of them were in great shape. I wondered if I should get into surfing, although 63°F didn't sound that warm to me.

Mitch handed Sebastian a garish red and yellow board, smiling kindly. It was then I remembered that Sebastian's own father had destroyed the blue surfboard I'd first seen him with.

I took some more snaps as they posed for the camera, and then watched as they sprinted into the water and paddled out beyond where the waves were breaking. I knew from my half-hour of research that this was called the line-up. They sat there, a gaudy flock, waiting for their wave. As the swell approached, they all started paddling, their arms stroking through the sea, the green water lifting them up, they raced down the shoulder of the wave, so graceful, so powerful. It took my breath away to watch them. Then, inevitably, the wave broke and they all dived off in different directions, bobbing to the surface seconds later.

After I'd watched for a while, Sebastian caught a wave that carried him into the beach, and he jogged over to join me, flicking his hair out of his eyes, skin glistening.

"You finished already?"

"I thought it might help if I explained some more—for your article."

"That would be great—it all looks kind of the same to me."

He laughed lightly. "Not really. See, Mitch is using a long board with a rounded nose. He can work the smaller waves with that, and do some hippy shit like hang ten. Ches is riding a short board, so he can slash across the wave, catch some air and do the more radical stuff."

I had no idea what he'd just said to me—it was like learning a foreign language, but for some reason his words made me smile.

"What sort of board do you have—have you borrowed?"

"This is a short board, a thruster, same as Ches and Fido. See how fast they're going there? You can't do that on a long board."

I began to see what Sebastian meant about the surfing styles as he patiently pointed out the differences, then named and described the different maneuvers. I made copious notes and was pretty sure I could turn this into a workable article.

"How many guys on the Base surf?"

"Quite a few: once you've got your board, the ocean is free. You can be an individual out here—you know, different from military stuff."

I understood what he meant immediately: there were no rules out here, no regulations, no one barking orders at you.

"Well, there are some rules," Sebastian said, seriously. "First, you don't drop in and steal someone's wave. That's bad etiquette. The guy who takes off first—that's his wave."

"And the second?"

"You go help anyone in trouble."

Obvious, when you think about it.

"Sebastian, don't let me keep you from your friends. I'm quite happy to sit here and watch."

He shook his head and looked at me intently.

"I can surf anytime, I'd rather be here with you."

I stared down at my notepad, unsure what to say, but absolutely certain that if I looked up I'd be caught in the net of his blue-green gaze. But I also needed to be clear.

"I wish you wouldn't say things like that, Sebastian. I'm a married woman. It makes me ... uncomfortable."

I still hadn't been able to look up. I dug my toes further into the sand, as if burying one small part of my body could hide me from him.

"I really like you, Caroline," he said softly.

I felt his hand touch my arm, he was trembling.

I had to look up. His face held such an expression of longing, mixed with anxiety. I slid my sunglasses from my hair to cover my face and stood up, abruptly.

Walking along the beach and breathing deeply helped restore some of my stolen equilibrium.

Why the hell did he have such an effect on me?

But I knew why: I was attracted to him. He was beautiful and sweet and kind —and he liked me. I had no idea why. I mean, I was nothing special—just an insipid, boring woman who lived down the road from him. What on earth was there to interest someone like him?

Why had he touched me like that? He said he *liked* me—what did that mean? What did he want?

I was irritated with myself as I stalked up the beach. It was beyond ridiculous. *I* was beyond ridiculous.

He's just a kid. Write your damned article and you won't see him again.

The thoughts were a warning siren blaring through my skull.

I was relieved when Mitch paddled toward the shore. I made certain I asked him endless questions, about surfing being so resolutely non-military and a way for Base personnel to relax. I wasn't giving anyone else a chance to talk to me—certainly not Sebastian.

"Well, the thing is, Caroline, there's just *no point* to surfing," said Mitch thoughtfully. "It isn't like skiing, you can't use it for anything. You might get military skiers like they have in those Nordic countries, but the military doesn't have any use for surfing. Plus there's a certain kind of rebelliousness to surfers. Call it individualism or what you will, but some people sure don't like it."

"Donald Hunter?" I said quietly.

Mitch's eyes narrowed and he looked around quickly to make sure Sebastian couldn't overhear him.

"He'd be on the list," he said shortly.

I knew better than to pursue that line of questioning.

I glanced at my watch and realized with horror that it was already 6 PM. I couldn't believe how the time had flown. David would be on his way home, he wouldn't be pleased to find an empty house. With a sinking feeling I realized that he'd also loathe the fact that I'd been spending time with a non-commissioned officer. He felt it reflected badly on him in some way.

"You okay, Caroline?" said Mitch. "You look kinda worried."

He was too observant.

"Oh, not really. I just realized how late it had gotten. Enjoying myself too much." I gave him a weak smile. He understood me instantly.

"We'll get you home, on the double," he said good-naturedly.

He yelled toward the ocean, parade-ground loud, and gave the time-honored time-out signal.

Ches was the last to surf in, complaining bitterly that he just wanted to catch one more wave.

"We've got to get Mrs. Wilson home," said Mitch, looking pointedly at his son.

The look and his tone was enough.

We walked back to the van together, Sebastian unnaturally quiet, while the rest analyzed the afternoon's surf, talking about tubes, green rooms and wipe outs. I turned my back while they peeled off their surf-shorts and dried themselves with old beach towels, pulling on t-shirts and jeans for the drive back.

I could barely listen to their cheerful banter, tension filling me up like an overflowing drain. I did manage to pull myself together enough to ask Mitch if he would read through my article once I'd written it.

"Oh no!" he shook his head laughing. "I don't do words, Caroline, not reading and writing words. You should ask one of the boys—that's more their thing."

"Sebastian will do it," said Ches, throwing a teasing look at his friend.

Fido snickered quietly while Sebastian scowled.

"Okay with you, Seb?" asked Mitch, restoring order swiftly.

"Sure," said Sebastian quietly. "Whenever you like, Caroline."

I felt bad, he looked so miserable, but better like this than ... I couldn't bring myself to think of the alternative.

Twenty minutes later Mitch dropped me off. I raised my hand in a quick wave and sprinted to the house. The small burst of speed didn't make any difference because David's Camaro was already parked in the driveway.

I fished in my beach purse for the key and tentatively unlocked the door.

"Caroline?"

Who else?

"Hello, David. Sorry I'm late getting home."

He was waiting for me at the kitchen table. He didn't look happy—irritation rolled off him in waves.

"Where have you been? Your car was parked out front."

"Sergeant Peters gave me a ride. He was helping me out with an article I'm writing for *City Beat*."

"Peters? Which one is he?"

"Um, he lives out on Murray Ridge. He's a Staff Sergeant. His wife is Shirley."

"You know I don't like you mixing with the non-coms, Caroline," he said, with finality. "When will you understand that it undermines my authority if my wife hobnobs with the enlisted men—and their wives?"

"I'm sorry, David, but he really was very helpful. He..."

"I'm not interested in your excuses, Caroline."

I felt the control on my temper starting to slip.

"I'm not making excuses. I'm very grateful for Staff Sergeant Peters' help today."

A chilly silence descended.

"I'll go make supper," I muttered.

"Don't bother," he said sharply. "While you were absent, I made other arrangements. I'm meeting one of my colleagues in the mess. Don't wait up."

He strode out of the house and I heard the Camaro screech down the road.

I knew what this meant: David was going on one of his rare drinking binges. He'd probably be falling out of a taxi at two in the morning, breathing his beery fumes in my face.

I was glad when he went, but I knew I'd have to face his wrath at some point.

I tried to settle down and type up my notes, but the yawning absence of his disapproving presence made me restless.

It was starting to get dark, with stars appearing in the east. I dug a coat from the closet, pulled on some sneakers and headed out for a walk.

I took a circular route, wandering toward the park, when I realized that it might not be the most sensible place to be as darkness approached. I looked across and could see a man sitting on one of the benches, his sweatshirt hood pulled over his head.

I was alert but not overly worried, not yet. The quickest way home was to walk past. I debated whether this was the smart thing to do and, in the end, decided that as he wasn't looking at me, I'd risk the most direct route.

As I got closer I realized the silent figure was Sebastian. What was he doing out here by himself? I almost walked past. I really didn't need another uncomfortable encounter with him. I had enough on my plate dealing with David's petulance. But he looked so alone, that I decided to risk a quick word and make sure he was okay. I wondered if he'd had another fight with his father. I hoped it wasn't because of me again. Or, rather, because of the surfing.

"Sebastian?"

His head jerked up and he looked directly at me before dropping his eyes to the ground.

I gasped. He had a bruise across one cheek, and his lower lip was split.

"Oh, my God! Are you all right?"

What a dumb question. Any fool could see he wasn't all right.

"What happened?"

He didn't answer, but hunched his shoulders and carried on staring at the ground, as if the answer would spring from between the scraggy blades of grass.

Without any conscious decision, I raised my hand and lifted his head carefully.

He jerked his face away. "Don't look at me," he whispered.

"Did your father do this to you?"

He nodded, and a slow burning anger began to build in me.

"Sebastian, let me see. I want to make sure you're not hurt too badly."

"I'm okay," he said in a hollow voice. "I've been hurt worse than this."

The pain in his voice was more than I could bear.

I stroked his face and felt tears beneath my fingertips.

"Don't cry, Sebastian. It'll be okay."

I didn't feel any force behind my words, we both knew they were empty.

I walked around to stand in front of him. Finally he looked up and met my eyes.

"Come back to the house. I'll fix you up and drive you home. Okay?"

My words seemed to sink in slowly. He stared for a moment longer, then stood up.

He walked as if dazed, in silence, unseeing. Twice I had to stop him before he plowed into the road at an intersection. His behavior was starting to make me really worried.

When we finally got back, the house was dark. I was intensely grateful for David's continuing absence, I was certain he would have insisted on phoning Sebastian's parents had he been there—and no way would anything good result from that.

I opened the door, switching on lights as I went and led him into the kitchen. I pulled out a chair and, after a moment's hesitation, he sat down.

I had to search through several drawers before I could remember where I'd put the antiseptic cream. More urgently, I needed a cloth to fill with ice to try and take down some of the swelling. I smashed the ice tray on the counter and saw Sebastian jump.

"Oh, sorry!" I said softly. He still didn't speak.

Gently, I placed the ice pack against his cheek and lifted his hand for him to hold it in place.

I pulled down the hood of his sweatshirt and an involuntary gasp escaped. Someone—Donald, I guessed—had hacked off chunks of Sebastian's hair.

"Your father?"

He nodded, his eyes flicking to mine briefly, then away.

Fury coursed through me.

"Because of the surfing?"

He closed his eyes and nodded again.

"Because of me?" I said, my voice a whisper.

His eyes blinked open. "No, it would have happened anyway. I'd already planned to go out with Ches and Mitch today. It's not your fault..."

But it felt like my fault—I felt guilty.

"Do you want me to fix it for you?"

He didn't seem to understand my question.

"Do you want me to turn it into a buzz-cut?"

It was the only viable option, short of shaving his head completely.

"Okay."

I led him upstairs, through the bedroom and into our bathroom, pulling out a chair for him to sit facing the mirror.

"I don't want to look at myself," he said, angling the chair away so he couldn't see his reflection.

David's shaver was in the cupboard. I'd trimmed up his crew cut many times and for once I was grateful that I could perform this simple task well.

The buzzing sound filled the small room as I ran the shaver over Sebastian's head. His sun-bleached hair fell to the floor in unhappy clumps. When I'd finished I took my towel and dusted away the small hairs frosting his face and neck.

He looked older, harder, and I didn't know if this was simply the result of his new haircut or something resolving inside him.

"All done," I said hoarsely, unshed tears making my voice rough.

His head sank to his chest as if a great weight pulled it down. I was desperately tempted to run my fingers over his short, soft hair, to soothe him in some way.

"It'll be okay," I murmured pathetically.

He looked up, his eyes meeting mine. "Will it?"

"Yes. When you leave home. You won't have to see him again—either of them."

He nodded slowly, as if the thought were difficult to process.

"Would you like me to get the ice?" I said gently.

He shook his head.

"Let me look."

Gently, I lifted his chin so I could examine his cheek, the bruise was coming through darkly but his swollen lip was looking better.

Then he laid his hand over mine and I felt the shock of his touch surge through me.

"Please don't," I whispered. But there was no force behind my words.

He stood, still holding my hand.

"I love you, Caroline."

He spoke softly but the words were clear, spoken without expectation and with little hope. His eyes were wide with anxiety and I could see the rapid rise and fall of his chest beneath the sweatshirt.

Whether it was these simple words, or the look on his face, his vulnerability, or my weakness, I couldn't say.

I lifted my empty hand and stroked his cheek, then ran my fingers over the fine bristles of his hair and around to the back of his neck, pulling his head toward me.

His lips were warm and soft and a small whimper escaped me as he increased the pressure against mine.

Tentatively I let my tongue explore, gently probing his split lip, and he opened his mouth gratefully. I felt his tongue enter and desire swept through me, fanned from small flames into a raging forest fire, greedy and unstoppable. I gripped his neck with my free hand and slid my fingers from his cheek, down his throat, to his chest.

His hands hovered over my waist, and then locked themselves around me, pulling me tight, closing me in.

Every piece of my carefully constructed restraint was washed away in the flood of unfamiliar sensations.

Abruptly, I pulled back from him, my heart thundering, caged by my ribs. Fear reflected itself in his eyes and his arms hung rejected at his sides.

Could I have stopped at that point? Perhaps. A very weak, stillborn perhaps.

I was married, yes, but it wasn't much of a marriage. Everything I did or said seemed to irritate David—his habitual expression was a frown of sour discontent, a tone of annoyance whenever he spoke to me—perhaps even dislike. If there had once been love between us, it was long gone.

Uncertain of so many things about myself, about my life, I knew that I wanted Sebastian. I wanted him very badly.

My hands fastened around the hem of his sweatshirt, my intention clear. Amazement flickered across his face, followed by a heated passion that I'd never seen, never experienced before.

He raised his arms willingly and I pulled the sweatshirt over his head, letting it drop where it may.

His white t-shirt hugged his chest snugly, and I indulged in a moment of sheer pleasure, feeling his muscles through the fabric beneath my bold fingers.

I let my hand drift down to the material's edge and gently skated my fingers over the smooth, warm skin of his stomach.

He inhaled deeply and rested his hands on my upper arms, his eyes wide and wondering.

I retraced my route upwards, this time my fingers tented under the t-shirt, enjoying the ripple of muscles and the undulations of his now shallow breathing.

I stroked his skin, my eyes still fixed on his, then let my hand steal downwards toward the waistband of his jeans. My fingers drifted around the edge and a shiver ran through him.

Taking a step back, I seized the hem of his t-shirt and ripped it upwards, pulling it over his head, and kneading it in my hands before dropping it to the floor.

I took a deep breath as I allowed my eyes to drink him in, his youth, his beauty, the desire flaring in his eyes. I reached out and hooked one hand into a belt loop and let the other trace the outline of his erection, so evident through the denim.

He swallowed and closed his eyes briefly. When he opened them, I took a step forward so my breasts brushed his chest.

One hand reached up to his bruised cheek, the other an adventurer in a foreign land, continued stroking him.

Tentatively, his hands crept around my waist, so gently that they barely touched me. I pulled his face down and kissed him again. And this time he kissed me back more urgently, his tongue driving into my mouth, and I felt his hands tightening around me. Encouraged, I slipped my hand inside his jeans, and his body tensed. I could feel his heat, his nakedness beneath the denim was doubly arousing. He moaned, a long drawn out sigh of desire.

"Undo my zipper," I ordered quietly.

Fumbling slightly, he pulled down the zipper of my dress. I shrugged my shoulders, watching with distant surprise as it fluttered to the floor.

For the length of a heartbeat, Sebastian paused, and then he stepped toward me again, his hands moving from my hips to my waist, then hovering uncertainly over my breasts.

"Yes. Touch me."

I threaded my fingers through his and slowly lifted his right hand to my breast, moving in a slow circle, showing him what pleased me, letting him explore my body as I shivered beneath his touch. The sensation of flesh on flesh.

He curled his left hand behind me, slowly drifting upwards, then pressed the palm flat against my spine, his right hand now cupping my breast. He kissed me again. My own heart rate escalated and I was aware that my whole being was responding to his touch.

"Kick off your shoes. I want to undress you."

He hesitated briefly, allowing the instruction to soak into his flooded brain, then he toed off his sneakers. His feet were beautifully bare.

I pulled him toward me again and undid the button on his jeans. His eyes were huge, gazing at me with unmistakable lust. I didn't dare stop to analyze how I felt. Boldly, I unzipped his jeans and pushed the denim off his hips. I surprised him by sinking down to pull the material from his legs.

His erection was freed, and I was surprised and slightly appalled. He was so much bigger than David. I'd never been with another man before or since my marriage. I was disconcerted, knowing that Sebastian was counting on me to continue taking the lead.

I ran my careful hands up his calves, behind his knees, over and between his thighs, then let my fingers drift through his pubic hair, stroking his erection softly. It was beautiful—soft and silky on the outside, but firm, too. I'd never wanted to spend time looking at David that way: this was different. Sebastian seemed so vulnerable standing there, trusting me. I continued stroking him, gently massaging him, rubbing my fingers along his tip.

His entire body quivered, and he squeezed his eyes shut.

I stood up and undid my bra as he watched me with stunned disbelief. I took a deep breath, then hooked my fingers into my panties, pulling them off my hips and stepping out of them.

For a moment, time seemed to billow outwards as we stood and stared at each other, drinking in our nakedness.

I held out my hand and Sebastian took a step toward me. Suddenly, it was as if a switch had been flicked on inside him and he wrapped his body around me—his hands on my breasts, my shoulders, my buttocks, my thighs, his tongue in my mouth, on my neck, between my breasts, overwhelming me everywhere.

I grabbed hold of him almost violently, pushing my fingers hard against his length, I heard his breath hiss through his teeth.

I pulled his erection once again, my fingers wrapped firmly around his sweet skin. He exploded suddenly, his body shuddering. I felt the dampness on my thigh and looked down to see the pale, creamy fluid.

A familiar feeling of disappointment trickled through me. But the look on his face halted my thoughts.

Crushed by the weight of further humiliation, he shattered, falling to the floor, weeping brokenly.

"I'm sorry! I'm sorry! I'm sorry!"

He heaved out the words again and again, his face hidden in his hands.

"No, don't. It doesn't matter. It's okay," I whispered, stroking the soft, golden skin of his back.

How many times had I said those words before without meaning them? Until now.

I sank to the floor and held him in my arms, rocking him to and fro, crooning wordlessly as his sobs wracked him.

Eventually he stilled but refused to look at me.

"Sebastian, it's okay."

There was no response.

"Sebastian. Look at me."

"I'm sorry," he muttered again, his face turned away.

I wasn't sure what to do, how to show him that it didn't matter, or, at least, that I didn't think any less of him because of what had happened, or rather, not happened.

I pulled one hand away from his tear-stained face.

"Come on."

He finally looked at me, utterly bewildered.

Gently, I tugged his hand.

"Come."

CHAPTER FOUR

Sebastian looked confused as I led him back into the bedroom.

I pulled the sheets away and tried to erase the thought that this was David's side of the bed.

"Lie down."

He lay back, his beautiful eyes watching my every move. I walked around the bed to lie on my side next to him, pulling the sheet up and around us, cocooning us, protecting him.

I reached out to stroke his cheek, and his lips parted. I traced the outline of his mouth with one finger and then leaned over to kiss him, tasting salty tears.

I moved down to his throat, gentle butterfly kisses, my hair sweeping across his chest. Hesitantly, he lifted one hand, skimming along my arm to my shoulder and then, more boldly, down to my breast.

His thumb circled my nipple and I gasped with pleasure. He immediately lifted his hand away.

"No, don't stop."

I continued kissing him across his chest and down to his stomach. His hand moved to my ass, stroking it carefully.

His erection was stirring again so I kissed him there, feeling his body tremble beneath my feather-light touch.

I lay back down beside him and moved his hand to my thighs.

"You can touch me."

I guided his hand closer. Folding my fingers over his, I massaged myself with his hand, tilting my hips upwards, sucking in a deep breath when he found my most sensitive place.

"Yes, that's right. Like that."

It was pleasurable for a few moments, but I wanted more. I took his hand, folding the shorter fingers toward his palm, and slid his index finger inside me.

"Slowly. Yes, in and out."

He followed my instructions carefully, the gentle assault making me moan and writhe. I angled my hips slightly, and moved his thumb so it made sweet circles around my clitoris. I let out a long sigh of pleasure. His warm lips kissed my throat as his hand continued its steady motion.

I didn't want to have thoughts of David in my overwhelmed brain, but I couldn't help comparing ... this love-making with the selfish sexual demands usually made of me.

I reached down and stroked him, now so firm and erect. I longed to feel him inside me, but I was afraid of rushing him again.

I trapped his hand between my thighs and sat up. He looked surprised and suddenly unsure of himself. I leaned over and kissed him, more forcefully this time, rocking onto him. With his free hand, he wound his fingers through my hair and kissed me back, letting himself go further and take more.

Then he ran his hand over my breasts, and gently pulled on one nipple. The sensation was overwhelming and shocking, an orgasm taking me by surprise. His fingers must have felt the ripples of my pleasure, and he could see the way my body arched and stiffened. So unexpected, so confusing. For me, orgasms were a solitary pursuit, this was new.

"Are you okay?" he asked hesitantly.

It took me a moment to find my voice. "Yes. Very okay. Very, very okay."

And for the first time that evening, he smiled.

I'd guessed, and I think I'd guessed right, that this was all new to Sebastian, but he made me feel things I'd never experienced before—love and passion. I just hadn't realized ... I didn't know it could be like this.

"Now your turn," I said.

A quizzical expression crossed his face. Then a look of understanding as I sat up and kneeled across him. I leaned down to kiss him as his hands snaked around my back, pulling me toward him. He moaned against my mouth, and I pushed myself upright again.

This time I raised my hips and used my hands to guide him inside me. Slowly, I sank down onto him, my eyes closed, I heard him gasp.

At last I could feel every inch of him inside. I took his hands and pressed them against my belly.

"Can you feel yourself inside me?"

His face was filled with amazement.

"Yes," he whispered. "I can."

I leaned forward again, my hands resting on his chest, moving my hips up and down in a steady rhythm. He pushed his head back into the pillow, his mouth open, absorbing the new sensation. I felt his body flexing into mine, pushing himself deep inside me.

He began to move faster, more confidently, more desperately, and I let the feeling carry me with him.

I opened my eyes to find his locked on mine, almost feral in their intensity. I moved faster, meeting each movement he made, grinding down as he squeezed his eyes shut, his hands locked over mine. He came quietly as his body quivered inside me. I fell forward onto his chest, breathless and relieved.

We lay peacefully for a few minutes, and I listened to the sound of his heart, slowing to its normal rhythm. Then I slid off him and lay on my back. I think I was smiling.

I felt the bed move, and I opened one eye. He was leaning on his elbow looking down at me.

"Hi," I said, almost shyly. "You okay?"

He nodded solemnly. "That was ... that was..."

"Yes, it was."

I stroked his cheek, and his eyes closed with a sigh. Then he turned his lips toward my hand and kissed the palm. The unexpected, intimate gesture took me by surprise.

"I love you, Caroline. I always have. My whole life."

I smothered a delighted laugh.

"That's a very long time," I teased him. "You're only 18—your whole life isn't that much, really."

He smiled. "It feels like it sometimes. Anyway, I'm not 18 for another four months, I'll let you know then."

As I processed his words, cold shock rushed through me, and a look of abject horror etched itself on my face.

"What?" I couldn't believe the words he'd just said.

He looked at me, puzzled.

"You ... you're *only seventeen?*"

He nodded, his expression anxious.

"For God's sake, Sebastian! *Seventeen?*"

Shit! Shit! Shit!

He looked at me nervously. "What's the matter?"

I threw my arm over my eyes, unable to look at him. *What had I done?*

"Please, Caroline. You're scaring me."

I took a deep breath and turned to glare at him, needing to take my sudden panic and anger out on him.

"The matter, Sebastian, is that you're a minor. What we've just done ... what *I've* just done ... it's against the law. It's a felony, for God's sake!"

"But I love you."

I wanted to scream.

"Sebastian: it's *statutory rape!* Do you know what that means? I could go to prison. If anyone found out..."

"I won't tell anyone. I love..."

"Don't say it! Do *not* say it!"

sI shouted the words and he flinched.

I ran to the bathroom, afraid I was going to be sick. I held my hand over my mouth as dry heaves raked me. Tears sprang to my eyes, and I felt him hovering uncertainly behind me.

"Caroline, please."

I held my hand out like a traffic cop, stopping him from coming any closer.

What had I done?

The words echoed emptily.

"Please!" His voice was begging, desperate, but I couldn't look at him.

My skin felt icy-cold then hot with shame, as a torrent of emotion engulfed me. I staggered to the bathroom door, plucked my robe off the hook and wrapped it around me, as if the thin material could hide my crime.

I tried to push past him to the bedroom, but he blocked my way.

"Oh, God, please, Caroline!" and he tried to pull me to him.

"No!"

I made it as far as the bed before my knees gave way and I sat down, gasping.

"What have I done? What have I done?"

I hid my head in my hands and tried to fight the rising panic.

I knew he was watching me but I couldn't look. Silently, he sat down next to me.

"I'm not sorry," he whispered. "That was the best experience of my whole life. I love you, I can't help it."

And he pulled me against his chest, wrapping his arms around me, taking care of me, soothing me.

Slowly the shock wore off, and finally I was able to sit up, pushing his arms away.

"I apologize, Sebastian. It isn't your fault. Please forgive my ... behavior." I spoke coldly, formally, afraid to give way to further emotion. "I think you'd better leave now."

"Please. Don't send me away."

His voice was husky.

When I didn't reply, he stood up and walked into the bathroom, his eyes downcast, searching the floor for an answer that wasn't there. I could hear the soft rustle of material and I knew he was getting dressed.

I hurried into the kitchen, needing activity to stop my hands from shaking. I cleared away a puddle of melting ice, and threw the antiseptic cream into the nearest drawer.

Then I leaned over the sink, trying to force some coherent thought into my befuddled brain. I heard his quiet footsteps on the linoleum and, taking a deep breath to calm my nerves, I turned to face him.

The expression on his face shocked me: he looked so broken.

"Oh, Sebastian!"

And I started to cry.

Half a heartbeat later I was in his arms, my cheek against his chest, and he was stroking my hair.

"Don't be sad, Caroline, I love you. It'll be okay."

I was crying and laughing and crying. How ridiculous. Of course it wasn't going to be okay. How ridiculously happy and terrified and happy I felt.

I lifted my head, aware that I was red-eyed and hideous.

He wiped my tears with his thumbs.

I thought he was going to speak, but then we heard the sound of a car outside.

"David!"

Panic lanced through me.

"You have to go! Quickly! Out through the backyard. Go!"

He turned to run to the door, then skidded to a halt. "When will I see you again?"

"I don't know! Go! Go!"

"Promise I'll see you again! Promise me!"

"Okay, I promise!" I said desperately, staring aghast at the front door.

He pulled me to him, kissing me fiercely. And then he was gone.

Trying to breathe naturally, I ran to the bedroom, straightening the sheets, plumping up the pillows where Sebastian had been just a few minutes before. There was no time to change the sheets and I felt faintly appalled by the thought of David sleeping where Sebastian and I had made love.

I heard his key in the lock, and then remembered that I'd shaved Sebastian's hair in the bathroom. I raced in and fell to my knees, sweeping up the sun-blond hair with my hands and tossing it down into the toilet bowl.

A sudden desire to have something of Sebastian made me pick up one lock and shove it deep inside the pocket of my robe. Then I pulled the handle and watched fascinated as the rest of the hair was swirled away. I splashed some water on my face and ran a brush through my knotted hair.

I heard a crash in the living room. As I'd expected, David was drunk.

"Car'line ... Car'line."

He saw me and licked his lips.

"Beau'ful Car'line. *Bella, bella!*"

I tried to lift one of his arms over my shoulder so I could help him to the bedroom, but he pushed me off, tugging open my robe. He ran his hands over my breasts as I tried again to steer him stumbling toward the bedroom.

"Come on, David, give me some help here."

"What I'd like to give you, Car'line. C'mere."

He tried to grab me again but missed and fell face first onto the bed. He was asleep instantly.

With relief, I straightened my robe and then pulled off his shoes and socks. His uniform would be un-wearable in the morning.

Glad of something to do, I hunted around in the closet until I found a clean shirt and the rest of his spare service summer whites. The pants would need pressing.

I'd tucked the portable ironing board into a closet in the utility room. I pulled it out, wincing when a mop clattered to the floor. But David didn't stir.

I set the iron to 'hot', finding some equilibrium in the familiar drudgery.

I was appalled by what I'd done. What part of 'forsaking all others' wasn't clear? And with a *child!* Dear God! I deserved to burn in purgatory for all eternity. But I couldn't think of Sebastian as a child, even though the law defined him as such. He'd made love to me, we'd made love together.

I knew it was wrong: I knew it was right.

I'd have to leave. I'd have to persuade David to take an assignment somewhere else. But what excuse could I give? That I missed my friends on the east coast? No, that wouldn't even give him pause for thought during the length of a coffee break. That I wanted to be nearer to my mother? No, he'd never believe that. My brain was empty of further excuses.

Maybe *I* could leave? Leave David, start again somewhere else—no job, no home, no money? It was a terrifying prospect. I'd never been alone my whole life, I didn't know how to do it.

Miserable, pathetic, *whore!*

And then a new fear threatened to derail me—I hadn't used any contraception.

"NO!"

I wailed out loud, then threw a hand over my mouth. "Shit! SHIT!" David grunted but carried on snoring.

I wasn't on the pill, I had no need—David was as infertile as the Gobi desert. But Sebastian ... oh God!

I tried to organize a list of urgent jobs for the morning but all I could think was, *what if I'm pregnant?* For the briefest of moments I imagined an alternative universe where I was the mother of a blond-haired child with eyes the color of the ocean, with a husband who loved me. But that's all it was: a moment.

Plan B Emergency Contraceptive—that was my priority. At least I could buy it over the counter. I'd have to drive into the city or somewhere I wasn't known.

How could I be so stupid?

Everything I'd done in the last 12 hours had been lunacy. What on earth was wrong with me?

I realized belatedly that I'd ironed David's pants to within an inch of their shiny-ass life. I let the iron cool and tiptoed into the bedroom to lay out the rest of the uniform. David was K-O-ed. I stared down at the man who was my husband, for better or worse. I gazed for so long, my eyes were dry. How curious. I couldn't put a name to what I felt when I looked at him. Maybe something, maybe nothing. My emotional gauge was running on empty, I think it had been that way for a long time. Until Sebastian ... no. Must not think. Must not think like that.

Back in the kitchen I fixed myself a coffee which I didn't drink, and waited solemnly for dawn.

As the sun's first light filtered weakly through the windows, I had resolved nothing. Go or stay? Stay or go? The devil I knew or the deep blue sea? Go or stay? Stay or go? Endlessly repeated through the torpor of my mind.

The doleful ring of the bedside alarm made me jump. David snorted awake, and I hurried to make breakfast. He liked it hot and greasy after a bender. Luckily, yesterday's sprint to the store had furnished the refrigerator with bacon and maple syrup. I whipped up some pancake mix and put a dab of oil in the pan.

He arrived at the breakfast table with military precision and in a full-on sulk.

"Nice to see some food for a change," he muttered.

"How many pancakes do you want?"

"Two."

Silently I served him the guilty-wife special: three pieces of bacon, two eggs sunny-side up, two pancakes, syrup on the side and coffee.

"This plate's cold."

"You want me to heat it up?"

"I haven't got time for that. Christ, Caroline! Can't you do anything right?"

No. Probably not.

He left the house without a word. I wondered how long his sulk would last—nine days was the record.

Belatedly, it occurred to me that Sebastian would probably come looking for me once he was sure David had gone to work. I knew it was cowardly and unfair, and I was *supposed* to be the adult—but I just couldn't face him.

I showered on the double and ran out of the house without bothering to dry my hair, scooping up my notebook from the hall table as I passed. I couldn't say why—perhaps some atavistic memory of needing to write, from a time when life was simple.

As I drove away, I refused to look in the rear-view mirror. I had an almost superstitious belief that if I looked, Sebastian would appear. Cowardly to the last, it seemed.

I was ridiculously grateful to find an out-of-town mall with a drugstore sign in cheerful neon, the 'Good Morning Pharmacy'. *Not for me.*

The woman serving was sympathetic until she happened to see my wedding ring, then the shutters of disapproval came crashing down and I slunk out, clasping my paper bag.

I hunted for a coffee shop and sat hunched in the corner to order a double espresso and a glass of water.

The Plan B Emergency Contraceptive packaging scolded:

'Side effects may include changes in your period, nausea, lower abdominal pain, fatigue, headache and dizziness.'

I don't care! Just don't let me be pregnant!

I swallowed the pill quickly, then tore up the packaging into postage stamp-sized pieces. My hands were shaking as I sipped the espresso. I probably looked like another caffeine junkie after my fix.

I had to find a way to channel the flurry of half-formed thoughts that gushed through me. Eventually I pulled out my notepad, trying to make sense of the scrawled words and phrases. Working slowly and carefully, I started to plan my article. It felt important, somehow, that of the complete fuck-up I'd made of my life, that I do this one thing well.

I realized I'd been working for over an hour when the irritated waitress asked me if I wanted anything else.

Yes, a life! Oddly enough, that's not something waitresses served up on a regular basis. I removed myself from her baleful gaze, leaving a larger than deserved tip. *Coward.*

I hid in my car and wondered what to do next. If I went home, I knew Sebastian would be waiting for me. I didn't know what to say, and I was afraid of how much more damage I'd done.

"Are you all right, miss?"

A worried looking man in a Padres baseball cap knocked on my car window, making me jump.

I wound the window down halfway.

"Oh, thank you. I'm fine, really."

"You were sitting there for so long I was starting to get worried. You sure you're okay?"

What was it about the kindness of strangers that made me want to weep?

"I've just got a few things on my mind, but I'll be okay. Thank you for your concern. That was very sweet of you."

He nodded, smiled uncertainly and ambled off.

The car engine started with a roar, and I was soothed by the familiar grating sound the gear shift made as I reversed out of the parking space. I drove without a destination, idly wondering what problems troubled other drivers locked in their glass and metal worlds, individual and isolated. Were they pondering the meaning of life, itemizing shopping lists in their heads, or simply idling in traffic, minds full of happy non-thoughts?

The June gloom of early morning had given way to hazy sunshine as I found myself driving along a quiet stretch of Pacific coast. It seemed as good a place as any to brood. The air was mild and a light breeze stirred the stubby grass that tried to maintain a foothold among the dunes.

I kicked off my sandals and felt the fine grit beneath my toes. My thoughts turned inward as I wrapped my arms around my knees and gazed out toward the ocean. Had I reached a turning point in my life, or was this merely a blip on a long and bleak horizon? Was leaping from a failed relationship to a doomed one the most sensible action for a woman of thirty? Rationally, no. But the feel of Sebastian's body against mine, inside mine, his sweetness, his gentleness. Could I really say that meant nothing? Were those feelings so abundant in my life that I could count them worthless?

The only real love I'd known in my life had been from my dear, chaotic father. Sebastian hadn't even had that. He was hungry for love.

Could I help him? Answer: I couldn't. I would only hold him back from all the wonderful things he deserved from life. So I had to let him go.

But where did that leave me? Contemplating leaving everything I had ever known because of one ill-advised hour of passionate lunacy. If I left David, I was well aware I would have nothing, not even my reputation. I had never lived on my own, never lived on what I could earn, never lived without the say-so of someone else. The unknowingness was terrifying.

I sat and stared until I realized with vague surprise that the shadows were beginning to lengthen around me.

I unclamped my hands and stood up stiffly, watching with fascination as blood flowed back toward my white knuckles. I'd wasted a whole day and resolved little—except that Sebastian deserved better than me.

Dread settled like a toad in my stomach. I didn't know how I could face David after what I'd done. I'd got away with it in so far as he hadn't caught us, caught me, last night, but I'd never kept a secret from him before—I had no idea how I was going to start. How could I school my face to stone in the next 30 minutes?

I made it home shortly before six, his usual home-time, unsure if I was relieved or disappointed that the house stood silent, untroubled by either friendly or malign presence.

I threw myself into cooking: spaghetti alla puttanesca—tomatoes, olives, chili pepper, capers, garlic. It seemed appropriate—the Whore's Spaghetti. Odd to think I'd planned that meal yesterday, when I was still an honest wife.

Hearing David's car in the driveway brought me sharply back to the present.

Set the table. Place the napkins. Open his beer. Pour it in a glass. Wash the salad. Act normal.

"Hi, supper is nearly ready," I said as brightly as I could manage, my voice sounding shrill and insincere to my ears.

He ignored me entirely. Oh, of course, he was still sulking. That made things easier.

We ate in silence. I cleared the plates without a word. He retired to his study. Not a syllable had passed our lips.

I was grateful to him. It made things so much simpler.

To my bemusement, I was able to concentrate on writing up my surfing story that I hoped *City Beat* would publish. The words flowed and it was therapeutic to spend the evening in a happier place.

At 11PM, David exited his study and headed for the bedroom. *I wish I'd remembered to wash the sheets today. Whore.*

I observed dispassionately that he deliberately balled up his clothes and flung them onto my side of the bed, knowing I'd have to get up early to press the pants —again.

He returned from the bathroom marching with stiff, military precision in his ironed PJs. I had an almost irresistible urge to laugh.

The sheets were thrown back with disdain and he turned sharply, hauling the bedspread onto his side. How marvelously childish.

Smiling to myself, I slid between the sheets and dared myself to feel hopeful.

~

By morning I knew I couldn't put off facing Sebastian any longer. I suspected that if I waited at home long enough, he'd appear. I probably had a few minutes to dash to the store to buy milk, vegetables and candy.

I didn't linger over my purchases, but even so, when I turned into the driveway, there he was, sitting huddled in my porch. At least he was hidden from the road.

My stomach flipped over.

His eyes lit up when he saw me, and he went to stand. I shook my head quickly and luckily he understood.

As soon as I opened the door, he slid inside unobtrusively. I still hadn't planned what I was going to say to him. I wasn't even sure it was possible to plan.

We stood looking at each other, the door unyielding against my back.

"Are you okay?" he said at last.

I nodded slowly. "I guess. You?"

"I ... I had to see you."

"Come in," I said, somewhat reluctantly, pointing to the kitchen. "Can I get you a coffee?"

He shook his head.

This was harder than I'd expected and I'd barely said a word. I sank into a kitchen chair while he continued to stand.

"I tried to see you yesterday. What happened after I went? Was it ... okay?"

His voice was low, hesitant.

"David didn't suspect, if that's what you mean."

By contrast my voice was unnecessarily harsh.

Sebastian's eyes reflected his hurt.

"Don't look at me like that," I said coldly.

You can do this. You can let him go.

"Caroline..."

"What?"

He took a deep breath.

"I've been thinking about you ever since..." His words came out in a rush. "We can go back east if you like, wherever you want. I can get a job."

I stared at him, stunned.

"We can be together," he whispered. "Forever."

I didn't know whether to laugh or cry, instead I continued to sit and stare.

"Caro?"

Caro? Oh, I liked that ... what a lovely dream.

"Caro!" he said, sounding panicked.

But just a dream.

I sat at the table and rested my head in my hands. This wasn't what I'd expected, it certainly wasn't how I'd planned the course of the conversation. Where was my resolve to end this?

I heard a chair scrape across the floor and he sat down next to me.

His beautiful face, so earnest, was just inches from mine. I straightened up and looked at him directly.

"Sebastian, I think you're very sweet but..."

He cringed as if I'd slapped him.

"Give me a chance—I know we can make it work, Caro."

"No, we can't. You're only 17 ... I could be arrested. I *should* be arrested! No, listen to me! The other night was..." I hesitated, unable to find the right word. "But the point is, it was wrong."

"Not for me."

I sighed. Again I recalled the sensation of his body against mine, how good it had felt. Good, bad, wrong, right.

"Then we'll wait until I'm 18," he said defiantly. "It's not so long. We can be together and no one can stop us."

Stupidly tempting.

"I'm married, Sebastian." *You were married two nights ago. Whore!*

"You don't love him, Caro."

My eyes darted to his. *How did he know?*

He sensed a small victory and pursued his advantage, grasping my hand.

"I love you. I'll ... I'll do anything, go anywhere. You can do your writing—we'll be happy."

So, so tempting. And his touch: flesh on flesh.

My traitorous mind filled with images of our sweet, gentle, glorious love-making. I'd never been touched like that before—it had been an education, a delicious, dangerous awakening.

He could sense the feebleness of my will. His lovely eyes were unclouded, free of all doubt, confident and reassuring. And when he leaned forward pressing his lips lightly against mine, it was a peaceful moment at the heart of a whirling pool of emotions. It was an electric moment, the eye of the storm.

I tried to understand the feelings that filled me, making me lighter than air. I felt beautiful for the first time in my life, safe and secure.

Loved.

Cherished.

He gathered me to him and I clung to the protective circle of his arms, feeling the warmth of his body, and listened to the steady beating of his heart.

Had David ever told me that he loved me? I couldn't remember that far back. I knew he was cold and controlling, and I knew that he didn't love me. Sometimes it felt like I was utterly despised.

And finally my poor, starved heart caught up with what Sebastian had been saying: he loved me. He'd always loved me. Such a balm to my shrunken soul. My damascene moment hit me with extraordinary clarity.

I loved him, too.

CHAPTER FIVE

A SUMMER OF STOLEN HAPPINESS—THAT'S HOW I REMEMBERED THE DAYS THAT followed. The storm clouds gathered in the distance while my days with Sebastian were filled with light.

We knew we had to be careful. The military was a close-knit family and, like all families, the whisper of disapproval was never far away.

Daytime was easier. David worked until 6PM most days and every third weekend, but now Sebastian had finished with school for good, his time was his own. Estelle had persuaded Donald of the benefits of a college education for their only child and, as far as they knew, Sebastian was due to start at UCSD in the fall. Only his mother had reluctantly attended his graduation, Donald being far too busy to attend such a trivial event, and Sebastian had shyly shown me the formal photograph of himself in his cap and gown. My own graduation seemed a shadow in another lifetime.

The hard part was knowing that we couldn't be together intimately—I was quite clear about that. But the more I saw him, the more I spent time with him, the harder it became. He was beautiful inside and out. I loved the way he looked at the world, with such zest and enthusiasm, despite the coldness of his parental home. He soaked up every smile, every hesitant touch that I could give him. But I knew he wanted more, and so did I. Pandora's Box had been opened, and it was proving very hard to keep the lid closed. No matter how hard I tried to ignore it, the intense memory of our night of love-making was ever present in my thoughts, I was pretty certain Sebastian felt the same.

We were sitting huddled together, sheltered by a sand dune, while a short shower clouded the horizon, a picnic blanket swaddling us.

"Caro, you know you talked about wanting to go back east—did you mean North Carolina or Maryland?"

"Not Maryland," I said, shuddering at the thought of being in the same state as my mother. "I was just thinking about getting as far away from here as possible. No, it doesn't have to be there or North Carolina. Why? Did you have somewhere in mind?"

"Well," he said hesitantly, "I was thinking maybe we could go to New York City. It should be easy to get work there, right?"

"I guess."

I wasn't sure I wanted to live in a city that size but after a moment's thought, I could definitely see the benefits. For one thing, we'd be harder to track. Sebastian was right about the increased chances of finding work. But I was also rather intimidated by the sheer scale of what we'd be undertaking. I'd been there twice, and each time had quailed at the speed at which everything happened. I was afraid I'd be lost. But ... with Sebastian? I wouldn't have to face it alone. I wouldn't have to face anything alone ever again.

"I looked at some courses at NYU," he said, in a voice that was just one shade too casual to be believable.

"And?"

"Nothing, really. I just thought it would be cool—you and me in the Big Apple."

"Sebastian, I don't mind where we go. If you want to go to New York, if you've seen some courses that interest you, then that's what we'll do."

"Really?"

He beamed at me.

"Of course! It's just as much your future as mine." *Or more.*

In secrecy, we planned for Sebastian to apply to NYU with his courses starting in the spring semester. We—and I delighted in that small pronoun—would leave California as soon as he was 18 on October 2nd, and hoped to hide in the anonymity of the gray metropolis. I would, of course, find work as a journalist, and undoubtedly we would be happy.

I was swept up in that delicious dream. I couldn't fully hide my happiness, someone was bound to notice.

"Caroline!"

Donna Vorstadt's voice interrupted my happy musings in the Kwik Shop.

"How are you? Johan and I are really looking forward to your little soirée tomorrow."

My brain lurched to attention. Had she seen me arrive with Sebastian? No, she was still smiling, acting normally—unlike me.

"Oh, yes, of course! Sorry, my mind was elsewhere."

So true.

"It must have been somewhere lovely—I called your name three times!"

I flushed uncomfortably and she raised an eyebrow, but was kind enough not to pursue the point.

"David told Johan that you'll be making some of your delicious little Italian delicacies."

She glanced, puzzled, at my cart. A milk carton and bottle of olive oil blinked back at her.

"I prefer to cook everything from fresh," I muttered, improvising wretchedly.

"Of course," she smiled. "Well, I'll leave you to it. Oh, look! There's the Hunters' boy over by the cold meat counter. He's cut his hair. Goodness! Sebastian! Yoo-hoo!"

A brief expression of horror swept over his face before he schooled his features into blankness. He walked toward us, warily.

"Hi, Mrs. Vorstadt." He paused. "Mrs. Wilson," he muttered.

"Hello, Sebastian," she said, eyeing his buzz-cut. "Are you shopping for your mother?"

"Um..."

"That's awfully good of you. I wish I could get my boys to do chores around the house. They think food just materializes into the refrigerator."

I laughed weakly and Sebastian smiled, giving a vague, non-committal answer.

"Can I give you a ride home, Sebastian?" Donna offered kindly.

"No, thanks, Mrs. Vorstadt, I'm good."

She smiled. "Well ... see you tomorrow, Caroline."

"Bye."

Eventually she disappeared behind the frozen goods and I let out a sigh of relief. I didn't realize I'd been holding my breath.

"We must be more careful," I whispered.

Sebastian nodded solemnly, but there was a glint of amusement in his eyes.

"What?!"

He shook his head, a small smile escaping. "Let's get out of here."

I abandoned my few goods with the shopping cart, much to the irritation of the staff, no doubt, and headed for the parking lot. Our exit was certainly more discreet than our shopping expedition.

I slipped into the driver's seat feeling elated and guilty at the same time.

Sebastian let his fingers drift down my neck, a shiver ran through me.

"Not here!"

"Where then?"

"Let's go to the beach."

He grinned. "Perfect."

As I drove, he fiddled with the radio and picked up a station playing cool, ambient jazz.

"Mom and Dad have been on my case about getting a summer job," he said casually.

My heart sank—if he worked all day, I'd never see him. I couldn't go out in the evenings, not without facing the inquisition from David.

"What sort of job?"

He shrugged. "Ches says I could get a job bussing tables at the place he works —the country club out at La Jolla."

"That sounds ... fun."

"Mostly evening shifts, Caro. I'll still be free during the days."

I smiled with relief. "By the way, I'd like you to read my surfing article, just to make sure it's okay."

"You finished it?"

He sounded surprised.

"Sure! What else is there to do in the evenings?" I said, teasing.

He scowled. "I hate you going home to that asshole."

I sighed. "Me, too, but it's not for much longer."

The truth was that I found David's brittle company almost unbearable. I honestly didn't know if I'd be able to last four months. I'd been turning over in my mind the possibility of moving out—but I was scared and had little money of my own.

I banished the thought of David: here and now was for Sebastian.

"Which beach should we go to?"

"There's a place I know not far from here. There's a beach shack, too, so we should be able to get some food."

I smiled to myself—the boy could *eat.*

No, not a boy, I snarled.

But the part of my brain where I parked all my miscreant thoughts was getting pretty damn crowded.

We drove with the windows down, Sebastian leaning back lazily, singing along softly to the radio, while the wind tangled my hair.

Sebastian was showing me a side of San Diego that I'd never seen before— the chilled out, laidback beach community that would have given David hives.

The girl working the counter of the beach shack eyed Sebastian with interest. I watched her follow his progress around the store. She was pretty, a stereotypical California girl with long, blonde hair, long tanned legs, and long, false eyelashes. To my amusement and delight, Sebastian didn't appear to notice her.

"What do you want to eat, Caro? They've got tuna on wheat or meatloaf on rye."

"I'll just have a soda and a small bag of chips."

He frowned. "That's not very healthy."

He looked so serious, standing there in his cut-offs and surfer t-shirt, I couldn't help a broad smile.

"Then I'd better have the tuna, kind sir."

"Are you laughing at me?"

"Just a little, but in a good way. You're so sweet!"

He looked like he wasn't sure whether or not that was a compliment, but shrugged it off.

I paid for the food, irritated with myself for recalling that the money came from the housekeeping David so grudgingly gave me. To hell with it! I earned every penny: cooking, cleaning, ironing his damn pants—even entertaining his colleagues.

The cashier loaded our purchases into a carrier which Sebastian tucked under one arm, with the briefest of smiles at her. Then he took my hand.

He took my hand!

David never held my hand. Well, perhaps once—the day of our marriage, when my father had given it to him. Not since then, not that I could remember.

It felt wonderful and terrifying, strolling along the beach, our fingers learning the lines and shapes of each other's hands.

We found the perfect dune, a concave dip among the marram grass. It gave us some slight protection from the prevailing wind, although it was gentle today, but, more importantly, it gave us privacy from anyone watching from the beach.

Shyly, I pulled a copy of my surfing article out of my bag.

"This is it."

He sank down to the sand and sat cross-legged. I watched his face anxiously as he read. It was the first time I'd shown anyone my writing. I badly wanted him to like it. I felt like I'd launched a baby out into the world and was waiting for someone to tell me whether or not I had an ugly child.

Once or twice Sebastian smiled as read through the pages, then he looked up.

"It's really good."

I looked at him, skeptically.

"It is! I really liked the joke about the Hawaiian Surfers Marine Corps storming up the beach to invade, but deciding to catch one more wave first."

"You really liked it?

"It's good, Caro."

"You'd say that anyway."

He smiled.

"Probably, but I mean it. It gives people an insight into surfing and the Military way of doing things. It's clever. There's just one thing..."

I knew it.

"You've got a spelling mistake there: you've put 'truster' instead of 'thruster'."

"Where? Show me."

He laughed. "Just kidding."

I raised an eyebrow. "Hmm, imagine getting the thrusting wrong."

He gaped at me as I lay back on the warm sand, basking in the sudden heat of his gaze.

"You are so beautiful, Caro," he whispered, unwinding his long legs so he was stretched out next to me.

I grinned stupidly at him.

"You are!" he insisted.

He was leaning on one elbow, his head resting on his hand. Out here, his eyes looked slate-green and his skin glowed gold in the sun.

"You're the beautiful one, Sebastian. Beautiful inside and out."

He blinked, surprised at my words, then smiled. Another chip of ice dropped from my heart.

"I think you should kiss me."

The words were out before I knew what I'd said. I really meant them.

"I thought we weren't going to ... you know ... until I was 18."

"That's right, but that doesn't mean you can't kiss me."

"Really?" He looked delighted.

"Perhaps you'd prefer a written invitation?"

"Not necessarily," he whispered.

I wrapped my arms around his neck and pulled his head down toward me, stroking his short, silky hair. His gentle lips touched mine and desire exploded inside me, rushing through my veins like quicksilver. A soft, wordless sound escaped him, and my tongue was in his mouth, savoring his taste, tasting his own desire.

My hands ran down his back and greedily pulled up his t-shirt. My fingers turned to claws as I raked my nails down his back, making him gasp. He leaned away abruptly and tugged the material over his head, then his naked chest was pressing into me, forcing me into the sand. Against my belly, his erection was taut.

God! How I wanted him. To renew the sensation of him inside me, to understand, to feel that I was desired and loved and needed.

He forced one leg between mine and ran his hand along my bare skin, up my knee, my hip, teasing the material of my panties, before moving up to my waist and then running his hand over my breast and squeezing gently.

I was desperate to take it further but I was held back by the thin edge of reason, and the knowledge that one more step would tip me into the darkness.

"We have to stop," I groaned against his lips.

"No," he gasped.

His hand moved determinedly under the thin fabric of my strappy t-shirt, stroking and caressing my breasts.

My breathing was becoming ragged, as if I was running.

Summoning my final ounce of will power, I pushed feebly against his chest.

"No, Sebastian."

He stopped instantly, and with a soft moan, rolled onto his back.

"I want you, Caro," he breathed out. "I want to make love to you. I want to make love to you forever."

My breath caught in my throat.

I want that, too. So much.

I didn't answer, but lay unmoving, feeling my body float back to earth.

Out of the corner of my eye, I saw him adjust himself. I felt guilty for making him uncomfortable.

Hell, was there anything I didn't *feel guilty about?*

"Is this what it's going to be like for the next four months?" he said, sounding aggrieved.

"Or I could join a convent," I muttered, almost to myself.

"I'd still find you," he said darkly.

I smiled.

"Okay, no convents. Or monasteries, come to think of it."

I fished around for a new topic of conversation.

"Tell me about this job you mentioned. When do you start?"

"I haven't applied for it yet."

"Why not?"

"I wanted to make sure it was okay with you first, Caro."

I was surprised. Yes, that was the word, surprised and plain amazed.

"You ... you were waiting for ... what, my permission?"

"Well, not exactly." He sounded puzzled. "So we could discuss it together and then decide."

Oh. Like a real couple.

David never discussed anything with me, I simply received his Decree from on high.

"And you'll be working the late shift? Well, that sounds fine to me."

"Great!" he said and turned on his side to look at me, smiling. "I'll have to do some day shifts, maybe. The pay is shit but Ches said the tips are pretty good, especially from older women."

I winced and his expression froze.

"I didn't mean ... I don't think of you like that! Caro, no!"

But the genie was out of the bottle, a vintage one at that.

"It's not far off the mark, Sebastian."

He sat up, his face alarmed.

"Don't say that! I love you so much, Caro. I ... what I feel for you ... I've never..."

He grabbed my hand and held the palm against his cheek.

I sat up, too, shaking sand from my hair.

"It is what it is, Sebastian."

We sat in silence for some minutes.

I could tell he was mortified, wishing his candid words unsaid.

"So," I said at last, my tone deliberately light, "no girls at high school who grabbed your attention? No cheerleaders waving their pompoms at you?"

He smiled ruefully, relieved, I thought for yet another change of topic.

"Not really."

"Not really isn't not at all. Tell me, I'm curious."

He sighed. "They didn't mean anything."

I couldn't help laughing. "I'm not jealous, Sebastian!"

But even as I said the words, I wasn't entirely sure they were true. I remembered the hungry look of the surf shack girl and how much I'd wanted to punch her vapid smile into the back of her throat.

"What do you want to know?" he said in a resigned voice.

"It's not important, honestly, I was just curious."

He lay back on the sand, his eyes closed.

"It's always been you, Caro. The first time I saw you, I thought you were the most beautiful girl that I'd ever seen. I thought you must be a princess, like Cinderella. It's only ever been you."

I was stunned by his reply.

Yes, a fairy tale. That's what this was—a lovely fantasy. But somehow I couldn't bring myself to care. I longed to run my fingers down his smooth skin, over his bare chest, across the defined muscles of his stomach. My gaze lingered on the waistband of his cut-offs.

"What about you?" he said, his eyes still closed.

"What about me what?"

"Did you go out with anyone before ... before David?"

I didn't really want to hear David's name and certainly not from Sebastian's lips, but it was a fair question.

"I dated a few times in high school—movies, bowling, that sort of thing. I met David when I was in my senior year."

"My age," he said softly.

"Yes."

Where was he going with this?

"Did you ... did you ... sleep with him then?"

I really didn't want to go there.

"Yes."

"But you won't sleep with me?"

"Oh, Sebastian! Please don't do this!"

"But I don't understand. You were my age. You just said so. How can it have been right then and wrong now?"

He sounded really angry and he turned his head away from me.

"Please don't, Sebastian."

My voice was suddenly hoarse with tears.

He didn't reply.

I swallowed and took a deep breath.

"Because we were in Maryland and the age of consent is 16. It wasn't illegal."

"And that's the only reason?" he muttered.

"Of course!"

He paused and then said,

"Are you still sleeping with him?"

"What?" I choked the word out.

His voice was barely a whisper. "Are you still sleeping with him? Now, I mean."

This was ghastly.

"We share a bed, Sebastian, but we haven't ... had sex. Not since ... you ... since us."

I thought that would be enough, but I was wrong.

"Are you going to sleep with him? While you're still living there?"

He turned toward me, his face desperate.

"Will you, Caro?"

Appalled by the direction of his interrogation, I closed my eyes and spoke with a cold, controlled voice.

"The thought of David touching me is utterly repellent, Sebastian ... but my husband is not a patient man."

I heard him gasp.

"You mean he'd *force* you?"

Sebastian's voice was horrified. I saw rage flare in his eyes, his expression scared me.

"No, not the way you mean..."

"You can't, Caro! You can't let him! Promise me you won't let him touch you."

How on earth could I keep that promise? I wanted to, desperately.

"I'll try."

He looked like he wanted to say more.

"Sebastian, it's a beautiful day, we have a few precious hours left, please let's not spend it fighting." *Or talking about David.*

He took a deep breath. "When I think of him touching you, I just..."

"Please, don't."

"I'm sorry."

We paused, our lives at opposite sides of a gorge, a delicate tightrope stretched between us.

He reached over and pulled me to him, so I was splayed across his chest.

"That's better," he said. "You were too far away."

I smiled sadly. His words were truer than he knew. But I was where I wanted to be, in the enchanted circle of his arms.

He nuzzled my neck, the tickling sensation making me squirm.

"You're all sandy," he murmured against my throat.

"I wonder why? Could it be because we're at the beach?" I tried to match his playful tone.

"You'll have to wash it off," he said, his voice soft and seductive.

"Mmm, I suppose I should."

He sat up quickly so I was cradled in his lap.

"I want to help with that," he said, his eyes glinting with mischief.

He stood up with me in his arms and started striding toward the sea.

"Sebastian! Don't you dare!" I half-screamed, half-laughed.

"I'm helping!" he said, smiling broadly.

And he dunked me in the sea, fully dressed.

"Aagh!"

The water was shockingly cold.

"Sebastian!" I gasped, spitting out seawater, "I'm soaking!"

"Mmm, I've always wanted to see a wet t-shirt competition."

"Sebastian!" I yelled, trying to maintain some shreds of dignity as I struggled back to the dry sand. "Just look at me! I'm furious with you!"

"What are you going to do, spank me?" he said with a wicked grin.

My mouth dropped open in shock.

"I'll think of something," I huffed ineffectually.

"Bring it on!" he replied, his tone amused.

I dripped back to our cozy dune and stripped off my strappy t-shirt and summer skirt, draping them across the long grass. The material of both was thin so there was a good chance they'd dry out before I had to go home. If not, well, David hadn't looked in the laundry hamper in the 11 years we'd been married.

I turned to watch Sebastian. He dove through the waves, swimming strongly. I caught glimpses of him, silvery in the sea as he bodysurfed back to the beach. He saw me watching him, waved once and disappeared into the ocean again.

I lay back in the sand, a strange sensation of happiness filling me.

My underwear, however, was uncomfortably damp. I slipped off my bra and spread it out in the sunshine, then lay on my front, the coarse sand doing a better job of exfoliation than any expensive beauty salon.

The sun was deliciously warm on my back and I began to doze, lulled by the rhythm of the waves.

"You look so beautiful like that."

Sebastian's words roused me gently. His hands, however, were chilly.

"Whoa! Cold hands!"

He laughed out loud, a happy carefree sound.

"Sorry, I couldn't help it."

"You didn't try," I muttered petulantly.

"No, not really," he admitted. Then his voice was serious. "I want to touch you, Caro."

"I know. I want that, too. But we have to wait."

He groaned. "I'm going to go crazy!"

"And it's not even a full moon."

"I'd love to see you in moonlight," he said, softly.

His sudden change of tone made me look up. *What his words did to me*. No one had ever spoken to me like that. It was all so new, I was adrift in a sea of unfamiliar feelings, as innocent as Sebastian in one way at least.

I shifted my shoulders and rolled them awkwardly, I'd been lying on my front for some time.

"Are you okay?"

"Just a little stiff."

"Should I give you a massage?"

"I don't think that's a good idea."

"Why not?"

"You *know* why," I said, patiently.

"I think I'll risk it," he said and reached out, sweeping my hair from my neck, massaging my shoulders and back, running his strong, supple fingers along my spine.

The feelings that his touch ignited.

Then he knelt across me and pressed down with more force, loosening my tight muscles but stoking the flames that burned within me.

Without warning he leaned forward, kissing the nape of my neck.

I groaned and his weight pinned me down. I could feel the cool skin of his chest on my back, the chilly dampness of his sea-soaked cut-offs against my backside.

"Oh, hell!" he said suddenly, throwing himself down next to me and squeezing his eyes shut.

"What's the matter?" I said, concerned.

"Nothing," he muttered.

"Tell me!"

"I have another boner," he admitted, sounding embarrassed.

I laughed with relief. "I did warn you."

"Yeah, yeah." He paused. "Are you sure we couldn't...?"

I groaned again. "Stop trying to tempt me. When you talk like that ... I feel like there should be a booming voice coming down from the sky pointing a fiery finger at me saying, 'The devil is at your elbow, my child'."

"Oh, come on, Caro! Four months, I mean ... *four months!*"

He had a point. But so did I, and the thought made me miserable.

"Let's eat something," I said brusquely. "Could you pass me my bra, please?"

He didn't reply.

"Sebastian?"

"No," he said.

"Excuse me?"

"I don't want to give you your bra."

"Oh for goodness sake. Fine!"

I sat up and brushed sand off my breasts, stomach and arms, aware that his gaze was pinned to me.

My bra was still damp and my nipples hardened automatically as I slipped it on. I glanced across to see Sebastian's eyes wide and wanting. It made me feel like a goddess.

"You might want to put your eyes back in before they roll down the beach," I said sarcastically.

"It would be worth it," he said, his tone matching mine.

I shook my head to hide a smile, he really was incorrigible.

We ate our subs which, by this time, were rather warm and limp. The sweet soda set my teeth on edge. A bottle of chilled Sauvignon Blanc would have been perfect. Then it occurred to me that Sebastian wasn't even allowed to drink alcohol for another three years.

His youth and our age difference kept booby-trapping my happy thoughts. Everything had a price: every glance, every kiss, every stolen touch. It seemed desperately unfair—I didn't want to live without love. Why should I?

"Hey, where did you go just now?" he said softly.

"Nowhere as nice as here and now," I said honestly, and sighed.

"It'll be okay, Caro, I promise," he said.

Don't make promises you can't keep.

"I think it's time to leave," I said sadly. "I have to buy some groceries and..." my words trailed off.

I didn't want to taint him with the dreary trivia of my life with David.

"Okay," he said, trying hard to keep his voice neutral.

He stood up and offered me his hand. But he took me by surprise when he crushed me to his chest and kissed me fiercely, an edge of desperation in the way his hands tightened around my waist. I kissed him back, matching his urgency, the specter of separation hanging over us, our own invisible sword of Damocles.

When he released me, when I could bring myself to let him go, there were no words. Solemnly I reached for my wrinkled clothes and Sebastian pulled his t-shirt over his head, then collected up the abandoned food wrappers to deposit in the nearest trashcan.

It was a strangely domestic scene, at odds with the sudden tension we both felt.

We walked back to my car, each wrapped in the emptiness of our thoughts.

"So, I'll see the guy about that job with Ches?" he said at last.

"Yes, good idea," I murmured, trying to dispel the image of large tips from *older women*.

"Do you still want me to read your ideas for some more articles?" he said hesitantly.

"Oh, yes, please. I'll email them to you."

I frowned.

"What?"

"Maybe that's not a good idea. What if your parents saw that I'd been emailing you?"

He shook his head. "Mom doesn't know how to program the washing machine, let alone check my email. And Dad," he glowered, "he doesn't know my password."

"Well, okay, then," I said, reassured.

"What about David?" he said. "Does he read your email?"

I had a horrible thought that he probably did and Sebastian saw the doubt reflected on my face.

"Bastard!" he said viciously. "Set up a Gmail account, Caro, and email me from there."

"Okay," I said faintly.

"And you'd better turn your phone off when he's there so I can still text you, or he'll want to know who's sending messages. Then check in when you can."

I was so bad at the practicalities of an affair. I wondered absently where Sebastian had learned such expertise. But then, I supposed, with two controlling parents, evasive tactics were fundamental to survival.

He looked at me, frowning.

"Are you okay, Caro?"

I nearly laughed.

"It's just that I've never ... done anything like this."

"Like this?"

"Had an affair." I blushed saying the words.

"Don't say that," he said heatedly. "That's not how I think about us, Caro."

I sighed. "Neither do I—but that's what people would call it, if they knew."

"I don't care about anyone else," he said, fiercely. "Just you."

I wrapped my arms around his neck and leaned my head on his shoulder. I felt his body relax slightly.

"It's going to be a long weekend," he muttered, "not being able to see you."

"You could come to our soirée." I laughed mirthlessly. "Your parents will be there. David has invited all the *right* people."

"Perhaps I will," he said, quietly.

I looked up at him, horrified. "No! I was teasing. You mustn't. I couldn't ... if you were there I know I'd give myself away."

"But I could make sure that the asshole doesn't touch you," he snarled.

"Sebastian, no. I mean it."

He scowled at me belligerently.

"I'm not afraid of him."

"Stop it!" I said, trying to pull away, but he wouldn't let me go.

"I can't wait four months, Caro," he said, almost desperately.

I felt panicky, but at the same time, aroused by his need.

"We have to," I said, barely able to think coherently. "You know what they'd do to me."

He sighed and pulled me closer.

We'd survived another 24 hours, but it was getting harder.

I drove back with one hand in his. That small connection meant so much.

As was fast becoming our routine, I dropped him off several blocks from his home. I hated that moment of desolation when he slammed shut the passenger door and I accelerated away from him: it felt so wrong.

David's sulk had finally come to an end. Whether this was because he was over his irritation or because we had a social engagement to live up to, I couldn't say. It made things both easier and harder.

I dreaded the nights the most, that moment when he sank onto the bed. If he picked up one of his journals I could relax, if he didn't...

After dinner and after he'd spent a couple of hours in his study doing God knows what, evening had passed into night.

I was already in my nightgown when he strolled out of the bathroom and eased himself onto the bed. The journal remained on his bedside table. He looked at me expectantly.

I tried to ignore him and he frowned.

"Is everything ready for tomorrow, Caroline?"

"I need to go to the store in the morning for a few things." *Everything, in fact.*

"That doesn't sound very organized."

"I wanted the ingredients to be as fresh as possible."

He grunted, then moved his hand down to his dick, pulling it out of his PJ pants and stroking it suggestively.

"I'm a little tired tonight, David," I said, trying to stay calm.

"So am I. I'll sleep better and so will you. Come here."

I took a deep breath. "No, David. Not tonight."

He looked irritated. "Well, the least you can do is relieve me, Caroline."

I closed my eyes, but closing my mind to the sounds and sensations was not so easy.

When he was finished, I walked into the bathroom to wash my hands and stared at my impassive reflection in the mirror. David was already asleep by the time I could face going back. I stood looking down at him, wondering: who was this man I'd married? Why had he married me? Had there ever been love? I knew I had never felt this way before, the way I felt when I was with Sebastian. Was David happy? I knew he was frustrated by not having climbed the career ladder with the speed and success of other men. He didn't have friends, he networked with people who could be useful.

I lay awake for a long time, refusing to cry. I'd made my bed.

Saturday started with a guilty dash to the large, out-of-town grocery store.

David had enticed his colleagues with promises of fine Italian cuisine—I doubted it was his sunny personality and winning ways that made so many people desirous of attending our supper party—so fine cuisine was what I had to supply. All homemade. David wouldn't allow anything pre-prepared—he liked to see me busy in the kitchen.

I checked my phone as soon as I left the house but there were no messages from Sebastian. I decided to text while I was out and hoped that'd he'd reply quickly while I dared to leave my phone on.

Am shopping but thinking of you. Cx

I was stupidly happy when he replied immediately.

I think of you all the time x

I read the simple message three times and then, with a sigh, deleted it. Now I had groceries to buy: I had to be *that* person—David's wife.

Ninety minutes later I staggered into the house, bowed under the weight of a multitude of loaves and fishes, and unloaded all the grocery bags into the kitchen. David was doing something in his study—he was too busy and important to help me. I hoped I'd bought enough for the 35 people I was expected to feed.

At noon I made him a quick sandwich and delivered it express. I surprised him. He snapped shut the lid of his laptop as I entered, but not before I'd seen that he was playing card games. Yeah, too busy to help me. Not that I cared anymore, but it was another irritant. I realized my tolerance levels were being eroded—every moment I spent with Sebastian made the long hours with David more unbearable.

By early evening I was exhausted. I'd been standing in the kitchen all day and I felt tired and bad-tempered. David wandered in fresh from the shower and eyed the buffet table with the air of a lord surveying his fiefdom.

"You're not ready," he said, gazing at me in my flour-stained, rumpled apron.

"I've just spent seven hours cooking, David."

"You look like it."

I turned on my heel. He couldn't even bring himself to say a simple 'thank you' or that the food looked damn fine, which it did. Bastard.

I thought again about Sebastian's words: *four months*. I was beginning to think I wouldn't last that long either.

Then I saw that the dress I'd laid out to wear tonight had slid off the bed.

David would have had to step over it three or four times as he'd moved around the bedroom, but he'd left it in a crumpled heap.

His pettiness filled me with sudden fury. I supposed his childish behavior was punishment for not fully attending to his *needs* last night. Whatever the reason, I felt a small kernel of real dislike hardening in the pit of my stomach.

I showered quickly, running through all the angry words I wanted to spit in his face, words that were getting harder to bite back.

Once I'd dried my hair, I swept it up into a simple chignon—one of the few arts of graceful dressing that I learned from my mom—then slipped on my favorite, if slightly wrinkled, terracotta cocktail dress, and cream pumps.

I was applying some gloss lipstick when I heard the first car pull up outside, followed by David's hysterical yell for me to be front and center in the living room.

Tempted as I was to keep him waiting, it just wasn't worth his prima donna overreaction later. He always found a way to exorcise his pique. It occurred to me that over the next few months it would behove me to be a model wife—it would certainly make life easier, but I severely doubted I was up to the challenge. But not when I felt like stabbing him with a pastry fork.

The early arrivals were a Commander Dawson and his wife Bette, a well-dressed couple in their mid-thirties who radiated curiosity, looking at me, the food, the house, our fixtures and fittings with such avid eyes, I wondered if they'd try to sell it on the home-shopping channel.

Then four people arrived together: two single officers and a couple called the Bennetts who were friendly and easy-going, greeting me kindly and ooh-ing and ah-ing over the food.

By the time Donna and Johan arrived, the house was filling up and people spilled out into the yard, the pleasant hum of chat drifting on the summer air.

"Darling Caroline. You look beautiful, as always," said Donna, kissing me on the cheek and holding my hands. "It's so good of you to have everyone over so soon after moving in."

I felt she was trying to convey some sort of message with her words, but I just smiled and nodded, and accepted a quick peck from Johan, whose eyes were fixed expectantly on the buffet.

Donna hooked her arm through mine and asked how I was settling back into the old neighborhood.

"I hear you're taking up your journalism again," she said.

"Oh?" I was surprised. I hadn't broadcast the fact and I doubted David would have mentioned it to anyone.

She winked at me. "No secrets on the Base, you should know that, Caroline. I just happened to run into Shirley Peters and she told me you'd been out with Mitch and the boys."

"Oh, I see."

Donna didn't mind mixing with the wives of enlisted men. Good.

The doorbell rang again and I was saved from having to move the subject away from Mitch and surfing.

"Duty calls," I said, rather too glumly.

Donna flashed a warm smile and released my arm, promising that we'd 'catch up' later. I was sorry that I'd have to avoid her instead—I liked Donna, but I couldn't afford to be friends with her. Not now.

Sebastian's parents were standing at the door when I opened it, Estelle's face set in the rictus smile she reserved for social occasions, Donald muttered some platitude and pushed his way inside.

Over Estelle's shoulder, I saw Sebastian sitting behind the wheel of the Hunters' car. I was caught off-guard and something about my expression caused Estelle to turn to see what I was looking at. She smirked.

"It seems that having a child can be useful after all," she said. "Who knew? Anyway, it saved us a fight over who got to drink tonight."

"Is he going to wait outside all evening?" I asked, the concern a little too evident in my voice.

"Oh no," she said, off-handedly. "He'll come when we call him."

He's not a pet dog!

She turned away and walked into the house, Sebastian and I were left to stare at each other across the expanse of driveway.

He gave me the briefest of smiles then reluctantly pulled his eyes away from mine. I watched until the car had disappeared from sight. My heart was racing and I felt dizzy. I took a deep breath to steady myself, and walked back inside.

I spent the rest of the evening being polite and a good hostess, but anxiety strained my nerves to the point where I felt I'd scream.

"Are you all right, Caroline?" said Donna sympathetically. "You seem a little out-of-sorts."

I laughed, trying to control the quaver in my voice. "It's just been a long day. I feel like I've been cooking forever."

It was a lame excuse and I didn't think she'd fallen for it. But, thoughtful as ever, she accepted my words at face value.

"Well, I'm afraid you've set the standard now. It's all absolutely delicious. I don't know how you do it: cook, write, and look after David."

She glanced over to where he was holding court, extolling the virtues of white Port over other fortified wines. I knew for a fact he'd looked up the salient points earlier that day on the internet ... in between playing cards. David knew nothing about wine. He hated the fact that I did. Was there anything he liked about me? Oh yes, my cooking.

I heard a loud crash and turned in time to see the remains of the food I'd so carefully prepared cascade to the floor in a shower of crumbs and broken pastry.

The worse for wear, Donald Hunter had blundered into the buffet table and was being supported by Commander Bennett and one of the officers whose name I couldn't remember.

The room was equally divided between those who stared at Donald and those who stared at me to measure my reaction.

"I guess that's what you call laying on the buffet," I said, with a resigned shrug.

A ripple of laughter eased the sudden tension in the room and Donald was escorted into the yard, presumably to sober up.

Donna squeezed my arm. "I didn't know you were mistress of the one-liner, Caroline."

Mistress? If only you knew.

"Let me help you clear that mess," she continued.

Several of the women and a few of the men volunteered to help shovel up the ruined food. Not David, of course. Nor Estelle, who stood with her back to the scene her husband had caused.

"What a waste," said Donna, sighing. "I admit I had my eyes on a box of take-out."

I smiled ruefully and was about to reply when we heard raised voices out in the yard. Donna's eyes hardened, and she shook her head with annoyance. I saw her exchange a look with her husband, who nodded slightly and headed outside.

"The Hunters," she said, confirming my suspicions. "Donald never could hold his liquor. I wonder how they're getting home."

"Estelle said that Sebastian was driving them." I answered a fraction too quickly and Donna threw me a quizzical look.

"Hmm. I'd better give him a call," she said, pulling a cell phone from her purse and scrolling through the numbers.

I couldn't control the riot of emotions that flooded through me: *I would see him. Soon.*

The argument outside ended abruptly. I suspected Johan had managed somehow to calm the situation, I knew it wouldn't have been David. He was far too cowardly to go up against a man like Donald Hunter.

During a tense few minutes while the Hunters snarled at each other across the barbecue pit, I chewed anxiously on my lip. I wasn't the only one—several guests looked dubious, as if the latent violence, so evident in the couple's venomous scowls, would erupt at any moment.

For different reasons, we were all relieved when the Hunters' car drove up and Sebastian climbed out.

Seeing his beautiful face, drawn for now with a serious expression, some of the tension left me. Just having him so close, albeit untouchable, made me feel safe.

"Well, if it isn't my son and heir," sneered Donald. "Although it's not son and hair anymore, is it, son?"

Donna snorted with disgust and my hands clenched involuntarily. I wanted to rip Donald's vile tongue from his head.

"Just get in the car, Dad," said Sebastian, quietly.

I was probably the only one there who could hear the tone of suppressed rage.

"Don't fucking tell me what to do!" snarled Donald, lurching toward his son, his fist raised.

Johan grabbed his arm but Sebastian didn't move an inch—he just continued to look at his father impassively.

"Take it easy, Don," said Johan. The note of authority in his voice might have had some effect on someone who'd had less to drink.

Donald just laughed mirthlessly.

"You're lucky you haven't got a fucking useless deadbeat for a son, Johan," he spat.

"Maybe that's because he takes after his father," slurred Estelle spitefully.

"It's all your fault!" shouted Donald. "You're too fucking soft on him! You've turned him into a fucking faggot! English Lit and Italian: that's what he wants to study at college, for fuck's sake!"

Johan gripped Donald's arm and, with the help of another guest whose name I couldn't remember, steered him toward the car. Estelle wobbled after him, still throwing barbed comments.

Sebastian's expression hadn't changed, but his cheeks burned with a tell-tale flush of anger.

"Show's over," said Donna. "We'll let these folks go take a nap."

But the ill-tempered display had cooled the party mood and the other guests started to make their apologies and leave. I wasn't sorry to see them go.

I stared at Sebastian, desperate to be with him, but unable to move. I simply hoped he knew how much I wanted to.

The ghost of a smile touched his beautiful mouth and then he turned to help load his inebriated parents into the family car.

Donna joined me, watching the unpleasant display as the senior Hunters continued to snipe and bicker.

"Gee, I'm sorry about your party, Caroline."

"At least no one will forget it," I sighed, shrugging my shoulders.

She smiled. "No, I guess not. You okay?"

"Yes, I'm fine. Really," I added, seeing the skeptical look on her face. "Please thank Johan for ... well ... everything. You, too."

She squeezed my arm. "Our pleasure, Caroline. You be well now."

It was only when the final guest had left and I'd cleared the last of the debris from the kitchen that I realized how drunk David was.

"What a fucking disaster, Car'line," he said, leaning against the door frame, watching me.

"It was fine except for the Hunters' little scene," I said reassuringly. "And no one will worry about that."

"You really are stupid, aren't you, Car'line? I'll be a fucking laughing stock. At least you're good for one thing."

He tried to grab me but I dodged out of his reach.

He frowned, trying to comprehend what had just happened.

"Come here," he ordered.

"I think you need to sleep now, David," I said, my heart beginning to sprint as adrenaline flooded through me.

"What I need, Car'line, is a fuck. And you're my wife."

I tried to swallow but my mouth was suddenly dry.

He took another step toward me. I turned and ran into the darkened yard, listening to his curses, a loud crash, and then sudden silence.

Cautiously, I peered into the pool of light spilling out from the kitchen. David was sprawled on the floor and across the doorway: out cold. I breathed a sigh of relief.

I tugged at his arm, trying to pull him across the threshold so I could close the door to the yard. He grunted, but his dead weight was too much for me. I stared down at him, wondering how the hell I'd move him.

Nervously, I stepped over his prone body then ran into the bedroom to get my cell. I hesitated briefly before pressing 'call'.

He answered instantly.

"Caro! Are you okay?"

My answer was a slightly hysterical laugh.

"Yes, I'm fine, but David is out cold and I can't move him. Will you come? Can you get away? Are Donald and Estelle...?"

"Sleeping it off," he said with disgust. "I'll be there in five minutes." He paused. "I'm glad you called me, Caro."

He hung up before I could reply.

With my adrenaline rush over, my knees gave way and I sagged to the floor and sat staring warily at David.

When I heard a car outside, I pushed myself up and staggered to the door.

I opened it, and without speaking Sebastian gathered me into his arms. I leaned weakly against his chest as he stroked my hair. I felt both calmed and reassured.

"Are you sure you're okay?" he said, his voice a soft murmur against my ear.

"I am now."

He sighed then straightened up. "Where's the asshole?"

I nodded toward the kitchen and followed him into the house.

David was snoring loudly.

"Just like my parents," he said, his voice hot with dislike. "Where do you want me to put him?"

"Can you help me get him to the couch?"

"Sure."

Sebastian rolled him into a sitting position and hooked his hands under David's arms. I grabbed his legs awkwardly and together we managed to half-carry, half-drag him into the living room and deposit him on the couch.

While Sebastian arranged my comatose husband into the recovery position, I fetched a spare blanket from the closet and threw it over him loosely.

"That's more than he deserves," muttered Sebastian. I wasn't sure if he meant for me to hear.

Then he looked directly at me, such a burning, scorching look that I couldn't breathe. He stepped forward.

"Not here," I whispered. "Not with him here."

Sebastian didn't take his eyes from mine but he nodded slowly.

"Where?"

I hesitated. "Can we take your car?"

"Of course. My parents won't miss it." His lips curled with distaste. "They'll be out for hours. As well as..."

He didn't need to finish the sentence.

Gently, he took my hand and led me to the car, opening the door and leaning across to fasten my seatbelt. He kissed me softly on the lips and grinned at my startled expression.

For the first time that evening, I smiled a genuine, happy smile.

"So, where to, ma'am?"

I shook my head. "Anywhere. Nowhere. Somewhere. I don't care—just as long as it's with you."

"The beach?"

"Perfect."

We drove in silence through the night, the tension slowly mounting between us.

Fate had thrown us together: who was I to deny it? No, that wasn't right. I simply no longer cared. I had chosen—willingly, knowingly, deliberately. I chose love over law. And I didn't care.

Finally, Sebastian stopped the car on a remote stretch of road and cut the engine.

"I always wanted to see you in the moonlight," he said softly. "I didn't think you could look more beautiful."

He reached over and touched my cheek, running one cool finger down the line of my jaw.

I captured his finger in my mouth and bit it gently, teasing him with my teeth. He gasped, then held his breath, his eyes closing.

"Oh, God, Caro!"

Air hissed through his lips.

The sound was beyond arousing. I wanted him. I needed him.

I unbuckled my seatbelt and his, sliding onto his lap, taking him by surprise again. I ran my fingers over the soft bristles of his hair as he wrapped his arms behind my back and pulled me to him. I kissed him deeply, my tongue pushing between his lips, stroking his, and he returned the kiss with ferocity. I felt him hardening beneath me and I knew I wasn't going to deny him again—or deny myself.

His tongue was urgent in my mouth, tension and ardor in equal amounts, pouring out of him.

When I pulled away I was breathless.

I couldn't, damn it! I'd already taken Plan B once, I didn't want to have to take it again—especially not so soon after the last time. Was I ever going to remember the basics?

"Caro!" he moaned.

"I know. I want you, too. But we can't. I'm not on the pill."

His eyes flared and he reached for me again, then stopped.

"You're not? But..."

"No ... I ... took care of ... last time."

"What?"

"I got some emergency contraception, Sebastian."

"Oh."

It was clear he didn't know what to say to that. I dropped my gaze and shifted uncomfortably. He winced.

"Sorry," I whispered.

I tried to move off him, but he broke the awkward silence first.

"I... I have condoms," he said, his voice uncertain.

I blinked in surprise. Had he been expecting this to happen—or just hoping? I decided either way, it didn't matter. I wanted him.

"Oh, right. Good."

I scrambled off his lap and leaned back on my seat, my eyes wide. He reached inside his jeans pocket and pulled out a small pack, then stopped again.

I didn't know what to do. I knew what I *wanted* to do but I'd never put a condom on a man in my life. My uncertainty turned to pity as I stared at the stricken expression on Sebastian's face.

I leaned toward him and ran my hand up his thigh, feeling the denim worn smooth with a thousand washes, then over his erection, tracing the outline greedily. He closed his eyes and took a deep breath.

I unbuttoned his jeans, and his eyelids fluttered but remained closed. I licked my lips, and slowly tugged down the zipper. He moaned softly as I let my hand explore through his boxer briefs. Then I pulled him free and ran my hand down his length. When I looked up, his eyes were burning into me, hot with desire.

Emboldened, beyond bold, I leaned forward, resting my hands on his thighs. I took him in my mouth and moved down, taking him deeper in my throat.

He cried out softly, his hands gripping my shoulders.

I sucked gently and felt his fingers tighten, but it wasn't enough for me, I wanted more. I sat up slowly.

"I want you inside me, Sebastian," I whispered.

He nodded, wordless, his eyes blazing and naked.

In the darkness I felt around on the floor until my fingers touched the packet of condoms that he'd dropped moments before.

"I've never done this," I said quietly.

I ripped open the packet and felt the smooth, slightly tacky, almost powdery texture. I frowned, wondering what that would feel like inside me.

"I'll do it," he said, his voice barely more than a whisper.

I looked up, surprised. "You know how to?"

He looked embarrassed. "Just ... you know ... for practice. Not with a girl or anything."

"Oh. Okay." I didn't know how to respond to that. Under the circumstances, being prepared was coming in handy.

He reached down to his jeans.

"Wait, I want to see you."

I tugged at the hem of his outer garments to emphasize my point.

I saw his throat move as he swallowed and he closed his eyes briefly, then with ones swift move he hauled his t-shirt and sweatshirt over his head, and tossed them onto the rear seat. He kicked off his sneakers, lifted his hips quickly and pulled his jeans and briefs out of the way.

His skin was silver in the moonlight and I longed to run my hands over every inch of him. But, patiently, if greedily, I watched as he pinched the nipple of the condom with one hand, placing it at his tip, then, he held it firmly in place, and rolled it down his length with the other.

He looked so beautiful and so vulnerable, gloriously naked and trusting. I reached under my dress, pulled my panties down, and wriggled out of them.

Taking a deep breath, I climbed awkwardly onto his lap, facing him, and rested my hands on his shoulders. The steering wheel dug in my back and I wondered briefly if this would be easier on the passenger side, but I didn't want to unsettle him, us, with more fumbling. And I wanted him. Oh, God, I wanted him.

I ran my right hand down his chest and he shivered under my touch. I could feel his heart beating a frantic tattoo and I knew he wanted me just as badly as I wanted him. God, what a feeling.

Moving as carefully as I could in the cramped conditions, I positioned myself over him. Our eyes locked for a second, then I reached down and gripped his erection with one hand, and lowered myself down onto him.

He groaned loudly but I was lost in the sensation of feeling him deep inside me once more. I clenched around him and he gasped, a fleeting look of astonishment on his face. I gripped him again and his eyes flew open.

"Oh, God, Caro!"

I kissed him deeply and his responding ardor scorched me. He ran his hands up my thighs, bunching the material of my dress around my waist so he was cradling my ass, caressing the flesh with his fingers.

Moving my hands to his shoulders, I raised myself off him and watched with delight as his eyes closed and he groaned again. As I slid back onto him, he flexed his hips upwards and I gasped as he thrust into me.

Every nerve ending in my body felt aroused and needy and grateful. I rose and fell again, more urgently, and with each movement he thrust into me.

Sweat broke out across my body as I moved faster and faster. My thigh muscles burned from the awkwardness of the position, but I was barely aware of the discomfort. My body began to tremble but then Sebastian called out, thrust deeply and stilled, burying his face against my chest, his hands still gripping my ass.

We sat locked together for some moments before his eyes opened and he looked up at me. He smiled. It was like seeing a sunburst in the darkness, and my heart leapt.

"Caro," he said.

Then, still smiling, he closed his eyes and leaned back, pulling me to him. We lay wrapped in silence.

CHAPTER SIX

Reluctantly, we disentangled ourselves and I shuffled back to my own seat, tugging my dress down to cover what wasn't left of my modesty.

Sebastian pulled on his jeans and reached onto the back seat for his t-shirt.

"Leave it off," I said. "I like to look at you."

"Yes, ma'am," he grinned back at me.

The windows were steamed up and the car smelled of sex. The moon cast a bluish light across the dunes and the ocean was an icy gray. I shivered.

"Are you cold?"

"No, not really. Are you?"

He shook his head, a wide grin threatening to break out again.

"Are you going to stop smiling at any point?" I asked, amused.

"Nope. Shouldn't think so."

"Do you want to go for a walk?"

"A walk?" He looked longingly at the back seat and I knew what he was thinking because I was thinking it, too. But there was something else I wanted to do first.

"Yes, a walk: perambulation, a stroll, an amble, a short journey made on foot."

"Oh. That sort of walk. Okay, I guess."

He half-fell out of the car and scooted around to open my door.

"My gallant knight."

"Your anything," he said seriously. "But I want to be your everything."

Oh, Sebastian. You already are.

"I want to make love to you again," he said softly.

"So do I." It was important to reassure him. "But I want to walk on the beach with you. I want to walk on the beach with you and hold your hand and to not be afraid that someone will see us."

My smile was sad and he leaned down to kiss me softly. He wasn't the only one who needed reassurance.

The breeze was cool in the night air so I insisted that Sebastian wear his sweatshirt, in spite of my selfish desire to watch the ripple and play of his muscles as he moved.

I'd left the house in just my summer cocktail dress but luckily the car had a picnic blanket in the trunk. Sebastian draped it carefully around my shoulders.

The tide was a long way out, the shoreline stretching almost to the horizon, we wandered along the cold, flat sand, under the moonlight, leaving the footprints of lovers. I couldn't help staring up at him as we walked hand-in-hand. His strong, clear profile, and soft, sensuous lips were thrown into relief by the moon's light, he was beautiful. And for now, he was mine.

"What?" he said, looking down at me, amused.

"You're so beautiful, Sebastian. And when I look at you I feel ... happy."

He swallowed and turned to face me.

"I want to make you happy, Caro. You look so sad most of the time."

"Do I?"

He nodded and ran his thumbs across my cheeks before leaning down to kiss me.

His lips were so gentle, his kisses so sweet. I pulled him closer, wrapping the blanket around both of us so were shrouded under the moon.

Desire blazed through me again. I hadn't known it could be so consuming, so devastating, so utterly impossible to think of anything but consummation. And seeing Sebastian so desperate for me, I was aroused beyond belief.

"Let's find our dune," I said.

He grabbed my hand and started dragging me up the beach.

"I can't keep up!" I shouted at him, half-laughing, unable to match his long strides.

But he didn't slow down, instead he swept me into his arms and staggered toward the nearest dune where he carefully stood me on my feet.

"Here," he said, his voice commanding.

"Yes, sir!" I threw him a quick salute and a reluctant smile spread across his face.

"Sorry," he said. "I just really want you."

I threw the blanket at him and he caught it one-handed.

"Don't be sorry," I said. "Let's have a picnic."

"We haven't got any food." He looked puzzled.

"I was planning on eating you."

His eyes widened with shock then a dazzling smile lit up his lovely face.

"Okay," he said shyly.

For a moment the blanket floated above the sand as he spread it out, a matador with his cape.

I sat down rather inelegantly and watched him sink down beside me. I lay back and held up my arms to him in invitation. Accepting, his heat and weight pressed me into the blanket, his hands greedy on my body.

His touch was becoming braver and more confident and I celebrated in that, because I'd been the one to teach him. And there was no doubt that I was learning from him, too. I was beginning to understand what it meant to be loved. It was terrifying.

He rolled onto his back and pulled me on top so he could unzip my dress. His fingers were hasty, fumbling deliciously. He pulled the dress open at the back and ran the palms of his hands across my bare skin. I groaned into his throat and slid my teeth to his neck, biting more sharply than I'd meant.

Suddenly the dress seemed constricting. I pushed away from him, knelt up and pulled it off. For the second time in a few hours it was thrown to the ground, this time I didn't care.

I unhooked my bra and dropped it to the sand, my nipples hardening in the cool air. He sat up, his eyes wide and needy, then tugged his sweatshirt over his head.

"You're still wearing too many clothes," I said, raising an eyebrow. "I think I should undress you. Lie down."

He obeyed immediately and I knelt across him feeling wanton with need. His hands skimmed up my thighs, over my hips, crossing my stomach until they rested on my breasts, stroking them, caressing them. A sound like purring came from deep within his throat and he sat up, the hard muscles of his stomach contracting, and he nuzzled his face between my breasts. Then, angling his head to one side, he sucked my left nipple, hard. I gasped and his eyes flickered up but his mouth didn't move away, his tongue teasing me, flicking from side to side. I arched my spine, throwing my head back. He ran his nails lightly across my skin then cupped my buttocks and squeezed them. His erection was hard, trapped by his jeans, pushing against the material as if it was trying to climb through the denim to reach me.

I pulled my breast out of his mouth and winced as I felt the sharp raking of his teeth.

I sat further back on his thighs and undid the single button of his jeans. I fixed my eyes on his, wanting to savor his expression as I unzipped his pants.

He leaned up on his elbows, his mouth slightly open, his breathing unsteady.

Almost more slowly than either of us could bear, I pulled the zipper down. Then, running my fingers over his sweet skin, I bent down to kiss him below his waistband.

He tasted different, not so good as before and I realized the odd, rubbery taste was from the condom we'd used earlier. *Oh well, live and learn. Now time for the next lesson.*

"Take off your pants and pass me a condom," I ordered, my voice low and brittle.

He reached into his jeans pocket and passed me a foil packet. I rolled to one side and examined the little packet curiously while he kicked off his pants.

"Weird things, aren't they?" I said.

"I guess," he replied, his mind obviously elsewhere, as he reached over to run his hand up between my thighs and pushing his thumb against my clitoris the way I'd shown him. I convulsed so hard I nearly levitated off the blanket.

"Oh, God!"

"You okay?" he said, his voice concerned as he looked up.

"Aah!" I gasped, utterly incoherent.

I saw his expression change from concern to lust. He sank two fingers inside me, pushing slowly in and out, and continued circling my clitoris. Definitely a fast learner. My hands clawed the blanket as his other hand pulled roughly on my nipple.

"Can I kiss you, down there?" he asked, hesitantly.

I didn't really want that. David had never showed any interest in performing oral sex on me—he'd made it sound dirty, sordid—unless, of course, he was the one receiving the pleasure. I wasn't sure I wanted to start now, but I couldn't say no to Sebastian either. If he'd asked me to fly to the moon naked on the back of a broomstick it wouldn't have seemed an unreasonable request.

"Okay, I guess," I said quietly.

He kissed my stomach, running his tongue down to my navel and biting my hip bone. Then he sat up, trailing one hand down my body and crawled between my legs. He pushed my knees up and curled his hands around them before his head disappeared between my thighs.

Dear God! The feeling of his hot mouth down there, kissing me, nuzzling my pubic hair. It was a strange, alien feeling, disconcerting almost. But then he slid his tongue inside me and my hips bucked involuntarily. His hands glided up to my thighs and pushed my legs more widely open. I ran my fingers over his hair as he kneaded my thighs, unsure if I wanted to pull his head away or push him more deeply inside me.

Then his tongue flicked against my sweet spot unexpectedly, and I exploded around him, calling out, sounds without words.

I had no idea. I had no idea!

My body continued to send a tsunami of tremors through me, the most powerful and unexpected orgasm I'd ever had.

"I want to be inside you, Caro," he said, his voice tight with urgency.

I couldn't speak, I think I nodded.

He leaned over me and picked up the condom packet from where I'd dropped it, my fingers nerveless. I watched mesmerized as he rolled the thin latex down his powerful erection, his own breathing equally rapid.

He grasped himself in one hand then positioned the tip.

"Please!" I gasped.

He thrust deeply into me and groaned, my name, I think.

I lifted my hips and wrapped my legs around his waist, crossing my ankles over his fine ass, and gripped him tightly.

Each powerful thrust pushed me further and further up the blanket, and further and further into another dimension. My nails raked his back, his shoulders and biceps. I forced my eyes to open and gazed into his face, contorted, stripped bare—there was just me, just him and the endless ocean.

I screamed his name as loudly as I could, needing to voice my love for him just once.

Too quickly, his body shuddered deeply inside me, his muscles contracting, sending waves of pleasure rippling through me.

He collapsed and I pulled him tighter inside, milking every last inch of him. He moaned and lay with his head nestled into my neck, breathing hard.

After several minutes locked together without moving, he reluctantly pulled out of me, making me gasp.

I was cold without the heat of his body and I shivered slightly.

He pulled the edges of the blanket around us and we curled up together, sated briefly. I half expected him to fall asleep, it was what David always did, but I was learning that they were different in so many ways.

Sebastian continued to run his fingers up and down my arm, gently stroking my skin. It was comforting.

"Sebastian, can I ask you something?"

"Of course—anything."

I was glad it was dark because just thinking the question, let alone asking it, was making me blush.

"What is it, Caro?"

"Well, I was just wondering ... that was really ... nice ... when you ... you know ... kissed me ... down there."

He nuzzled my shoulder.

"Good."

"How ... how did you know what to do?"

His body was suddenly still, and his hand froze on my arm. I regretted my impulsive question immediately.

"It's okay. You don't have to tell me. I was just wondering..."

"It's not what you think, Caro," he said, quietly. "I've never ... you know I've never been with anyone else. I've never ... done that before."

"So, how did you know? Because it was amazing."

"Amazing? Really?"

He sounded pleased.

"Oh, believe me: I know what 'amazing' means, and that definitely qualifies."

He chuckled quietly.

"Cool!"

"So ... come on ... how did you know what to do? Or maybe you're just a natural."

I sensed there was something he wasn't telling me.

"Come on, Hunter. Fess up. Other than being God's gift to women..."

"Okay, but promise not to laugh."

"Cross my heart."

He sighed heavily.

"I looked it up."

"Excuse me?"

"Online. I looked it up. There are websites where you can ... find out stuff."

I was astonished. It would never have occurred to me in a million years.

"So ... did you just do an internet search on 'oral sex'?"

I heard his quiet laugh again.

"Kinda, yeah. A couple of years ago me and Ches were on my dad's computer when he was out, he'd only turned off the screen so when we turned it on again it was on some porno site. Someone had posted a question about ... that. I think it freaked us out at the time but I was thinking about it the other day after we ... and I just thought ... I just wanted ... if we did it again ... I just wanted to please you. I know I'm not very good at this and ... well ... after what happened that first time, I thought it might be good to ... you know ... pick up some tips."

I was so overwhelmed—not only had he done this for me, to please me, but that he was so open and honest.

"Sebastian ... I think you're a wonderful lover. The things I feel when I'm with you ... the things you make me feel ... I've never, *never* felt like that."

I pulled his mouth to mine, trying to show through my kiss that I meant every word.

"You're very special, Sebastian," I murmured onto his lips.

"I love you so much, Caro," he said huskily.

We lay quietly for some minutes and I began to drift off to sleep. But then, in a hesitant voice, he spoke again.

"Caro, can I ask you something?"

"Of course. What is it?"

My brain was happily disconnected from my body, and my voice sounded dream-laden.

He hesitated and I stroked his chest to reassure him.

"Why did you change your mind?"

"About what?"

"About us."

"I haven't. Oh, you mean ... this."

"Yes. I mean, I'm glad you did—I was just wondering why."

I wasn't sure I knew how to answer that. In fact I didn't want to be reminded that this was ... wrong.

"I didn't really change my mind: it's still ... dangerous for us, for me."

He wrapped the blanket more tightly around us as if that could protect me from the disapproval of the world.

"I was too weak to stay away from you," I whispered. "And today was so ... I've never felt like this before. You make me feel alive. But that doesn't mean it isn't wrong and..."

"How can you say that?" he said angrily, his body suddenly too still. "How can you say it's wrong? How..."

He stumbled, trying to find the words, and I gasped with pain.

"Don't be angry with me, Sebastian."

I couldn't bear it if you left me now.

"Just ... just please don't say it's wrong. I can't hear you say that."

His hands were bunched into fists against the rough blanket.

I sat up alarmed.

"I'm sorry! I'm so sorry, I didn't mean it like that but *nothing has changed.* You're still only 17 and I'm ... still breaking the law. In the eyes of the world, I'm some disgusting, depraved sexual predator ... a vile, awful..."

"Don't!" He shouted, his eyes furious.

Abruptly, he pulled away from me, his fists pressed against his forehead.

His sudden anger scared me. I was used to anger from David and it rarely touched me—but this ... I felt torn in half.

"Sebastian!"

I tried to pull his hands away from his face, but he was too strong and refused to look at me.

"Sebastian," I spoke more gently. "You asked me why and I've tried to explain. This isn't going to be easy. You know this."

I stroked his shoulder.

"Please?"

Eventually he turned toward me, although he still couldn't meet my eyes. He let me take one of his hands in mine.

"Sorry," he muttered softly.

"Me, too."

He moved gently, wrapped me in his arms again and pulled me down so we were lying, a tangle of arms and legs and coarse wool.

He kissed me with sudden ferocity, covering my face and throat with hard, burning kisses. His weight pinned me down as I ran my hands across the taut muscles of his back and shoulders.

"I love you," he growled. "That's all that matters."

I badly wanted to believe he was right, I knew he was wrong.

But I let his words, his hands and his body sweep me away. I realized with dim surprise that he'd grown hard again and his erection was probing between my legs. I wished I could just allow him to slide inside me without fear or consequence but the small, unquiet voice of reason was just about audible.

I felt his wet tip push again against my thighs. I laid my hand firmly against his chest.

"Sebastian," I said, a warning in my voice.

He groaned and rolled onto his back, then fumbled around while I waited, growing impatient.

"I can't find the fucking condoms!"

"What?"

"They were in my jeans' pocket, but I can't find them now."

What?

We scrambled around in the dark, frustration mounting. I grabbed handfuls of sand, sieving it through my fingers, trying to find the small packet.

"Oh, for fuck's sake!" he yelled suddenly and threw himself back down on the blanket.

He looked so wretched and, well, kind of uncomfortable, that I couldn't help smiling. I was really trying hard not to laugh but the situation was so ridiculous.

"Oh dear," I said, the humor obvious in my voice. "What are we going to do now?"

He ignored my tone. I really hoped he wasn't going to sulk. But I had a solution in mind.

I stroked his satiny skin, still stretched tight over his erection. He groaned and turned his eyes toward me.

I held him firmly, sliding my hand up and down him several times. His hips arched underneath me while his hands lay limply at his sides.

Slowly, my intent now obvious, I knelt at his side and stared down at him.

"Oh, fuck!" he breathed.

Well, not quite, but this will have to do for now.

Gently, I pulled his erection back toward my mouth and ran my tongue around the skin. I tried to ignore the rubbery flavor and hoped it would wear off soon. I decided to do some more wearing off using my tongue and teeth and, with great satisfaction, I watched him writhe and pant under my touch. I massaged his balls with one hand and spread my other hand out on his stomach, pressing him down into the blanket.

"Caro!" he moaned.

Hearing my name on his lips was extraordinarily arousing. For the first time ever, I really wanted to do this, to take him all the way.

I moved my mouth faster and sucked harder. I could feel him all the way to the back of my throat so I made sure I relaxed, then stroked my mouth up and down him rapidly. I felt Sebastian's hands weave themselves through my hair and with a sound that was more animal than human, he shuddered and stilled.

I swallowed quickly, trying not to think about the salty taste too much, then crawled over to curl up next to him. I was cold and the heat of his body was welcoming. I pulled the blanket around us and felt his arms sweep down my back.

As I snuggled up to him, I felt something dig into my hip.

I pulled out the packet of condoms that had gone AWOL, and held it up.

"Look what I found."

Sebastian's eyes opened sleepily. "What? Are you kidding? Oh well, that was pretty fucking amazing anyway." He laughed in astonishment. "I mean, just fucking sensational!" Then he paused, "But keep that packet where we can find it."

Now it was my turn to be amazed. "You want more?!"

His voice was suddenly serious, all humor gone.

"It could be weeks, months even before I get to spend the whole night with you again, Caro. Whereas that fucking asshole..."

I held my finger over his mouth then kissed him. "But tonight is still ours."

And I didn't want to waste the hours by uttering David's name.

~

As dawn began to leak through the darkness, Sebastian slept. His head rested on my chest and his arms and legs were wrapped around me. I could feel his warm breath on my skin as my fingers rhythmically stroked his back.

It was a peaceful moment tinged with sadness for me. I didn't want it to be over, but with each minute the dark faded, and I knew it was time to go.

I'd never known a night like it, I'd never known it could be that way. I finally understood what my dear Papa had tried to tell me when I'd announced that I was marrying David.

"You're so young, *mia cara*. You have so much life ahead of you. You don't have to decide now. See a little of the world first."

Of course I hadn't listened. Children never listen to their parents, do they? Not about life, not about love ... or what I'd thought was love.

"Sebastian," I whispered, rubbing his arm. "We have to go."

He mumbled something and tightened his grip. His reaction made me smile.

"Come on. Wake up."

"I *am* awake," he said, and to make his point he took my nipple in his mouth and tugged gently.

I swatted his shoulder even as my body shuddered with desire.

"Stop it! We have to go."

"Yep, I'm ready," he said, pushing his growing erection into my hip.

Good God! He really was insatiable, I'd always thought that must be a myth. I was very grateful that David had always been easily appeased. The thought spoiled my good mood.

"No, it's time to go," I said, feeling grumpy and turned on at the same time.

Sebastian sighed. "We're out of condoms anyway," he said sadly.

We got through a whole box of condoms? No wonder my legs felt like I'd never be able to cross them again. Yes, well used—that was the sensation. I wondered idly if Sebastian felt the same. I didn't know though, could men be sore from, um, extended usage?

I was about to ask him when I realized the sky was lighter with pink streaks glowing in the east. I sat up in a panic, looking around for my clothes, I *had* to get back before David woke up.

"What's the matter?" said Sebastian, sitting up, frowning.

"I really have to go!" I hissed, feeling angry and tearful at the same time.

"Caro!" Sebastian tried to capture my hand.

"No! What part of that don't you understand?" I snapped.

He didn't reply but his hurt expression said it all. He stood up and pulled on his jeans and sweatshirt in silence, then shook the sand off the blanket and folded it under his arm.

I'd found my dress, which looked more like a rag than anything else, but my bra was missing in action. The panties, well, I assumed they were still somewhere on the floor of the Hunters' car.

I stepped into the dress and almost jumped when I felt Sebastian's hands on my spine, pulling up the zipper. He kissed my neck quickly and held out his hand.

I took it, feeling rather ashamed of my outburst, but too anxious to apologize.

When we reached the car, I fished out my panties from under the driver's seat, shyly stepped into them and wriggled them up my hips. Sebastian was gentleman enough to turn his back during this awkward procedure. How ridiculous of me, after everything we'd done several times last night and twice this morning.

Sebastian drove barefoot, but I tried to brush sand off my feet and push them into my pumps. The sky grew lighter each minute and I was terrified that someone would see me get out of the Hunters' car or, worse still, that David would be awake and waiting for me.

Sebastian pulled up outside the house and gave my hand a quick squeeze. "Text me later? Let me know you're all right?"

I nodded and pulled my hand away.

I stumbled up the driveway and crept around to the back of the house, peeking in through the window. I breathed a sigh of relief: David was still asleep on the couch and snoring loudly.

I took off my pumps and tiptoed through backdoor, feeling all colors of guilty, but oddly exultant at the same time.

In the bedroom, everything was as I'd left it, a lipstick on the dressing table and a comb abandoned by David's side of the bed, which hadn't been slept in.

It was nearly 7AM and although my body ached for sleep, and really just ached from using muscles that had never before seen the light of day, I ignored the bed and headed for the bathroom. I badly needed to pee. Sebastian had had no qualms about wandering off into the dunes during the night to relieve himself, but I hadn't quite been able to be that free. Luckily, I hadn't drunk much during the evening, so I'd been able to hold on.

I showered quickly, enjoying the hot water on my skin, and washed off the last of the sand that had managed to work itself into a number of interesting crevices.

I wondered if Sebastian's parents would comment on his absence—or the fact that the car had been missing all night. But then again, the state they'd been in when he'd taken them home, I doubted they would have noticed much at all. I hoped that was the case.

As I dressed, pulling on a pair of jeans and old shirt, I heard David stirring next door. I didn't know how I was going to do this—to go on deceiving him, to carry on living the lie. I wondered again if I could contemplate the alternative, or could I weather the next four months.

I took a deep breath and walked into the living room. David peered at me through bleary eyes, grunted and rolled into a sitting position.

"Coffee?" I said, a little too brightly.

He eyed me suspiciously. "Where have you been?"

"Showering," I said, breezily.

My hands shook slightly as I put the water on to boil.

"Bacon? Pancakes?"

From the corner of my eye I saw David pull a face and he didn't reply. I couldn't help feeling a sharp sense of satisfaction that he was suffering with a hangover. If things ran true to form, he'd spend the rest of the day in his study.

I hoped Sebastian would be able to get a couple of hours sleep—he started his new job today. It was only bussing tables at a country club outside of La Jolla, but it would keep him out of his parents' way and meant he'd eventually have enough money to buy a car—especially if tips kept up, as Ches had promised.

I had the interesting task of cleaning the house and erasing the evidence of occupation so it would pass David's undoubtedly close inspection later on.

The day dragged almost unbearably. The only bright side was that David stayed out of my way. I managed to send Sebastian a quick text halfway through the morning. David was in the shower and I was vacuuming his study. I had just a few minutes.

I'm ok. Hope all good with you?

I waited anxiously for his reply but my cell stayed ominously silent. When I heard David dressing in the bedroom, I turned it off.

Throughout the day, I checked it intermittently, my anxiety increasing with every hour that passed. I finally got a reply late in the evening.

Sorry, baby. Got called in to start work early. Weird place! Tomorrow? Please say yes

He called me 'baby'!

I wondered why the place was weird. Yes, tomorrow. God, that seemed a long time from now.

I felt better after reading his message, but was sad that I had to delete it immediately. But my sense of well-being evaporated when it was time to go to bed. With my husband.

I was reading a book: well, I was trying to concentrate but the words swam in front of my eyes. I switched off the light and turned on my side, hoping this would protect me. My breathing was shallow and I tried to slow it down to appear as if I were really resting. I felt the bed shift and couldn't help holding my breath. David leaned over and ran his hand over my hip.

"Not tonight, David," I said, trying to speak naturally. "I'm tired. Last night was very late."

Especially for me.

"You're not menstruating—what's wrong with you?"

"Nothing. I'm just tired."

"Hmm."

He didn't say anything else but rolled to his side of the bed. I breathed slowly. Soon he was snoring, but it was much later when I was able to relax enough to sleep.

I was awake before the alarm—occasionally David liked to be jerked off before breakfast and I wanted to avoid that particular scenario.

I made sure his uniform was laid out, coffee was waiting, bacon and pancakes delivered with military precision on a hot, fucking plate.

But it wasn't enough to earn sos much as a 'good morning', he was making it very easy for me to leave him.

As soon as he was out of the house, I texted Sebastian.

Meet you at the park—30 minutes?

He texted back seconds later.

Not soon enough but I'll be there

My heart lightened immediately.

I ran into the bedroom and dug out the knee-length floaty skirt and strappy top that I'd planned to wear. I'd shoved my hair into a ponytail before breakfast, but now I shook it out and brushed it vigorously. I'd noticed that Sebastian liked to run his hands through it when we made love.

I didn't bother with colored lipstick, just a little gloss, as I wasn't planning on wearing it for long. Just thinking about kissing Sebastian made my heart race ... and other things. Yes, I definitely felt a little moist—best to concentrate on finding sandals that matched.

He was waiting for me. I'd barely stopped the car before he was opening the door and climbing in, a huge smile on his face.

"Hi!"

His eyes glowed with love and something darker. He took my breath away.

"Hi!" I grinned back at him. "So, where do you want to go?"

I pulled out into the road, happiness flooding through me.

"I don't care. Anywhere, as long as it's with you."

"Should we go to our coffee shop in Little Italy?"

He raised his eyebrows. "That's a little public for what I had in mind."

"Which is?" I asked innocently.

He smiled wickedly and without speaking leaned across to bury his head in my lap, biting me softly through the thin material of my skirt and running his hands along my bare legs and up to my panties.

"Sebastian! I'll crash!" I whimpered.

He let his fingers stray a little further and I gasped. Then he sat up slowly, leaving my skirt bunched up around the tops of my thighs.

My breathing had accelerated and my hands were clenched into fists on the steering wheel.

"That was really stupid and reckless!" I said, my voice shaking. "I could have had an accident."

"You were fine," he said, arrogantly.

I shook my head, really rather angry with him.

He just grinned.

Two could play at that game.

I stopped the car, letting it rest at a crazy angle, half-on and half-off the curb. I got out, standing with my hands on my hips.

"Caro?"

He looked at me anxiously then came and stood next to me, worried that he'd really upset me.

I passed him the keys.

"You drive."

"Okay," he said softly, still concerned.

Without speaking, we got back into the car and he pulled away from the curb. I let him drive a short distance before I reached over and squeezed his balls, hard.

The car swerved across the lane and the truck behind honked loudly.

"Fuck!"

"Not so easy to concentrate, is it?" I said.

I'd just contributed an important lesson to his portfolio of life skills and safety while driving. They should cover it in Drivers' Ed.

Sebastian glanced at me then, as we passed a weed-covered, overgrown and empty lot, he pulled over suddenly.

He cut the engine and the sudden silence whispered out between us.

I felt a tremor of apprehension—I had no idea what he was going to do.

"I have a whole box of condoms."

His voice was quiet but his eyes were blazing. I think my mouth dropped open. *Another whole box? Wow!*

Two long seconds ticked by as we stared at each other. I don't know who moved first, but suddenly we were tearing at each other's clothes.

"Back seat!" I gasped.

I clambered over the seats and felt him bite my ass. Then he forced me down onto the seat, tugging his t-shirt over his head. I ran my hands greedily over his chest and stomach, then pushed my right hand into his jeans pocket and pulled out the condom packet. It was still wrapped in cellophane so I used my teeth to rip it open. It exploded apart and condoms showered down around us.

Sebastian caught one and kneeled up, tearing the foil. I yanked down his zipper.

"Ow! Careful, Caro!"

"Sorry," I breathed. "Let me kiss it better."

There wasn't much room to maneuver in the backseat but I managed to take him briefly in my mouth before he pulled back and shook his head.

"Caro, I'll come in about three seconds if you do that—and I want to be inside you."

"Okay, but let me do the condom, you have all the fun."

He stared at me as if he couldn't believe what I'd said, but passed me the little piece of latex. I pinched the nipple like I'd seen him do and then carefully rolled it all the way down to the hilt. It didn't seem to want to stay in place so I tried tugging it.

Sebastian pushed my hands away, groaning loudly.

"Fuck, Caro!"

The slippery little sucker wouldn't stay put but Sebastian eventually wrestled it into submission, pulling it down. Seeing him touch himself like that drove me crazy.

His eyes were wild as I grabbed his jeans and dragged them down, running my hands over his firm ass-cheeks.

He groaned louder then clawed at my panties, tugging them roughly down my trembling legs. They were still hooked over one sandal, waving like the flag of a defeated army when he plunged into me.

He buried his head in my neck and I clutched him inside and out.

"Ssh, Sebastian. Let me feel all of you."

He drew back slowly and I clenched tightly, making him moan again.

"Yes, like that," I breathed, running my nails over his back.

Twice more he moved inside me slowly, luxuriously, letting me enjoy the delicious sensation, watching my face as I gazed at his. Then he squeezed his eyes shut.

"I can't! I can't!" he moaned. "Please, Caro!"

Without waiting for my reply he started pounding into me. I felt his whole body stiffen suddenly and he cried out softly.

For a second I felt his full, crushing weight, then he propped himself up on his elbows and kissed me deeply, lovingly.

I stroked the short, soft bristles at the back of his head then ran my hands down the length of his spine.

"Sorry," he said, at last, looking shamefaced.

"What for?" I was genuinely confused.

"Well, mostly because I wanted that to last longer for you ... but for nearly making you crash, too. Although you got me back."

I smiled up at him. "Consider it a life lesson, Sebastian."

He kissed me again. "I like your lessons, ma'am."

"Don't call me 'ma'am'," I grumbled at him. "That makes me feel even older."

He silenced me with another kiss then pulled out carefully.

His face was suddenly chalky under his tan.

"What?" I said, struggling to sit up.

"I can't find the condom!" he said, gazing at me in panic.

"What do you mean you can't find it?"

"I mean ... it's not here!"

He pointed to his erection which was still very worth looking at. But he was right: no condom.

"It must have come off when you pulled out," I said, not feeling too worried yet.

"I think ... I think it must be still inside you!" he said, shock and horror mingling on his face.

Oh, what?

"Just ... just close your eyes, Sebastian," I ordered.

"What? Why?"

"Just do it!"

I wasn't going to go searching around *up there* with him watching. But search as I might, I couldn't find anything that felt rubbery.

My cheeks must have been a brilliant, flaming red.

"I think I'm going to need the ladies room," I muttered quietly.

"Do you want me to...?" he offered.

"No!" I said quickly.

But I couldn't help a small laugh escaping.

"What?" he said, half-relieved, half-puzzled.

"We never seem to get a break, do we?" I sighed.

He pulled a face, twisting his mouth into the semblance of a smile. "Other than meeting you in the first place, not really, no."

He finished buttoning up his jeans and gallantly passed me my panties.

"Thanks," I said, a wry expression on my face.

"At your service," he said, trying to stifle a smile.

At this point I decided I was going to have to start taking the contraceptive pill—I couldn't afford anymore fuck-ups, so to speak.

Sebastian drove a couple of miles down the road and we found a mall that had a restroom.

"Are you sure you don't want any help with the ... um ... situation?" he said, a salacious gleam in his eye.

"No, thank you," I said primly.

He laughed and I stalked off to the restrooms.

It was some minutes before I was able to locate the missing condom. Who would have thought it could disappear so far ... um ... up. At this rate I was going to have dreams about my ovaries being tied in knots by miscreant latex.

When I finally emerged, Sebastian was wearing an expression of dismay. His face cleared instantly when he saw me.

"Everything okay?"

"It's all in hand," I smirked at him.

He squeezed my fingers and whispered, "Next time, *I* want to play hunt the rubber."

I shook my head in disbelief. "Can we please go and get that coffee now?"

He draped his arm around my shoulders, possessively. "Sure, baby."

God, he made me feel like a teenager. Except that I wasn't. I banished the thought and we headed off to Little Italy.

Papa Benzino kissed me warmly on both cheeks and swept Sebastian into a huge bear-hug, which he returned a little shyly. Mama B came running from behind the counter, dabbing at her eyes with an apron as if we were her long, lost family. They chattered away in Italian and I could tell that Sebastian was picking up more of the conversation than before. Perhaps I was doing him some good after all.

The *nonna* issued forth from her room over the shop and held my cheeks while she kissed me and told me I was glowing with love. Then she slapped Sebastian on the chest, felt his biceps and winked at me, repeating something that translated as, 'a fine lover is like a good salami' and threw me a knowing look.

Sebastian blushed, whether from her words or her touching, I couldn't say, but it made me laugh out loud and he gave a grin that was embarrassed and amused at the same time.

A crowd of people on their lunch break came in to order food, sending the family scampering back to work, so we sat outside under a sun umbrella and sipped our coffees: espresso for me, regular for Sebastian.

"You didn't tell me how your first day at work went?"

"Oh, that," he said frowning.

"Was it bad?" I said, surprised.

"It ... well, it wasn't really what I was expecting," he muttered, and for some reason he looked embarrassed again.

I rubbed the tip of my finger over his hand. "Tell me."

"No, it's just dumb."

"Sebastian, you just watched me go fishing for a stray condom, it can't be any dumber than that!"

He smiled wryly. "Yeah, that was pretty funny!"

"It won't be funny if I get pregnant." I reminded him.

He gaped. "Could you?"

"Well, of course I could, but don't worry, I'm going to take care of it. I've decided it's going to be safer to start taking the Pill. I can't afford any more ... accidents."

Sebastian looked totally out of his depth at this sudden conversational segue. I steered us back to less controversial topics.

"You were saying about your first day at the country club?"

He frowned again, and I could tell he was wondering whether or not he should pursue the more serious subject. He shook his head and chose to follow my lead.

"Well, I thought I'd just be bussing tables but ... they wanted me to do other stuff, too."

"Like what?"

He hesitated, drawing patterns on the palm of my hand with his index finger.

"Sebastian?"

"It's just kinda lame."

"Tell me anyway, I won't tell anyone," I said, raising an eyebrow.

"They had me waiting tables," he said finally. "Carrying food and drinks."

"Okay. That doesn't sound so bad. And...?"

"I had to wear a uniform."

"That wasn't a surprise, was it?"

Surely he didn't have a problem with uniforms, he was the son of a Navy officer.

"Shorts and a polo t-shirt, they were a little ... tight."

I was beginning to get the picture.

"Okay: shorts and a tight t-shirt. And...?"

He closed his eyes, a pained expression on his face.

"The women there ... they ... they grabbed me ... *a lot!*"

And I laughed out loud, I couldn't help it.

"So, basically, you're telling me you're a cabana boy—and that all the women were feeling you up."

"I was supposed to be bussing tables!"

He sounded so indignant, it just made me laugh harder.

"I can't blame them." I teased. "Did you get any offers? Any phone numbers dangled in front of you?"

His cheeks reddened, and he stared at the table.

"You did! Sebastian!"

"I said no!"

He grimaced at me and I took pity on him.

"*Tesoro*, I'm not the least bit surprised—those places are notorious for hiring good-looking young men as eye-candy for the diamond-wife brigade. I bet your boss is a woman, right?"

He nodded unhappily.

"And she took one look at you and saw dollar signs. That's all. You'll just have to put up with a bunch of horny, older women shoving dollar bills in your back pocket for the summer. You think you can do that?"

"I guess. It's not as much fun as I thought it would be."

I fell a little bit more in love with him.

I stroked his cheek and rested my free hand on his knee.

"You can always get another job, Sebastian. Besides, they shouldn't really have you serving drinks at your age. Do they know how young ... how old you are?"

He raised his eyebrows. "They do, but I guess I look older than my age."

It was my turn to blush, especially when I remembered my comment about 'horny older women'. On the other hand...

"I think I'll join."

"What?"

"The country club."

"Why?"

"I heard there are a lot of horny, older women there—I thought you might need some protection. Besides, it could be fun."

A slow smile spread across his face.

"Yeah! That would be fun."

"I'd tip well."

"Would you throw me your phone number?"

"I think that could be arranged."

My cell phone rang, interrupting us. It was a number I didn't recognize, which made me nervous.

"Hello?"

"Caroline Wilson?"

"Yes, speaking."

"This is Carl Winters, the editor at *City Beat*. I was just calling to say that I loved your 'Base Line Up' article. I'd like to run it in Thursday's issue. You got some great photos there, too. The fee would be $325. And I'd love any other articles you've got on life out at the Base. Folk around here are real interested in stories on life from a military point of view. Between 1,500 and 2,000 words."

"Wow! That's great! Thank you! Yes, I'm sure I could write any number of articles on military life."

"You've got a very nice writing style, Mrs. Wilson—really draws the reader in. I'm surprised I haven't run across you before."

"Oh, thank you. We just moved here from the east coast."

"I guess that explains it. Well, drop by the news desk sometime and we'll sign you up to one of our standard freelance contracts."

"I'll do that. Thank you, Mr. Winters."

"Call me Carl. It'll be great to meet you, Caroline. And maybe next time we could send out one of our photographers with you."

We hung up and I threw my arms around Sebastian's neck. "*City Beat* is going to print the surfing article." I said into his chest.

To the surprise of both of us, I started to cry.

"Hey! What's the matter? This is good, isn't it?"

"Yes, yes, of course. I'm just being stupid."

He hugged me tightly. "I don't understand."

How could I explain? I wasn't even sure I understood myself.

He stroked my back and kissed my hair, his touch soothing me. When my sobs finally ebbed, he leaned back and brushed the salty tears away with his thumbs, his face lined with concern.

"Caro? Why were you crying?"

I took a deep breath and tried to order my thoughts.

"It's just ... getting one of my stories printed. You know, someone saying that I'm actually *good* at something. I'm ... not used to it. David never..."

I stopped mid-sentence as his face hardened.

"It was just a nice surprise," I finished lamely.

He picked up my hand from the table and kissed it softly. "Yeah, I get that."

We sat in silence for some moments.

"Come on," he said at last. He stood up, still holding my hand.

"Where are we going?"

His expression softened. "To our place."

"Our place?"

"The ocean."

I smiled up at him. "Okay."

CHAPTER SEVEN

There's something so restful about the ocean. Why is that? Perpetual motion, never still and yet it's a soothing, peaceful, rolling, restless movement. Even the rage of a winter storm has a quality that strips away troubles, if only for a short time.

And it was *our* place—it was where Sebastian and I went to be ourselves for a few, brief, uninterrupted hours.

Even so, we had to be careful.

We walked in silence, away from the vacationing crowds that were beginning to populate the beach, until the nearest were mere pinpricks on the horizon.

Then, hand-in-hand at last, we stopped to find a secluded dune. I sank down into the warm sand and Sebastian pulled me to his side.

"Are you okay now?" he asked, anxiously.

"Yes. Sorry about that."

I was embarrassed by my most recent loss of control. It seemed to happen around him a lot, as if some emotional levee had been breached after a decade, a lifetime of holding back.

Sebastian stroked my hair and said in a low voice, "Don't be sorry. I just hate seeing you unhappy."

I didn't know how to reply so I just let him hold me.

For 19 years I'd been someone's daughter and, for the next 11, someone's wife. But what was I now? Could I have the chance of a career after all? Could I be something different, something else?

"What are you thinking about?"

I shook my head and smiled. "Not much. But I'll have to come up with some more ideas for the *City Beat*—if he really meant what he said."

"Of course he did. You're a brilliant writer."

"Well, thanks, Mr. Bernstein."

His face fell and I immediately regretted my words.

"Sorry, I'm just a little freaked. Maybe you could help me come up with some ideas about life in a military family."

He pulled a face. "Depends on the family."

That was true.

"How are Mitch and Ches?"

It seemed an innocent enough question but Sebastian looked away.

"Okay, I guess. I've only seen Ches at work."

"And?"

I waited for him to continue but he just carried on watching sand run through his fingers. "Sebastian, what's the matter?"

He took a deep breath. "Ches said that he knew I was seeing someone."

I felt the blood draining from my face.

"How?"

Sebastian looked at me anxiously.

"He was ... when I wouldn't tell him anything he started saying that there must be a reason and what was the problem. He kept on and on at me. He was just horsing around but... "

Sebastian didn't need to finish the sentence.

"What made him ... suspect?"

"Well, at first it was because I haven't been hanging out that much. He's been asking me to go surfing with him and the guys, and when I kept on saying no ... I guess he worked it out."

"Then what ... you said 'at first'?"

His expression was evasive.

"Tell me!"

He sighed. "Ches saw me getting changed into my uniform at work."

"So?"

"He noticed ... scratches down my back."

Oh! I remembered doing that.

"What did he say?"

Sebastian shrugged, unable to meet my worried gaze. On second thought, I didn't need to know what Ches had said, I could probably imagine how *that* conversation had gone.

"I told him to drop it but he wouldn't. I got so mad at him..."

"We're not very good at this, are we?" I said softly.

"It's harder than I thought," he agreed quietly.

My heart lurched painfully and I felt a little nauseous.

"Do you want to end it?"

He looked at me, horrified.

"No! Caro, no! Of course not! That's not what I meant! How can you say that?"

"Just ... if it's getting too hard..."

He pulled my face to his and kissed me roughly.

"Don't say that! Please don't say that! We'll work it out somehow. Promise me you won't give up on us, Caro. Promise!"

I felt the edge of desperation in his voice so I kissed him back, trying to pour reassurance into my touch, words that I couldn't say out loud because I was afraid they might not be true.

He pulled me down onto the sand so I was half-lying across his chest. One hand was tangled in my hair and the other pressing into the small of my back. My lips crushed his and he forced his tongue into my mouth, locking us together.

I had to break off the kiss before we went too far, it was still mid-afternoon and I was hyper-aware that someone could stumble across us at any time.

Sebastian was reluctant to let me go and I had to push hard against his chest to make him release me.

I was breathless when we rolled apart. He threw an arm over his face and groaned.

"Fuck, Caro," he said softly, and he turned to stare at me, his sea-green eyes accusing.

"We have to get back," I said, cowardly as ever. "You'll be late for your shift."

I started trudging back up the beach and, reluctantly, he followed me.

"Don't forget to bring me an application form for the country club," I said, trying to lighten his somber mood.

He smiled slightly. "I guess I could take some day shifts, if you're going to be there."

"And maybe you'd better arrange to go out with Ches a few times."

"What for?"

I sighed in exasperation. "To throw him off the scent and..."

"And what?"

"Well, if our plans work out, you won't be seeing him again."

His eyes widened in surprise. He clearly hadn't thought about what he'd be giving up if we did make it to New York.

I looked at him steadily, watching him regain his equilibrium.

"Ches is a good buddy—but I love you. Ysou're where I want to be."

And that was it: his alpha and omega.

~

I drove us back, torn between joy and fear, and wishing the night would race past so we could be together again.

A few blocks from his house, I pulled the car to the curb. He brushed his lips over my hand and got out quickly. "Tomorrow," he said, and his words were not a question but an answer—and a promise.

The house, my so-called home, seemed empty and unwelcoming. It didn't bother me, not really, not anymore, but I couldn't help noticing the emptiness a little more each day.

I set up my laptop at the kitchen table and sketched out some topics for articles. I was pleasantly surprised by how easily the ideas flowed. Then again, after 11 years of being a military spouse, there wasn't much I didn't know about Base life. And David talked so often about the hospital that I pretty much wrote out an entire article in one go.

I was enjoying myself too much because I didn't realize how late it had gotten. Suddenly David was standing over me inspecting the kitchen for evidence of a meal, when he realized nothing was ready, his already chilly look became glacial.

"The least you could do is to prepare a meal when I come home, Caroline, instead of playing around on your computer. I should throw the damn thing away."

"I wasn't *playing*," I said sourly. "I'm working on some articles for *City Beat*—they've accepted the one I wrote on surfing and they're publishing it on Thursday with my photographs."

He frowned. "What for?"

"Because they thought it was *good*. It may be a surprise to you, David, but there are some people out there who think I can actually do something useful."

"What would be useful would be for my wife to cook a fucking meal when I come home in the evenings." He paused, staring coolly at me. "I don't know what's gotten into you lately, Caroline. You're forgetful, distracted, disorganized. In fact, I'd say that you've been acting very strangely for some time."

He paused, waiting for his words to sink in. I stared back, afraid he suspected something. For all his faults, my husband was not a stupid man. At least, not in that way.

"I think you should see a doctor. I've made you an appointment to see Dr. Ravel," he said at last, his tone carefully neutral.

"What? There's nothing wrong with me! Who's Dr. Ravel?"

"A competent gynecologist, Caroline. I suspect you're experiencing an early menopause."

I couldn't help gaping at him. He was really unbelievable.

"David, I'm only 30! Most women don't reach the menopause until they're 50."

"Don't be obtuse, Caroline. Early menopause is not uncommon and you have all the symptoms."

"What symptoms, for fuck's sake?"

"Don't use language like that, Caroline. It's unpleasant and unnecessary."

"What symptoms, David?"

"Mood swings, irritability ... loss of libido. Dr. Ravel will undertake a colposcopy to ascertain which stage you're at. They are expecting you at OB-GYN Reception at 10AM. I've already checked that our insurance covers the exam."

"David, I've never heard anything so ridiculous. I..."

"Maybe I should make you an appointment with a psychiatrist instead!"

I was outraged. "How dare you!"

"Then you tell me why you refuse intercourse with your husband!" he snarled.

He turned away from me, his ferocious temper barely in check.

Gingerly, I closed my laptop. My hands shook slightly as I prepared a cold pasta salad, but my brain was working feverishly, desperately trying to come up with a suitable reply, some convincing words. As usual, his molten anger silenced me.

I was furious with myself for not standing up to him. Then again, he'd had 11 years' practice making me feeling inconsequential, there was certainly no reason for him to stop now.

Although he didn't suspect the truth, I couldn't help thinking it would be a case of when, not if. My life, once so gray and certain, was now on shifting sands. Whatever the catalyst, no one had forced me to go in the direction I'd chosen. I wasn't sure what choices I had now, other than to wait until Sebastian was of age. If I went to a lawyer about a divorce tomorrow, how long would it be before my 'affair' became known? That was the crux of the problem. I was committing a crime, David's only crime was to be born an asshole and just grow bigger.

We ate in silence and he didn't speak to me again that evening. Nor did he try to touch me, which was a blessing.

Breakfast passed with the same cheerless routine. Perhaps we both breathed a sigh of relief when it was time for him to go to work. He flung down my appointment card as he left.

At 9.45AM, I presented myself at the OB-GYN reception. The waiting room was already full of pregnant women, toddlers and babies, each trying to make themselves heard above the din. I felt conspicuous and ill at ease. One of the women smiled kindly and raised her eyebrows in acknowledgment of the noise. She probably assumed I was newly pregnant.

What the hell was I doing here? I'd had a Pap smear just six months ago and that had come back clear. I had no menopausal symptoms and I knew David was just using this as a means of exercising his power: and I was letting him. Again.

I was ashamed of myself for being so weak. Part of me wanted to get it over with to appease him for a few more weeks, but another, newer, bolder part was telling me to stand up to him.

Somewhere a door opened and the moving air caused posters tacked to a bulletin board to flutter colorfully. The notice for a women's rights group caught my eye: 'However we dress, wherever we go—yes means yes, and no means no'.

There was something about the simple wording that resonated—perhaps it was my turn, at last, to say no.

I took a deep breath and stood up. The appointment receptionist looked irritated to see me standing in front of her window for a second time.

"Yes, may I help you?" she said curtly, clearly having no wish to help me whatsoever.

"Yes, you may. I had an appointment for 10AM with Dr. Ravel, but I've decided to cancel it."

"Cancel it?"

"That's right. I apologize for wasting Dr. Ravel's time." *But not yours, you sour-faced bitch.*

"Well, that's most irregular. Dr. Ravel is a very busy woman."

"Hence the apology."

"Hmm, well. I can give you another appointment in five weeks and..."

"No, there's no need. No appointment necessary. Thank you."

And I left, leaving her puzzled and annoyed.

Damn, that felt good! Even though I knew I'd have to face David's ire later. What the hell: I was a habitual irritation to him anyway. For the first time, it occurred to me that he might even be a happier man without me in his life. I wasn't sure he'd see it that way, without his cook, cleaner, party organizer and occasional sexual toy, but it might even be true.

I drove out of the hospital parking lot feeling elated and jittery. I'd taken my first baby steps toward independence.

On a roll and feeling unusually daring, I headed out to the country club. I knew Sebastian had taken a double shift. He hadn't been happy at not seeing me in the morning, but when I said I was having a doctor's check-up, he'd acquiesced at once and said he'd work to take his mind off 'things'. He promised to text me on his break but now I was hoping to see him before that: a surprise.

The country club was located at the end of a long, private driveway, fringed by an avenue of mature palm trees. The single story was old Spanish-style—white with tall arches, a wide, cool veranda running around three sides, and frothing with bougainvillea in rich magenta. Wides steps led up to an impressive frontage, and green lawns flowed down toward an 18 hole golf course. Behind the building, I could see the ocean stretching to the horizon, breakers rumbling in the background. Whoever had picked the location had done half the job of selling memberships.

My old Ford looked so out of place I dumped it in the rear parking lot, deftly avoiding the valet service as I walked to the entrance.

It was clear that the dress code was more than advisory: men wore polo shirts with collars, and women's skirts were of a decent length. I couldn't spot an un-tucked shirt anywhere. A handsome young man in uniform smiled at me as I walked up the steps. Sebastian had hinted at the way staff were selected: those I could see were young and attractive, wearing Navy blue shorts and plain, white t-shirts with the club's logo discreetly positioned.

I was glad I'd dressed up for my abortive hospital appointment, otherwise I'd have felt even more intimidated by the grand surroundings.

"May I help you, ma'am?" said the well-dressed young woman at the reception desk.

"Yes, I'd like a membership form, please."

"Certainly, ma'am. Would that be an individual membership, associate member, executive or junior executive member, non-resident membership or social membership?"

"I ... I..."

"The individual membership starts at $1,000 per month, with an initial fee of $4,000 or for a social membership, if you don't wish to play golf..."

"I believe Mrs. Wilson is entitled to the Active Duty Military Membership."

The voice made me jump.

"Of course, Mrs. Vordstadt," said the receptionist, rummaging through her files, then passing over a thick sheaf of paper.

I turned to find Donna standing behind me, smiling at my surprise.

"I didn't figure you for a country club type, Caroline. Or perhaps this is more David's thing?"

I tried to wipe the shock from my face but I don't think I was entirely successful.

"Donna, how ... how nice to see you. Yes, I, um, just came to pick up a membership form—I had no idea there were so many different types." *Or that it would be so expensive.*

"One of the few benefits of military service—and it puts the fee down to a more manageable $500 a month," she whispered conspiratorially.

She took my elbow and led me out to a seating area at the rear. Several women were sipping cocktails, even at this early hour. The view of the ocean was stunning and the club had a large pool overlooking the waves, peppered with sun loungers and fringed umbrellas. I was far from enjoying it though—foolishly, it hadn't occurred to me that I'd bump into anyone I knew here. And now Donna was ordering coffee for the two of us.

"I'm so glad you're here, Caroline. We haven't had a chance to chat and I did so want to thank you for inviting us to your home on Saturday. I really should have called before now."

"Oh, no, that's fine..."

There was an awkward pause—perhaps we were both remembering how the evening had ended—or our different versions of that.

"Is David a golfer?" she asked at last.

"A little, in Florida," I said, flustered. He'd played a couple of times that I could recall.

"And you?"

"I prefer the beach," I said, truthfully. "Swimming, sailing—anything like that."

"Have you tried surfing?"

I'm sure I blushed beet red: I was thankful that my tan covered it up a little.

"No, I've never tried."

"You should get the boys to teach you," she suggested.

I nearly choked on my coffee.

"I'm sure Mitch Peters wouldn't mind helping out."

I smiled weakly. Clearly the 'boys' she was thinking of were quite different from the ones—the one—I had in mind.

"I thought you might have been tempted," she continued.

I was ready to crawl through the floor—her words laced with unintentional double entendres.

And then I saw Sebastian.

He looked so handsome in his crisp, snug uniform, no one would have guessed he was still only 17. Certainly not me—he looked more like early twenties. It was easy to see how the club could get away with allowing him to serve alcohol. It seemed I suffered from the same hypocrisy.

Donna turned to see what, or rather who, I was staring at.

"Oh, there's the Hunters' boy. I remember Shirley Peters mentioning that her son was going to get him a job here."

She waved to attract his attention, as I sank lower into my chair.

He hesitated for a moment, then strode over.

"Good morning, ladies," he said smoothly.

His audacity brought a small smile to my lips.

"Hello, Sebastian," said Donna.

"Hi," I said, shyly.

"How long have you been working here?" asked Donna.

"Just a few days. Ches Peters got me a job."

"And how are you liking it?"

"It's getting better," he said, glancing at me.

Donna raised her eyebrows and I could tell she was trying not to smile.

I frowned. Sebastian's recklessness was hardly helpful.

"Can I get you ladies anything?" he asked, sounding a little flustered as he correctly interpreted my cool expression.

"No, we're good, thank you. We're just having coffee."

"Well, okay, then ... I'd better get back to work..."

Donna waved him on his way and with a last flicker of his eyes toward me, he headed off.

"He's such a nice boy," said Donna thoughtfully. "Amazing he's turned out so well when you consider..." She paused. "I was very impressed with how he handled his parents last Saturday."

"Yes," I agreed quickly, wanting to get her off the subject but not sure how.

"Of course," continued Donna, "you knew him as a child. What was he like then?"

I couldn't help smiling. "Oh, he was so sweet. He used to come to our house after school. My father was particularly fond of him."

Dear Papa. My smile faded. How he would have loved Sebastian the man, as well as the boy he'd known.

Donna touched my arm. "Sorry, Caroline."

I shrugged.

"So, do you think you and David will join?"

Now that I realized how popular the club was with Base families, I was a lot less keen, but I didn't know how I'd get out of it.

"Maybe. It's quite pricey. I'll have to see what David says."

Secretly, I had no intention of telling him I'd been there.

"I know what we'll do," said Donna, enthusiastically, "I'll ask Johan to suggest it to him."

"Oh, that's not necessary." I said, feeling a little panicky.

"It's no trouble," said Donna, decisively. "Besides, it'll be much more fun coming here with you. Do you play tennis?"

~

My trip to the country club hadn't gone exactly as planned. In fact, it was hard to imagine how it could have been worse. Despite my feeble objections, I had Donna's cast iron promise that her husband would speak to my husband about a membership.

I sat in my hot car in the club's parking lot, surrounded by expensive foreign cars, and rubbed my forehead, trying to ward off an incipient headache.

The whole situation was ridiculous—even hilarious—although not to me.

I sent Sebastian a quick message.

Sorry. Not the surprise I'd planned. Cx

I waited a few minutes but there was no reply—he was probably still working. I drove home, determined to sketch out some more ideas for *City Beat*. There was no point in letting the day be a complete wash-out.

As the hands on the kitchen clock crept toward 6PM, I put away my laptop and notebook, and turned my thoughts to making dinner. Risotto wasn't David's favorite but it was quick and easy.

The moment the hands on the clock were aligned vertically, I heard David's Camaro pull up outside. I hurried to set the table and waited anxiously. Would he fight with me about the missed colposcopy before or after we'd eaten?

His face was impassive although I'm sure mine was a little paler than usual.

"Something you want to tell me, Caroline?" he said, his voice unnervingly even.

I felt my courage shrivel under his chilly gaze.

"Such as?"

"Don't be obtuse. I was talking to Captain Vorstadt today," he said, emphasizing the title 'Captain'.

I frowned. Where was he going with this?

"Apparently you were out at the country club this afternoon."

"It was just a silly thought, David," I said, hurriedly.

"You have many silly thoughts, Caroline, but if people like the Vorstadts are members at the country club, we should certainly join. I'm glad to see you're making more of an effort for a change."

I gaped at him.

"In fact, Captain Vorstadt suggested we dine there together tomorrow night," he continued smugly, "so I can see the facilities."

David looked sickeningly pleased with himself, presumably because a senior officer had invited him—or rather us—to dinner.

He tossed his cap onto the couch and didn't even ask about the exam I'd skipped. I knew the reprieve was temporary but I was happy to take what I could get.

I spent the evening with anxiety twisting my stomach but nothing more was mentioned. When David finally headed to the bathroom to get ready for bed, I switched my phone back on. Sebastian's response made me smile:

You always make my heart beat faster. Tomorrow?

Yes, tomorrow.

CHAPTER EIGHT

David was almost cheerful as he left for work. The prospect of dinner with a superior officer had put him in a good mood and kept him there.

"Wear something nice tonight: a cocktail dress. And heels, of course. In fact, buy a new dress."

"David, that's really not necessary. I've dry-cleaned the green one."

I'd thought he'd be pleased with my frugality, but, as usual, I was in the wrong.

"For God's sake, Caroline! I can't have the Vorstadts thinking I can only afford to buy my wife one decent dress. Get a new one."

"I had plans for this morning..."

"Such as?"

"Well, writing..."

"You can do that anytime. Buy a new dress. But no more than $150. You don't want to look like you're trying too hard."

Like you're *trying too hard, you mean.*

I sighed. There went my plans to spend the morning at the beach with Sebastian. Well, maybe if I went to the mall, I could be done in an hour.

I watched David drive off then picked up my phone to text Sebastian.

I have to go clothes shopping. Pick you up later? Sorry. Cx

Immediately my phone started ringing.

"Why are you going shopping? Don't you want to see me?"

"Don't be..." *Rephrase.* "It's not that—the Vorstadts have invited us to dinner tonight. David is insisting I buy a new dress."

"I wish you wouldn't say that."

"Say what?"

"When you talk about you and ... him. You say 'us'."

There was a long silence as I tried to frame a response but Sebastian spoke first.

"Can I come with you?"

"Where?"

"Can I come clothes shopping with you?"

I was nonplussed. "Well, I guess ... if you like."

"Great! See you at the park at our usual time. Love ya!"

I shook my head as he ended the call. I couldn't help thinking of all the times I'd seen pitiable men, waiting outside women's changing rooms, looking for all the world as if they'd been there since the dawn of time. But I was also intrigued, and if Sebastian wanted to come with me, well, I wasn't going to argue.

He was sitting on the curb with the hood of his sweatshirt pulled over his head, as if he was some punk looking for trouble. The thought made me smile—it was the polar opposite of Sebastian's personality which was so warm and thoughtful and caring, although I was beginning to recognize a reckless streak in him, too.

"Hi!"

"Hi yourself!" he answered happily as he scrambled in and fastened his seatbelt.

I longed to lean over and kiss him but we couldn't risk it here.

"So where are we going?"

I shook my head. "I don't know: a mall somewhere."

"Mom goes to Mission Valley. They've got all those brand name stores out there."

I screwed up my face at the suggestion.

"That's not really me. Besides, I want to avoid going somewhere I might run into your mom!" What a horrifying thought. Sebastian clearly agreed because I saw him wince.

"I thought maybe we could head up toward Miramar—there's that mall at Westfield UTC."

"Whatever."

"So, do you make a habit of this?"

He looked puzzled.

"Going shopping for women's clothes?"

He grinned widely.

"It's my new hobby, especially if you're buying underwear?"

I laughed, blushing slightly.

"Well, I ought to—I seem to keep losing mine."

He sniggered. "Yeah! That's fun."

His happiness spilled over and I felt my spirits soaring—six uninterrupted hours with the man I loved. Six stolen hours.

"Did I tell you I was a member of the surf life-saving club at school?" he asked, changing the subject.

I could tell he had something on his mind.

"No, but I guess I'm not surprised."

"Well, my manager at work, Miss Perez, she said that they'd get me certified for CPR and First Aid so I could be a trainee lifeguard at the pool. And I can start studying for the Open Water course, too, although I won't be able to take the test until I'm eigh— until later. It'll make it easier to get work in NYC."

"Oh. Okay."

"And I was thinking," he continued quickly, "if I take a course to be a personal trainer, I could earn maybe a hundred bucks an hour once I'm qualified. You know, while you're getting your journalism career going. I was looking at some apartments on the internet: they're pretty expensive. I couldn't find anything less than $2,000 a month unless we live in one of the outer boroughs, and we'd take a train or a ferry to get to work and school. It's a little slower, I guess, but a lot cheaper. But by the end of the summer, I'll have enough for the first month's rent wherever we live."

He looked at me anxiously.

A powerful swell of emotion swept through me. Here he was, 17 years old, planning for our future, determined to make it happen—and what had I contributed? Nothing. David had steered my life over the last 11 years, now I was letting—expecting even—that Sebastian would do the same. I felt ashamed.

"What do you think, Caro?"

"I think you're extraordinary," I said honestly.

He blinked, surprised by my unexpected answer. Then he grinned.

"Extraordinary, huh? I can live with that. And you called me 'God' the other night—that was okay, too."

"I like your plan," I said, deliberately ignoring the second half of his reply. "But we need to make sure you can fit your college courses in, too. I don't want you giving up a university education. Besides, I could look for some translation work or maybe even teaching Italian—conversation classes—nothing too formal as I'm not a qualified teacher."

"Well, you know, I looked at that, too. You could be a translator for the courts in NY—you can get $125 a day. Federal Courts pay even more." He reached out and took my hand, then kissed it. "I can't wait for us to be together."

Neither could I.

"Well, that's definitely a plan. If I could earn that sort of money ... although they probably wouldn't want Italian interpreters that much, but even so ... are you still planning on a joint major in English Lit and Italian?"

"Sure!"

"Do you know what you want to do after?"

He nodded slowly. "I'd like to go to Europe. I have this image of you and me on a motorcycle traveling through Italy. I don't know, teaching English, picking grapes—I don't care. I've never been outside the US."

"That sounds wonderful! We could go to Capezzano Inferiore—it's a small village in the hills above Salerno—where Papa was born. I've always wanted to go."

"Then we'll go," he said, simply.

I was grinning from ear to ear, smiling from the inside out.

"Do you have family there?" Sebastian asked thoughtfully.

"I'm not really sure—some second cousins, I think. Why?"

"We should try to find them," he said. "If they're as crazy as your dad, it could be pretty wild."

I laughed out loud, delighted with the picture he was painting. And I decided that as soon as I went home, I would start planning our escape in earnest—no more taking a back seat in my own life.

"There's the sign for Westfield," said Sebastian, bringing my attention back to the road.

I took the exit ramp and followed the signs.

The mall was a vast sprawl of boutique shops and places to eat with a Sears at one end and Macy's at the other.

"Where do you want to start?"

"I have no idea. Let's just make it quick."

"I thought all girls liked shopping?"

"Not this one."

"You look beautiful whatever you wear."

I stared at him. "You always say the sweetest things! How do you do that?"

He shrugged and looked embarrassed. "What about this shop?"

"You're changing the subject."

He smiled and towed me inside.

"May I help you, ma'am, sir?"

Seeing as it was a women's clothing store, I wasn't entirely sure how the sales assistant was going to help Sebastian, although going by the look on her face, I could make a damned good guess. And, of course, she was younger than me.

An unaccustomed desire for sudden violence flooded through me.

"I'm looking for a black cocktail dress," I said coolly. "Size four."

It occurred to me that I'd never once been jealous of another woman looking at David—maybe that should have told me something. I couldn't work out how much of what I was feeling now was to do with my own insecurities. I didn't want to spoil today, so I pushed the wretched thought aside.

The assistant picked out a couple of dresses and I took them into the changing room.

I could hear her chatting to Sebastian through the curtain. Well, I could hear her trying to hit on him.

"Are you from the Base?" she said.

"Yeah, but..."

"Are you, like, a pilot?"

"No, I..."

"But you're a Marine, right?"

I pulled back the curtain sharply, and the assistant jumped.

"What about this one, honey?" I said, throwing a few poses, for her benefit as much as Sebastian's.

"Wow! You look great, Caro!"

I had his full attention. From my peripheral vision I saw the sales assistant pout. Hmm, shopping was proving a lot more fun than I'd expected.

"You want to see the other dress, honey?" I said, doing another slow turn.

"Yeah!"

I smirked and ducked back into the changing room, throwing a look at the assistant that dared her to resume her conversation with Sebastian. Sensibly, she declined the challenge.

The second dress was even more fitted and skimmed the top of my knees.

"Can you zip me up, honey?" I whispered through the curtain, still enjoying my performance.

I gazed over my shoulder at Sebastian, trying to play seductive. His presence alone made me feel sexy. His expression immediately heated, and suddenly the confines of the changing room seemed unbearably hot. He pulled up the zipper with aching slowness, brushing a soft kiss over my bare shoulder.

"You look beautiful, baby," he said quietly.

Suddenly, we weren't playing anymore. The assistant coughed, embarrassed.

"How's the size, ma'am?"

"Fine, thank you."

"It's perfect," said Sebastian in a low tone.

I wandered out of the shop in a daze. Sebastian insisted on carrying the bag and wrapped his free hand around my limp fingers.

"You want to get some lunch?"

"Sebastian, it's only 11.15AM!"

"Yeah, well I'm hungry."

"You never stop eating. You're going to be enormous when you get older."

"Nah. I'll have you to keep me fit."

Dear God, I hoped I was up to the challenge. A few hours with Sebastian was yoga, Pilates and aerobics all rolled into one delicious workout.

"Donna said I should get Mitch to teach me to surf," I commented slyly.

Sebastian wasn't pleased.

"I can teach you! You don't need him."

"Are you pouting at me?" I laughed. "You are! You're pouting."

I brought our twined hands up to my mouth and kissed his fingers.

"I'm just teasing you."

He still looked hurt and I rather regretted trying to make him jealous. I suppose it was a childish tit-for-tat—that sales assistant had upset me more than I was willing to admit. But it wasn't fair to take it out on Sebastian. It wasn't his fault girls were throwing themselves at him.

"Come on, I'll buy you coffee and a Danish."

He settled on pastrami, lettuce and tomato on ciabatta bread, a regular black coffee with two sugars, and a Danish pastry, as promised. I had a large espresso and watched him wolf down the food. Our grocery bill in New York was going to be huge.

"Where else in Europe would you like to go?"

He swallowed his mouthful and drank some coffee while he thought.

"Well, everywhere, but I'd really like to go to Southern Spain—see all the Moorish stuff. I saw a picture of the Alhambra palace once—it looked, I don't know, like 'One Thousand and One Nights'."

I was surprised and I realized how little I knew of him, his hopes and dreams. The more I learned, the more fascinated I became.

"You've read 'Arabian Nights'?"

He cocked his head to look at me. "You don't remember, do you?"

I was confused. "Remember what?"

"You gave me the book to read—when I was a kid. I must have read it a hundred times. I used to think you were Scheherazade."

Scheherazade: the princess who told a different story every night to keep the king from beheading her. I wasn't very keen on the comparison. Except then he fell in love with her and married her.

"Just because you were such an amazing storyteller," Sebastian said, intuiting my reaction. "I guess I'm not surprised you became a writer."

I smiled gamely. "I'm trying to become a writer."

"You will," he said, certainty coloring his voice. "You are."

I struggled to hold back the tears that threatened to betray me. His encouragement, his certainty that I had the ability to achieve my dream, it meant more to me than I could ever express.

"What about you?" I asked, trying to speak naturally. "After our road trip..."

He shrugged. "I don't know. Mom and Dad always expected me to go the military route."

"Is that what you want to do?"

I managed to suppress a shudder at the thought of being pulled back toward living on military bases.

"No, I don't think so. I mean, parts of it would be great—but I'd like to travel."

"Traveling isn't a job," I laughed. "Unless you want to work on a cruise ship."

"Maybe," he said smiling. "You could be a travel writer and I'll ... carry your bags."

"That sounds like a plan."

He leaned over and kissed me so I could feel the smile on his lips.

This kiss was different somehow: more relaxed, less desperate—just sweet and loving. I stroked his cheek and he sighed happily, leaning into my hand.

"I know," he said, suddenly sitting up. "I'm going to take you surfing. You said you wanted to learn..."

"No, no! It was Donna who said I should..."

"Are you chicken?"

"Yes! The water's too cold."

He laughed. "They've invented wetsuits. You'll be fine. I know a place just north of La Jolla where we can rent boards. Come on! We've got a couple of hours. You can drop me off at work on the way back. We've got time."

I really had no desire to immerse myself in chilly Pacific waters but his enthusiasm was contagious. Maybe it was his recklessness that was catching, his unbreachable zest for life. Maybe I was just no longer afraid to live.

"Okay, let's go!"

We abandoned the car next to a shabby-looking surf shack that perched precariously above a small, secluded cove. The water was turquoise, and I imagined it to be the color of the Mediterranean, wondering if that was something I'd ever see—the sea my dear Papa had lived by as a small child.

"Hey, man," said the owner of the shack. "Long time no see."

I immediately felt anxious. It hadn't occurred to me that Sebastian would take me somewhere he was known. My eyes flickered to him nervously and he squeezed my hand reassuringly.

"Yeah, can we get a couple of shorties, rash vests and a spongey board?"

"Sure, man. Come on through."

Sebastian let the owner go ahead then whispered in my ear.

"Don't worry. He says that to everyone. He hasn't got a clue who I am. It's cool."

I tried to relax, but the shot of adrenaline was still working its way through my body—I smiled wanly.

The owner sized us up expertly and handed over a couple of cropped wetsuits, silky rash vests to wear under the neoprene and a large, heavy foam-covered surfboard. I was glad that Sebastian tucked it under his arm—it was too wide for me to be able to carry easily.

"That'll be twenty bucks," drawled the owner.

Before I could stop him, Sebastian pulled out his wallet and handed the man a couple of bills.

"And I'll need a credit card for security, dude."

Sebastian's eyes flickered uncertainly to me. I knew he didn't have a credit card and I wasn't really keen on the idea of handing one over that described me as 'Mrs. Carolina M. Wilson'.

"How about we give you our car keys?" said Sebastian, thinking quickly. "We're parked right over there."

He pointed at my old Ford.

"Dude, that piece of shit isn't gonna pay for anything!"

"Ah, come on! What are we going to do? Go running down the highway carrying a spongey?"

The owner held up his hands in defeat. "Okay, okay, but only because your girlfriend has such a cute smile, man!"

I thanked him quickly as I dragged a suddenly angry Sebastian out of the door.

"He was hitting on you," he grumbled.

"Hardly!"

"He was."

I shook my head. "Are you going to teach me to surf, or what?"

Sebastian grinned. It really didn't take much to put him in a good mood—how very different from David.

Neither of us had swimming costumes. I just tugged on the wetsuit over my panties, sand unhooked my bra when I'd pulled on the rash vest, so I was half-dressed. Sebastian watched in fascination. I didn't think it warranted *that* close a scrutiny. He caught my expression and winked, pulling his borrowed wetsuit over a pair of tight-fitting gray briefs that soon had my mind wandering.

He carried the board down to the sand and gave me a quick lesson on how to pop up using a rocking motion. He made it look easy—probably something to do with his well-developed upper body strength.

The heavy beginner's board was covered in soft foam to help prevent injuries among the uninitiated, but it was also impregnated with sand, and the palms of my hands soon began to feel sore.

"You're getting it," said Sebastian encouragingly. "Let's try you on a few waves. I'll push you onto them and tell you when to pop up."

The waves in the cove were small and well ordered—perfect for learning on. I lay face down on the board and felt the cold water splash around me.

"Get ready! Paddle, paddle, paddle. Now!"

Sebastian pushed me onto a small wave and as the board began to tip down onto the green-water, I popped up, wobbled for a few feet then fell off sideways. I managed to close my mouth but felt seawater gush up my nose. My head broke the surface of the water as I coughed and rubbed my eyes. My long hair hung like seaweed over my face.

Sebastian was laughing but he looked at me proudly.

"Wow, Caro! You just rode your first wave! That was awesome!"

He kissed my salty face and hugged me tightly as the water rippled around our waists.

"Try again!"

We spent another hour playing in the ocean and, by the end, I'd managed to ride a wave for several seconds and even put in a small turn.

Sebastian hadn't got bored or shouted at me or shown any signs of impatience. I was slightly in shock, but elated, too.

"So, how do you like being a surfer dude?" he said, smiling at me proudly.

"I love it, but I'm exhausted. It's almost as tiring as spending the night with you," I teased him.

He laughed happily then sighed. "I'd like to do that again, but we can't, can we? Not for a while." He frowned and squinted at the sun. "I have to get to work soon—we'd better head back."

We hadn't planned the surf trip so I didn't have a towel in the car. Instead we had to pull our clothes back on over damp, salty bodies, and my hair dripped chilly drops of water down my shoulders.

It was easier for me to get dressed since sI was wearing a skirt, but I enjoyed my private ogling as Sebastian pulled off his boxer briefs, only partially hidden by the car door, and grabbed his jeans. I loved watching the flex and ripple of his muscles under his golden tan, the way his jeans dropped down from his waist to hang on his hips, and the way two tiny lines appeared between his eyebrows when he was concentrating on something.

He grinned as he saw me watching him, and with deliberate slowness pulled his t-shirt over his damp chest, so the washed-out fabric clung to him.

I really wanted to pull it off him again but he had to get to work and I wanted to spend a couple of hours working on my next *City Beat* story.

I'd decided to write about what it was like for military families to move around the country from base to base. I had some experience of that, and I knew that Donna had lived in at least three other states. She and Johan had also been stationed overseas twice already with the possibility of another stint in Germany on the horizon.

"Time to get back to the real world," Sebastian said wistfully. "Maybe I'll see you tonight?"

"I rather hope not," I said, truthfully.

Sebastian looked hurt.

"It's too hard to act normal when you're there," I explained softly.

He nodded slowly. "I know what you mean ... but I'd still like to see you."

I sighed and shook my head.

"Well, can I come to your house tomorrow?"

"Sebastian, I don't think so. You know what people are like around here—all it would take would be for you to be seen coming in or leaving. Or if someone came to the door because they'd seen my car in the driveway and I ... we..."

He knew what I was saying and he knew as well as I did which risks were acceptable and which weren't. We were making up the rules as we went along, but there were still rules.

"When *can* I see you?" he said, sulkily.

"I'm still free tomorrow. Maybe we could go surfing again?"

"I want to make love to you, Caro," he muttered, gazing at my fingers as he squeezed them gently.

I took a deep breath as the familiar flickering tongues of love and lust swept through me.

"We could find a motel," I said, softly.

He looked up, his eyes wide.

"Do you mean it?"

"Yes," I said. "I want to be with you, too."

He closed his eyes and breathed deeply, a glorious smile spreading across his face.

He pulled me into a hug and leaned his head into my neck. I reached up and stroked his hair, which was nearly dry already.

I dropped him off at the end of the long driveway leading to the country club and watched as he waved once, then jogged along the avenue and out of sight.

I drove home with the sun beating down and all my car windows open. A brief glance in the mirror told me I looked like a cavewoman, with wild, salty hair hanging in clumps. I don't know how Sebastian managed not to laugh at me.

I showered quickly and sat in my robe to tap out the first few hundred words of my article, keeping one eye open for David's return.

As soon as I heard his car in the driveway, I snapped the laptop shut and headed to the bedroom to at least look like I was spending time getting ready. David imagined that all women took hours doing their hair and makeup before going out—it was one of his favorite stereotypes. It came in useful when I wanted an extra half-hour of peace and quiet.

I slipped on the new dress, remembering Sebastian's scorching look as he'd zipped it up. It was a soft chiffon hung over a fitted bustier top and clinging skirt, so plain, it was almost severe, but also elegant and sophisticated.

I dug out my simple, gold necklace that my father had given me and matched it with a pair of plain, gold hoop earrings.

I was just sweeping my hair back to pin it up when David walked into the bedroom.

He stopped and did a double take.

"Is that it?"

"My new dress? Yes."

"We're going out to dinner, Caroline, not attending a funeral."

Once his words would have hurt me, that evening I just stared at him impassively in the mirror.

"It's a classic little black dress, David."

"It's dull."

"It's all I have."

He scowled.

"For fuck's sake, Caroline. Do I have to supervise everything you do? You can't even buy a fucking dress that's appropriate for dinner."

I didn't reply. There was no point. Unfortunately, it meant the evening would now start on an awkward note. I hoped he'd be able to hide his annoyance from the Vorstadts—I didn't want Donna throwing any more pitying glances my way.

Johan's car arrived outside with typical military precision. David was wearing a dark blue suit with matching tie. If it hadn't been for his permanently sour expression, he would have been good-looking.

Johan stepped out of the car to open the door, and blinked when he saw me.

"Good evening, Caroline, David."

"Hello, Johan. Hi Donna."

"Caroline, darling. Don't you look gorgeous," gushed Donna. "Johan, doesn't she look amazing?!"

"I'll say!" agreed Johan enthusiastically.

I saw David frown. It was going to be a long evening.

David sat up front with Johan, while Donna and I chatted in the back. I freely grilled her about her experiences of moving around the country, explaining it was for a new article.

"I can introduce you to some of the other wives," she said. "Well, you know Shirley Peters—she's moved around even more than I have."

"I've spoken to her on the phone, but never actually met her," I admitted.

"I'll set something up," she said. "Shirley is a member of the country club, too. Why don't we all meet over there tomorrow afternoon? I'll drive."

Oh no! Not tomorrow—I'd promised Sebastian.

"Could we make it Friday? I have one or two things on tomorrow."

"Why sure! I'll phone Shirley and set it up."

I found myself looking forward to it and I was curious to meet Mitch's wife. The fact that David would be torn between his disapproval of Shirley and his desire to encourage my friendship with Donna only added to my pleasure. *But how the hell was I going to get through the next three-and-a-half months with this man?*

First we had to get through dinner.

Johan gallantly offered me his arm as we walked up the front steps, much to Donna's obvious amusement and David's sullen irritation.

The maitre d' fussed around our table, pulling out chairs for Donna and me before introducing our waiter for the evening—a familiar face was grinning down at us.

"Oh, hello, Ches," said Donna, pleasantly. "What a nice surprise! So you'll be our waiter. How are you?"

"Very well thanks, Mrs. Vorstadt." Then he turned to Johan. "Hello, sir. Hi, Caroline!" he grinned at me.

I smiled back. "Hi, Ches, how are..."

But before I could finish the sentence David snapped, "Her name is 'Mrs. Wilson'."

Ches's smile vanished, while Donna and Johan looked embarrassed.

"David," I said softly. "I've met Ches before: he and his father were kind enough to help me with my surfing article."

"I know who he is, Caroline," said David sharply, "and it's not appropriate that he addresses you by your first name."

Donna hid a look of disgust behind her menu, and I saw a hard look pass over Johan's face. David had screwed himself royally this time. I didn't care about that, but I was mortified by the way he'd treated Ches.

"Perhaps you can tell us what the specials are, Ches?" said Donna coolly.

"Sure, Mrs. Vorstadt," said Ches, with a chastened tone.

We placed our orders and I tried to think of some way to apologize for David's appalling rudeness.

"By the way, Ches," I said, "the surfing article will be published in *City Beat* tomorrow. There's a photo of you and your dad in it. I'll buy a copy for each of you. Will you tell your dad for me? And Sebastian and Fido. I never did find out his real name."

He grinned at me. "Okay, thanks, Mrs. Wilson, I'll do that."

He walked away smiling but David pursed his lips. "Don't be over-familiar with the wait staff, Caroline."

"He's our neighbor," said Donna, raising her eyebrows to make the point.

"Of course," said David after half a beat.

Johan cleared this throat and threw a warning look at his wife.

It was a wonder we didn't all have indigestion before we started. But then our wine waiter arrived and the talk devolved into a discussion of how well New World reds stacked up against Old World. I kept my mouth firmly shut—now was not the time to irritate David even further.

Johan picked a soft Californian Merlot and ordered a jug of iced water.

Our entrées were very slow arriving and Johan's eyes began flicking back and forward toward the kitchen. The maitre d' came out to apologize, saying that two members of staff had suddenly gone sick and that they were short-staffed but trying to remedy the situation.

That's when I saw Sebastian.

He wasn't in his usual sports assistant uniform. Instead he was dressed in long, black pants, a white button down shirt with a black bow tie. He was walking purposefully toward our table, carrying a basket full of small bread rolls.

No! No! No!

I then had to endure the hideous spectacle of my lover serving my husband, while I tried to stop myself from screaming and running.

Donna smiled as I studied my linen napkin.

"Hello, Sebastian. We've already seen Ches this evening. It looks like you boys are running the place tonight."

I didn't dare look up to see his face but I could tell from his voice that he was nervous as he tried to laugh.

"Not really. They're just very short-staffed—I haven't done this before."

"I'm sure you'll be fine, dear. You look very handsome, doesn't he, Caroline?"

My head jerked up at the sound of my name.

"Oh, yes. Very."

There was a pause that felt long enough for the world to end.

"Would you like some bread?" Sebastian asked awkwardly.

I shook my head while David reached across me to take two rolls. Donna also declined but Johan looked hungry enough to eat all the rolls and the basket, too. Luckily Ches was close behind bringing out our entrées. I had no idea how I was going to eat anything, my stomach was so tied in knots. And I still couldn't look at Sebastian.

The men dug into their food with gusto. I glanced up to see Donna give me a small wink, I had no idea what she was referring to but I tried to smile back. I probably just looked sick. From the corner of my eye, I could see Sebastian waiting on other tables and Ches hurrying to and fro.

"I wonder if those boys will both enlist," said Donna, musing aloud, "you know—following in their fathers' footsteps."

"The Hunter boy is going to," said David confidently. "I don't know about the other one."

"Really?" said Donna. "I'm quite surprised—I rather thought Sebastian might do something else."

"No," said David with finality, "Donald told me. Estelle has talked him into letting the boy have a year at college first," he sniffed disdainfully, "but that's all he's prepared to pay for, the boy will enlist after that."

"That seems a little harsh," said Donna frowning. "Surely they'd let him get his degree once he's started?"

David shrugged. He really wasn't that interested.

I was shocked yet again by Donald and Estelle's callousness, I knew for a fact that Sebastian was unaware of this plan. I was even more determined that he'd get his degree if I had anything to do with it.

The conversation moved onto other people we knew in common and for me at least, into safer territory.

"Where did you get your fabulous dress, Caroline?" Donna asked while Ches cleared away the entrée plates.

"Westfield. I went this morning."

"Oh! I wish I'd known. I was there this morning, too. We could have gone together. What a pity I didn't see you."

I shuddered internally at the thought of a disaster had so narrowly been avoided.

"I don't know why she had to pick black," David complained. "It's so funereal."

Donna stared at him in astonishment then turned her sympathetic eyes to mine. I glanced away and caught Sebastian watching me. He looked angry—he'd obviously heard David's unkind comment.

"Do you have any plans while David is away?" said Donna.

"Excuse me?"

"While he's at the conference ... you know, the thoracic surgery symposium in Dallas?"

I stared at her in bafflement.

"For God's sake, Caroline!" muttered David. "What is the point of me filling in a schedule if you never look at it?"

"When are you going?"

"They're flying out on Friday evening and back Sunday night," Donna added helpfully.

Johan nodded to David. "Have you read the papers yet?"

I barely listened as they discussed the speakers—my mind was racing through the possible ways I could spend my 48 hours of freedom.

"What will you do with yourself, Caroline?" asked Donna.

"Oh, I don't know. I guess I'll be able to get on with my writing."

"And you'll come to the beach barbecue on Sunday?"

She immediately answered my blank expression.

"It's for all the Service families. It's usually pretty good fun and, as you're by yourself ... do say yes."

With everyone staring at me, I had no choice.

"Yes, of course I'll come," I said.

I felt like some weird internal elevator was rushing up and down with its cargo of emotions—from elation at the thought of David being away for two nights, to come crashing down because precious hours when I could have been with Sebastian would now be squandered at a military picnic. Someone sure had a lousy sense of humor.

***s

I deliberately took my time getting ready for bed once we got back from the country club. I hoped that if I was slow enough David would have fallen asleep by the time I slipped under the covers. So far I had managed to avoid any further confrontations about sex, but I knew it was only a matter of time before David would insist on his conjugal 'rights'.

I closed the toilet lid and sat down with my head in my hands. I couldn't go on like this—the stress was beginning to get to me and it had only been three weeks. *Was that all it had taken for my life to change so completely?* I wasn't cut out for infidelity. Or maybe it was simply that Donna's comment about having been at the mall at the same time as us that had made my anxiety levels spike.

The choices were stark: leave David and set divorce proceedings in action—stay away from Sebastian for another 13 weeks and save money from my writing so we could disappear to NYC together at the end of September—and hope no one put two-and-two together to make four.

Either way people would work out the truth when we both disappeared at the same time—I hoped that once Sebastian was 18 and there was no *proof* of wrong doing, they'd leave us alone. That was my grand plan. And money was going to be an issue. David had his salary paid into a savings account and gave me $1,000 a month for groceries, gas for my car and utility bills. It was only just enough. I had no money of my own. When I'd had my job back east, David had insisted that my wages went into the communal pot. That's what he called it, although I never saw the money again. I didn't even know how much was in our savings account. What a humiliating admission.

But if I could get an article published in *City Beat* every week for the next three months, I'd have over $4,000—enough for seven or eight weeks rent in NYC. It was going to be tight, but when it came down to it, what price freedom?

Although the fact that the age of consent was 17 in New York was reassuring, I tried not to dwell on it. It didn't change the facts of what I'd done in California, and what I planned to continue doing.

The rumbling sound of David's snores broke through my grim thoughts: it was safe to go to bed.

I slipped carefully under the sheets and tried to think positively. Tomorrow was a new day: my first ever piece of professional writing was going to be published—and I had a promise to keep to Sebastian.

CHAPTER NINE

I COLLECTED SEBASTIAN FROM OUR SPECIAL PLACE NEAR THE PARK AND DROVE off quickly. He was unusually subdued.

"Are you okay?"

He shrugged.

I really hoped he wasn't going to sulk for long—I'd had enough of that in my life, and in particular from David during the last 24 hours.

"Sebastian, talk to me!"

He sighed. "I *hated* seeing you with that asshole last night. How can you stand it?"

I blanched at the anger in his voice.

"I've got used to it, over the years," I said quietly. "But it's getting harder."

I could feel Sebastian's eyes on me as I drove.

"Sorry," he mumbled.

It was my turn to shrug. He didn't need to apologize—if it was anyone's fault, it was mine. I looked for a way to change the subject and diffuse the tense atmosphere.

"I need to buy a half-dozen copies of *City Beat*. My article is published today—you and Ches will be in it."

"Oh, yeah! I can't wait to see that!" he said, sounding happier.

I pulled up at a convenience store and we both jumped out, racing each other to the stand of newspapers, suddenly light-hearted.

I tore open a copy of the paper, my heart beating rapidly with excitement. I didn't have to look far—my article was printed on page five with a huge photograph of Sebastian, Mitch, Bill, Ches and Fido.

I felt a sharp pain in my chest as I stared at the photograph of Sebastian. In the picture his sun-lightened hair was still long, and he looked the epitome of young and carefree. I'd taken it just a few hours before his father brutally hacked off his hair, and a few hours after that we had slept together for the first time. But I also felt a great welling up of pride—seeing my article in print with my name beneath it was the first real sense of achievement I'd had since getting my degree at night school three years ago.

"They've spelled your name wrong," said Sebastian frowning.

I scanned the page quickly. "Where?"

"There," he said, pointing at the small, bold type under the heading.

"No, that's correct," I said, looking at him puzzled.

"Your name is 'Carolina', not 'Caroline'?"

"Carolina is the Italian," I said softly, emphasizing the long vowel in the middle. "David—and my mother—preferred the Anglicized version, but the name on my birth certificate is Carolina Maria."

I couldn't help noticing that Sebastian's lips were pressed tightly together and his knuckles where he gripped the newspaper had turned white.

"Why are you so upset?" I asked hesitantly.

Sebastian took a deep breath.

"That bastard has taken everything from you," he growled, "even your name!"

I sighed.

"That's not really true, Sebastian. Everything he's done, I've let him do. Look, this isn't really the place to have this conversation—let me just buy the papers and we'll go. Please."

Sebastian waited outside while I paid for six copies.

When I came out with my newspapers tucked under one arm, he was leaning against the brick wall with his eyes closed. I gazed at him anxiously.

He opened his eyes and looked down at me, forcing a smile.

"Come on, let's go celebrate your first article, Ms Reporter!"

I smiled back, relieved that he was attempting to lift his mood.

"We've got something else to celebrate. David is going away to a medical symposium. He leaves Friday night and doesn't get back until Sunday evening."

A huge and genuine smile spread across Sebastian's face. "*Two nights?!*"

I couldn't help laughing at his obvious happiness.

Without warning, he pulled me into his arms, hugging me to his chest. My free arm wrapped around his neck and I pulled his head down. His lips were warm and soft, his kiss gentle and sweet. Then I felt his lips part and his tongue swept into my mouth. I shivered with desire and I could feel his growing arousal through his jeans.

I tried to remember that we were in public. Reluctantly, I pushed him away from me.

"Let's go to a hotel ... like you said."

His voice was low and rough and he rubbed his hands over his short hair, with evident frustration. But before I could answer, I heard someone calling his name.

My head swiveled to see Ches walking toward us and my cheeks flushed with guilt. *How much had he seen?*

"Hey, man! What's up? Hi, Mrs. Wilson."

I tried to smile. "Hello, Ches. And please call me Caroline. I'm sorry about last night—I hope I didn't embarrass you."

He frowned slightly then laughed it off. "Nah, *you* didn't. It's cool."

Then he turned to Sebastian, a puzzled look on his face, his eyes flitting between us.

"Caroline's article has been published," said Sebastian, pointing at the pile of newspapers still tucked under my left arm.

"I was going to deliver them," I said smiling more naturally, "but now you're both here."

I handed a copy to Ches and another to Sebastian.

"Awesome!" said Ches. "Dad is going to be stoked when he sees this!"

"I've bought copies for Bill and Fido, too. Can you get these to them for me?" I handed the spare copies to Ches. "By the way, what *is* Fido's real name?"

Ches laughed. "It's Arnold. But don't use it, because he won't answer, and it'll just make him want to break my face if he finds out that I've told you."

His attention returned to Sebastian. "So what you doing, man? I'm going to take off and get a surf in before work—they'll probably want us to start early anyway because they're still short-staffed—whatever, it's more gas money for the van. You want to check out some waves or are you *busy* again?"

There was a brief, uncomfortable pause.

"Well, you guys have fun," I said, forcing a smile. "I have some errands to run."

"Are you going to the club later?" said Sebastian, a little too quickly.

I saw Ches's eyes flicker over to him.

"Oh ... I don't know. I'm not a member yet, although Donna Vorstadt suggested we might go there for coffee, but I'm not sure if that was supposed to be today or tomorrow. Maybe I'll see you both later. *Ciao*."

I tried to convey a message with my careful words but it was hard to tell if it had got through: Sebastian looked pretty pissed off.

I walked away with my copy of *City Beat* under one arm while my stomach played hopscotch.

I was bereft. I'd counted on a few hours with Sebastian and they'd been ripped away. But I wasn't going to waste my time either: not any more.

I pulled out my cell phone and dialed the number for *City Beat*.

"Hi, this is Caroline Wilson. Could I speak to Carl Winters, please?"

I was put on hold for a few seconds before I heard the editor's voice.

"Hi, Carolina, how are you?"

He pronounced my name the Italian way—just like in my article.

"Good, thank you, Mr. Winters. I wanted to say that I thought the article looked really great. Thank you so much for giving me the opportunity."

"Not at all, and please, call me Carl. I was going to call you. Do you have something for the next issue?"

"Yes, I do. I have 1500 words on the work of the Base hospital and I've nearly finished one on military families and what it means to them to move around a lot. That might be a little longer, if it's okay. I have some interviews with other wives set up for that."

"Excellent! Can you email them to me or, better still, can you come on in? It would be really good to meet you in person."

I made a quick decision.

"I'm free now. I could be there in thirty minutes?"

"Great! I'll look forward to it, Carolina."

Next I phoned Donna.

"Hi, Donna, it's Caroline."

"Hi! How are you?"

"I'm good. I just wanted to thank you for last night. It was ... very pleasant."

She chuckled. "I'm glad you enjoyed yourself. Johan was very taken with your dress—I think I should be jealous."

I laughed a little uncomfortably. "I was wondering if you and Shirley were free for coffee later today after all?"

She sounded surprised. "I'm free, but I'd have to check with Shirley."

"It's just I have a meeting with the *City Beat* editor now and it would be great to be able to tell him that I have another article almost ready."

"Wow! That's great! Good for you, Caroline. Look, let me call Shirley and I'll get back to you."

~

The offices of *City Beat* were housed in an orange-stucco, art deco building a couple of blocks from Lincoln Avenue. I managed to park nearby and hurried in with my laptop and notebook. I'd decided to show Carl some of my photographs of Base life. I knew they were pretty amateurish but there were three or four that I thought had come out well.

As I was walking into reception I heard my phone beep. There was a text from Donna arranging coffee at the country club and two missed calls from Sebastian.

I texted him back quickly.

Hi mtg at City Beat. Very exciting. Will meet Donna and Shirley at cc 3PM. Hope 2 cu. But wkend just for us

I turned my phone off quickly and introduced myself to the cheerful receptionist.

Carl Winters was much younger than I'd expected—in fact he was probably only a couple of years older than me. Here he was running a whole newspaper in a major city. It made me feel inadequate. But he was friendly and seemed to go out of his way to put me at my ease.

"It's nice to meet you at last, Carolina," he said shaking hands. "We've had some really good feedback already on the article. What else have you got for me?"

I opened my ancient laptop and while it was slowly cycling through its warm up, Carl started asking me questions about myself. I'd answered three or four before it occurred to me that I was being interviewed.

"How long have you been a military wife?"

"Eleven years."

"Eleven! You must have been a child bride."

"Well, not quite, but pretty young I guess. I know that's not in fashion these days, although you find it more among the military."

"Why do you think that is?"

"Rules!" I said, laughing lightly. "If you want to be able to follow your spouse around the country, you have to be married first. Or, if you want to live in sin, you have to live off base."

"It's quite different from civilian life, isn't it," he said thoughtfully.

"In all sorts of ways, big and small," I agreed.

I showed him the article on the Base hospital and he nodded as he read through it, which I took to be a good sign. Then I showed him my photographs.

"These are really good," he said, sounding surprised. "You didn't say you were a photographer."

"I'm not. I mean, I enjoy taking pictures, but I've no training. I just use my dad's old SLR. It's not even digital—I have to get the films processed at the drugstore."

"Well, they're really good: they definitely capture that sense of ... organized chaos, I guess. Well, Carolina, if we're going to use your photos, too, there'll be an additional fee for you: $450 for an article and photo. How does that sound?"

"That sounds wonderful. Thank you."

He glanced at his watch.

"I'm going to head out and get some lunch now. Maybe if you're not busy I could buy you a sandwich and a coffee?"

"Oh! That's very kind of you, Carl, but I've set up interviews with a couple of wives from the Base and, as I'm sure you'd guess, none of us do 'late'."

He laughed but looked a little disappointed. "Another time then?"

I smiled without answering, thanked him again, and left. He'd seemed very friendly. I hoped that's all it was.

Despite that slight awkwardness, I was walking on air, thrilled with the response to my articles and with a new sense of purpose. For a few brief moments, I allowed myself to be happy and in love.

Driving out to the country club, I ran through the questions I wanted to ask of Donna and Shirley. Carl Daniel's assessment of my work had given me confidence—newborn and weak, but it was confidence—of a sort.

I parked around the back, as before. It was only two o'clock and I hoped, really hoped, that I'd be able to snatch a few, private moments.

Am at cc

I sat for a minute but there was no reply. I didn't even know if Sebastian was allowed to carry his phone while he was working. I'd just have to be patient.

At reception, I handed in a completed membership form and a check, signed by David, for our first month's membership. David had felt that last night's dinner had gone well—he seemed to be oblivious to how much he'd annoyed Johan and Donna. Empathy was not one of my husband's qualities. I almost felt sorry for him. Almost.

I changed into my bikini and headed out to the pool with my notebook, sketching out some more ideas and refining my questions. I was so absorbed in my work—my work, not my hobby—that it was several moments before I realized that someone was standing over me.

"Your mineral water, ma'am."

I looked up to see Sebastian smiling down at me.

"Hi," I whispered.

"Hi, yourself. Meet me in the women's locker room in five minutes. There's a door at the back that says 'Private'. I'll be waiting."

My mouth was still hanging open as he walked away, desire shooting through my body. I took a sip from the frosted glass and stood up as casually as possible on shaky legs.

The locker room was mercifully empty. I made my way to the back, glancing over my shoulder every other second, my heart rate accelerating with every step.

I pushed open the door marked 'Private' and peered into the gloom of a large storage closet. I gasped when Sebastian's hands pulled me inside.

He didn't speak, not with words.

His lips burned on mine and I felt his hands everywhere, drinking me in, pulling me in, heating my blood.

I ran my hands down his chest and then around to his back, pushing them up under his t-shirt to feel his taut muscles and the warm, smooth texture of his skin beneath my fingertips.

He gripped my hair jerking my head back, running his teeth across my neck. I don't know if it was the dark, or the confined space, or the sense of danger, but Sebastian's movements were more confident, more assured than ever before, and I was swept away.

I felt the straps of my bikini top suddenly loosen, the thin fabric falling away. His mouth moved from my neck, across my chest and then he ran his tongue between the valley of my breasts and down to my stomach, where he knelt.

He hooked his fingers into my bikini bottoms and tugged them down. I stood naked before him in the dim light while, in his own way, he worshipped my body.

He stood up slowly, kissing me all the way.

I gripped his shoulders, feeling his muscles bunch under my hands as pleasure shot through me. I tugged on the material of his t-shirt, desperate to connect flesh with flesh. He stood quickly and pulled it over his head then crushed me to his chest and kissed me with increasing urgency. I had never felt so desired, never wanted a man as much as I wanted Sebastian at that moment.

He pressed himself into me and I knew that he was as aroused as I was.

My fingers scrabbled at the front of his shorts and I heard his soft gasp. With one, swift movement I pushed his briefs off his hips and reached down to grip him in my hands.

He groaned again, then abruptly brushed my hands away. He bent down and pulled out a condom packet from his shorts. The sound of the foil tearing seemed so loud, I half expected someone to bang on the door and demand to know what we were doing.

Sebastian straightened up and fastened his hands on my hips, lifting me up suddenly. I wrapped my legs around his waist as he thrust into me, making me cry out. I clung onto his shoulders as he pushed me back against the wall, moving hard and fast, his face buried in my neck, his breathing becoming ragged.

Behind my bare back, I felt the doors of a cupboard. The contents rattled alarmingly as Sebastian pounded into me.

The rawness and urgency of our love-making pushed me over the edge and I climaxed around him, made breathless by the extraordinary turn of events. Four minutes ago I had been working quietly by the pool.

I felt Sebastian slam into me one last time and he cried out softly then sank to the floor with me cradled on his lap.

I stroked his face in the dark. I thought I felt tears on his face but I couldn't be sure.

I laid my hand on his chest, feeling the rapid beating of his heart slowly return to normal.

"I love you," he breathed, placing gentle, loving kisses on my lips. "I love you so much."

We lay there for some minutes, cocooned by the dim light creeping through the cracks around the door.

"You have to get back to work," I said softly.

He sighed. "I know."

"We have the whole weekend to look forward to."

"I have to work all day Friday and Saturday," he said sadly.

"The nights are still ours."

"All night."

"Yes."

I felt his lips turn upwards in a smile and he kissed me.

I slid off him, wincing slightly. I'd enjoyed his aggressive love-making, more than enjoyed, but I was feeling a little sore. I didn't care: it was a small price to pay.

We both had to scrabble around in the dark to find our clothes. I couldn't help laughing to myself—there certainly wasn't much dignity in it, but damn, it was hot!

We listened carefully at the door but at that time of the day the locker room was still empty. I don't know what we'd have done if it had been busy—we could have been stuck there for hours! Hmm, that didn't sound so bad.

Sebastian quickly pressed his lips to mine then snuck out first. He looked his usual, handsome self, although perhaps a little more flushed than usual.

I, on the other hand, looked as if I'd just had rough sex up against a cupboard door in the dark. I stared in the mirror at my reddened face, neck, chest and back, and at my once neat ponytail which was lopsided with half my hair coming loose.

I spent a few minutes splashing myself with cold water, trying to return my skin to its usual olive tones, and combed my hair out with my fingers. Eventually I felt composed enough to leave the locker room. As I walked back to the pool, I imagined that everyone I saw knew *exactly* what I'd been doing. I felt as if I had a sign pointing at me shouting 'Locker-room Slut!'.

I slid onto my sun lounger and gratefully took a long drink of my mineral water. I picked up my notebook and pencil and tried to concentrate but my thoughts were well and truly scattered. I couldn't believe what I'd just done. It had been so intense and exciting and so completely out of character for me. Although I wasn't entirely sure what my character was anymore. I'd meant it when I'd told Sebastian that it wasn't David's fault, that I'd let him take control and allowed him to take away the essence of being me. I'd been a sleepwalker through my marriage: we both deserved better—David as well as me.

I wondered again what David saw in me—had he seen something when I was 19 that was no longer there? Or did he simply prefer a submissive, compliant, bovine wife? And what about Sebastian? Why did he want me? Was it more than just sex for him, or was I being naïve? He said he loved me but...

"I see you've been catching some sun—my, you're looking a little red, Caroline."

Donna's kind face was looking down at me.

"Oh, hi Donna," I said, my voice sounding a little more high-pitched than usual.

"And this is Shirley."

"We've spoken on the phone—it's nice to meet you in person."

I stood up to give Donna a quick hug and to shake hands shyly with Shirley Peters who was short and dark haired, and had mischievous hazel eyes—the resemblance to Ches was obvious.

"It's good to meet you, too, Caroline. I've heard so much about you already. You've made quite an impression on the boys. Ches couldn't wait to show me your article."

She laughed lightly. "My son is certainly a fan and I have my suspicions about Sebastian."

My face froze as she winked at Donna. "It's like having a second son—I swear Sebastian spends more time at our house than he does at his own. Hmm, well, not so much lately: Ches thinks he's got a girlfriend, although I don't know why it's such a secret." She sighed. "Well, maybe I do—I can't imagine him wanting to bring a girl home to meet Estelle and Donald."

Donna nodded sympathetically and settled herself in a deckchair under the large, colorful sun umbrella. Shirley headed for the locker room to change into her swimsuit.

"How was your meeting at *City Beat*?"

I couldn't help smiling at Donna—she really was interested in my writing. I showed her the article and watched her face as she read it in detail.

"You've really caught the spirit of surfing, Caroline," she said. "And that's a super photograph. Oh, look! Sebastian still had his long hair there. I wonder why he cut it? I suspect that his father had something to do with that."

Shirley returned wearing a purple and orange tankini.

"What are you suspecting?" she asked, her voice laced with curiosity.

"Oh, we were just talking about Sebastian's buzz-cut."

"Oh, that," said Shirley darkly. "He wouldn't say anything to Ches, but we definitely had the impression it wasn't voluntary. All the girls at school were crazy about Sebastian, according to Ches. I think if they weren't such good friends he would have been a little jealous—well, more than a little. There was even something in the yearbook about Sebastian's long hair, if you can imagine that." She frowned. "And did you see that bruise he had on his cheek last week?"

She sucked her teeth.

"Hey, Mom!"

Ches was walking toward us in his shorts and polo-shirt uniform. He grinned at his mother and gave her an affectionate kiss on the cheek.

"Chester, honey! Just in time—Donna and I are about to expire from thirst."

"Hi Donna, Caroline," he smiled, but whatever he saw behind us made his smile falter. "Hello, Mrs. Hunter."

Sebastian's mother weaved her way toward us—it was clear she'd spent some quality time at the bar.

"Donna," she slurred. "And friends." She looked at me, "the won-der-ful Caroline Wilson. I almost expected you to be walking across the water in the swimming pool, not lying next to it."

"You've been drinking, Estelle," said Donna sharply. "Perhaps you should rest on the veranda where it's cooler."

"Yes, let's put the embarrassing drunk where she won't bother anyone, let's hide her out of the way," sneered Estelle. "You sound just like Donald."

Donna turned to Ches and spoke in a quiet voice. "Is Sebastian here? Can you get him, please."

Ches nodded and walked away quickly.

Estelle picked up my copy of *City Beat* and tried to focus her eyes on the photograph. Suddenly she tossed the newspaper into the pool.

"You don't fool me, *Mrs. Wilson*," she snarled. "You were a stuck up bitch nine years ago and you haven't changed, have you? You've just polished up your act. But you don't fool me."

"Estelle! Keep your voice down," ordered Donna, as other people around the pool began to stare. I was frozen on my sun lounger, terrified of what Estelle might say next.

She scowled at me then turned her glazed eyes to Donna.

"You don't tell me what to do, Donna. I don't even know why you like her. She pretends to be so sweet and pure—but she isn't. Flaunting herself everywhere, ingratiating herself. Well, she doesn't fool me. She's nothing but a..."

"Mom!" Sebastian's voice was tight with anger as he walked toward us. "What are you doing?"

Ches stood behind him, one hand on his shoulder, seeming to restrain him.

"Mom, you're embarrassing yourself," he said, coldly. "I'll drive you home."

Estelle whirled around and slapped him hard. I couldn't help gasping as my hand flew to my mouth and I started to stand up.

Sebastian's eyes were almost black with fury. Ches gripped his arm and tugged him backward.

"Come on, buddy, walk away."

A sudden silence descended, horrified eyes staring at Estelle.

Slowly she came to her senses and her cheeks flushed with embarrassment as she took in the shocked faces turned in her direction. She straightened her purse over her shoulder and staggered off.

"What the hell was *that* about?" whispered Shirley.

Donna sighed. "I don't know: but her drinking is getting worse. Donald will have to do something."

Shirley scoffed at the idea. "Donald doesn't give a shit about her—word is that he's been seeing some young civilian nurse. *Seeing to her,* probably."

Donna shook her head slowly. "God knows those two should have divorced years ago. It would have been better for Sebastian if they had. Poor boy, I hope he's okay."

"He's got Ches with him," said Shirley softly. "He'll be okay, he's used to it."

My heart lurched painfully. I desperately wanted to wrap my arms around Sebastian to comfort and protect him, but I couldn't. It hurt so much. And then a more painful thought crossed my mind—maybe he wasn't running *to* me, maybe he was just running away from *that*. And if he was, I couldn't blame him. Besides, wouldn't he say the same thing about me and David?

I didn't want to believe it, but once the thought was there, it seemed more plausible than to believe that Sebastian would want to be with me.

He had opened my eyes to a world of possibilities, to a world where I could be loved for myself, but would my new life be with him? I was afraid to hope.

After a moment, Shirley stood up. "I'll just go check on the boys."

Donna exhaled deeply and looked at me. "Are you okay, Caroline?"

I nodded, still feeling shaken. Did Estelle *know?*

"That wasn't really about you," Donna continued, "she's just jealous."

"Jealous? Of what?"

Donna smiled sadly. "Never mind, it doesn't matter. Now, what were those questions you had?"

I shook my head. "They seem rather insignificant now." I stared at the sodden sheets of newsprint that some helpful children were fishing out of the pool.

"Please ask me," said Donna. "I need something to take my mind off that awful scene."

We chatted about our shared experiences of living on different bases for several minutes, before Shirley reappeared.

"How's Sebastian?" asked Donna, her concern evident. "Did you see Estelle?"

"Ches and Sebastian got her into the car, he's driving her home."

She shook her head. "If there are any more incidents like that, Estelle will have her membership suspended."

"I'll speak to Johan," said Donna. "Maybe he'll be able to persuade her to ... seek some help. She won't be the first Navy wife to ... well, she won't be the first."

A subdued Ches returned with thee orange juices. Shirley rubbed his arm and they swapped brief smiles. It was refreshing to see the close relationship they had—especially after the unpleasant scene that had played out between Estelle and Sebastian.

I bit my tongue as Ches went back to work—I wanted to ask him if Sebastian was okay, but I couldn't.

I turned my attention to finishing my article, as Donna had suggested.

Shirley was incredibly helpful, offering fascinating insights into the world of the military wife.

"Of course, it's hard leaving friends behind, and hard for Chester starting new schools every couple of years, but it's made us closer as a family, too. And the Marine Corps is a second family, we're all pretty tight. It's made Chester good at making friends and he's a very resourceful boy, very self-sufficient. But we did make sure that his last four years of high school were consistent—we felt that was important for his education. I like traveling and the challenge of new places—new countries. To be honest, I'm dreading the day when Mitch retires: I don't know what he'll do with himself. He's so used to the structure and routine of the Marines, I'm not sure how well either of us will adapt to civilian life.

"But what about you, Caroline? If David decided to quit the Navy, what would you do?"

I twitched uncomfortably, not wanting to have the spotlight turned on me.

"I don't think his routine would change that much: he'd still work in a hospital, still work his clinics. It wouldn't make that much difference. Just a different sort of uniform."

Donna smiled. "Yes, you're right. Medicine imposes its own set of regulations and routines. Being the wife of a doctor isn't such a huge leap."

I'd enjoyed talking to Donna and Shirley—it had been a lot like having friends—but I realized the sun had shifted in the sky and I leapt up.

"Oh, I'm so sorry. I have to get back and pack for David. He's taking everything with him to the hospital tomorrow morning. I have a mountain of ironing to do."

Shirley laughed and Donna smiled sympathetically.

I thanked them again and waved quickly.

CHAPTER TEN

DAVID MANAGED TO FIND FAULT WITH EVERYTHING THAT EVENING: MY cooking, the clothes I'd packed for him, the way I'd ironed his shirt and pants, probably even the amount of air I was inconveniently breathing.

I tried to think if he'd always been so difficult. I honestly couldn't remember.

He was particularly annoyed because I refused to come to bed with him, insisting instead on finishing my interview notes. During his bombastic huffing, I realized that he didn't have a coping mechanism for dealing with my refusal—he wasn't used to it and he didn't know how to handle it. The thought was oddly liberating.

When he left the next morning, he didn't even ask how I was planning to spend my weekend. Not that 'screwing the brains out of my young lover in your bed' would have figured high on my list of responses to that particular question, but I did think he might have pretended to take an interest.

I'd had one brief text from Sebastian simply saying that he was looking forward to the weekend. He hadn't answered when I'd asked if he was okay.

I spent the day writing and also took a moment to look up possible photography classes I could take at NYU. Carl Winters had praised my snaps—it made me wonder if I could take that side of my work further.

During the afternoon, Donna telephoned to invite me to supper. I appreciated her kindness but I wasn't going to be as alone as she thought. I simply told her I was enjoying the peace and quiet—she understood at once, checking only that I'd be at the annual Base picnic on Sunday.

I felt strangely nervous. I hadn't seen Sebastian since yesterday's ugly scene.

It was also the first time that we'd been able to plan to be together for more than a few hours.

It was nearly midnight when I heard his light tap on the backdoor. I'd been dozing on the couch while I waited for him to finish his shift at the country club.

I made sure the kitchen light was off before I unlocked the door.

"Hi."

"Hi, yourself."

We stood staring at each other, and he frowned slightly.

"Can I come in?"

"Of course."

I stood back to allow him to pass, then I closed the door and locked it again. When I turned around he was still staring at me.

"I want to kiss you," he said, sounding uncertain.

"Do you?"

I didn't know why there was so much tension between us.

"Caro, what's wrong?"

"Nothing. Just kiss me."

He hesitated for less than a second then slowly walked forward. He held the palm of his hand against my cheek and lowered his face to me. He kissed me twice, his mouth lightly touching mine, then he wrapped his arms around my waist and leaned down to rest his forehead against mine.

"I've missed you," he whispered.

I smiled and felt my body relax.

"Have you?"

"Yes." He pulled me in more tightly. "I'm really sorry about yesterday, about ... what my mom said."

I straightened up abruptly and his hands dropped to his sides as he gazed at me warily. We needed to have this conversation—now.

"Does she know? About you and me?"

He shook his head vehemently. "Of course not!"

I looked into his eyes. "Because she said some things that made me think she did."

Sebastian looked horrified.

"What did she say?"

I shrugged.

"Please!"

I let out a long sigh, closing my eyes against the unpleasant memory.

"She said I'd been 'flaunting' myself and that I wasn't 'pure', that she *knew better*. Sebastian, what does she know? She must know something or why would she have put it like that?"

He ran his hands over his hair looking angry and upset, but stayed resolutely silent.

"For God's sake, tell me!"

My voice was louder than I'd intended.

He blinked and looked away. "I promise she doesn't know anything, Caro. It's just that..."

He paused.

"Just what?"

"Just some shit my dad was talking. It's nothing."

"Tell me!" I said forcefully.

Sebastian looked at me angrily.

"My dad said you were a hot piece of tail and that you wouldn't be such an uptight bitch if *your husband* had been fucking you properly."

I felt sick.

I walked to the kitchen sink, and leaned over it.

"Is that ... is that what people think of me?" I murmured.

"No! God, no! My father is an asshole, Caro. No one thinks that. Mitch, Bill, Ches—they all think you're great. I mean, yeah, they think you're gorgeous, who wouldn't? But I promise they've never *ever* said anything like that."

I straightened up slowly and turned around to face him. He was standing with his arms out-stretched as if he wanted to touch me but was afraid to.

"Are you hungry?"

He was confused by the sudden change of topic, away from my self-flagellation.

"Hungry?"

"Yes. Did you eat at the club tonight?"

His hands fell to his side and for a second he closed his eyes tiredly, before walking toward me and taking me into his arms.

I tried to resist, still raw from his father's words.

"Caro, don't push me away."

He wrapped his arms around my shoulders and held me.

"I'm sorry, okay. I'm sorry I told you what that asshole said. Hell, you should hear what he calls me sometimes ... well, maybe not. I don't listen anymore. All that matters is that we're together, okay?"

I didn't answer.

"Okay?" he said again, more forcefully.

I took a deep breath.

"Okay," I agreed, quietly.

He kissed my hair and smiled down at me.

We stood there for some minutes, just enjoying a moment of peace.

"So, are you hungry?" I said at last. "Did you eat tonight?"

He rolled his eyes at me and I had to smile.

"No, we were slammed—I didn't have time."

"I'll fix you something to eat: linguini, pesto and pine nuts okay?"

"You don't have to cook for me, Caro," he said frowning slightly.

"I want to. Besides, you haven't eaten ... and you'll need your energy."

I grinned up at him and he gave in with good grace.

"Well, in that case, yeah, I'm starving."

He pulled out a chair and sat at the table watching me.

"So, how was work? Anything interesting happen today?"

I was determined that we would have some normal conversation.

"I did that First Aid training certificate this morning. It was all stuff I'd done at the surf lifesaving club, so it was pretty easy. I'll be mostly working poolside with Ches from now on."

"You don't like waiting tables?"

"Not so much—I'd rather be outside."

"Are you sure it's not just a chance to impress bored, horny Navy wives with your gorgeous body?"

"There's only one woman I want to impress," he said, returning my smile.

"How's that going for you?"

"Well, it was touch-and-go for a while, but she's making me dinner, so I guess it's going okay. How was your day?"

"Good. I finished another article and have planned out three more. I was afraid I might run out of material, but I have enough ideas to write a whole book, I think. Oh, and I looked up some photography courses at NYU. Have you decided which classes you want to take in the spring?"

When he didn't answer, I looked up from the chopping board—Sebastian was sitting, rocking back on the chair, a huge smile on his face.

"What?"

"I love it when you talk like that?"

It was my turn to be confused.

"Like what?"

"When you're talking about stuff we're going to do together: about our future."

I dropped the torn basil leaves and looked directly at him.

"Sebastian, I didn't *have* a future until you got me thinking about one. God knows how long I'd have carried on drifting. But you have to promise me something..."

"Anything: I'll promise you anything."

I took a deep breath.

"I want you to promise me that when you ... when you start thinking about a different future ... without me..."

His expression changed and his eyes darkened with anger.

"Jesus, Caro! How can you say that to me?"

"No, please! Let me finish. We can't ignore our age difference and one day, when it starts to ... change things, I'll understand. I don't want us to sink into indifference and dislike. Been there, done that. When you decide to go, just ... just give me some notice. That's all I ask."

He stared back.

I was glad I'd said it—I'd needed to say it, but Sebastian looked really angry.

"Caro, don't you understand how I feel about you? I love you: you're all I want. I want a future with you—I want our lives to be together. I'm not a kid—I've had to grow up fast. I've been taking care of myself for a long time now. And I want to take care of you."

"I'm just saying that I'll understand when that changes."

"Don't patronize me, Caro," he said, sounding even angrier. "You think I don't know what it means to make this commitment, but I do. You think I'm giving up everything and that I'll regret it later, but you're wrong. I've seen what a bad marriage is like, I've seen how miserable my parents have been. But when I'm with you, I feel ... so incredibly happy, like the world is worth it after all. I know how rare that is, I've *seen* how rare that is. Don't dismiss how I feel just because ... just because I'm younger than you. You're beautiful and kind and talented and you have a gift ... people are drawn to you—and you don't even see it. And it's just one of the things I love about you."

I sighed, feeling his anguish in every word.

"And what about children, Sebastian?"

He blinked several times.

"What about children?"

"Well, do you really want to be saddled with children when you're twenty? No, I don't imagine you do. Well, what about when you're in your thirties and you like the idea of having a couple of kids running around the house and I'll be in my late forties and *too old*."

He shrugged, trying to look casual but I could tell that he was rattled.

"If you want kids we can have kids."

I smiled sadly and shook my head.

"It doesn't work like that, Sebastian: we'd both have to want them—and time isn't on our side. Do you see what I'm saying?"

"Yes, I see what you're saying—and I see what you're doing: you're trying to think of every reason under the sun why we shouldn't be together. But none of that matters—if you want to be with me." He took a deep breath. "Do you, Caro?"

I sighed. I wanted him more than air, but I had to make him think, *really think*, about what we were doing.

"Sebastian, how long do you think these *physical* feelings will last? Six months? A year? Two, if we're lucky. And then what? What about when you make friends at college and you introduce them to your *older* girlfriend? What about..."

But he interrupted me.

"None of that matters. And I think you're wrong anyway—I can't imagine not wanting you—not ever. You're smart and funny and I enjoy being with you even when we don't ... when we're not ... making love. When I was eight years old, I used to imagine that you were my girlfriend and that we'd run away together. And then you left and I'd lost my best friend, too. I used to dream about you coming back. As I got older, I ... I began to understand the ... my feelings for you better. I didn't think dreams could come true—but they have for me, Caro. Why are you so scared? I mean, forget all that legal bullshit ... why do you keep trying to ... I don't know, make me change my mind? What do you think I have here that I wouldn't give up in a heartbeat to be with you? There's nothing to keep me here. I'll go anywhere, do anything to be with you." He sighed. "I know you have more to lose and I hate, *hate* that I'm responsible for that, but ... do you want to be with me? Forever. *Sempre*."

I didn't have any words of opposition or defiance left in me. The future was unwritten—maybe one day I would be too old for him and he would leave me—it seemed inevitable. But wouldn't two or three years of love be worth having, regardless? I knew my marriage was over: it had been over for a long time before I'd met Sebastian—I'd just been too much of a coward to admit it.

Was I prepared to take a chance on the future ... a chance on love? I looked into his lovely face, tension and fear and anxiety holding him rigid. I thought again about the question he'd asked me: did I want to be with him?

"Yes. I do."

He exhaled deeply as if he'd been holding his breath.

"That's all that matters."

He pushed his chair back and walked over, draping his arms around me. He rested his chin on my shoulder and nestled his face in my neck, his breath warm on my skin.

We stood like that for some moments, allowing the fear and tension to drain away.

"You'll have to let go if I'm going to finish making you supper," I said gently.

I felt his smile as he tightened his grip momentarily and then let his hands slide away. He sat back at the table and grinned at me.

"It's good to know you want food more than you want sex," I couldn't help commenting.

He laughed. "It's about even at the moment, but you told me that I'd need my energy so I'm just following your advice."

I loved to see him like this, happy and relaxed, teasing me. I felt guilty for causing the tension in the first place, but relieved we'd talked it through—for now, at least.

I finished making the pesto and served up the linguini with toasted pine nuts and freshly grated parmesan.

"Aren't you having some?"

I shook my head. "I had mine hours ago."

"It smells great."

He ate rapidly, shoveling in huge mouthfuls. He was clearly ravenous. I thought it was rather poor that the club hadn't ensured that their young staff had had a proper meal break.

"What's this photography course that you're interested in?" he said, between mouthfuls.

"When I met up with Carl Winters at *City Beat* he really liked my photos of Base life. I thought I might try and take a course in photojournalism. What do you think?"

"That sounds great. I haven't seen your photos—I'd really like to."

"Would you?"

He rolled his eyes at me as he chomped through another enormous mouthful.

"Okay, well, I'll show you later if you like."

"Later, like tomorrow," he said assertively.

A thrill of anticipation ran through me at his words. Yes, later.

"I'm going to have a glass of wine. Would you like one?"

"Isn't that illegal," he smirked at me. "Plying a minor with liquor!"

I glanced over my shoulder at him as I retrieved the bottle of red wine I'd opened earlier.

"If I'm going to go to Hell, I may as well do it thoroughly."

He laughed. "I'd rather have a beer, if you've got one."

I pulled a face. "Beer doesn't go with pesto. Here, try this."

I passed him a small glass of red wine.

He tasted it hesitantly then smiled. "That's really good. What is it?"

"It's a ten year old Barolo. It's better when it's not too fruity. Most people like the oakier-tasting ones but I guess I get my old-fashioned ideas from my dad."

Sebastian looked impressed.

"Do you know a lot about wine?"

"A little. Well, only what Papa taught me. His family used to grow Moscato grapes." I shrugged. "Maybe they still do."

"Let's find out!" he said, his eyes sparkling with adventure, "when we take that road trip."

"Can you ride a motorcycle?"

"Sure! Well, I don't have a completion certificate from the motorcycle training course, but I took a few lessons, and I've ridden Ches's. It's cool."

I saw that he'd cleared his plate and was eyeing the fruit bowl.

"Help yourself."

"Thanks!"

I stood up and carried away his empty plates. I liked listening to music when I washed dishes so I put on a CD of my favorite arias.

"Puccini?"

I smiled. "Of course. Do you know this opera?"

Sebastian shook his head. "I recognize it but I can't remember what it's from."

"It's *'O Mio Babbino Caro'* from *Gianni Schicchi*."

"Caro! Like your name, except that's the male way of saying it, isn't it?"

"I don't mind. I like that you're the only person who calls me that."

His answering smile was huge.

"Papa used to call me *'mia cara'*."

The music swirled around us and I was swept up in a deluge of memories.

"What's this song about?" asked Sebastian after a couple of minutes.

"It's an aria sung by a girl to her beloved father, begging him to let her marry the boy she loves."

"It sounds very Romeo and Juliet."

"Yes, except it's a comedy."

He raised his eyebrows. "Yeah, right!"

I laughed at him. "It is!"

He listened to the music some more. "I can pick out some of the words—something about buying a ring?"

"That's right, and if he doesn't let her, she's threatening to throw herself off the Ponte Vecchio bridge."

"Sounds over the top."

"Well, it is opera."

"I'd like to buy you a ring."

He sounded so serious I turned around from the sink. Sebastian was staring at me.

"I want to marry you, Caro."

I gasped and dropped the glass I was holding. It slid down into the soapy water but didn't shatter.

"Sebastian..."

"I mean it. I want to marry you. Will you, Caro? Will you marry me?"

I shook my head. "Sebastian ... I can't talk about this now. I *am* married—to David. And anyway, I wouldn't do that to you—you're too..."

"Too young? Is that what you're going to say, because if you are, don't bother."

He rested his head in his hands then looked up again.

"In just over three months, I'll be 18. I could enlist and a few months later I could be sent to the Middle East. I'll be old enough to fight, to die for my country, but you don't think I'll be old enough to marry you?"

He didn't sound angry, just determined.

My brain had ceased to function—I simply carried on staring at him.

He looked at me accusingly.

"You met David before you were 18—and you married really quickly."

"Yes, and what a disaster that's been," I said, bitterly.

Sebastian looked like I'd slapped him.

I immediately regretted my words.

"I'm sorry, but..."

"But what?"

"Sebastian, we've been together for just a couple of weeks—under the most intense circumstances. Can't we just ... spend some time together? Get to know each other properly. Sometimes I feel that we hardly know each other at all."

"I love you and I want to marry you. What else do you want to know?"

"Everything! What's your favorite book? What's your favorite movie? What was your best subject in school? Who was your first crush? What CD have you got in your player at home right now? What do you eat for breakfast? Do you prefer football or baseball? Were you a jock at school? Did you ever date a cheerleader? Do you remember your dreams? What's your favorite color? Have you ever cried watching a movie? I don't know—everything!"

He let out a deep sigh.

"Okay, I get it. I'm rushing you."

I frowned.

"That's not it—well, not entirely. It's just ... we've done everything backward."

I walked over to him and laid my hand on his chest. "I want to know everything: inside as well as out. I want to know *you*."

He held my hand and played with my fingers but he still couldn't look at me. He was really upset. I guess being turned down when you ask someone to marry you would get you that way. I'd hurt him—and he was the last person in the whole world that I wanted to hurt.

I pulled my hand free and held his face until he had to look at me.

"Sebastian, I feel like you've woken me from a dream. But I barely know who *I* am, let alone ... I'm sorry I hurt you. I would never want to do that."

I rested my lips on his, two, three times, trying to convey a message with my light touch.

He pulled away and looked at me.

"Old Yeller."

"Excuse me?"

"That was a movie that made me cry ... when he had to shoot his dog."

"How old were you when you saw it?"

"Ten, maybe. I'm not sure. I always hoped we'd have a dog, but Mom said they made too much mess. Do you like dogs?"

"Yes. When I was growing up a neighbor had a little Jack Russell terrier called 'Tano'. He said the name meant 'number five' but I don't remember what language that was. She was so sweet. I cried for three days when she died. Dad wanted to buy me a puppy but Mom wouldn't let him, so I got a goldfish instead."

"A goldfish?!"

I grinned at him. "Yes, not quite the same thing! I called him 'Splash'—not very original."

"We could get a dog."

"What, and take him on the back of our motorcycle through Italy?!"

"Yeah! A biker dog! That would be awesome!"

I laughed.

"What's your favorite movie?" he said.

"I can only think of animal movies now. I don't know, 'White Fang' maybe or 'Call of the Wild'. Oh, but I love 'Gone with the Wind'."

He pulled a face.

"What was the last movie that made you cry?"

"I cry at most movies. Um ... 'Edward Scissorhands'—that always makes me cry."

"Who was your first crush? It had better be a movie star though or I might have to hunt him down."

"Better get your gun then!"

"Why?"

"Anthony Kiedis."

"Who?"

"The vocalist from the Red Hot Chili Peppers."

"You like rock?"

"I like all sorts of music."

He laughed happily.

"God, I love you!"

I couldn't help smiling back at him. "What?"

"Just when I think I know you, you surprise the shit out of me."

I sat on his lap and put my arms around his neck.

"Okay, your turn: favorite book?"

"Heart of Darkness."

"Ugh! Why that? It's a horrible story!"

"I guess because it shows how ... how far a man can go when he's in a place without limits."

"Hmm, I don't think you'll turn me into a Conrad fan. Okay, first girl you ever kissed?"

He reddened and looked down.

"Go on, tell me. I won't be jealous. Well, maybe a little."

"Brenda Wiseman."

"And how old were you?"

"Sixteen."

I couldn't help thinking that wasn't so very long ago for him. And then my overactive brain imagined him making out with her and...

"What happened to her?"

"Nothing."

"Well what happened *with* her?"

He shook his head, clearly embarrassed. I was intrigued.

"Come on, tell me. It can't be that bad."

"We dated for a while..."

"And..."

"We broke up."

"When was this? When did you break up with her?"

He shifted uncomfortably beneath me.

"Four months ago."

I felt like I'd been punched in the stomach.

"You went out with her for two years?"

He shook his head. "No, not ... about ten months."

"Oh."

I stood up and he looked at me helplessly.

"I'm sorry, Caro..."

"No, don't apologize. I'm just ... surprised. I got the impression that you hadn't..."

"We didn't sleep together."

"Why not? Most teenage boys..." the words burned my throat, "most teenage boys would have been desperate to..."

He shifted uncomfortably.

"We were going to—then I heard that she'd been screwing Jack—that guy you met once." He shook his head. "But I'm glad I didn't—with her. I didn't love her. You're the only woman I've ever loved: it's always been you."

I found it hard to take in. Where did his certainty come from?

"Caro?"

"I'm okay. I'm just ... surprised." There was that word again. "What would you have done if I hadn't come back?"

He shrugged. "I don't know."

But I knew. One day he would have met someone his own age, someone special, and he'd have fallen in love, he'd have had a chance of a normal relationship. And if *I* hadn't met *him*? I'd still be sleepwalking through my life.

But I *had* come back and we *had* met again. And I couldn't go back to the way I was. I didn't want to.

I held out my hand to him.

"Come on, it's late. Let's go to bed."

We walked up the stairs, hand-in-hand. He stood awkwardly in the doorway while I turned on the small bedside light.

"You want to use the bathroom first?"

"Okay."

"You can use my toothbrush if you want. The blue one."

He fidgeted for a few seconds then went into the bathroom. I turned down the sheets, wondering if it would have been better if we'd gone to the guest room. But then again, what difference would that really make?

We swapped over and as I cleaned my teeth with the damp brush, I stared at my reflection in the bathroom mirror—the face was familiar but that was about all. Everything else had changed.

When I came out Sebastian was sitting on the edge of the bed, still fully dressed.

"By the way, where do your parents think you are tonight?"

He blinked and looked up, clearly his thoughts had been somewhere else entirely.

"They won't notice I'm not there. They've probably passed out drunk again."

He sneered the words.

"Ches dropped me off at home and I jogged over here—that's why I was late. I didn't want him to know where ... he's picking me up at 10.30AM, so I'll have to be back by then." He sighed. "That doesn't seem very long from now."

"What if your parents see your room is empty and that your bed hasn't been slept in?"

I felt panicky at the thought.

Sebastian gave a half-smile. "I didn't make my bed this morning. If they look in—which they won't—they'll just assume they missed me. Honestly, they won't notice." He scowled. "They never notice anything about me anyway—except my fucking hair."

Unconsciously, he ran his hands over his head as he spoke.

"But it got us here, didn't it," I said quietly.

He looked at me seriously and nodded slowly. "Are you sorry?"

I shook my head. "No. You make me feel ... alive."

I leaned down and kissed him—a soft, gentle, loving kiss. He responded immediately and passionately, kissing me until we were both breathing hard.

"I ... I have to go downstairs," he said, standing up.

"What? Why?"

"I left the condoms in my jacket pocket," he mumbled, embarrassed.

"Oh, well, I meant to say something about that."

He flashed a nervous glance at me.

"I told you I was going to start taking birth control pills—and I did, I have. We don't need to use condoms anymore."

"Really? You're sure?"

I smiled. "Yes, no more playing hunt the lost condom."

He laughed softly. "I kinda liked that game."

"Well, *I* didn't. Anyway, we're good to go," I said, arching one eyebrow. "Oh, but I should mention ... I don't know if this will bother you ... but I got my period. That's why I know it's safe for us to stop using condoms. Does it bother you? I mean, *will* it bother you?"

I felt suddenly anxious—we were reaching for a new level of intimacy and I wasn't sure what his reaction would be.

"Can you? I mean, is it okay to ... while you're...? I don't want to hurt you..."

I stroked his cheek. He looked so worried.

"Yes, we can still make love. I was just checking that you were okay with ... a little sblood."

His eyes were huge. "I want to make love to you, Caro. God, I want to."

"Then I think you're wearing too many clothes."

He responded immediately, kicking his sneakers off his bare feet and tearing his t-shirt over his head. I thought I heard one of the seams rip.

"Hey, it's okay! We've got all night. I want to take it slow with you."

He looked confused for a moment, then smiled shyly.

"Okay."

I pushed him down so he was sitting on the edge of the bed again, and sat astride him. His arms encircled my waist, pulling me toward him.

"Mmm," I said, nuzzling his chin as I wrapped my arms around his neck, "this is my happy place."

Using my teeth, I tugged gently on his earlobe and was rewarded with a soft moan. I let my fingers ripple across his back, enjoying the feel of his skin and the tautness of his defined muscles. I used my fingertips to massage him lightly and he groaned again.

"What's your favorite color?" I whispered against his neck.

"What? Um ... blue. No, green. Red—maybe."

"That sounded definite! So, football or baseball? Or maybe basketball? Hockey?"

"Basket ... base... um..."

"Are you finding it difficult to concentrate?" I teased him.

"Caro, I can barely remember my own name when I'm with you!"

I chuckled quietly. "What do you like for breakfast?"

"Jeez, I don't know!"

"Tell me!"

"I don't usually eat breakfast."

"Well, what would you like tomorrow?"

"You!" he said.

He stood up suddenly, taking me with him, then threw me down on the bed.

"Enough with the slow," he said, his eyes dark and serious.

A pulse of desire and lust and need surged through me.

I sat up slowly, hooking my fingers into his belt loops and pulled him toward me. He trembled as I ran the tips of my fingers under his waistband. With bold hands, I traced the outline of his erection through his jeans. He inhaled sharply.

Watching his face the entire time, I opened his jeans, one button at a time, and pulled them down his long, strong, tan legs. His eyelids fluttered closed and he breathed deeply as I pushed the jeans past his knees.

They tangled around his ankles and he nearly fell over trying to kick them off. I smothered a laugh. Sebastian didn't have an arrogant bone in his body, but he was a man, and all men have their pride.

"Come and lie down next to me," I said, still smiling.

I wiggled out of my skirt and tossed it onto the floor. Tonight was not a night to worry about creased clothing.

We lay facing each other: he in his briefs, me in my t-shirt and panties. He scooted down the bed till our faces were at the same level and he smiled at me.

"Hi."

"Hi, yourself."

"What's *your* favorite color?" he said.

"I have absolutely no idea."

He laughed happily and ran his warm fingers down my arm.

"You're so beautiful," he breathed.

"So are you," I countered, "and so sweet."

He frowned slightly and let his hand drift over my body until he was cupping my backside. He squeezed gently and I responded by hooking my leg over his hip.

He flexed automatically, pushing himself into me and another delicious shiver ran down the entire length of my body.

He rolled gently so I was on my back, and he was hovering over me.

"You still want to go slow?"

I nodded, stifling a chuckle.

He smiled reluctantly. "Okay, I'll try."

He slid down the bed and used his teeth to pull my t-shirt up off my stomach. He ran his nose across my body and kissed me slowly on every exposed inch of skin while he supported himself on his arms.

I ran my fingers over the front of his briefs and he groaned.

"I won't be able to go slow if you do that again," he said in a warning voice.

I laughed quietly, unsure whether or not I wanted his slow, delicious torture to continue.

"I want to get this t-shirt off you."

I sat up briefly so he could pull it over my head. When I lay down again, he nuzzled my breasts, running the tip of his tongue along the junction between my skin and the fabric of my bra.

I stroked my hands over the bunched muscles of his biceps, luxuriating in their hard tension.

Carefully he fastened his teeth over the fabric of my bra and pulled the cup down, then ran his tongue over my nipple, sucking hard. The sensation was exquisite, almost painful.

I pushed the waistband of his briefs over and down his hips. He rolled off me to kick them free and I sat up to undo my bra.

"No, I'll do that," he said confidently.

For several seconds he tugged futilely on the elastic straps. "Fuck! Turn around—I can't see what I'm doing."

Smiling to myself, I turned my back to him. A heartbeat later, my bra was dumped on the floor and I shimmied out of my panties, tossing them down with the rest of our clothes.

"How slow?" he whispered as his body loomed over mine again, lightly pressing me into the mattress.

"How slow can you go?" I asked teasingly.

I pulled my knees up and slid my hand along his erection. He trembled and bit his lip.

"You're not helping!" he said, accusingly.

But I didn't care anymore: I wanted to feel him inside me—all of him.

I pulled him toward me and I felt the mattress move as his weight shifted on the bed. He used his knees to open me wider, then, with aching slowness, he sank into me, pulled out, then sank in again, circling his hips, stimulating me everywhere.

I tilted my hips up to meet him—the movement seemed to push him too far.

"I can't! I can't!" he suddenly gasped and started moving faster.

I wrapped my legs around his waist and gripped his arms with my hands.

His eyes were squeezed tightly shut and I felt his body turn rigid then he collapsed onto me with a soft moan.

"Sorry," he mumbled into my neck a long moment later.

I stroked his hair, smiling to myself. "It's okay. Practice makes perfect. And we've got all night."

He raised himself up and kissed me softly and sweetly. Then he pulled out gently and rolled off of me.

"Oh, wow!" he said, looking down at the blood on his dick. "That really didn't hurt you?"

I shook my head, suppressing a smile. "Do you want to take a shower?"

"Um, yeah, if you don't mind."

He looked stunned.

"I don't mind—not if you let me scrub your back."

He grinned and looked up at me. "Oh, definitely up for that."

I turned on the hot water and led him into the shower.

"Did you have a long day at the office, dear?" I said as I ran a soapy sponge over his back.

He chuckled, stretching out his arms.

"God, that feels so good!" he sighed.

He rested his hands on the tiled wall and let the water rain down on his head and back. When I reached around and ran the sponge over his front he jumped slightly. Gently, I swirled the sponge over his stomach and thighs and everything in between, he groaned loudly.

I felt his erection stir again. I guessed that's what they called a fast re-loader. I was impressed—and shocked.

He turned around and kissed me hard, his tongue demanding access to my mouth. He pushed me back against the chilly ceramic tiles and I almost slipped.

"Careful!"

"Sorry! God, sorry," he muttered, barely moving his mouth from my lips.

I was slipping and sliding all over the place—suddenly shower sex didn't seem like such a good idea.

I left the hot water running and pulled him after me. He looked confused as I leaned over the sink and grasped the rim with both hands.

"From behind," I whispered.

I heard the breath hitch in his throat then a second later his hands were gripping my hips. When he entered me it felt amazingly deep. Truthfully, I'd never felt anything like it before.

"Oh fuck!" he hissed.

I glanced up into the mirror—his eyes were wide with wonder and his lips were parted. Our eyes met—and locked on each other's.

I clenched around him and watched his face as he cursed again.

He rotated his hips slowly and this time I was the one who cried out.

"Hand!"

"What?" he grit out between his teeth.

"Give me your hand!" I half-gasped, half-yelled at him.

He leaned onto me, his weight pressing me into the cold, hard porcelain, and I groaned but he gave me his hand. I pushed it between my legs and against my clitoris. He caught on fast: the thought crossed my mind that he must have got good grades in school. My orgasm began to gather and I felt the delicious trembling inside.

I knew Sebastian felt it, too, because he swore again and started moving faster, his hand in rhythm with his thrusts.

I screamed out his name. The sheer relief of being able to be as loud as I wanted, to show vocally how much he was pleasing me: it felt fantastic.

He kept moving, his hips grinding into me. I could barely stand, my thighs were shaking with the effort of staying upright.

What? No? Surely not! I couldn't believe it! My eyes opened wide as a second orgasm began to build. I was shocked to my core—I didn't even know I *could* have two orgasms so close together. And then I lost all train of thought as my body became nothing but sensation.

I was vaguely aware that Sebastian had stopped moving and that we were both lying on the floor, gasping.

It was desperately uncomfortable on the hard surface but I felt too weak to move. A giggle escaped me—I was, quite literally, well fucked. That expression would never again have the same resonance for me now I'd actually experienced it.

I started laughing.

"What's so funny?"

But I couldn't reply, I was laughing so hard. I pushed up onto my hands and knees, vaguely aware that there was blood on the floor.

"What are you laughing at?" said Sebastian, sounding aggrieved.

I crawled into the shower, slightly hysterical.

"What?!" he said, starting to laugh despite himself.

"I. Am. So. Thoroughly. Well. Fucked!" I finally managed to spit out.

Sebastian was laughing, too, as he came and joined me in the shower.

We sat in the shower tray and I leaned back between his legs, letting the hot water soothe and restore us.

Eventually I managed to stop laughing but I felt too weak to stand.

"That was amazing," Sebastian whispered into my hair.

He sounded slightly awestruck.

"It certainly was. But I can't stand—you'll have to help me up!"

Sebastian laughed and stood up easily, pulling me up by my hands.

I managed to turn off the shower as I staggered out. I grabbed a clean towel and tossed one to him. I made a few quick passes with the towel and, still half-soaked, collapsed face down on the bed.

"Hey," said Sebastian, following me to the bedroom. "You're all wet."

Gently, lovingly, he dried me with the towel, doing his best to get the moisture out of my hair as well.

"I'm so tired. I can hardly keep my eyes open," I mumbled.

"Go to sleep, baby," he said softly.

I rolled onto my side and felt Sebastian's warm, slightly damp body curl up behind me. He wrapped his arm around my waist and I was asleep in seconds.

CHAPTER ELEVEN

AT SOME POINT, NOT LONG AFTER DAWN, I WOKE.

Sebastian's arm was still draped over my waist but I must have turned in the night because now I was facing him. His lips were slightly parted and he was breathing softly. I thought he must be dreaming because his eyelids fluttered and he frowned.

A pale gold stubble covered his cheeks, upper lip and chin. It was soft, nothing like five o'clock shadow and he looked so young and very beautiful.

His tan was deep over his arms, back and chest, then vanished completely, leaving his buttocks and hips a creamy white that changed again to gold on his legs.

The low angle of the sun cast long shadows that highlighted the definition of his muscular chest and stomach and I reveled in the thought that for a few more hours—and for another whole night—he was mine.

I hardly dared to imagine how it might feel to wake up like this every morning, feeling such peaceful joy. And I refused to think about what would happen when our weekend was over.

I spent another minute drinking in his beauty before I tore myself away to use the bathroom.

"Where are you going?" he asked sleepily, blinking up at me.

"To pee," I whispered. "Go back to sleep."

But when I returned to the room, the bed was empty. For a heart-stopping moment, I thought he'd left. Then I saw his sneakers, t-shirt and briefs, all still strewn on the floor. Only his jeans were missing.

I stared with some distaste at the blood on the sheets. At least I didn't get really heavy periods and they didn't last long. Even so...

I heard soft footfalls behind me and turned to look. Sebastian was carrying two glasses of orange juice and wearing, well, half-wearing his jeans.

He'd pulled them over his hips but only bothered to fasten half of the fly buttons. He was beyond sexy, I felt my face getting hot—and then I remembered I was standing there naked—and blushed everywhere.

I scooted back into the bed and under the sheet.

Sebastian looked at me like I was a little crazy.

"I wanted to make you breakfast," he said, shrugging slightly, "but I can't cook. I can, however, pour a mean juice."

He passed me a glass and I took a long drink.

"Why, Mr. Hunter, you can indeed pour an amazing orange juice."

He smirked, then tipped the rest of his drink down his throat in one swift gulp. How the hell did men do that? It was a complete mystery to me.

"Well, let me make you some breakfast. What would you like? Eggs, pancakes, bacon, omelet?"

"I already told you yesterday," he said.

I frowned.

"You. I want you for breakfast."

He put his glass on the bedside cabinet and slowly walked toward me, his eyes never leaving my face. His expression made me breathless.

"Sex rather than food today?"

"Yes, ma'am."

I looked at the alarm clock. It was 6.45AM.

"We've got about three hours before I have to drop you off. Do you think that's enough time?"

He shook his head.

"Not really."

Then he leapt on the bed, making me shriek with surprise. I spilled orange juice down my chest and onto the sheets.

"Sebastian!"

He ignored me and started lapping the juice from my bare skin. I nearly melted from the heat of his touch, but just about managed to place my somewhat emptier glass on the bedside table.

I scrabbled to pull off his jeans but he was too intent on working his way down my body. It was neck and neck who was going to have their way first.

Sometime later, some *considerable* time later, the alarm went off.

We were both lying on our backs breathless. Again. I felt like I'd just gone ten rounds with Mike Tyson: every muscle ached and I was bathed in sweat. Sebastian had been tossing me around the bedroom for nearly two hours. He lay with his eyes closed and a blissful expression on his face.

The alarm clock had inconveniently been knocked out of reach. I struggled to sit up, crawling the length of the bed and fumbling on the floor to find the obnoxious electronic box.

Sebastian tried to bite my ass, which didn't really help my coordination.

"We need to get up!" I moaned.

He didn't reply.

"Up!"

"I am up," he mumbled against my skin.

Again? Oh, my God!

"Time for a shower. Go! Now!"

He grumbled a little more but eventually rolled off the bed, allowing me to get up and pull on my robe. I glanced around to see him stumble into the bathroom. It was true: he was up.

Smiling to myself, I headed down to the kitchen and rummaged around in the refrigerator. As he hadn't managed to express a preference, I decided to make a cheese omelet with bacon on the side.

I was still grilling the bacon when I heard him running down the stairs. There was a huge thud and I guessed he'd jumped the last three or four steps. His exuberance made me smile. And where the hell did he get all that energy?

He wrapped his arms around my waist without hesitation and nuzzled my neck. I nearly dropped the spatula.

"What can I do?" he said.

I was surprised. No man had ever said that to me in my kitchen before. I turned and smirked at him.

"Just sit there and look decorative."

He threw me an amused look and stretched his long legs under the kitchen table, rocking the chair back on two legs, just like he had last night.

To have him sitting at my breakfast table felt wonderfully new and wonderfully natural, all at the same time.

When I served up the food, I put most of the omelet on his plate and four out of five of the pieces of bacon. He didn't even seem to notice the uneven distribution, he was so intent on getting the food into his stomach in the shortest time possible.

I was still chewing when he pushed his plate away. He glanced around to see if there was anything else to eat. Really, his appetites were enormous in all sorts of ways. The last ten hours had been a revelation.

"Toast?"

"Please!" he said happily.

I cut four slices off a new loaf and shoved them all in the toaster. "Do you want jelly?"

He pulled a face. "Nah, just butter, please."

"Don't you have a sweet tooth?"

"Only for you."

I rolled my eyes.

"Where do you stand on chocolate? I'm serious! It's an important question!"

"You like chocolate, Caro? What sort?"

I could see what he was thinking. Sometimes he was so easy to read.

"I don't want you to buy me any, Sebastian."

"Why not?"

He pouted and I wanted to laugh.

"Because we're saving our money for more important things."

He sighed. "Yeah, I guess."

"Mind you," I said, slyly, "I wouldn't mind licking some melted chocolate off you—I bet that would taste really good."

For a moment he looked a little shocked, then a huge grin spread across his face.

"Yeah! That sounds *hot!*"

"I'll see what I can do for tonight."

He groaned.

"What?"

"I'll have that image in my head all day now! I'll be a walking hard-on!"

"It's one way of increasing tips at work," I said, laughing at him.

He shook his head and looked embarrassed. He was so easy to tease. I really wasn't being very fair.

I glanced at my watch. It was nearly ten o'clock.

"Time to go," I said, trying not to sound too bereft.

He scowled.

"I'll call in sick."

"You can't do that," I said patiently. "For a start, Ches will be knocking on your door in about 20 minutes, and secondly, word is sure to get back to your mom—do you *really* want her asking awkward questions about where you've been?"

He sighed. "I guess not."

"Come on. Go be a lifeguard."

I cursed the day I'd left those empty packing crates in the garage. Instead of being able to drive my car inside it, so Sebastian could make a discrete exit from the house, I had to reverse the car right up to the front door so he could sneak in the passenger side with the least chance of being seen. By now it was broad daylight and I was anxious. I tried to come up with some excuses just in case—some reason as to why Sebastian was in my house at this time in the morning. Nothing sounded convincing. I just crossed my fingers. How very mature.

Luckily, very luckily, we arrived to the park without incident.

"Text me later?"

"Okay," he promised. "See you tonight. Love you!"

He slammed the door and waved goodbye. I watched him jog across the park and with a last glance, I made an illegal U-turn and headed off to the store. I wanted to make him something special for our last night together. And to buy some chocolate.

I'd just parked outside the store when my phone beeped. Sebastian hadn't wasted any time before texting me. But when I checked the message it was from David.

Flight lands 2115. I need dress uniform dry-cleaned for formal on Monday

And hello to you, too.

The message put me in a bad mood, reminding me that by tomorrow evening I would have to be *that* person again—loyal wife, spineless factotum. I didn't know how the hell I was going to do that.

"Hello, Caroline. How are you? You look a little tired."

Donna stood behind me with a piled up cart and a kind smile on her face. She patted my arm as my brain attempted to click into gear.

"I know, dear," she said. "I never sleep well when Johan's away either. I think I miss his snoring!"

I tried to smile and her face creased with concern.

"Are you all right?"

"I'm fine, thank you, Donna. I just got a message from David—he wants his dress uniform dry-cleaned for Monday. Now I'll have to go back to the house to get it."

"Oh my. Did you forget to look at the schedule again?" she teased me.

I couldn't help laughing.

"Yes! You'd think I'd have learned by now."

"Well, I'm glad I caught you. I was wondering if I could ask you to bring something for the picnic tomorrow. Maybe some of your delicious cold pasta? Just for our group."

"Oh, of course! I was going to bring some sandwiches, too, if you like?"

"How wonderful! Yes, please. I think it's going to be a fun day, and it looks like we'll be blessed with the weather. Would you like me to pick you up? There isn't a huge amount of parking, and the organizing committee has asked us to carpool. Besides, you haven't met my boys yet. They're back from college now."

"Oh, yes, that would be lovely," I stuttered, feeling under pressure. "Thank you!"

"I'll pick you up at 11AM then. And do try and get some sleep tonight, dear. You're far too young to look so tired. You don't want to end up with bags under your eyes like mine. Well, I have suitcases rather than bags."

Truthfully, I wasn't planning on getting much sleep during the night, but maybe I could take a nap later. I wondered briefly if I should let Sebastian get some more sleep—he'd probably only had about four hours last night and he was working all day. But then again, he was young—and I couldn't imagine him agreeing to sleep when I was fairly certain he would have other things on his mind. The thought made me smile.

Damn it! I'd forgotten to ask Donna how many people were part of the 'group' that she'd mentioned.

Moving slowly up and down the aisles, I filled the cart with focaccia rolls, cold cuts and some fresh pasta. I felt guilty buying store-made pasta but figured no one but me would be any the wiser. I also bought some lamb chops, potatoes and salad for Sebastian. And a jar of chocolate sauce. Although that was more for me.

As an afterthought, I picked up a few of David's favorite foods, too. He was always more amenable on a full stomach.

It was getting harder to buy 35mm film, especially in black and white, but I managed to find a few rolls. I wondered if I'd be able to buy a digital camera when we moved to New York. I had no idea how much they cost. I'd be sorry to stop using my dad's SLR, but the price of buying and developing film was an additional cost I could well do without. A cost *we* could well do without.

As I was happily daydreaming about a new life in a new city, my cell phone rang.

"Hi, Carolina! Carl Winters, here. How are you?"

"Well, thank you, Carl. And you?"

"Good, good. Look, I heard that the folk at the Base are having a family fun day on the beach tomorrow. Are you going?"

"Yes, I am."

"Great! I was wondering if you could take some photographs for the paper. We'd need them dropped off on Sunday evening."

"Oh, I'd love to do that but I think I mentioned to you—I don't have a digital camera. I wouldn't be able to get the film developed that quickly."

"No problem. We have a lab on site—just drop off the film and I'll have one of my technicians develop it."

I was silent.

"Carolina! Are you still there?"

"Oh, yes. I'm here."

"Is there a problem?"

"It's just ... what if they're not good enough? I'd hate for you to be relying on me and..."

He laughed.

"Carolina, it's a family fun day. I'm sure the snaps will be just fine. We'll get something usable—we can do a lot with cropping images. Don't worry about it."

"Well, okay. Thank you! I'm really flattered."

"Good. That's settled. I'll see you tomorrow."

He ended the call leaving me puzzled. He was the editor of a weekly paper and he was going to be there on a Sunday evening? Go figure.

Shopping bags filled the trunk of my car, including a jar of chocolate sauce, and I drove home with an unaccustomed smile on my face. It took a while to unload all the extra food I'd bought for the picnic.

But when I went into the bedroom, it looked like a bomb had hit it. With a sigh, I scooped up the sheets lying in a tangled heap on the floor, and wearily stripped the bed. Then I trudged downstairs and loaded them into the machine. I didn't know that having an affair meant more housework.

And then I remembered David's damn dress uniform. Muttering bad-temperedly, I shoved it into a plastic bag and drove to the dry-cleaners.

I nearly fell asleep at the wheel driving back and when I stumbled into the living room, I couldn't help thinking that the couch looked inviting. Perhaps just five minutes...

My cell phone alerted me that I had a message, waking me from a very interesting dream that involved a shower of chocolate instead of water ... and a naked Sebastian.

Feels like a long day. Missing you. Can't wait for later. Did you get chocolate? Sxx

I smiled and sent a text back.

Yes to choc. But how slow can you go?

He replied immediately.

Let's find out x

I had a huge grin on my face when I flipped my phone shut. But then I glanced at the time and was horrified to see I'd been asleep for more than three hours. I had a mountain of food to prepare for the picnic tomorrow and I sure as hell wasn't going to be wasting my time doing it while Sebastian was here.

Despite the rude, very rude awakening, I felt better for my extended nap and set to work with a will. I had so much food, I had to drag out some cardboard boxes that I had stashed in the garage and stack it inside. I couldn't help thinking about the morning Sebastian had come over to help me empty our moving-in crates. It seemed a lifetime ago—I wondered how it seemed to him.

I hunted through the kitchen cupboards for some candles. I'd bought them in case of a power outage—they'd certainly never been used for a romantic interlude with David. I wanted what I'd never had. I wanted tonight to be perfect.

The table looked so pretty, laid with proper linen napkins and decorated with candles and a small posy of flowers that I'd picked in the yard. I headed up to change into the little black dress that Sebastian had helped me choose, and matched it with elegant, suede pumps—I wanted to look beautiful for him.

After I unlocked the kitchen door, I curled up on the couch with a book. I must have fallen asleep again because it was dark when I next looked up. I was shocked to see that it was nearly one o'clock in the morning. *Where was he?*

The first thing I did was to check my phone, but there were no messages and no missed calls. Uncertainty vied with panic—had something happened to him or had he just had enough of me? I wondered if I should risk calling him. In the end I decided to send a text—just in case. And it was also our more usual form of communication.

r u ok? I'm worried

I sat on the edge of the couch, anxiously waiting for a reply. When I couldn't take the tension anymore, I stood up and started pacing.

Another half an hour passed and I still hadn't heard from him. I was pondering the wisdom of getting in my car and going to look for him when I finally, *finally* heard a soft knock on the door.

I flew into the kitchen, yanked the door open and, to my dismay, I burst into tears when I saw him standing there smiling at me.

"Hey! What's wrong? I'm sorry I'm late. Don't cry, Caro. Please don't cry, baby!"

He held me in his arms, stroking my hair, letting me cry myself out, all the fear and unreasoning anxiety, the stress of having to split myself in half, the intensity of the last three weeks, the hope for more that was so tender and fragile—it all poured out of me.

"Sorry," I choked out. "I was just so worried. You didn't answer your phone and I didn't know how to contact you."

"We got a flat on the way home," he said, soothingly. "It took forever for me and Ches to put the new tire on in the dark."

"I texted you!"

"I couldn't charge up my phone yesterday—it died on me a few hours ago. I didn't think it would matter. You were really worried about me?"

I nodded miserably. I felt such a fool getting myself into that state because of a dead phone battery and a flat tire. I wanted to yell, *keep your phone charged, you jerk!* But I didn't—I was just glad he was here with me and safe.

He wiped my tears away with his fingers.

"I like that you were worried about me," he said, softly.

He glanced over my shoulder at the kitchen table.

"Is this for me, too?"

I nodded again and tried to smile. "Surprise!" I muttered.

He laughed quietly. "I love it. Thank you. And ... you look beautiful, Caro."

"Red-eyed and hideous is more like it, but thank you for saying so."

"You always look beautiful to me."

"Yes, well that must be because you're wearing those rose-tinted glasses again."

He sighed and shook his head. I couldn't tell if he was irritated or amused—maybe a little of both.

"Are you hungry?"

"God, yes! Right now my stomach is thinking that someone cut my throat."

"They really ought to feed you at work," I grumbled.

He shrugged. "We were busy. But I have tomorrow off."

He looked at me expectantly but when he saw my dismayed reaction, his face fell.

"I thought ... I just hoped we could spend the day together, but ... it's cool ... if you're busy."

I swore. He looked surprised, I wasn't much given to cursing.

"Oh, I wish I'd known! I've told Donna I'd go to the family fun day at the beach—you know, the big picnic?"

He scowled. "Can't you tell her you've changed your mind?"

"I wish! But I've agreed to take photographs for *City Beat*, too. They're counting on me. Oh, Sebastian, I'm so sorry! If I'd known you had the day off..."

"It was a last minute thing," he muttered. "They gave Ches the day off, as well. Probably because so many people will be at the fun day."

The possibilities presented by being able to spend a whole day alone with Sebastian now drifted through my mind, as substantial and certain as mist.

I wrapped my arms around his waist and laid my head on his chest again.

"There'll be other days," I said, my voice sad.

"Yeah, I know. It's just that every day ... every moment with you..."

"...is precious," I finished the sentence for him.

"Very."

I kissed him softly. "I'll go make dinner."

"I'll light the candles."

I was surprised when he pulled a lighter out of his pocket, I'd never seen Sebastian smoke and I'd certainly never smelt tobacco on him. Odd.

I switched off the overhead electric lights so the only illumination in the kitchen was from the candles. The flickering lights threw weird images onto the walls, like some freakish shadow play. A shiver ran through me—someone must have walked over my grave. I shook off the superstitious notion and concentrated instead on the way the candlelight played across Sebastian's face, highlighting his cheekbones and making his eyes glitter. He smiled up at me and in the dim light, his irises looked coal black. I could lose my train of thought just by looking at him.

I served up the grilled lamb chops and Sebastian ate heartily, I merely picked at my food. I felt resentful of tomorrow's wasted opportunity and, stupidly, I was letting it spoil this evening, too. I made an effort to pull myself together.

"How was work today?"

"Busy. There was some big golf tournament: a lot of out-of-towners."

"Any pool-side incidents?"

He laughed as he remembered something.

"Yeah! One of the guests dropped her cell phone in the deep end. I dove down to get it for her."

"Was she grateful?"

"I think she was more pissed, but she gave me ten bucks ... and her cell phone number."

"You're kidding me!" *How dare she? Was she pretty? How old was she?*

Those were the questions that I couldn't ask.

"I mean, how dumb can you get?" continued Sebastian. "She just dumped her damn phone in the pool and that's the number she gives me!"

"Sebastian," I said, pointing out the blindingly obvious, at least to me, "the number will still work—she'll just have to buy a new handset."

He looked at me.

"Really?"

"Yes!"

He shook his head. "Well, it doesn't make any difference—I threw her number away."

"You did?"

"Of course I did!"

He looked annoyed. "I wouldn't cheat on you, Caro!"

I couldn't bear to point out the irony in that statement. Instead, I changed the subject.

"Do you want some dessert?"

His expression changed in an instant—from righteous indignation to the most scorching look of lust.

"Chocolate?" His voice was low and seductive.

"I ... I made a polenta cake ... but I bought chocolate sauce, too."

He didn't take his eyes off me and his voice didn't waver.

"Just the chocolate."

He stood up, his chair scraping across the kitchen floor, and he held out his hand to me. I took it wordlessly and Sebastian pulled me into his arms, then kissed me until I stopped breathing.

"I want to make love to you," he said, his voice hoarse. "I've been thinking about it all day. Fuck! I couldn't think of anything else." He blinked and his eyes danced with amusement. "People could have been drowning in that pool and I don't think I'd have noticed."

"Let's go to bed."

"Oh, yeah, baby!"

Suddenly he scooped me up off the floor and flung me over his shoulder. The surprise made me cry out. He practically ran up the stairs and threw me on the bed. I couldn't help laughing at his eagerness, at the sheer joy I saw on his face.

"Damn! We forgot the chocolate."

"No, we didn't." I pointed to the bottle of chocolate sauce by the alarm clock and watched his eyes light up.

He twisted the lid and the jar made a soft popping sound as it opened. He stuck his index finger in and pulled it out covered in chocolate. He held it out toward me.

"Suck," he said.

So I did.

~

At some point in the night we must have fallen asleep. It hadn't been a conscious decision, more a sort of acknowledgment of sheer exhaustion.

Waking up was a struggle. My eyes were gritty with tiredness, and my body ached so much, I didn't know which muscle to favor first. *And there was chocolate everywhere!*

Oh, the chocolate! Mmm, that had been good. No, that had been *great*. That had been *fun*.

We'd laughed so much. I couldn't remember laughing so much, not ever.

And the way we'd explored each other's body. I remembered again the touch of his fingers, the way his skin warmed against mine, the soft, wet heat of his lips, everywhere. The passion that had smoldered for hours, blazing suddenly into flames that burned.

I rolled over to find his eyes open, a smile of wonder on his face.

We didn't speak, we just gazed at each other. I think I was smiling, too.

His fingers stroked my arm slowly, rhythmically.

I reached up to rest my hand on his cheek, but he pulled it to his lips and kissed the palm. I nestled into his body and his hand moved down to stroke my bare back.

I listened to the quiet, steady beat of his heart.

"We have to get up," I said, sadly.

He nodded slowly but neither of us moved.

"When will I see you again?" he murmured.

"Today, at the picnic," I said, trying to sound upbeat.

"You know what I mean."

I sighed. I did know what he meant, I just didn't have an answer. There was no tomorrow for us.

"We'll figure something out," I said, trying to sound reassuring.

"I hate this," he said sulkily. "All the sneaking around, all the lies. I want everyone to know we're together."

"Fine!" I snapped. "Go ahead! Tell everyone! And then I can spend the next God knows how long in prison, or stuck on the sex offender registry and not able to get a job."

I knew I was behaving badly, childishly, but I couldn't seem to stop.

He gasped in shock. "I didn't mean it like that," he mumbled.

"Then what did you mean?" I said, my voice beginning to rise in volume. "Do you think I find this easy? Do you think I enjoy betraying people, lying to decent people like Donna and Shirley? Deceiving everyone? Do you think this isn't hard for *me?* This isn't a game, Sebastian!"

"I know that!" he yelled back. "It's my life, too!"

I closed my eyes and took a deep breath. "I'm sorry. I'm just ... a little tired. You've worn me out."

That brought a slight smile to his lips but his eyes were still hurt and angry.

I knew I shouldn't take my constant anxiety out on him.

"I'm sorry, it's frustrating for me, too."

"I don't want to fight with you, Caro. I just want to be with you all the time. You're all I think about."

We lay there for a few more minutes, wishing the hands of the clock to slow in sympathy.

"Donna will be here in an hour," I said quietly. "We have to get up."

Our shower was over too quickly and my hands reluctantly let him go. We dressed in silence, the ache of separation already billowing between us.

I glanced at the bed where he had made such sweet love to me, the chocolatey sheets a reminder of a carefree night.

"Do they have other flavors?" asked Sebastian, following my gaze.

"I don't know. Probably. Maybe we should investigate?"

"I like peanut butter," he said, wistfully.

I raised my eyebrows. "Crunchy or smooth?"

He laughed, a little sadly, and pulled me into a hug.

"I'd better get going."

"You don't want breakfast?" I was surprised.

"You can't risk driving me to the park today—half the neighbors will be outside in their yards. I'll go through the back."

At least one of us was thinking clearly.

"I'll see you later?" he said, tentatively.

"Yes," I said simply.

He smiled.

We walked down the stairs in silence.

In the kitchen I pulled him toward me and we kissed hungrily. I held him as long as I could, but too soon, it was time for him to go. He kissed me lightly on the forehead and then ducked out through the kitchen door.

I'd forgotten to remind him to charge his phone.

Feeling miserable, I threw the chocolatey sheets in the washing machine and made up the bed with clean ones. I removed every piece of evidence, every trace that there'd been anyone in the house but me—the doormat wife of a bullying man.

I was disgusted with myself—and the list of reasons was endless.

CHAPTER TWELVE

DONNA WAS ON TIME. OF COURSE.

"Good morning, Caroline. How are you today?"

"Just fine, thank you, Donna. Are these your sons?"

Two attractive men in their twenties with Johan's Nordic looks were getting out of Donna's station wagon.

"Kurt, Stefan—Caroline Wilson."

"Hello, nice to meet you. I hear you're down from college for the summer break?"

We chatted easily while the boys loaded up Donna's trunk with the boxes of food stashed in my kitchen.

"My goodness," she said. "There's enough here to feed the five thousand!"

"Too much?" I asked anxiously.

She laughed. "I'm sure it'll all be eaten, it looks delicious."

I grabbed my notebook and camera, shoved the spare films in the pockets of my shorts and we headed off.

"How many people do you think will be there today?"

"Oh, well, probably a couple of thousand in total—it's mostly folk from the Naval Medical Center but quite a few families come from the Marine Corps, too. The Peters will be there, and I think Shirley said the boys had been given the day off work, so I expect they'll tag along ... especially if they know you'll be there—with food."

I stared out of the window, hoping my burning cheeks wouldn't give me away.

I hadn't realized the picnic was quite such a big deal. Of course, if I hadn't been so preoccupied, I might have been a little more aware. But then again, I'd never gone out of my way to be involved with family life on the Base, not having had a family.

I'd been to Harbor Beach just once before. It was a wide, flat esplanade of fine sand, perfect for families. Lifeguard towers ran the length of the beach between the jetties, where a couple of surfers were catching some small waves. A playground on the sand was a major attraction for the younger children and Donna informed me that some of the older ones—and their parents—would be making use of the volleyball courts: just supply your own ball and net.

The beach was already getting crowded, the military personnel stood out a mile with their crew cuts and buzz-cuts. The parking lot was a cheerful, chaotic crowd with mountains of food being ferried to the fire pits that ringed the beach.

The tide was way out, it would be quite a hike for anyone wanting to go for a swim. But most people seemed intent on playing and eating their way through the day.

I saw volleyballs, soccer balls, Frisbees, footballs, numerous body boards, and lots and lots of kids carrying colorful kites—several in the shape of airplanes. One group of mothers was organizing a sandcastle-building contest for the kids—and whichever of the adults felt like joining in, and a group of Marines was planning a pie-eating competition. Something I personally found rather gross—watching grown men shove as much pie in their faces in the shortest amount of time was unpleasant, to say the least. I couldn't understand why anyone would want to do it. It seemed a waste of good food.

Despite the fact that alcohol was not allowed on the beach, I saw several men openly carrying six-packs. It wasn't really taking that much of a risk—I knew that you would be hard-pressed to find a police officer willing to give a ticket to someone in the service. I suppose you'd call it a sort of brotherhood. I'd lost count of the number of tickets David had gotten out of because of his 'Fly Navy' license plate and his military service window stickers.

There was a real holiday feel to the day—I felt cheerless by comparison despite knowing that I'd see Sebastian later. Nevertheless, I had a job to do, such as it was. I pulled out my camera and started snapping some candid shots of the military at play. To my surprise, I began to enjoy capturing the varied scenes of happiness: games of football that seemed to be rule-free, small children chasing their burly fathers, kids running around in swimsuits, and enough food to feed an army—which it was, of course.

Although it had been advertised as a 'family' fun day, there were lots of singles there, too, men (and a few women) adopted into the family of the unit they served with. There was no doubt that putting your life in the hands of the other guys in your unit created a bond.

It dawned on me that I was one of the 'singles', and that Donna had adopted me into her family for the day. There were worse ways to be treated.

I heard Ches's van before I saw it, but I studiously kept my eyes on the boxes of food that Kurt and Stefan were carrying to the spot where Donna had staked her claim.

She looked up at the noise and waved furiously to attract their attention. The van rumbled to a stop nearby and I saw that Mitch was driving, with Bill and Shirley sharing the front seat.

My heart began to beat a little faster because I knew that Sebastian was now just a few feet away from me, although he may as well have been on the moon because I wouldn't be able to touch him. I would hardly dare to look at him.

I didn't know which was worse—to see him and not touch him, or to not see him at all.

Shirley jumped out first followed by Bill who winked at me, much to Donna's amusement. Mitch went around to open the back of the van. I kept my eyes on the trunk of Donna's car and continued unpacking.

"Can I help you with that?"

Sebastian's soft voice made me jump. He was wearing a fresh white t-shirt and colorful board shorts, with a pair of wrap-around sunglasses pushed up onto his short hair. He'd also shaved. I felt dizzy just seeing him, but quickly dropped my eyes.

"Oh, thank you!" I managed to mutter.

He grinned at me and took the box from my nerveless hands, following the convoy of Donna's sons, Bill and Mitch. I picked up the polenta cake, still untouched from last night, and gingerly joined the line.

"I really liked your article, Mrs. Wilson."

I turned around to see Fido smiling at me. I was surprised, I'd never heard him speak before.

"Thank you! I'm glad you enjoyed it—and please, it's Caroline."

Sebastian must have overheard because he turned around and frowned, throwing an angry look at Fido. Fido merely grinned back and insisted on carrying the polenta cake. I tried to keep my smile bright, but inside I was dying—wasn't this day going to be hard enough without worrying about whether or not Sebastian would be jealous of anyone who spoke to me?

I didn't think it was a coincidence that Sebastian chose that moment to pull off his t-shirt, baring his chest, flaunting his golden skin, naked in the sunshine. He knew I wouldn't be able to stop myself from having a quick ogle. Of course, the other men immediately followed suit and I was soon surrounded by a surfeit of taut, tanned and toned flesh. I pulled my sunglasses over my eyes and tried to think cooling thoughts.

We settled in a loose group around our fire pit, Sebastian securing a spot opposite me, but every time I stood up to get some more of the food, or pass something around, he'd stand up, too, and 'help'. Then he'd brush up against me: seemingly innocent little touches. Each time my skin blazed with need and I wanted to yell at him to stop—or to not stop but do something about the heat that was rising within me. Somehow I managed to follow a conversation with Shirley about her idea to keep chickens as a way of making some extra money. I knew nothing about poultry so it was a fairly one-sided discussion.

Bill and Mitch kept up a friendly banter of profanities as they proceeded to char vast quantities of meat. I resolved to stick to cold cuts and salad as I helped to lay out the rest of the provisions.

Several Marines from Mitch and Bill's unit wandered over to pass the time and help reduce the mountain of food. All the men were eating like their lives depended on it, and my concern that there was too much quickly vanished.

Donna introduced me to all the visitors and I could read surprise on the faces of several when she explained I was the wife of Lieutenant Commander Wilson. Clearly, David's reputation had gone before.

Kurt and Stefan regaled us with tales of college life, each trying to outdo the other. They were attractive, intelligent young men, good company and entertaining. Stefan was following in his father's footsteps and studying medicine at UCLA. Kurt had chosen civil engineering and went to school at McCormick in Chicago. Unfortunately, the brothers seemed to have a well developed rivalry which, on this occasion, they were using to take turns flirting with me. It was beyond embarrassing, particularly as I could see Sebastian's murderous looks from across the fire pit, and Ches's amused expression. Fido just stared at me, which was more than a little unnerving.

During the course of the afternoon, Sebastian became quieter and quieter, and I sensed that his temper was beginning to fray. Worse still, Fido's dog-like devotion to me was also becoming more apparent. Every time I reached for something, he leapt up to hand it to me. I had never been so popular—and it had never been less well timed.

I couldn't help wondering if all the sex I'd been having was giving off some sort of invisible signal, some sort of scent, a pheromone, perhaps. Could that happen? I'd never before been in a position to need to ask the question.

As unobtrusively as I was able, I stood up, determined to slink away by myself for a while.

"Are you okay, Caroline?" asked Donna.

I cringed as every eye focused on me.

"Oh, I'm just going to go and get some shots of the volleyball game and sandcastle competition," I said lightly.

"I'll come with you," said Sebastian immediately.

"No, no! I'm fine. Stay and enjoy yourself," I said, just one shade too forcefully.

His eyes darkened with anger and he slumped back to the sand, a surly expression on his face.

Honestly! Did he want *to make it so obvious?*

I hurried off to take some photographs, including the ghastly pie-eating competition. Even though I ached for Sebastian's company, there were too many eyes everywhere. I returned half an hour later, when my blood pressure had returned to normal, and avoided meeting his too ardent gaze. But I did see Donna raise her eyebrows and smile. The woman was just too damned observant. It made me nervous.

Ches was interested in my old SLR so I showed him how to change the focus and how to read the built-in light meter. I let him take a few snaps of our group. Bill, of course, bombed the photograph, scooping me up into a huge hug, which earned him a furious look from Sebastian. Then Ches insisted on taking one of me. I didn't mind—it wasn't like I'd have to look at it—all the photographs would be developed at *City Beat*.

"I had an old SLR once," said Bill. "I wonder what happened to it—I used to love taking photographs."

"First I've heard of it," said Mitch, raising his eyebrows.

"Hey! I do have one or two secrets, buddy!" replied Bill, raising a bottle of beer in salute. "So, what else do you like taking photographs of, Caroline?"

"You mean other than pictures of fine figures of men like you, Bill?" laughed Shirley.

"Too right!" said Bill, flexing his biceps. "You want to take some photos of me, Caroline? *Private* photographs? Anytime, honey—but you'll need a long lens!"

I laughed, trying to seem as if I was enjoying the joke. It was kind of hard when Sebastian looked like was about to punch Bill.

"I do like taking photographs of people," I said, trying to change the direction of the embarrassing conversation, "but when they're not aware I'm watching—just candids of people carrying on with their lives. I'm not into landscapes that much—I always admired people like Robert Capa and Cartier-Bresson and..."

"Oh, I love it when you talk French to me, Caroline!" said Bill, winking at me.

This was getting beyond embarrassing.

Ches's head was swiveling between Bill and Sebastian as if he was watching some sort of tennis match.

I saw Shirley throw Bill a warning look. His only reply was to smirk at her and take another swig of beer.

I wondered if he was deliberately trying to tease Sebastian. Heaven forbid, but it seemed to be some sort of open secret that Sebastian liked me. It was obvious from the way that everyone's eyes were drawn to him whenever I became the subject of conversation that they knew *something*. Thankfully, no one had guessed that his feelings were more than reciprocated.

I wanted to shake him or send him for acting lessons or something that made it less damn obvious how he felt about me.

Not only did it make me anxious, but it made me question how successful my own attempts were to act like I didn't notice him, or didn't give a damn. The whole thing was giving me a headache and I longed for the picnic to be over. It really wasn't living up to its billing of a 'fun day'.

I began to have quite violent thoughts toward Donna—I wished more than anything that I hadn't accepted her misplaced kindness and instead gotten here in my own car.

The mountain of food continued to diminish and Donna was encouraging me to serve up the lemon polenta cake when I became aware that the eyes of every male in our group had swung to a spot just behind my right shoulder.

"Hi, everyone," said a female voice.

"Hi, Brenda," said Ches, his tone friendly but cautious.

I saw him glance at Sebastian.

Oh. The ex-girlfriend.

Brenda Wiseman was undeniably lovely: a perfect, willowy figure, stick-straight blonde hair that she flipped over her shoulders, pale blue eyes, and the smallest bikini I'd ever seen outside of a men's magazine. Irritatingly, she certainly had the figure to wear it to its best advantage.

While everyone stared at Brenda, Bill's eyes about popping out of his head and Donna's lips pursed in apparent distaste, I saw Sebastian glance nervously toward me. I dropped my eyes to the polenta cake and continued to cut it, gripping the handle of the cake-slice tightly. It was bad timing on Brenda's part that I happened to have a weapon conveniently at hand.

"Hi, Sebastian," she said.

"Hi."

His reply was short and unenthusiastic.

I couldn't help wondering if that was solely for my benefit.

She hesitated for a moment, as if waiting for an invitation. When none was forthcoming, she sat down next to him anyway, stretching out her long tan legs and leaning back on her hands.

"I haven't seen you since graduation."

Sebastian stared at the sand. It was clear he had no clue how to handle this.

It was quite funny—if you weren't me.

"Where have you been hanging?" she persisted, her voice unnaturally cheery.

I wondered if she'd been rehearsing.

"I've been busy."

"Ches said you guys have jobs out at the country club," she prompted him.

Sebastian glared at Ches who guiltily shrugged his shoulders.

"So, what do you do there?"

"Lifeguarding," replied Ches quickly, "and some waiting on tables when they're short-staffed."

"Cool!" said Brenda, flipping her hair over her shoulders *again*.

I wanted to leap across the barbeque pit and make her eat sand.

The men looked amused as Sebastian became increasingly and obviously uncomfortable, his cheeks reddening with each awkward second. Shirley and Donna looked sympathetic and politely tried to maintain a separate conversation. I hated to think what expression was leaking out onto my face.

"Hey, you cut your hair," said Brenda, reaching out to run one hand across the nape of his neck.

I wanted to snap her fingers off at the wrist.

Sebastian flinched away from her and looked annoyed. I hoped that Brenda would take the hint but she hadn't deployed her primary weapons yet.

"Well, it suits you," she said, hitching up her bikini top.

I could have sworn her tits had magnets attached to them the way the men's eyes seemed to be drawn toward her impressive cleavage. Even Sebastian's.

"Although I always liked your hair long, but then you already knew that, didn't you?"

"I cut my hair, too," said Ches in a farcical attempt to protect his friend from Brenda's relentless onslaught.

She glanced at him with humiliating brevity.

"Nice."

"Have you decided where you're going to school in the fall?" asked Stefan, trying to attract her attention.

"I've been accepted at UCLA—and UCSD," she said, her eyes fixed on Sebastian.

"You should go to UCLA," said Stefan. "It's a really great school. What's your major?"

But she completely ignored him and he crashed in flames, much to his brother's amusement. Brenda drew up her knees and nudged Sebastian's arm with her thigh.

"Can we talk?" she said softly.

"I thought you'd be *talking* to Jack," he said coolly.

She blushed.

"Please, Sebastian? In private."

The sudden timidity in her voice made me look up. She was staring at Sebastian, a worried little pucker between her eyebrows. I had to hand it to her: she was good. And she had guts. She was making a very public statement that she still had feelings for him. In fact, speaking from recent experience, I'd say she was crazy about him.

The burn of jealousy in my throat got worse, running all the way down to my gut. She was gorgeous, sweet, rather brave, *extremely* determined, and had her eyes on the prize. Oh, and they were the same age. She was perfect for him, she was the sort of girl he ought to be with—assuming she wasn't really the man-eating tramp she seemed to be channeling.

It was unfair of me to hold onto him, it was wrong.

I felt my eyes began to fill with tears. I hoped I was near enough to the smoking barbeque pit to have a believable excuse.

I waited for Sebastian to tell her that there was nothing to talk about.

Except he didn't.

He pushed himself to his feet in one graceful move.

"Okay," he muttered.

I don't know if he looked at me because my gaze was locked on that damn cake—I'd never be able to eat lemon polenta ever again.

"She's a nice girl," said Shirley sympathetically, as Brenda walked away with Sebastian. "I was so surprised when they broke up." She glanced at Ches, who wouldn't meet his mother's eyes. "I don't know what happened between them."

I stabbed the cake viciously.

"She's a hottie!" declared Stefan.

"I remember when she was skinny and wore braces," said Kurt. "Now look at the size of those bazookas!"

"Kurt!" said Donna in a warning voice.

Mitch and Bill laughed.

I handed around the cake, a painful smile plastered to my face. I told myself that it was wrong to watch Sebastian and Brenda and that I wouldn't try to see what was happening—it was just coincidence that when I sat down again after helping everyone to cake, I had a clear view.

From what I could see she was using every trick in her well-thumbed manual. Nice girl, my ass!

She pretended to stagger slightly, losing her balance so she could bump against him and take his arm, she played with the strap of her bikini to draw his gaze and show him what he didn't necessarily have to go on missing. Then she tossed her hair over her shoulder and tucked a strand behind her ear. I was desperate to know what they were saying. Sebastian was shaking his head and she was standing too close and stroking his arm. Then they seemed to be arguing. She was pleading with him, her arms outstretched, he was shaking his head vehemently, his hands on his hips. I don't know how it happened but then she had her arms wrapped around his neck, her cheek on his bare chest, and he was holding her, rocking her gently, the same way he'd held me last night.

"I have ten bucks says we won't be seeing Seb till tomorrow morning," said Stefan, gesturing obscenely with his hands.

"You won't get any takers on that bet!" laughed Kurt. "She's all over him!"

Ches looked disgusted, and threw the remains of his sandwich into the fire pit.

"Boys!" said Donna in a warning voice.

I'd seen enough. Seen enough and heard enough.

"Caroline? Are you going somewhere?"

Donna's attention was directed back to me.

I smiled stiffly, forcing the words out.

"I'm just going to go and take some more photographs before I lose the light—I want to make sure I have everything covered." *And to get the hell away from all of this.*

I wandered along the beach, feeling numb even though traitorous tears were leaking from my eyes. I snapped photographs at random, barely aware of what I was looking at. There was only one picture in my head—the one where Sebastian held his ex-girlfriend. His beautiful, sexy, *young* ex-girlfriend.

I was angry! So it seemed my hypocrisy knew no bounds. I was angry because Sebastian had left me and gone off with Brenda—the slut who'd screwed his friend Jack. Yes, I was cheating on my husband; yes, I was an unfaithful wife. But I'd risked everything for Sebastian—everything. The life I'd known, jail time, a record.

I had to watch him walk away and smile and smile while he played the villain. I was choked with jealousy and anger and more hurt than I could easily take.

I found myself at the ocean's edge. The tide had turned and was beginning its slow journey back across the sun-warmed sand. The gentle lapping of water at my feet was soothing. I let my mind wander among the dizzying memories of the last three weeks—a ridiculously short amount of time during the course of a life. And yet ... and yet I had never felt so alive. Fear—as much as hope—had colored those weeks but I realized I didn't have to go on like that.

I had expected too much from Sebastian: it wasn't fair. He was so young ... too young to be expected to take on everything I represented, with all my ridiculous insecurities and emotional baggage. If I truly cared for him, I would make it easy for him to go. Of course, it didn't seem as if he'd need my blessing, the way Brenda had clung to him and the way he'd held her, too.

Much as my body, my whole being ached for his touch, I had a revelation—I was strong enough to make it on my own. He'd shown me how to be strong. Perhaps he'd given me his own strength, I didn't know. One thing was certain—I couldn't be with David anymore. And if Sebastian didn't want me, there was no reason for me to stay.

But it hurt. It hurt badly. I'd opened myself to the possibility of love and now love had slapped me down. Down, but not out: not quite.

I felt a dull tearing inside my chest—part of my heart was breaking, knowing that in all probability I wouldn't see Sebastian again. I took a deep breath and stared toward the horizon—time for me to grow up at last.

I glanced at my watch. I hoped Donna was ready to leave because I needed to get over to *City Beat* and drop off the films. Oh, and pick up David's dry-cleaning. I quailed at the thought of facing him, or rather, telling him that I was leaving. I needed to clear my head and decide how I was going to do that. Just thinking about it made me feel sick. So much for being strong. I was definitely going to have to work up to it. Somehow.

By the time I'd wandered back to the barbeque pit, Donna and Shirley were alone, slowly packing up the remains of the food—women's work, it seemed. I hurried to help them.

"Did you take all your photographs?" asked Donna.

"Yes, I think so. Are you heading back now? It's just I need to drop these films in at *City Beat*?"

"Tonight?" Donna was surprised. "The paper doesn't go out until Thursday."

"I know, but the editor asked for them, so..."

"Well, Shirley and I are heading back now anyway. The boys are getting a ride with Mitch. I expect they'll be rather late."

She raised her eyebrows and shook her head in a way that suggested *boys will be boys*.

With everything piled into Donna's station-wagon, we drove away from the beach. I glanced over my shoulder once, as the sun had begun its slow descent toward the horizon. I don't know what I was looking for—a soft hiss of steam as the sun touched the ocean, or perhaps a glimpse of someone silhouetted on the sand. Of course, there was neither.

It felt like the end of something, but maybe it was a beginning, too.

"That went well, didn't it?" said Donna, cheerfully.

For a moment I couldn't think what she was talking about. Oh, the fun day. Right. So much fun.

My lonely thoughts burned like acid. I was so stupid to have expected anything different.

Shirley smiled. "Yes, I think everyone had a good time. Of course, the boys are planning on extending the fun. I hope Mitch keeps an eye on them."

I didn't want to think how Sebastian might be extending the fun at this very moment.

Donna smiled, "I'm sure he will."

For a moment I wasn't sure if she was answering my unspoken thoughts.

"Hmm, well, he won't let them drink too much, but I dare say there'll be a few sore heads in the morning. Mitch did say that there was a possibility they were going to sleep in the van tonight if they didn't make it back, although I'm not sure how they'll all fit now Stefan and Kurt are with them."

Donna shook her head and smiled. "I doubt they'll care. You know what they're like when they all get together." Then her serious look was back. "Although they really shouldn't be drinking on the beach—Chester is still under age. And Sebastian. And that other boy—Fido."

Shirley laughed. "Don't you remember when you were that age, Donna? You've told me you bent a few rules in your time—in fact, I distinctly remember you saying that Johan climbed in your dormitory at that private girls' school of yours."

I threw a surprised look at Donna. She was a lovely lady, but she'd always struck me as rather formal.

"Oh, yes," said Shirley, smiling at me, "Donna has her fair share of secrets, don't you?"

"You'll be giving Caroline the wrong impression of me."

"Or the right one," laughed Shirley. "Yes, Johan used to climb into her dormitory to steal a kiss or two. She nearly got expelled, didn't you, Donna?!"

"Yes, I admit it all," smiled Donna.

"Well, now you know where your boys get their wild streak from," said Shirley with a wink.

"Yes, well ... and who would you say Chester takes after?"

"His father!" asserted Shirley. Then she sighed. "I don't know who Sebastian takes after—luckily the poor boy isn't like either of his parents. I sometimes wonder if Donald is really his father."

"Shirley!" said Donna, looking shocked.

"Well, you've said yourself he doesn't take after either of them—he certainly doesn't *look* like either of them. Then there's Estelle's *reputation*. And it would explain why they're always so ghastly toward him."

"Well," said Donna, quietly, "I don't think we should speculate on that. Not without facts."

Shirley shrugged and for a moment there was an awkward silence in the car.

"You're very quiet, Caroline. Are you okay?" asked Donna, her eyes inquiring.

"Just thinking about the week ahead," I replied, my words deliberately bland.

The week. The month. The rest of my life.

In truth, I'd been fascinated to hear Shirley's speculation about Sebastian's heritage. I wondered if there was any shred of truth in it, or perhaps it was just the useless, baseless gossip that percolated through so many military facilities.

With a painful jolt I reminded myself that in all reality, it wasn't any of my business, Sebastian wasn't any of my business. But I couldn't resist torturing myself a little more.

"What happened to Sebastian this evening?" I asked innocently, while nearly choking on my words. "They'd all vanished by the time I came back."

"I think he left with Brenda," said Shirley, confirming the thoughts that tormented me.

"Oh, I don't know," disagreed Donna. "He was talking to Chester for a while, wasn't he? Or was it before that girl arrived? I thought she was rather ... underdressed."

I definitely agreed with that point of view. Tramp.

Shirley smiled. "All the young girls dress like that, Donna. And, frankly, if she wanted to catch Sebastian's attention, which she obviously did, she certainly went about it the right way!" She paused. "Although, to be fair, I was a little surprised, she'd always seemed rather sweet when they were dating, hardly the siren of today's little show and tell. But who knows: they're probably off having mad, passionate sex behind the pier."

I could have quite cheerfully stuck Shirley's head in the passenger door and slammed it several times. It wasn't that she was saying anything I hadn't been thinking, but to hear it confirmed by a third party was a new source of humiliation and hurt.

"I should hope not!" said Donna, severely.

"Oh, come on, Donna. You were young once. You've got two sons: you know what teenage boys are like. They think about sex every other second—or more often than that. You saw their faces when Brenda arrived—and what she wasn't wearing. I wouldn't be surprised if every dick within a hundred yards leapt to attention and saluted when she fiddled with her bikini strap. Which of them can say no when it's offered up on a plate like that? I mean, I've tried to talk to Ches about waiting until he's in love and respect for women and all that, but I'm definitely swimming against the tide there—I'm probably too late anyway. Mostly, I hope he's being safe. I don't relish the thought of being a grandmother just yet."

Donna shook her head but it was clear she didn't agree with Shirley's more liberal views. "I think I'd be a nervous wreck if I'd had daughters instead of sons. And their father would have kept them locked up until they'd graduated college ... or possibly longer."

Just then my phone beeped. I decided to ignore it. Donna glanced at me, a quizzical expression on her face.

"It's probably David making sure I've collected the dry-cleaning," I said, trying and failing to keep the bitterness out of my voice.

She smiled.

"Yes, Johan said something about a formal dinner at the mess tomorrow. I don't think he was very keen, having been away for two nights. But who expects the military to be sympathetic to us poor wives?"

Shirley nodded in agreement, and the topic moved on to other wives and partners who had dropped by to say hello during the course of the afternoon.

"I think Bill enjoyed himself today," said Shirley. "I haven't seen him like that since before he and Denise divorced."

"How long have he and Mitch been friends?"

"Oh, ever since we came to San Diego, so it must be at least four years—we wanted Ches to have some consistency through high school."

I leaned back in my seat as the conversation continued, letting the tiredness wash over me. I was almost asleep by the time Donna pulled up outside my house.

"Did David mention that I was picking them both up at the airport?"

"Oh, I probably should have read David's text," I said, guiltily.

"Never mind," she said, smiling at me. "You've got enough on your mind remembering the dry-cleaning."

I laughed, although I knew the tone was a little off.

"And I have to get into town. Well, thanks for a lovely day, both of you. And thanks for the ride—and for looking after me."

I gave Donna a quick hug and blew a kiss to Shirley.

"Our pleasure, Caroline," said Donna.

"We must have another coffee soon," agreed Shirley. "Maybe at the country club?"

I had no intention of ever going near the place again but I smiled wanly. I waved goodbye and watched them drive out of sight. They really had been very kind to me. I'd be sorry to leave them behind.

Tiredly, I got into my own car and headed to the dry-cleaners. My phone beeped for a second time but I ignored it.

David's uniform was ready, the woman at the dry-cleaners proudly informing me that it was their patriotic duty to give precedence to the military. I smiled thinly and thanked her, tossing the plastic-wrapped uniform into the trunk. I was so tired I was about ready to fall asleep at the wheel.

I parked as close to *City Beat* as I could and jogged the block and a half to the offices.

The reception was in darkness and the door was locked. I rang the buzzer for the intercom and was just considering the wisdom of dropping the films into the mailbox when I saw Carl striding toward the door.

"Carolina, hi! Good to see you! You look well—you've got some color on your beach day."

I realized too late that appearing in a shorts and a skimpy t-shirt wasn't the most professional attire.

"Oh, yes," I agreed awkwardly. "It was a lovely day—everyone enjoyed themselves."

"Did your husband enjoy it?"

His question threw me off balance.

"Um, well, no. He's away at a medical symposium at the moment."

"Oh, that's a pity," said Carl, although if his expression was anything to go by, that was the opposite of what he really thought. "Well, perhaps you'd like to join me for a quick drink? I was just about finished here anyway."

I'd definitely given him the wrong impression by wearing my beach shorts.

"That's kind, Carl," I replied quickly, "but actually I have to go pick him up at the airport now."

He looked disappointed.

"Are you sure you haven't got time for one quick drink?"

"Sorry. I really have to go."

"Okay, well ... I guess I'll see you."

"Sure. Have a good evening. I'll be interested to see how the photographs turn out."

"Drop by any time."

I waved hurriedly and made my escape. My beat up old Ford made a good stand-in for a sanctuary.

I decided I'd better check my phone to see what commands from on high David had sent this time.

But the texts weren't from David, they were from Sebastian. My heart shuddered, an intense mixture of pain and pleasure. With trembling hands I opened my phone. To my surprise, there were three texts, each one more urgent than the last.

Where are you?
I need to talk to you. Where are you?

And the last one.

I'm going to your house NOW

I gasped and, although I tried to beat it back, hope flared suddenly and brilliantly. It was so confusing—I was still burning with anger and jealousy. *He'd left me at the picnic for that girl.*

I glanced at my watch—it was just after 9PM. Donna would be at the airport by now. Another 30 minutes and David would be walking through our front door. It would take me more than 20 minutes to drive home. I did the math.

Fuck.

By now my hands were shaking so badly it took me three attempts to scroll through to find Sebastian's number on my cell.

The phone rang, and rang, and rang. And then it switched to voicemail.

I hung up and tried again. This time it went immediately to voicemail. This time I left a message.

"Sebastian, do not, repeat DO NOT go to my house. I'm downtown and David will be home any minute. Please, please don't go."

I had no idea if he'd get the message or, if he did, whether he'd do as I asked. And then I started to feel angry—really angry. *He* was the one who'd gone off with his ex-girlfriend, *he* was the one who was threatening to go to my home just as David was due back.

Maybe my anger was unreasonable but it didn't feel like it, and right there and then, I needed it.

I drove home as fast as I dared. I didn't have those get-out-of-jail-free military plates on my car, and I couldn't risk getting stopped for speeding now.

I screeched onto the driveway, relieved that the house was dark and silent. I'd beaten David home, at the very least.

I nearly leapt out of my skin when I heard Sebastian's voice in the darkness.

"Where were you?"

"Sebastian!" I hissed. "You can't be here! David will be home any second!"

"I'm not going anywhere until you *talk* to me."

His voice was tight with anger.

Well, fuck him! I was pretty damned angry, too!

I shoved the key in the lock and pushed the front door open.

"Get in!" I snarled. "Before someone sees you!"

He pushed past me and I slammed the door shut behind him.

"You can't be here!" I repeated.

He didn't answer but suddenly grabbed my waist and pulled me toward him. Without warning, he kissed me fiercely, forcing his lips against mine.

My body started to respond, but anger and fear had the upper hand. I shoved him hard in the chest. He let go, his hands dropping to his side, his face shocked.

"Caro!"

"I mean it, Sebastian. I want you to go. Now!"

His voice turned pleading, the words tripping over themselves.

"I need to talk to you, Caro. You just disappeared. I didn't know where you were. I know how it must have looked ... with Brenda ... but it was *nothing*. I promise. She was upset and I couldn't ignore her, could I?"

Yes, you could! I wanted to yell at him.

"Why did you just go? Why didn't you talk to me? You could have called me! Please! I love you!"

I didn't know what to believe. I did know what I'd *seen*.

Blue-white car headlights suddenly flooded the hallway and I heard the sound of Donna's station wagon pulling up outside.

"For the love of God, Sebastian! Just go!"

"When will I see you? Caro, please!"

"I don't know. Just go. Just get out!" I yelled.

He gave me one, last, tortured look, then turned and ran into the kitchen. I heard him fumbling with the lock on the back door as I moved swiftly through the house turning on lights.

My heart was hammering so loudly in my chest that I barely heard the sharp rap on the front door.

Breathless, I snatched it open.

"You *are* in then, Caroline. I was beginning to wonder."

His tone was brusque. It was just what I needed to hear—and I snapped out of my funk.

"I haven't been in long—I had to drop off some films I took at the fun day to *City Beat*. How was your flight? Can I get you a coffee?"

"You know I can't drink caffeine at this time of night, Caroline."

"A glass of wine, then?"

"I don't need to drink every day—not like you."

I blinked. This was a new and interesting development. Now I was an alcoholic? I almost laughed. And then I had an epiphany: I wasn't scared of him anymore.

"Well, I'm glad to see the flight didn't affect your good mood, David. I'm going to have a glass of wine. Let me know if I can get you anything."

I left him gaping in our hallway.

Eventually, I heard him stomp up the stairs with his bags. My adrenaline rush over, I felt a little shaky. I hadn't eaten much at the picnic but now I was ravenous.

Scrabbling through the fridge, I found a jar of peanut butter. I'd bought it for David, not really being a fan, but right now it was just what I needed. I found a dessert spoon and dug in.

I remembered that only this morning Sebastian had told me that he liked peanut butter. Was that really just this morning? It seemed a lifetime ago. In some ways it was.

I started to feel bad for the way I'd spoken to him. I'd thought he was behaving recklessly to insist on coming to my house and taking such a huge risk. Yes, that was foolish, but, truthfully, I was the one who'd behaved badly. He looked so hurt when he left. No, damn it! I was right to be angry.

My emotions whirled around, reeling from sadness to anger and back again. It was sometime later when I realized that David was being unusually quiet.

I walked upstairs and found him already under the sheets, his dirty clothes scattered on *my* side of the bed.

When it came down to it, I had to admit that David had Sebastian beaten in childish behavior.

I headed for the guest room. It was cool and calm and untainted by any association with David or any memory of Sebastian. Before I set my phone alarm to wake me in the morning, I wondered briefly about texting Sebastian, but I wasn't sure what I wanted to say.

I fell asleep with the pain on his face burned into my eyes.

CHAPTER THIRTEEN

David was sulky at breakfast. What a shocker.

Without comment, I served him bacon, pancakes and eggs, pointed out his dry-cleaned uniform and calmly sat down with a slice of toast at my laptop.

I could feel his eyes on me, a silent castigation. Well, as long as it remained silent, that was just fine by me.

True to form, he flounced out of the house without speaking to me. I noticed he took his dress uniform so, with luck, I wouldn't see him until tomorrow. A twenty-four hour reprieve I could definitely use.

Before I faced David, it was time to man up and face Sebastian. I sure as hell wasn't going to apologize for what I'd said last night but we needed to talk. At least, I thought we did. Whatever had happened between him and Brenda, or not happened as he'd insisted ... whatever the rights and wrongs of him risking our exposure by coming here last night, I was supposed to be the adult in this relationship. I decided I was going to let him go with a few shreds of my dignity intact.

I pulled out my phone to text him.

Texts were such a useful medium: they could say so much or so little—and yet they side-stepped all the screwed up emotions of a face-to-face encounter. I could see why dumping someone by text was so popular. It was the coward's correspondence method of choice. Well ... perfect for me, then.

I was about to type a message when I heard a soft tap at the back door. It seemed Sebastian had beaten me to the punch. At least he wasn't going to dump me by text. I supposed that was a good thing.

God, he was so beautiful. I couldn't help taking one long, last, devouring look.

Even if this was goodbye, I felt lucky to have had him in my life. Knowingly or not, he'd been the catalyst for changing my life. I'd always be grateful.

"Hi. You want to come in?"

He nodded silently and I pushed the door open wide to let him through.

"I'm just having a coffee. Do you want one?"

"Why are you being like this?" he whispered.

"Being like what?" I said, coolly.

"Like ... *this!*" he gestured helplessly.

His voice pierced my carefully constructed façade—he sounded so bruised. I sat at the table, warming my cold hands on my coffee mug. I began my pre-prepared speech.

"I'm sorry I disappeared without saying goodbye. I didn't mean for you to worry. I saw you with Brenda and ... I thought it was better for me to go."

"I knew it! I knew that was it! Fuck, Caro!"

He sat down opposite me and rubbed his hands over his face.

"It was nothing with Brenda. Nothing! Why are you being like this?"

Oh no, he didn't get to be the injured party.

"It didn't look like nothing," I hissed, my careful control sliding away. "You say you love *me* and then you just walk off with Brenda? Do you have the slightest idea how much that hurt? Do you? You entered into a relationship with me knowing that I'm a married woman. But it's okay for you to get mad with my husband, and it's okay for you to sulk when Bill pretends to flirt with me, and you tell me how upset you are that you can't be with me in public at the stupid fun day ... but you know what, Sebastian? This is what you signed on for. With me. I sure didn't sign on to see you going off with some girl. Did you really think it was okay for you to take a nice, romantic stroll along the beach with your ex-girlfriend who obviously has feelings for you and wants you back? Did you? Because it isn't okay. It really isn't."

"Wow. You're ... you're really angry. Caro..."

No shit!

I glared at him and he dropped his eyes to the table, sighing heavily.

"I'm sorry. I am. It's just ... Brenda is ... was ... I guess I knew she might be there yesterday. Her dad's a buddy of Mitch. I should have said something ... I get that now ... but I didn't know what to say ... I mean, I broke up with her months ago before I even met you again so I didn't think it would matter if she did ... but I didn't know she was going to... I'm not interested in her, so it didn't ... how can you..."

He took a deep breath.

"Caro, I've said to you over and over again that I love you. You never say ...

why don't you believe me? Why don't you trust me? I'd never, *never* do anything to hurt you. I love you."

"You did hurt me, Sebastian," I said, gravely. "You hurt me a lot. You say you'd never do anything to hurt me but then you go ahead and do something like this."

I thought he was going to reach out for me, but then he closed his eyes, shaking his head slowly.

"God, Caro, I'm so sorry. I didn't mean to hurt you. I just ... I didn't know what Brenda was going to say and I didn't want you to have to sit there and listen to it. I thought ... I thought I was doing the right thing—getting her out of the way. And ... she was upset and I guess ... I felt like I owed her or something. She's been having a really tough time since..."

He stopped. It was probably the look on my face. I *so* didn't want to hear him telling me how he owed his slutty ex-girlfriend and that he still cared enough about her not to want to upset her. But it was okay to upset me.

I sighed. I knew that wasn't what he'd intended. He'd obviously thought that getting her out of my way was the best solution if she was going to start babbling about wanting him back. Sometimes he was just too damn nice for his own good.

"Caro, I'm sorry. Please, please don't be mad at me. I love you."

His voice trembled and his eyes begged me to believe him. And I did. I just wasn't sure I believed in us.

I reached over and took his hands in mine, my resolve a little shaken by his renewed declaration.

But it was a mistake: the warmth of his skin, the touch of flesh on flesh—my whole body flushed with desire. The prepared speech died on my lips.

"You looked so good together." I choked out the admission.

He shook his head slowly, his scared eyes fixed on mine.

"And then ... the others were saying how nice she was—and pretty—and that you'd made a great couple and ... I couldn't help agreeing with them. And I *saw* the way she was with you. She made it pretty damn obvious she wants to get back with you. I guess I couldn't blame her. Or you. And ... you don't need all ... all my emotional baggage. You *should* be with Brenda—or someone like her ... someone your own age. And ... I *saw* you! I *saw* you with her—how you were with her—holding her like that."

He pulled my hands to his face and kissed the palms gently.

Then slowly and deliberately he sucked the tip of each finger. He could see on my face what that did to me.

"I want to make love to you," he whispered.

I tried to snatch my hands back but he held onto them.

"Don't give up on us, Caro. Because I haven't."

I tugged my hands free and this time he let them go.

"Sebastian, I'll be honest with you—I don't know what to do for the best so I'm kind of making this up as I go along. But ... all this ... this craziness—we're getting swept away by it. Making love with you is extraordinary. I've never, *never* felt anything like this my whole life. But it was wrong of me to ... to start this relationship with you—and I don't mean because of what the law says, although that's certainly an issue ... but because it's not fair to you."

He tried to interrupt me but I was determined to finish.

"Please, I need to say this. I've had a lot of years of feeling inadequate, of not being good enough—I don't need to paint a picture, I'm sure you can guess why. And every time, *every time* I see you with a younger woman, whatever the circumstances, it's going to rip me up. I don't want to see the best thing I've ever known soured by my insecurities—I couldn't bear that. You've brought me to life—and you'll never know how much I owe you because of that. But you're only just starting out in your life. It's not fair to burden you with me. You deserve better than that. I *have* to let you go."

He stared at me in silence for some seconds as if to make sure I really had finished. He took a deep breath—and I held mine.

"You want honesty? Well, answer this: if I was 25 and you were 38, would we still be having this conversation?"

I shrugged helplessly.

"About you going off with your ex-girlfriend? Yes. Definitely."

He shook his head impatiently.

"No, the age thing."

"Maybe," I said, cautiously.

"No, I don't think so and nor do you—not really. That's what I'm saying, Caro. Nobody would blink twice. It wouldn't matter. It *doesn't* matter. Don't you think that I don't feel the same, that I'm not good enough for you? Hell, what can I give you? A shitty apartment and working two jobs while you try to put me through school. You think I feel good about that? Because it fucking kills me! I want to take care of you, not ... I don't care about going to college, I don't care about leaving San Diego. I only care about being with you. And we have this same fucking argument over and over. You're driving me crazy! I love you! If you left me now..."

But he couldn't finish the words. He scrubbed away tears from his cheeks and looked down.

"Every time something goes wrong, you give up on us. You're killing me, Caro."

I sat with my hand over my mouth, unable to move or speak, appalled at what I'd done to him.

He looked up.

"You want honesty? Well, I don't know what will happen ... but neither do you. Maybe we'll make it ... maybe we won't. But you're giving up before we've even tried. I don't understand. Why won't you take a chance?"

Is that what I was doing? Had I found yet another way to be a coward? I'd thought I was setting him free, but he saw it as my refusal to take a chance ... on him, on us, on love—maybe even on myself.

"What do you want to do?" I said, softly.

"Try. Just try."

Yes. I could do that.

"Okay."

"Okay?"

"Yes, I'll try."

"You've got to mean it, Caro. *Promise* me."

"I promise I'll try."

His shoulders slumped with relief.

"I missed you last night," he said.

I tried to smile but my face still felt stiff from our most recent fight.

"Should we go to our favorite coffee shop?" I suggested, thinking neutral ground might be a good idea.

He shook his head.

"I don't want to share you."

We stared at each other across the kitchen table.

"Can we go to bed?" he asked. "I ... I really need you, Caro. To touch you ... to show you how much I love you. Please."

It was breaking all my carefully constructed rules. What if someone saw my car in the driveway and came around? What if someone had seen Sebastian arrive? What if they saw him leave later? What if? What if? But I was tired of being afraid, and right now, I didn't care. I needed him, too.

I stood up and held out my hand. For a second he continued to stare at me, then a huge smile lit his eyes.

We walked up the stairs hand-in-hand, each step measuring the distance from our argument.

He was surprised when I turned left into the guest room. He threw me a questioning look.

"I sleep in here now," I said simply.

I saw him try to suppress a triumphant smile. He almost managed it.

Slowly we undressed each other, taking our time to reconnect.

He unbuttoned my shirt, pausing to kiss my chest, a little lower each time. He undid the cuffs and kissed my wrists, then let the material slide over my shoulders. I ran my hands down his chest, then tugged lightly on the hem, pulling his t-shirt over his head. I slid my hands over his skin, burying my face in his chest, breathing him in. He smelled of sunshine and the ocean.

He watched me, his eyes dark, filled with desire, as I slowly unzipped his jeans. He pushed them down his legs and stepped out of them, quickly sliding his briefs over his hips, so he stood naked before me, his love exposed.

He sank to his knees, and rested his hands on my waist, his eyes still fixed on mine. Then his eyes closed, and he kissed my stomach, nuzzling me gently.

I rested one hand on his shoulder, and stroked his head with the other.

He smiled up at me then turned his attention to my zipper. Carefully, he helped me step out of my jeans and panties. He kissed my body briefly, then stood up and pulled me into a tender hug.

"Do you know how much you mean to me, how much I love you?" he whispered into my hair. "I hate fighting with you."

"I hate it, too. Just kiss me."

His mouth rested gently on mine and I felt the softness of his lips as they moved against me. His fingers drifted over my shoulders and down my spine where both his hands cupped my behind.

My hands trailed up over his ribs until they were twisted behind his neck, pulling his head down to deepen our kiss.

Here in this room, with our bodies entwined, I felt that I could trust this fierce love that had shattered and rebuilt my life. But outside, the world was a cold and dangerous place. I didn't know if love would be enough, but I'd promised to try.

He bent down suddenly and quite literally swept me off my feet so I gasped. He cradled me in his arms and kissed me again.

"I've been meaning to do this for ages," he said, his voice a soft murmur.

"Sebastian, you swept me off my feet our very first night together."

He grinned.

"Yeah, but I've been wanting to do it properly ever since."

Gently, he placed me on the bed and stood looking down at me, his gaze soft and loving.

"I want to kiss every inch of you," he said.

"That sounds nice: which end are you going to start?"

He laughed lightly.

"Hmm ... choices, choices. Today, I think I'll start with your toes."

"My toes?!"

"Sure, why not? You have beautiful feet."

And, to make his point, he picked up my left foot and sucked my big toe, nipping the end playfully.

Why that was so erotic, I couldn't say, but it made me desperate to feel him inside me. I reached out for him but he leaned away.

"Nope! You're always saying you want me to go slowly ... your wish is my command."

"But...!"

"Nope—slowly."

He kissed the front of my foot and ran his tongue up my shin. He sucked my knee, gazing up at me through his lashes, a wicked gleam in his eye. Just when I thought he'd be moving up to my thigh, he put my foot back on the bed and started again on my right foot.

Why the hell had I ever asked for 'slow'? This was torture. Slow, delicious, unbelievable torture. Boy, he was a good student.

This time he didn't stop at my knee, but hooked my leg over his shoulder and kept on going. And going.

My back arched and I gasped as his tongue flicked up to my sweet spot, then circled around and around.

I moaned his name and clutched at his shoulders but he just pressed harder and I felt myself begin to build.

"Sebastian," I moaned again. "Please!"

I wasn't even sure what I was pleading for: me, him, us.

Then he started teasing me with his fingers, slowly circling, massaging me inside and out. I didn't think I could take much more and tried to push his hands away but he was relentless. My body shuddered and he sat up. I glimpsed a satisfied expression on his face between my frantic breaths.

"Slow enough for you?" he muttered, as he continued his kisses up my body, finally reaching my breasts, which he sucked and teased with playful bites.

I pulled my knees up and felt his erection pushing between my thighs, but he didn't try to enter me. I ran my hand up and down him and he squeezed his eyes shut, momentarily losing his concentration.

"Don't," he said.

"But, I..."

"You have to wait, Caro."

"Why?!"

"You wanted slow. I'm giving you slow."

"I've changed my mind," I whimpered. "I want fast. Please. Now."

He arched his back away from me and grinned.

"No. I like slow. Who knew?"

And to make his point, he grabbed both my hands and held them above my head so I couldn't touch him and he carried on kissing my breasts.

That made me mad. I didn't like not being able to touch him.

"Let go my hands!"

He ignored me so I bit his neck and pushed against him with my feet.

"Wow, you want to fight me? I like it!"

"Stop teasing me!"

"I thought you wanted slow?"

"No!" I said forcefully, and he laughed.

"What do you want then?"

I shook his hands off me and grabbed hold of his erection, placing it at my entrance. *If that wasn't enough of a clue, I really didn't know what was!*

Thankfully he took the hint and allowed himself to slide into me. I was so turned on it was a relief and pain and pleasure when he was finally inside me. And that's when his plans to go slow completely unraveled.

"Oh, fuck!" he hissed. "You feel so fucking amazing! Oh, Caro!"

I tilted my hips up and he started to really move—long, hard strokes that rocked the whole bed and sent the headboard banging against the wall.

I clenched around him, and that tipped him over the edge. He rammed into me urgently one last time, his muscles rigid, his breath hot and rapid on my neck. He rested his head on my shoulder and gently pulled out of me, collapsing onto his side.

Breathlessly, I inched back down the bed and nestled into him. He wrapped his arm around me and we lay there wordlessly.

Finally, we lay peacefully. My head was on his chest, listening to his heart beating, his breath rising and falling, and the distant sounds of the world outside our window. His fingers drifted rhythmically up and down my back.

I felt so content, I began to fall asleep. Then Sebastian brought me crashing back to the here and now.

"Did David say anything to you when he came home?"

I sighed. I really didn't want to talk about him.

"Not much."

"He must have said something."

"He implied I drank too much."

"What? Why?"

I laughed mirthlessly. "I think, because I offered him a glass of wine. I was trying to be ... civil."

Sebastian muttered an oath under his breath.

Well, now that he'd started this line of questioning ... here was my starter for ten.

"How did you get home last night? I understood from Shirley that everyone was sleeping in the van."

"Hitched," he said, shortly.

And now for the six million dollar question.

"What did Brenda say to you, when you went off with her?"

He sucked some air in through his teeth. *Yeah, should have seen that one coming.*

"She wanted us to start dating again."

I'd guessed as much. Hell, she couldn't have been more obvious if she'd sky-written it with scarlet letters, then ripped his clothes off and mounted him on the sand in front of everyone.

"And what did you say?"

"I said I didn't feel the same ... I told her I'd met someone else."

I inhaled sharply. "Was that wise?"

He shrugged. "I thought that would make her back off."

"But it didn't?"

He shook his head. "Not at first. She kept on and on asking me who it was."

"And?"

"She kept naming all these girls we knew in school..." he sighed. "Then she said the thing with Jack was a mistake ... and she started crying."

All those girls...

I couldn't help feeling he wasn't telling me the whole story. Did I want to know? If he didn't tell me, I'd probably just imagine something worse.

"How did you leave it with her?"

"What do you mean?"

"Well, when she started crying, what did you do?"

"You *saw* what I did," he said, sounding annoyed.

"Yes, but after that. sShirley and Donna said you'd been gone ages."

He didn't answer straight away.

"We went for a walk," he said at last. "Brenda was ... embarrassed. She didn't want to go back to her friends looking like she'd been crying."

"She's very pretty."

He looked uncomfortable. "Yeah, I guess."

"What happened next?"

"That's it. I walked her back to her friends. She seemed fine. I went back to the fire pit, but you'd already packed up and gone. I texted you," he said accusingly.

"I didn't look at my phone."

I could see he wasn't fully convinced but he didn't press me either. I was grateful for that.

"Why were you downtown so late?"

"I was dropping off the films I took of the fun day."

"On a Sunday?"

"Yes, the editor wanted them early. I don't know why." *Although I had a pretty good suspicion what the reason was.*

He paused. I was glad he'd decided to let it go.

"Bill's an asshole."

Ugh. He wasn't letting *everything* go. Now I was the one who should have seen that coming.

"You shouldn't let him wind you up so easily."

"I hated the way he spoke to you!"

"I know how that feels," I said, calmly.

We lay quietly for a few minutes, letting the twin specters of our jealousy spiral further away.

I think Sebastian must have finally decided to try and put yesterday behind us, because he suddenly said, "I never asked: have you ever been to New York before?"

"Yes, a couple of times. You?"

"No. Mom and Dad went sometimes but they always left me with a neighbor."

His voice was bitter. I wondered again if Shirley's speculation about his parentage was accurate.

"What made you want us to go there then?"

He shrugged.

"Same reason you want to go back East—to get as far away from here as possible."

"What should we do when we get there?" I said, happy to try and imagine our future. "I mean, is there anything special you'd like to do?"

"Have sex. A lot."

I rolled my eyes. "That's a given. Anything else? Perhaps of an outdoor nature?"

"Have sex outdoors."

I laughed.

"I don't think they have a lot of beaches in New York City."

"Yeah, they do! I checked. Well, not the city exactly but there's a surf community at Rockaway Beach. If we lived in Brooklyn or Queens, we'd be less than 10 miles from it."

I had to smile. "You've been doing your research."

"Sure! And a guy I know who used to surf Long Beach said that it can get pretty gnarly."

"I think you should write me a glossary of surfing terms so I know what you're talking about."

"Well, you've gotta know about Sex Wax, baby."

"What?!"

"Yeah, you rub it on your stick."

"Okay, you've got about five seconds to explain that or..."

"Or what?"

"No peanut butter for you!"

"Wow! You really do play rough!"

"You'd better believe it."

He laughed and tugged my hair gently.

"Sex Wax is a brand name for the kind of wax you put on your board—your stick. It helps give you traction. Not as much fun as it sounds."

"*Preferisci una inceratura a caldo ... o a freddo?*"

"What does that mean? Because it sounded really dirty!"

"I said, 'Do you like it coated in hot wax ... or cold?'"

"Oh man! That sounded so hot!"

"*Si è alzata l'onda, o sei proprio contento di vedermi?*"

"Huh?"

"Is the surf up or are you just pleased to see me?"

"Fuck! It makes me so horny when you say stuff like that."

"Sebastian, I could read a bus timetable and you'd say it made you horny!"

He smiled. "Yeah, you're right. I have a tide table in my jeans' pocket. Will you read that to me?"

"You want a bedtime story? Does that sound good?"

"*Supra la luna!*"

"You're learning!"

"You're a good teacher," he murmured into my hair.

His stomach rumbled loudly, interrupting the mood somewhat.

"Are you hungry?"

"Hungry for you."

"That is *such* a cheesy line, Sebastian!"

"Yeah, but it's still true."

I kicked the sheets off the bed and pushed him away, grabbing my robe.

"Come on. I'm going to feed you. A little lesson in Italian cookery."

"Pizza?" he said hopefully.

"That's not proper Italian food. Papa would turn in his grave! No, we'll make some fresh tortellini."

"Will it take long?"

"It can be a little tricky."

He sat up, propping himself with a pillow.

"We don't have that much time," he said, his tone solemn. "I have to be at work at 2PM."

I held back a sigh as I pulled on my robe.

"Oh well. Something quick then. How are you going to get there? Ches?"

When he didn't reply I looked over at him.

"What's wrong?"

"I was going to ask Mom to drive me."

"Oh, why?"

He blew out a lungful of air and fiddled with the sheet.

"Ches is kind of mad at me."

"I can't imagine that. He seems so easy going."

Sebastian looked uncomfortable.

"I guess. But ... he doesn't get why I won't tell him who I'm ... dating."

I couldn't help sniggering. "I'm sorry, really. It's just ... dating?!"

He gave a half-smile and ran a hand over his hair.

"Whatever. He said that I shouldn't expect him to cover for me with my folks if I don't trust him with the truth."

I felt a shiver run through me.

"Has he had to cover for you?"

He didn't reply.

"Tell me!"

He grimaced.

"Mom ... she noticed that I wasn't there for two nights. She ... she kind of made a big deal out of it."

I groaned. "I knew it!"

"She phoned Ches's mom and Ches said that I'd stayed over. I guess Mrs. Peters is covering for me, too. She knew I hadn't been there."

"We'll just have to be more careful," I whispered.

"Maybe ... maybe I could tell Ches. He'd keep it a secret, I know he would."

I was appalled. I understood why he wanted to tell his friend but I couldn't let that happen.

"We can't risk it, Sebastian. *I* can't risk it. And ... if anyone found out, he'd be complicit in ... in a crime. You do understand, don't you?"

He shrugged and looked down. "Yeah, I guess."

He obviously wasn't happy with my answer.

I sighed. "Do you want me to run you to the country club? I could drop you at the entrance and get there before you. No one would be any the wiser."

"Okay," he muttered. "Thanks."

A thunderous knocking at the front door made me jump.

"Fuck!"

I heard Sebastian's oath as if from a great distance but I couldn't move.

The banging on the door started again.

"Caro!"

Sebastian's panicked voice unfroze me. He was thrashing about, dressing as quickly as possible. There was nowhere to hide. He couldn't get down the stairs and out through the back without being seen. This was every nightmare I'd imagined, played in fast forward.

I pulled my robe around me more tightly.

The pounding started again.

"Caro! Get the fucking door!" mouthed Sebastian.

I ran down the stairs and stumbled to a halt. I took a deep breath and pulled the door open.

"Delivery, ma'am," said a man in a red and yellow DHL uniform as he handed me a large parcel. "Sign here, please."

I started giggling. I couldn't help it.

"Are you okay, ma'am?"

"Yes!" I gasped, wiping tears of relief from my face.

He gave me a strange look and headed back to his van shaking his head. *Hysterical woman alert: just walk away.*

I sank to the floor and began to cry in earnest, more from shock than anything else. Sebastian came down the stairs and sat on the floor next to me.

"Fuck! That scared the shit out of me! Don't cry, Caro. It's okay."

He wrapped his arms around my shoulders and rocked me slowly.

Eventually, he pulled me up off the floor.

"Come on. Let's get some breakfast. I'll make you one of my special omelets."

"I thought you couldn't cook," I said, my voice still shaky from the rush of adrenaline.

"I can't—that's why it's special."

He sat me at the kitchen table and started rummaging through the fridge.

"How many eggs do I need?"

"How hungry are you?"

"Starving!"

Of course.

"Then get six. And you'll need to add a drop of milk in the mixture."

He peered at me from around the door.

"Really? Milk? Oh, okay."

He frowned and disappeared back inside the fridge.

I stood up to fetch the frying pan and mixing bowl but he waved me back to the table.

"I can manage," he said, confidently, as he turned on the stove and placed the frying pan on top.

I waited for a moment, twitching in my chair. I had to speak.

"Um, Sebastian?"

"What?" he said, staring intently at the eggs as he whisked them sloppily.

"The frying pan is getting really hot and you haven't put any oil in it..."

"Oh, fuck!"

He pulled the pan off the stove and swore as the hot metal burned his wrist.

"Quick! Run your hand under the faucet!"

He stood with his hand under the running water cursing softly. He really was adorable and I couldn't help grinning at him.

"What?"

"Will you let me help you now?"

"Okay," he said reluctantly. "You can help."

In a calmer, more organized fashion, I showed him how to make a plain omelet, seasoning it with black pepper and a little salt, fried some tomatoes to go on the side, put on a pot of coffee, and then breakfast, or rather brunch, was ready.

"By the way," I said, a thought occurring to me, "what were you planning on doing—you know, if it had been someone ... else at the door?"

"Fucked if I know," he said honestly. "Climb out the window, hide under the bed? Any suggestions?"

"Not the window—you could fall and get hurt. Besides, that window is right above the front door—it would have been kind of obvious."

"I could have flattened the bastard," said Sebastian easily.

While I went back upstairs to shower, Sebastian insisted on clearing away the dishes, which was a novelty for me. I hoped he would manage not to break anything.

I'd just finished rinsing the conditioner out of my hair when the shower door opened and Sebastian pressed his chest against my back.

"Mmm, you smell great," he said approvingly.

"Sebastian!" I said, my voice a warning, as he ran his hands over my breasts and kissed my neck. "We don't have time for this."

"I'll be quick," he mumbled into my skin.

I didn't even try to resist him.

Which made us horribly late.

"I told you!" I said crossly, as the highway traffic congealed in front of us. "You're going to be late *and* get fired!"

"It was worth it," he grinned, reclining his seat all the way back and pulling his sunglasses over his eyes.

He was acting like he hadn't a care in the world. *How did he do it?*

"Look, I'll drop you around the back of the country club, you haven't got time to run down from the entrance."

"Whatever," he said, carelessly.

I shook my head, a little irritated, even though I was just as much to blame.

I drove too fast down the avenue leading to the club and skidded into my favorite parking lot at the back.

"When can I see you again?" he said, curling his fingers into my hair.

"Tomorrow morning?"

"That's ages away. Can't you sneak out tonight? I mean, you're in the guest room—he'll never know, right?"

"Sebastian, I don't think so. It's too risky. We've just got to be careful for three more months and that's it. After that you'll see me every day and you'll soon be sick of me."

"That's not funny," he said frowning.

"Sorry. Bad joke."

He sighed. "Okay, tomorrow, then."

Instead of getting out of the car, he pulled me toward him and we kissed with the desperation of our imminent separation.

For a moment, he leaned his forehead against mine, and then pushed open the passenger door. And froze.

Ches was staring right at us—and from the shock on his face it was obvious he'd seen everything.

The floor dropped away and I stared back at him in horror.

"Fucking luck," said Sebastian bitterly. "Let me go talk to him—it'll be fine, Caro, I promise."

My hands locked on the steering wheel as Sebastian walked toward his friend. For three of the longest minutes of my life, I watched them talk. Well, Sebastian seemed to be doing most of the talking, in fact it looked like he was pleading with Ches. It was a twisted replay of yesterday's scene with Brenda, except this time it was Sebastian who was doing the begging.

Ches's body language was hostile, his arms folded across his chest, his face stiff and angry. Eventually,s I saw him nod curtly then stalk off in the direction of the clubhouse.

Sebastian looked upset as he climbed back in the car and pulled the door shut.

"He's cool," he said, an expression of pain on his face.

"What did he say?" I whispered.

"He promised not to say anything."

"He didn't look very happy about it."

Sebastian sighed. "He wasn't."

"What did he say?"

Sebastian shook his head.

"Please tell me," I said softly. "I'd rather know."

"It doesn't matter—the important thing is that he won't tell anyone."

"Please tell me," I repeated, quietly.

"Why?" said Sebastian, angrily. "What difference does it make? He's just pissed at me generally."

"I thought you wanted us to be honest with each other," I reminded him gently.

His temper exploded.

"Why do you do this, Caro? Why do you have to drag out every last fucking, miserable word? Why can't you just let it go?"

"How the hell am I supposed to 'let it go'?" I snarled, my fear and anger getting the better of me. "I'm the one who'll be prosecuted if Ches tells anyone!"

"He won't!" shouted Sebastian.

"Well, I'm glad you trust him so much!" I yelled back, "Because he's the loose-lipped idiot who told Brenda that you got a job here!"

"What the fuck has Brenda got to do with this?"

"Nothing! Everything! I don't know! Just tell me what Ches said—I *need* to know!"

"He said I was a stupid fucking asshole for screwing a married woman who probably just wanted to get her rocks off for the summer, and he hoped the fucks were worth it because my dad would beat the shit out of me when he found out. Happy now?"

He looked away from me and slammed his fist against the car door.

I dug my fingernails into the palms of my hand, refusing to cry.

We sat there in silence for several minutes, the atmosphere tense and angry.

"You'd better get to work," I said at last in a low voice.

He stared at me coldly then flung open the door and stormed off.

I kept waiting for him to turn back or turn and look at me—some slight acknowledgement. But he didn't.

Bile rose in my throat and I hurriedly leaned out of the car and vomited, watching my brunch slowly sink into the gravel.

I drove home feeling weak and shaky.

All afternoon I waited for Sebastian to text me, but he didn't. A dozen times I picked up my cell to send a message, but I didn't.

When I couldn't stand it anymore, I tapped out five letters.

Sorry

Why had I forced Sebastian to repeat Ches's angry words? Why did I continue to allow my pathetic insecurities to spoil the best thing that had ever happened to me? Was it some form of deliberate self-destruction, some way of proving that I didn't deserve Sebastian's love? And it must be love—why else would he put up with my ridiculous outbursts and lead-weighted emotional baggage? Because it sure wasn't for the *fun*.

Feeling wretched, I tidied up the guest bedroom, *my* bedroom, and contemplated the sorry state of my life. I really had an amazing talent for making a complete fuck-up of everything. If the military could bottle that negative energy, they'd have one helluva weapon of mass destruction.

As I hung up my robe, a thought occurred to me—something I'd forgotten about in the whirlwind of the last three weeks. I reached into the pocket and pulled out the lock of Sebastian's hair that I'd saved from the bathroom floor the night I'd found him at the park, the night we'd made love together that very first time. His hair was light brown near the root, bleached by the sun to a golden blond at the ends—the surfer boy he'd been when I first met him.

I took an envelope from David's study and carefully sealed the lock inside, simply writing Sebastian's name and the date across the corner. Then I placed it between the pages of my copy of *Lolita*—a book so profane that I knew David would never so much as touch its dust jacket, it was also my private joke—not that I felt like laughing. In fact it was everything I could do to keep from crying.

And I knew I was on borrowed time with David—he wouldn't take another night of me sleeping in the guest room without some sort of explanation.

I had two choices. I could lie:

'I'm fine, I just need some space'.

Or I could tell part of the truth:

'Our marriage is over and I want a divorce. No, there's no one else'.

Either way, I was scared of what he'd do. His temper was so unpredictable, I didn't know what would happen if I pushed him to extremes. Discussing divorce certainly constituted 'extreme' in anyone's book.

I wandered into the kitchen to make something for his supper. Without even being aware of my movements, I threw together a lasagna and tossed it into the oven.

It was a quarter after six and I was beginning to wonder where David was when I suddenly remembered it was his formal dinner at the officer's mess. He was right: I really should check the schedule more often.

I pulled the lasagna out of the oven and dumped it on the side. I considered throwing it in the garbage but I hated to waste food. David could have it reheated in the microwave tomorrow. He was going to have to get used to microwaved meals once we were separated—I figured he may as well start getting in some practice now.

The thought made me feel a little better. I decided to risk checking my phone. Maybe there would be a message from Sebastian, or maybe I could just torture myself a little more by seeing that he hadn't responded.

But he had.

Me 2

God, I loved this man.

I sent another quick message.

Can I c u tonite? I can get away for a while if u can. What time u finish? Pick u up?

His reply was immediate.

10
I'll be there
:)

With those few words, happiness flooded through me.

And then I remembered Ches—I hoped I wouldn't have to face him again today. It had been bad enough seeing the look on his face this morning, and it had been beyond horrible fighting with Sebastian. I just wanted to be able to see him and touch him and have him hold me and utter the sweet lie that it was going to be okay.

It really wasn't my day.

He was waiting for me: 'he' being Ches, not Sebastian.

He was leaning against his van in the rear parking lot where he'd seen us earlier in the day. He folded his arms as I drove up and threw me a look of such contempt and loathing that my stomach gave an unhappy lurch. I wanted nothing more than to hit the accelerator, drive in the opposite direction and get the hell out of Dodge.

Gathering strength from some unknown place, long hidden, I took a deep breath and got out of the car to face him.

"Hello, Ches."

"Mrs. Wilson," he said, emphasizing the 'Mrs.'.

He scowled at me, challenging me to speak.

"I can guess what you think of me," I said softly.

"Can you?" he said coolly, raising an eyebrow in disbelief and disgust.

"You think I'm just using Sebastian, but it's not like that."

"Then tell me what it is like," he sneered, "because I'd really like to know. Seb is my friend and you..."

"I don't want to hurt him," I said, forcing the words out as my throat began to constrict.

"Yeah? Well, you're doing a really great job there! His head is completely spun, he doesn't know what the fuck he's doing. You've messed him up real good."

I choked on my reply but he wasn't going to give me time to recover.

"You've met his dad. Do you know how many times he's beat the shit out of him? Have you any idea what he'll do to him when he finds out about this?" His voice was bitter. "Yeah, the military hero will really freak out, his son bringing shame on the good family name of Hunter and all that crap, by banging a married woman."

I had no words.

He glared at me.

"And what about when your husband finds out? I suppose you'll dump Seb so fast that..."

"I'm leaving David."

I spoke so quietly I wasn't sure he'd heard me at first.

"What?"

I looked up. "I'm going to ask David for a divorce."

He stared at me, then shook his head.

"I don't believe you."

"It's true. We ... I ... as soon as Sebastian turns 18."

"You're full of shit."

"No, she's not."

Sebastian's voice came out of the darkness and I closed my eyes in relief. He walked up and put his arm around my shoulders, kissing me quickly on the lips.

"Hey, baby."

Then he turned to his friend.

"We're just waiting till I'm 18 and then I'm legally free of my family. We're going to go to New York." He pulled me closer and nuzzled my hair. "I've found us an apartment. It's in Bensonhurst—it said on this website that they call it Brooklyn's Little Italy. I thought you'd like that."

He smiled at me then looked back at Ches who was staring in outrage and astonishment.

"What the fuck you talking about, man? New York?"

"Yes, as soon as we can, and as far away as we can get."

"But ... *New York?*"

"Caro's going to work while I go to school. And I'll get a job, as well. We've got it all worked out."

"Are you crazy, dude?"

I thought Sebastian would lose his temper, but he just carried on talking, his voice even.

"We know it won't be easy but we want to be together. It's the only way."

Ches blinked, opening and closing his mouth several times. "Why didn't you tell me, man?" He sounded hurt.

"We didn't want to tell anyone because ... we couldn't. Caro is breaking the law by being with me."

It was clear Ches was in shock. He stood and gaped at us.

"I'm under age," continued Sebastian softly. "If anyone found out ... if anyone reported us, it's a felony—because of ... the age difference." He shrugged. "Caro could go to jail. That's why I couldn't tell you."

"Wow, I'm sorry, man. I didn't know!" said Ches helplessly.

"She's taking a huge risk. She wanted us to wait but ... I couldn't stay away from her. So if anyone is to blame, it's me." He looked Ches directly in the eye. "I think you owe her an apology."

I touched his arm. "It's okay, Sebastian. He was just looking out for you. I understand."

Ches looked mortified. "I didn't know! I just thought ... is it that serious? I mean, what could happen to her?"

He seemed to be having a hard time taking it in. I couldn't blame him—I still had a hard time with the concept of being loved so much, of being so much in love that it hurt.

Sebastian nodded, and I stared at the ground feeling a mixture of pride and shame in our confession.

"I'm sorry, Caroline," said Ches, shaking his head. "You guys ... wow ... I..."

"Thank you," I said quietly. I looked up at Sebastian. "I'll go wait in the car."

They talked for a few more minutes while I sat and waited and watched. Eventually Ches pulled Sebastian into a bear hug and then patted him on the arm. I guessed he was telling him it was going to be all right.

Sebastian opened the passenger door and slumped down onto the seat.

"Everything okay?" I asked, tentatively.

"I guess," Sebastian said wearily, rubbing his eyes. "He ... he gets how much you mean to me but..."

But?

"He still thinks it's kind of crazy. He's cool though. He won't tell anyone."

I hoped he was right.

Sebastian raised his hand to my cheek. "Don't worry: Ches is my best friend —he's my brother," he said simply.

I leaned against him, feeling the warmth of his body through his thin t-shirt. I stared out at the stars in the night sky, wondering if one of them might be our lucky star.

I traced Sebastian's silhouette in the darkness, his straight nose, his full, sensuous lips, his strong chin, the graceful profile of his head.

He leaned back in the seat and turned to smile at me.

The most incredible feeling of love welled up inside me. I was so lucky. He was kind and thoughtful and caring. He was fun to be with, beautiful inside and out. I didn't know a lover could be a friend, too. And he loved me.

Me.

But was I really strong enough to follow my heart and to hell with the consequences? Could I expect a 17 year old boy ... man ... to be strong enough for this? No, that wasn't right. I was the one who had to be strong for both of us.

And at that moment, I knew the question and the answer. Was I strong enough? Yes, I was.

CHAPTER FOURTEEN

"I NEED TO HOLD YOU," SAID SEBASTIAN, SOFTLY.

I scrambled onto his knee and we clung to each other in the dark of the country club's parking lot.

All our hopes and fears had been explored in those tense few minutes with Ches. Sebastian was strong in so many ways, but he was also so young. And now he needed me and I wanted to give him comfort, to reassure him, to protect him from the world. He needed me—and I needed him.

I held him tightly, pulling him closer. Gradually his body began to relax, the tension leaking away.

"So," I said, breaking the heavy silence, "you found an apartment in Little Italy?"

I felt him smile against my neck.

"Yeah, I thought you'd like that."

"I do. Tell me about it."

He let out a long breath and settled me more comfortably in his arms.

"It's got one bedroom and one bathroom and is on the fourth floor of an apartment building on 82nd Street. We've even got an elevator."

I smiled. I didn't care how many elevators it had, I just wanted it all to be real.

"From the top of the building you can see Staten Island and the Statue of Liberty. We can walk along the Belt Parkway Promenade, or ride bikes—people go kite-flying there, too..." he paused. "And the rent is only $1,250 a month, but that's unfurnished, and we get 875 square feet."

"So much room."

I couldn't bear to tell him that despite the tiny size of the apartment, the rent was still more than twice the amount I currently had in my checking account.

"Yeah, well..." he continued. "But it says it's near the train and we can walk to Coney Island in about 30 minutes. Oh, and it's only four blocks from a park."

"It sounds perfect."

He sighed. "I almost phoned the rental agency but..."

"Too soon."

"I know," he sighed again. "Jesus, Caro. How the hell are we going to get through three more months like this?"

"Because we have to," I said in a steady voice. "And we will."

A look of admiration flickered across his face.

"God, I love you!" he said.

He kissed me lightly on the lips but his touch was like an incendiary device going off inside me. I kissed him back deeply, pouring all the angst and fear and passion I could into that one moment, showing him how much I loved and needed him, too.

His body responded immediately and I felt his arms tensing around me.

"Let's go somewhere," he said, his voice low and rough.

"I don't want to go to my place," I said, a shiver running down my spine. "I don't know what time David will be back. We can't risk that."

"Where is the bastard?" Sebastian spat the words out.

"At a mess dinner."

"Oh, yeah. I forgot about that—Dad went, too. They're usually pretty late though," said Sebastian thoughtfully.

I shook my head. "No, I'd rather go to the beach. Anywhere but *home*."

The word sounded like a lie on my lips. It wasn't my home, not anymore.

"We could drive out to the beach? But it's pretty cold tonight—no cloud cover. I guess we could stay in the car."

He sighed. I knew what he was thinking. After the luxury of a bed, neither of us really wanted to revert to an awkward backseat fumble.

"We could find a cheap motel," he said doubtfully.

"We can't afford it," I reminded him. "Let's just drive out to the beach and..."

"We could go to my place," said Sebastian suddenly.

"Excuse me?" *Had I heard him right?*

"Yeah! Dad's out at that officers' mess dinner with the asshole. He always stays over—he usually passes out in a bachelor room," he said, the disgust clear in his voice.

"What about your mom?"

He pointed to the clubhouse with his chin. "Drinking."

"How's she getting home?"

"Like I give a damn? Taxi, probably. But she won't come in my room. She never does—she stopped coming in my room when I was ten." He paused, his lips curling with contempt. "Anyway, she usually can't even make it up to their room—she just sleeps on the couch in the den."

"I don't know, Sebastian..."

I felt freaked at the thought of being in Donald and Estelle's house, but now Sebastian had suggested it, I was burning with curiosity to see his room.

"How will I get in without being seen?"

"There's an empty lot next door and we'll go in through the backyard. No one will see us."

He sounded excited.

"Okay," I said, shaking my head in wonder at what the hell I'd just agreed to.

He grinned at me, a beautiful, wide, beaming smile.

We drove back listening to *Lucia di Lammermoor*—the tale of a girl caught in a feud between her own family and that of another powerful clan. And then she went mad. I hoped it wasn't portentous.

I parked my car behind the vacant lot, making sure it was as well hidden as it could be on a public street.

"Okay?" said Sebastian, squeezing my hand.

I laughed nervously at my own recklessness.

He led me through the darkness, following the line of a high fence. When we arrived at a large and beautiful Japanese maple that grew close beside, he stopped. The tree partially obscured the fence.

"How are you at climbing?" he grinned at me.

"You're joking?" He just smiled at me. "You're not joking?!"

"I'll help you."

He climbed the fence easily, his strong arms pulling him up and over. He'd obviously done it many times before. He disappeared from sight briefly, then reappeared, balancing his torso on the fence as his arms reached down for me.

"Jump! I'll pull you up!"

I took a deep breath and ran at the fence, jumping as high as I could. Sebastian grabbed my wrists and pulled me up but our combined momentum was too much, and we were pitched over the fence, crashing down onto the turf below.

The air was forced from my lungs and I lay there winded for several seconds. Sebastian struggled to sit up, which wasn't easy as I'd landed mostly on him.

"Caro! Are you okay?"

I couldn't answer.

"Caro!"

I gasped for air and started to giggle.

"Shit! You had me worried there for a minute. Seriously, are you okay?"

"Ow!" I sat up slowly, still slightly hysterical. "If I have to come in through your backyard again, I'm going to buy a ladder."

Suddenly he pulled me to his chest and kissed me fiercely.

"What ... what's that for?" I gasped.

"You're just so ... brave!" he said, in awe.

I was pretty certain he had me confused with someone else.

"You are!" he insisted. "You always take that leap, whatever it is. God! I love that about you!"

I flushed at his unexpected praise—I really didn't think it was justified, but I loved that he'd thought it, and loved it even more that he'd said it.

"Come on," I whispered. "I want to make out in your bedroom."

"Definitely up for that," he agreed, laughing quietly.

He pulled me to my feet.

"Wait here a sec. I'll make sure there's no one around."

I watched as he climbed onto a water barrel outside one of the rooms and levered himself in through a narrow window. I had the distinct impression that he was enjoying himself.

I stood alone in the darkness, knowing that I was being swept along by all the craziness, or maybe, finally, I'd just dove right in and stopped fighting it.

I saw a light go on upstairs and a moment later Sebastian was unlocking the back door.

"Coast's clear," he said grinning. "There's no one in."

From what I could see in the gloom, the Hunters' kitchen was sleek and modern and well equipped. But everything had a pristine look about it, as if most of it had never been used. I remembered Sebastian saying that his mother never cooked. I could have gone to town in a kitchen like that—it was almost to a professional standard. I wondered why a woman, why anyone, would want to have a show-kitchen like that and not be tempted to use it. Maybe the answer was in the description: a show-kitchen, a kitchen for show—like everything else in Estelle Hunter's life. Despite excessive opulence of design, the room had a neglected air: the trash can was overflowing with pizza boxes, and a large number of empty wine bottles, beer cans and hard liquor bottles had been tossed haphazardly into the recycling box.

Sebastian towed me quickly down the hallway and up the stairs, eager to get me into his room. An unpleasant thought crossed my mind—how many times had he brought Brenda here, maybe to make out in his bedroom?

I tried to ignore it, but the idea was like a worm in my brain, wriggling, wriggling, burrowing away.

On the upper floor, we passed several empty rooms that looked like guest suites before Sebastian opened a door at the end of the corridor. From the layout of the house, I guessed that this room, his room, must overlook the backyard. The fact that his parents had put their son as far away from their own room as possible had worked out well for Sebastian—in the end.

He'd turned on his bedside light and drawn the curtains, I could feel the suppressed excitement coursing through him.

His bedroom was small, barely bigger than a box room, with a narrow, single bed pressed against one wall. Several old surfing posters were tacked to the only free wall space, the rest were covered by unmatched bookshelves, crammed with a mixture of CDs, paperbacks, a few hardcover books, with what looked like surfing trophies jammed in among them.

There was a large chest with one of the drawers partially open, and a couple of t-shirts hanging out.

My eyes were drawn back to the bed, currently strewn with a pair of jeans, shirts and the boardshorts he'd worn to the beach yesterday. The sheets and cover, however, were neatly folded, almost with military precision. I shivered as I imagined Donald 'teaching' his son how to do that.

Sebastian cleared away the clothes hurriedly, tossing them onto a small, wooden chair that was festooned with t-shirts.

"It's pretty small," he said, sounding embarrassed.

"It's very you," I said, watching him throw more clothes on the chair. I turned to examine some of his books. I always thought you could learn a lot about a person by the kind of books they had on their shelves. David didn't have any books, he only read the newspaper and occasionally medical journals.

Sebastian had a whole shelf of Conrad, several Allan Quatermain paperbacks, Jack London's *The Road*, countless travel books. *The Red Horse* by Corti in translation caught my eye.

"Wait, what's this?" I pulled out a heavy book, bound in cloth, and ran my fingers over the cover. I stared at him in disbelief. "You still have this?"

He nodded, his face serious.

I flicked through the pages depicting Hansel and Gretel, Rumpelstiltskin, Rapunzel ... all the gruesome stories from the Brothers Grimm.

I turned to the frontispiece, knowing what I'd see,

> *To Sebastian, from Caroline*

And a date, nine years in the past.

"You kept it."

"Of course," he said simply. "You gave it to me."

I didn't know what to feel, standing there with the evidence of his childhood in my hands, the grown man in front of me.

"It's always been you, Caro."

I continued to stare at the book, at my handwriting, evidence in black and white, of our innocent and childish friendship.

His voice became anxious.

"It doesn't mean anything, Caro, not like that."

But it did, to me at least. It had been a horrible mistake coming here.

"I think I'd better go now," I said quietly.

"It's just a book, Caro, just a damn book. Please don't go!"

He grabbed me by the shoulders and forced me to look at him.

"Caro! Stop it!" he said, almost roughly. "I was a kid, we were friends. That's all. You haven't done anything wrong." He shook me, making me grab onto his arms. "I'm younger than you: so what?! It doesn't mean *anything*."

Suddenly my knees gave way and I sat down on the bed hard. I felt sick. I hadn't eaten anything since the omelet I'd made earlier, and that had ended up on the gravel of the country club's parking lot.

"Caro?"

"Could I have a glass of water, please?" My voice was shaky.

"Sure! Sure!"

I heard him running down the stairs. I put my head down and tried to breathe deeply.

He was back a moment later with a large tumbler of cold water. I took the glass from him and drank a few sips gratefully.

"Are you okay?" he asked anxiously.

"Yes, I'm fine. Sorry. It was just..." *Disturbing? Shocking? A devastating reminder?*

My hands were still trembling and I was in danger of tipping the rest of the water onto his pillows. He took the glass from my hands and placed it on the tiny bedside table.

"Come and lie down with me," he said, tugging gently on my hand. "Just lie with me. I'm not going to do anything you don't want, you know that."

He pulled me down and held me in his arms, softly stroking my hair. We lay there peacefully. Somewhere in the room I could hear a clock ticking—my life was passing with every second.

He continued to soothe me, kissing my hair, stroking my back and my arms, threading his long legs through mine.

"Do you want to hear a bedtime story?" he said, quiet humor in his voice.

"Not funny," I muttered into his chest.

He laughed gently. "You'll like this one. It starts with a girl and a boy, a motorcycle and a full tank of gas."

"Very romantic."

"Told you you'd like it."

"Well, the boy says to the girl, 'Hey, baby, let's go see the world.' And do you know what the girl says?"

"'I'm washing my hair'?"

"Ha! No, not quite. She says, 'Let's go see Italy because the whole world starts there'."

"She sounds like an idiot."

"Hey! This is *my* bedtime story."

"Okay, I'll be quiet."

"Is that even possible?"

I punched him lightly on the arm and he laughed.

"Okay, so the boy says, 'I have an idea. Let's fly to Switzerland...'"

"On the motorcycle? Because I should explain to you..."

He put his hand over my mouth, so I kissed the palm and snuggled in some more.

"'Let's fly to Switzerland, drive over the Alps and then we'll go to Milano and see *Il Trovatore* at La Scala'."

"That's the opera where everyone ends up dying."

"You said you'd be quiet."

"Sorry."

"So, then they stay at this amazing hotel where they have breakfast in bed, served on silver plates..."

"And they *scappati* in the morning because they can't pay the bill?"

"Yeah! Then they ride off on their trusty motorcycle and go to Verona, one of the most romantic cities in the world..."

"It's not romantic—that's where Romeo poisons himself and Juliet stabs herself to death."

"Shh! Then they drive down the spine of Italy, stopping to eat pasta ... and have *a lot* of sex..."

"This story is NC-17."

"Yeah, that's because it's *my* bedtime story. Then they ride to Salerno and take this little mountain road to a tiny village called Capezzano Inferiore and they meet all these wonderful, crazy people who turn out to be cousins and aunts and uncles of the girl, because she's kinda crazy, too..."

"And then what?"

"They live happily ever after."

I sighed. "Okay, that was a pretty good story after all."

"Told you you'd like it."

I felt very comfortable lying in his arms and my attack of guilt and disgust was slowly passing.

He didn't speak after that and neither did I. We drifted to sleep, wound around each other.

A loud crash woke me suddenly. I sat up, disoriented and panic-stricken in the darkened room.

"Oh, fuck. Mom's home," said Sebastian sullenly. "Are you okay, Caro? Don't sweat it, she won't come up here."

My heart was pounding, it was so loud I felt certain he must be able to hear it knocking against my ribs.

"Are you sure? Is your door locked?"

"I don't have a lock—I put the chair up against it when I want some privacy."

I couldn't believe how casual he sounded. I almost leapt out of my skin when he reached out to stroke my hair.

"I'll go see if she's passed out," he said, reading my mood.

I nodded, nervously twisting my wedding ring around my finger.

He frowned, then rolled off the bed and gently opened his bedroom door. He was gone for less than a minute while I waited anxiously.

"She's out cold—like I said. No problem."

He pulled the chair up against the door, letting all the clothes slide off into a heap, then wedged its wooden back tightly under the handle.

He turned slowly, staring down at me.

From the look on his face, I guessed he wanted to cash in the rain check on the make-out session I'd promised him. I definitely wasn't on the same page, the adrenaline rush caused by Estelle's noisy return had freaked me out.

I pulled my cell phone out of my jeans pocket and flipped it over to check the time; it was after 1AM.

"It's late," I whispered. "I should get back."

"Stay. Please."

He sat down next to me again and ran the tips of his fingers down my arm.

"We don't know when we'll have another night together," he said persuasively, kissing my shoulder. "What difference does it make if you go now or in a few hours?"

When he didn't meet any resistance, he pushed me gently back onto his bed and used his body to press me into the thin mattress. I could feel that he was already aroused. Boy, it didn't take much. I still felt shaken, but at the same time it thrilled me that I could make him feel that way, make his body respond that way.

"Stay," he whispered as he ran his tongue up my neck and tugged at my ear lobe with his teeth.

His right hand rode up under my t-shirt and cupped my breast, circling his thumb over my nipple. "Please stay."

For that moment, his touch pushed away all my concerns, all the dull considerations of a rational mind and I wrapped my hands around his neck to pull him closer.

My tongue swept into his mouth and I raked my nails down his back, making him cry out.

"Ssh, you have to be quiet, *tesoro*," I reminded him.

I tugged on the hem of his t-shirt and he immediately yanked it over his head, throwing it across the room. Mine soon followed and the cold metal of his pants button pressed into my belly making me shiver.

I lay on my side so he could unhook my bra, this time he didn't fumble—within seconds it had joined my t-shirt on the growing heap. In fact, there wasn't any floor space that *wasn't* littered with clothes, his and mine.

He knelt up to watch me as I undid my zipper and shimmied out of my jeans and panties. He ran his hands down my body and then slid his fingers back up along my inner thighs. I closed my eyes and sighed deeply with pleasure and desire.

His body hovered over mine again and I enjoyed the rough feel of his denim against my bare flesh. I pulled his waistband toward me and slipped my hands inside, running my fingers over his fine, sculpted ass. A tremor ran through him and he leaned down to kiss me again.

Hastily I unzipped his jeans, pushing them down over his hips. When he sat up to kick off his pants, I reached up to run the nail of my index finger from his chest to his stomach, watching the faint white mark I left behind quickly fade. His eyes fluttered closed and he sucked in a deep breath as his body quivered.

"Now you've got me here," I said teasingly, "what are you going to do with me?"

His eyes opened wide with surprise. "What do you mean?"

"Well, what do you want to do?"

"I want to make love to you," he said, sounding confused.

I laughed gently. "Yes, I can see that! But will you be on top, or should I be on top, or maybe you'd like to do it from behind again? Or perhaps I'll let my mouth do the talking? You choose."

He licked his lips as he hesitated, his eyes blazing.

"From behind," he whispered.

"Your wish is my command."

I knelt up on the bed and, with deliberate slowness, turned around and sank to all fours. Then I glanced at him over my shoulder, flicking my hair out of my eyes.

I heard him suck in a deep breath and the springs of the bed protested loudly as he climbed up the mattress. He knelt behind me, holding my hip with one hand and positioning himself with the other. He sank into me slowly and groaned loudly.

"Fuck! Oh, fuck!"

I pushed my hips back toward him and his whole body convulsed.

I could tell he was trying to control himself, to move slowly, but his body was winning the battle over his mind. I wasn't even trying for control. I wanted all of him. Now.

I ground back against him again and Sebastian lost it completely, gripping my hips with both hands and pounding into me. The bedsprings squeaked loudly with every thrust. A breathless giggle escaped me—it couldn't have been more obvious what we were doing if there had been a neon sign over his door saying, 'sex in progress: do not enter'. Although I was rather enjoying the entering. And exiting. And entering.

His hand moved to my sweet spot the way I'd shown him before, and, at that point, I lost all cogent thought as exquisite and uncontrollable sensation lanced through me. He'd gotten so good at finding my weak spots: mentally and physically. He was a hell of a fine student. I let my elbows fold, taking our combined weight on my forearms, so I could sink my face into his pillow, attempting to muffle my increasingly loud moans. Between us, we were making enough noise to wake the dead—luckily not enough to wake Estelle.

I felt Sebastian shudder into me with one last, powerful thrust—he gasped, biting back a mangled sound that could have been my name.

We sank down and lay full length on his narrow bed together. After a moment, he shifted onto his side and pulled me with him so my back was half-resting on his chest.

"That was ... fuck, Caro! I didn't know..."

He paused.

"Didn't know what, *tesoro*?" I asked, still breathless.

"Nothing."

He sounded embarrassed.

"Go on. I'm curious now." I stopped and shook my head. "Sorry ... I'm doing it again, aren't I?"

"Doing what?"

"Forcing you to speak when you don't want to. Sorry."

"Fuck! Don't be sorry, Caro. I was just ... okay, but don't get mad at me. I just didn't know girls really liked it like that."

For a moment I was taken aback and then I started to laugh. "What? You thought only porn stars liked it from behind ... doggy style?"

"Well, yeah!" he sounded rather shocked.

I turned around awkwardly in the narrow bed so I could look at him. I stroked his face, but I couldn't stop grinning.

"Sebastian, women like sex just as much as men ... if it's good."

He tried to smile but still looked uncertain, his forehead creasing with worry.

"Am I...?"

He bit his lip.

I knew what he was trying to ask me.

"Yes, you're good. In fact I'd say you're amazing in so many ways." I didn't mean to tease him—well, maybe just a little. He was just so unbelievably sweet. "Besides," I continued, "the whole orgasm thing is a clue that the woman is really enjoying it. In case you were wondering."

"Yeah, I was. Kind of. I mean, it always feels amazing with you, but I wasn't sure if you thought so, too."

"Well, I do. So stop worrying." I considered for a moment. "I could make score cards if you like: grade you on required elements, presentation, and technical merit—like in ice skating."

He laughed. "Okay! So how did that score?"

"Three sixes."

He didn't reply for a moment, then said quietly, his tone hurt, "Only six?"

I nearly choked, I was laughing so hard. "The score is out of six!"

He laughed, too, but the sound was a little embarrassed. "Oh, okay then."

He reached down and pulled a sheet up to my shoulders. I was warm and comfortable in his little bed and could easily have fallen asleep.

When I felt my eyes closing I nudged his chin with my nose. "I should go now. It'll be getting light soon."

He pulled me tighter. "Five more minutes."

"Okay, but I'm going to count: 300, 299, 298..."

"Okay, okay! I'm moving."

He pulled back the sheet and shivered slightly. He knelt down, fumbling around on the floor trying to find our clothes.

"Hey, can I keep your bra?"

"Excuse me?"

"I haven't got anything of yours, Caro, please!"

"Sebastian!" I shook my head in disbelief.

"Please, Caro!"

"Fine! But you owe me, Hunter. That's the second bra that's gone missing in action on your watch."

He grinned and threw my t-shirt at me.

When we were both dressed, he pulled open the door and we tiptoed down the stairs. Well, I tiptoed, he walked normally, glancing at me and shaking his head like I was a little crazy. I'd never snuck out of a boy's bedroom before—it was more fun than I'd imagined.

Once we were out of the confines of the house and in the yard, I began to breathe a little more easily. Sebastian insisted on rolling the water barrel over to the fence to make it easier for me to climb over.

There was the faintest hint of gray light in the east, and the air was cool and scented with pine.

We leaned against the car, holding each other before the inevitable division that always came.

"Your buzz-cut is growing out," I said, absentmindedly running my fingers through his hair.

"Yeah, I guess."

It was clear his mind was elsewhere. "Can I come over tomorrow morning before work?"

"It *is* tomorrow," I reminded him.

"Can I?"

"I guess so, but let me text you." I frowned when it occurred to me that I had to face David now—or at some point soon. "Just in case."

He sighed. "Okay. Love you, Caro."

I hugged him more tightly then let him go. "I'll see you later."

"We're always saying goodbye. I hate it, Caro."

"It won't be for much longer," I said, with as much conviction as I could muster.

Getting in my car and driving away from him was one of the hardest things I'd ever done.

A few minutes later I was home—or rather, at the house where my soon-to-be-ex-husband slept. I certainly hoped he was asleep as I crept through the back door.

But then I froze. From the kitchen I could see a leg hanging off the end of the couch, it was clad in dress uniform.

Shit!

I took off my shoes and slunk past him barefoot, hardly daring to breathe. His snoring remained deep and regular, so when I reached the top of the stairs without incident, I gasped, feeling faint with relief.

Glancing into our ... *his* bedroom, I noticed that the bed hadn't been slept in. He'd come home so drunk he'd never even made it up the stairs.

Just like Estelle.

The clock on my bedside table informed me that it was 6AM, I still had an hour before the alarm. I peeled off my t-shirt and jeans and slid under the cold sheets. I missed Sebastian's warm body next to mine and couldn't relax, instead of sleeping, I found myself staring dry-eyed at the ceiling for the best part of an hour.

Five minutes before the alarm was due, I gave up and headed for the shower. The hot water soothed and revived me, and then I spent a few minutes rubbing in moisturizer and body lotion. I'd better start looking after my skin more carefully if I was going to have a boyfriend who was so much younger than I was. It didn't seem likely that a little palm oil could help *enough*, but I was prepared to try pretty much anything—anything that I could afford—which wasn't saying a lot.

As I stared in the mirror, examining the fine lines around my eyes and searching for any gray hairs, I noticed a small, oval bruise above my left breast. Oh, my God! A hickey! I hadn't had one of those in years! Well, make that over a decade. In fact I wasn't completely sure that I'd *ever* had one. What was that boy's name who'd asked me out the semester before I met David? Kevin? Colin? I remembered he'd tried to make out with me in the movie theatre, but I'd been more interested in watching the screen.

I made a mental note to remind Sebastian that biting was out until we'd got to New York. Pity.

When I'd finished drying my hair with the towel, I laid out David's uniform for work. I hoped it would avoid, or at least delay, the next fight for as long as possible. Needs must.

He was just beginning to stir when I started making breakfast. I banged around the kitchen as loudly as possible, taking out some of my frustration on the frying pan and kitchen sink, feeling his whiskey-soured eyes glaring at me balefully.

"Good morning, David. Are you feeling up to some breakfast?" I asked breezily.

"Just coffee," he said sulkily, then added, "Thank you."

I nearly dropped the plate I was carrying, staring at him in disbelief. I couldn't remember the last time he'd thanked me for anything. I wondered what had brought on that outbreak of civility. It was too weird. Still, it was better than being snarled at, which was usually how he behaved when he was hung-over. Wonders would never cease.

The polite entente was fairly short-lived. He left the house without speaking to me again, for which I was inordinately grateful.

The sun had broken through a layer of thin cloud and the gloom of San Diego in June was promising to be another glorious day. My heart felt curiously light—and I knew what would be perfect. I texted Sebastian immediately, knowing he was waiting to hear from me.

Park in 20? Bring your boardshorts!

His reply made me laugh.

Isn't it bedtime?
No! 20 mins?
ok :)

I changed into my bikini and pulled on a pair of shorts and strappy t-shirt, then ran downstairs to make an *enormous* picnic. I knew he wouldn't have gotten himself any breakfast or, even if he had, he'd still be starving by lunchtime.

As an afterthought I picked up my laptop and notebook and tossed them in the trunk of the car. I still had some notes to type up and, more than ever, I needed the money from the articles that *City Beat* was prepared to pay me for. Besides, now I had a membership to the country club, I may as well use it. Of course, there were also the ancillary benefits of the locker room to be considered, if it happened to be empty again, well, who knew what might happen.

Sebastian was sitting on the curb in his usual place, my dear sweet punk.

"We're going surfing?"

The hope and surprise were equally evident in his voice.

"Why not? It's a beautiful day. Maybe you can teach me some more moves."

"I liked the moves you taught me last night."

"Sebastian!"

He shrugged. "It's true."

"Well, maybe. We'll have to see if that locker room is free later."

He groaned. "Oh, man, that was hot!"

I couldn't disagree with that assessment.

We drove with the windows down and Sebastian chose another jazz station to listen to. I was fairly sure that his interest in opera was just to please me. It was really rather cute.

I parked next to the same surf shack just north of La Jolla. It was aptly named, being so ramshackle, it looked as if it might tip over the cliff with the faintest gust of breeze.

The owner recognized us immediately—either that or he used the same patter on everyone.

"Hey, sugar, long time no see! You want to rent another board?"

"Yes, please," I said politely, elbowing Sebastian in the ribs as he scowled at the man. "And two shorties."

"I'm good," muttered Sebastian. "Just a shortie for her."

"Aw, that sucks," said the owner, sizing me up, "I bet you look great in a bikini."

I paid quickly, leaving my car keys again as surety, and pushed Sebastian out of the shop before he decided to start something. The owner grinned at me and winked. When he slid me my change, I saw that he'd written his phone number on one of the bills.

Classy. Ugh.

What kind of guy hit on someone when they were with their boyfriend? You wouldn't find a woman doing ... and then I thought of Brenda. Yes, she was definitely the kind of woman who would do *exactly* that.

I wondered if it was worth keeping the surf shack man's number to pass on to her, he was quite attractive in that so-laidback-he-was-almost-horizontal sort of way. And I knew for a fact she liked surfers. I really wished he hadn't written his cell number on a ten dollar note. Oh, well, I'd just have to use it for a tip somewhere. A large tip.

Sebastian carried the heavy board down to the beach and swam out with me. I didn't know how he could stand the water without a wetsuit—it felt cold to me. He just laughed and said he was used to it.

I wobbled about and fell off more times than I could count, but I also managed to get several rides where I rode the board all along the green water in front of the breaking wave. Sebastian was wonderfully encouraging and I felt very proud of myself.

We'd been playing in the surf for nearly an hour when a familiar looking van parked alongside my battered old Ford and Ches strolled down to the beach, his sleek, lightweight twin-tail thruster under one arm.

I nudged Sebastian and his happy expression vanished.

"Let's go say hi," I suggested.

He shrugged, but followed me as I caught a wave to the beach.

"Hi, Ches," I said pleasantly, as I dragged my heavy board onto the sand.

"Hi, Mrs. ... Caroline," he said, looking warily at Sebastian. "I didn't know you could surf."

"Sebastian is teaching me."

"Yeah, we don't spend all our time fucking," Sebastian said aggressively, folding his arms across his chest.

I cringed and felt my cheeks redden. Apart from anything else, he was such a hypocrite.

Ches winced and fiddled with the leash on his board.

"I still have trouble making the turns," I said, desperately trying to lighten the tense atmosphere.

"Yeah, well, you were looking pretty good out there," muttered Ches.

"Why don't you guys go have some fun, I'm ready for a rest. Sebastian, take my board."

I thrust it toward him, giving him very little choice in the matter. He gazed at me mulishly then snatched up the board and paddled out.

Ches stared helplessly for a second, murmured something inaudible, and followed him. I watched for a while, hoping that they'd work it out somehow, then peeled off the wetsuit and stretched out on my beach towel. The sun was deliciously warm on my chilly skin and I was soon dozing peacefully, full of happy non-thoughts. Besides, I hadn't been getting a lot of sleep lately.

I was woken abruptly by something very cold dripping on me. I squinted into the sun to see Sebastian grinning down at me. My heart lurched suddenly—it was so much like the first day we'd met. So much had happened since then. I was barely the same person. Was he?

At least Sebastian looked happier now.

"Hey, baby, did I wake you up?"

"Sort of—not really. Did you have fun?"

He shrugged. "It was okay. Waves aren't great today. Wind's onshore, so it's pretty mushy. It was more fun with you."

I shivered as he lay down next to me.

"Ugh! You're all cold and clammy!"

"I could warm you up," he said suggestively, running his hand across my stomach and leaning over me.

I pushed him off.

"Not here!"

I glanced up to see an embarrassed Ches desperately trying to find something else to look at other than his best friend getting it on with a married woman.

"Behave!" I said severely, frowning at Sebastian.

He just grinned at me with the same irritating air of insouciance. God! He could be infuriating.

I sat up and flicked his wrist away as he tried to lay a possessive hand on my thigh. I reached into my bag and pulled on my t-shirt. I thought Ches might feel slightly more comfortable if I was wearing a few more clothes, and there was that damn hickey, too. In truth, Ches's level of comfort mostly depended on whether or not his friend would quit behaving like an ass.

"Ches, would you like some sandwiches? I've made more than enough."

"Yeah, that would be great, Caroline," he replied quietly.

His eyes flickered nervously to Sebastian who was acting like a sulky teenager. Okay, maybe he wasn't acting—he *was* a sulky teenager. I sighed. He was spoiling our lovely day. It wasn't Ches's fault that he'd turned up at the same beach as us. We should just be thankful it was Ches and not any other of Sebastian's surfing buddies.

Over lunch, relations began to thaw. Sebastian stopped trying to show off, and Ches began to relax. Food was proving to be a universal panacea for men's ill tempers. I was relieved—the last thing I wanted to do was come between Sebastian and his best friend. And, if things went badly, he'd need all the friends he could get. I shivered at the thought.

After our increasingly enjoyable picnic, Sebastian insisted on returning my board and shortie to the surf shack, and *I* insisted that he ride to the country club in the van with Ches.

"I'll see you there soon enough," I pointed out, cutting off his protest. "Please, *tesoro*!"

He kissed me hungrily and this time I knew it wasn't an act. When we could bear to stop, he leaned his forehead against mine.

"Bye, Caro," he said softly.

I kissed him on the lips and watched him climb into Ches's van.

He was right about one thing—we were always saying goodbye.

When I arrived at the country club, my grim mood turned into something much darker. A girl in a *very* skimpy bikini was lying on a sun lounger by the pool.

Brenda fucking Wiseman.

CHAPTER FIFTEEN

Brenda looked up and frowned as I settled myself at a table under a sun umbrella and fired up the laptop.

It was clear from her confused expression that she recognized me, she just couldn't remember from where. I didn't have any plans on helping her out with that—the less she connected me with Sebastian, the happier I'd be. In fact, the smart thing to do would be to pack up and go home for that very reason.

Even though I'd only just arrived, I should leave—maybe if I could just pretend that I'd forgotten something, I could go without drawing too much attention.

Quietly, I closed the laptop's lid and slipped it into my shoulder bag even though the poor machine was still grumbling through its start-up routine. I stood up to go but I was ten damn seconds too late. Sebastian was walking toward me in his country club uniform, a huge smile on his face. You would have thought he hadn't seen me in days, not just a few minutes. I felt exactly the same.

I flicked my eyes to Brenda then stared at the floor, but he didn't seem to be able to read my mind, which, at that precise moment, was extremely inconvenient of him.

"Hi!" he said, happily. Then he frowned. "Are you going somewhere?"

I was like a deer caught in headlights from the juggernaut that was Brenda Wiseman—and I was about to get squashed flat. Her eyes swiveled toward us and, from the look on *her* face, I was pretty certain that *she* had super-powers, probably X-ray vision, the way she was ogling his body.

"Hey, Seb!" she sang. "Oh, I *love* your uniform! It's, like, so cute!"

Her hysterical cheerleader whine made me want to hold her head in the pool's deep end and watch until her pedicured feet kicked out a tarantella.

Sebastian's expression morphed from happy to irritated and then to slightly worried. He was right to be concerned—his acting abilities were even worse than mine. The two of us being in the proximity of the preternaturally observant Brenda, was a sure recipe for disaster. Possibly hers, as I might be forced to rip her tongue out of her head and feed it to the nearest tiger shark as bait.

I still thought that my best plan was to exit stage left at a convenient moment, although that meant leaving Sebastian in the clutches of the harpy. Unobtrusively, I sank back down in my seat and retrieved the confused laptop from my bag.

"Um, no," I said softly, trying not to look too befuddled, "I was just going to get ... a coffee."

For a second Brenda glared at me then her gaze became rather condescending.

"Oh, I thought I recognized you—you were at the picnic on Sunday, Mrs....?"

"Caroline Wilson," I supplied politely. "And you are...?"

"Brenda Wiseman," she said, raising her eyebrows, clearly believing she was unforgettable. How right she was.

Sebastian's haunted eyes pedaled between us.

"Nice to see you again, Brenda," I said, matching her for insincerity.

She adjusted her tiny bikini top, her tried and tested method for attracting Sebastian's attention. This time it failed spectacularly, he was still staring intently at me. God, I hoped somebody tried to drown themselves soon—maybe that would snap him out of it—although it was doubtful.

Brenda's eyes narrowed—she sensed competition, so now she was going in for the kill. While Sebastian's gaze was still fixed on me, I saw her fiddle with one of her earrings and slip it into her purse. What was she up to?

I was about to find out.

"Seb?" she whined. "I lost an earring, I think it came off in the deep end. Would you, like, dive down and find it for me?"

Wow, she really was shameless! She'd deployed the poor, helpless female act to get her own way *and* she was about to make him take his shirt off—all in one short sentence. I would never have thought of that: I had a lot to learn.

Sebastian frowned at her.

"Are you sure you lost it in the deep end?" He stared at her accusingly. "Your hair is dry."

She flushed. "I've been here a while ... I was swimming when I noticed it had gone. Please, take a look?"

"Okay," he said, staring down into the pool.

I saw a look of triumph in her expression which soon changed to lust as Sebastian pulled off his t-shirt and stepped out of his flip-flops.

It was really hard to imagine that they'd dated for ten whole months. Even harder to imagine that she hadn't ripped off his clothes and stolen his virginity at some point during that period. Had she only become so obviously desperate once he'd broken up with her or had she always been like this? I reminded myself of the reason why they'd broken up in the first place—she'd slept with someone else. Perhaps Sebastian had a good grasp on his self-control when he was with her—just not with me, I concluded smugly.

Across the pool, I saw two women of Shirley's age nudge each other and adjust their sunglasses for a better look.

Big tips from horny, older women.

Jealousy was such a new and unaccustomed emotion, that I had to remind myself my homicidal thoughts were something of an over-reaction. Except, perhaps, where Brenda was concerned.

I was relieved that the nail marks I'd inflicted on Sebastian last night—or very early this morning—had, mostly, faded. Hes wasn't the only one who had to be careful not to get carried away.

With a grace that took my breath away, he dived into the deep end and stayed under for half a minute, searching for the earring that Evil Brenda pretended she'd lost. He came up for air then dove down again. Twice more he swept the bottom of the pool but, of course, found nothing.

Eventually he gave up and pulled himself out of the pool, right next to where Brenda was sitting, the vixen trying to look all helpless and grateful. His swim-trunks clung to his body as the water poured off him, and his skin sparkled in the sun, droplets reflecting light off his chest and arms.

Brenda looked like she'd died and gone to heaven. Although ... a thought occurred to me, hadn't she seen it all before? Hadn't he ever taken her surfing with him? I'd have to remember to ask him. Then I slapped the idea down—I'd promised myself to quit plaguing him with questions that were only going to piss off both of us.

The two women across the pool were grinning at each other and I swear they gave each other a high five. I could see Sebastian was going to have a long afternoon of being asked to retrieve lost jewelry from the pool. Or maybe, if those cocktails the women drank were alcoholic, he'd end up having to save them both when they threw themselves in the deep end, hoping that he'd give them mouth-to-mouth resuscitation.

"I'm sorry," he said at last, "I couldn't find it. It probably got sucked into the filter system. I'll report it to the manager and he can ask the pool guy to look out for it. But it won't be until tomorrow morning now."

Brenda shrugged.

"Whatever. So, did you decide which school you're going to go to yet? UCSD, right? What classes are you taking?"

"I'm working, Bren," he said, not very subtly.

She pouted. "It's not *that* busy."

He frowned. "I'm not supposed to chat to members."

"I won't tell if you won't," she said, smiling up at him.

I felt desperately sorry for Sebastian, he was utterly hopeless at trying to blow her off. He really didn't have a clue. He was far too nice for his own good.

I wondered if he'd appreciate my help—maybe if I attacked her with a pool chair and beat her into putty, she'd be distracted enough to leave him alone. On the other hand, that would definitely draw unwanted attention.

Instead, I tried to focus on the small screen in front of me, but I couldn't help noticing that Sebastian's eyes kept flicking nervously in my direction.

Brenda was getting irritated that her wiles weren't working, and she was bound to notice that he kept looking at me, not her.

At that moment Ches walked over to Sebastian and spoke to him quietly. Whatever he said, Sebastian was hugely and obviously relieved. He picked up his uniform polo-shirt and pulled it over his still-wet body, slipped on his flip-flops and walked off, glancing just once at me and smiling.

But it was enough: Brenda had seen the look.

Her eyes narrowed dangerously and I couldn't help a nervous swallow. Then I straightened my back and decided that I wasn't going to roll over and let her walk all over me.

"Where's he gone?" Brenda snapped at Ches.

"We've been told to swap duties," he lied casually.

I knew for a fact that Sebastian was supposed to be poolside his whole shift.

"They want him in the gym," continued Ches, sounding utterly convincing. I was glad he was on our side—on Sebastian's side.

Then he looked at me and grinned, "Hey, there, Mrs. Wilson! How are you?"

"I'm just fine, thank you, Ches," I said, smiling at him gratefully. "How's your mom and dad?"

We slipped into our double act as if we'd been practicing it all our lives.

"Good, thanks. Are you writing another article?"

"I thought the staff weren't supposed to chat to members," Brenda muttered in a sulky tone.

Ches pretended not to hear her and spoke to me for several minutes before taking up his place in the lifeguard's chair.

I was totally unprepared for Brenda's next line of attack.

"So, you're, like, a writer?" she said, coming and standing next to me, one hand on her hip.

I glanced up and saw Ches's fleeting look of sympathy.

"Trying to be," I said politely.

"Aren't you, like, kind of old to be starting out?"

I was astonished by her rudeness.

"I don't think it's ever too late to try something new."

She sniffed and started reading my notes over my shoulder. I'd had enough.

I closed the laptop and looked her in the eye. "Is there something I can help you with, Barbara?"

"It's *Brenda!*"

"Oh, is it?"

"You knew Seb when he was a kid, right?" she said, not the least bit perturbed by my overt hostility.

"Slightly," I acknowledged.

"So, you've known him, like, forever?"

If she said 'like' again, I might have to beat her over the head with a book of English grammar. Or I might just do it anyway—the idea was undeniably attractive.

I smiled coolly at her and she looked a little confused. "Oh, sorry, Barb ... Brenda. Was that a question?"

She nodded briskly.

"No, not really," I replied shortly. I wasn't going to give her any information I didn't need to.

"You know his parents, right?"

"Slightly," I repeated, knowing that would aggravate her more than anything.

"Seb and I have been dating since tenth grade," she lied blandly.

"How nice," I said, grinding my teeth. "Dear me! Shirley must have been mistaken when she told me you two had broken up."

She flicked her honey blonde hair over her shoulder. "We were on a break, but he wants to get back with me."

She spoke with such an air of conviction that I was rather in awe of her. How did she lie so easily and with such confidence? I should take lessons from her—especially as I had another three months of living with David to get through.

The reminder was a sharp one, and I'd had enough of her games.

"How nice for you. Well, it's been lovely chatting, but if you'll excuse me, I have deadlines."

Now she looked mad. It turned out that I was much better at blowing her off than Sebastian was. What's more, *it had been fun*.

She huffed angrily, grabbed her towel and headed indoors. I suspected she would be stalking Sebastian in the gym. I looked up at Ches. He shrugged and shook his head helplessly. Nope, he didn't know what to do about Barbara ... um ... Brenda either.

I decided to wander in to get that mythical coffee after all. I left my laptop on the table and Ches cheerfully acknowledged that he'd keep an eye on it. Pulling on my t-shirt and shorts I headed for the bar area but before I got there I could hear a woman's angry voice.

"It's not appropriate for you to be chatting to your girlfriend while you're working, Mr. Hunter."

"She's not my..."

A middle-aged Hispanic woman in a neat pant-suit was chewing a piece out of Sebastian. My immediate reaction was to rush in and defend him. Instead, I watched silently from the sidelines. Story of my life.

"We have rules here for very good reasons. We don't want our members injuring themselves when they're in the gym—that's why we have staff on hand to instruct them in the correct use of the equipment. If you're chatting to your girlfriend, Mr. Hunter, that's when accidents will happen. I take a very dim view of that ... a very dim view indeed."

"She's not my girlfriend, ma'am, she's a member and..."

"Well ... I've made my views clear, Mr. Hunter. And should any other of your *friends* decide to come and chat, I'm sure you'll dissuade them from that. Am I making myself clear?"

"Yes, ma'am."

"And may I ask why you are working the gym right now and not Mr. Peters?"

Sebastian flushed and dropped his gaze to stare directly over his manager's shoulder.

"I ... I asked to swap, ma'am."

"*I* arrange the rosters, Mr. Hunter, not you. Kindly go back to your lifeguarding duties and send Mr. Peters to see me, please."

"But Ches..."

"*Now*, Mr. Hunter."

"Yes, Miss Perez."

Sebastian turned on his heel and strode back out to the pool area.

Luckily, he was unaware that I'd overheard the humiliating little scene. I could cheerfully have smacked Brenda into the middle of next week for causing so much trouble.

I lingered to order a coffee and the young barista offered to carry it out to the pool for me when it was ready. Now Sebastian was back outside, it was the only place I wanted to be.

Happily, Brenda seemed to have disappeared. Which was lucky for her, the way I was feeling.

Sebastian was slumped in the lifeguard's chair when I emerged into the sunshine from the gloom of the clubhouse, but beamed at me as I resumed my seat under the sun umbrella. I really was going to have to talk to him about playing it cool. I gave him a quick smile and went back to my laptop. Now Brenda had gone, I had a reasonable chance of actually managing to put some words on the page.

It was surprisingly soothing to have Sebastian sitting there while I worked. I wrote steadily for some time, sipping at the thin coffee that had been brought to my table, becoming more and more absorbed in describing life on a military Base, with its odd mixture of discipline and play, rules and separation that marked us out as different from the world beyond the walls. It made me realize how much I'd come to rely on that sense of orderliness, togetherness, of family, even. I'd felt so alien in this world for so long, I hadn't even noticed my slow absorption into this isolated, alternative way of life. I wondered if I'd miss it once I left. I didn't think so, but it was all I'd known for 11 years. Now, at last, Sebastian was offering me something different.

I looked at my wristwatch, astonished that it was already after 5PM. I had to get home—and face David. Twelve more weeks of feeling like this, I didn't know how I'd manage. And I'd be without the warmth of Sebastian's body beside me tonight. That thought alone made me feel bereft.

I looked up to see him watching me, a small frown creasing his forehead. I smiled quickly and subtly tapped my watch. The corners of his lips turned down and he nodded fractionally.

With a sigh, I packed up my notebook and laptop, and left him behind.

At 6PM I heard David's car pull up. I made sure that his dinner, reheated lasagna and salad, was ready.

As he walked in, I fixed a smile to my face and pulled his steaming plate out of the microwave and placed it on the table next to the salad bowl.

But he didn't look at the food—he looked right at me, his face stiff and angry, sitting bolt upright at the table.

"Have you got something to tell me, Caroline?"

I'm sure my face was drained of color, because I suddenly felt very faint. I tried to speak but the words wouldn't come out.

"Well?"

"I..."

"I saw Dr. Ravel today," he snarled at me, "who reported to me that you *missed your appointment!*"

I felt a sudden desire to laugh. Was *that* all that was bothering him.

"That's right," I said, feeling brave now that I was sure it was nothing to do with Sebastian.

"Would you like to explain that?" he hissed.

"I felt no need for an appointment, David. You made it without consulting me. If you had, I would have reminded you that I had a Pap smear six months ago and that there were no problems. And I certainly am *not* experiencing an early menopause—I'm quite sure of *that*."

Silence filled the room and our eyes locked.

"And what the hell is Dr. Ravel doing discussing me—her patient—with you? Hasn't she heard of HIPPA?"

"If it's not physical, it must be psychological," he said, coolly ignoring my comment. "I'll arrange for you to see the Base psychiatrist and..."

"No, you won't, David," I replied, trying to match his sanguine tone, but with little luck. "I am not seeing a shrink, there's *nothing* wrong with me."

"Then why are you sleeping in the guest room?" he yelled, all attempt at any control gone. "*That* is going to stop tonight. I want you back in my bed where you belong!"

"No!" I yelled back. "I fucking well won't!"

David's face was comically shocked. "Yes, you will," he said, with far less force.

I stared back at him and folded my hands across my waist.

"No."

We glared at each other across the kitchen table.

"What the fuck is wrong with you?" he shouted suddenly, making me jump.

Adrenaline and mounting anger sharpened my tone.

"Nothing! There's nothing wrong with me! I wash your fucking clothes, I iron your fucking pants, I cook, I clean, I..."

"That's your job! That's what you're here to do!"

"I'm NOT a fucking servant!"

"You're being hysterical, Caroline, I think..."

"I don't give a rat's ass what you think, David! I'm tired of you bullying me, putting me down, patronizing me, treating me like some sort of simpleton. I was supposed to be a *partner* in this relationship—that's what I signed up for. *Not this!*"

"You're acting like a child, Caroline."

"Then stop fucking treating me like one! I'm thirty fucking years old!"

"And please stop using that vile language."

"Aaaaaaaagh!" I screamed at the top of my lungs. For a moment he actually looked scared.

Then he stood up abruptly and forcefully shoved the lasagna and salad away from him. The plate slid right across the kitchen table and crashed to the floor, sending a shower of steaming hot sauce and scalding vegetables over my bare feet and legs.

I cried out and jumped back, trying to scrub off the burning food.

"You bastard," I screamed at him. "You fucking bastard!"

He looked shocked.

"Caroline ... I ... I didn't mean for that to ... are you hurt?"

I ran to the sink, trying to splash cold water over my burning legs and feet.

"Caroline!"

Tears sprang to my eyes and my voice was shrill.

"Go away, David. Leave me alone."

Instead, he hovered guiltily while I cleaned myself up in silence. The hot food had left blotchy, red burn marks down my thighs and shins and across the front of my feet. I thought I'd got the hot sauce off quickly enough to prevent any blistering or real damage.

David watched me helplessly. It was clear he hadn't a clue what to say or do. Just as long as he didn't try to touch me—if he did, I wouldn't be responsible for my actions. The great doctor didn't even offer to get the First Aid kit.

Carefully, I rubbed large dollops of antiseptic cream over my legs and, without a single glance in his direction, I left the room. The pool of lasagna was still spread out over the floor like a crime scene.

I walked upstairs stiffly and lay down on the bed in my room. I wanted to curl into a tight ball but my skin was too tender to stretch like that. Instead I lay on my back and stared at the ceiling. David had never ever hurt me before—not physically. I knew it was an accident but the hate I felt for him at that moment raged through me. All the years of being belittled and bullied, all the times he'd made feel stupid and inadequate, it all came boiling up inside.

The fury I'd felt when Brenda had flirted too openly with Sebastian was nothing, an insignificant annoyance, compared to the way I felt now.

I was *glad* I was having an affair behind his back. I was *glad* I'd taken a younger man into his bed. I was *delighted* thinking of the humiliation he'd suffer when he finally knew the truth. I wanted to yell it to his face and watch his whole fucking world fall apart.

Even after I heard the front door slam and his car screech out of the driveway, I continued to imagine the fierce joy I'd feel when I finally told him what a pathetic little man he truly was.

I lay on the bed as the house sank into darkness. Outside I could hear the small sounds of the day's end, people's lives continuing down the same, certain paths. I'd been like that once—moving from hour to hour, sleepwalking down a road that had been chosen for me—not awake, not aware.

It was all ashes and dust.

~

I must have fallen asleep because when my cell phone buzzed with a text message, I jerked awake. I struggled to sit up, wondering why I felt so sore and then the memories came flying back like locusts. The skin on my legs felt raw, or rather, the hot tightness of bad sunburn. I was astonished to find that my face was wet. I didn't know it was possible to cry in your sleep. It wasn't from the pain—at least, not the physical pain.

I turned on my side to reach the bedside light. The little alarm clock told me it was after 11PM, I'd been asleep for nearly four hours.

I expected the text to be from Sebastian and it was—but not the goodnight message I'd anticipated.

Am outside. Is he there? There's no car? Can I c u?

I leapt out of bed and immediately regretted moving so quickly. Even in the weak pool of light from the little lamp, my legs looked horrible. I needed to find something to cover them up. I found an old hippy skirt at the back of the closet. It was dated and faintly ridiculous, but it was the only fabric I could tolerate right now. Best of all, it was floor length.

Moving carefully, I made my way down to the kitchen. I stared in disgust at the vomit-like pool of cold lasagna on the tiled floor. That bastard hadn't even tried to clear it away. I hesitated, thinking I should clean up before I let Sebastian in—he'd only ask questions which I wanted to avoid. But it was too late, he'd seen my silhouette as soon as I'd walked in the kitchen and I could see his shadow rocking impatiently on the balls of his feet.

His smile vanished as soon as he saw my face. My attempt to fool him for even a second had obviously been in vain.

"Caro, what's wrong?"

I just shook my head and he pulled me into a tight hug. His jeans pushed against my legs, rubbing my skirt fabric against my burns. I winced and he felt me shudder.

"What's the matter? Did something happen? Tell me!"

I sighed into his chest.

"David and I had a fight," I said.

He froze as soon as I'd said the words.

"He knows?"

I shook my head slowly. "No. It was nothing to do with you—just a stupid fight."

He breathed a sigh of something like relief.

"What was it about then?"

He wasn't going to let this one go.

"He was pissed because I refused to sleep with him—I mean, sleep in his bed, not ... I told him I'd be staying in the guest room."

"That asshole! Fuck, Caro! I really want to..."

He didn't finish the sentence but it didn't take a genius to figure out what he was thinking.

"Has he ... gone out?"

I nodded. "Yes, he's been gone a while. I've no idea when ... or if, he'll be back."

"Can I come in?"

His voice was hopeful.

"Okay, for a minute."

He frowned at my unenthusiastic reply. I was so tired and wrung out, I couldn't handle a jealous and angry Sebastian right now.

He halted in his tracks when he saw the mess on the floor.

"Did *he* do that?"

I nodded silently and fetched a cloth to start clearing it up.

Without speaking Sebastian took the rag from me. I was too weary to argue even though I wanted to. It was just all wrong to have my lover clear up the mess my husband had made in our kitchen over a fight about the matrimonial bed. My brain was tied in knots just trying to keep all the pieces in the right place. Somehow everything had gotten so mixed up and confused.

Finally, the floor was clean and the remains of David's dinner had been dumped in the trash can. Sebastian washed his hands and dried them on the back of his pants.

He sat down at the table and put his arm around me. I leaned my head against his shoulder and closed my eyes. He wrapped his other arm around my waist and pulled me to his chest, just holding me. Every now and then I felt his light kisses in my hair.

His kindness was the thing that broke me, and tears began to slide down my cheeks.

"Don't cry, Caro," he said softly, his voice aching with sadness. "Don't cry, baby."

He repositioned one arm under my knees and gently lifted me up. I whimpered once from the pain, then bit my lip to stifle any more sounds.

Slowly and carefully, he carried me up the stairs and laid me down on my bed, placing his body alongside mine.

We lay together as I sobbed quietly. We didn't speak.

When my tears finally dried, he kissed me on the cheek.

"Come on, let's get you undressed."

His hands rose to my waistband but I pushed them roughly away.

"No, don't!"

He looked hurt. "I wasn't going to do anything, Caro. You're exhausted. You need to get some rest. Come on, let me help you."

I tried to push him away, but my body felt like I weighed a thousand pounds, and he'd pulled up the hem of my skirt before I could stop him.

I heard his gasp and then he swore.

"What the fuck, Caro? What happened? Did ... did *he*...?"

"It was an accident," I said tiredly. "He didn't mean to."

Sebastian was furious, as I knew he would be. I could see cords of tension on his neck, his eyes were blazing with fury.

"That *asshole!*"

He bounced off the bed and balled his fists as if he wanted to hit something

—or someone. He was trying to rein in his temper, but he wasn't having much luck with that. Then he saw my face, fresh tears breaking out.

"Shit, I should take you to a doctor!"

I shook my head slowly. "I'm okay. They're just ... mild burns ... from the pasta sauce. I'm okay."

"You should fucking report this! You can't let him get away with doing this to you!"

"It was an accident," I repeated quietly. "Please, Sebastian, just drop it."

"Drop it?!" he shouted. "Look what that sack of shit has done to you! Fuck, Caro!"

I put my hands over my ears and squeezed my eyes tight shut, trying to stop the new tears from leaking out. His rant stopped in midstream.

"Oh God, Caro."

I felt the mattress tremble and he lay back down on the bed and hugged me to him. That was all I needed, his arms around me.

After a long while it was Sebastian who broke the silence.

"What do you want to do?"

His voice was soft, unnamed emotions making his tone raw.

"I don't know."

"You can't stay here anymore, Caro. You know that, right?"

I let my breath out in a long sigh.

"I don't have anywhere to go."

"Maybe Mitch and Shirley? They'd help, I know they would."

I shook my head slowly. "I'm not taking my troubles to their door." I sighed. "I'm still ... in an illegal relationship with a minor—I wouldn't do that to them."

He didn't argue so I knew he'd taken my words seriously.

"What about your mom's? I know you're not close, but..."

"No. She practically kicked me out when I was 19," I said bitterly. "Why do you think I married David so quickly?"

He was silent for a moment but I felt his body tense, he did that every time I so much as mentioned David's name. Some sort of primal response, I guessed.

"What about friends back east?"

"Same problem," I whispered. "I'd be involving them in ... well, you know."

He hugged me closer and I could feel his warm breath on my neck.

"There's a women's shelter near Park West ... I ... I heard Mom mention it once. Maybe..."

"I can't because..." My whispered words shuddered to a halt.

"Because of me."

His voice was bitter.

"You can't go to any of the places that would help you ... because of me."

I knew why he thought that, why he would say that, but I couldn't let him blame himself.

"It's not your fault, Sebastian," I said gently, stroking his arm. "You're the one good thing I have in my life. I wouldn't change that for anything. Not for anything. I finally feel ... alive."

I heard him gasp and he pulled me closer.

"I feel the same, Caro. You've taught me everything I know."

I blinked in surprise.

"You have. You've taught me who I can be, you've made me stronger. You make me want to see the magic in the world. I ... I didn't know falling in love could be ... like this."

Was that really how he felt? Is that how he saw me—someone who could make him stronger? How did that happen? I was so weak and cowardly. But, and I felt a small flowering of hope inside me, I *had* changed, hadn't I. I was getting stronger—not yet strong, but getting there.

It felt as if he'd been the one to teach me. Perhaps we had learned together.

He held me carefully, making sure his legs didn't accidentally brush against mine.

"I don't know what to do," he said softly. "I want to be with you so badly, but you just end up getting hurt every time I come near you. Why is it so hard for us to be together? It's so fucking unfair!"

"I know, *tesoro*."

He was so hurt and confused and there was so little I could do to help either of us.

I let out a long sigh.

"I think you'd better go now."

"No!" he gasped. "No way!" He raised his voice. "I'm not leaving you alone with that asshole!"

"I can't fight with you, too, Sebastian," I whispered. "I don't have the strength."

"No! I didn't ... what if he ... I *can't* leave you here alone!" he said, desperately.

I turned carefully to look at him.

"This isn't something you can fix, Sebastian. I'm the one who's screwed up, I have to fix it. But you're right about one thing—I can't stay here." I took a deep breath. "There are lots of empty rooms around the university now all the students are on vacation. I'll check out the listings for people wanting roommates. There are places for less than $500 a month. I can manage that."

I didn't tell Sebastian I had no idea how I'd afford to eat and put gas in my car at the same time.

"And there's a Motel 6 up by San Ysidro that's only $50 a night. That can be my last resort, if necessary."

Sebastian's face was grim. "I have nearly $700. That'll buy another month, food and gas."

Maybe he could read my mind.

I stroked his cheek. "I can't take your money."

"Yes, you can! I want you to, please, Caro. Let me help you. I want to take care of you. This is all my..."

I laid a finger over his lips. I couldn't bear to hear him so desperate, trying to look after me the way a man looks after a woman.

He kissed my finger and pulled my hand away from his mouth.

"You should go see a lawyer, Caro. Take half of everything that bastard has."

I shook my head. "No, Sebastian. I won't be doing that."

"Why not?" he said, hotly. "You deserve..."

I interrupted him gently.

"I don't *want* anything of his. Do you understand? Nothing. But there's another reason ... if I make David fight a divorce, I'm afraid he'll find out about us. I *know* him: he'll keep digging and digging and digging until he finds the reason why I left him after all this time. His ego will demand that there's a reason other than ... other than himself. And then he'll take me down."

I could feel the tension and stress in Sebastian's body—all his muscles were rigid and he was only just holding onto his temper. He pulled me tighter against his chest, his hands trembling, but he couldn't speak. He buried his face against my neck and we held each other as the night slipped past.

I stroked his back and gradually his body began to relax, his breathing becoming deep and even.

I couldn't sleep but I was glad that Sebastian did. I listened to the soft sounds of breath on his lips, and watched his face relaxed and peaceful. I felt such crushing guilt when I looked at him, so beautiful, so sweet and young. All he'd done was to love me and now he was in danger of being swept away in the floodwaters of my failed marriage.

The right thing for me to do was to leave quietly and head for New York. That way David and I could conduct our divorce with some dignity—I hoped—and my relationship with Sebastian would stay hidden. Once he was 18, and with me already on the east coast, he'd be able to escape. People would talk and maybe even guess the truth, but there would be no proof—and we'd be safe.

Two things held me back from making that decision: firstly, I knew that Sebastian would never agree and it would mean another fight, and secondly, I felt responsible for his fragile soul and I didn't want to leave him unprotected.

I knew Shirley and Mitch would look after him as much as they could—they already thought of him as a second son—but they didn't have the legal power to support him against the wishes of Donald and Estelle. Not unless they were prepared to swear to the historic and ongoing abuse. And, despite everything, Donald was one of *them*—part of the military family. That worked two ways. The military looked after their own, but the other mantra that was drilled into them had a darker side: 'snitches get stitches and wind up in ditches'.

I couldn't see Mitch wanting to go down that road—it would be the end of his career. If Sebastian had been younger, then maybe, but not now he was so near his eighteenth birthday, legal adulthood and emancipation.

So that was the reasoning behind my plan—spend the next couple of days finding a room, then work up the courage to tell David I was leaving him.

I knew my husband well enough to feel confident that his guilt over my accident would keep him silent for the few days I needed.

At least, that's what I hoped.

CHAPTER SIXTEEN

At dawn, I gently shook Sebastian awake.

I'd listened all night for the sound of David's return but the house had stayed silent and kept its secrets.

He yawned and stretched, giving me the most glorious smile.

"God, I love waking up with you, Caro. I want to do it for the rest of my life."

His words squeezed my heart painfully. I badly wanted to believe them.

Then his smile faded and I saw the weight of memories flood back. He frowned.

"How are you? How are your legs?"

"Not too bad. Pretty good really."

In truth, they were more than a little sore, particularly so when I flexed my knees, but nothing I was going to worry about. The worst area was the top of my right foot and that *was* painful. From a few exploratory prods, I could feel that it had blistered over night. It was going to be hellish trying to wear shoes, even flip-flops would rub in all the wrong places.

He looked at me skeptically.

"Really?"

"Sure," I said, not meeting his eyes and sitting up.

He reached out and pulled me back down, forcing me to look at him. "Really?"

"My right foot is a little sore," I conceded. "I just need to put a band-aid on it, that's all."

This time he let me get out of bed and lay there watching me.

I couldn't help noticing that he'd kicked off his jeans in the night and was wearing just a t-shirt and boxer briefs—with a large bulge showing clearly. Although my body tingled with Pavlovian response, I really wasn't in the mood to do anything about it, and Sebastian didn't even seem to be aware. Perhaps he woke up like that every morning. I smiled to myself, considering that soon I'd be in a position to answer that interesting question.

When I came back from the bathroom, he was fully dressed. He'd even taken the time to make the bed and turn back the sheets nicely.

I crept downstairs in the pale, gray light of dawn, checking that David's return wasn't imminent. We'd have about two minutes after hearing his car in the driveway—just enough time for Sebastian to make an escape through the back door. I'd liked to have made breakfast for him but there was a good chance that David would return soon to get a change of clothes.

We stood in the kitchen, the scene of so much drama, so many key moments in our lives, and held each other.

"I'll miss you every minute," he said, softly.

I sighed into his chest.

"I'll see you at the park at 9AM?"

"Yes," he said, simply.

And then it was time for him to go. It seemed to me like it was always time for him to go. I knew he felt the same.

But David didn't return. Instead I spent the hours before I could be with Sebastian again wandering around the empty house, letting my fingers drift over the old, familiar furniture and through the old, familiar memories.

I decided what I would take with me from the marital home. When it came down to it, there was very little: my clothes, the jewelry my father had given me, my ancient laptop, a few books, and my favorite CDs which were already in the car. The ugly wedding china that my parents had bought us had been my mother's choice—I was more than happy for David to keep it. It wasn't much to show for 11 years of marriage, but with a new life ahead of me, I didn't care either. That, by itself, said everything.

When I'd still lived in North Carolina, some friends and I had had a rather drunken evening and we'd all had to choose which three things we'd save in a house fire. One woman that I didn't know very well said, and I remembered this clearly, "My dog, my handbag and my wedding album."

"What about your husband?" we'd asked, laughing.

"He can get his own damn self out," she'd replied.

I had one other job to do before I left the house—I scoured the rooms-to-rent websites and made a shortlist of five places to check out. I didn't much care what the room was like so long as it was cheap and reasonably clean. It wasn't going to be for long.

Despite my lack of sleep, I was filled with a nervous, restless energy. I'd made my decision and now I was ready to get on with my life. The last month had raced by, but the next few days seemed destined to drag.

I headed back up to the bathroom and gritted my teeth through a tepid shower that stung my too sensitive skin. All the burn marks were ugly but only my foot really bothered me. I dug in the closet and eventually located a pair of long, loose pants and found some old sneakers that were bearable once I'd made a gauze pad to cover the large blister. Not my most elegant look but hell, Sebastian wouldn't care. And that was all that mattered.

He was waiting for me, of course, and just seeing him made my day a little brighter.

"How are you?" he said again, peering anxiously at my face.

"I'm ... surprisingly good," I said, honestly.

He smiled that beautiful smile and I saw his shoulders relax.

"How are you?" I grinned back at him. "Are you hungry?"

"Yeah, starving!"

"Did you skip breakfast again?" I admonished.

His smile died. "Yeah, I guess."

"What is it?"

He shrugged. "No food in the house."

I felt so bad for him, knowing I'd sent him away hungry. "Is ... is it usually like that?"

He carried on staring out of the window. "I guess. Although it's gotten worse lately. All they do is fight. I don't know why they stay together—it damn well isn't for me. Probably to protect their reputations—as if that were even possible. God, I can't wait to get out of there."

I reached over and gently squeezed his thigh. He looked down and a moment later carefully twined his fingers through mine.

"I thought we could go to our coffee shop," I said, softly.

He was still gazing at our joined hands, when he replied.

"Yeah, that would be good."

"I'll spring for breakfast," I said, hoping to make him smile. "I saw on their menu that they do fresh *zeppole* and three different *crostata*."

"Only three?" he said, his lips lifting upwards at last.

"Hmm, well! I think a taste test might be in order."

The Benzinos welcomed us back with open arms, berating us vociferously for having stayed away so long. I made the mistake of mentioning that Sebastian had skipped breakfast and the little old *nonna* scolded him for five minutes solidly, rattling off her rebukes in quick-fire Italian while Sebastian wilted under her stern gaze—then she turned her attention to me, wagging her finger and telling me I was a bad wife for not feeding my man. I agreed with every word. If only she'd known.

Almost every item on the menu was soon delivered to our table and I couldn't help smiling as Sebastian's eyes bugged out at the vast quantity of food. But then I remembered the reason he was always so hungry, and my smile faded.

He ate everything in sight with the exception of one *crostata* that he insisted I have for myself.

"Oh wow, that was amazing!" he said, replete at last. "I'm going to get so fat when we go to Italy."

"If you carry on eating like this you'll be enormous long before we make it to Italy," I laughed at him. "There's nothing on the menu here that I can't make."

"You're kidding? Wow, really? Jeez, I knew there was a reason I loved you!"

And he leaned forward to kiss me.

The little *nonna* clapped her hands together with feeling, then darted over and peppered me with questions, her quick, squirrel-brown eyes darting between us. I shook my head, more than a little embarrassed. She sighed heavily, pointed at her watch and shot off to serve some newly arrived customers, still shaking her head.

"Was that about what I think it was about?" said Sebastian, raising his eyebrows.

"How much did you pick up?" I asked, curious to know how good his Italian was getting—as well as avoiding answering the question.

"Something about babies and the time?"

"Well, yes," I agreed, feeling flustered. "She wanted to know when we were going to start a family." I tried to smile. "She was pointing out that time waits for no woman."

He lifted my hand from the table and frowned as he stared at my wedding ring. "I'll do whatever makes you happy, Caro. I reckon I could handle the idea of a couple of *bambinos* running around. We'd make a helluva better job of it than my folks, that's for sure."

I tried to smile but I didn't want to dare let myself think that far ahead. What was the point? He was far too young to be talking like this. And when he *was* old enough...

The conversation was making me feel despondent so I thought quickly how to change it.

"What time are you working today?"

"Not till 4PM," he said, smiling again. "What would you like to do?"

"Not much," I admitted.

"Do you want to go to our beach?"

My smile faded. "I don't think that would be a good idea—I don't want to get my feet wet or sand in my blister." My words stalled, seeing the venomous look on his face.

He made a visible effort and reined in his rising temper.

"Maybe we could check out some of these rooms to rent that that you've seen advertised?"

"No, that's okay, thanks. I'll do that this afternoon while you're working."

He thought for a moment.

"There's a jazz band playing down in the Gaslamp Quarter today. We could go listen if you like?"

"Jazz again!" I teased. "And here was me thinking you were devoted to opera."

"I like both," he said, looking a little sheepish.

I smiled at him. "Me, too."

He stood up, stretching his tall frame and held out his hands to pull me up.

We hid some bills under our plates and tried to sneak away before the Benzinos saw us but the *nonna* must have had her eagle eyes trained our way because she sent her son darting after us with the money, remonstrating about our underhand trick and reminding us that family didn't pay. Then he kissed us both, thrust the notes into Sebastian's hands and hurried back to his business. How they ever made any profit was beyond me.

We wandered through the Gaslamp Quarter, admiring the Victorian architecture and old world charm, enjoying the sun and warm air, people-watching and relaxing in a way that was new and rather wonderful to me.

We heard the sounds of jazz filling the summer morning long before we saw the band. Strolling out of an alleyway into a large plaza, I could see that one side had been converted into a mini stage where the musicians performed, decked out in black jeans and t-shirts, and wearing dark sunglasses, presumably to show that they were jazzmen, if the music didn't already prove it. They looked young enough to be students and were playing a sort of hyped up version of Dixieland jazz mixed in with a more modern, fusion sound and some Latin rhythms. A couple of girls in their late teens were already dancing, losing themselves in the music. Soon, other people were joining them and the crowd steadily grew.

We didn't want to waste any money by sitting at one of the café tables that ringed the plaza, so we joined a group sprawled out on the sidewalk. Sebastian gallantly pulled off his sweatshirt so I wouldn't have to sit on the dusty ground.

He did these things so naturally, with no fuss or embellishment that my heart expanded with delight and pain each time. Sebastian always put me first. I wasn't used to that.

We sat shoulder to shoulder and he casually draped his arm around me, turning every now and then to kiss my hair. I wished the moment could last forever.

I couldn't help noticing that his feet and hands moved constantly with the music, keeping up a contrapuntal rhythm, his fingers drumming on my arm.

"Have you ever learned a musical instrument?" I wondered.

He smiled. "No, but I always wanted to play guitar."

"We should get you one when we get to New York. Not electric, though, please! An acoustic guitar."

"I thought you were a rock chick at heart. Which reminds me—I still have to go beat up Anthony Kiedis!" He paused. "Did you ever learn to play anything?"

"Not really. I had piano lessons when I was eight. I hated them. Mom wanted me to do it but I begged Papa to stop the torture and he did."

He hesitated for a moment. "Will you tell your mom...?" His words trailed off.

"When I leave David? Yes, I suppose so. Eventually."

He held my hand tightly and kissed my fingers. "At least you had your dad—that's one more good parent than I had." He considered for a moment. "But I have Shirley and Mitch—they've been more like parents to me than my mom and dad. I hate not being able to tell them about you."

He frowned and I stroked his arm, trying to soothe away the hurt, or, if that were impossible, to show that I understood.

"I know, I hate it, too. But when this is all over, if ... if they forgive me, maybe we can..."

He lifted my chin with his fingers to make me look into his eyes.

"There's nothing to forgive," he said, his voice forceful. "We fell in love: it's not a crime."

But I still felt like a criminal. Sometimes.

He kissed me on the lips, trying to lighten our suddenly bleak mood.

"Come on," he said, pulling me to my feet. "Let's dance!"

"What? You can't dance, can you?"

"Oh, yeah? Is that what you think? Let me show you, baby!"

And he could, he really could!

He placed my arms around his neck, wrapped his around my waist and pushed his right leg between mine so we were joined at the groin. If it hadn't been for the fact we were practically welded together, I would have fallen over from shock. No one had *ever* danced with me like this before. It was so good I was sure it must be illegal. In fact the way he wove our bodies together I was quite certain it would have been banned in several states.

David's idea of dancing was to sway slowly, usually to a different tune from the one that was being played, and circle carefully on the spot. The only other man I'd danced with had been Papa—and that had been a waltz. I hadn't even gone to my high school prom because I was already dating David so I hadn't seen the point.

But this! This was more like sex to music but without the messy sheets. And in public.

He ground himself against me, our bodies undulating with the music. Then he spun me around and pulled me tightly against him again. I caught glimpses of envious faces of other women as we moved. Then his hands slid down to my ass and he pushed my hips into him, fingers splayed out over my buttocks.

When the tune finished I was red-faced and hyperventilating and so damn aroused! He grinned at me wickedly, knowing exactly what he'd done. He dipped me almost to the floor, then swept me up and kissed me hard.

The watching crowd gave us an ironic cheer and several yelled at us to get a room. It was the best suggestion I'd heard all day. Instead, Sebastian saluted the amused audience and grabbed my hand, towing me in the direction of the car.

"Where ... where did you learn to do that?" I gasped.

"Shirley and Mitch," he said, walking so fast I had to trot to keep up.

"You're kidding me!"

"Nope! Base salsa champions, four years running."

He pulled me down the street, a determined look on his face. When we got to the parking lot, I saw his eyes scanning the rows of parked cars until he found my Ford. I tried to fish my keys out of my purse but he was walking so quickly, it was hard to keep up and do anything else.

When we got to the car, he slammed my back against the door, his hands in my hair, his teeth on my throat .

"I want you so bad," he breathed into my skin.

"Empty lot."

"What?"

"That empty lot—you remember."

"Fuck, yes!"

With shaking hands, I climbed into the driver's side and fiddled with my seatbelt. Sebastian reached across me and snapped it into place, letting his fingers drift across my stomach as he did so, his heated expression made my mouth dry up.

I don't know how I drove without having an accident—my whole body was on fire for him. Sebastian leaned back in the passenger seat, his eyes closed. He looked calm, but his too rapid breathing gave him away.

I swung into the weed-covered space of the empty lot, slammed on the brakes and the car screeched to a halt. I'd only just managed to take off my seatbelt before Sebastian was unzipping his pants and showing me just how much he wanted me. I was so turned on seeing his need. I crawled onto his lap and thanked my lucky stars I'd chosen to wear loose pants with an elasticized waistband. I pushed them over my hips, ignored the pain from my sore skin and sank down on to him.

There was no finesse, no gentle touches—it was hard and raw and urgent. Sebastian grabbed my hips, pumping me up and down even faster. His eyes were tightly closed and his head was buried in my chest, every muscle rigid. He came hard, shuddering into me. I whimpered as my body exploded from the inside out and, without meaning to, I bit down on his neck.

His arms tightened around me and we sat there, trying to adjust our shattered breathing.

Finally, the pain from my sore skin broke through the post-orgasmic miasma and I shifted awkwardly back to the driver's side.

I glanced over to see Sebastian zipping up his pants, a huge grin on his face.

"We should name this empty lot," he said.

"Like what? 'Emergency Room'?"

"Yeah!" he laughed out loud. "I hope they never build on it."

"Maybe they'll build one of those Japanese Love Hotels and put a plaque on the wall in our memory."

"What's a Love Hotel?"

"Places where courting couples can go for some privacy. You can pay by the hour."

His eyebrows shot up. "Seriously? Do they have them in San Diego?"

"I can see what you're thinking, Hunter, and the answer is no way!"

He narrowed his eyes and then with a lascivious leer, leaned toward me. He ran his finger down my throat, over my t-shirt, between my breasts and all the way down to my stomach.

"You sure about that?"

My eyelids fluttered. I couldn't remember what my reasoning was.

Suddenly he swore. "Fuck!"

A police officer was walking toward us.

He tapped on my window and I rolled it down. If he'd been two minutes earlier ... I really didn't want to think about that.

"May I see your license, please, ma'am?"

He was stocky, in his fifties, and had a weathered face that was not unkind.

"Yes! Yes, of course!"

I reached over to the back seat to grab my purse. I felt a little shaky, Sebastian just looked pissed.

The officer glanced at my ID and then over at Sebastian. "You from the Base, too, son?"

"Yes, sir."

"Hmm, well. This is private property. So you and *Mrs. Wilson* should find somewhere else to ... park."

"Yes, sir. We'll do that. Thank you, sir."

The officer handed me back my license and watched while we buckled ourselves in and I drove off.

Sebastian blew out a long gust of air and grinned at me.

"That was *so* embarrassing," I whined.

He laughed and shook his head. "It was worth it."

"Where should we go now?" I said, still feeling grumpy.

"Somewhere we can get some food."

"You're hungry *again?*"

He gave me a wicked smile. "Sure! It must be all the ... exercise."

I slapped his leg. "You are a bad influence!"

"Yeah, baby, but you love it."

I couldn't argue with that.

I drove us back to the I-5 and then took a turning toward Mission Beach, heading north up the coast road until Sebastian told me to pull over.

"There's a place here we can get some food," he said, quietly. "This cove is real pretty—we could just sit and chill for a while."

"Sounds great," I said smiling at him. "Although I'm more thirsty than hungry."

"You should eat something," he said seriously.

I just adored the way he tried to look after me—so, so sweet.

"Okay, I'll have a sandwich. Anything, whatever they've got."

I wandered down the steps to the small cove and cautiously laid out the picnic blanket as near to the concrete steps as possible, without being so close that people would actually trip over me.

It was soothing being by the ocean. I imagined how blissful it would be to hear the sound of the waves rolling in until they were as familiar as breathing. I felt so full of hope for the future—I hadn't even realized it had been missing from my life until Sebastian had opened my eyes.

I didn't need to turn around to recognize his quiet footsteps coming down behind me. He had a bottle of water and a can of Coke in one hand, and two packages of sandwiches in the other. He flopped down next to me with a grin and kissed my shoulder.

"Tuna or BLT?"

"Tuna, please."

He handed me the package and I took a huge bite. It was freshly made and very good.

"Hungry?" he said, raising an eyebrow.

"Must be all the exercise," I said, glaring back with my mouth full.

He laughed and unwrapped his own sandwich.

He finished before me, of course, and pulled off his t-shirt to lean back on his elbows and soak up the sun. His smooth skin gleamed in the sunlight, utterly distracting me from finishing my sandwich. I ran my eyes over his flat stomach and muscled chest and decided I'd much rather eat him.

I laid the remains of the sandwich to one side and pushed him down onto the picnic blanket.

His eyes flashed open in surprise and then he let out a long sigh as I kissed his chest and teased his nipples with my tongue. Mmm. He tasted way better than any sandwich, no matter how freshly made.

I stroked the flesh just below his waistband, running my fingers along the edge of the denim, knowing that he was primed and ready for action. He groaned.

"Caro, what are you doing to me?"

"Saying thank you for the sandwich," I murmured against his stomach.

"You're driving me crazy! How am I supposed to think about anything when you've got me like this?"

He gestured weakly toward his zipper.

"That's the point," I said, smiling against his chest. "You're not supposed to think about anything."

"It's working," he muttered, then ran his hands down my back, pulling me closer.

I wanted him very badly and I only had myself to blame. I wondered briefly if the storage closet at the country club's locker room had a 'vacancy' sign on it. But he had work to do and I had room-shares to check out.

I ended our mutual torture, planting a loud kiss on his belly button, then snuggled into his shoulder, resting my head on his chest.

"When did you get to be such a bad girl?" he asked, stroking my hair.

"Oddly enough, around the time I met you," I said, digging my fingers into the ticklish spot around his waist.

"Okay, okay! I give in! Jeez, you play rough."

"I got the distinct impression you like it rough," I said, leaning up to look at him.

His anxious look was back immediately. "Oh, God, I'm sorry, Caro! I didn't hurt you, did I?"

"Of course not! And believe me, I enjoyed our illicit car sex just as much as you."

"You're sure?"

"Yes! How many orgasms do I have to have for you to believe me?"

He smiled and looked smug. "Five is the record."

"What?! You've been counting?"

He shrugged and looked a little embarrassed, as if he'd been caught out in a naughty secret, which he had.

"Can't help it—it's a guy thing."

"You ... you haven't said anything to Ches, have you? Because if you have I wouldn't be able to look at him..."

"Of course not!" He sounded angry. "I would never say anything to anyone about us. Ches knows as much as he needs to."

"Has he said anything else?"

Sebastian sighed. "He's worried, I guess, but he won't tell anyone."

I decided to let it drop. If he trusted Ches, well ... there was nothing I could do about it one way or another.

"By the way, did Brenda find you again yesterday?"

He scowled. "That stupid bitch nearly got me fired."

While I wasn't sorry that Brenda was annoying him, I was shocked to hear him talk about his ex-girlfriend like that.

"Did she ... um ... try again after I left?"

He sighed. "Kind of, but..."

"But what?"

"I told her I was seeing someone and that there was no way I was getting back with her after..."

Now he had my complete and undivided attention.

"After what?"

"Nothing," he mumbled.

I bit my tongue, determined not to press him if he didn't want to talk. But, wonder of wonders, my silence seemed to have the opposite effect.

"Ches told me some stuff ... after I broke up with Brenda, she started hanging out with some of the guys we used to surf with. She was ... partying a lot."

"Oh."

From the expression on his face I guessed that was a euphemism for sleeping around. I could see Sebastian wasn't impressed with that.

I sighed to myself. Men were so good at double standards—here he was, having an affair with a married woman, and he was dismissing his ex-girlfriend because she'd slept with other people *after* they'd split up. I knew he didn't think of what we had as an affair, but that was just his insider view, and if he'd have asked Ches to tell it like it was, that's exactly what his friend would have said.

I felt almost sorry for Brenda. Almost.

"You know, I just don't see you two together. Was she always so ... pneumatic?"

"Pneumatic?!"

He smirked then a shadow crossed over his face.

"Not always. I mean, she could be pretty full on—she liked being the center of attention, Homecoming Queen, all that kinda shit. It wasn't really my scene—it was one of the things we used to argue about. But she could be really sweet and fun, too."

It was my own fault for asking, but I really didn't want to hear her described that way. My sympathy for her took an early bath.

"What happened?" It was none of my business but now I *really* wanted to know. "Why did she change?"

He shrugged and lay on his back, folding his hands under his head.

"Some of her friends were sleeping with their boyfriends and she thought we should, too. I just thought it was lame to do it just because her friends were."

"And you were never tempted?"

"Yes and no. I thought about it a lot..." Then he smiled. "Not as much as I think about having sex with you, but yeah, I thought about it. We got close a couple of times. I'd pretty much made up mind I was going to..."

"Hence practicing with the condom?"

He reddened and didn't reply.

"So what stopped you?"

"Ches told me he'd seen her making out with some other guy. He wouldn't tell me who so I figured it was probably someone I knew ... I thought maybe Jack ... she denied it—at first, then blamed it on having too much to drink. But that just finished it for me. I thought ... I thought I must be something special if she wanted to ... with me, but ... I guess not."

I leaned over and kissed him gently on the lips.

"Well, I think you're *very* special, and Brenda's loss is my gain. Although, I'm surprised she thought you'd take her back after that."

He smiled. "She said she didn't believe I was seeing anyone—that I was just making it up to get back at her."

"Well, hopefully she'll go on thinking that."

He frowned. "Why?"

"Because as long as she's thinking that, then she's not suspecting me. I mean, let's face it, you couldn't have been more damned obvious yesterday!"

He looked hurt. "I hardly even spoke to you!"

"Sebastian, you were staring at me the whole time. Even when she heaved up her enormous tits in her bikini top, you didn't look at her. She must have thought you'd gone blind."

"Enormous tits!" He laughed loudly. "Yeah, I guess they are kind of hard to miss. But I prefer yours."

"I thought all men liked women with big breasts?"

He nuzzled my hair. "I'm more of an ass man," and he ran his hands over my backside, squeezing gently, to emphasize his point.

"Well, I'm glad to hear it, because I definitely can't compete with her on ... chest volume."

He chuckled quietly and continued stroking my back as I snuggled closer.

Then his hands stilled and he seemed deep in thought.

"I was wondering," he said softly, "can I ask you something ... about you and David."

Uh oh.

"What were you wondering?"

"How you got together in the first place. You don't seem to have much in common."

Or, in fact, anything at all.

"He was stationed at the Base near where I lived. I'd gone to the drugstore to pick up something for my mom and he drove up in this cute little sports car—a Corvette—electric blue. He was in uniform and he just came up and started talking. I couldn't believe he was interested in me—sophisticated older man."

I rolled my eyes.

"I just saw what I wanted to see—and I was desperate to leave home."

He nodded. "I totally get that."

"I was in my senior year, so ... when he proposed, I said yes."

"Did ... did you love him?"

"I convinced myself I did—at first. But I soon realized I'd made a mistake. I just didn't have anywhere to go back to. Mom made it pretty clear I'd made my bed, and Papa—he just did as he was told. Besides, I got to travel some."

He was silent for a moment but I could tell he still had more questions. Eventually he cleared his throat and tried to sound casual.

"When did you and ... him first ... um...?"

"First have sex?"

"Well, yeah."

He had a right to know—he'd told me all about Brenda.

"It was a week before my eighteenth birthday. There'd been some event up at the Base—my first big formal. I'd loved all the dressing up—it seemed so glamorous to me." I took a deep breath. "We did it on the passenger seat of his car. It was ... unpleasant. It hurt."

"Have you...?" He bit his lip, unable to finish the question.

"Have I what?"

"I know I have no right to ask, Caro, but since ... since me and you ... have you ... slept ... with him?"

I could tell this was a question he'd wanted to ask me for a while.

"No, *tesoro*. I haven't let him touch me since our first night together."

I didn't think he needed to hear that I'd jerked David off instead.

"Sorry."

"Don't be sorry, *tesoro*. It's only since I've met you that I've known what it's like to make love, *really* make love."

And I kissed him, desperately, passionately, to show him that I meant every word. He held me to him, our mouths locked together, breathing each other in.

"Don't go back to him tonight, Caro, please."

"I have to, Sebastian. After I drop you off at the club, I'm going to check out those rooms. I'm sure one of them will do. I'll put down a deposit and move my stuff in tomorrow. Then, when I have somewhere to go, I'll tell him that I want a divorce—tomorrow evening. I'll be able to go straight away."

"I don't like leaving you with that asshole! You don't know what he'll do! He could hurt you again!"

Sebastian's body filled with tension and his hands were balled into fists at his sides.

"He won't hurt me. Yesterday evening was an accident. Yes, he's a bastard, but he's not like *that*."

It was clear that he didn't believe me. Perhaps he needed David to be as big a bastard as his father.

"I can come over tomorrow morning and help you pack," he offered, rubbing his eyes with his knuckles.

"There won't be much—just my clothes and a few bits and pieces."

"I want to help."

"It's probably best if I do it myself after he's gone to work tomorrow. I'll meet you after I've moved into the new place."

He scowled, unhappy with my plan.

"Sebastian, I have to do this by myself. It's my mess—I don't want you anywhere near him."

"If he lays one finger on you, I'll fucking crucify him!"

"He won't. I promise. I'll be fine." I glanced at my watch. "Look, we should go now. You have to be at work in half an hour."

"I mean it, Caro, I'll rip his fucking arms off!"

I didn't think there was any point replying so I picked up my empty bottle and Sebastian's can and shoved them in my purse, and waited for him to get off the picnic blanket so I could fold it.

He stood up and pulled his t-shirt on but his expression was still angry.

"Hey, come here!"

I dropped my bag on the floor and wrapped my arms around him, willing his tension and anger away.

"We've just got one more day to get through and then I'll be free of him. One more day, *tesoro*. Just one more day. We can do it."

After that we walked back to the car in silence but I could tell his mind was still mulling over everything I'd told him. I hoped it would be busy at the club to help distract him.

As I drove, my right foot started to feel very sore. I glanced down and noticed that the dressing was wet. Damn. The blister must have burst. I really needed to re-do it before I started traipsing around the city or it would be a lot worse. I decided to ask at the club's reception to see if they'd let me use their First Aid Kit, once I'd dropped Sebastian at the parking lot. I really didn't want to give him another reason to imagine doing violence to David.

"Can I see you tonight?" he said, his eyes already knowing my answer.

"No, I need to pack and sort out a few things. I'll text you tomorrow when ... I've moved."

He sighed and got out of the car, then stood, waiting for me to leave.

"I ... have to go and check up on something in reception," I said. "I'll text you later."

"Promise?"

"Yes, I promise."

He walked away, his hands jammed in his pockets. I could tell he felt miserable from the set of his shoulders—and because I felt exactly the same way.

I waited for him to disappear out of sight, then headed to reception where I explained my predicament.

"Of course, ma'am," said the helpful receptionist. "I'll just send for one of our first aiders."

"Oh, that's not necessary, I can do it myself."

"Sorry, ma'am," she said, not sounding at all sorry. "I have to call it in."

She made a call and a few moments later Ches came striding over, a look of surprise on his face when he saw me.

"Hi, Caroline. How are you?"

"Good thanks, Ches. You?"

"I got a call that someone needed first aid?"

"Yes, this lady here needs some help," said the receptionist, obviously having one ear tuned to our conversation.

"It's nothing, really," I said hastily.

"I'll take Mrs. Wilson to the med room, Nancy," said Ches, to the receptionist.

She nodded and returned to her computer screen, having already lost interest.

Reluctantly, I followed him. If I'd known what a fuss was going to be made, I'd have waited until I could have gotten to a pharmacy in town.

It felt awkward being alone in the small room with Ches. He looked uncomfortable, too, shifting around from foot to foot. Maybe he thought I was going to leap on him.

"I just need to change a dressing on my foot," I said quietly. "Do you have some gauze and tape?"

"Sure. You want me to do that?"

"No, that's fine, thank you, Ches. I'll be fine."

I sat down on the low hospital bed and rolled up my pants leg to my ankle, then tugged gently on the gauze. It was stuck fast. I was going to have to yank it off—and it was going to hurt.

I took a deep breath and pulled hard—a huge flap of skin came away with the gauze. My foot looked like raw meat.

"Wow! That looks bad," said Ches, his eyes anxious. "I think maybe a doctor should see that."

Then he blushed, remembering that I was married to a doctor.

We heard voices outside and Sebastian burst in, a worried looking Nancy hot on his heels.

"Caro! Are you okay?"

Damn it! Hadn't he listened when I'd told him to be more discreet?

"I'm fine, thank you," I said as calmly as possible. "Ches is looking after me."

Perhaps noting my chilly reception, or Ches's panicked look, Sebastian took the hint and closed the door in the face of the nosey Nancy.

"Dude, that looks pretty bad to me," Ches said quietly to Sebastian, pointing at my foot.

"I'm fine," I repeated, not at all happy to be the subject of their combined attention. It was like being a particularly ugly zoo exhibit.

"What happened?" said Ches.

"Just a silly accident."

"It wasn't an accident," snarled Sebastian. "Her bastard husband did that to her. Show him the rest of your burns!"

He yanked up my pants leg and Ches's eyes scrunched up in horror.

"It was an accident," I whispered again, pushing his hands away.

I couldn't take the pity I saw on Ches's face and the anger on Sebastian's.

To the accompaniment of their silent stares, I cleaned the wound with some saline, applied a thick layer of antibiotic cream and covered it up again. Sebastian's eyes watched every move I made. Ches was desperately ill at ease, I decided to help him out—and reduce the excess of tension in the room.

"Ches, could you give us a moment, please?"

"Sure, sure. Seb, I'll see you later, man."

Sebastian nodded but didn't look at Ches as he ducked out of the room.

"I want to kill him!" he said between gritted teeth.

"Sebastian, please don't."

"Don't what?" he snarled.

"Make things harder for me."

He blinked, his expression changing from fury to hurt.

"How am I making things harder? I just want to help. I love you!"

"I know that, but right now what I need is for you to be calm and in control. If you keep charging in on your white horse to save me, people will start to notice." *If they haven't already.* "And the last thing, the *last* thing I need right now is for *anyone* to see you treating me as anything other than just another member here. Do you understand?"

"Of course I understand—I'm not a fucking idiot!"

"Good. Then please tell me why you're here, making a scene in front of that receptionist, when Ches was looking after me?"

Every emotion was transparent as it scrolled across his face: surprise, anger, hurt—again—and then understanding and shame.

"I'm sorry. It's just ... I go a little a crazy when I think you're hurt."

"I know, *tesoro*. I understand, but can you see how that makes things harder for me?"

"Yeah, I get it. Sorry."

"Okay. Then just hold me."

He pulled our bodies together and we stood in silence, feeling the tension ebb and flow.

"Okay?" I asked, stroking his cheek.

He took a deep breath. "Yeah, I'm fine."

He didn't look fine: he looked stressed out and worried.

"Okay. I'll text you later—hopefully to tell you that I've found a room."

He forced a smile.

"Stay out of trouble till then?" I said, softly.

"I'll try," he said, forcing a grin, "but I'm not making any promises."

I kissed him gently and walked back through the lobby, avoiding the over-curious eyes of Nancy.

I was so distracted that I narrowly avoided colliding with Brenda as she sashayed through the main doors.

"Hi, Barbara!" I called cheerfully as I walked down the steps.

"It's *Brenda!*" she snarled.

It really is the little things in life that matter.

CHAPTER SEVENTEEN

THE FIRST ROOM TO RENT WAS A SHITHOLE THAT I WOULDN'T EVEN HAVE LET David sleep in. Well, probably not.

Apart from the fact that the landlord answered the door in a knit undershirt that looked like it had last month's breakfast down it, and talked to my cleavage rather than my face, the room he showed me smelled of cabbage and cat wee, and the carpet was tacky under my shoes. I didn't even want to think about the stains on the bare mattress that was introduced to me as the bed but in fact was nearer to something that had been plucked from a landfill site sometime during the last year.

The second room in a hip part of downtown was perfect—small but clean, in a house shared with two mature law students, Phyl and Beth. I put down a $60 retainer and drove away two parts happy, promising I'd be back tomorrow.

They hadn't probed too hard into why I was looking for a room, but they were bright women and I was sure they'd put two and two together during our brief conversation.

When I got home (and I wouldn't be using that word for much longer), I was surprised to see that David had been back—the evidence being dishes in the sink and a full basket of his dirty clothes next to the washing machine. He'd obviously waited until I'd gone out to make a stealthy return. That made two of us then. Two cowards locked in a loveless marriage.

But not for much longer.

I ignored the laundry, faintly amused to think he'd have to learn how to clean his own damn clothes, or continue living in some hotel, as I guessed he must be doing.

I filled my suitcase with all the clothes I could squeeze into it and shoved everything else into black garbage bags. What I removed from the house made almost no difference—it was only if David looked in my closet that he'd notice any major changes. That my 11 years with David had made such a small indentation was a sobering thought. I hadn't been a bad wife, but I hadn't been a companion to him either. Although it seemed doubtful that he'd ever wanted one. Still, it was a lonely way to live—for both of us.

Six o'clock came and went—still no sign of David. I wasn't quite sure how I was going to tell him I was leaving him if he wasn't even around himself: leave a note, send a text message, call his office, or even ... drop by in person? None of them seemed particularly palatable. When I'd imagined telling him, I'd always assumed it would be in the privacy of our own front room.

Just after 10PM I got a text from Sebastian.

How's it going? Did u get a room? Is the a$$hole there?

I knew if I told Sebastian that David was AWOL, he'd want to come over. But without knowing where David was, or his intentions, it was risky. The smart thing was to wait another 24 hours. But being smart and being in love, well, that was oil and water.

By myself. Can Ches drop you downtown? Need to get out of here.

He replied immediately, as I knew he would.

30 mins, jazz plaza. r u ok?

I didn't know how to reply so I just sent a quick text agreeing to meet him where we'd seen the jazz band earlier in the day.

The city felt very different at night. Once the sun had disappeared the laidback aura was tinged with a frisson of excitement, and an intangible air of possibilities. I was so close to being free, so close to restarting my life—it was a heady feeling. I was dizzy with unaccustomed recklessness—and I was going to see Sebastian.

We had three more months before we could escape to New York—it was going to be a time of austerity, not that I cared about that, but I thought we deserved one night to really celebrate. So when I found myself outside a low- to medium-priced hotel, I hesitated less than the length of a heartbeat, reserved a room, paid cash and put the keycard in my purse with a sense of abandonment.

My impulsive decision made me slightly late getting to the plaza. My phone started ringing just as I spotted him scanning the crowds and running a hand through his hair.

I watched him from a distance, enjoying that moment of seeing before touching. Dressed simply in washed-out denim and a plain, black t-shirt that emphasized his strong, slim build, he was a still point of light, surrounded by the swirling crowds.

"Hi!" I said into my cell phone.

"Where are you?" he said, sounding worried.

"On my way," I said, softly as I snuck up behind him and ran my hand over his toned ass.

He jumped and turned around with a scowl on his face which broke into a huge, sexy smile when he saw me.

"I have to go now," he breathed into the phone, "a beautiful woman is feeling me up."

"Is that right?"

Hidden by the crowd I ran my hand up the front of his jeans.

"Yeah," he said into his cell phone, "I don't know what she wants."

"She hasn't given you a clue?" I asked, rubbing my hand over him again and feeling his body respond.

"I think I'll have to call you back," he said, and snapped his phone shut.

We stood staring at each other as I slowly lowered my cell phone.

He took a pace forward so our bodies were nearly touching then he ran his hands lightly over my arms and rested his mouth on mine. I felt his warm breath wash over my face and his lips parted.

It was hard to remember we were in a public place as he deepened the kiss, his tongue sweeping into my mouth. Tasting him, touching him, losing myself in him—the world fell away. Eventually I pulled back, aware that there was a time and a place—and tonight we had both.

"God, Caro!" he whispered and closed his eyes, just holding me to his chest.

"Come on," I said, after a long moment, "let's go for a walk."

He frowned, looking puzzled. "Are you okay?"

"Sure, why?"

He shrugged. "I just wasn't expecting to see you tonight. I mean, I'm glad you're here, but..."

"Well, I have everything packed up in my car. I ... I just need to tell David. I was going to do it in the morning, but, well, he didn't come home. And I wanted to see you."

"Good," he said happily.

I smiled up at him.

"Are you hungry or is that a dumb question?"

He laughed. "Yeah, I could definitely eat something."

"Let's head to Little Italy."

"Yeah! We can pretend we've got that motorcycle and we're on our road trip!"

We didn't get quite that far before we found a small Sicilian café serving *couscous al pesce*, one of my favorite dishes—I was finding it hard to walk on by.

"I don't know, Caro," said Sebastian, scanning the menu hanging up outside, "it's not that cheap."

"I know it's not, but tonight I don't care—tonight I start my life over. Thanks to you."

He smiled down at me and his eyes glowed with love.

"Really?"

"Truly. We're celebrating ... and I have another surprise. But that's for later."

I tried to tug him into the café but he resisted. "Tell me!" he said his voice suddenly husky.

I shook my head and smiled. "No, it wouldn't be a surprise if I told you."

"Caro, you're driving me nuts! Please!"

"Well, okay, as I don't want to be the cause of your insanity ... I've reserved a hotel for us."

His breath hitched in his throat and his eyes widened. "A hotel?"

I nodded and had to swallow when I saw his expression change from love to lust.

"Let's go now," he said, pulling on my hand.

"No, I want to eat—and you said yourself that you're starving."

"We'll get take-out!" he growled, tugging me down the street.

I planted my feet and tugged back. "Sebastian, no!"

He stopped, staring at me in hurt surprise.

"Why not?"

I couldn't help but smile at the expression on his face, but my voice was serious. I'd spent quite a while thinking about this.

"Because after tonight we won't be able to afford to do this again for a while, and for tonight, at least, I don't want to hide. I just want to have a nice meal in a nice café ... I just want to have ... a date. With you."

He grinned. "A date? Yeah, I'd like that. With sex after?"

I laughed. "Oh, yes. *A lot* of sex after."

We sat at a table in the window and the elderly waiter lit a candle and stuck it in an old wine bottle encrusted with wax.

I spoke to him politely in Italian and he smiled hugely.

His accent was very strong and he explained he was from Trapani on the toe of Sicily. I could tell Sebastian was finding it hard to follow the conversation so I switched to English.

"We hope to visit Sicily one day soon," I said, throwing a quick glance at Sebastian who grinned back.

"Ah, then you must visit my home town and wish her well for me," said the old man, "and you will weep before the beauty of our Madonna di Trapani."

He wandered away, happily chattering to himself, as he reminisced about his home town. I smiled at Sebastian as he held my hand across the table, but then his eyes widened in shock.

"You took off your rings," he whispered.

I nodded silently.

It was true: earlier, while I was pacing around the house, I happened to glance down at my hand and saw the rings—I mean really saw them, and everything they stood for. I slipped off my engagement ring, three small diamonds in a channel setting, and then took off the plain, gold wedding band. I held them in my hand, wondering what to do with them. I considered leaving them on the kitchen table, or on the cabinet next to David's side of the bed, but in the end, I dropped them into my change purse.

My hand felt so light without my wedding rings, it was as if it could float away, but Sebastian held my left hand to his cheek and closed his eyes. When he opened them again, his eyes glistened with unshed tears.

"You're really leaving him," he said and I wasn't sure if it was a statement or a question.

"Yes. You didn't think I would?"

He looked ashamed. "I did and I didn't. I kept hoping but ... I knew how much you'd be giving up. And ... and I knew I couldn't offer you anything..."

I held up my hand to stop him.

"That's not true, Sebastian. You've already given me so much—you just don't realize it."

He shook his head impatiently. "Don't try to make me feel better because..."

I interrupted him again. "I'm not! You've given me back my self-esteem and you've given me hope for the future. You've given me love. You've given me yourself. There's nothing else I want."

He reached across the table and held his hand against my face. I leaned into him and closed my eyes.

"I love you," he said.

The waiter interrupted us with a polite cough, a smile and a wink at Sebastian who grinned back.

Sebastian refused to order *antipasti* and I couldn't tell if it was because he was anxious about the cost or because he wanted to get back to the hotel as quickly as possible. Either way, I couldn't persuade him to change his mind so I had to abandon my thoughts of *caponata* and ordered the couscous for *secondi* with half a carafe of the house red.

I didn't mind. He wasn't the only one who was thinking about a king-size hotel bed with crisp, white sheets and a double shower. Hmm, sheets I wasn't going to have to wash—what a treat. Hmm, soapy, wet Sebastian in a double shower. Wait! Wasn't there a large bath, too, or did I just dream that? Damn! I couldn't remember. That was really going to bug me.

"What's the matter? You look kinda pissed," he said, worriedly. "I don't mind if you have a starter."

I looked up, confused, then I smiled at him.

"No, that's fine—I was just trying to remember whether or not there was a bath in the room."

"That's what you were thinking about?"

For a second he looked slightly shocked then a wicked grin lit up his face.

"Cool!"

I was distracted momentarily when I caught sight of someone turning away from the window, a glimpse of long blonde hair...

"What were you thinking of doing if there is a bath?"

I raised an eyebrow. "Well, I thought I'd start with getting really dirty. And then getting really clean."

He swallowed and blinked several times. "How dirty?"

Now he had me on the back foot because I really didn't know. David was nothing if not traditional. It was only over the last few weeks with Sebastian that I'd begun to explore the possibilities of pleasure.

I looked directly at him. "Let's find out together."

His answering smile was glorious.

The waiter arrived with our half carafe and poured a glass for each of us. I could see Sebastian was taken aback and then I remembered his age. How ridiculous that I could forget it, given the unusual circumstances of our relationship. Clearly the waiter was quite prepared to believe that Sebastian was over 21—he hadn't even given us a second glance. It made me feel—hopeful.

Sebastian picked up his wineglass and ran his finger around the rim. For a second I imagined him dressed in a black tux and white shirt, sitting in a private box at La Scala. I picked up my glass and angled it toward him.

"Salute!"

He smiled and clinked his glass against mine, "To us."

A much better toast.

I leaned across the table toward him and whispered conspiratorially, "Of course, you're too young to drink that legally."

He smiled and took a long sip.

"I'm too young to do a lot of things," he said, then dipped his finger into his wine and held it toward me.

I took his finger in my mouth and bit it gently then sucked hard.

A hiss escaped him and he closed his eyes. When he opened them again the black of his pupils had eclipsed the sea-blue irises.

I shivered, releasing his finger.

He smiled, a slow, sexy, seductive twist of his lips. I wanted to run my tongue over those lips, feeling their softness, their fullness, their wetness when he parted them. I imagined letting my tongue taste every inch of his firm, taut body, drinking in his scent and tasting the salt on his skin.

He hadn't taken his eyes off me and I'm sure mine revealed each and every thought. He licked his lips and swallowed.

The waiter broke the spell by discreetly placing our dishes in front of us and ignoring our heated gaze. Perhaps it was something he saw all the time although if he did, I couldn't imagine why the restaurant hadn't gone up in flames.

Sebastian leaned back in his chair and I took a deep breath.

"Is it always like this?" he said, suddenly looking lost and vulnerable.

I knew what he was asking me and I didn't have an answer. I shook my head. "Not for me ... not until now, until you."

What did I know of the kind of love that made it hard to breathe, where your body ached day and night for that connection with another, physically, mentally, spiritually? It was utterly new and terrifying and exhausting and wonderful. I was dazzled by the light that spilled from him into the shadow of my previous existence. He eclipsed everything, erased everything that had gone before. I was reborn—not just to him, but to myself. And I was ready for the adventure.

I took a deep breath and pointed with my chin toward his food.

"Eat: you'll need your energy."

Without breaking eye contact, he picked up his fork and lifted some pasta, holding it out toward me. "Want to taste it?"

I took the food in my mouth and felt the creamy sauce drip down my chin. Sebastian grinned and cleaned up the drip with his finger, putting it into his own mouth.

The rest of the meal went the same way, tasting each other's food, turning ourselves on, stoking the flames, with each new sensory assault. I wanted to crawl over the white tablecloth, tear off his shirt and take him where he sat. I imagined running my hands through his hair and thrusting my tongue into his mouth, clenching on his body when it was inside my own. I licked my lips.

He threw down his fork suddenly and rubbed his hands over his face.

"I can't concentrate on eating when you look at me like that!" he complained.

"Like what?" I said, feigning an innocence I most definitely wasn't feeling.

"Like *that!*"

Tauntingly, I pushed my fork into the couscous and carefully lifted it to my mouth, chewing with insolent slowness, as I kept my eyes on his face. Then I licked my lips and sucked the fork clean.

He made a sound deep within his throat that was halfway between a moan and a growl and my eyes opened wide.

"Caro, I mean it! If you do that again..."

His warning amused and aroused me. I wanted to know his limits—and I was curious about mine.

Again, I pushed my fork into the couscous, again I lifted it to my mouth and slowly sucked the fork clean, a challenging look on my face.

He slammed his chair backward, startling the waiter and the elderly couple who were sitting across the room from us drinking their after dinner Sambuca. He strode around the table and pinned me to the chair, one hand on each side of my seat and kissed me roughly, his frustration and ardor all poured into that one, spellbinding moment.

My hands reached up to his chest and fastened into his t-shirt. I didn't know if I was pulling him toward me or pushing him away. My whole body was flushed and heated.

I was dimly aware that the waiter was hovering over us and Sebastian stood up reluctantly.

"Ah, sir," the poor man said nervously, "we have other patrons, sir ... ah..."

"Wrap the food to go," Sebastian ordered.

"Certainly, sir," replied the waiter, gratefully scuttling away with our dishes.

"You're impatient tonight," I said, taking a much needed drink of wine.

He scowled at me. Jeez, even his anger turned me on.

"How the fuck can I eat a plate of carbonara when you're looking at me like that and I'm sitting there with a boner that's as hard as Mount Rushmore?"

I nearly spat my wine out and couldn't help laughing.

"Mount Rushmore?"

A reluctant smile made his lips twitch but I could tell he was still a little mad.

"Come on, then, let's go. You can finish your cold carbonara later." *Ugh.*

I paid for our abandoned meal with cash, disappointed that our date hadn't quite gone as planned, although it was my own damn fault. I should have realized that Sebastian wasn't the kind of man who played games. I didn't think of myself as that kind of woman either—I just hadn't realized that a little flirting with food would have such a gratifyingly immediate effect.

Once we'd left the relieved waiter behind and were strolling down the street, Sebastian draped his arm possessively around my shoulders, every now and then stooping to kiss my hair.

"Maybe I should just buy you energy bars next time and skip the whole dinner-date idea," I teased him. "I could tie you to the bed and feed you Gatorade."

He stopped so suddenly, I almost skidded past him. He turned and stared at me, then swallowed, his expression burning.

"What would you tie me up with?" he said, his voice full of unexplored longing.

I blushed beet red as he pulled me to his chest and stared down into my eyes.

"Stockings?" I whispered uncertainly.

He squeezed his eyes closed and tightened his grip on me almost painfully.

"And garter straps?" he choked out.

"If you like."

"In black?"

"*Tesoro*, for you I'll wear a different color for each day of the week."

He let out a low moan.

"Where's this fucking hotel?" he muttered, then towed me down the street at the quick march.

It took a moment to orientate myself and remember the direction for the hotel. Sebastian was so frustrated I was half expecting him to toss me over his shoulder and make a run for it. He was a man on a mission and he'd had as much foreplay as he could take.

When we reached the hotel, he yanked open the glass door and hauled me across the lobby while the bemused reception desk clerk blinked in surprise.

"Which floor?" he snarled, his fingers drumming impatiently next to the elevator's call button.

"Fourth," I stuttered, a little awed by his suddenly commanding behavior.

The doors slid open silently and I almost ran to the back, gripping the handrail, certain I needed something to hold on to. Sebastian took one step inside and let the doors close an inch behind him. He glanced over the buttons and stabbed number four with his finger.

My heart rate spiked as he stared at me, a hungry, desperate, utterly focused look on his face. I licked my lips but my mouth was suddenly dry.

I struggled to think of something to say but my mind was blank, totally without thought—just a raging need to consume.

The elevator started to rise and Sebastian took a pace toward me. Then another. And another. Until he was standing in front of me but still our bodies weren't touching. Then he reached out and placed one hand above my left shoulder, and his other above my right. I was trapped between his arms. And *still* he didn't touch me. He leaned forward and I held my breath. Then slowly, deliberately he nuzzled my hair out of the way and ran his tongue up the side of my neck.

I could feel his warm breath on my cheek, his wet tongue teasing my ear. I took another, deep lungful of air and breathed in his scent: some spicy soap, salt, and his own sweet smell.

Perhaps he was getting his own back for my distractions in the café or perhaps he was learning to take his time, I couldn't say.

I pushed my hands into the back pockets of his jeans and heard his breath catch in his throat. He let out a long sigh and let the full weight of his body rest on mine.

The doors hissed open, an almost welcome distraction.

He stood up straight and I pulled my hands out of his jeans' pockets, then he stepped back so I could exit the elevator first.

The corridor was silent and our feet sank into the plush carpet soundlessly.

The gilt sconce lights cast pale shadows on the patterned wallpaper, and twenty wooden doors stretched in each direction. It took me a moment to remember which way to turn. I fished in my purse and pulled out the keycard.

"It's room 429," I said, softly.

Wordlessly, Sebastian took it from me then led me by the hand down the corridor, his eyes glancing at the discreet numbers on each door.

Toward the end of the corridor, he stopped, pushed the keycard into the lock, and let the door swing open.

I'd left one small sidelight on and my overnight bag was still on the large bed.

I heard Sebastian turn the catch on the door, locking it behind us. When I turned around, he was standing watching me.

He kicked off his sneakers and tugged his t-shirt over his head as he padded toward me barefoot. I stood limply, frozen to the spot, mesmerized by his predatory gaze. When he reached me, he rested his hands on my arms and breathed in deeply, his fingers tightening around my biceps.

I laid my head on his chest and kissed him just above his heart. He sighed and wrapped his arms around my back. We stood there in silence, just holding each other.

Then I kissed his chest again, and ran my tongue across his torso, remembering that I'd wanted to taste every inch of him. I let my hands drift down, pushing them inside his jeans, beneath his briefs, stroking his skin and digging my fingers into the flesh of his buttocks. A soft sound escaped his lips and his hips pushed forward.

Still without speaking, I pulled my warmed hands free and stepped back, giving myself room to undo the button of his pants and pull down the zipper, opening his jeans and pushing them over his hips. I ran my hands lightly over his briefs and felt his body quiver, his erection evident beneath my gentle fingers. Carefully, I pushed the briefs down so he could step out of them.

He was beautifully, gloriously naked and I drank in his beauty and his strength as he stood before me, unembarrassed, eyes soft with love.

"You are my world, Caro," he said.

"And you're mine."

He smiled and pulled me into his arms then walked me slowly backward toward the bed.

I sat down and wrapped my arms behind his thighs, pulling him closer. I placed a soft, wet kiss on his tip and watched as his eyelids fluttered.

"Do you still want me to tie you up?"

He blinked several times then smiled again and shook his head.

"Not tonight. I want to be able to touch you—all of you."

He grabbed the hem of my t-shirt and gently pulled it over my head.

"You're so beautiful."

He kneeled in front of me, resting his hands on my hips. He leaned forward to kiss my breasts, playful little nips, and then his tongue was washing over me, laving my cleavage. I arched my back, letting my head hang backward and suddenly his hands were urgent. He pushed me onto the bed and leaned over me, his mouth, breath, tongue, hot against my skin. He groaned loudly then stood up. I struggled to sit but he slid one arm under my knees and the other behind my back, picked me up bodily and slung me higher up the bed. I was so surprised, the breath whooshed out of my lungs. He stretched out alongside then reared up to hover over me, his erection pointing confidently toward my belly. Before I could reach out for him, he knelt across me, lifted me up with one hand and with the other expertly unhooked my bra. *Jeez! Had he been practicing?*

I knew what was coming next but before he could reach for my pants, I pushed him away and rolled onto my side, struggling to turn off the bedside lamp. The curtains were still open but the dull, orange illumination of the streetlamps was the only light.

"What are you doing?"

His tone was surprised.

I had my reasons. The marks on my legs were no longer painful, with the exception of my right foot that throbbed relentlessly, but they were unsightly. And I didn't want him distracted, not by that. I had other distractions in mind.

I shimmied out of my pants and panties while he watched me, and tossed them randomly, not caring where they landed.

I could see his silvery gold outline on the bed next to me as my eyes adjusted to the dim light. I sat up and found that my skin was too tender to kneel across him. Instead I seated myself in his lap and stretched my legs out in front of me.

"Sit up," I said, my voice high from tension.

I wrapped one hand around his neck as he raised himself off the bed, and then held his length in my hand to position myself over him. I stroked him several times and he took a deep, faltering breath. As I sank down onto him, he groaned and I felt him tremble.

It was an extraordinarily intimate moment as our bodies joined together, our faces just inches apart.

His eyes were wide and wondering and I pulled his head toward me, breathing a soft kiss onto his lips. Then his mouth locked onto mine and our tongues moved in a new rhythm as our bodies thrust together. I pulled my knees up slightly and he did the same, almost lifting me off the bed with each powerful movement of his hips. He wrapped his arms behind me, pulling me still closer.

I needed to take a breath and Sebastian mirrored my actions. His eyes were fixed on mine and in a moment of utter stillness, I stroked his face, letting my fingers whisper across his cheek, his eyelids, along his soft eyebrows, down his nose, across the slight flare of his nostrils, along his jaw and fluttering across his lips, where he kissed them.

We were joined together as one, it was impossible to be closer, more intimate

—all the barriers between us were finally down. We were equal and open and unafraid.

I ran my hands down his back and felt him move inside me. I pulled back and leaned away from him, changing the angle of connection, and he groaned again and began to pump faster.

I clenched around him, unable to control the waves of sensation pulsing through me.

He called out and I felt him shudder into me with one, deep thrust. He gasped, pulling in lungfuls of air and then he gathered me to him, crushing me to his chest so hard I could barely breathe myself.

We sat like that, still joined together, and I felt a small giggle bubble up as I wiped a bead of sweat off my forehead.

"Who needs gym classes," I said, stroking his face.

He laughed softly. "You don't need anything, Caro, you're perfect."

"Oh, I'm far from perfect, but I'm very happy that you think I am. I'll have to keep you in a darkened room forever."

"Suits me."

"You might get hungry," I pointed out. "You'd starve to death."

"We'd order take-out," he said pragmatically.

I eased myself off him gently and lay back in his arms as he stroked my hair.

"Hey, did you check out the bath situation?" he said.

"Hmm, what? No. I was too busy checking you out."

He laughed. "Seriously! We could take a bath together."

"Oh, okay," I said, reluctant to move from my semi-comatose position. "If you go run it. See if they've put out any bubble bath."

He kissed me quickly and leapt off the bed. He had so much energy. I was exhausted already and I sensed it was going to be a long and wonderful night.

I heard the sounds of the faucet running as if from a great distance while I felt myself drifting asleep. But then a strange, unfamiliar sound reached my ears and suddenly, unexpectedly, I was wide awake: Sebastian was singing to himself. I strained to hear the words. When I did, my heart broke open, filling with the love that poured from those faint, heartfelt words. Peace and joy and a sense of wholeness that I'd never known utterly overwhelmed me and I began to cry softly.

> *When I hear her voice, the world disappears*
> *When I hear her voice, I have no more fears.*

I had never believed it was possible to cry from happiness.

Quietly, I slipped off the bed and moved silently to the bathroom door, standing half hidden, watching him. He was leaning over the tub, testing the water with his fingers, the steam weaving through the air like ghosts.

He'd switched on the light above the shaving mirror and the yellow glow bathed his skin with gold. I watched the ripple and play of his muscles as he continued to reach into the bath, drawing pictures with his fingers in the hot water.

> *She takes away the sadness, she takes away the pain*
> *She takes away the darkness, she takes away the rain.*

He stretched up to pull down two white towels, placing them carefully at the side of the bath.

> *When I'm traveling from so far away*
> *She's my path, she's my sun, she lights my way.*

Then he turned and saw me standing in the shadows.

"Caro! Why are you crying?"

"Because I love you."

CHAPTER EIGHTEEN

He stared at me, then one, long second later he strode toward me and took my face in his hands, kissing the tears as they trickled down my cheeks.

And there we were, two fools in love.

"I waited and waited and waited," he stammered. "You never said it ... you never told me ... and now you have. I love you I love you I love you. Oh, Caro, so much."

A sob escaped his throat and I felt ashamed of having held back for so long, not realizing how much he'd needed to hear me say the words.

I wrapped my arms around his waist as he took long, shuddering breaths. My own tears soon dried, overwhelmed as I was by my own happiness and my need to protect and comfort this beautiful man-child who had known so little love in his life.

Skin to skin, my head to his shoulder, we stood, drinking each other in. Finally his breathing slowed and he kissed the base of my neck. A smile lifted my lips and I opened my eyes.

"Sebastian, the water!"

The bath was nearly full and in danger of overflowing—like me.

"Oh, crap!"

He leaned down to turn off the stream of water and pulled out the plug to let some escape. He continued to stare into the water and I sensed he was using the time to compose himself.

When he looked up again, his focus was slightly to the left of my shoulder. He couldn't meet my eyes and the expression on his face was sheepish.

"Sorry for spazzing out on you."

I laid my hand on his cheek, forcing him to look at me.

"No, Sebastian! Don't *ever* be embarrassed about how you feel—not with me. Not ever. I love that you're so open with me, I love that you show me how you feel every moment of the day and night, it drives me crazy when you do it in front of other people but I love it, too, because it's part of who you are. I've never known anything like it and I don't want it to stop. Because I feel the same."

He gasped slightly then beamed at me.

"Okay," he said softly.

I smiled back and all the tension drained from the room leaving us calm and replete.

"Should we have a bath now?"

He nodded, then his forehead creased as he glanced at my right foot that was still swathed in thick gauze.

"Can you? You don't want to get that wet," he said, and his expression darkened to something quite intimidating.

"I'll hang it over the side," I said, trying to stop him from brooding on my injury, "but I'll need to lean on something: I had you in mind."

He smiled. "You think I'll make a good pillow?"

"Well, you're a little hard..."

He grinned at me salaciously, then looked down at his dick.

"Not at the moment, but I could be..."

"Can't you get your mind off sex for two minutes?!"

"Nope, don't think so."

I sighed, pretending to be annoyed, but it was hopeless—a huge smile cracked my face.

He grinned back and even as I looked at him, his dick twitched. It really did have a life of its own.

"Oh no! I'm not ready for round two yet! I want a nice, relaxing bath. I've used muscles that I didn't even know I had."

"Okay," he said, still smiling, "but it'll have to be a quick one."

"'Quick' and 'relaxing' aren't words that really go to together," I pointed out.

"Oh, I don't know—I can think of an occasion when they'd go together."

His eyes seemed to darken and I couldn't help it as my gaze dropped to below his waist, it was apparent that he wasn't just having a rush of blood to his head.

"Can I take a rain check?" I said, my voice a little shaky.

"Nope, don't think so," he repeated, pacing toward me.

"I want to take a bath."

"We will. Later."

I backed into the vanity unit and had nowhere else to go.

He caught me by my hips, pressing himself against me and nuzzled my neck.

"I really want to take a bath," I gasped, gripping onto his wrists.

"Mmm," he replied, as my body arched at his touch. "You're definitely not dirty enough yet."

I watched, speechless, if not completely soundless, as he slowly sank to his knees. His mouth followed the general downward direction and I swallowed hard.

His tongue traced around my left nipple then he bared his teeth and pulled against the heated flesh, tugging not very gently while his hands continued to knead my hips, his fingers digging into my ass. Then he turned his attention to my right breast, sucking and kissing and grazing it with his teeth.

My blood was thrumming through my veins and my knees began to tremble. Then his right hand slid down from hip to my calf, and started a slow ascent back up to my inner thigh. My breathing sounded loud and seemed to echo around the bathroom. The volume was almost embarrassing but it seemed to turn Sebastian on even more because he began to bite harder, making me shudder and call out. Then he began to rub me, gently at first and then harder, circling around and in and out.

He glanced up, giving me one quick look, a slight smile on his face, then his head disappeared between my thighs and I felt his tongue and fingers working me, playing with me, stroking me inside and out.

I thought my legs would buckle but then he hooked my right knee over his shoulder and pushed his tongue deeper inside me. I could barely stand on two legs, let alone one, I hung onto the vanity unit behind me for dear life.

I came loudly and had a brief glimpse of his grinning face before my eyes squeezed shut. He placed my right leg back on the floor and spun me around so I was facing the mirror. I was still quaking from my orgasm when he bent me over and pushed in from behind. He circled his hips, pulled out slowly and plunged in again. My face in the mirror was unrecognizable, my mouth hanging open, my eyes wide, my breasts seemed larger, the nipples flaring outwards, engorged, standing rigid. He pulled out again and sank in achingly slow, rolling his hips, massaging every part of me, all the way in and in. Just as the thought flashed across my mind, *He's learned to do slow*, he started moving hard and fast, increasing the pace as his breathing began to turn to gasps.

He reached around to the front of my legs and pressed hard, sending me plunging into the deep end where I couldn't even remember my own name. I think I actually passed out for half a second because when awareness trickled back, his arm was around my waist holding me up as my hands flapped limply by my sides. His hips pumped hard and he bit the back of my neck as he came.

We sank to the floor and I lay curled up on my side, grateful for the bathmat beneath my hip. Sebastian's chest was against my back and his knees flexed behind mine, his arm still around my waist.

Neither of us could speak for several minutes.

I felt lightheaded and flushed all over, superheated from the inside out.

"What is it with you and bathrooms?" I gasped.

I heard his quiet chuckle. "I think it's the mirrors—I fucking love watching your face when you come—I can see you from all angles. And I can see myself fucking you." I felt his shoulders shrug. "It turns me on."

I wasn't quite sure what to make of that. I realized we still had a lot to learn about each other—and I was so ready for that voyage of discovery.

I pressed my hand to my chest, feeling my heart rate beginning to return to normal.

I struggled to sit up—Sebastian was still lying on the floor, curled around me. I reached down to stroke his hair and a wicked sea-green eye blinked up at me.

"Can I have that bath now, please?" I said in my most persuasive voice.

I would have got up and crawled into the bath myself—except I didn't think I could stand.

Sebastian bit my ass-cheek making me yelp then he pulled himself to his feet.

"You'll have to help me up," I mumbled petulantly.

He grinned then bent to scoop me into his arms.

"Bed or bath?" he said, raising one eyebrow.

It was a tough choice but I was half afraid that if I said 'bed' it would mean more sex and I really needed a rest.

"Bath," I said, at last.

He grinned and carefully lowered me into the hot water, making sure that my right leg hung over the side, keeping the dressing on my foot dry.

It felt wonderful. Not that I needed to relax—my body was so limp I was nine-tenths unconscious already. Two orgasms in two minutes might have had something to do with it.

"Are you going to join me?"

"In a minute—I want to wash you first."

Slowly and methodically he soaped me all over using the small bar provided by the hotel, cupping his hands to rinse me off. No one had washed me like that since ... well, I guessed the last time must have been when I was a young child because I couldn't actually remember it ever happening.

His face was serious as if he was concentrating hard, revealing a small frown as his eyebrows pulled together. He moved my hair off my shoulders and massaged soap into my neck.

"Your eyelashes are really long," he said quietly.

I squinted up at him and waved my fingers indicating that he should come and join me, I was almost too tired to talk.

He smiled and helped me scoot forward so he could climb in behind me. The water lapped perilously close to the edge as he sank down.

I leaned back against him and he kissed the top of my head, letting his left arm rest on the ledge alongside the bath while the right wrapped around my shoulder and across my chest.

"This is nice," he said softly. "I could get used to this."

"We might not be able to afford an apartment with a bathtub *and* a shower in New York," I pointed out.

"I'll get an extra job to pay for it," he said casually. "It'll be worth it."

His optimism made me smile, it made me a little sad, too. I didn't think life was going to be as easy as he seemed to expect. We might be moving across the country but we'd be taking a whole heap of our problems with us. *No, time enough to think about that tomorrow.*

"What will we name our first child?" he said, in a dreamy, offbeat voice.

"Excuse me, what?!"

I was so shocked I jumped, causing a small tidal wave to cascade over the side of the bath. Sebastian didn't move, he just kissed my hair again.

"If it's a boy, we could call him Chester—Ches would get a kick out of that. Or maybe Chesney if it's a girl."

I struggled to sit up but he wouldn't let me go.

"What are you talking about?" I said, my voice rising about four octaves. "We can't have children!"

"Why not?" he said challengingly. "You said you wanted to have kids, so let's do it. We'll find a way."

My head was about to explode with the impossibility of what he was saying. We had nowhere to live, no jobs, no money, he'd only just got his high school diploma and was thinking about going back to study at college and *he was still only 17!* And then, that sneaky little voice in the back of my head said, *Why not? What are you waiting for? He's got all the time in the world but you haven't. You want to wait till you're middle-aged to be pregnant?*

His body had tensed up and I could tell he was waiting for my reaction. I tried to make light of the situation.

"Fine. But let's talk about it when you've got your degree. I'm not going to rob you of a chance to go to school. We can wait three years—we're not in *that* much of a hurry. Besides, we want to see Italy first, don't we?"

I felt his body relax again and he kissed my shoulder.

"Yeah, I wouldn't want to miss that. Okay, when I'm 21. That would be cool. Hey, do you like the name 'Orlando'? I went to school with a kid who was named that—he said it was after some character in a play."

I smiled.

"What's so funny?"

"You are. The name 'Orlando' is the Italian form of Roland. It's also used in Shakespeare's 'As You Like It'—but I always think of the book by Virginia Woolf."

"What's that about?"

"A time-traveling man who becomes a woman."

Sebastian was speechless for exactly three seconds—then he started laughing.

"You're kidding me! Seriously?"

Small waves started washing over the side of the tub as laughter rippled up through him.

"Sebastian! You're causing a flood!"

But he couldn't stop laughing. I twisted around to look at him, adding to the water spilling over the edge.

Tears were squeezing themselves from the corner of his eyes and there didn't seem to be much chance that he'd gain control of himself anytime soon. I shook my head, a smile pinned to my face. *Hopeless!*

I climbed out of the tub awkwardly. Sebastian made a half-hearted grab for me but was too weak from laughter and I slipped out of his grasp.

I picked up one of the towels he'd laid aside and started drying myself while he lay helpless in the now tepid water.

"Are you quite finished?" I said, raising one eyebrow, as his laughter turned to wheezing.

He grinned up at me then slid completely under the water and sat up quickly, rivers of bathwater pouring off his face.

He leapt out of the tub and tried to grab me again.

"Oh no! You're all wet, mister, and I only just got dry!"

I threw a towel at him which he caught before it hit his chest.

He made a few quick passes then tossed it on the floor where it started to soak up the spilled water.

The look on his face had me backing up into the bedroom.

"Sebastian! It's nearly 2AM. We have to be up in less than six hours."

"Plenty of time," he said, his voice a growl.

Unbelievable!

When I finally woke up Sebastian's heavy arm was pinning me to the bed and daylight was pouring into the room. I screwed up my eyes to see the time by my wristwatch. It was already 10AM: check-out time.

"Damn it!"

I pushed his arm off and sat up in alarm.

"Caro! What's wrong?"

He was awake immediately.

I threw myself back on the bed helplessly, angry with myself and frustrated at the lateness of the hour. No, I was angry with *him*. If he hadn't kept me up half the night—if he hadn't *been up* half the night—I wouldn't have slept in: not today.

"Caro!"

"I wanted to get home early," I grumbled.

He pulled me over to face him.

"Why? What's the big rush?"

"I just wanted to catch ... David ... before he went to work. Assuming he went home last night. Now I'll have to put off telling him *again* ... unless I go to the hospital. I guess I could do that."

Sebastian scowled.

"Why don't you just leave him a note? You don't owe that asshole anything."

I disagreed but I didn't want to get into a fight over it either.

"I guess I'll find him later," I said almost to myself.

"Can we talk about something else?" said Sebastian, mirroring my own thoughts.

I forced a smile.

"Sure. What do you want to talk about?"

"Well," he said, suggestively flexing his hips, "I woke up feeling horny and I have this beautiful woman in my bed..."

"Sebastian!" I whined.

But he was already burying his face in my chest and nuzzling my breasts.

"I have to pee!" I moaned.

"Later."

I guess that answered my question about whether he woke up every morning with a hard-on. There were definitely dangers to having an inquisitive mind.

Ten minutes later I had my head thrown back while Sebastian reared into me.

"Fuck!" he hissed, collapsing back onto the bed. "That was so intense! Jeez, Caro! You just about wrung me out there! What *was* that?"

"I told you I wanted to pee!"

He looked at me, utterly bemused.

"Yeah, and?"

"Well," I said blushing a little, "it makes the, um, orgasm more intense if you have to, you know ... don't look at me like that—I read it in *Cosmo*."

"Wow! Really? Have you got any more trade secrets?"

I slapped him on his chest and stomped off to the bathroom, listening to his laughter roll out behind me.

Damn him!

I insisted that we get dressed, fearing the hotel staff would come at any moment to throw us out, so I put an absolute ban on shower sex on the basis that: a) I'd probably slip and knock myself out or break something, especially as I had a plastic bag covering the gauze on my right foot, and b) I just couldn't take any more.

Sebastian had a full on pout, which made me laugh, and a full on erection, which didn't. But we found a suitable compromise that satisfied us both, although my knees were red and sore afterwards.

I turned over the room key to the clerk as we checked out, embarrassed to think of the state of the place and grateful that I wouldn't have to face whoever had to straighten it up.

I'd tried to tug the sheets into better order and mop up the worst of the spilled bathwater, but it still looked like a wild animal had been rampaging through the room, which, when I thought about it, rather summed up the way Sebastian had behaved all night.

I smiled, remembering the way our bodies moved together, the way his eyes told me he was mine and I was his, the love that my starved heart had craved for so long. The way love had turned to lust, and lust turned to need—raw and ready, sometimes soft, sometimes hard, sometimes gentle, sometimes rough. Our bodies coming together, melding as one, two pieces fitting together, over and over.

I remembered.

It was a beautiful day as we strolled out of the hotel, the early morning gloom was long gone and the heat of July was beginning to build. As usual, Sebastian was hungry and even though he'd eaten the cold carbonara and the remains of my couscous sometime between my fourth and fifth orgasms, he was ready for more food.

We grabbed coffee and rolls to-go and wandered along to my car feeling relaxed, if a little tired. Maybe that last bit was just me because Sebastian seemed to be fizzing with energy, talking happily about all the things he'd got planned for us in New York (going to baseball games seemed to figure rather more than I was expecting), but also walks through Central Park and, of course, checking out all the east coast beaches.

Here on the west coast, the surf was pumping and Sebastian gazed longingly at the barreling surf as we drove along the ocean road.

"Why don't you call Ches and see if he wants to catch some waves?" I suggested.

Sebastian's face brightened.

"Really? You don't mind?"

"No, go ahead. I'll meet up with you later. What time do you have to be at work?"

"I'm on four till ten again."

"Okay, well, I could pick you up after? We can go to my new place—you can meet my roommates."

"Sure, that would be great. You really don't mind?"

"Course not! Go have some fun."

And I had some business to take care of, too.

Sebastian picked up his cell.

"Battery's almost dead but I should have enough juice for one call." He scrolled down to find Ches's number and dialed. "Hey, man, what's up? No, I'm with Caro. We've just driven past Silver Strand and it's pumping. You wanna go take the boards out? No, she's cool." He grinned over at me. "We'll hook up later. Yeah, okay." Then he frowned. "What? No, we didn't yet. Yeah, okay, okay. See you in twenty.

He ended the call. "Ches says *City Beat* printed your article. I dunno, he sounded weird."

I'd forgotten about the article. It was rather irresponsible of me—after all, it was supposed to be my future source of income.

"I'll pick us up a copy on the way back. Where are you meeting Ches?"

I dropped him off on Seacoast Drive. Ches was leaning against his van waiting for us. I smiled and waved but stayed in the car. Things were still a little tense between me and Sebastian's best friend—I didn't want to push anything.

"I'll see you later, baby," said Sebastian kissing me hard.

I kissed him back and felt the now familiar electricity surge through me. I pushed Sebastian away and tried to calm my pulse rate.

"Fuck!" he breathed, closing his eyes. "I just can't get enough of you, Caro."

I smiled and shook my head to clear it.

"Go, before Ches drives off in disgust. I'll text you later."

He kissed me quickly and leapt out of the car, a huge grin on his face.

"And charge up your cell phone!" I called after him.

He waved and jogged over to Ches.

~

I stopped by a convenience store and picked up half a dozen copies of *City Beat*. As soon as I turned to my article I could see why Ches had acted a little weird. As well as six pictures of different events from the Base's fun day, there was a half-page photograph of me—with Bill's grinning face, his arms wrapped around my waist, and kissing my cheek. *Shit!*

That must have been one of the pictures Ches took when he was messing around with my camera. No wonder he was acting weird: *he damn well should!* Worse still, the way the photo was captioned made it look like Bill was my husband: 'The author, wife of Lieutenant Commander David Wilson'. *Double shit!*

Carl had known damn well that David hadn't been at the fun day. Was it a mistake, or was this his way at getting back at me for refusing to go for a drink with him?

I was getting paranoid. I was sure it was just an honest mistake, probably the sub-editor wrote the caption—nothing to do with Carl at all.

But an ominous feeling chilled me. I was about to leave David and, looking at this photograph, people would assume I was having an affair with Bill. But ... just maybe I could work this to my advantage—it would certainly deflect attention from Sebastian. Probably too well.

I drove home chewing on the inside of my mouth, deep in thought. I'd do one more check of the house to make sure there was nothing else I wanted and then I'd go find David at the hospital. That was the plan. It seemed callous to just leave a note although a large part of me would have preferred it. Come to think of it, maybe David would prefer that, too.

But when I got home, I was out of choices—David's car was parked in the driveway.

I sat in my car and took several deep breaths to calm myself. It didn't help in the slightest—my heart was still slamming against my ribs.

Pull yourself together, Venzi. You can do this.

My legs were shaking as I got out of the car. I dropped my key twice before I managed to open the front door.

David was sitting at the kitchen table as I walked in, his face tight with anger ... and a copy of *City Beat* laid out in front of him.

I felt like running.

"Hello, David."

My voice was so soft I could barely hear it myself.

"Would you care to explain this ... this nonsense, Caroline?"

His tone was clipped, his anger under control—for now.

I sat down at the table opposite him and tried to stay calm.

"I assume you're referring to the article, David, there's nothing in there that needs explaining."

His face was a dangerous shade of purple.

"And this ... *man* who seems to be draped all over you! Are you *trying* to make a fool of me?"

I took a deep breath.

"David, he's just a friend of the Peters. He was fooling around—the newspaper editor got the wrong idea, that's all. Look, this isn't important..."

"It most certainly is, I have a reputation at the hospital and..."

I interrupted him quietly but I was proud that my voice didn't tremble.

"No, David, it's not important. But we do need to talk. At least, I do have something to say to you."

"I can't think of anything more important than finding out why *my wife* is flaunting herself in this disgusting way ... and where she slept last night!"

"I might well ask you the same question, David, but I dare say we would both answer 'in a hotel'."

"Don't you fucking start that!"

I paled at the undisguised anger in his voice but I'd gone too far to turn back now.

"I want a divorce."

He stared at me in shock, his face draining of color as the words sank in.

"What? Are you crazy?"

You mean, crazy not to want a controlling bully like you?

"No, David. I'm not—just unhappy. I've been unhappy for a long time and ... I know I haven't made you happy either. I think it's best if we both just go our own way."

"Because of this ... this *ape!*" he snarled, jabbing his finger at the newspaper.

I sighed. The picture of me with Bill was an unnecessary distraction.

"No. I was telling the truth about him. He's just someone who happened to be there that day. I've only ever met him twice in my entire life. David, this is about us. Well, there is no 'us', there hasn't been for a long time—if there ever was. Look, I'm sorry this seems to have come out of the blue, but surely it can't have escaped your attention that our marriage has been over for a while now..."

He glared at me and gripped the table until his knuckles were completely bloodless.

"*Are you screwing this man?*"

I looked him in the eye—I was so grateful he'd asked *that* question. I wouldn't have to lie to him. Yet.

"No, David, I'm not."

He took a deep breath and it seemed as if he believed me.

"This is about that silly accident the other night, isn't it? For fuck's sake, Caroline, it was just an accident!"

He sat back, his arms folded across his chest, a supercilious expression on his face. I could tell what he was thinking—the storm was blowing over. If anything, this was the eye of the storm.

"I know it was an accident. But the fact remains: I'm leaving you and I want a divorce."

"Don't be ridiculous! You can't leave me!" He stared at me then added, "You haven't got anywhere to go—your mother certainly won't take you back."

God, he was arrogant.

I was beginning to get angry: angry was good.

"I've already moved my things out. I guess you haven't noticed yet. I've rented a room downtown until ... until we get everything sorted legally. Then I'm going back East."

He stared at me, utterly speechless.

"I won't make it difficult," I continued, "I don't want anything from you."

He looked like I'd punched him, he was deflating in front of me, all bombast gone.

"You're leaving me?"

"Yes, David. It's for the best."

His head sank to his chest and I felt an unfamiliar pang of pity for him.

And then there was a loud and insistent banging on the door. I tried to ignore the knocking, but it was relentless.

Who the hell was this? What absolutely appalling timing.

With the habit born of a decade of domestic drudgery, I was the one who walked to the front door and pulled it open.

"There you are, you little bitch!"

Estelle pushed past me into the main room and Donald followed close behind. I could smell alcohol on his breath as he leered at me. The door hung open as I fell back weakly against the wall.

There could be only one reason for them coming here, only one reason for Estelle to speak to me like that...

They knew.

"What's going on?" shouted David, his temper fraying with this new incursion.

He stood up and glared at Donald and Estelle.

"Estelle, this isn't the time or place. Donald, what's going on?"

"Your little whore of a wife has been fucking my son!" spat Estelle. "My *underage* son!"

David recoiled and stared at her as if she'd grown two heads.

"Don't be ridiculous! Have you been drinking again, Estelle, because from the look of you..."

"Ask her!" she taunted him. "See if she denies it!"

David's disbelief turned to shock: one look at my face was evidence enough.

"Caroline, is this ... is this true?"

My knees gave way and I sank onto the couch.

David stared at me, his mouth opening and closing like a goldfish.

"You're such a limp dick fucking pencil pusher, Wilson," snorted Donald. "If you'd been servicing your wife properly she wouldn't have come sniffing around my son."

David was helpless to reply, adrift in a scenario he didn't understand.

"Caroline?"

David's voice pleaded with me to deny what Donald was saying—but I couldn't.

"Caroline?" he stuttered again.

"Come on, Wilson," sneered Donald. "Be a man for once in your life—if you can remember how."

"I just wanted to see you deny it," Estelle hissed at me. "I knew I was right about you, pretending you're so prim and proper. People like you make me sick. Who are you to judge *me* when you go around getting your kicks with *children*? Sneaking around behind your husband's back—or did he know?"

"It's got nothing to do with David," I said, tiredly. "He and I are getting a divorce."

"Oh, so that's the plan, is it?" sneered Estelle. "Trying to blame my son! My *seventeen-year-old* son! Do you think I'd let you implicate him in your divorce? Do you think for one moment we'd let even a hint of a scandal like that sully our reputation? Or maybe you think you can *blackmail* your way out of this? Over my dead body, you stuck up little slut. I suppose you'll say that he attacked you now? Is that it? Blame someone else? Pretending you're so much better than everyone when you've really been putting it out for all the boys, no doubt you've fucked half the Base by now. Well, no, missy! You're not ruining *our* name."

"Shut up, Stell," said Donald coolly. "I'm running this show, not you."

Estelle fell silent, her eyes narrowing at me, her expression vicious.

Where did so much hatred come from? I felt myself drowning in their ugly accusations. I didn't have the strength to think about that: all I could do was try to protect myself. I had to go—now.

"I'm leaving anyway," I said, quietly, leaning forward in a weak effort to get up off the couch even though I was afraid I was going to be sick. "I won't bother you. You'll never see me again."

David's head jerked up. I saw hurt and pain in his expression along with something else. Was it fear?

I needed to get away—I'd done enough damage already.

I could go straight to New York, Sebastian could catch up with me later. It was only three months—only three months.

I was vaguely aware of the sound of car doors slamming outside and angry voices.

"Oh, that's much too easy!" snapped Estelle.

She marched over and slapped my face hard. My head rocked back and tears sprang to my eyes. She raised her hand again. I didn't try to stop her.

"Mom! Leave her alone!"

Suddenly Sebastian was standing in the room, placing his body between me and his mother who still had her hand raised to hit me. I didn't understand where he'd come from. I felt sick and confused and so dizzy I was afraid I might faint.

At first I thought Estelle was going to hit Sebastian instead, but she backed away when she saw the appalled faces of Ches, his parents and Donna standing at the entrance of the room watching the ghastly drama unfold in front of them.

Sebastian sat down next to me and pulled me into his arms.

"It's okay, baby. I'm here now."

I leaned against him, a half-sob escaping from my chest. It felt good to be held: it felt safe, protected.

"How ... how did you know...?"

"My *mom*," he sneered, "she called Shirley to tell her good news."

"And how did she...?"

His head dropped.

"Brenda told her. She saw us ... last night at the restaurant. She followed us."

The blonde at the window.

"Yes, apparently you were very cozy going into a hotel last night," Estelle added, triumphantly. "And he was missing for two nights without a word. And you," she said, pointing to Shirley, "you hypocritical bitch—you lied to my face to cover it up! I wouldn't be surprised if you knew about it all along."

Shirley gasped and Mitch looked angry.

"Not to mention the box of condoms I found in his room," continued Estelle, enjoying her moment in the limelight. "And a woman's bra—yours, I presume. In my son's bedroom! Slut!"

Sebastian stared at her, his face curiously blank.

Silence crept across the room like ice. I started to shiver and seemed unable to stop.

David's face was frozen in a mask of shock.

"This boy?" he whispered. "You're leaving me for this *boy?*"

Sebastian shot him a look of pure hatred, while Donna held her hand over her mouth as if trying to push back words that sprang to her lips. Mitch shook his head and Shirley took a step forward seeming to reach out toward us. Ches looked as if he wished he could be anywhere but here—I understood that emotion very well. I was watching my life implode in slow motion.

"It's okay, Caro," Sebastian crooned, kissing my hair over and over. "It's okay now. I love you, baby."

It was Donald who broke the spell.

"It isn't fucking okay," he said in a low voice, full of loathing. "It really isn't fucking okay. She's been screwing half the Base and now she's got her claws into you. You're so fucking naïve you can't even see it. Christ! Why did I have to have a son with shit for brains?"

Sebastian was on his feet in seconds.

"Don't you dare talk about her like that! You're so fucking wrong! You think everyone is like you, but they're not! You think it's a secret that you've been fucking that little nurse all those nights you've been working late, *Dad?* You're just a fucking joke and you don't even see it!"

Donald hit him so hard that Sebastian flailed across the room and crashed to the floor. He struggled to his feet, blood pouring from his nose and launched himself at his father.

Ches and Mitch ran forward trying to pull him off. Sebastian had got in several good body blows before they peeled him away. He was incoherent with rage, shouting and swearing at his father.

Donald rubbed his ribs, and seemed to grow calmer as Sebastian's fury increased.

"Sebastian!" I breathed. "Don't, please."

He turned and stared at me and his face softened. His body went limp but Mitch and Ches hung onto him.

"*Tesoro*, please!"

I reached out for him and he stretched his hand toward me. Cautiously, Mitch let him go and nodded at Ches for him to do the same.

Sebastian swept me into his arms and pulled me to his chest.

"Don't listen to that fucking asshole, Caro," he mumbled, his bloodied nose making his voice thick. "He's nothing. Nothing."

"Is that right?" said Donald, nastily. "I've supplied your life with everything you've got: the clothes on your back, the roof over your fucking head! I'm the poor sucker who has a half-wit for a son, but that's the point, isn't it? You're still *my son*—and that whore of yours has been fucking an underage boy. All I have to do is call the police and that bitch will be in jail so fast, she won't have time to say a prayer."

There was a horrified silence and I closed my eyes, fear and disgust burning through me.

"Hey, come on, man," said Mitch, quietly. "There's no need for that."

"No, indeed," said Donna, sounding appalled. "There's no need to involve the police. I'm sure we can sort this out without resorting to anything so ... so serious."

But Donald was too far gone in his anger and hatred to listen. Or maybe he was finally saying what he'd come to say, to find another way to bully and belittle his son, to control him.

"And you know what?" he said, viciously, "She *will* get jail time—I'll see to that. Corrupting a minor at *her* age: that's not a misdemeanor, it's a felony. She's been plying him with alcohol, too, did you know that? And when she finally gets out of jail, after being finger-fucked by every hairy-assed lesbian in the slammer, she'll have a reputation as a pedophile. Try getting a job with *that* tag around you, bitch! I'm going to make you fucking pay."

The whole world came crashing down. All my worst nightmares coming true in one foul-mouthed rant from an evil man who had bullied and beaten up on his son for years.

Sebastian's face was chalky white under his tan.

"You can't do that!" he whispered.

"Just watch him!" sneered Estelle, her eyes glittering. "Your little whore of a girlfriend will get what she deserves."

I hung my head, unable to shake off the weight of her despising words.

"Just because you hate me," said Sebastian, his voice tight with emotion, "there's no need to take it out on her."

He wiped the blood from his face with his jacket sleeve

"Oh, listen to you!" spat Estelle. "Do you think you're some sort of white knight who can charge in and save the day? You're so pathetic! You ruined my life from the day you were born, mewling and puking, always hanging around my neck, a pathetic child! You don't know anything!"

Shirley gasped and Mitch grabbed her arm, Donna was pale with shock and anger, the horror of Estelle's admission washing over them both.

"I'm not a child!" yelled Sebastian. "I've been looking after myself since I was eight years old because *you* were too drunk to look after your own kid. How many times did I have to help you up the stairs because you were too shit-faced to walk, *Mommy*? How many times did strangers drop you at the door because you couldn't even manage to call a cab? And as for *my father*, you're just a fucking joke. Everyone here knows that you're just a pathetic hole-chaser with an alcoholic slut for a wife. Caro is the best thing that ever happened to me. We're going away together and you'll never see us again."

Sebastian stared at his parents triumphantly. Estelle looked winded and turned to Donald.

"No, you're not," said Sebastian's father, with chilly finality. "You're not going anywhere with that whore."

"You've said that enough times now, buddy," Mitch interrupted with a warning tone. "No need to say it again. And you reel it in, too, Seb."

"Butt out, *Sergeant*!" snarled Donald. "This has fuck-all to do with you. It's hanging around with your loser family that started all this in the first place. He's *my* son and what I say goes. So listen good, *boy*: if you go anywhere near that bitch, I'll call the police and she'll be finished."

Sebastian tried to throw himself at Donald but Mitch and Ches held his wrists and Shirley wrapped her arms around his waist trying to calm him down.

Donna gasped. "Donald, no! Think of the scandal!"

Donald smiled and turned to me.

"If you contact *my son* in any way: email, text, phone, letter, flying fucking carrier pigeon, we'll prosecute. It's a felony—you'll go to prison. At the very least, you'll be on the sex offender's register for the rest of your fucking life—you'll never work again. And the same goes for that fucking asshole of a son of mine if he tries to contact you." He turned his eyes back to Sebastian. "Ever."

Sebastian was yelling obscenities, trying to get to his father, Mitch, Shirley and Ches were desperately holding him back.

"And as for you, *son*," Donald continued, "you can kiss goodbye to any idea about going to college, I'm not wasting another penny on you. But I'll tell you what you will do—as soon as you turn 18 you'll be enlisting. Do it, or your bitch will be facing jail time."

I was still sitting on the couch, white-faced and shocked, body trembling, barely able to take it in.

Donna spoke in a shaky voice.

"Donald, really! There's no need for this. Surely if Caroline promises to leave quietly, we need say no more about it. Sebastian will be 18 in a few months and..."

"You're such a fucking hypocrite, Donna. You'd really do anything for the reputation of this shit-hole of a Base, wouldn't you?"

Donna's mouth opened and closed several times but she seemed unable to speak again.

"And another thing, you fucking whore," said Donald, glaring at me again. "The statute of limitations is three years: *three years*. You come anywhere near my son in that time and you know what will happen to you. Same goes if he contacts you. *I'll know!* If you're so much as in the same *state* I'll make sure you get what's coming to you."

Three years. Oh, God.

I turned to Sebastian, love and loss filling me as my eyes started to blur with tears.

"Don't listen to him, Caro!" gasped Sebastian, desperately. "He won't do it, he won't! He doesn't care enough about me to bother. Don't listen to him!"

"You're right, you little shit," smirked Donald, rubbing his ribs again. "I don't give a damn about you, but believe me, it would give me a great deal of pleasure to send your little bitch to jail, if only to wipe that smug look off your fucking face."

Shirley gasped and Donna looked disgusted.

David was lost and shattered, his gaze drifting around the room as if he couldn't recognize anyone.

But it was Sebastian's face that I couldn't take my eyes off. All the fight had gone out of him and he sagged in Mitch's arms.

I did this. I did this to him. All my rehearsed excuses flew away: I despised myself. And it was time to let him go.

"No, Caro!" breathed Sebastian as he read the decision on my face. "Don't let him win."

Like a sleepwalker rising to Judgment Day, I stood.

Mitch dropped his hands, releasing him, and Sebastian was in my arms for one last time. He held onto me so tightly I could hardly breathe, burying his face in my hair.

"I have to go now, *tesoro*," I said softly, stroking his neck.

His grip tightened around me. "No!" he gasped as if he was in great pain.

"Yes. Sebastian, listen to me. I want you to have a good life, *tesoro*, a big life. I want you to be happy, to fall in love..."

"No, God, no, Caro! Don't say that!"

"Yes! Do it for me."

"I'll always love you, Caro. Don't give up on us. Please don't give up. I'll wait for you. It's only three years. I love you!"

But it wasn't just three years, was it? I knew that now.

"I love you, too," I whispered so softly I didn't know if he'd heard me. "*Ti amo tanto*, Sebastian, *sempre e per sempre*."

I tried to peel his hands away from my body but he wouldn't let go.

"No!" he cried over and over again. "No!"

"Oh, for fuck's sake!" snarled Donald in disgust.

Somehow Mitch and Ches managed to pull Sebastian off, he tried to fight them but his spirit was broken.

I turned to Shirley and Donna, their faces filled with pity.

"Look after him," I said softly. "Ches, I ... just be his friend."

Ches nodded, unable to speak.

"Oh my dear, dear child," said Donna, tears in her eyes.

I looked at my husband, whose silence was more eloquent than a thousand words.

"Goodbye, David," I whispered. "I'm sorry..."

He stared at me blankly, then dropped his head into his hands.

I turned to go, my eyes sweeping over Estelle's malice, David's bewilderment, Donald's triumph, the sadness in the expressions of Donna and Shirley, and the anger darkening the faces of Ches and Mitch.

Then my eyes rested on the man I loved, the man I vowed I would never see again because he'd been hurt enough—by me.

"Caro, no!" he cried again, tears falling down his face, mingling with the blood.

"I love you, Sebastian. So much, *tesoro*."

And then I walked away, leaving behind all the goodness and beauty that I'd ever known in my life.

~

Despite what happened that day, despite what happened later, I can't bring myself to regret the events of that summer, because Sebastian taught me how to love.

END OF PART ONE

THE EDUCATION OF CAROLINE

The Education Series: Book 2

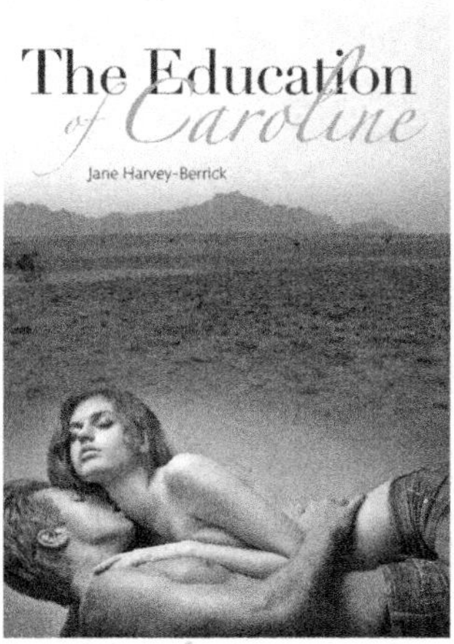

PROLOGUE

When a woman turns forty she is no longer young, but not yet old.

At least, that's what I was told by friends who had reached that milestone some years ahead of me. I wasn't concerned, although perhaps I should have been: my work as a freelance journalist was always uncertain, my mortgage large, my pension minute, with the future unwritten. So, yes, turning forty should have bothered me, or at least sparked my interest a little, but you can't force yourself to feel, can you?

I never dreamed that my past would catch up with me, and that I'd be drawn back into the erotic madness of a decade ago.

But then again, perhaps life is what happens when you least expect it.

CHAPTER ONE

I GAZED AROUND THE TABLE AT THE FACES OF MY FRIENDS, BATHING IN THE warmth of their love.

Nicole smiled back at me and raised her glass.

"Well, today's the day," she said, winking at me. "The big 4-0! Not that you look it, beotch! Happy Birthday!"

Jenna and Alice lifted their cocktail glasses and clinked across the table.

I smiled wryly.

"Well, some days I certainly feel forty. But not today—it's so great that all you guys made it."

"Are you kidding?" said Nicole. "Of course we made it—and I *never* go to Brooklyn, so you should feel really honored, Venzi!"

"Here we go," muttered Alice, "the 'I never leave Manhattan even to see how the peasants live' speech."

"Yeah, yeah," snorted Nicole.

I laughed, happy to hear their bickering, which was as familiar and innocent as air.

These were my friends, but I thought of them as family. And they had all come to my favorite Italian restaurant in Brooklyn to celebrate with me.

"So, you're leaving us again," sighed Alice. "Up, up and away on your travels."

"It's not exactly a vacation," retorted Nicole.

She would have raised her eyebrows except she'd been for her monthly Botox treatment, and the upper part of her face was currently immobile.

It was true: it wasn't a vacation—I was going away for work. And I was living my dream.

I'd come a long way since arriving in New York ten years ago, penniless and unhappy, fleeing a failed marriage and a doomed affair.

It hadn't been easy, although I doubt that moving to the Big Apple is easy for anyone. But for me, it meant living by myself, by my own efforts, for the first time in my life. I was scared and adrift in a city I didn't understand, where I knew no one.

At first, I'd lived in a horrible, low-rent hostel, before finding a tiny apartment in Brooklyn's Little Italy—a place that became my home for the next eight years. I cleaned people's apartments to earn money for food and rent, while saving what I could to go back to school to study journalism and photography.

I'd been in New York for less than two months when 9/11 happened. The world changed on that day: everyone's lives were different, as if we'd lost our innocence. The smoke and ash had hung in the air for days after, the feeling of shock and despair lasted much longer. And then came the anger—it was so strong, it was like a nightmarish creature that haunted our waking dreams. You couldn't see it, but you could feel it, glimpsed in the faces of people around you—those expressions you caught out of the corner of your eye, that showed the rage was still there.

But there was also a sense of togetherness, maybe of shared experience. It was as if the whole city came together to care for each other. We mourned together, we tried to pick up the pieces together. It was as if we were one big family, living through a crisis together. It was just a different atmosphere. Everyone wanted to help out, everyone had some sort of connection to those buildings.

Somehow, selfishly, it fit in with my own sense of loss: not just the life I'd left behind in California, but also because I'd lost who I was.

A year passed before I opened my eyes, shook myself from my torpor and found a way to live again.

An old acquaintance from San Diego had helped get me some ad hoc work on local newspapers and, from there, I'd managed to begin my freelance writing career. At first, it was just small features: a food festival in Brooklyn, a music festival in Queens, but gradually the scope of my writing became more wide-reaching, adventurous even.

It was shortly after that, when a piece I wrote called 'The New Immigrants' about asylum seekers, had caught the eye of a national newspaper editor and suddenly and unexpectedly, I was on my way. For the past six years I'd been lucky enough to earn my livelihood as a foreign correspondent, working freelance for several major newspapers.

Two years ago, I'd even saved enough to put down a deposit on a tiny, 1920s bungalow in Long Beach. My mortgage was scarily large, but I wanted somewhere of my own: somewhere I could come home to as driver of my own destiny, and queen of my own castle.

I'd loved living in Brooklyn and was sorry to say goodbye to my favorite coffee shops and restaurants. There was a real sense of community in the neighborhood, and the area thrummed with the vibrancy of the constantly changing wave of people that passed through.

By this time, I was working mostly from home—'home' being wherever my laptop was—so the commute into the city didn't bother me, and I was ready for another change. For much of my life I'd lived near the ocean, certainly during the most significant parts, and I loved that sense of space and peace that living by water gave me. Above all things, I loved to walk down to the shoreline when a big swell came and watch the surfers like so many seals, clad in black neoprene, bobbing behind the line-up, then charging down the barreling green waves. Sometimes, in the summer, I'd take my surfboard out and join them. It brought back happy memories and I felt carefree for an hour or so.

My new home in Long Beach was a fascinating and diverse community. I loved the mix of people, and spent many happy hours just watching the world go by, often finding inspiration for new stories. My neighbors included an elderly Jewish lady, Mrs. Levenson, who used to walk side by side with her close friend, Doris, a Hispanic mother of three small children. Then there were the teenage beach bums, quietly smoking pot all day, hanging out on the boardwalk or by the mall, quiet and inoffensive. They all had their presence in the town, all part of the diverse culture, color and life.

In recent years, it had become popular with Manhattanites to come for the weekend, no doubt finding it friendlier and considerably cheaper than a few days in the Hamptons. Long Beach's renewed popularity might have had something to do with the recession, of course, but I liked to think it was for its unique identity and sense of freedom.

My new home was surrounded by delis, bagel shops, and diners. Brunch was my favorite meal of the day, and on weekends, the colorful variety of eateries was packed with people placing orders to go, or waiting for a table to get breakfast. Even on weekdays it could be busy, but I was more likely to be able to get a table to myself and spend an hour or so staring out the window or working on my laptop. An Italian coffee shop on the boardwalk was—for all intents and purposes—my second home, the older members of the family chatting to me in strongly-accented Italian, the younger ones in English, of course.

One of the main commuter rail branches went directly from Long Beach to Manhattan, so it was handy for when I had meetings in the city, which seemed to happen with increasing frequency once I'd quit Brooklyn. Of course.

But the weekends were all about the beach. Even in the winter, when it definitely wasn't lay-out-in-the-sun weather, people still liked to parade. The boardwalk spanned the entire town and every type of person seemed to take a Sunday stroll, although perhaps I was the only one who still enjoyed walking in the rain.

On a nice day, families mingled with the athletic-types taking a break from the overcrowded and sweaty gyms to go for a run or bike ride in the open air. Elderly couples would sit at one the many benches, gazing out toward the water. I liked to fantasize that they were contemplating their youth and memories of earlier days when running and jumping came as naturally as breathing, but perhaps they were just planning what to eat for lunch.

Perhaps they were thinking about their families: children who lived in different states or different countries, long-lost friends, dear, departed parents.

I had been close to my father, but my darling papa had died more than 12 years ago. I was not close to my mother. She did not like her daughter.

I didn't like to look back that often.

My most precious memories were closely guarded secrets and I only looked at them occasionally, taking them out of my Pandora's Box of the past, to treasure and enjoy, then carefully replace and lock away. As the years passed, I looked less and less, because, perhaps, I felt there was more to look forward to. And this was new.

As far as my friends were concerned, I barely had a past. They recognized that I preferred not to talk about it, and they respected my wishes, or else they knew better than to ask.

I'd dropped my married name the moment I'd left my husband, and I'd even hacked my Christian name into small pieces, choosing just one short syllable, a new identity for my new life. Instead of Mrs. Caroline Wilson, I was now Carolina Venzi—pronounced the Italian way—but known to my new friends as 'Lee'.

And funny enough, it turned out to be very handy: people often made the assumption that 'Lee Venzi' was a man. There was one editor who had bought my freelance features for five months before he'd discovered that it was a woman writing articles about crime in the city. I'm not sure I'd have gotten the commission if he'd known the truth, but by then it was too late and, he had to admit that he'd liked the job I'd done—which was all that mattered, in my opinion.

It amused me, but it suited me very well, too. I was eager to retain a level of anonymity in my work, more particularly, some distance from my past.

And now I was forty. More confident than ever before in my life, believing in my abilities, and comfortable in my skin, I had a career that I enjoyed. True, it was an itinerant lifestyle that could take me away from home for weeks or even months, but it was one that suited me. I'd spent the first thirty years of my life dormant and static, now I liked to be on the move. Besides, there wasn't much to go home to other than a shelf of books, and a closet full of clothes from my old life that I no longer wore.

A few men, very few, had drifted in and out over the years, but there was no significant other, there was no significant anything at all—and I was quite happy to keep it that way. I had the company of my friends, and that was more than enough.

Nicole, in particular, found my casual celibacy hard to understand. She was forever trying to set me up with 'cute guys' that she knew. It became something of a game between us: her vowing that one day I'd meet someone who'd sweep me off my feet, and me promising it would never happen.

What I didn't tell her, what I had no plans for her to know, was that I *had* been swept off my feet once before, and that the trail of devastation I'd left behind me after that event was still too painful to examine. The memories stayed carefully locked away.

My current assignment would take me away for an unknown number of weeks—perhaps as long as two months. I'd been hired by *The New York Times* to write about US servicemen and women being deployed to Afghanistan.

My friends were supportive, but they didn't really understand why I wished to take the risk. It was hard to explain. Perhaps it was about being master of my own destiny and being able to do what the hell I wanted for the first time in my life. Perhaps it was something to do with having arrived in New York with no more than a few hundred dollars, and an ancient and worn out Ford Pinto that died shortly after crossing Verrazano Bridge. Perhaps it was a need to empathize with people who took risks. I couldn't say.

It had taken me years to afford a way of living that many women my age were able to take for granted. Maybe those were the reasons that I seemed drawn to document the lives of those who had significantly less.

My first foreign assignment came about because my agent knew a little of my background—eleven years of living on military bases had certainly given me an insight. I was sent to several camps near Mosul and Baghdad to report on the living quarters of military personnel—and, for once, a woman's point of view was wanted.

So my latest assignment wasn't the first time I'd been paid to go somewhere dangerous, but it was certainly going to be one of the most challenging.

"I'm going to miss you, Lee," said Nicole, sadly. "Who am I going to hang with on the weekends?"

"You'll manage," I smiled, "and I'll be back long before the summer. "Besides, you have the keys to my place, so you can all go and do what you usually do—check out the cute surfer guys."

"Yeah, but it's not the same without you," complained Alice, "even though you never notice any of them."

"Maybe you'll meet a hunky soldier," said Nicole, with a leer. "God, I love men in uniform."

"They're not in them very long around you," snarked Jenna.

Nicole just winked and threw me a challenging look.

I shuddered. My ex-husband had been in the military—I definitely wasn't going down *that* particular route again.

My flight was the following morning, even though the newspaper was still fighting the bureaucrats in DC to get my visa and travel documents approved. An additional set of hurdles had been erected by the Department of Defense, in the form of requiring me to attend a 'hostile environment' training program for journalists, specially put on by the military in Geneva, before traveling on to the Middle East—or South Asia, depending on your point of view or political affiliation.

I'd never been to Switzerland before, although I'd flown over it a number of times. It was something new.

Before dawn, I was ready and waiting at the front of the bungalow for the headlights that would announce my taxi. I'd tucked my passport into my back pocket, packed up my small travel bag, tugged and pushed and pulled at my heavy, wheeled suitcase, and slammed shut the door to my home.

I'd become used to living with the minimum of necessities, and dressy clothes were very low on the list. When on assignment, I lived in jeans and lightweight walking boots, and had a no-frills haircut that required low to zero maintenance—I just pulled it all into a rough ponytail. Makeup? Not really. I had an old lipstick and tube of mascara somewhere in the bottom of my bag, but a fully charged smart phone and laptop were more important, and I never went anywhere, not even to the bathroom, without a small notebook and pencil. I had some of my best ideas in the bathroom. Probably too much information. I'd even perfected the art of making notes to myself in the dark to save the hassle of turning on a light when I woke in the night with an idea—of course, reading my scrawl in daylight was another story.

I did, however, have a set of my own body armor that weighed a ton, and cost me a fortune in excess baggage charges.

My cab driver, who was just finishing his shift, was unusually quiet for which I was grateful. He dropped me off at the international departures terminal, and I began the first leg of my long journey.

~

I rolled over in bed and groaned. The six-hour time difference between New York and Switzerland meant that I was wide awake at four in the morning, and the prospect of sleep seemed slim.

I tried to force my eyes shut, but they soon drifted open of their own accord and I lay staring at the ceiling.

My hotel was one of those nondescript blocks of concrete that you could find in any city, in any country, the world over. But it had a central location, functional rooms, free Wi-Fi, and boasted a tiny swimming pool and gym. I'd stayed in far worse places and probably would again—in fact, as I was headed to Afghanistan sooner rather than later, that was a given.

Feeling gritty-eyed and grumpy, I climbed out of bed and gazed out of the window. My room was just high enough up for me to see Lake Geneva glittering darkly in the distance. I was tempted to go for a walk, to stretch my legs and try to wear myself out enough for sleep to take me again. But wandering the streets of a strange city in the early hours was asking for trouble, even somewhere as safe and well-ordered as Switzerland. I wouldn't have lasted long in my present job taking those sorts of unnecessary risks.

Turning from the window with a sigh, I wondered if the swimming pool or fitness center would be open: it seemed unlikely. Frustrated and sleepless, I pulled out my laptop and spent a couple of hours reading news stories online.

I finally managed to get an hour's sleep before my alarm dragged me awake at 7AM.

The face that stared back at me in the bathroom mirror made me want to shatter the glass with my hairbrush. Today, I looked every one of my forty years. I felt like draping a black cloth over the mirror to blot out the view. Instead, I turned to the shower and contemplated the creamy-white tiles, as my tired brain stuttered into action.

The shower was marvelous, so powerful, it almost pinned me to the back wall. It was like having hundreds of little fingers massaging me, and definitely provided the shot of vigor I needed to face the day ahead. I was very grateful for the deep pockets of my employer in providing for my current comfort.

I pulled on a pair of jeans, not caring that I was woefully underdressed compared to the rest of the hotel's clientele. Hungry, I enjoyed a leisurely breakfast comprising of *zopf*, a rich, white bread baked into the shape of a braid, and served with butter, different jellies, honey, *emmental* cheese and a selection of cold meats. There was muesli, too, of course, but that didn't interest me. Too much like the granola I usually had at home.

I was just contemplating whether or not to order a third coffee when I heard someone calling my name.

"Hey, Lee! Yo, Venzi! What the bloody blue hell are you doing here?"

I looked up and grinned.

Bearing down on me was Liz Ashton, an indomitable British bulldog of a woman in her late fifties. She was rather famous in our field, an English Marie Colvin you might say, having been to every war front since Chad in 1979, every civil unrest since Uganda in the 1980s, and every guerrilla action since El Salvador in 1981. She'd reported on every atrocity from Croatia to the Congo, and was as tough as nails: probably tougher. She didn't take shit from anyone.

Liz was a senior reporter with *The Times* of London. We'd become friends over the course of the last five years when we'd run across each other in a variety of low-rent hotels, pitched together among the testosterone-rich world of the foreign correspondent.

"Hi, Liz! Good to see you!"

She swept me into a hug that almost cracked a rib.

"You, too. So, what's cooking, Venzi?"

"I'm in town for a hostile environment training course," I replied. "I'm supposed to be flying out to Camp Leatherneck in four or five days. You?"

"Hmm, well good luck with that. A little bird told me that your top brass are being tricky customers over non-military personnel visiting their precious Base since that last blue-on-green incident..."

Incidents where our so-called allies attacked US personnel were increasing.

"Who are you with on this one?

"New York Times."

"Well, tell them to kick some arses or you could be stuck here for weeks. My insurers are demanding that I attend some sodding training course for journos, too: how to wipe my bleeding nose in a 'conflict area', that sort of thing. I'm shipping out to Bastion next week, so we'll be neighbors. Just got to jump through the usual hoops first."

Camp Leatherneck was the US Marines' base in Afghanistan, and Bastion was the equivalent for British forces. I wasn't delighted to hear that my travel plans were likely to be disrupted, but Liz's information was invariably accurate: forewarned was forearmed in this job. Liz had spent years, decades even, developing her contacts, and she had fingers on the pulse of the beast that was international news. I made a mental note to contact my editor and see what strings he could pull to get me on my way.

"Is your training at the InterContinental by any chance, Liz? Because if it is, then I'm on the same one."

"Excellent news, Venzi! We can go and get pissed afterwards."

I really didn't think that was a good idea: Liz's drinking sessions were legendary. I definitely wasn't in that league.

"No way! I can't keep up with you. You'd be carrying me home."

"You're such a lightweight, Lee."

"That is true—and I intend to keep it that way, so stop trying to lead me astray."

"Ha! All work and no play makes Jill a dull girl. Come on, let's go and see who they've sent to whip us into shape this time."

Outside, the air was clean and crisp, the faintest whisper of spring penetrating the crystal clear morning. The city felt very European, the architecture reflecting the mix of French, German and Italian influences, and, in the distance, I could see the dominating summit of Mont Blanc, snow lying thick on the top like frosting.

Liz linked her arm through mine and we strolled through the city, behaving like a couple of tourists. I had to drag her away from an upscale chocolate shop where they sold crystallized lemons dipped in dark, milk, and white chocolate. We could have easily spent a week's salary in there and gorged ourselves stupid under the supercilious eye of the sales assistant.

There was a time when the piercing eye of someone like that would have reduced me to a nervous wreck, but not anymore. I wasn't twenty and married to a bullying man; I was forty, myself at last, and doing a job I was passionate about.

Less than a half-mile from the Palais des Nations and its long avenue of national flags, the InterContinental was an ugly, 18-story tower in the center of the diplomatic district. In the distance, the Alps outlined the horizon, reminding me, if I needed it, that I wasn't in Kansas anymore.

The receptionist directed us to a nondescript, beige-colored conference room, where coffee and croissants awaited us.

Liz dug in with gusto and I decided one more cup of black coffee wouldn't go amiss.

I thought about what she'd told me, and the probable delays I'd experience. I suspected this was the old Washington two-step. It had happened five years ago when I'd been trying to get to military bases in Iraq. I was shuffled around between departments, each one denying the delay was anything to do with them. I would try to be stoic, but it wasn't always easy.

For now both Liz and I had to play the game to get where we wanted to be. As we waited, six other journalists from various European nations joined us, a couple that I knew by sight, as well as my friend Marc Lebuin, a freelance writer who sold his stories to French language newspapers.

"*Chère* Lee, and *ma bonne* Liz! This is a most pleasant surprise. How are you, my dear ladies!"

He hugged us warmly and kissed us on both cheeks.

"Keen as mustard, Marc, and as excited as a wet weekend in Wigan. Where are you off to?" asked Liz.

He shrugged. "I do not yet know. I am here waiting for assignment. I think it is to pass the time. Perhaps I will learn some Farsi. I understand there is a language specialist here to train us. It might be useful, who knows? *Ça fait bien.*"

A young-looking British lieutenant entered the room, and looked around him rather nervously.

"New kid on the block," said Liz, grinning. "I think we can have some fun with him."

I groaned inwardly. Liz's idea of 'fun' didn't match mine. But there was no stopping her, not even a Sherman tank could change her mind once it was made up. Her mantra, 'compromise is the sign of a third-rate mind', summed up her general attitude to life.

The young lieutenant disappeared. I wondered idly if he'd noticed Liz's gorgon gaze and gone for backup.

As the scheduled starting time came and went, an irritated muttering rippled through the assembled journalists.

"Damn all this waiting around!" snapped Liz.

I cast an amused glance at my friend—she really didn't do waiting very well—which was ironic, because a good chunk of our work involved sitting around: waiting for the people we needed to talk to, hoping they would acknowledge our presence, waiting for flights, waiting for rides, waiting for visas, and waiting for permission to cross borders into war zones. It was rather similar to the military adage, 'soldiering is 99% boredom and 1% sheer terror'. I didn't mind the boredom.

The room was chilly, overly-air conditioned and similarly soulless. I hunkered down in my chair at the back of the room, and wrapped my long, cashmere scarf twice around my neck so it covered my chin and part of my nose.

Liz, as I said, was made of sterner stuff. She marched to the front of the room and fiddled with the thermostat, while the British lieutenant watched her anxiously. I could tell he was dying to tell her not to touch it, but had quailed beneath her withering gaze. She had that effect on most people—especially men. I wondered if I'd ever acquire that chilling, thousand-yard stare. Probably not.

The lieutenant kept stealing glances at his watch, and it became apparent that he was waiting for someone who was late. I imagined it was probably a journalist who was a no-show. That happened a lot: missed planes, changed schedules, visas refused, or even assignments cancelled at the last minute. As it turned out, I was wrong about that.

Very wrong.

Eventually we were joined by a much older man with the crown insignia of a British Major embroidered onto the epaulettes of his khaki uniform.

His cap badge was the tiny figure of Mercury—winged messenger of the gods—which meant he was from the Royal Signals Corps. I enjoyed the British whimsy embodied by that image.

The Major was a strong-looking man of about 50, with kind, hazel eyes that crinkled when he smiled. He wasn't smiling now. In fact he looked more than a little irritated and as he entered the room, shutting the door behind him, I heard him mutter something that sounded uncannily like "bloody Yanks".

I shifted uneasily in my seat while Liz winked at me.

"Well, good morning, ladies and gentlemen," he began. "My name is Major Mike Parsons and my colleague here is Lieutenant Tom Farley."

He indicated toward the young lieutenant, who was trying to appear relaxed and doing a very poor job of it.

"I apologize for the slight delay in starting, our American colleague has clearly been held up. However, we'll press on and begin with the basics. I'll be talking about prep and planning and what you need to have in your exit plan—primarily how you'll be repatriated in the event of injury or illness. Then I'll hand over to Lieutenant Farley, who will discuss making use of local knowledge and getting around in a dangerous place. In the afternoon sessions we'll cover coping with gunfire, keeping safe in a crowd, and emergency first aid. Tomorrow we'll be covering landmines, IEDs, chemical dangers, and what to do in the event that you are taken hostage. We'll be joined by our colleague from the US Marines for some of the sessions, and for an introduction to Dari and Pashto—the two official languages of Afghanistan." And then he muttered under his breath, "If he bothers to turn up."

Liz nudged me and I felt irritated that my compatriot, whoever the hell he was, was making the US look bad. I had to remind myself that such tardiness was not restricted to press training, after all, it was Washington officials who were deliberately delaying my paperwork.

The Major began his lecture, and although the advice was good, I'd heard it all before and my mind began to drift. I made a few desultory notes for the sake of appearance, but I already knew what to pack in an emergency grab bag for immediate evac (passport, solar-powered phone charger, first aid supplies, dried food, water for a day, flashlight, pocket knife—which I was always having confiscated at airports along with my matches, emergency contact list—known as the 'call sheet'), as well as basic safety messages such as arranging a code word for whoever arrived to pick me up at my destination. Obvious, when you think about it, but a tip that had come in *very* handy on a number of occasions. I'd passed that one to Nicole for when she met her frequent internet dates in unfamiliar places.

The Major went on to remind us about leaving the call sheet and next of kin details with our agency or a trusted third party. That bit always left me feeling sad. My next of kin was my mother, but we hadn't spoken in nearly ten years—not since she'd made it crystal clear what she thought of me when I told her my marriage was over and that I was getting divorced.

I was vaguely aware that she'd moved to a retirement community in Florida, but we weren't in touch. I certainly had no plans to name her in the event of an emergency. My real family were my friends, and I left my important numbers and my Last Will and Testament with my agent in New York.

Major Parsons then reiterated the importance of not having an Israeli stamp on our passports when traveling into Afghanistan or any other Muslim country. Yep, checked that box—we all had.

Then he handed over to the lieutenant who was competent, but far less polished in his delivery. I got the impression that this was the first time he'd delivered his talk.

The Major stayed for a few minutes to make sure his man was going to be okay, and then sidled out of the room. I was a big fan of sidling, and wondered how obvious it would be if I slunk out, too. But I knew the two-day training was compulsory for the newspaper's insurers, and there would be new things to learn after they'd gone through the basics.

I sighed softly and hunkered down a little more.

I woke up slightly when the lieutenant lost his train of thought for a moment, and became aware that someone else had entered the room. I craned my neck, wondering if the Major had come back. But it was someone else entirely.

A man, extraordinarily beautiful with a deeply tanned face, and blue-green eyes the color of the ocean.

A jolt of recognition shocked me. There was no doubt. Ten years older, but still stunning.

Sebastian Hunter.

Oh. My. God.

CHAPTER TWO

My breath caught in my throat.

Sebastian: the reason my marriage had ended, the catalyst for my becoming a journalist. The man I'd loved more than any man, before or since. The man I hadn't seen for ten long years. My beautiful boy, my lover, my friend. The man I thought I'd never see again.

Sebastian.

Yes, it was definitely him. He was slightly taller, his shoulders were a little broader and his face a touch more angular, but otherwise he was unchanged. Except his eyes. Yes, they had changed, their sweetness hardened with the years.

Our affair, if you want to call it that, had begun when he was just 17 and I was already 30. As we were living in California at the time, it had been a criminal act. I'd fallen deeply, hopelessly, ridiculously in love. For his part, he'd been infatuated with an older woman, but his zest for life, his enthusiasm, support and belief in me, had opened my eyes to the dismal state of my marriage.

Our secret was discovered and dismembered in the most painful of ways. In a scene that still haunted my nightmares, I'd been forced to leave or face the cruel wrath of his parents. Even though Sebastian had been only months from his eighteenth birthday, my crime was a felony, and his parents had threatened to have me arrested if I ever contacted their son again. And, with California's statute of limitations being three years, I'd been forced to comply.

Since the day I'd walked out of my marriage ten years earlier, I hadn't seen or heard of Sebastian.

I'd thought of him often, wondering what he'd made of his life, where he'd gone, what he'd become, wishing to believe he was fulfilled and happy. And now, here he was, standing in the same room as me again, dressed in the khaki Service Uniform of the US Marine Corps.

I slumped lower in my chair, glad that my face was partially concealed beneath my scarf. My heart was beating so fast I was afraid I might pass out.

Liz nudged me.

"Are you okay?"

I nodded silently. She threw me a puzzled look, but shrugged it off, leaving me to dwell on remembrances of things past.

The door opened again and Major Parsons returned. He waited for the lieutenant to finish his point, throwing an irritated glance at Sebastian, who slouched at the side of the room, a bored expression on his face.

"Thank you, Tom. We'll take a short break now, ladies and gentleman, and meet back here at 1100 hours. Refreshments will be served in Les Nations lounge. And we're very glad to have our colonial colleague Sergeant Hunter to join us. I'm sure his insight will be invaluable."

I doubted I was the only one who heard the note of sarcasm.

The other journalists stood up to go, following our military escort out of the room, but I was incapable of standing, afraid that my legs would give way.

"Ah, the infamous Sergeant Hunter," said Liz, in a stage whisper. "Well, he certainly looks the part. Quite the lady-killer, I hear."

"Excuse me?" I said, faintly.

"The American ... he has something of a reputation. I'm surprised you haven't heard."

"Why would I?" I managed to choke out. "Heard what?"

She gave a conspiratorial chuckle and leaned toward me. If there's one thing journalists the world over have in common, they do love to gossip.

"Oh, I came across our Sergeant Hunter in Paris two years ago, although he was a humble corporal then. Well, not that humble, you understand! Yes, a rather notorious lothario: it was something of an *amour célèbre*. They say he was tupping the wife of his CO, although nothing was made public, and it was all hushed up."

"Surely that's just gossip?" I said, weakly. "I mean—if he had—it would have been a federal felony, a court martial, and then he'd have been thrown out of the Corps."

"I'm just telling you what I heard," said Liz, with a leer. "Suffice to say he was shipped out of Paris PDQ. Whatever the reason, they say he's got an eye for the ladies." She nudged me, a wicked look in her eye. "I imagine you'd be quite his cup of tea, Lee."

"Oh no, I don't feel like joining a harem," I laughed, a little faintly. "I'm sure Sergeant Hunter has a parade of young women following him."

I remembered that feeling *very* well.

If Liz noticed that my tone was off, she politely ignored it.

"Well, perhaps, but I believe his tendencies run in another direction—he's known to like his women older ... more experienced."

I winced.

"They say he's brilliant in the field," she continued, unaware of the impact her words were having on me. "That's why they put up with his behavior off the field. I heard a whisper that he was headhunted by military intelligence, but you know how close-mouthed your lot are about that. I wouldn't be surprised if he were one of those men who's a complete nightmare when he's not doing something dangerous. You know the kind: reckless, a bullet magnet." She tapped me on the arm. "They say he drinks."

Her comment cut through me like a knife. *Oh no. Not like Estelle—not like his mother.*

With some bitterness I remembered her drunken rant the night I'd left San Diego. She'd called me a 'whore' and 'slut' and various other unpleasant names. And she'd slapped me hard enough to make my teeth rattle. She would have hit me again if Sebastian hadn't stopped her.

The memories, long since locked away, came flooding back.

"Do you want to get coffee, Lee?" asked Marc.

"Sorry, what?"

"Coffee, Venzi!" snapped Liz. "Yay or nay?"

"Oh, no, I'm fine. You guys go ahead."

I wrapped my arms around my knees, physically holding myself together, as the intensity of my feelings floored me.

I took deep breaths and tried to keep calm, but my body was swamped by a rush of adrenaline and the desire for fight or flight overtook me. Right now I was favoring flight—except for the inconvenient fact that if I'd tried to stand up I'd have fallen over.

I heard someone return to the room and the blood drained from my face.

"You look a little pale, Lee," said Marc, a hint of concern in his voice. "Are you okay?"

"Yes, I'm fine. Just cold."

He gave me a look that showed he wasn't convinced, but accepted my explanation.

When the others filed back into the room, I hunched over my notes and hid as best I could. I was ashamed of myself. Why on earth couldn't I get up, walk over to him and say 'hi, hello, how are you' like a normal person? I would do it, of course, I told myself: I would do it during the lunch break, when we weren't surrounded by curious eyes.

Liz was the last to return, by which time I'd managed to pull myself together a little more, or, as my father might have said, a horseman galloping by at a hundred yards wouldn't have noticed anything wrong.

"Ready for round two?" Liz whispered loudly.

I could tell that she'd had more than coffee during the ten minute recess. I wasn't surprised—drinking was one of the hazards that beset our way of life.

And then my plans to reintroduce myself to Sebastian with a modicum of privacy and dignity were blasted out of the water.

"Just a quick roll call before we go on," said Major Parsons, "now everyone is here ... so we all know who's who." And he proceeded to call out our names. I was last.

"Lee Venzi?"

I nodded and raised my hand.

I saw Sebastian's eyes flicker across to me, then widen with shock as recognition set in, and, for the briefest of moments, he looked like the 17 year old I had known.

"You're Lee Venzi?" he blurted out.

Everyone turned to stare at me, alerted by the tone of his voice, so I was the only one who saw his expression turn to something darker, almost hateful—before he controlled his features and looked away.

My heart lurched uncomfortably. He looked like he really hated me. I hadn't expected that, although I suppose I couldn't blame him. It must have been a difficult time for him after I'd left. Even so, to have such a residue of dislike after so long ... I began to feel a little sick.

I took a deep breath and tried to focus on my notes.

Marc nudged me to attract my attention.

"You know that guy? Mr. Sullen-but-beautiful?"

"Yes, we've met," I said, dryly.

"Hmm, I think there's a story there, Venzi. Care to share?"

"Some other time."

He eyed me narrowly, but I twitched a small smile and returned my waning attention to the talk.

Unwillingly, I glanced at Sebastian, but he was staring out of the window, a faraway expression on his face. I wondered if he was remembering, as I was, how we'd met, and our brief but stormy summer of love. Or lust. Depending on your point of view.

Even as I tried to beat away the images, they filled my mind. Even now I remembered the intensity of our lovemaking, the way we could never get enough of each other—his hands, his lips, his tongue sweeping across my body.

As the lieutenant continued to lecture us on precautions against carjacking and criminal attacks, shatterproof windows and tracking devices, I was devoured by a series of increasingly erotic images that brought a warm flush of color to my cheeks.

"Because most attacks occur on reaching home," the lieutenant droned on, "always ensure that you can drive right into your garage or compound, and secure the door or gate behind you."

Liz looked bored, utterly clueless as to the helter-skelter of emotions that disturbed the equilibrium of my mind. She began to whisper an amusing tale to me, the gist of which was that she'd ended up ramming her car into the garage wall not once but twice, during a posting in Cairo, doing exactly what the lieutenant was suggesting. Her *sotto voce* comment was more *voce* than *sotto*, and caused several titters among the rest of the journalists.

The young lieutenant looked annoyed at Liz's too-loud interruption to his lecture.

"This is serious, madam. What I tell you today may save your life."

Uh-oh. Wrong thing to say to Miss Ticking-timebomb.

She inflated like the turkey float on the Macy's Thanksgiving Parade.

"Listen, sunshine, you may think you're something special with a weapon of mass destruction dangling between your legs, but let me tell *you* a thing or two: I've been to the frontline of every war since Uganda in 1979, before you were bloody well born." She started ticking them off on her fingers. "Angola, Croatia, Rwanda, Bosnia, Iraq, Kuwait, Afghanistan, and ... bloody hell, places you've never even heard of. And this woman," she pointed her chin at me, "has been in more hot spots than you've had hot dates."

I could have predicted Liz's response, although I didn't agree with her: to me the next assignment was always like the first—and experienced correspondents were just as likely to get hurt as the newbies.

The lieutenant's ears turned red, and he looked flustered. I thought I detected a small smile on Sebastian's lips, but it immediately disappeared, so I couldn't be sure.

Major Parsons stepped in to retrieve the situation and the poor lieutenant was allowed to continue.

Several times, during the rest of the lecture, I felt Sebastian's eyes on me, but every time I looked up, he'd glance away with a sneer on his beautiful face.

By lunchtime, I'd worked up enough courage to speak to him. But Sebastian, it seemed, had other ideas. He disappeared out of the door before I had the chance to utter a single syllable. I sighed. It looked like he wanted to avoid me.

Marc, however, more than usually sensitive to the emotions of others, was on the trail of a story.

"Come on, Lee, spill your beans. How do you know our Sergeant Hunter?"

"And how come you didn't say you know him?" Liz asked, sounding annoyed.

"It was a long time ago," I said, trying to sound casual, and failing miserably.

"And?"

"And nothing," I insisted.

"Oh, come on, Lee!" said Liz, accusingly. "You get me to tell you all the scandal I know about our mysterious Sergeant Hunter, and you don't even mention that you already know him. You're holding out, I can tell."

"Yes, *chérie*," agreed Marc with a smile, "I, too, think you are keeping secrets."

They knew me so well. Plus, they were journalists, which made them the nosiest people on the planet.

"I met him when I lived in California," I said at last. "When I was married."

"Ah," said Liz, knowingly. "Fair enough, Lee."

They both knew I was divorced and didn't like to talk about my marriage. Thankfully, they didn't ask any further questions.

I spent an uncomfortable lunch hour wondering what to say to him. What could I say? *Sorry about that—I hope I didn't ruin your life—how are you?*

In any event, I didn't have to say anything because Sebastian didn't return after lunch. His departure wasn't commented on by his British colleagues, and they stoically ignored his absence.

The afternoon session continued with little to inform or interest those of us who had sat through these lectures several times before. The only part I was really interested in would come on day two and covered questions specific to Kabul and, to a lesser extent, Kandahar.

I wondered why Sebastian hadn't come back. Surely it couldn't have anything to do with me? That would just be ridiculous.

When we were finally dismissed for the day, Liz wandered off to catch up with some sources, or so she said. I suspected these were more sauces—and of the alcoholic type. Marc muttered something about a prior engagement and I was left to my own, tangled thoughts.

Irritated with myself and perplexed by Sebastian's behavior, I spent a dreary evening in my room. I amused myself by writing long emails to Alice and Jenna. I didn't bother writing more than a few words to Nicole because I knew she only read the first and last paragraphs, unless the messages were from a guy.

I thought that I was at least tired enough to manage a reasonable amount of sleep, but my dreams were haunted by a memory of sea-green eyes, golden skin and naked flesh.

I was rudely awoken shortly after dawn, by an orgasm ripping through me. My back arched and my legs were rigid as I rode out the waves of sensation.

I sat up gasping, shocked at the way my body had betrayed me.

What the hell was that? An orgasm in my sleep?! That definitely hadn't happened before.

I staggered into the shower, trying to wash away the memories that continued to torment me.

The second day of the training began much like the first, except Sebastian's continuing coldness toward me became apparent to the others.

"The beautiful Sergeant Hunter is staring at you again, Lee," said Marc, unnecessarily. "He does not look happy with you."

Sadly, I had to agree.

Today, the lectures had started off with how to spot a minefield. Dead animals were a big clue, but it was also looking out for areas avoided by locals, particularly if the surrounding area was turned to agriculture, where anything overgrown stood out. Pieces of waxed packaging were something to look out for, too—explosives often came wrapped in them.

And then, for the language section of our training, we were in Sebastian's capable hands—something of which I'd once had considerable experience.

"Yes," said Liz, agreeing with Marc's assessment, "young Sergeant Hunter narrows his eyes every time he looks at you."

I sighed and smiled at her. "Maybe my Dari pronunciation is lacking."

I'd been more than a little impressed to find that at some point over the last ten years, Sebastian had become fluent in Dari, a dialect of Afghan Persian, as well as Pashto and Arabic.

He was teaching us how to introduce ourselves and give our name, job title and nationality in the languages we'd need, as well as a useful passage from the Koran for emergencies.

I remembered how quickly his Italian had improved when we'd first started dating. Ugh, 'dating': that seemed such a deeply inadequate word for our tumultuous and passionate affair.

"Perhaps Ms. Venzi can answer that question."

Sebastian's voice cut through my bedraggled thoughts.

"Excuse me? Um, what was the question?" I stammered.

He didn't even bother to answer, but looked away, an expression of disdain on his face.

"Oh, dear! He'll have you staying behind after class," chuckled Liz.

Then he told us that a typical answer to a question an Afghan couldn't answer would be for them to say, 'because the sea is green and the sky is blue'.

"Tell them that and they'll think you're clever," he said, gazing condescendingly at me.

I felt flustered and annoyed—no matter what had happened ten years ago, there was no need for him to be so unpleasant. I decided I'd have it out with him at the first opportunity.

Sebastian's habit was to be the first out of the door as soon as a break was announced, dodging ancillary questions from any of the other journalists: either that or to dodge me. After the morning coffee break, I'd taken a seat near the exit so he wouldn't be able to continue avoiding me as we all left for lunch. And I made sure I paid attention during the rest of the language section so he'd have no reason to pick on me again.

Sure enough, as soon as Major Parsons called a break, Sebastian headed for the door.

"May I have a word, please, Sergeant Hunter?" I said, as he shot past me.

He almost skidded to a halt, but before he turned to look at me, an expression that I couldn't catch flitted across his face.

"I'm rather busy, Ms. Venzi," he snapped.

"Too busy to say 'hello'?" I shot back.

He stared at me for a long second.

"Yes, I'm too busy for that," he replied, then stormed out of the door.

Well, fuck you, too!

Unfortunately, I could see that our little *tête-a-tête* had been far from inconspicuous.

"Bloody hell, Venzi! What did you do to the poor bastard? He looks as pleased to see you as a fart in a teacup."

I shook my head in frustration.

"I have no clue," I lied.

"He is a rude man," concluded Marc. "He is certainly no gentleman."

I had to agree, but the thought saddened me. Ten years ago, Sebastian had been the gentlest of souls. I couldn't help thinking back to his many acts of kindness toward me. That had been a long time ago; it was obvious that he detested me now.

I decided that I'd done as much as I could. If he didn't want to talk to me that was his prerogative. I wouldn't push it. Besides, this wretched training would be over soon, and I hoped to be on my way to Leatherneck within the next two or three days. I'd contacted my editor, and he'd promised to make some calls on my behalf to get things moving.

It seemed my last chance to talk to Sebastian had gone already, because he didn't return after lunch for the end of the training. No comment was made about his absence, but I had the feeling that the British officers were relieved he'd disappeared.

"So, I hope you found the last two days useful, Ms. Venzi," said Major Parsons, as I was packing up my bag.

"Most informative," I said, blandly.

"Glad to hear it," he said, a twinkle in his eye. "Did you actually learn anything new?"

"I have doubled my vocabulary in Dari and Pashto," I replied.

He looked puzzled.

"I didn't know you had spoken any before?" he said.

"I hadn't."

He grinned as he caught the gist of my meaning.

"I see! Well, perhaps I can make up for your lack of progress by buying you a drink tonight?"

Oh. I wasn't expecting that.

"That's very kind of you, Major, but I have some notes to prepare. It has been a pleasure meeting you."

He took my rejection well, returning my handshake with just the right amount of pressure.

"Good luck out there," he said seriously. "Keep your head down. I'd hate to hear that anything had happened to you." He hesitated for a moment. "Perhaps we could meet up—next time you're in Geneva—or in fact anywhere in Switzerland. I'll be in this post for the next six months at least."

"Well, thank you. I don't have any plans to be in the country again, but I'll certainly make a note of that."

At which point he resigned the field, and left with his dignity intact—and my opinion of him rose even higher.

"You are not interested, Lee?" said Marc, a knowing look on his face.

"What's the point?" I sighed. "I won't be in Switzerland again for months, if ever."

"You could just take him for a quick ride—see what his rising trot is like," Liz smirked.

I rolled my eyes. One-night stands had never been my thing, and what I'd said was true: there was no point in starting such a long-distance relationship. Apart from which, I'd have been a fool to get mixed up with another military man after my disastrous marriage.

We headed to the bar and spent the evening with several of the other journalists, swapping tall tales about some of the locations we'd reported from. Liz's tales were by far the tallest—although in her case, I was willing to bet they were all true.

Shortly before midnight, I headed back to my hotel, feeling in a much better mood. I still hadn't heard back from my editor during the day, but I was hopeful I'd be on the move soon.

I threw off my clothes and showered quickly, before checking my emails again. Still no word about my ride to Leatherneck. Annoying—but I wasn't going to worry just yet.

I programmed my cell to wake me in the morning and turned off the light, hoping against hope that I might actually get some sleep.

I was woken abruptly when someone banged on my bedroom door. I scrunched up my eyes and peered at my phone. Jeez! Two in the morning. Who the hell was knocking on my door at this hour?

Grumpily, I switched on the bedside lamp, squinting against the light, and fumbled for my robe.

"Who is it?"

"Let me in, Caro."

No one had called me 'Caro' in years, in fact, only one person had *ever* used that version of my name. And I knew his voice—except the tone was off.

Surprise and shock made my heart rate spike suddenly.

"What do you want, Sebastian?" I called through the door.

"Let me in," he mumbled again. "I need to talk to you."

Now he wanted to talk?

He banged on the door again. "Caro!"

At this rate he'd been waking up the entire hotel. His timing was lousy.

Reluctantly, but curious nonetheless, I pulled the door open.

Sebastian was leaning against the door frame, deliciously rumpled in old jeans, black t-shirt and a brown leather jacket. Irritating *and* gorgeous.

"Caro," he said, a leer on his face.

Oh hell. And also *very* drunk.

"What do you want, Sebastian?"

He didn't answer, but pushed past me into my room.

"What are you doing?" I asked again, my temper rising.

"Catching up with old friends," he smirked

"How did you find me?"

He grinned and tapped the side of his head with one long finger, "Military intelligence."

I closed the door, hoping that no one had seen or heard his noisy entrance into my room. But the hotel corridor was silent.

He fumbled out of his jacket and tossed it toward the chair, missing by a mile. I couldn't help noticing that his t-shirt was snug on his body in a way that brought back too many memories.

He sat down on the bed, and patted the space next to him, suggestively.

"Come and sit with me, Caro," he slurred.

Oh, I really didn't think so.

I folded my arms across my chest and stayed standing. His gaze drifted up and down me in a way that heated my whole body. I hadn't blushed like that in a long time.

"Why are you here, Sebastian? You had your chance to talk to me earlier today, but you preferred to ignore me."

He blinked up at me, his sea-green eyes puzzled. It was strange seeing him so far from the ocean. Then he smiled again.

"You still have a great ass, Caro."

Enough was enough.

"Okay, I think you'd better go now. Whatever you have to say to me can wait until you're sober."

He just sat there smiling at me. I decided to make the hint more obvious. I walked forward to pull him off the bed, but instead he leaned forward, wrapped his arms around me and buried his face in my chest. This was getting ridiculous. Couldn't the man take 'no' for an answer? And I certainly didn't want to be part of any harem.

"Sebastian, stop that," I said forcefully. "I want you to go. Now!"

But he increased his grip, and his shoulders started to shake. With something like horror, I realized he was crying.

"Why didn't you come back?" he sobbed. "I waited and waited for you, like I said I would, but you never came back! Why? Why didn't you come back? I love you I love you I love you."

I was stunned. No. This was not what I'd expected at all. And then I wondered if all his apparent dislike, all the rudeness he'd shown me, was just a wall protecting him from the pain I'd put him through, a rejection that had lasted years. He still loved me?

Oh no.

He couldn't mean it. No, it was the alcohol talking.

"Sebastian..." I began.

He clutched me tighter and started kissing my chest, pulling open my robe and exposing my breasts. He fastened his mouth over my nipple and began to tug gently with his teeth.

I tried to push him away.

"No!"

But he didn't stop. He pulled me onto the bed and pushed himself on top of me, kissing my throat and breasts over and over. He was so strong, I couldn't fight him off, his arms held my wrists and his body was heavy, crushing me into the mattress.

"Get off me!" I yelled at him, dragging my hands free and pushing at his chest with all my strength.

With a long sigh, he rolled onto his back and was still.

I sat up, shocked and afraid. I pulled my robe together and stared at him. He was fast asleep, passed out drunk and snoring softly.

I was shaking from a fear-fueled adrenaline rush.

I shoved him with my hand.

"Sebastian, wake up! Wake up!"

He mumbled something and rolled onto his side.

Shit. Just what I didn't need.

I wondered what the hell to do. If I phoned for help, everyone would just assume we'd slept together. I didn't want to ruin my already dented reputation, and if I reported his assault, he'd be arrested and court-martialed, with the distinct possibility that our illicit past would be uncovered.

No matter how far I traveled, no matter how hard I worked, I was never able to outrun my past. The thought made me cold with fury.

In the end, I decided the simplest thing to do was to leave him as he was. He certainly wasn't going to be making any more passes at me in that condition, and a small but insistent part of me remembered that we'd once been in love.

I wrestled his heavy biker boots off his feet and pulled the duvet over him. I definitely wasn't going to sleep naked like I usually did, so I hunted down a loose t-shirt, pulled on a pair of panties and crawled back into bed.

It felt so strange to have him lying next to me again after all these years. I lay awake for a long time, listening to the sound of his breathing, a flood of memories stirring my brain and warming my flesh.

When my alarm woke me the next morning, for the briefest moment, I couldn't remember what had happened. I froze when I realized I wasn't alone in bed, and then it all came back to me: Sebastian banging on my door, his fumbling kisses, his strange admission—drunken Sebastian passing out in my bed.

I felt his body shift on the mattress and he flexed his hips, lightly pushing his very noticeable morning wood into my back. Some things never changed.

Cautiously, I moved away from him and sat up.

A sleepy blue-green eye blinked up at me. He looked puzzled.

"Caro?"

"You're awake then," I said, sharply.

He looked embarrassed and confused when he realized where he was.

"Did we...?"

"No, we most definitely did not. You woke me up in the middle of the night by banging on my door, and then passed out on my bed."

"Oh, right."

He leaned up on one arm and looked down at the clothes he was still wearing, assessing the truth of my statement. Then he grinned at me.

"Sorry about that. We can make up for it now if you like?"

I couldn't believe him. Who the hell did he think he was?

"Astonishing as this may seem, Sebastian," I said in a cool voice, "your charming offer doesn't thrill me."

His smile slipped and for a moment he looked hurt: I remembered that look. Then his arrogant expression was back.

"Whatever."

He swung his long legs out of the bed and sat up. He didn't seem to be experiencing any hangover effects whatsoever. *God, he was annoying!*

"Where are my boots?" he muttered.

"Under the chair," I said, pointing. "Along with your jacket."

He stood up and I was a little amused to see he had to rearrange his pants. He picked up his jacket and I realized he was leaving. I was surprised to feel a pang of disappointment.

"Why did you come here last night, Sebastian?"

He frowned, then shrugged. "I don't remember."

He strolled toward the door and glanced over his shoulder once.

"See you around, Caro."

And then he was gone.

I sat there for several minutes, trying to process what had just happened. He'd always been so easy to read, but now I didn't have a clue what was going on with him.

I shook my head and made a mental note not to open my door to strange men in the middle of the night, no matter how hot they were or how well they filled a pair of jeans.

After my unusually stimulating wake-up call, the day dragged. My editor had emailed during the night to say that my travel documents had definitely been delayed, but that he was hoping to get hold of someone who could help as soon as possible. The small print was: expect to be stuck in Geneva for at least a few days.

Liz commiserated with me over breakfast.

"Sorry to hear that, Lee. I got my papers couriered over from the Embassy first thing. My flight leaves in a couple of hours. Maybe see you out there."

"Maybe," I said, wearily. "Look after yourself. Keep your head down and watch your back."

"You know me, Lee, I wear brass knickers—utterly indestructible."

We hugged briefly, and she was off again.

I texted Marc to see if he was free. I couldn't face a day wandering around pointlessly by myself. I much preferred pointless wandering with company. I was relieved when Marc said he'd be happy to meet up. We spent a peaceful day examining a photography exhibition in the Sonia Zannettacci gallery, and strolling along the Quai de Seujet toward the lake.

By early evening, I was starting to feel hungry and Marc offered to keep me company over a plate of pasta in a small, family run bistro that I'd discovered just around the corner from my hotel. I was digging into a very tasty *pizzoccheri*, a tagliatelle-type pasta made from buckwheat flour and cooked with asparagus and diced potatoes—a local specialty—when Marc's phone beeped to tell him he had a message.

"I am afraid, *chère* Lee, that I will be leaving you alone after this night. My papers and assignment have come through."

I was pleased for him but a feeling of despondency washed over me. How could the British and French governments expedite visas for their nationals, while my own was so inept?

As we discussed his imminent departure to Fayzabad in the north of Afghanistan, we made vague arrangements to meet up, should we find ourselves within spitting distance.

We'd nearly finished a carafe of house red, when I became aware that someone was hovering over us. To my astonishment, and more than a little dismay, I saw it was Sebastian.

He looked as though he was barely managing to rein in his temper, his eyes blazing.

"We need to talk," he said from between gritted teeth.

Before I could frame a reply, he grabbed my arm to pull me up.

Marc stood immediately. "Let go of her, *m'sieur*, or you and I will have a problem."

Sebastian scowled at him and for a moment I thought I was going to be breaking up a fight, but then he dropped my arm.

I wanted to know what the hell Sebastian was playing at. Whatever his problem, I'd had enough of this game of hide and seek where he was the only one who understood the rules.

"It's okay, Marc," I said, quietly.

He raised his eyebrows, stared at Sebastian, then back at me. "Very well, but I will be phoning your mobile in 15 minutes to check on you, *chérie*."

I smiled and blew him a kiss.

"Who the fuck does he think he is?" snarled Sebastian as I left the bistro with him.

I stared at him in amazement. "A friend! What's it to you?"

He didn't answer.

I trailed along beside him as he marched down the street in furious silence. I didn't know whether to be amused at his petulance, angry at his rudeness, or wary of his apparent temper. All three, probably.

He ducked into a small *bierkeller*, holding open the door for me. Well, that was a small improvement in manners. The barman nodded at him in recognition, and Liz's words came back to me: *they say he drinks.*

He ordered without asking my preference.

"*Deux* whiskies."

He had a damn nerve!

"*Non merci, je préfère du vin rouge, monsieur.*" I'd always preferred red wine to whiskey.

Sebastian looked enraged. *Well, fuck him.*

The barman poured our drinks, then wandered off to serve a couple of tourists at the other end of the bar.

Sebastian tossed the whiskey down his throat, and turned to face me.

"What are you doing here, Caro?" he said, a scowl marring his lovely face.

"That's a good question, Sebastian," I replied calmly. "Right now, I'm wondering why the hell I'm listening to you order me around."

"Oh, for fuck's sake!"

His reply was almost amusing. Almost.

"Seriously, what is it to you?" I asked, genuinely interested in an honest answer.

He ran his hands over his hair, a gesture, I remembered, that expressed extreme frustration.

"It's dangerous out there, Caro. In Afghanistan, I mean. I know that's where you're going—obviously."

What?!

I took a deep breath.

"Sebastian, apart from the fact that I've already had assignments reporting from Iraq and Darfur—which weren't exactly summer camps—*it's none of your business.*"

"It *is* my business!"

He really was unbelievable.

"Based on what?"

He was silent.

"You know, Sebastian," I said, my voice rising with anger, "I spent 11 years being told what to do by my ex-husband—I don't need *you* to do it as well. You of all people should understand that."

He blanched, his expression wounded. It was the first time either of us had referred to the past or what had happened between us.

"Caro, that's not it, I..."

But I'd had enough. If these were the pearls of wisdom that I'd come to hear, thereby screwing up my last evening with Marc, I'd had enough. I stood up to leave.

"Caro! Don't ... don't go."

His expression and voice were pleading.

"Why did you bring me here, Sebastian? And I'd *really* like to know why you assaulted me last night."

He gaped at me.

"Assaulted? I didn't! I'd never..." his words trailed off and he stared at me in anguish, as he saw the anger on my face.

"Actually you did—you were just too drunk to remember it. You're damn lucky I didn't report you. Although I'm fairly sure you can work out the reason why I didn't—why I couldn't. Good night, Sebastian."

I took a step away, then turned and looked back at him. "I hope you have a nice life, I really do. And while you're at it—quit drinking before you really do something stupid. More stupid."

And then I turned on my heel and left.

CHAPTER THREE

I WAS FUMING AS I STRODE BACK TO MY HOTEL. WHETHER IT WAS THE CHILL night air or the memory of his hurt expression as I walked out, my anger began to cool.

And no matter how inappropriate his behavior, I realized it was because he was concerned about my well-being. I shook my head. I really couldn't figure him out. One minute he was either ignoring me or just plain rude, the next trying to sleep with me, then acting like a jealous boyfriend when he found me with Marc. And *how the hell* did he find me in the first place? Twice.

I wished we could have talked like two normal human beings. That seemed unlikely. There was too much history, too much turbulent water under the bridge.

By the time I slid the keycard into the door of my hotel room, my ire had leached away. Instead, I felt restless and irritable. I checked my cell to see if I'd had an email from my editor, but although he'd written to say he was still chasing his contacts in the Defense Department, there was no other news. Worse still, it was beginning to look like the delay would be numbered in weeks, not days.

I threw the phone onto my bed in disgust, and decided a hot shower might relax me. It was a futile hope.

I'd just wrapped myself in a towel when I heard a knock at my door. My instincts told me it wasn't going to be room service.

"Yes?"

"Caro, it's me. Can we talk?"

"I think we've said everything, Sebastian."

"Can I come in? Just to talk."

"Is that a joke? No, you can't."

There was a pause, then his voice became quieter and more strained.

"Caro, please. I won't ... try anything. I just want to talk to you. Please."

His voice sounded so desolate, my resolution began to waver, buckle, and give way entirely.

"Okay," I sighed. "Listen, I'll meet you in the lobby in five minutes. That's my best offer."

"You ... you don't trust me?"

I didn't reply.

"Okay," he said, softly, "I'll be waiting."

I ran a comb through my wet hair and pulled on a pair of jeans, t-shirt and jacket.

I half expected him to be waiting outside my door, but the corridor was silent and empty.

The elevator slid to the ground floor, exhaling with a soft hiss as the doors opened. My eyes scanned the room and I saw him at once. He was sitting on a long, low sofa, his head in his hands.

When he looked up and saw me, his expression cleared, a small smile appearing on his face. He stood up politely as I approached, but my own gaze, I'm sure, was wary.

I sat on a chair next to the sofa, and waited for him to speak.

"You came," he said, quietly.

"Evidently. What do you want now, Sebastian?"

My voice was cool and distant, although inside I felt anything but.

"Would you like a drink?"

I raised my eyebrows. "Is that supposed to be funny?"

"No ... I..."

He looked longingly toward the bar, then dropped his gaze to his hands.

I crossed my arms and waited for him to speak.

"What you said earlier..." He took a deep breath, and that simple action seemed to raise some sort of emotional barricade.

"I didn't really assault you, did I," he said, confidently. "You were just saying that to get back at me."

Is that why he'd begged me to come here? To call me a liar? A fantasist?

"No, Sebastian, you really did," I replied with some heat. "You were drunk ... I couldn't ... couldn't stop you."

I closed my eyes, and shivered at the memory.

"If you hadn't passed out when you did ... you scared me," I said, looking him in the eye. "It reminded me of your..."

I bit my lip to stem the flood of my hasty words, but it was too late. He gasped.

"I reminded you of ... of my father?"

I nodded, and his expression was stricken.

"You were really afraid to let me in your room just now? I scared you that much?"

I didn't reply, leaving an appalled silence hanging in the air.

"Oh God! Caro ... I never ... I couldn't..."

I stared at him doubtfully. The boy I'd known would never have hurt me—but he was long gone. I didn't know who Sebastian was anymore—he was a stranger.

"Fuck, Caro! I'm so sorry."

He dropped his head into his hands again.

I beat back a long-dormant urge to comfort him, to hold him and tell him it would be okay. Instead I continued to stare at him, tracing the memories of ten, long years in the past.

My cell phone rang, which was a very welcome interruption.

"*Chérie!* I have been calling and calling you! Are you all right?"

"Oh, shit! Sorry, Marc. Yes, I'm fine. Really. You don't need to worry."

"Hmm, okay, you are still with him?"

"We're just sitting in the lobby at my hotel. I'm good, really."

"*Bien, ma chère*. If you say so. Call if you need me."

"I won't, but thanks, Marc. Have a safe flight and look after yourself—I wouldn't want anything to happen to you. *Ciao*."

Sebastian frowned. "Was that your *friend?*"

I rolled my eyes.

"Is he your boyfriend?"

I laughed, but without humor.

"Marc is a good friend. He was just ... being concerned."

"Yeah, right."

"Actually, I think you're more his type."

Sebastian looked surprised. I'd known for years that Marc was gay, but he didn't broadcast the fact—it wouldn't have been good for his career.

"Did you ... tell him about me?" he asked, quietly.

"Which part?" I sighed. "It doesn't matter: the answer is no—it's not anyone's business but mine."

I looked pointedly at my watch.

"Sebastian, it's late and I'm tired. If you've got anything else to say to me, say it quickly. Otherwise I'm going to bed."

He stared at his hands again.

"I'm sorry I've been such a jerk," he said, his voice quiet, almost humble. "It was just ... a shock ... seeing you again."

"For me, too," I said, softly.

He looked suddenly hopeful, and I regretted giving him a reason.

"Let me make it up to you, Caro. Let me take you out tomorrow. I could show you the city. I've been here for months—I know my way around pretty well."

"I don't think so..."

"Caro, come on. I'll be on my best behavior, I promise—I know your travel permit hasn't come through."

I narrowed my eyes. "How do you know that?"

"Well..." He paused. "That was just the impression I had. You'd have been packing otherwise."

Again, there was something off about his tone, but I couldn't put my finger on it. On the other hand, this whole conversation had been more than usually fraught.

"Please, Caro, I know some great Italian restaurants. It'll be like..."

He hesitated, so I finished the sentence for him, "...old times?"

He gave a small smile. "Do you have anything better to do?"

I sighed, giving in. "No, I don't. Fine. But one false move, Hunter, and you'll regret it."

He grinned hugely. "Yes, ma'am!"

I couldn't help smiling back.

I was exhausted by the heated emotions that had been superabundant lately. A glass of wine sounded damn fine. I looked over toward the bar.

Now we'd talked and he'd apologized, I was able to relax a little.

"I think I will have that drink now."

Before I could stand up to go to the bar, he was on his feet.

"I'll get it. A red wine?"

"Yes, thank you."

I slumped in my seat, watching him lean against the bar while waiting to be served. The last time we'd spent time together like this, he hadn't been old enough to buy alcohol.

I was surprised when he returned with two glasses of wine, I'd assumed he'd be hitting the whiskey again. I was very glad to see he wasn't.

"I got you a Barolo."

"Mmm, my favorite."

"I know. I remembered you liked it."

I stared at him in amazement. How on earth did he remember something like that?

"Oh, well ... thank you."

I suddenly felt awkward again, his gaze was too intense. I sighed. It was time to have *that* conversation.

"How was it ... after I left?"

He leaned back on the sofa and closed his eyes, as if in pain. When he opened them again the old wounds were raw.

"Bad."

He swallowed, and I could tell he was trying to find the words.

"Mom and Dad were ... in the end Mitch went to see them—I didn't know what he said at the time but he and Shirley took me to live with them. Later, I found out that Mitch had threatened to go to my dad's CO and tell him that he'd been ... beating up on me."

My hand fluttered to my mouth, trying to block the rising nausea.

"On my eighteenth birthday, I enlisted in the Marines." He looked up. "That's pretty much it."

"And Mitch and Shirley? Ches?"

"Mitch and Shirley were posted to Germany soon after that. Ches was studying at UCSD so when I had leave, I used to hang with him and his college buddies." He smiled briefly. "He's married with two kids now."

"You're kidding me? Really?"

I tried to imagine happy-go-lucky Ches as a responsible father of two. And then I remembered a time when Sebastian and I had thought about having children. An impossible dream.

"Did he enlist?"

"He was going to, but then he met Amy at college and she talked him out of it. He's the manager at La Jolla Country Club now."

I had memories of the country club, the brief few weeks of my membership while Sebastian had worked there as a lifeguard. In particular I remembered one very steamy session of illicit sex in a changing room storage closet, of all places.

From the heat in Sebastian's eyes, he was currently on the same page. I had to look away.

"Are Shirley and Mitch still out in Germany?"

"No. Mitch got sent to Parris Island as an instructor. But last time I saw them, they were talking about going back to San Diego. I guess they want to be near their grandkids."

"Where did Donna and Johan go?"

An odd expression crossed Sebastian's face. "How did you know they went away?"

I hesitated, wondering if an honest answer was in anyone's best interest after so many years. But, perhaps, after all, it needed to be said.

"I wrote to them."

He leaned forward, staring at me.

"When?"

"Around the time of your 21st birthday, Sebastian. And to Shirley and Mitch. My letters were returned to sender, unopened. I assumed they'd either gone away or..."

I didn't need to finish the sentence. He let out a lungful of air in a long sigh, as if he'd been holding his breath for a very long time.

"So, you did try to contact me?"

"Yes and no. I wanted to believe that you'd gone on with your life and I didn't want to ... disrupt anything. That's why I tried to contact Shirley and Mitch. I wanted to find out if my approach would be a positive thing—or not. When my letter was returned..."

I looked up at him. His expression was skeptical and I felt both hurt and annoyed: he didn't believe me.

"Everyone said I should just forget about you," he said, his voice deep with regret. "As if that was even possible. I tried to find you, Caro, but I didn't know your surname—your unmarried name—and the only person who knew..."

Was my ex-husband.

"I left messages everywhere I could think of," he continued, quietly. "I asked the new tenants at your house, at Shirley and Mitch's, and Donna's—I asked them to forward any mail to me ... I guess that didn't happen. Fuck, Caro, we would have been..."

He couldn't finish, his voice becoming choked and indistinct. I noticed his hands were shaking slightly as he took a long drink of his wine.

"You thought I didn't care."

He shrugged. "I didn't know what to think at first. Later ... yeah, I guess I thought you'd ... moved on."

I sighed. "I did move on, Sebastian. I had to. When those letters came back ... and even before I sent them, I thought you'd be better off without me. I hoped that your life would be ... different. More like Ches's. I guess that explains why you were so unpleasant the last few days."

He winced and looked apologetic.

"Shit, I'm really sorry about that. It was just such a fucking shock. I didn't know what to think. It sent me into a real tailspin."

"It was a shock for me, too, Sebastian, but I didn't behave like a dick."

He glanced at me, surprised, then gave a small, contrite smile.

"Not your style, Caro."

His smile faded and I could tell he wanted to ask me something, but wasn't sure if he should. I could probably guess...

I leaned back in my chair.

"Just ask me, Sebastian."

He blinked a couple of times, then shook his head slowly, an admiring smile lifting his lips.

"You're so fearless, Caro, I love that about you."

His words caught me by surprise, leaving me speechless. Again.

"I was wondering ... if you were seeing anyone."

Yes, that's what I'd thought he was going to ask.

"No, I'm not."

He seemed to relax one degree. "But you were? I mean ... since..."

"I dated a couple of times, but no, there was nothing serious. Besides, I travel too much to sustain a relationship. And I definitely don't want to get tied down again."

He frowned, but didn't comment.

"What about you? Any significant other?"

He snorted and rolled his eyes. "Fuck, no!"

I raised my eyebrows. "That's not what I heard."

"What? What did you hear?" he said, almost angrily.

I was rather taken aback by his tone, but as we seemed to putting it all out there...

"About your CO's wife—in Paris? Maybe it was just gossip."

He grinned wickedly. "Oh, that. Guy was a first class bastard—he deserved it."

I shook my head in admonishment. "And did she 'deserve' it? His wife?"

"Yes, she did."

I hated to see such an ugly expression on his beautiful face.

"And the possibility of getting court-martialed and thrown out of the Corps ... that didn't matter to you either?"

He shrugged arrogantly. "I don't give a shit."

I didn't like this aggressive, macho-bullshit side to him. I decided I'd done enough strolling down memory lane for one evening.

"Well, I think I'll call it a night now, Sebastian."

His startled expression met my cool one.

"Don't go, Caro! We've only just started talking again. You haven't finished your wine, you..."

"No, I'm tired."

I started to stand but he laid a restraining hand on my thigh.

"Caro, I really want you."

What? He was unbelievable! Why was I even listening to this crap?

"For God's sake, Sebastian! We have one civilized drink together and you think I'm just going to fall into bed with you?"

"You used to."

I felt like I'd been slapped—and I really, really wanted to hit him.

"How dare you!" I hissed.

The realization of what he'd said and how I'd interpreted it sank in, painting his face with disgust. At himself, I hoped.

"I didn't mean it like that," he said, sullenly.

I stood up to leave and he grabbed hold of my hand.

"Caro, wait! Shit! I'm sorry."

I shook him off.

"Sebastian, we can't just roll back the last ten years and pretend it never happened. Too much has happened—too much time has passed."

"Come on, Caro, don't say that."

"Good night, Sebastian."

I didn't bother with the elevator—I needed to burn off some of the angry energy that coursed through me. I couldn't help feeling that his clumsy pass was some sort of attempt to punish me—to add me to his list of conquests so he could reach some closure maybe, seal shut the door to his past.

Just when I'd started to feel...

No. Not going there. Definitely not going there.

To add insult to serious irritation, there was still no news from my editor. I stormed around my hotel room, finding insignificant jobs to do, then hammered out more emails to Jenna and Alice as an attempt at distraction. It was a futile attempt.

I didn't know what the hell was going on with Sebastian. Some moments I could sense the presence of the sweet boy he had been, whose thoughtfulness and kindness had swept me off my feet, as much if not more than his physical presence. But at other times, I saw nothing more than a bitter and predatory manwhore whose aim was to bed as many women as possible, and whose primary weapon was his ridiculous good looks.

I was half expecting him to come knocking on my door again, and I had a few choice phrases on standby, but the corridor was eerily silent.

Annoyed with myself, annoyed with him, I flung myself into bed and spent a sleepless night fighting with the duvet.

Before dawn, I gave up and headed to the hotel's pool, swimming a few dozen laps before other guests arrived to make it unpleasantly crowded.

I staggered out of the pool and wrapped myself in the bathrobe provided by the hotel, before padding back toward my room.

Rounding the corner, I heard his voice before I saw him, his angry tones echoing down the corridor.

"For fuck's sake, Caro! Can we please just talk?"

He thumped on my door again, and then I heard him mutter to himself, "This is fucking crazy."

"That's one of the words," I said quietly, and saw him flinch.

He turned around and had the grace to look ashamed.

"Oh. I thought you weren't talking to me."

"That certainly would have been one of my better ideas."

He sighed, and rubbed the light brown stubble on his chin.

"Look, I'm sorry. I mean it. Around you, I just seem to open my mouth to change feet."

"You can say that again."

"I will if you let me buy you breakfast," he said, raising one eyebrow and grinning at me.

"Are you stalking me, Sebastian? I thought we said everything we had to say to each other last night?"

His face fell and he looked hurt.

"I just want ... can't we be friends?"

"Friends? I was under the impression you wanted to fuck me, out of some sense of revenge."

I glared at him.

"No!"

"Are you sure about that? Because last night you told me that's exactly what you did to your CO's wife. Why should I be any different?"

He stared at me in disbelief.

"Just go," I said, wearily.

I really didn't want to fight with him again, it was too tiring.

He took a deep breath.

"I know I'm saying everything wrong but ... we used to have fun, didn't we? Let's just spend some time together—get to know each other again. You're right—we can't pretend the last ten years never happened. Just ... give me a chance. I'm not the heartless bastard you seem to think I am. I'm still me, Caro."

He was still beautiful, but the same? I didn't think so.

I stared back at him, remembering how two nights ago, he had cried in my arms. Was that the real Sebastian, or was it the cold predator who preyed on women? I desperately wanted to believe that the former was the real man.

He must have seen in my eyes that I was weakening.

"We could start with breakfast," he said, almost hopefully. "Who knows, I might be able to get through a whole meal without making you mad at me."

"It seems unlikely," I replied, a reluctant smile creeping across my face.

He grinned back.

"You gonna wear that robe? Not that I give a shit—you could go naked for all I care. In fact..."

I groaned. "I'm going to take a shower. I'll see you in ten minutes."

"Want me to scrub your back?"

"Sebastian, I thought you were going to try and make it through breakfast before making me mad at you—right now your adolescent flirting is just annoying."

He grinned at me, but held his hands up in a gesture of defeat. "Okay, I get the message. I'll see you downstairs."

He turned on his heel, and strode off toward the stairs, whistling to himself.

God, he was annoying. And cute. But mostly annoying.

I took my time getting ready, I wanted to test his threshold of tolerance. I dressed slowly, checked my messages and took a moment to email my editor—again. It was nearly half an hour before I made it down to the hotel's restaurant for breakfast.

He was gazing out of the window, an untouched cup of black coffee in front of him.

I took a moment to drink in his beauty, which seemed almost otherworldly in the low light of early morning. His eyes were softer than I'd seen them in the last few days and had a faraway expression that suggested he was lost in memories. His short, Marine-style hair was golden blond, no doubt bleached by a foreign sun, and his full, sensual lips were slightly parted. His long legs were stretched out in front of him, his hands relaxed in his lap.

When he saw me, his eyes brightened and he stood up politely.

"You look great," he said.

Yeah, in old jeans and a t-shirt.

I rolled my eyes at him, and his smile slipped a notch.

"Did you order yet?"

"No, just the coffee. I was waiting for you."

"I usually have the continental breakfast."

He waved to the waitress, who was unusually attentive. I had the impression she'd been watching us. Well, watching him.

Plus ça change.

"Was there anything in particular you wanted to see in Geneva?" he said, once the waitress left with our order.

"You have to make it through breakfast without being irritating first," I reminded him.

"Yeah, well, I like a challenge," he said, smiling. "Seriously, anything you want to see?"

"Not really. I saw a lot wandering around yesterday. The Russian Church, maybe? I hear that's pretty amazing."

He fiddled with his napkin, then looked up.

"I had an idea of something we could do—if you like."

"Which is?"

"How about a trip to Chamonix? It's only an hour away—or just a little longer if we take the scenic route through Lausanne. It'll be a really great trip through the Alps." He grinned at me. "I'll have you back before bedtime."

Nope. Still annoying. But I couldn't resist his enthusiasm and playfulness. Plus, I'd heard that the road to Chamonix was particularly stunning, and I liked the idea of getting out of the city.

"And you absolutely *promise* you'll bring me back here by evening? No accidentally running out of gas or getting lost."

"I wouldn't dream of it," he said, with a look on his face that made me doubt every syllable.

"Okay, but I'm serious about getting back. I'm waiting for my travel permits and I can't afford to miss them."

He shifted uncomfortably in his seat. "Caro, I'll get you back here tonight, I promise."

Our breakfast arrived and Sebastian proceeded to chow down on anything that didn't move. Something else that hadn't changed.

"Tell me about Ches's kids," I said, trying for some relaxed conversation, but also genuinely curious.

Sebastian smiled.

"They're great. They call me 'Uncle Seb' ... well, Simone, the youngest one, she calls me 'Zed' because she still gets her words mixed up sometimes. She's nearly three. Ben is four and he's a little surf-rat already. I see them as often as I can, but every time they seem so much more grown up. Jeez, they grow fast."

"What's Amy like?"

"Yeah, she's okay."

I raised my eyebrows—his tone was distinctly lukewarm.

"Let me guess—she doesn't approve of you?"

He looked surprised. "What made you say that?"

"First, because you're single, and married women get nervous that their husband's single friends will lead them astray; second, because, from the sound of it, you've had more women than most men have hot dinners, and *that* will make her nervous because she won't want you reminding Ches of what he's missing out on, and..."

I stopped mid sentence.

"And what?"

"Well, the drinking, Sebastian. She wouldn't want that around her husband and kids."

He grimaced. "Yeah, I guess that about sums it up."

"When did you start drinking?" I said, gently.

"What do you mean? I don't drink that much, not like that bitch mother of mine."

I stared at him. "Well, twice in as many days you've been so drunk you've either passed out or made inappropriate comments to me."

Sebastian's face darkened perceptibly.

"I think my question stands," I said, holding his gaze.

He looked at me, hesitating to reply immediately.

"When I was 21," he said at last. "That's when I started drinking."

And then it hit me, fool that I was. The drinking, the womanizing, the reckless disregard for his career: it had all begun when he was 21. It had all begun because he'd given up—given up hope of love ... of me.

"Sebastian, I'm so sorry. I had no idea."

My words seemed deeply inadequate.

He shrugged and looked away. "Old news, Caro, don't worry about it."

I struggled to think of something neutral to say.

"Do you like living in Geneva?"

Lame, but it was the first thought that came to mind.

"It's okay, but I miss the ocean."

"Ah, no famous Swiss surfing beaches."

He grinned, his equilibrium restored. "I haven't found any yet."

I smiled back.

"Are you done eating?" he asked impatiently. "Let's go."

"I just need to go back to my room and pick up a jacket and, I presume, my passport, but otherwise, yes, I'm good to go."

He frowned. "You're a journalist: you should always have your passport with you. Hell, that was in that fucking tedious lecture that Parsons gave the day before yesterday."

"So you were listening."

He shook his head and smiled.

"Yeah, yeah, just grab a sweater, too—it's going to get cold."

I nodded as I left him at the table, but I was puzzled. It was mid March, it wasn't *that* cold. But when I saw him waiting for me at the front of the building, I understood why he'd told me to dress warm.

"Are you kidding me, Hunter? You expect me to get on that thing?"

Sebastian was standing next to a large, black Japanese motorcycle with French plates, his eyes dancing with amusement.

"Sure! It'll be fun."

I eyed the monster warily. It didn't look like *fun*: it looked dangerous and cold.

"Do you know how to drive it?" I asked suspiciously.

"Caro, I rode it from Paris—I think I can manage 88 kilometers to Chamonix," he said, grinning widely.

"I don't know," I muttered, shifting from foot to foot. "I've never been on the back of a motorcycle before."

He looked surprised. "Really? Because we used to talk about riding from..."

He stopped abruptly.

Was it ever going to get easier to talk about the past?

"Oh, what the hell," I said, shaking my head.

"Such faith in my abilities, Ms. Venzi."

"If I get killed on this thing, I'm going to come back and haunt you!"

"Promise?"

"Oh, you'd better believe it, Hunter!"

He smirked, then passed me a heavy, leather jacket that was obviously one of his. It was old and battered and so enormous that my hands disappeared inside the long sleeves. It had that pleasant musty smell of old leather, and a faint trace of Sebastian's own delicious scent.

He pulled up the zipper for me, and turned back the cuffs so I could free my hands.

"Suits you," he said, raising an eyebrow.

Then he handed me a shiny, black helmet that matched his own. He swung one long, denim-clad leg over the seat and held out his hand to help me mount the machine.

The seat tipped me slightly forward so my thighs automatically gripped his.

"Hold on tight," he said, his voice muffled through the helmet.

I could tell from the tone that he was enjoying himself. I would really have liked to ignore the suggestion, but I was so terrified of falling off, that I wrapped my arms around his waist and hung on tightly. I could feel the hardness of his body beneath the leather and I knew for certain that agreeing to this trip had been a bad, bad idea.

The engine started with a gravelly roar that crescendoed as Sebastian revved the accelerator.

He started forward at a gentle pace, mostly for my benefit I had to assume, and soon we were traveling steadily through Geneva, before taking the lakeside road north-east to Lausanne.

The lake was a steely green-gray and flecked with white. It was serene and timeless and I felt my body start to relax. Irritating as it was to admit, I was beginning to enjoy myself.

Sebastian must have felt the change in my body because he accelerated smoothly, bending forward slightly, weaving his way past the patchwork fields as we continued to circle the lake. I snuggled closer, grateful for the warmth of his body as the cool air flowed past us.

He slowed as we reached Montreux, giving me time to appreciate the chocolate-box prettiness of the old town with chalets and fairytale granite castle, and the contrasting modernity of the concrete and glass buildings, and hotels that looked like chateaux.

"Do you want to get a coffee?" he called over his shoulder.

I nodded enthusiastically, bumping my helmet awkwardly on the back of his, and gave him a thumbs up.

He drew up outside a small café that looked out onto the lake, then kicked down the stand and cut the engine. The sudden silence was very welcome and I gazed out across the water, feeling peaceful, at peace.

Sebastian pulled off his helmet and grinned at me.

"How was that?"

I struggled out of my own helmet and hoped my 'hat hair' wasn't too scary.

"That was ... surprisingly okay!"

He laughed at my bemused expression, then his eyes darkened in a way I remembered. It was a look of lust and need and deep, burning desire. Yes, I remembered.

I scrambled off the bike hastily and rubbed my hands trying to get some warmth back into my fingers.

"Are you cold?"

"Just my hands."

Without saying a word, he took my hands in his and lifted them to his lips, heating them with his warm breath and rubbing them gently.

After a moment, I pulled free.

"That's fine, thank you."

He continued to stare at me, his expression serious. I looked away, confused and ill at ease.

"This café looks good," I said desperately.

I heard his soft sigh, but refused to look at him. Instead, I strode into the café and found a table by the window.

Sebastian followed more slowly, sliding into the chair opposite me.

"*Un espresso et un caffé americano, s'il vous plâit.*"

"You speak French?" I asked curiously.

He shrugged. "Enough to get by. I never studied it."

"And the Dari? The Arabic? How did that come about?"

"My first tour in Iraq. I was playing soccer with some of the local kids who used to hang around the Base. They taught me a few words and I just started picking up some phrases. My sergeant heard me talking to the kids and sent me on a couple of training courses. When we started pulling out of Iraq, they figured I should learn Pashto and Dari so I could be useful in Afghanistan. I found I could just *hear* it, all the different cadences." He sneered. "Finally found something I was good at. Who knew."

I was shocked by his dismissive tone.

"You were always good at lots of things, Sebastian. You picked up Italian really quickly."

"That's because I had an Italian girlfriend," he said.

"Really? When was that?"

He rolled his eyes as if I was missing the obvious.

"Oh, right," I muttered, embarrassed. "And you taught me to surf, don't forget."

He grinned, breaking the tension of his odd outburst.

"Yeah, that was fun. Did you ever keep it up?"

"I go quite often in the summer," I said. "I bought a place in Long Beach and..."

I ground to a halt, worried by his stricken expression.

"Sorry," he said, shaking his head, as if to cast off some grim thought, "It's just ... well, we used to talk about going to Long Beach and checking out the surf spots."

"I didn't have any other plan," I said, quietly. "When I left you ... when I left San Diego, I drove for eight days until I arrived in New York. That old Pinto I had, died crossing Verrazano Bridge. I got an apartment in Little Italy because I didn't know anywhere else and you'd mentioned it once. I lived there for eight years. You were right, I did like it."

He closed his eyes and let his head drop into his hands. He looked so vulnerable. How such ordinary words can hurt us, I thought.

"God, Caro, when I think about how things could have been ... it makes me a little crazy."

"I know what you mean," I said, softly. "But there's no point thinking like that."

The waitress returned with our coffees. I stared into the dark liquid, losing myself in the wisps of steam.

"I'm glad you went there, I'm glad you did the things we said we'd do."

"Not all of them," I amended.

"Fuck, if only..."

"Stop, Sebastian," I said, forcefully. "No 'what ifs': what if we'd never gone to that Sicilian restaurant that night, what if Brenda hadn't seen us, what if she hadn't told your parents ... there's no point thinking like that. Like you said, it'll just make us crazy."

"I know you're right, it's just that..." He ran one hand over his hair in frustration.

"Hey, stop," I said, grabbing his fingers. "It is what it is. We can't change anything."

He held on tightly, then rubbed his eyes with his free hand.

"Mind you," I said, "if I ran into Brenda again, I might have to give her a quick slap."

He smiled slightly.

"Yeah, I'd like to see that." Then he frowned. "She felt really bad about what happened."

I released his hand, and leaned back in my chair.

"You spoke to her about it—what she did?"

I was amazed. Maybe even hurt. Brenda the Slut was the only memory I had of her. Yes, she'd certainly lit the fuse that had led to our explosive separation. I knew, deep down, that it would have happened anyway, but still. To hear that Sebastian had spoken with her, maybe even stayed in touch with her. Maybe even *slept* with her—I really wasn't ready to hear *that*.

"Well, yeah. She kept bugging Ches until I agreed to see her. By then it was kind of obvious why she'd done it."

"Obvious how?"

He sighed.

"She was pregnant—knocked up by that bastard Jack Sullivan. You remember that older guy who used to hang out at the beach? Yeah, well, when she found out she was pregnant, she freaked. Had this crazy idea in her head that if she could get back with me, she'd get me to sleep with her and pretend the baby was mine."

He shook his head in disbelief at the screwed up behavior of a scared 18 year-old girl.

"She thought if you were out of the way, we'd get back together. She had no idea what she'd done. Until after—and it was too late."

"And did you? Sleep with her?"

"For fuck's sake," he said, his anger evident. "I told you. I didn't even touch another woman for three years."

"Sorry."

"Yeah, well," he said, continuing with the grim little story, "she had to face her parents eventually. Jack wouldn't have anything to do with her, and she wouldn't say who the father was. Everyone assumed it was me anyway."

He rubbed his forehead tiredly. "But when Kimberley was born, she had all this dark brown hair and dark eyes, it was kind of obvious I wasn't the father."

"Kimberley?"

"She's a great kid. I see them sometimes when I'm on the west coast. Brenda married a car salesman a couple of years back. He's a pretty nice guy and good with Kimberley."

I nodded slowly, finding I couldn't dislike Brenda as much as I'd wanted to.

"Well, I'm glad it worked out for her—in the end." I paused. "You didn't tell me what happened to Donna and Johan. They were always kind to me."

"Shirley's stayed in touch with them. I saw them a few times after ... Johan retired a couple of years back, and they moved to Phoenix. I heard he was pretty sick—leukemia, I think."

"I'm sorry to hear that, they were a nice couple."

Oh, poor Johan. Such a decent man. Poor Donna. Maybe I should write ... no, they wouldn't want to hear from me.

He nodded but didn't reply.

"What about that funny little friend of yours—Fido? What was his real name ... um ... Alfred? Albert? Arnold! What happened to him?"

Sebastian didn't smile, which was never a good sign.

"He enlisted just before me. He joined the Rakkasans, 187th Infantry. He died eight years ago in Iraq—IED. Poor bastard never stood a chance. He didn't even make it to twenty."

"Oh no, I'm so sorry!"

And I remembered that sweet kid who used to try and flirt with me: dead. All those young men gone.

We finished our coffees in silence, each lost in the past.

Every time I thought we'd finished our stroll down memory lane, something else came along to hijack us, tugging us back to our turbulent history. It was like being on an emotional carnival ride—including the nausea, but seriously lacking the fun.

"Ready to head for Chamonix?" asked Sebastian.

I smiled at him, grateful that he'd interrupted my musings.

"Yes, ready as I'll ever be. Actually though, it's more comfortable riding on that motorcycle than I thought it would be. I just wish I'd worn something warmer."

"Put your hands in my pockets this time," he said. "That will help. And there's a shop in Chamonix where we can get you some good gloves."

"That's not necessary."

"I can buy you some fucking gloves, Caro!" he said, crossly.

"Fine!" I snapped, matching his irritated tone, "Although I have no idea what 'fucking gloves' are: made of latex?"

He laughed loudly. "God, I love you, Caro!"

He stopped when he'd realized what he'd said.

"Slip of the tongue," he mumbled.

I ignored his comment and waited until he mounted the motorcycle, before clambering on behind him.

Gratefully, I pushed my hands into the pockets of his jacket, winding my fingers into the soft leather.

~

We crossed into France at the quaintly named village of Saint Gingolph. A border guard glanced at our passports, looked again when he realized we were American, sneered a few questions that Sebastian answered in fluent French—which seemed to annoy the man even more—then he waved us across.

The road on this side of the lake was more thickly wooded and less inhabited than the northern side. Small farmhouses dotted the hillside and winding roads threaded their way up into the Alps.

"This road leads to Italy," Sebastian yelled over his shoulder. "How about a quick trip over the border?"

"Two countries in one day is enough!" I shouted back, but the thought that I was just miles from my father's homeland tugged at my heart.

Chamonix soon appeared out of the low mist that had settled in the valley. To my left, I could see the awe-inspiring presence of Mont Blanc, thick snow capping the summit.

The town itself was empty—the winter skiers long gone, the summer tourists not yet arrived.

The ride through the Alps had been sensational, as promised, and Chamonix was lovely: a picture-perfect Alpine town, with an abundance of bijou shops selling everything from skiwear to expensive, designer jewelry.

Sebastian pulled up outside one of the former, and dragged me inside.

"We'll get you some ski gloves to wear," he said. "Best I can do for now."

The sales assistant was overly helpful. I couldn't decide if that was because she was delighted to have a customer so close to the end of the ski season, or because she got to stare at Sebastian's ass as he wandered around the shop.

As far as I was concerned, he had a very fine ass and, having been wrapped around it for the last couple of hours, I felt I was in a position to voice an expert opinion.

And then a very erotic image sprang unwelcome to my mind, as I recalled the numerous occasions when I had reason to know Sebastian's naked ass very well indeed.

I did my best to banish the memory, but I wasn't entirely successful. I wondered if all US Marines were in such good shape.

"How about these?" asked Sebastian, handing me a pair of black ski gloves.

"Ninety Euros! Are you kidding me? That's $115! For a pair of gloves!"

"Just try the damn things on, Caro," Sebastian growled.

"No. That's ridiculous. There must be something cheaper."

"If you don't try them on, I'll buy them anyway," he threatened.

"No! It's a waste of money."

He turned to the sales assistant and handed them over. "*D'accord. Je les prends.*"

"Wait! *Attendez!*"

I snatched them back from her and pulled them on over my hands. They fit perfectly.

Damn!

He grinned at me wickedly.

"You argue too much, Caro."

"I can't imagine why," I said, dryly.

We left the shop with my ridiculously expensive gloves tucked into my jacket pocket. Sebastian looked annoyingly pleased with himself.

"Should we find somewhere to have lunch?"

"What, you're actually asking me, Hunter? As in, seeking my opinion?"

He grinned at me. "Sure!"

"In that case, yes, but only if I treat you—non-negotiable."

"I love it when you tell me what to do, Caro," he leered at me. "Brings back memories."

And this time I couldn't help the blush that rose to my cheeks. I knew *exactly* what he was talking about. Other than Italian, the one thing I had taught Sebastian was how to give me an orgasm. And he had been a *very* good student.

He laughed out loud when he saw my blush. I couldn't think of a single comeback. Not one. Not a word. Not a single response, answer, reply, witticism, quip, jest or jibe. I was utterly mute.

He wrapped his arm around my shoulders and pulled me to him, kissing my hair lightly.

"Just teasing you, Caro."

I shuffled away, trying to look offended, but he knew better and just grinned.

"Do you want to try fondue?" he asked, still trying not to laugh.

"Fine," I muttered sulkily.

I regained some of my rumpled poise over lunch.

We both ordered the cheese *fondue* and were given a basket full of different rolls: *foccacia*, olive breads, breadsticks, and a *fondue* made up of *mozzarella*, *dolcelatte* and parmesan. It was the perfect winter warmer, especially on a chilly day in the spring.

"Mmm, this is good. Have you been here before?"

He nodded nonchalantly. "A couple of times."

"Ever bring your women here?"

He frowned, and looked irritated. "You make it sound like I had a fucking parade of them."

"Didn't you?"

He threw down his fondue fork angrily.

"What do you want me to say, Caro? I fucked everything I could get my hands on when I realized you weren't coming back. It was years before I trusted a woman enough to be able to make love to her, and even then..."

He stopped mid-sentence, scowling at me.

I'd done it again: forced him to say words that only brought pain to both of us.

"I'm sorry," I murmured. "I didn't mean..." I looked into his eyes. "It's none of my business, Sebastian. I apologize."

And it really wasn't. I was the one who had insisted that we couldn't change the past, and here I was, surgically opening old wounds, one by one.

"I'm sorry, too. I didn't mean to yell at you," he said, his voice aching with regret.

Then he took a deep breath and shook his head to clear away the anger and recriminations.

We sat silently for several minutes. I searched around for a more neutral topic of conversation.

"How long have you had the motorcycle?"

He leaned back in his chair.

"This one, about two years. But I've had one on and off since I was 19. Bought my first bike as a birthday present to myself. It's still in Ches's garage."

"Really? Well, there's another reason for his wife to think you're leading Ches astray. Or is he the responsible father-type now?"

Sebastian smiled.

"He's a great dad—really patient. He fucking loves those kids of his. But we still take the boards out and catch some waves when I'm there."

"Uh-huh, and how many meals have you made him late for, just catching 'one more wave'?"

He smiled knowingly.

"Too many! But he goes out when Mitch visits, too, so she can't blame me for that."

"I think I'd like her—a woman immune to the Hunter charm."

Sebastian laughed. "She's immune all right. But yeah, she'd like you. I'll introduce you when we're stateside."

"In case you'd forgotten, I live about 3,000 miles and ten states from San Diego."

"Yeah, well, in case *you'd* forgotten, they've invented airplanes."

"*Touché,* Sergeant Hunter."

He smirked at me, and raised his glass of water in a toast.

"What happened to that friend of Mitch's—Bill—the one who was at that wretched 'fun' day Donna dragged me to at the beach?"

"Why are you asking about him?"

Sebastian frowned at me and I rolled my eyes. Surely he wasn't *still* jealous because Bill had flirted with me once?

"Just wondering. He was in your surfing crowd, wasn't he?"

"Oh, right," he said, rather huffily. "He married again a few years back, I think. He was sent to Quantico. Mitch keeps up with him—Christmas cards—something like that."

Thank God Bill's story had a happy ending. I didn't think I could take any more bad news today.

"It felt good having you on the bike with me today, Caro," said Sebastian, thoughtfully, as if he was testing the water before adding something more.

"Hmm," I said, the sound filled with skepticism.

He laughed. "Well, I've had an idea about that..."

"Oh, another of your ideas? That sounds dangerous."

He grinned at me, a gleam of mischief in his eye.

"You know how we always talked about traveling through Italy? I just thought, while we're both here, why don't we?"

I frowned at him, not sure I understood what he was suggesting.

"Why don't we what?"

"See Italy. We could take the motorcycle and go see all those places we talked about: Milano, Verona, Capezzano Inferiore—see if your dad's relatives still live there."

Oh, he'd definitely found my weak spot.

"Don't you have work to do?" I replied, avoiding answering the question. "How come you've have all this time off?"

"I'm on leave," he said, quietly. "I'll be shipping back out to Afghan—in about three weeks."

"Oh," I said, feeling the blood drain from my face. "I didn't realize ... I thought you were stationed in Geneva."

He shrugged.

"I was, but they need interpreters, and they're getting antsy about using locals. Too many green-on-blue attacks." He brushed the thought away. "So, what do you think?"

I shook my head.

"I can't, you know I can't. My papers could come through any moment and I'll be on my way out there myself. Besides," I said, trying to lighten the moment, "three weeks with you—that's definitely a dangerous mission."

"Don't you trust me?" he asked, trying and failing to look wounded.

"No, not particularly."

He grinned, completely unabashed.

"Oh, don't say that. I'll be good. Scout's honor."

"You were never a boy scout."

"True," he said with a smirk. "What if I promise I'll behave myself: separate bedrooms and everything?"

"No way, Hunter. I've heard about your *reputation*, remember? Besides, I don't know how soon I'll get a flight to Leatherneck. I don't want to risk losing my slot."

"It won't happen for at least two weeks."

I narrowed my eyes at his tone.

"You sound very sure of that."

He just grinned at me.

And then realization dawned.

"What did you do, Hunter?"

His grin grew wider.

"Let's just say I know people in the right places."

I couldn't believe his arrogance.

"Are you telling me you've blocked my application?"

My voice started rising, and he had the grace to look almost contrite.

"It's not blocked, Caro, not entirely. I ... just threw a few well-aimed monkey wrenches in the works. It'll take at least a week to sort out—probably two."

Unbelievable!

Now I was really angry.

"This is my *work*, Sebastian," I said, the fury in my voice more than obvious. "This is how I get *paid*. How dare you interfere like this! You're unbelievable."

He scowled at me.

"You can't butt into my life like this!" I half yelled at him. "I'm not the insipid little woman I was ten years ago!"

"You were never that," he said, his expression burning.

Oh, how well I remembered that look.

"You'd better damn well get that monkey wrench out, Hunter! I mean it."

He sighed, looking disappointed.

"I can't, Caro, it's out of my hands now. But I promise it's temporary. I just ... after all this time ... I wanted us to be able to spend more than a few hours together." He stared at his hands. "I don't know when I'll see you again," he mumbled. "I've already waited ten years."

His admission was so astonishing and he looked so miserable, that my anger began to ebb. I was still annoyed, furious at his interference in fact, but I couldn't hold the same level of rage when he looked like that and, more importantly, once he'd explained his reason for doing it—that he still had feelings for me. But what the true nature of those feelings really was, I remained deeply unsure.

"Will you at least think about it?" he asked softly.

I nodded, still too angry to speak.

I let Sebastian have all the fondue, my appetite having vanished. He kept throwing me guilty glances, but it didn't stop him finishing both his plate and mine.

We spent the afternoon wandering through the town, stopping to look in shops and gazing up at the stormy face of Mont Blanc.

I was still irritated by his high-handed behavior, but there was nothing I could do about it, besides I was used to waiting, and I'd waited in a lot worse places.

"I wouldn't mind coming back here in the winter," said Sebastian, "try out the snowboarding."

"That's something else I've never done," I grimaced, trying to imagine hurtling down the steep, icy face of the lowering mountain on a piece of wood not much bigger than a skateboard.

"I'll teach you," said Sebastian, confidently.

"Oh, something you can teach me, Mr. Hunter?"

He raised an eyebrow and grinned at me.

I glanced at my watch. "I think we should be heading back now. I can't get a signal on my phone here. My editor might have been trying to contact me."

I threw him a challenging glance. Sebastian didn't look happy, but he didn't argue either.

We walked back to his motorcycle and I pulled on my very lovely, and very expensive new gloves.

Sebastian took the autoroute back to Geneva and we arrived in slightly under an hour. I didn't like to ask what speed we'd been traveling at—one that exceeded the limit, I suspected.

I climbed off the bike, and handed him back my helmet. He stowed it in one of the empty saddlebags and stared down at me.

"I really enjoyed today, Sebastian. Most of it, anyway. Thank you."

"You're welcome, Caro."

We stood gazing at each other. Without knowing why, I felt awkward, the tension rolling in waves between us.

"Okay, well, thanks again," I murmured, turning to go.

"Can I see you tomorrow, Caro?" he asked, his voice filled with intense longing. "Will you think about the Italy idea?"

I stared at him, certain the anguish was etched on my face.

His eyes darkened as he continued to stare at me.

"I want to kiss you, Caro. Very badly."

The breath caught in my throat as he took a step toward me. I knew I wanted that, too. *Very badly*.

I raised my hand to his cheek and he sighed softly as he leaned into it, closing his eyes. I ran my fingers down his neck, feeling the warmth of his skin.

He took another step toward me, and rested his hands on my waist. I pulled his head toward me and felt his lips on mine. So soft, so sensuous. I could feel his breath stroke my face, then his lips parted and his tongue swept into my mouth.

My God, the feelings that burned through me, scorching away every sorrow, every moment of regret. Instead, I remembered how his hands had learned every curve and hollow of my body, how our love had melded us into one, how his body had fit inside mine.

He pressed himself into me, his mouth hungrily devouring every breath.

"God, I want you, Caro. I want to make love to you," he whispered on my lips.

"Yes," I said. "I want that, too."

CHAPTER FOUR

SEBASTIAN HAD TO GO AND PARK HIS MOTORCYCLE IN THE HOTEL'S SECURE underground garage.

His absence gave me ample time to consider the consequences of what I was about to do. I still wasn't sure I trusted him, I had about a minute to decide whether or not to change my mind. But, in truth, there was no decision to make. My body ached to be touched, it had been a long time, too long perhaps, since I'd allowed a man this close to me. And the way I felt when Sebastian was near me, it was as if every nerve ending was sensitized simply by his presence. I hated it and I loved it and I hated it.

I waited for him in the lobby, sitting on the same sofa where he'd sat last night during our fractured heart-to-heart. The receptionist's curious gaze bounced off my back: I didn't have room in my mind to consider anyone else at this point, and I cared even less what she thought of me, if she thought anything at all.

And then he had returned and it was too late.

Watching him walk through the automatic doors into the lobby was extraordinarily arousing. I longed to feel his body intertwined with mine, to feel as I had felt once before. I could see the tension and expectation on his face, and the old insecurities began to worm their way to the surface. Ten years ago, I had been the experienced one and I had led the way, even though my 'experience' had been limited to my uncreative husband. Sebastian's experience, at the time, had been zero, but now? By his own admission, he had fucked every woman who'd let him. I had no doubt that his charm, superficial or otherwise, combined with his extraordinary good looks had gained him entry to a large number of bedrooms.

By contrast, the number of men I'd slept with since him could be numbered on one hand. I was afraid he would find me ... boring.

He crossed the lobby with long strides until he was standing in front of me, searching my face. He held out his hand, and I didn't hesitate. If it was a mistake, then it was one I made willingly.

A relieved smile flickered briefly across his face.

He pulled me to my feet and braided his fingers through mine, leading me toward the bank of gleaming elevators.

All were busy, crammed with tourists returning from day trips, politicians and businessmen retiring to their suites for the evening. Sebastian and I stood off to one side, wedged among a throng of men in suits. He wrapped his arms around my waist and pulled my back into his chest, bending down to place soft kisses in my hair.

Two men smiled knowingly, but Sebastian didn't so much as glance at them.

Several other people got off at the same floor, following us along the corridor, chatting noisily. Sebastian and I were silent.

I pulled the keycard out of my wallet with shaking fingers, and pushed the door open. I stepped inside, my heart racing, my nerves taut. I moved around the room, turning on the side lights, pulling the curtains and shifting my laptop from the neatly made bed. In other words, doing everything rather than look at him.

He hovered by the door for a moment, then walked in slowly and sat on the edge of the bed, his eyes following me around the room. He caught my hand as I fluttered past on another pointless circuit.

"Hey, it's okay. I'm nervous, too."

I stared at him in amazement.

"*You're* nervous ... why?"

"Because it's you," he said, simply.

He raised my hand to his lips and kissed it courteously, a sweet, old-fashioned gesture.

"Only if you want to, Caro."

"I do ... I just feel, I don't know, embarrassed. It's so stupid."

He lay back on the bed and gently pulled me down next to him. He began kissing my throat, his hands moving up from my waist.

I felt him everywhere, all over me, suffocating me, and I froze.

"No, Sebastian."

I pushed him away, and he stopped immediately.

I was half expecting him to get up and leave in disgust, but he surprised me again.

Suddenly, he rolled away from me to the other side of the bed.

"Let's just make out," he said, grinning at me.

"Make out? As in..."

"Lie on the bed, watch trashy TV in French or German—your choice—and make out."

He raised his eyebrows as he sat up, then he shrugged out of his jacket and dropped it on the floor, unbuckled and levered his feet out of his biker boots, before peeling off his socks.

He grabbed a couple of pillows, piled them against the headboard and launched himself back onto the bed.

"Where's the remote?"

I pointed to the cabinet on my side of the bed and watched as he stretched over me to retrieve it, exposing a delicious sliver of taut, naked stomach as his t-shirt rode up his body.

Oh, I really wanted some of that.

He surfed through a few channels before he found some badly-dubbed TV show, then grinned up at me, patting the space on the bed next to him.

I followed his lead, unlacing my boots and dropping them in the corner with my socks. I crawled up on the bed next to him, and he pulled me into his arms so I was resting against his chest. He kissed my forehead and settled back on his pillows with a sigh.

I snuggled into him, feeling surprisingly relaxed.

"This feels good," he said, happily. "Should we order room service?"

"I'm not hungry."

"Would you mind if I ordered myself a beer?"

Just one beer?

"No, I don't mind."

He pulled the hotel telephone toward him to order a beer and a sandwich, then settled back with his arm around me.

With typical Swiss efficiency, the beer arrived within five minutes, the 'sandwich'—an enormous French baguette—was stuffed with cold meats, lettuce and tomato.

Sebastian's eyes lit up.

"Food instead of sex?" I couldn't help saying, reminding him of a running joke we'd once had.

He grinned at me, and licked his lips.

"For now. I'm still kind of hoping the sex comes later."

"How's that going for you?"

"Not sure: she's playing hard to get. I was going to ply her with alcohol and have my wicked way with her, but I guess she's wise to my game."

"Women!" I said, rolling my eyes.

He laughed, and started to work on demolishing the sandwich.

When he'd finished and brushed the crumbs from his t-shirt, he lay back with the bottle of beer, and wrapped his free arm around me again. He sighed contentedly and stretched his long legs out in front of him, crossing his bare feet at the ankle.

"I could get used to this," he said, nuzzling my hair.

"What, badly dubbed reruns of 'Frasier' and TV dinners?"

"You know exactly what I mean, woman."

"Oh, 'woman', is it?" I said, thumping him on the chest.

"Yes, a beautiful, amazing, talented, gorgeous woman," he said, his voice serious.

The mood shifted immediately, from relaxed and playful, to heated tension.

He placed his beer on the bedside table, then pulled me gently into his chest. With his fingertips, his free hand caressed my ear, gently sweeping my hair aside. His eyes studied my face carefully as he leaned in to kiss me, the lids fluttering closed at the last moment, before his lips touched mine.

His mouth drifted across my face, sweet, gentle kisses, as light as butterfly wings, hovering over my eyelids, brushing over my chin, then returning to rest on my lips.

My hand crept across his stomach, and slowly up toward his chest, pausing for a moment just over his heart. Then I lifted my hand to cup his cheek, and he turned his head to kiss my palm.

He pulled me in more tightly, so I was half-lying across him, and he ran his hands up my spine while he kissed my neck. His kisses grew more urgent, and I felt him run his tongue over my throat. Then his teeth tugged on my lower lip, and his tongue dove into my mouth. I could taste beer and hot, delicious Sebastian.

I moaned into his mouth, and heard an answering growl from deep within his chest. I hooked my leg over his thigh, pulling our bodies closer together. Through his jeans I could feel that he was aroused, and the knowledge sent a jet of heat spiraling through my body.

His hands stroked my back through the thin cotton of my t-shirt as his kiss deepened. Then they dropped to the waistband of my jeans and he pulled the material free, running his strong fingers along my bare skin, toying briefly with the elastic of my bra, before dropping back down to cup my ass.

I shivered with desire, and his hands stilled.

"Are you sure, Caro?" he whispered.

I leaned away so I could gaze down into his beautiful eyes, softly massaging the small frown line between his eyebrows with my finger.

"I'm sure." I sat up and pulled off my t-shirt to add emphasis to my words.

His eyes were dark with desire and he swallowed quickly before sitting up and hauling his own t-shirt over his head. His silver dog tags chinked quietly as they settled back on his chest.

I reached over to touch him, needing to feel the warmth of his silky flesh, then stopped.

"You got a tattoo?"

He smiled slightly.

"Standard Marine issue."

I studied the delicate artwork and misty colors while Sebastian slowly stroked my back.

"The Marine insignia."

"Yep. The eagle represents the nation, well, protecting the nation—see the way its wings are spread out? The globe is our worldwide presence, and the anchor is because of our naval heritage."

The eagle was carrying a ribbon in its beak: I was just able to make out the tiny words.

"*Semper fidelis*—always faithful."

He nodded, his eyes serious.

I kissed his shoulder gently and lay back on the bed, pulling him toward me. Without speaking again, he pressed me down into the mattress, kissing me hard. His right hand roamed over my breast, gliding his fingers under my bra-cup and teasing the nipple until it was sensitized and rigid.

Then he slid his hand under my back, snapping open my bra, and pushed the shoulder straps over my arms, tossing the flimsy fabric onto the floor.

He moved his head to my breasts, his tongue dancing around the nipples, grazing his teeth over my aroused skin.

I moaned, arching my back, and he hooked one hand underneath me, half-lifting me off the bed. I responded by dragging my nails down his spine, making him cry out. He ground his hips into my pelvis and sucked the skin on my shoulder, biting so I could feel his teeth.

I ran my hands over his biceps and forearms, then slid my fingers inside the front of his jeans, feeling the large bulge pushing through his briefs. He groaned loudly, and I squeezed him through the material.

"Fuck, Caro!" he said, his voice hoarse with need.

Matching me move for move, he pushed his hands underneath my waistband, caressing my ass, pushing his fingers into the cleft between my buttocks. Then he pulled his hand out and toyed with the button on the front of my jeans, before twisting it open. He didn't bother with the zipper, but simply pushed his fingers under my panties, pulling gently on my pubic hair, massaging my mound in slow circles, before letting his index finger drift lower.

I knew I was wet, desperately aroused, and as soon as his fingers found me I cried out. He'd always known this part of my body so well, and he definitely hadn't lost his touch. In and out, in and out, torturing me, confined as I was by my jeans. My back arched, and I cried out again.

He sat up quickly and unzipped my jeans, hauling them roughly down my legs, before catching his fingers through the fragile fabric of my panties and tossing them to the floor.

I quivered as he splayed out his fingers and ran them from my chest, down across my stomach, down across my pubic bone and along my thighs. His hand rose upwards again, finding my sweet spot with his index finger, he began to press hard, back and forth.

I groaned, and pushed his hand away.

"No. You. I want you."

He smiled briefly, then unzipped his pants and stood to let them drop to the floor, kicking his feet free.

I knelt up on the edge of the bed, pushing my breasts into his chest, and running my hands over his ass. Then I peeled the briefs over his hips and his erection leapt free.

Wow! I'd honestly forgotten how well endowed he was. Truthfully, I'd not realized until after our ways had parted, that he was considerably above average.

I licked my lips and ran one hand over the length, gently cupping his balls in my other.

He breathed in deeply through his nose, his nostrils flaring slightly. I repeated the gesture and he swore lightly under his breath.

A bead of moisture glinted at the tip, and I swirled it around with my thumb. His body trembled.

"Are you on the pill?" he said, his voice rough.

I shook my head, a smile threatening to break out. "I don't usually have a need for it. Please tell me you have condoms, otherwise 'making out' is all we're going to be doing."

He smirked, and bent down to rifle through the pockets of his leather jacket.

"Just wondering," I said, casually, "but when did you buy them, or are they old stock?"

He grinned at me, and shook his head. "Nope, new packet. Check it out."

He tossed me the small box and I saw that it was true: the seal hadn't been broken.

"So, no need to practice putting one on then?"

I was teasing him—ten years ago, he'd admitted, somewhat shamefaced, that he'd practiced putting on a condom so he'd know what to do when the time came.

Sebastian laughed.

"Well, I haven't practiced recently, but I think I can remember what to do."

"You're avoiding the question," I said raising my eyebrows. "When did you buy these?"

"Second day of the hostile environment training."

"But you were still mad at me then!" I said, very surprised.

"Didn't stop me wanting you," he replied, grinning back at me.

"Hmm, well. Let me see if *I* can remember what to do," I said, raising one eyebrow.

His grin widened and he stood in front of me with his hands on his hips, his erection heading in my direction.

I tore open the box and pulled out a foil packet, running it down his length, and tapping him on his tip lightly.

"Whoa, careful!" he breathed out.

"Wimp! I thought you were a Marine not a mouse."

"Just be careful with my weapon," he shot back.

"Close your eyes and relax."

"Why, what are you going to do?" he asked warily.

"Don't you trust me?" I said, smiling innocently.

"Not with that look on your face," he said, but closed his eyes anyway.

I ripped open the foil and pinched the end between my thumb and forefinger, but before I rolled it on, I leaned forward and took him in my mouth.

"Fuck!" he hissed between his teeth, as I stroked my mouth up and down him.

He rested his hands on my shoulders and flexed automatically, sending him deeper into my throat. I pulled back slightly and bared my teeth, making him shudder.

I sucked hard, and he groaned.

"No, baby. I want to be inside you."

I gave another not-so-gentle tug, and released him.

He shook his head, his eyes amused but heated.

I smiled up at him and ran my hands over his ass, enjoying the defined dip where hip met muscle.

"Just put that fucking thing on," he said. "You're killing me here."

"Oh, don't be such a baby, Sebastian. We've waited ten years, you're not going to expire in the next 30 seconds."

"I wouldn't be too sure about that," he muttered.

I held the condom at the tip of his penis, and as slowly as was humanly possible, I rolled it down him, making every second, every millimeter count.

He brushed my hands away as soon as I was finished.

"My turn," he said, his voice allowing no argument.

I lay back on the bed, and raised my arms to pull him down to me.

"Oh, I don't think so," he said. "My turn, remember? Pull your knees up."

"Yes, sir!" I barked, and threw up a salute.

"Are you mocking the US Marine Corps, lady?" he snarled.

"Why? What are you going to do about it?"

The expression on his face changed subtly, and I had a feeling I was going to regret my challenging words.

I slid my feet up the bed as commanded, and watched with a mixture of anticipation and delicious foreboding as his head disappeared between my thighs.

His tongue flicked up and I was so aroused I nearly came on the spot, my body bowing to meet him.

For a second, he pulled back to glance up at me, grinned wickedly, and continued with his erotic assault that had me moaning at an embarrassing volume.

Then he hooked his shoulders under my knees and lifted my whole lower body off the bed, so my weight rested on my upper back.

And he was merciless.

My orgasm began to build quickly and even as the waves tore me apart, he didn't stop until every bone in my body had turned to liquid.

I couldn't help the nasty little thought that darted through my brain: practice makes perfect.

But he didn't give me time to think too deeply because he laid my hips back down on the bed, and positioned himself over me.

"I've waited a very long time for this," he said.

Then he slid into me, inch by slow inch, as my body adjusted to his invading presence.

"Fuck, you feel so good, Caro. I can feel you all around me. *So fucking tight!*"

And I could certainly feel every inch of him. My numb brain began to fill with memories, the times, the places, the many, many times he'd made love to me before. Many times, but somehow too few times.

I ran my nails down his back again, then pressed the tips of my fingers into his tight muscles.

He groaned, continuing to stroke slowly in and out.

Ten years ago, the boy he'd been had been unable to stop himself from racing to the finish line. Now I was benefiting from his experience.

He held his weight on his forearms, and gradually increased the speed. I felt the cool metal of his dog tags on my skin over my heart, which was beating furiously fast, as my body began to respond again and again.

Death by orgasm—what a way to go.

I moaned out his name, and he seemed to lose a fraction of his careful control because he started to move faster. Soon his hips were plunging fiercely, and I absorbed every delicious thrust as he ground into me.

His eyes were wide open, staring down at me, almost wild in their intensity, then his mouth was on mine, our tongues twisting and twining together.

I tilted my hips up to meet him and felt his body go rigid, he flexed deeply once more then stilled, his breath coming in rapid gasps.

I wrapped my legs around him, locking my ankles behind his waist and clenched inside, milking every last bit of him.

Then he let his arms give way, burying his face in my shoulder.

A slow minute passed, and gradually, our breathing began to return to normal, and I felt his lips pressing lightly into my neck.

He lowered his hand to where we were joined, making sure that the condom hadn't gone missing in action, and pulled out of me carefully.

He rolled onto his back, and peeled off the thin rubber, pulling a face as he tied a knot in the end of the condom before dropping it into the garbage can. Then he leaned up on one elbow to look at me, resting his free hand on my stomach.

"Are you okay?" he asked, tenderly planting a gentle kiss on the tip of my nose.

I wasn't sure how to answer that question.

I'd *promised* myself I'd never get involved with another man in the military, I'd been *determined* never again to be attracted to a younger man, I *knew* that revisiting the past was a bad, bad idea, and I sensed that Sebastian was a volatile mixture of intense emotions and unexamined anger at the past.

And yet, my reckless body sang every time he touched me.

"Yes, I think so," I replied, my voice carefully neutral.

I pushed his hand away and sat up, ignoring his confused expression.

"Where are you going?"

"Just to get some water," I said, without looking at him.

I felt his eyes on me as I walked into the bathroom, brutally aware that my forty-year old body couldn't match the exquisite perfection of his.

I pulled on the bathrobe and drank some water from the faucet. The bathroom mirror reflected my flushed face and tangled hair. I'd picked up my hairbrush to resolve one of the issues when I heard Sebastian, and turned to see him standing in the doorway behind me.

"Caro, what's the matter?"

"Nothing," I said, too brightly. "I'm fine."

His eyes met mine in the mirror and I could see that he didn't believe me, but he didn't challenge me either. Silently, he took the brush from my hands and slowly, carefully, brushed my hair until it hung in tidy waves down my back.

"You have beautiful hair, Caro. I'm glad you kept it long."

His tone was gentle, almost loving.

I shrugged.

"Every now and then I decide to cut it, especially after I've been somewhere I haven't been able to shower for a couple of weeks."

"That would be a crime," he said solemnly.

"You can talk!" I said, pointing my chin at the haze of golden hair that clung to his skull.

His lips twitched in a small smile.

"Believe me, babe, I'd grow it if I could. Maybe I should go to my CO and tell him my girlfriend wants me to..."

He stopped abruptly.

I sighed. "It's okay. I keep forgetting which decade I'm in, too. It's so strange."

He nodded in relief.

"Yeah, this is so weird, I feel the same. It's as if nothing's changed but everything's changed. It's like being in some crazy time machine. I keep expecting your husband to be banging down the door."

I winced.

"Fuck, sorry. I'm doing it again."

I smiled, painfully.

"Oh well, I imagine you've had some experience with husbands banging on the door."

"Don't, Caro."

I stared at him for a fraction of a second, then pushed past him, back into the bedroom.

I couldn't believe he'd mentioned my ex-husband. Didn't we already have enough painful memories between us? Apparently not.

I heard the faucet running, and he followed me, carrying a glass.

He handed it to me silently, and I took a small sip before placing it on the cabinet next to the bed.

"Thank you."

He sat back on the bed, covering his lower half with the sheet.

"Caro, I know this is fucking weird but it's good, too, isn't it? I mean, not everyone gets a second chance."

Is that what this was, a second chance? But a second chance at what? A second chance to rip ourselves apart again?

"Today was fun," I said, trying to think it through, "and tonight was ... good, but the reality is I'm based in New York and spend between three and six months of the year away from home. You're a Marine and go wherever they send you. Presumably this next tour of Afghanistan will be six months or maybe longer? And then where, because let's face it, Sebastian, the chances of you getting posted to the Corps' Division of Public Affairs in New York is slim to none—especially with your record. So I'm not sure what sort of 'second chance' you have in mind."

Sebastian's body went rigid with sudden, suppressed rage, and then he leapt off the bed, glaring down at me, gloriously naked—and very angry.

"Christ, it's like listening to an old record, Caro! You *always* try to think of reasons why we can't be together!"

"What do you mean 'always'? I haven't seen you for ten years!"

"That's the whole fucking point, Caro! You used to say this shit to me when I was 17, and you're still doing it now. We wasted *ten years* and you're worried about a few thousand miles? Hell, we've got airplanes, we've got email, they've invented fucking cell phones. Jesus, if it comes down to it, I'll even write you a fucking letter!"

I bit back a rather hysterical giggle that began to bubble up.

"You write letters?"

His shoulders relaxed slightly, but his eyes were still tight with emotion.

"I'll write you on both sides of the fucking paper, Caro."

"How can I refuse such an astonishing offer?"

"Are you laughing at me?"

"Are you shouting at me?"

"Yes!"

"Then, 'yes' to you, too." I sighed. "Look, today, tonight—it's been fun. But like I said to you before, I'm really not looking to get tied down again. I work *a lot* and I love what I do. I'm still mad at you for screwing up my travel papers. I won't be paid until I've filed a story, and I won't be able to do *that* until I get to Leatherneck. All this time, I'm not earning—and I have a *very* expensive mortgage to finance."

He rested his hands on his hips, and looked me in the eye.

"I'm sorry about the money, Caro, and I'm sorry that I made you mad at me again, but I'm not sorry about what I did. I hoped I'd get a chance to spend some time with you, but I would have done it just to keep you safe."

I sighed. "This is getting us nowhere."

He sat down on the edge of the bed with his back to me, and rested his elbows on his knees.

I had the opportunity to study his finely muscled back, sculpted shoulders and glowing, gold skin—my golden boy.

"Caro, I have 17 days before I ship out. I'd like to spend them with you. That's all. If you don't want to see me after that ... well, I guess that's it."

CHAPTER FIVE

WHEN HE PUT IT LIKE THAT, WHAT DID I HAVE TO LOSE? I COULD SEE ITALY with him or spend a pointless two weeks kicking around Geneva on my own. And, despite what I'd said to him about the sex having been 'fun', 'spectacular' and 'mind-blowing' would have been more appropriate adjectives. Plus, it was the most orgasms I'd had in one evening for a decade.

"I'm going to need a cushion to sit on if you expect me to ride on that motorcycle of yours all the way to Salerno."

His expression lifted at once.

"Really? You're sure?"

"Well, to paraphrase you, 'what the hell'." I paused. "But I reserve the right to fly back if you're being too much of an ass."

"Huh, well, you'd better give me a sliding scale of assaholic behavior, just so I know."

I raised an eyebrow. "That could be quite a long list."

"Try me."

"Okay," I said, sitting up straight, and diving straight to my mental list of his most assifying and irritating moments since we'd met up again. "First, no getting drunk and passing out in my bed; second, no more interference in my career *of any kind*—that's a deal breaker; third, no territorial displays of adolescent jealousy; fourth..."

But I didn't get to finish my list—he jumped on me, pinning me to the mattress, and kissed me hard.

I was breathless and aroused when he let me go, and I could also feel his renewed erection poking my hip through the bathrobe.

Of course—fast reloader. I'd forgotten.

"What was that all about?" I said, pushing him off me.

He shrugged.

"It sounded like a very long list, I thought I'd try to distract you."

"Diversionary tactics?"

"Yeah, we're schooled on that in the Marines," he smirked.

"I bet you are! And by the way," I said, pointing to his fully erect dick, "you can put that away—I'm exhausted. Somebody dragged me all over Switzerland and half of France today."

"Sure I can't persuade you?" he said, leaning down to bite my thigh.

"Quite sure, thank you. This forty-year-old woman needs her beauty sleep."

He scowled. "I wish you wouldn't do that, Caro."

"Do what?"

"Keep going on about your age. You're older than me—I get it. And guess what? I don't give a shit. I never did. I just wish you weren't so hung up about it. It's kind of annoying."

I was annoying *him? In what universe?* Oh, this one, probably.

I realized my mouth was still hanging open in a most unattractive way.

"Feel free to say what you really mean, Hunter."

He grinned at me. "Okay."

I shook my head, half-amused, half-irritated.

"So, we can go tomorrow? Start our road trip?" he said, his eyes glowing like a kid at Christmas.

"Well, I suppose so. But I don't know how we'll get my case on the back of your motorcycle."

"Don't worry about that. We'll just take what you need, and leave your case at my place till we get back." He paused, his expression turning challenging. "So, can I stay the night, or are you going to kick me out into the cold, dark world, all alone in a strange city, where foreign women might try and have their evil way with me?"

"That's a sob story, if ever I heard one, Sergeant Hunter, although I strongly suspect it's a highly edited one."

"Is that a yes?" he asked hopefully.

"It's a yes, providing sleep is what you had in mind."

"Mostly. Good enough?"

I shook my head. He really was incorrigible.

"Fine. You want to use the bathroom first?"

"No, go ahead."

As I brushed my teeth hard enough to remove several layers of enamel, I wondered how I'd got railroaded *again*. I really didn't seem to have the ability to say 'no' when it came to Sebastian. Had it always been like that between us? I thought back to some of the outrageous risks we'd taken ten years ago. Yes, I had to admit—it had always been like that.

When I'd finished, Sebastian took his turn in the bathroom, and I climbed wearily into bed. I'd forgotten what a workout it was, having sex with him. My thirty-year-old self had trouble keeping up, there seemed even less chance I'd be able to keep up now. I reminded myself that according to the consensus of opinion, a forty-year-old woman was in her sexual prime, while a man's was at the age of 19. Which meant Sebastian was already past his prime, although there was no evidence that anyone had told him that. Even so, it cheered me up slightly.

I enjoyed the floor show as he strolled out of the bathroom, unembarrassed by his nudity, wearing just his dog tags and a big smile. He was either very comfortable with me, or he was just used to wandering around naked—did they have open showers in the Marines? Hmm, maybe some research was in order—strictly on the grounds of professional integrity, of course.

Instead of walking around the bed, he deliberately sat on my side, then climbed over me.

"Sebastian, what are you doing?"

"Taking a shortcut," he said, as his body hovered over mine, and he dipped down to kiss me.

He tasted of mint.

I reached up and pulled him deeper into the kiss before pushing lightly on his chest.

"Sleep! Now!"

"Sure I can't change your mind?" he said, eyeing yet another erection, which was growing at an alarming rate.

"Oh, put it away! I'm tired."

He grinned at me and gave in, sliding under the duvet on the other side of the bed.

I stretched to turn off the bedside light and the room was plunged into darkness. I felt Sebastian's hand drift over my waist, and he kissed the back of my neck.

"Night, baby."

He fell asleep quickly, his arms wrapped around me, warming me and weighing me down. I listened to the sound of his quiet, even breaths, wondering if our differences would bring us together or push us apart.

~

It was barely light when Sebastian shook me awake from a confused and disturbing dream.

"Caro, are you okay?"

I rubbed my face as his worried eyes gazed at me.

"Oh, sorry, did I wake you up? I was dreaming."

"It sounded more like a nightmare."

"Sorry. Yes, I'm okay."

In truth, I'd been dreaming about Iraq again. It wasn't something that happened often, but it was always frightening when it did. The recurring images stemmed from the time I'd visited Victory Base near Baghdad's airport: the medical team had just heard that three 'Category Alpha' injuries were on their way. In my dream, it was the distinctive thrum of the medivac helicopters that filled me with fear.

Sebastian definitely didn't need to know what my nightmare had been about.

I shivered and sat up, the duvet slipping down to my waist. Sebastian's expression changed, and I realized his eyes were hungrily fixed on my breasts.

"Your eyes are going to fall out, Hunter," I muttered.

He grinned guiltily, acknowledging that he'd been caught staring.

"Just looking, boss," he said.

I didn't bother to reply. Instead, stretching stiffly, I shuffled off to the bathroom with the bathrobe pulled tightly around me.

I contemplated the bags under my eyes and frazzled hair, searching for any gray ones that I could ruthlessly root out. And then I realized the truth: this was as good as it gets. I was never going to be younger, or more toned, or less wrinkly. And maybe there would be a day, sooner rather than later, when Sebastian would want younger flesh under his expert hands. And if that happened, there was nothing I could do about it. But right now, he wanted me. It was *my* body that made his eyes pop out of his head, and *my* body that had so aroused him last night. He'd said again that he didn't care about the age difference, so what was my problem? Maybe I should just sit back and enjoy the ride, so to speak.

Perhaps I was having a breakthrough: *he didn't care*, so why should I?

I prodded my puffy eyes again. Nope, still luggage-laden. Then I remembered something: something Sebastian had said to me ten years ago, something we'd never done.

Hmm. That had interesting possibilities. I wondered if he'd let me ... one way to find out.

It would certainly take my mind off my inadequacies and, well, hopefully it would take Sebastian's mind off of everything.

Sebastian was lying back on his pillows with his hands behind his head.

"Hi," he said, his eyes glowing.

"Hi yourself."

"You seem better."

"Why, Sergeant Hunter, what masterful skills of observation you have."

He grinned at me. "Yeah, much better."

"Well, now you mention it, I am in a much better mood, although I'm rather hungry."

"Do you want to go down for breakfast or should I call room service?"

"Let me think about that for a minute."

Slowly, I untied the belt to my robe and pulled it out of the loops, winding it through my fingers.

I dropped the robe to the floor, and watched Sebastian's eyes as he followed its descent.

"I was thinking about eating you, Sarge, but as you're such a stubborn, annoying man, who makes me pissed with every other sentence he utters from between his beautiful, badly-behaved lips, I thought I should tie you up first. What do you say?"

Sebastian's mouth dropped open.

"I'd say, where is Carolina Venzi and what have you done with her?"

I smirked at him. "I'm just taking your advice, Sarge."

"I don't know what advice I gave you, but it must have been damn good."

"Let's find out. Put your hands on the headboard."

"Yes, ma'am."

He wrapped his hands through the metal framework, and I crawled up the bed and across his body. Kneeling over his chest, I threaded the belt through the headboard and tied both his wrists tightly.

"Have you done this before?" he breathed out, his gaze heated.

"Only in my dreams, Hunter. Now, be quiet, or I might have to gag you, too."

"Fuck!" he whispered.

"Maybe later."

I whipped the duvet from him in the same way that I ripped off wax strips from my legs. I wasn't surprised to see he was beautifully erect.

"Now that's a sight for sore eyes, Sebastian. Maybe I should just leave you here—the hotel maids might appreciate that. Or, better still, maybe I'll take a photograph of you on my phone. Don't worry, I won't post it on the internet, it'll just be my screensaver."

"Caro!" he said, a serious warning in his voice.

"Spoilsport," I said, pouting at him. "No sense of adventure."

He grinned back, but his expression was slightly wary. He flexed his arms, testing the knots. I was delighted to see he couldn't move them. I placed a gentle kiss on each of his biceps before sliding back down his body.

Oh, I was going to enjoy being the one giving the orders. Maybe I'd teach him how to be a good soldier and take them.

I knelt down on the bed, and ran my tongue from his balls to his tip, he groaned loudly. Nope, that wasn't going to work.

I clambered off the bed again.

"Where are you going?" he asked, rather nervously.

"Back in a minute," I called, as I wandered into the bathroom. I rooted through my toiletry bag trying to find a hair-tie.

"Caro!" he yelled. "What the fuck?"

"Are you getting impatient, Sebastian?"

He swore again and I heard him tug on the headboard, making it creak ominously.

I strolled back into the bedroom, pulling my hair into a ponytail. "Couldn't see what I was doing," I explained.

"There's going to be payback for this, Venzi," he said, his eyes dark and amused.

"Bring it on, Sarge."

I knelt back on the bed and ran my hands over his fabulous chest, enjoying the smooth tautness of his pecs, every ripple of his abs and washboard stomach. I took his dog tags in my mouth and sucked hard.

He closed his eyes, and breathed in deeply.

I smiled to myself. I was enjoying having him at my mercy—I suspected he was, too. Well, it was more than a suspicion, I had the evidence to prove it. Yes, about that evidence...

I kissed, nipped, bit, licked and sucked my way downwards. I must have found a ticklish spot, because his hips bucked uncontrollably and he swore again.

"Sebastian, your language!"

I ran my tongue down his full length, and gently held his balls in my teeth. His body was rigid, and I think he stopped breathing. I released him carefully, and heard the breath rush out of his lungs. I felt the urge to laugh, but thought better of it. I held his erection at right angles to his body, and leaned down. I planted a soft kiss on the tip, feeling his body quiver, and then I took him in my mouth, all of him, all the way up and all the way down. I used my tongue, teeth and lips to give him sensation in as many different ways as possible.

His skin was soft and silky to the touch, his erection hot, hard and delicious. I massaged his thighs and balls as I rode up and down him with my mouth.

He flexed his hips upwards, and moaned softly. That was my cue to increase the pressure and ramp up the speed.

I felt so turned on having him in my complete power. I'd never done anything like this before in my life, and I'd lied to Sebastian when I'd told him I'd dreamed about doing it. But there was something about his honesty and openness that made me feel strong and almost fearless. It was *me* giving him pleasure and making him writhe underneath me, not some nubile twenty-year old. Forty, and with fewer inhibitions: it wasn't a bad place to be.

With a feeling akin to triumph, I felt him come in my mouth as he cried out my name. I swallowed quickly, aware of the warm, salty fluid in the back of my throat. *Really don't want that going down the wrong way.*

I sat up, feeling a little stiffness in my neck and shoulders. Oh, well, it was worth it.

His eyes were still closed and his breathing was rapid. I watched him for a moment, then leaned over to the bedside table and drank some of the water that he'd left there last night.

I glanced at my phone to see the time, wondering if he'd regain the power of speech anytime soon.

I lay back on the bed and cuddled up on his chest, pulling the duvet over us.

"Jeez, Caro! That was ... that was ... wow!" He paused. "Are you going to untie me now?"

I shook my head sleepily. "Don't think so. I like having you as my beck-and-call boy."

He chuckled lightly, then rattled the headboard again. "Seriously, I want to hold you."

Grumbling quietly, I untied his arms and he flexed his hands. He worked the fingers a little, which made me wonder if I hadn't tied him a little too tightly. Oh well, live and learn.

"Where did you teach yourself to do that?" he asked teasingly, once I'd settled back on his chest.

"Night school," I said, with a yawn.

He laughed and kissed my shoulder. "Is it my turn now?"

"I thought you wanted to take me on a road trip."

"Yeah," he said, a salacious gleam in his eye. "But I could be quick..."

Hmm, fast, hard sex ... with Sebastian.

No, my muscles were still feeling the sting of last night's activities.

"I'll take a rain check, Sarge."

His expression was rueful.

"Okay. In that case, I guess we should get going."

But his hands weren't obeying the words his mouth was speaking.

"What are you doing?" I asked suspiciously, my eyes still closed.

"Nothing," he said softly, as his fingers skated a little lower.

Then I gasped, and my eyes flew open. He was grinning at me, a devilish expression on his face.

"Sebastian!" I moaned.

"Shh, baby," he whispered, then covered my mouth with his.

It seemed it was my turn after all.

~

I showered quickly, shooing him out of the bathroom when he tried to join me. I knew if he did, our road trip would begin and end with this bedroom, which didn't sound so bad, but now, after all my arguments, I found I was looking forward to seeing Italy with Sebastian.

His shower was even briefer than mine, and he dressed quickly while I packed up my clothes, cell charger, laptop and notebooks. Carefully, I wedged my camera case in among my t-shirts to give it as much protection as possible.

The camera was a Nikon D2Xs and it meant a lot to me. It had been one of the first things I'd bought myself, once I started making some money from writing. There were other, better digital cameras out there on the market, but this one had accompanied me all over the world, and it had never let me down.

"Do you want to get breakfast here?" said Sebastian. "You didn't eat anything after lunch yesterday."

His thoughtfulness was endearing. Yes, I remembered that: those brief moments when someone had put my needs before their own. Sebastian had been the first person to do that.

"No, it'll take too long. You must know some little café we could stop at? Maybe on the lake?"

"Yeah, okay. But I need to swing by my place first and pick up a few things."

We headed down to the lobby, and while I settled my bill, pushing the receipt in my pocket, glad that my newspaper was paying for this expensive hotel, Sebastian went to retrieve his bike. I still wasn't sure how he was going to get my case onto his motorcycle, even for the short distance to his apartment.

I realized I had no idea where he lived. It was going to be fascinating seeing his private world.

I heard the bike's engine before I saw it, the throaty roar surprisingly familiar already.

God, he looked gorgeous in his leather jacket, and denim stretched tightly over his toned thighs. I could daydream for hours about those. And the black helmet made him look dangerous.

He lifted up the visor.

"Give me the case, Caro."

"Where are you going to put it?"

I handed it to him, feeling puzzled, but he just wedged it in front of him between the handlebars, and jerked his head at me to get on behind him.

Yes, sir!

I'd definitely have to tie him up again—he liked being in charge too much. Or maybe I should stop encouraging him by calling him 'Sarge'.

Certain that carrying luggage like this was highly illegal, we headed off into the city. I decided that if we were stopped, I'd try the innocent-and-clueless-tourist-abroad card.

Luckily, we made it to Sebastian's place without incident.

His apartment, if you could call it that, was in an older part of the city where the architecture looked more Italian than Swiss. The cobblestone street was narrow and very quiet.

Sebastian's apartment was in a tall, thin building, with peeling stucco and weathered shutters. It wasn't at all what I'd expected. I'd imagined some chic bachelor pad, all glass and chrome—somewhere to take his conquests.

I pulled off my helmet, and clambered inelegantly from the mean machine. Sebastian swung his long leg over easily, smirking at me.

"Nothing to laugh at, Hunter. Just because you're about a foot taller than me."

"Shrimp," was his generous comment.

I tried to swat his backside, but he dodged out of the way.

"You're feisty this morning. I think I like it."

He pulled an old-fashioned key out of his pants' pocket and grabbed my case with the other.

The door creaked open and I peered into a gloomy passageway.

"Sorry," said Sebastian, "no lights."

He led the way up three flights of dark, narrow staircase, and slid the key into another lock when we reached the top.

"This is it," he said,shortly.

As I stepped inside, a feeling of sadness welled up through me. The room was small and white, with a narrow single bed pushed against one wall. An ugly military-style blanket was neatly folded over the top, as if ready for inspection. A dozen, well-thumbed paperbacks lay on a plain, wooden bookshelf. The only color in the room was provided by his dress uniform, which had been arranged on a hanger inside a dry-cleaner's bag, and hung from a hook on the wall.

A wooden chair sat silently underneath the window, and a small chest of drawers stood sentry next to the door.

There was no carpet and no rugs, just bare, wooden boards; there were no pictures, nor photographs, just his iPod and laptop, which looked lost and oddly out of place in the Spartan room.

Sensing my shock, Sebastian pointed toward the window.

"It's got a great view," he said, defensively.

"Yes," I agreed, looking out over the tiled rooftops toward the lake, "very pretty."

He shrugged. "It's all I need."

I turned to flick through his books, needing a moment to blink back the tears that threatened. He wouldn't want my pity.

"Still the Conrad fan," I said, trying to control my voice, although my throat was tight with unshed tears.

"Sure," he said.

"You should get yourself an e-reader," I said, trying to find a normal tone of voice. "The whole of Conrad for two bucks."

"Yeah, I guess I should," he replied, his voice muffled as he reached under the bed for a small overnight bag, "if I knew there'd always be somewhere to charge it up when I'm in some shithole, Stone Age village."

He stood up and tossed his bag on the bed, then rifled through the chest of drawers, pulling out half-a-dozen white t-shirts, and some of his gray briefs and black socks.

"What happened to all the colors?" I blurted out.

He threw me a puzzled look.

"Sebastian, the most colorful thing in this room are your Dress Blues," I pointed out helplessly. "The first time I met you, you were wearing those ridiculously bright red board shorts."

He laughed lightly. "Oh yeah. I've still got those somewhere. In a box in Ches's garage, I think."

"It sounds like Ches has all your worldly possessions."

"Pretty much," he said, shrugging. "I didn't take a lot when I left my parents' place. But what the hell—it's easy to pack up and move on when you're not laden down."

My heart swelled with emotion. My poor, beautiful boy—his entire family was Ches's. He owned nothing, lived nowhere, and had no one.

Except, perhaps, me—if I let him. If he wanted me.

"Caro, how much of this stuff in your case do you need?" he asked, pulling me away from my forlorn thoughts.

"I definitely need my laptop and notebooks..."

"I mean clothes, Caro. I wouldn't dare suggest to a reporter that she goes anywhere without the tools of her trade."

"That's right, Sergeant. You'd just stop her going where she needed to go in the first place."

He pouted and I couldn't help smiling. He was so cute when he did that. I wondered how many other Marines used pouting as their primary weapon.

I picked out some t-shirts.

"See," I said, arranging a palette of pink, green, blue, yellow and orange t-shirts. These are called 'colors'. They're what you get when you're not wearing black, white or gray."

"My jeans are blue."

I rolled my eyes. "So they are, Sebastian. Way to go."

"I could maybe get into colors," he commented, holding up my favorite, lacy bra, which was a deep magenta.

"I don't think it would suit you."

He added it to the pile of clothes I was taking with me.

"No, but I'm really looking forward to taking it off you."

"That's assuming you get lucky, Hunter. You promised me separate rooms, remember?"

He looked like I'd just told him Christmas was cancelled.

"You're not going to hold me to that, are you, Caro?"

I smiled at him.

"I don't know—depends how irritating you are."

"What if I promise to be on my best behavior, ma'am?"

"Mmm, maybe. I was impressed how well you took orders earlier today."

His eyes darkened dangerously, and he licked his lips.

"Yes, and there'll be payback for that, Ms. Venzi."

I tried to step away but he caught me in his arms, running his nose down my neck and kissing my throat.

"And I'm looking forward to collecting. Maybe we should christen this bed."

"Christen it? I would have thought it had seen plenty of action."

He stilled and looked up at me.

"No, you're the first woman I've brought here. It's ... private."

I wrapped my arms around his neck and pulled his head down, kissing him softly on the lips.

"We'll christen it when we get back," I whispered.

I felt his smile on my skin.

"Something to look forward to."

I pulled away and continued with my packing.

"Okay, I'm done. By the way, where exactly are we going? It's a pretty long way to Salerno, so I presume we're going to stop somewhere *en route*."

"Yeah, it's just over 1100 kilometers, so..."

"Give me that in good, old-fashioned US miles, Sarge."

He chuckled. "Seven hundred miles. I thought we'd stop at Genoa tonight—that's just under 200 miles—take us about four hours."

Or less, the way he drove.

"How come you know all these distances off the top of your head?"

He hesitated, and I saw that he was stuffing a map of Italy into his jacket pocket.

"I've been planning to do this road trip for a while."

Oh. So not something special to do with me after all.

"You and I talked about it once, you remember? All the things we were going to do, all the places we were going to see? I just figured that as I was here, I'd go anyway. And ... I remembered that you said your dad came from that village near Salerno. I thought I might find ... I don't know what I thought. I just wanted to see it."

I shook my head. Every time, *every time*, he surprised the hell out of me.

"Then let's get going," I said, smiling up at him.

As I made my way down the gloomy stairs, I heard the lock click as he closed the door. I still felt sad that this was the only place he had to call home. But when I tried to imagine him in my tiny bungalow at Long Beach, somehow the picture didn't fit. I shook the thought away, concentrating instead on the here and now.

"We could go straight to Genoa, using the Mont Blanc tunnel," he said, pulling me from my maudlin thoughts again, "but I really like the idea of going up through the high pass. There'll still be quite a lot of snow around—you up for that?"

Hmm, snowy roads, two wheels: I didn't like the math. On the other hand, long tunnel and large trucks.

"I vote for the route over the Alps," I said, sounding a lot braver than I felt.

Sebastian dropped our bag to the ground and picked me up, swinging me around. I laughed delightedly, happy that he was happy. When he finally put me down, he kissed me sweetly.

"God, you're amazing, woman!"

"Wait, I should write that down," I replied, making a grab for my notebook.

"No way! You might use that against me in court. Do I have the right to an attorney?"

"Get on the damn bike, Sebastian, before I change my mind."

He grinned and stowed our overnight bag in one of the saddlebags. I was impressed how light we could both travel, something we had in common after all.

We had a quick breakfast of sweet rolls and coffee in a café overlooking the lake, then headed up into the mountains. I was very glad I had my expensive ski gloves to wear, because we hadn't gone far before I started seeing heaps of snow at the sides of the road. Some were as high as six or seven feet. I assumed they'd been piled up as snowplows cleared the road. A couple of miles later we really began to climb, the blacktop disappeared and we were riding on compressed snow. Sebastian dropped the speed as the hairpin bends began to live up to their name.

The bike wobbled dangerously, and Sebastian pulled to the side of the road. He twisted around and lifted up his visor.

"Baby, you're going to tip us over if you do that, and I don't know about you but it looks like a helluva long way down to me."

"What ... what did I do?" I asked, nervously looking down the sheer drop.

"You're trying to sit upright on the bike: don't. You have to lean into it or the balance goes for shit. Don't try and do anything, just sit real tight and hang onto me."

"Okay, good safety tip, Sergeant. Glad you mentioned it."

His eyes crinkled in a smile, and he snapped the visor down again.

We took off slowly, zigzagging our way up the mountain. The views became more spectacular the higher we climbed, but commensurately more terrifying. My arms were wrapped around Sebastian's waist with a death-grip that was probably crushing his ribs. I was thankful he couldn't see my face because half the time my eyes were closed. So much for being fearless, so much for enjoying the view.

Twenty minutes later we reached the highest point of the pass, and Sebastian stopped again. He pulled off his helmet and grinned at me.

"It's really something, isn't it?"

Awkwardly, I clambered off the bike, tugging at my helmet and shaking my hair loose. Then I turned to look at the view.

"Wow," I breathed.

Geneva was spread out below us, the lake mirror-like in the chilly sunshine. Disappearing into the valley, I saw the Z-bends that we'd just driven up. Even here, from the safety of the summit, they looked hair-raising, and I still had to make it down the other side. But it was beautiful, too—the air was crystal clear and the sky too blue to be real. I felt grateful to be here, enjoying this moment with this man. Second chances didn't come any better.

"Thank you for this, Sebastian. Thank you for bringing me."

I leaned against him and he wrapped his arm around my shoulder, kissing me softly. I twisted in his arms so I was facing him, and gave his kiss the attention it deserved, expressing my gratitude wordlessly, pouring all my happiness into that one moment.

When I pulled away from him, my face felt flushed, along with other parts of my body. Sebastian's expression told me that outdoor sex at the top of a mountain pass in the snow was suddenly on his 'to do' list.

I stroked his cheek.

"Save it, Sergeant. We've got a long way to go yet."

He smiled reluctantly and waited while I snapped some photographs, then helped me climb back on the mean machine. We started the descent down through the Alps and toward a new country.

A short while later, Sebastian pointed to a road sign: *Italia*. I felt a thrill of excitement ripple through me. At last I was in the country where my dear papa had been born. The idea was fanciful, but in an odd way it felt like coming home.

The border guard gave our passports the briefest of examinations before waving us through with a cheerful smile. I really was in Wonderland.

We traveled onwards, and I felt almost sleepy on the back of Sebastian's motorcycle. I wondered if it was possible to fall asleep in this position.

I was beginning to feel the need to stretch my legs when we passed a sign that announced, 'Genova 20km'—and I saw the sea. It was calm and of the deepest ultramarine, fringed by delicate, white villas. Italy's Mediterranean coast.

Sebastian took us along the shore road, and it became apparent that Genoa's seafaring tradition was not just historical. We passed dock after dock lined with every kind of yacht, boat and ship I could imagine, from sleek motor-cruisers to enormous, ugly cargo vessels.

Modern Genoa seemed to be thriving, with housing creeping higher and higher up the sides of the mountain that loomed behind us.

Sebastian aimed for the towering beacon of the Torre della Lanterna as we headed into Genoa's bustling center. Skimming past the Piazza de Ferrari, we passed palatial buildings built at the time of the Renaissance, and up on the hill I could see a medieval castle. I drank in the history as we roared past.

I thought Sebastian would stop soon, but he cruised on and soon Genoa had fallen behind us. Was he going to try and reach Salerno tonight after all?

I was relieved when he finally pulled over, but when he didn't cut the engine, my hope that we'd finished for the day evaporated.

"Just checking the directions, baby," he shouted over the noise of the engine, and waved the map at me. "Not far now."

I gave him a quick thumbs up, and we took off again, climbing back up the mountain that seemed to have grown directly out of the sea.

He stopped once more to check the map, then turned off the main road, and we bumped up a steep, gravel track. A sign next to a small, whitewashed villa welcomed us to 'Casa Giovina'.

He stopped and let the engine idle.

"This is it. It only has one guest room, but it's out of season ... want to try it?"

Sebastian's expression was wary. Perhaps he thought his simple tastes didn't compare with the upscale hotel where I'd stayed in Geneva. We still had a lot to learn about each other—and I didn't mind at all.

"It looks charming. Let's go and see, but if the owners have a pretty daughter, we're out of here."

He rolled his eyes, and chose to take my words as a joke, which they were. I think. Sort of.

An elderly woman in the severe, black clothing of a widow opened the door.

"*Posso aiutarvi*?"

"I hope you can help us," I replied, in Italian. "We were wondering if you had a room for the night?"

I could see her eyeing Sebastian's 6'2" of solid muscle and evaluating how much trouble he was going to be. I could have saved her wondering and just answered 'a lot'.

"Are you married?"

As I stuttered out a surprised answer, a man in his fifties came stomping down the corridor.

"Mama! You can't ask people questions like that! I apologize—my mother is very old-fashioned. Are you French?"

"No, American."

"But you speak *Italiano*! Americans never speak our language."

Sebastian decided it was time to demonstrate his own linguistic abilities, if a little less fluent than mine.

"We mean no disrespect to your mother—this beautiful woman is my fiancée," he said pointing to me, "but if your mother would feel more comfortable, I will happily sleep in a separate room."

Oh really? Two lies in one sentence, Sebastian: see you creeping into my room after dark.

"No, no, that won't be necessary," said the owner, as his mother rolled her eyes to heaven and crossed herself twice. "Besides, we have only one room."

A fact which Sebastian already knew.

"Please, come in. Let me show you the room."

The room was airy and simply furnished. A pine wardrobe stood in one corner, and a matching chair was the only piece of furniture besides the large, old-fashioned bed. A mosquito net hung in a pool of lace above it, making it look like a rustic boudoir. But the views out toward the coast were spectacular.

I smiled happily at Sebastian, and he nodded his agreement.

"The bathroom is across the hall, *signore*, it is to share."

He shrugged helplessly, as if to apologize for the smallness of his establishment, but I didn't care. I imagined making love to Sebastian in that bed looking out over the Mediterranean.

"Breakfast is at 8AM, *signore e signorina*. There is a *ristorante* just two kilometers up the road. It is very good—run by my brother."

"That sounds great," said Sebastian.

"Ah, *signor*, one more thing: if you would mind not riding your motorcycle after dark. My mother doesn't sleep well, you understand, and she has the room next to yours."

"That won't be a problem," I muttered, once he'd gone. "I'm not getting on that thing again tonight if you pay me."

"Feeling a little tender, Ms. Venzi," said Sebastian, grabbing me and rubbing my ass soothingly.

"Not really. It's more the feeling that I'm still in motion."

"I know something that will cure that," he said, wickedly.

"Would that have anything to do with taking off our clothes and making mad, passionate love on that bed?" I said, frowning at him.

"It might have," he said, eyeing me warily.

"Oh, all right then. I'll try anything once."

His double-take was almost comical. "Is that a yes?"

"Yes, that's a yes. But you'll have to hurry, Sarge—the *ristorante* probably closes before midnight."

He glanced at his wristwatch, completely confused. "It's only five o'clock?"

"Like I said—you'll have to hurry."

Understanding brought a smile to his beautiful lips.

"Well, in that case, woman, you're wearing too many clothes."

Finally, he was on the same page as me.

"By the way," I said, before he got too caught up in the moment and knowing from experience that he could only concentrate on one thing at a time when sex was on the menu, "your *fiancée?*"

He grinned. "Seemed like a good idea at the time."

"Hmm, well, I like *my* idea better—the one where we commit as many sins as possible in the shortest amount of time."

And, to make my point, I unzipped his jacket and ran my hand down his chest, before tracing a finger around the waistband of his jeans.

I was interrupted in my further exploration by a knock at the door.

Looking irritated, Sebastian pulled it open.

"*Ah, mi scusi, signore e signorina*. I have just telephoned my brother: he is closing at 7.30PM tonight. If you wish to eat there, it would be best if you leave now."

"Thanks," said Sebastian shortly, and the little man darted away, not knowing how close he'd just gotten to a *very* pissed off Marine.

I couldn't help laughing at his expression. "Rain check, Sarge?"

He sighed, "Looks like."

"Never mind. Come on, let's get you fed and then I can have my wicked way with you."

"How wicked?"

"Not that wicked, so stop drooling. Just moderately naughty—it's been a long day."

CHAPTER SIX

Hand in hand, we climbed up the steep lane to the *ristorante*. I couldn't imagine how a place that was so out of the way could attract much business, but when we poked our heads through the door, I saw that my assumption was very wrong.

It was thronged with families, and children of all ages were sitting at the long, trestle tables like little adults.

The happy noise tailed off when they saw us, and an unsubtle whispering began. I heard the word '*Americani*' several times before a man in a white shirt and black pants, whom I assumed was the owner, came hurrying over.

We agreed that yes, we were the Americans and yes, it was an astonishing thing that we both spoke Italian and yes, we'd have whatever was on offer. No, we weren't fussy, and yes, we were happy to have the locally made *dolcetto* red wine.

We were seated at the corner end of one of the trestles, wedged in next to a family of seven. At first, our neighbors seemed a little shy, but then Sebastian shrugged out of his jacket and pushed up the sleeves of his t-shirt. A little girl in the party, a dark haired ragamuffin aged about five, noticed his tattoo and asked her mother about the 'picture'.

Her mother tried to hush her, but Sebastian smiled and explained to her that it was because he was a sailor and a soldier, and the 'picture' reminded him of his work.

"Is that because you forgot?" asked the child, clearly puzzled.

The whole room burst into laughter. I joined in, but seeing how at ease he was with the little girl made me sad for things that might have been.

It was clear the child was completely smitten with him, because she asked her mother if he was an angel, then reached up to stroke his short-cropped hair.

The meal finished with a small bowl each of *gelato di miele* honey ice cream, a local specialty. Sebastian ate most of mine, as I'd already eaten enough. He really was a bottomless pit when it came to food.

By the end of the evening we were practically family, and all on first-name terms. It had been a wonderful evening, full of laughter and quiet enjoyment, Sebastian chatting to his new, little friend. But I also couldn't help noticing that Sebastian had drunk almost a whole bottle of wine by himself, although it didn't seem to have had much effect. On the other hand, I was feeling a little lightheaded after two glasses.

"Having fun, baby?"

"Do you realize this is our first dinner-date?"

He frowned. "What about back in San Diego—that Sicilian place?"

"That doesn't count—you wouldn't let me finish our meal because you wanted to drag me back to the hotel."

"Oh yeah, I definitely remember that!"

"Besides, your *friend*, Brenda, was spying on us. I'm half expecting to see her now, tossing her hair over her shoulder and thrusting her boobs in your face like she used to."

His expression was amused. "She thrust her boobs in my face?"

"Don't pretend like you didn't notice. Anyway, if any boobs are to be thrust in your face, they'll be mine. Right, Hunter?"

He laughed. "Anything you say, boss. Looking forward to it."

"But then I was thinking," I went on, "if this is our first date, I probably shouldn't sleep with you. I don't want you thinking I'm easy."

Sebastian gazed at me appraisingly, then pulled out his phone and started scrolling through the numbers.

"Who are you calling?"

"Well, my date just told me she wouldn't sleep with me, so I thought I'd see if I had Brenda's number on speed dial."

Ouch. He was much better at this game than I was.

"Fine, fine. I'll sleep with you. But if my reputation is in ruins, it's all your fault."

Sebastian grinned at me, then stood up to pay the bill.

I realized we hadn't discussed how we were going to split up the costs for this vacation. Maybe if he paid for one night and I paid for the next—that would be fair.

We left the *ristorante* with the good wishes and prayers of our new friends, the little girl blowing kisses to her 'Angelo'.

But the angel proved he had a devilish streak because the moment we left the *ristorante*, he pushed me up against the wall and kissed me hard, holding my waist with one hand, and running his other hand up between my thighs.

He pressed his body up into me and I could feel his arousal by my hip. I was seriously considering taking him there and then, when the ristorante started emptying, and we were very nearly caught *in flagrante delicto*.

The women looked envious, and the men called out several coarse suggestions. I was very glad the darkness hid my embarrassment.

"Should we try and make it back to our room this time?"

"Good idea," muttered Sebastian. "I don't think I could take a third interruption in one evening."

The moon lit our path as we strolled back down the hill. The air was mild, much warmer than chilly Geneva, but, of course, we were at sea level on this side of the Alps. I marveled again that in just a few days, we would be in the town where my father had been born. I don't know why that filled me with expectation, but I was looking forward to walking where he'd walked, looking at the views that he'd seen, maybe even talking to people he'd known. Italy was changing, but there were still places where the old folks lived and died in the villages where they'd been born.

When we got back to Casa Giovina, the villa was in near darkness. One, small lamp glowed in the hallway, and we crept up the stairs as if we were naughty teenagers.

I grabbed my toiletry bag before Sebastian could distract me and dashed into the bathroom, scrubbing the wine stains from my teeth, and then massaged a little moisturizer into my face with hope, rather than expectation, that it would erase any wrinkles.

When I returned to our room, Sebastian was already barefoot and shirtless. I dropped my toiletry bag from nerveless fingers, and he laughed at me.

"Seems like *your* eyeballs are the ones in danger of falling out, Ms. Venzi."

"That is true, so hurry up and get your ass back in my bed."

"Yes, boss!"

I stripped off my clothes, tossing them onto the chair, and threw myself into bed. Instead of it being the fairytale boudoir with the lacy net curtains that I'd imagined, the bed creaked alarmingly with every movement. I was horribly aware that the owner's mother was in the room next to ours *and didn't sleep well*. I stifled a giggle: it was not our night.

Sebastian returned, looking all hot and predatory. I was getting aroused just looking at him. But the thought of our noisy bed was making it hard not to laugh.

"What?" said Sebastian, annoyed that his entrance hadn't had quite the effect he'd anticipated.

"Nothing," I said, snorting back a giggle.

"What's so funny?"

I shook my head, holding a hand over my mouth.

Huffily, he pulled down his pants and kicked them off, then slid his briefs down his slim hips. For practically the first time, there was no hint of an erection. My laughter obviously had a dampening effect.

He threw the sheets back on his side of the bed, looking sulky, then sat down and started to slide over to me.

The bed creaked loudly and his eyebrows shot up. I laughed out loud.

"Sorry! I think we got the you're-not-married-so-you-damn-well-won't-be-getting-any bed. It's got a built-in anti-screwing alarm."

Sebastian smirked at me. "You think a noisy bed is going to stop me?"

"The old lady is right next door! She 'doesn't sleep well'—remember?"

"I can't help that. Besides, it'll bring back happy memories for her."

"Huh, you think you're that good?"

Uh-oh, wrong question.

He gave me a dark smile, and then his head disappeared under the sheets. I really wasn't laughing now. I tried to stifle a groan as a powerful sensation, beginning at my toes, raced up through my entire body. I pulled a pillow over my face and moaned into the soft mound of feathers.

"Oh, God!"

"Yes, baby?" said Sebastian, his amused voice muffled by the sheets.

I heard him crawling back up the bed, the mattress articulating every movement, and he tugged the pillow from my face and grinned down. His long, skillful fingers continued to dip in and out of me, bringing me to the edge of orgasm. When he fastened his teeth over my left nipple, I fell, spiraling down and choking out his name.

"Still embarrassed by the bed?" he said, smiling at me wickedly.

The question was unfair. I wasn't capable of speaking, let alone forming a rational answer.

The mattress creaked again as he slid off it to dig a condom out of his toiletry bag.

"You want to do this, baby?" he said, holding out the condom toward me.

He waited for all of two seconds before he gave up trying to get an answer. As if from a long way away, I heard the foil being ripped and the distinctive sound of a condom being tugged up an impressive erection.

"Roll over, baby, I want you from behind."

When I didn't move, Sebastian sucked my right nipple until he was guaranteed a reaction.

"Give me a minute," I grumbled.

But this Marine had waited long enough. He picked me up bodily and tossed me face down on the bed, before hauling me onto my knees so my ass was pointing to the ceiling.

He stroked my cheeks and then I felt his hot tongue between the cleft of my buttocks.

Oh, that was new.

I wiggled, not sure I was liking that. Hmm, okay, maybe.

But then he pulled away and I felt him position himself before sinking into me.

"Fuck, Caro!"

He groaned loudly. Maybe it was the alcohol, or maybe it was because he'd finally gotten around to fucking me from his favorite position, but he seemed to have less control than usual. He started pounding into me and I could feel him unraveling rapidly. The bed creaked in sympathy, the antique springs urging him on.

Oh! Not another orgasm! I forced my face into the pillow and moaned into it. We were racing toward the finish, and I was afraid the bed was going to collapse before I did.

But then Sebastian shuddered into me and stilled, and I gasped out some wordless sounds.

"Oh fuck!" he hissed, pulling out of me roughly.

My body gave way, and I lay splayed on the bed, thoroughly fucked.

And then, through the thin wall that separated us from the owner's mother, I heard the sound of someone clapping, and her reedy voice called out, "*Bravo! Bravo!*"

"What the fuck?" said Sebastian, still breathless.

I started to laugh. "I think ... I think we just got a round of applause!"

"You're fucking kidding me!"

I shook my head weakly. "That's what it sounded like. I guess she was impressed by your performance."

I heard the bed creak again as Sebastian sat up and called out loudly, "*Grazie, signora!*"

"*Prego!*" she replied.

He lay back on the bed, his hands behind his head. When I rolled onto my side to look at him, he seemed very pleased with himself.

"Something making you smile, Hunter?"

"Yeah! I never got a round of applause before."

"Maybe she was applauding me."

"Nah, she thinks I'm a stud, I can tell."

He peeled off the used condom as if to emphasize his words.

"Well, it's a good thing you don't have performance anxiety, that can put a man off his stride, so they say."

He smirked at me, then his smile faded and he looked serious.

"Do you ever think about the first time we were together? You know, when..."

"Sebastian," I said, softly. "You don't have to remind me—it's not something I'm likely to forget."

"Sorry. It's just ... I thought about it a lot at the time and, seeing you again this past week, well, it's brought it all back."

"For me, too."

He smiled and leaned over to run a long finger down my cheek, before lying back again.

"Do you know how amazing you were that night? You took care of me after my dad had beaten the shit out of me." He closed his eyes. "I thought my heart was going to fucking stop when you undressed me and you took your clothes off. And then you touched me and my cock just exploded. I thought you'd laugh at me or something. It was so fucking humiliating." He paused, remembering that awful and wonderful and dreadful night. "But you didn't. You made me feel like a man. I remember every word that you said. You told me it was going to be okay, and I didn't know how it could be, but somehow you made the world go away, like it was just you and me."

I was silent, remembering how crushed he'd been that night, how broken, and how the act of making love had somehow healed him. I wondered, now, if it had been the same for me. It was certainly the moment when my life took a completely different road from the one I'd been on.

His admission touched me deeply. I'd forgotten how painfully honest he could be. Even though he'd been so young when I'd known him before, or maybe *because* he'd been so young, he'd never held back with me. I couldn't help thinking that in some ways I'd had the best of him then, before life had made him bitter. Although his early life had been far from perfect, he'd been the sweetest, kindest person, the gentlest, most thoughtful and selfless lover—and a good friend.

"That's how you make me feel, Caro, like the world just goes away and it's just you and me. I ... I didn't think I'd ever feel like that again. All those other women, I know it bothers you, but it was just sex. It wasn't ... this."

"So, there was never anyone special, where it was more than just sex?"

He looked thoughtful.

"There was one girl, Stacey, that I sort of dated for a while. She was ... okay, but I wasn't interested in anything long-term."

"What happened?"

He shrugged and looked away.

"I heard her telling her girlfriend that she'd 'tamed' me."

I winced inwardly.

"Oh, I can guess how much you enjoyed hearing that. What did you do?"

He twitched his shoulder in an irritated gesture.

"I slept with her best friend."

I took a sharp intake of breath. "I see."

He didn't look guilty or upset, and I felt a brief frisson of sadness for Stacey and the way he'd treated her, especially when I knew he was capable of such gentleness.

"You asked me why Ches's wife didn't approve of me, and that's the reason," he went on. "Stacey was a friend of hers. And before you ask, no, I didn't sleep with Amy—it was another girl. I would never do that to Ches."

I took a deep breath.

"Well, I'm not surprised Amy doesn't like you after you did that to her friend ... and it's not very reassuring to hear that you've shown your dick to half the female population of California—and Paris, or so I've heard—but that's your business. But surely you see that you made things difficult for Ches."

"How's that?" he said, rather testily.

"You put him in the middle, making him choose between his best friend and his wife."

"What?" he said, angrily. "How was I making him 'choose'?"

"Well, I bet you anything Amy would have said she didn't want you in the house if you were going to treat her friends like that, and Ches would have had to find some way of defending what was, frankly, indefensible behavior."

I paused, wondering if Ches would have explained about Sebastian's history—our history—as a reason for his friend's actions. I hated the thought that Sebastian had used 'all those women' because he'd imagined that I'd left him without a backward glance. It was such an ugly distortion of the truth.

"You get on your fucking high horse damn quickly, Caro," he snapped.

I was taken aback at his angry tone. "I'm just saying..."

"What? What the fuck are you 'just saying'?" he said, his voice growing louder with each syllable. "You were a fucking journalist, Caro! You could have found me any time if you'd wanted to. It would have been so easy for you. So easy! I didn't even know your fucking last name. I was so desperate to find you that I even tried to see that prick of a husband of yours, but he slammed the door in my face and called my CO. I was on fucking punishment duties for weeks after that. But you didn't give a shit, did you? It's just lies. You just tell me what you think I want to hear. How can I ever trust you?"

"Sebastian, I..."

"I really want to hear this, Caro. I really want to hear how hard you tried to find me," he jeered. "You knew my fucking father was forcing me to enlist *because of you*, but you didn't even bother to make a few fucking phone calls. *Three years* I waited for you, Caro. *Three fucking years*, while you were off building your career and having a great life traveling all over the world. So yeah, I fucked some women who deserved it, because I'd already been fucked over once and I wasn't going to let it happen again."

I felt sick. All that hatred and anger pouring out of him.

"It wasn't like that, Sebastian. Just listen to me for a moment! Let me explain, because I..."

"Go tell it to the Marines," he sneered, "because I'm not listening."

I needed to get some space and t he bathroom seemed like it could be a place of refuge until he'd calmed down. His anger was scaring me and I didn't want to say anything that I'd regret later, although it was clear he wasn't having the same reservations.

I sat on the edge of the bed and reached for my t-shirt.

"Where are you going?" he shouted. "Running away again? Yeah, well, it's what you do best, isn't it? Run away. Fuck that! I'll save you the trouble."

He leapt out of bed, pulled on his jeans, thrust his bare feet into his boots and scooped up his t-shirt and jacket.

And then he walked out.

A moment later I heard the throaty roar of his motorcycle.

I pulled the sheet around me tightly, wondering what the hell had just happened. It was hard to believe that the man who'd made such sweet love to me could talk to me like that. Or rather, yell at me like that.

So much anger at me.

It seemed clear now that the gentle side he'd shown had simply been a mask that hid his true feelings.

But he'd gone and I had no idea if he was coming back. Well, *fuck him!* He wasn't the only one who'd suffered, he wasn't the only one who'd had to struggle. Oh sure, my life had been so easy: I'd cleaned other people's toilets for nearly three years before my writing earned me enough to give it up. *How dare* he speak to me like that!

I jumped out of bed and whirled around the room shoving everything into his small overnight bag. I knew his phone and passport were in his jacket, so he hadn't left anything that he needed. *Not even me*, said the sad, little voice in my head.

I thought through my options: I could book a cab to take me into Genoa, and from there, take a flight to Geneva. Then it was back to Plan A: wait for my permits to come through for Leatherneck—assuming Sebastian didn't try to screw that up again, although the odds didn't look good, given his current rage—do my job and get on with my life. And then I'd write off this episode to experience. Or something.

But it hurt. It really hurt. Just as I'd begun to trust him and let him back into my life...

And then I wondered if he'd be back after he cooled off. I really didn't want to face very-angry-and-scary Sebastian again tonight. But if I wedged the chair under the door, I wouldn't be the least surprised if he'd just decide to kick it in. Not that we'd be welcome staying at Casa Giovina after tonight's stunt anyway, but I didn't want to add a broken door to our troubles.

In the end, I pulled on my t-shirt and panties and tried to get some sleep. After thrashing around for several hours and replaying the whole horrible scene over and over, I finally lapsed into unconsciousness about an hour before dawn.

My alarm pulled me awake at 7AM and I immediately looked over to the other side of the bed: it was cold and empty—like me.

Fierce disappointment mixed with relief washed over me. At least I didn't have to face his recriminations again. Wake-up arguments definitely didn't do it for me.

I headed for the shower, but the tepid water did little to relieve my heavy mind. I didn't feel much like breakfast, but the least I could do was apologize to the hosts for our behavior. His behavior.

I wandered out to the patio and saw that the little table had been laid for two. I felt hot tears prick my eyes and I angrily scrubbed them away.

When I heard footsteps behind me, I turned hopefully. But it wasn't Sebastian and it wasn't the owner, instead the little grandmother was walking stiffly toward me, carrying a pot of coffee.

"Sit, young woman," she said. "And don't worry: it will all seem better once you have eaten. He'll be back."

I swallowed and tried to smile. She patted my shoulder sympathetically and left me alone.

The coffee was very good: rich and strong and just the shot in the arm that I needed. I drank almost the whole pot, then managed to eat a small plate of *fette biscottate* with salted butter. And I did feel better. And angry. *Really fucking angry.* How dare he talk me into this road trip, then drop me in the middle of nowhere the minute it suited him!

Or maybe this was his plan all along: maximum humiliation. *Screw him!*

I marched back to my room, scooped up the overnight bag and went to find the owner.

"Ah, *signorina*," he said, worriedly.

"Please accept my apologies for last night's disturbances," I said, with polite formality. "How much do I owe you for the room?"

He twisted his fingers unhappily. I could tell he felt bad about charging me, but I was determined to pay my debts. I pulled out my wallet expectantly.

He sighed. "Forty Euros, *signorina*."

"Thank you, *signore*. You have a very pleasant establishment."

"*Grazie, signorina*." He bit his lip and tried to smile.

"Can I get a cab to pick me up and take me to the airport?"

"Ah, regretfully, *signorina*, taxis do not like driving up my narrow road, but if you walk two kilometers toward Quinto Al Mare, you will find a taxi office."

I thanked him, hefted the bag over my shoulder, and strode out into the beautiful spring morning.

I'd reached the main road when I heard Sebastian's bike roaring up behind me.

My stomach lurched, twisting with anxiety. When I heard him cut the engine, I put my head down and walked as quickly as I could.

"Caro, wait!"

He jogged up behind me and grabbed the handles of the bag, forcing me to stop.

"Caro, I'm sorry. Okay? Are you going to talk to me?"

"I think you've said enough—for both of us."

"Fuck, Caro! It was the alcohol talking, that's all."

"It was more than that and you know it, Sebastian."

"Can't you take a fucking apology?"

"I don't know—can you make one?"

We stood staring at each other, both hurt, both angry.

He ran his hand over his hair and scowled. "Can we just go somewhere and talk? Or are you going to walk back to Geneva?"

I folded my arms and glared at him. "Yes, frankly. I was going to get a cab to drive me to the airport. I'm sure I'd have no trouble getting a flight."

"Don't leave like this, Caro," he said, in a slightly less aggressive tone. "Let's just talk. If we can't ... fix this, I'll take you to the airport myself."

Damn him!

I nodded coldly and let him carry the bag. Silently he passed me my helmet, and stowed our solitary piece of luggage in the saddlebag.

He climbed on the bike and held out his hand to help me, but I preferred to scramble on by myself. And, instead of fastening my hands around his waist, I held onto the small grab-bar at the rear of my seat. It was uncomfortable and I didn't feel very safe, but it was preferable to touching him.

He swung the bike around in a slow U-turn and headed southeast, away from the airport, following the coast road. After a few miles, he pulled into a parking lot next to a beach café in the small town of Bogliasco.

"Do you want a coffee?" he asked stiffly.

"An espresso and a glass of water, please."

He placed the orders with a bemused waiter, who clearly hadn't been expecting any customers so early. In fact, I suspected that we'd interrupted his morning gossip with his cronies, a group of grizzled old men who eyed us curiously, but relaxed when they heard Sebastian speaking in Italian. The waiter ambled away with reasonably good grace.

I stared across at Sebastian's beautiful sullen face, wondering why we were even bothering. I realized his eyes looked rather red. Obviously he'd chosen to dive straight into a bottle of whiskey last night, or *grappa*, perhaps. He stared out at the water, refusing to look at me or to speak. Not a great start to 'talking'.

Our coffees arrived along with a basket of rolls, and I wondered who was going to break the silence first.

He pushed the basket toward me.

"No, thank you. I've already eaten."

"Did you check out of that place?"

"Yes."

"Did you pack up my stuff?"

I blinked at him. "Of course!"

"Okay, thanks. What do I owe you for the room?"

"Nothing. Forget it."

"Just tell me what I owe you, Caro."

"Seeing as you didn't stay in it, I don't see why you should pay."

"Is this how you're going to be?"

"How would you like me to be, Sebastian? Because, honestly, I just don't know."

He grabbed a roll and started tearing it into pieces.

"Look, maybe we should just cut our losses," I said. "I'll get a cab to the airport and you can ... do whatever you want, Sebastian."

For a moment I thought he was going to agree, but then he looked down at the crumbs on his plate.

"I don't want you to go," he muttered.

I waited for more, an explanation for his behavior, perhaps. But he was silent.

And then realization hit me with the force of a Sherman tank, why he was struggling to find the words: he'd never done this before. Ever. He hadn't had a girlfriend in any real sense of the word since he was 17, and that relationship had ended abruptly without any desire for reconciliation on his part. From there, he'd plunged into a turbulent affair with me, which hadn't exactly honed his relationship skills either. By his own admission, he'd fucked Stacey's best friend as his version of solving their problems. He had no clue how to cope with the complex emotions of an adult relationship. Last night, his first reaction had been to run and hide in a bottle. No wonder he was finding this so difficult. As far as relationships went, he was on virgin territory.

I considered the fact that he actually wanted to talk to me was a step forward.

I'd been married for 11 years, and although that had ended in dismal failure, at least I had some vague idea of how relationships worked, or should work. And I'd dated two guys since Sebastian. Sort of. Sure, those hadn't panned out either, but for quite mundane reasons. Bob had moved to Cincinnati with his job, and Eric had traded up to a younger, wealthier model. I didn't count the one night stand with Allessandro, a reporter I'd met in Mexico. We were still in touch, occasionally.

"Sebastian, you're going to have to tell me why on earth you'd want me to stay," I said, gently. "Last night you said some pretty unpleasant things, and I'm not going to accept your explanation about drinking too much. It's pretty clear that you've been hanging on to a lot of anger—toward me. And I don't know what I can do about that."

He slouched down in his chair, looking for all the world like a sulky teenager. He seemed to be waging some sort of internal battle, but eventually he straightened up and looked me in the eye.

"Caro, did you really try and find me when I turned 21?"

And here we were again.

"I'll tell you exactly what I told you before: I wrote to Shirley, and I wrote to Donna. But no, I didn't try and find you directly, because I simply wanted to know that you were okay. When both letters were returned unopened, I took it as an omen that it wasn't to be. I didn't feel I had the right to interrupt your life and risk doing further damage. I felt a great deal of guilt at the devastation I left behind me: I didn't want to remind you of all that, or make you feel any obligation toward me. It never occurred to me that you ... that you'd be waiting for me."

He leaned forward, his eyes intense and angry. "But I *said* I'd wait for you. I promised I'd wait. Hell, Caro, it was the last thing I got to say to you. And you ... you said..." he bit his lip, hesitating.

I'd promised to love him forever.

An ugly wave of guilt rushed through me, and finally I could see how it had looked from his point of view: I hadn't tried hard enough—I'd let him down.

"Oh, Sebastian ... I'm so very sorry."

What could I say that would wash away so many years of hurt?

His voice dropped to a whisper. "Did you mean it, Caro? Did you mean it when you said you loved me?"

"Yes, *tesoro*, I did. I loved you very much. But you're not the person I knew ten years ago. The Sebastian I knew was sweet and gentle and loving, but you ... you can be like that, but your anger scares me. The hatred I saw in your face and heard in your words—that was hard for me. I can see that you think I let you down badly ten years ago, or seven years ago ... and I can't tell you how sorry I am for that, but I can't fix it either—I can't change the past."

He turned away, staring out at the sea.

"I'm confused about what you want from me, Sebastian. One minute you say we've been given a second chance and that we should try again, and the next minute you're blaming me for every bad decision you've taken in the last ten years. If you hate me that much, if you resent me that much, why am I here?"

"I don't hate you, Caro," he murmured.

"Sebastian, you called me a liar, you said you could never trust me."

He winced, but I was determined to see this out.

"You asked me to come with you on this trip, and then the first time something goes wrong, you fling the past in my face. If you really believe I did what I did because I didn't care, then I don't see how we're going to get past that."

I hoped he'd offer something, some insight as to what he was thinking, but his lips remained pressed together.

"Listen, I wouldn't be who I am now if I hadn't met you—that's the truth. I'd probably still be locked in a loveless marriage. But that's only half the story."

Finally he looked at me.

"It was really tough for me in New York. I had almost no money, no contacts, nowhere to live, no job. Do you want to know how I survived? I cleaned people's houses, I scrubbed their toilets. For three years. Until eventually I earned enough from my writing."

"I didn't know," he said, softly.

"No, because you didn't give me the chance to answer you last night."

I wondered if he could see how cruelly he'd behaved, but his next question took a different turn.

"You said you dated a couple of times."

"Excuse me?"

"The first night we talked. I asked you if you were seeing anyone, and you said you'd dated a couple of times."

"Yes, so?"

"When?"

"What, you want dates?"

"Yes."

I sighed. "I met Bob on my 35th birthday when I was having drinks with friends. We dated for three months and then he was transferred to an office in Cincinnati. Eric was a couple of years later: we dated for about six weeks before he dumped me for a younger woman."

"That's it?"

Oh, what the hell.

"I had a one night stand with a reporter when I was on assignment in Mexico. That's it. Now you know my entire sexual history. Although I very much doubt you could be as succinct about yours."

For a moment, he looked angry, then he gave a wry smile. "I deserve that."

I closed my eyes and leaned back.

"Are you okay?" he said, quietly.

I shook my head slowly. "Not really."

He sighed. "I am sorry, Caro. I just get fucked up in the head sometimes."

"You can't deal with it by lashing out at me. And *I* can't deal with it if you keep blaming me for something I can't change."

He put his head in his hands. "Don't give up on me, Caro."

"Last night I thought *you'd* given up on *me*."

A pained expression crossed his face.

"Can we start again, Caro? I promise I'll try not to fuck up again."

I took a deep breath.

"Sebastian, it's not a case of 'starting again', it's about working things through when we have a problem. Funny enough, it was you who taught me that, ten years ago: you made me face up to things. You can't promise me you won't fuck up, because you will. And I can't promise you that I won't fuck up, because I will. We can deal, and we can move on. Or, we can say it's been an interesting few days, and go our separate ways."

He reached over and tentatively took my hand.

"I want to go on. With you."

I wasn't even sure why I was agreeing to this. My head was screaming for me to get out now, but my heart had gone in another direction entirely.

I nodded my agreement. "Okay, then. Let's try."

"And I promise not to sleep with your best friend, especially if it's that scary British woman I saw you with in Geneva."

I could see he was trying to lighten the mood, but I wasn't quite ready to joke about it.

"Sorry," he said, quietly. "Another foot-in-mouth moment."

I tried to smile, but I probably just grimaced at him.

I pulled my hand free, and sat back to sip my lukewarm espresso.

He picked up some of the pieces of his eviscerated roll and chewed solemnly.

"Did they say anything about last night? The people at the villa?"

"Not really. They were mostly embarrassed. I think we've managed to ruin it for any other Americans who might want to stay there. But the old lady told me that you'd be back."

Sebastian looked surprised. "Really?"

"Yes, and I'm pretty certain it was me not you she was applauding last night. She probably thought I should get a medal for putting up with you."

"Yeah," said Sebastian, smiling softly, "a Purple Heart."

"Wounded in action?"

His smile slipped away. "I'm really sorry about what I said."

"We're moving on, remember? But, for the record, apology accepted."

He shifted uncomfortably in his chair and ate some of his roll, more for a distraction than anything else, I guessed.

"I got drunk and fell asleep on the beach," he muttered. "In case you were wondering."

His voice was so quiet, I could hardly hear him.

"Well, thank you for telling me."

"I panicked when I woke up and I thought you might have gone. And then I saw you walking along the road. At first I was relieved but then ... I just thought you'd walked out on me. That's why I was..."

"...such an ass?"

His smile was rueful.

"Yeah, that about sums it up."

"Well, like I said, thank you for telling me. Now, what's the big plan for today?"

He smiled his first, genuine, relieved smile of the day.

"I thought we could go to Pisa—take a look at that big, old leaning tower. It's about two hours away."

"Sure, that sounds fun."

I'd always found it hard to fake enthusiasm—something my ex-husband had pointed out on numerous occasions. But I was trying. For Sebastian's sake. For our sake.

He finished his breakfast, threw some Euros on the table and stood up to go. He held his hand out to me and, a little awkwardly, I took it.

His hand was warm and dry, the skin across the top, soft, while the palms were slightly rough, as if he'd done some manual labor recently. I hadn't noticed that before. I wondered why I did now.

When we got to the bike, he fiddled with the zipper on his jacket.

"I really want to kiss you," he said, gazing at me, a mixture of anxiety and need etched on his face.

I hesitated, and it was just long enough to see his expression change to hurt.

"Okay," I said, quietly.

He rested his hands lightly on my waist and I raised my face to his. He touched his lips to mine and I felt the familiar tug of desire. I pulled back quickly.

"Caro..."

"Just hold me, Sebastian. Just hold me."

I laid both my hands on his chest and leaned my cheek against his shoulder. He wrapped his arms around me, hugging me tightly.

"I'm sorry," he whispered. "I'm so sorry," and I felt him kiss my hair several times.

Eventually, he let me go and I gave him a brief smile.

"We'll get there," I said, quietly.

Whether I was reassuring Sebastian or myself, I didn't know.

CHAPTER SEVEN

If I hadn't known that Pisa was a university town before, I knew it as soon as we drove along the main thoroughfare. The streets were packed with twenty-somethings, all casual-chic in that way foreign students do so effortlessly. By comparison, I felt scruffy, dusty and well-traveled. Being dog-tired didn't help either. I was looking forward to finding accommodation where I could have a long, hot shower and sleep in a quiet, comfortable bed—alone.

It was clear that we'd arrived during some sort of festival, because music blared from every café and *ristorante*, competing with the street entertainers and musicians who seemed to be performing on every street corner.

Sebastian carefully steered his bike into the corner of an overwhelmed municipal parking lot, surrounded by battered Fiats and old Renaults. I was a little nervous about leaving my laptop, but at least I had all my notes stored on a flash drive in my wallet, if worst came to worst.

"Are you taking your camera?" Sebastian asked me.

"Might as well. Who knows, maybe I'll be able to sell a travelogue of motorcycling through Italy."

Sebastian raised his eyebrows. "It's got to beat reporting from shitty military camps in fucked up countries."

I shrugged, not feeling in the mood to explain my obsession. Sebastian caught the hint and wisely let the subject drop.

The famous leaning tower was only one of a number of architectural marvels. The central plaza, the Piazza del Duomo, was also home to the beautiful Romanesque cathedral and the 900 year old *Battistero* or Baptistry.

It was a strange feeling, wandering among such antiquity while surrounded by irreverent youth, one of whom kept trying to hold my hand. I was glad that I had my camera as a chaperone. I didn't feel ready for the level of intimacy Sebastian clearly felt was needed. It was hard to explain to myself: I'd said I'd try, but I felt on edge being near him, as if I was waiting for him to explode again. Our earlier, relaxed mood was going to take some effort to achieve. Instead, I felt tense and ill at ease.

After an hour of wandering, I could tell he was beginning to get bored just ogling old buildings, although he did his best to hide it, which I appreciated. I recognized that he preferred action to introspection, but right now I needed to let my mind rest on the centuries of mysteries I saw all around me. I found it soothing and I couldn't help wondering if my father had ever visited Pisa. There was no particular reason why he should have, but still, he might. I liked to imagine that he wandered around here as a young man before deciding to try his luck in the New World. After all, in the sixties, he'd have heard the siren call of Janis Joplin, Bob Dylan and Woodstock. By comparison, Italy would have seemed dull and dreary, dragged down by postwar depression.

"A penny for your thoughts," Sebastian asked quietly, interrupting my musings.

"I was just thinking about Papa—wondering if he ever came here."

Sebastian's eyes lit up and he smiled.

"I really loved your dad, Caro. I was kinda jealous of you when I was a kid—I wanted so badly to have a dad like him, not the sack of shit I was saddled with."

He scowled at the memory.

"Do you ... keep up with your parents at all?"

He shook his head.

"Last time I saw the old bastard was at my graduation from boot camp."

"Oh," I said, surprised, "that was ... nice of him."

"Are you fucking kidding me? He only did it because he knew it would piss me off to have to salute him."

"Oh, right. What about Estelle?"

He shrugged. "She's still in San Diego. Ches sees her around now and again. He banned her from the country club—drinking."

He raised his eyebrows as he looked at me. I didn't say anything, but I hoped he was aware of the parallels in their behavior. Of course, being in the military didn't make for many teetotalers.

"They divorced a few years back. Dad shacked up with some stripper. I don't really know. What about your mom? Do you see her?"

I shook my head. "No, we're not in touch. I know she's living in a retirement home in Florida, but that's all."

"Why aren't you in touch? She couldn't have been as bad as my mom."

"Don't be too sure about that."

He hesitated, but I could tell he was curious. "What did she do?"

"She didn't do anything, Sebastian. That's the point. When I ... when I left David, she told me I'd 'made my bed so now I could lie in it'. She didn't want anything to do with me. Wouldn't lend me a red cent to help out when I went to New York. She wouldn't even send me any photographs of Papa. I only have a couple of old pictures of him."

Sebastian tried to pull me in for a hug, but I resisted him without even being aware of it. He shoved his hands in his pockets.

"Do you see anything of him ... David?"

"No. We had to correspond over the divorce papers, but that's all. I believe he stayed in the Navy. You said you tried to see him ... when was that?"

Sebastian frowned and stared off into the distance.

"About four months after you'd left. It was killing me not knowing how you were, or where you were, or how to get in touch with you. Dad had already trashed my computer and deleted all my email accounts before I went to live with Mitch and Shirley. I didn't even think the bastard knew how to do that stuff. Took my cell off me and smashed that, too. Anyway, I was getting pretty desperate, so I went to your old house—but it was a waste of time. The asshole yelled at me that I'd ruined his marriage, I told him he didn't deserve you and was a bastard for the way he'd treated you. He threatened to call the police. That was it."

I sighed.

"You don't feel sorry for him do you, Caro?" Sebastian said angrily.

"A little. He just married the wrong woman, but he wasn't a bad man."

I could tell from Sebastian's expression that he disagreed strongly.

"But you didn't ruin my marriage. David and I managed to do that all by ourselves. You ... freed me."

His angry expression dissolved, and his eyes gazed at me with wonder.

"Please let me hold you, Caro. It's driving me crazy that you won't let me touch you."

He reached out, but I stepped away from him.

"Just ... just give me some time, Sebastian. I don't deal with rejection well."

"Is that how you see it? That I rejected you."

I stared at him. "Of course. There's no other way to see it."

He ran his hands over his hair in frustration.

"Fuck, Caro! Last night was about my shit, not about you. Don't you see that?"

"No, I don't. Not really. But I don't want to go over that again. I'm trying to put it behind us ... I just need time."

He sighed and his shoulders sagged slightly. "Okay."

There was an awkward silence, but I'd learned that there were two ways to guarantee Sebastian's good humor—and sex was off the menu.

"Do you want to go find somewhere to eat?"

He gave a small smile.

"Yeah, I was hoping you'd say that. Do you feel like Italian?"

"Oh, very funny. You should be on 'Saturday Night Live'."

We wandered through the crowded streets, trying to enjoy the party atmosphere. I began to relax—a little.

"What about that place over there because...?"

Suddenly, I was shoved from behind and I lost my balance. Sebastian caught my elbow but my camera strap had been tugged off my shoulder.

"My camera!"

I pointed at the fleeing figure but Sebastian was already off the blocks and running. The would-be thief made it a hundred yards down the road before Sebastian tackled him, knocking him to the ground.

By the time I arrived, the man had blood pouring down his face from where Sebastian had punched him—more than once, by the look of him.

"Sebastian, no!" I gasped, as I ran up behind him.

At the sound of my voice, he uncurled his fist and stood up, handing my camera back to me. An angry crowd had started to gather, and without knowing what had happened, their sympathies were with the bleeding man.

"We'd better get out of here," Sebastian muttered.

"What about the police?" I gasped, my eyes mesmerized by the blood fountaining from the man's nose.

"Fuck them!" he snorted, and grabbed my hand, towing me through the ring of people who were watching the show with grim fascination. There were a few angry voices aimed at our backs, but no one tried to stop us.

Sebastian darted down a side-alley, pulling me after him and a moment later, we emerged into a wide piazza. I began to breathe normally again, but I was feeling shaky. I knew it was a combination of an adrenaline rush on top of an empty stomach.

"Are you okay, Caro?"

"I'm fine," I lied, weakly.

He didn't look convinced.

"Come on," said Sebastian. "You should eat something."

I nodded, and didn't argue when he led us into a small café that looked like a fifties diner, with high stools ranged along a Formica bar.

"Thank you for saving my camera," I said, quietly.

Sebastian looked surprised, then pleased. "I was waiting for you to chew me out for hitting that guy."

"Well, I'm glad you stopped punching him when you did, obviously, but I'm very fond of my camera. I worked hard to afford to buy it. Thanks, Sarge."

"You never cease to amaze me, Caro," he said, shaking his head.

I didn't know what he meant, but right there and then, I didn't really care either. I reached over and took his hand. "How are your knuckles?"

He chuckled quietly. "Much better now," he said, running his thumb over the back of my hand.

The waitress sauntered over to take our order and I could see her taking a keen interest in Sebastian. He saw the direction of my gaze and smirked at me.

"Not my type," he whispered.

"I'm glad to hear it. She's not mine, either."

For just a moment, Sebastian was caught off balance, then he smiled wickedly at me.

"Not interested in threesomes?"

"I don't know," I replied, casually. "Do you have friends in the Marines who are as cute as you?"

He frowned. "No. I don't."

I laughed. I'd finally won a round of verbal teasing. Things were looking up.

Over dinner, we began to talk naturally with each other again. Sebastian told me more about his life in the Marines and the work that he did—although I sensed there were things he couldn't tell me, as well.

He asked me about my assignments, and more about Liz and Marc, when and how I'd met them. And I told him about my little bungalow in Long Beach, and about Jenna, Alice and Nicole, and how they'd been among the first people I'd met when I'd arrived in New York.

I was relieved to see that he stuck to just the one bottle of beer, which also helped me to relax. I was putting off the moment when I'd have to tell him how much he scared me when he'd been drinking. But not now.

I stifled a yawn.

"Are you tired, Caro?"

"Yes, definitely ready to head for bed, Sebastian. To sleep."

He smiled, but didn't comment.

"Okay, let's see what we can find. There were a couple of streets I saw online that are mostly *pensiones*. Should we try one of those?"

I liked the idea of staying in one of those small hotels. They were usually family run and, although modest, friendly and fun, too.

"Sounds good."

Sebastian paid for the meal, waving away my suggestions that we take turns to pay, or split the bill. I was too tired to argue, but added it to my mental list of 'things to talk about'. It was quite a long list.

There was, however, a tricky subject that I wanted to bring up, and I didn't know how he was going to react.

"Sebastian, don't get mad at me, and don't read too much into this..."

His expression was already worried as I plowed on.

"...but I'd really like to have separate rooms tonight. Just..."

My voice trailed off as a kaleidoscope of emotions flitted across his face. The predominant emotion seemed to be hurt, but there was anger and frustration mixed in there, too.

My body tensed, a primal fight or flight reaction, but he nodded his head slowly.

"Whatever you need, Caro."

I let out a long, relieved sigh.

"Thank you."

But our relaxed banter had, predictably, vanished, and we walked in silence.

"This is the street," he muttered, pointing toward a long line of narrow townhouses.

The first two *pensiones* were full, and the third could only offer a single room. It wasn't looking too good.

"We could try going more upscale," said Sebastian, obviously irritated, although whether that was with me or the accommodation, I couldn't tell.

"Well, we have to walk along this street to get back to the main hotel area, so we may as well try a few more on the way," I suggested.

"Yeah, okay."

At the fifth *pensione*, we struck gold. Sort of.

"I'm sorry, *signora*," said the owner, a stout lady aged about sixty. "I have one room with two single beds, but that's all. It's the Festival, you see," she said, gesturing helplessly. "You're lucky—I had a cancellation."

I could see out of the corner of my eye that Sebastian was willing me to take it. I turned to look at him.

"Pajama party," he mouthed.

I couldn't help smiling. "*Si,* we'll take the room. *Grazie*."

The *pensione* was narrow and old-fashioned, but clean and welcoming, too. Our hostess went by the name of Signora Battelli, and when Sebastian informed her that my surname was 'Venzi', she went off into paroxysms of joy that 'Mr. and Mrs. Venzi have come home', meaning we'd returned from America to the mother country. She had delightfully misunderstood him.

Our room looked like it was last refurbished in the 1970s, decorated with an astonishing clash of vivid patterns, and garish pictures of saints. But I was so tired I didn't care. There was a small sink in the room, and the shower was down the hall, shared, she assured us, by just one other couple.

She bustled off, calling over her shoulder that breakfast was at 8AM.

Sebastian threw himself down on the bed and it groaned slightly.

"Not as noisy as last night," he said, smiling up at me.

"I don't think that's even possible," I agreed.

He unpacked our overnight bag and tossed my toiletry bag onto the second, narrow bed.

"Thanks for packing up my stuff," he said, looking over at me. "I thought I'd probably seen the last of these shirts."

"What a tragedy," I said, cattily. "You might have had to do something shocking, like buy t-shirts in different colors."

He smirked at me, but didn't reply.

The bedroom window had old-fashioned slatted shutters instead of curtains. Sebastian leaned over to open the window, and the sounds of revelry drifted up on the night air.

"Listen to that," he said, dreamily. "Sounds like being in Italy."

I stood and listened for a moment, a smile on my face. "Yes, it sounds, I don't know ... happy."

He turned and looked at me. "Are you happy, Caro?"

I nodded slowly. "Getting there."

"Good," he said, quietly.

I collected my toiletry bag and headed for the shower. As I glanced over my shoulder, he was still staring out of the window.

When I returned, he was leaning out as far as he could, soaking up the mild, night air. He looked relaxed and had a serene expression on his face. I didn't often see him like that: it reminded me of how he'd been when I'd known him in San Diego.

"Back in a minute, baby," he said, smiling at me.

While he was gone, I pulled on a baggy t-shirt that I used for sleeping in, and pulled out my laptop to catch up with emails.

My editor was fuming, still unable to expedite my travel documents. With a frisson of guilt, I realized that I hadn't even told him I was on the move. I tapped out a hasty email of explanation, and offered him a light travel article as a bonus.

Jenna and Alice had sent long and chatty emails about a new gallery they'd been to see in Manhattan, mentioning how the cheap wine had been undrinkable. I wrote to tell them I was traveling through Italy with an old friend, and that I'd finally seen the Leaning Tower of Pisa for myself. It made me feel comfortable to be connected and have news from home.

True to his word, Sebastian returned quickly from the shower. He seemed relieved when he walked back through the door. Perhaps he thought I'd run away while he was gone.

"You doing your writing?" he said, nodding at the laptop.

"No, just catching up with my girlfriends."

"Did you tell them about me?"

"I told them I was traveling through Italy with an old friend."

He looked disappointed, but didn't question me further.

"So, what do you want to do tomorrow?" he said. "Look at more old buildings?"

I was amused by his tone—he was obviously trying to please me, but the look on his face screamed *no more old buildings or I'll want to stab my eyeballs with a fork!*

"Whatever. This is all a bonus anyway. Where would you like to go?"

"There're a couple of surf spots I'd like to check out, if you don't mind," he said, looking hopeful.

"I don't mind, Sebastian. I could use some beach time—sleeping in the sun sounds perfect about now."

"Okay, cool!" he said, clearly relieved. "The surf isn't great in the Med, but there are a few breaks that look like they might be rideable."

He peeled off his t-shirt while he was talking, and I couldn't help my eyes drifting over his chest. *Damn, he was in good shape.*

I dropped my eyes back to my laptop before he caught me staring.

I heard, rather than saw, the rustle of fabric as he tugged off his jeans. I couldn't help glancing up, and noticed that he'd kept his briefs on. That was thoughtful. I knew I wanted him in my bed again, but not yet. This time last night, he'd been yelling at me, calling me an untrustworthy liar. Memories like that took some swallowing.

He jumped into his bed and lay back with his arms behind his head, smiling across at me.

"Are you going to tuck me in?"

I laughed. "I think you're old enough and ugly enough to do that yourself."

"Ugly?"

"Hideous. I can hardly bear to look at you."

"You could close your eyes."

"I could, Sebastian, but I might get the urge to peek.

He thought about it for a moment. "Well, can I get a goodnight kiss?"

"Sure. I'll ask Signora Battelli if she's available."

He pulled a face. "I've never kissed a woman with a mustache."

"First time for everything, Sebastian."

"Please, Caro," he said, pouting cutely at me. "I'll be good. Promise."

"Hmm, I've heard your promises before."

He looked so sad and sort of lost, I couldn't resist him anymore.

"Okay, one kiss. But that's all!"

He grinned at me, delighted to have his own way.

I stowed my laptop back in its case, and sat on his bed. He wrapped his arms around me and pulled me down gently.

I snuggled next to him and lay my head on his chest while he stroked my back.

"We're okay, aren't we, Caro?"

I could hear the anxiety in his voice.

"Getting there."

I wriggled free of his arms and planted a quick kiss on his lips. He held me briefly, then let me go, an expression of regret on his face.

"Night, Sarge."

I turned off my bedside light and heard him murmur.

"Night, boss."

The helicopter was so loud I had to hold my hands over my ears. The whirling blades kicked up plumes of yellow dust that coated my nose and throat so I could taste it. A man in desert fatigues was yelling at me, but I couldn't hear the words. And then his face disappeared in a bloody mist.

"Caro, wake up!"

Sebastian was shaking me hard. I sat up, wide-eyed and trembling.

"Fuck, Caro," he said, more quietly. "Another nightmare?"

I nodded silently.

"Come here, baby."

He wrapped his arms around me and pulled me tightly into his chest.

I gulped in air, my lungs burned as if I'd been holding my breath for a long time, and I could almost taste the acrid dust in my mouth.

Damn, that had been a bad one.

"What was it about, baby?"

I shook my head. "Just a nightmare."

"You can tell me anything, Caro," he said, rocking me slowly.

No. Not anything. Not that.

But he didn't press me, and I was happy just to have him hold me.

After a few minutes, my heart rate had returned to normal.

"Scoot over," he whispered. "I'll just stay till you go back to sleep."

"Thank you."

He slid down next to me and I felt his warm body press into mine. There was no anger, no ugly accusations, no tension, just his gentle hands around me.

Finally, the nightmare drifted away, and I slept.

When I woke up the next morning feeling happier and refreshed, bright sunshine was filtering through the shutters, and Sebastian's body was still twined around me in the narrow bed. His breath was hot on the back of my neck and his heavy arm pinned me down.

I tried to wriggle out from underneath him, but he mumbled something unintelligible and pulled me in more tightly.

It felt good waking up in his arms. Hell, it felt better than good, it felt right. We still had some issues to resolve—pretty important ones—but I began to feel hopeful that we were getting there. Like I'd said.

I stroked his long fingers that were resting across my stomach, and I felt him move, stretching out in the bed like a big, old sleepy cat.

I shifted around so I could look at him.

A slow, sexy smile appeared on his face as he rubbed the sleep out of his eyes.

"Wow, I have this beautiful woman in my bed. I really like this dream."

"Actually, Sebastian, you're in *my* bed."

"Oh, yeah. You must be one of those fast women I heard about at boot camp."

"Hmm, well, I think that lecture was supposed to warn you off them."

"Oh, I guess I didn't hear it right. I suppose that explains why I didn't get into Officer Candidate School."

"Did you try?"

He shook his head slowly. "Nah, not really. Not my thing. I took some college classes for a while, but then ... I was already fucking around. Guess I pissed off the wrong people."

"You'd make a good officer, Sebastian. Maybe you should think about it."

He shrugged. "I'm a Master Sergeant—three ranks up from Sergeant." He correctly interpreted my expression. "Yeah, you know that stuff. Sorry. I did get asked to join the Navy SEALs, though."

"Really? That's great! I mean, that's a real honor, isn't it? You'd like that—all that super-macho stuff."

He smiled, and ran a finger down my arm. "I turned them down."

I gaped at him. *Nobody* turned down the chance to join the Navy's elite team. "Why?"

He looked at me as if the answer was obvious.

"Caro, there's no way I'd join the same service that my father is in. Fuck that! Can you imagine if we ended up at the same Base? I'd end up killing the bastard."

"Shh," I said, resting my finger on his lips, as his voice started to get louder. "We're in Italy, it's a beautiful day, and we're going to go and find some waves for you to surf."

He took a deep breath and smiled. "Okay," he said, happily.

Then his hand drifted down to my thigh and he circled, slowly, his fingers tugging at the material of my panties.

"You know what would make this day even better?" he said, suggestively.

"Oh no, Sebastian. I'm not falling for that. I'm going to take a shower, and you'd better have some damn clothes on by the time I get back."

I rolled out of bed before he could stop me, and stomped around the room picking out clean clothes to wear.

"Are you sure?" he said, smiling lasciviously, as his hand disappeared under the sheets. I could tell he was stroking himself, and the thought of what I could do with the result was very arousing.

I shook myself out of my reverie. No, I'd promised myself that we had to get through at least another 24 hours without having another major meltdown before I'd give in. It was just being smart. If I let him in any further without some sort of proof that I could trust him with my heart, I was a damn fool, and deserved everything that happened to me.

I headed for the shower, cursing myself for not having taken a photograph of him lying there in my bed, all hot and wicked. I'd need something to entertain myself with during the dark, lonely nights when I was an old woman, and boring anyone who'd listen about that summer vacation where I'd had more sex than Madonna. Well, maybe—I was still thinking about it.

The shower was cool enough to put out the flames of passion that Sebastian had been stoking in me.

Twenty-four hours I chanted to myself.

When I was back at our room, he'd gotten as far as pulling on a pair of jeans, but that was all.

"You shouldn't wander around like that," I admonished. "You'll give Signora Battelli a coronary."

He winked at me but took no notice whatsoever, as he sauntered out of the room.

While he was gone, I searched through his jacket pockets until I found his map. I scoped out the beaches that might have enough swell for surf, then Googled them on my laptop. There were two possibilities within an hour's drive. We'd already gone past one of the best surf spots at Levanto. The next best spot was outside Rome, but that was a five hour drive. I decided we could save that for another day.

"Whatcha find?" said Sebastian, as he wandered in from his shower, still only wearing his jeans.

He knew damn well what that was doing to me!

"We seem to be in between surf spots here, but about 30 miles away, there's a place that looks like it might be okay. There's a big campsite there and it says they rent out boards, so it seems like a good bet. Want to try it?"

"I'll try anything with you, baby."

"Sebastian, focus."

I pointed at the map.

"Sure, baby," he said, smiling. "I just need to fill up the gas tank, but otherwise we're good to go."

He wrapped his hands over my shoulders and kissed my hair.

"Come on then, Hunter," I said, throwing him one of his ubiquitous white t-shirts. Let's go see what Signora Battelli has for breakfast."

Breakfast: the word was deeply inadequate for what Signora Battelli had laid out. It was more like a banquet of breakfast foods: fresh oranges and wild berries, *panini*, sweet rolls, *fette biscottate*, muesli, three different homemade yogurts, *caciotta* and *pecorino baccellone* cheese, and a chef's delight of *salumeria*—cold meat—including the local specialty of wild boar.

Sebastian's eyes glowed, and he completed at least three circuits of the buffet table before he was satisfied, or possibly too embarrassed to go around a fourth time. Maybe not: I didn't think Sebastian did 'embarrassed'.

At the next table sat a couple of American students who were wide-eyed at the spread in front of them. One of the girls was asking Signora Battelli's opinion on different types of fresh pasta.

"But how much should I give guests at a meal?" she said. "How will I know how much to buy back home?"

"Young woman," said Signora Battelli, swelling with knowledge. "You buy a half pound of fresh pasta per person ... except for my son: he eats one pound of pasta!"

I was rather hoping the son would appear so I could see if he lived up to expectations, but we were to be denied that pleasure. Signora Battelli explained that her son had taken a job in Rome.

It was the same story everywhere: young people leaving their small towns and villages to seek their fortunes in the big city. But wasn't that always the case?

As soon as they realized that we were Americans, too, the girls were determined not to leave us alone. Well, I'm sure I could have disappeared in a puff of purple smoke and they wouldn't have noticed—their eyes were welded to Sebastian instead. I couldn't blame them, and I was sort of curious to see how he behaved with them.

One of them reminded me of his ex-girlfriend, Brenda. Maybe it was her propensity to toss long, shiny hair over her shoulder, and gaze at him from beneath her long lashes.

She was flirting with him right in front of me like I didn't even exist!

Sebastian answered their questions pleasantly. It was obvious they were angling for a ride with us, and it was almost comical how far their faces fell when he told them we were traveling by motorcycle.

"I've never ridden a motor-sickle," said the one called Lydia.

And today won't be the day either, lady.

"Well, I'm sure you'll enjoy it when you get the chance," said Sebastian, evenly. He stood up to go, and held out his hand to me. "Come on, baby," he said.

I placed my hand in his and he pulled it to his lips, kissing the inside of my wrist. A warm feeling traveled up from my feet, and settled somewhere in the area of my groin.

He was delicious and dangerous and my resolve to wait another 24 hours crumbled away.

The girls looked like they were in agony, and I couldn't resist smiling at them as Sebastian and I walked away hand in hand.

"What?" Sebastian asked, catching my eye.

"Sometimes you can be very sweet."

I heard his breath catch in his throat, he looked so raw and vulnerable as he stared down at me.

"*Tesoro*, what did I say?"

He looked into my eyes, then let his forehead rest on mine.

"I love you, Caro," he said.

CHAPTER EIGHT

STANDING OUTSIDE SIGNORA BATTELLI'S BREAKFAST ROOM, MY WORLD changed.

"I love you, Caro, so much."

I couldn't believe he was saying these words to me.

"I haven't changed how I feel. I still love you—I've always loved you. It's only ever been you."

I thought my heart would stop beating.

Ten years ago he'd said these words to me, told me that he loved me. I'd believed they were the words of a lonely, infatuated boy: real, but not lasting. Now the same man was standing before me, saying that he'd loved me all this time—and that it was real. He didn't care that I was older than him, he didn't care that I was ridden with insecurities, and he'd forgiven me for doubting him.

Was I brave enough to accept his love? Could I accept that he wasn't perfect, that he had his own problems to deal with, that he drank too much, and his hot head led him into trouble more often than not? Could I accept that he did a dangerous job in a dangerous world, and that we would be apart for months on end?

He'd asked me once if I was brave enough to take a chance on love. I finally knew the answer.

"I love you, too, Sebastian. More than you'll ever know."

He gasped, staring at me with wonder. And then he kissed me.

Not the boiling, surging kisses that heated my blood and shredded my resolve, but a kiss so sweet and gentle, so honest and simple, that my heart cracked open and filled with love.

He pulled me to his chest and we stood in silence, our arms wrapped around each other.

I was vaguely aware of the continuing quiet tide of humanity flowing around us, but for that moment, we were the only people in the whole world.

"You mean everything to me, Caro." Sebastian spoke softly into my hair.

"You're so brave, *tesoro*," I said, quietly. "You've never been afraid to love."

I felt his smile. "That's because I learned from you."

I shook my head.

"It's true," he said, gently.

I sighed and pulled my arms a little tighter around him.

He laughed softly and stroked my cheek.

We continued to stand there, basking in a love that came from within, warming us and filling us.

Eventually, Sebastian rubbed my arm and stood up straight.

"I guess we'd better get going before Signora Battelli decides to start vacuuming around us."

"Okay," I said, smiling up at him.

At that moment, I'd have followed him to the four corners of the Earth and the very gates of Hell.

We walked back to our room in blissful silence, and every now and then I felt Sebastian's fingers squeeze mine.

"I can't stop smiling," I said, stupidly. "I think I've pulled a muscle in my mouth."

"I know what you mean," said Sebastian, grinning back. "Although I have some ideas about how you could do that for real later."

I slapped his arm.

"You don't change, do you, Hunter!"

He threw himself back on his bed and grinned up at me.

"Do you want me to change?"

"Oh, you could do with a little polish here and there, but otherwise, no, you'll do."

"I'd like you to polish me right now," he said, smiling wickedly.

"Well, I'd love to oblige, but Signora Battelli is going to be knocking on our door in about two minutes."

He pouted. "We could make it quick."

"Oh no, I want to take my time."

"How much time?" he asked, his gaze heated.

"Hours, possibly days ... whole months even," I said, staring back at him.

He groaned and closed his eyes. "Months?"

"Years," I said, softly. "A lifetime."

He sat up, his gaze serious. "Do you mean it, Caro, a lifetime?"

"Yes."

He closed his eyes, breathing in deeply. Then his head sank to his chest. Slowly, he opened his eyes and looked up at me. His smile was glorious.

"Okay," he said, his face glowing with happiness.

Yes, I did mean it. There was no doubt. And I could tell from Sebastian's reaction that he was overwhelmed with happiness. I felt the same way. Overwhelmed, over-brimming, over-full, flooded with joy.

We packed up our small bag, moving easily around the room, touching each other as we passed, as if there was a physical necessity to express our happiness somehow.

Sebastian paid a relieved Mrs. Battelli. We'd taken so long, she was obviously wondering if we were planning on moving in permanently.

Sebastian thanked her beautifully for her delicious breakfast, telling her that he'd never enjoyed a *pensione* more. Then he kissed her hand, and the stout widow blushed.

"You are so smooth, Hunter!" I scolded him as we headed out to get the bike.

"I was just telling her the truth," he said. "I think we should come back here, and book the same room every year—then spend the night fucking."

"You're such a romantic."

"Yeah, I know, baby."

Sebastian's motorcycle had survived the night. I pulled on the now familiar black helmet and settled myself onto the seat, enjoying the comforting smell of old leather, with my thighs pressed into Sebastian. I'd almost go so far as to say I felt comfortable—although a car with a roof and doors also had a lot to be said for it. Hmm, hot, steamy car-sex with Sebastian. On the other hand, now beds had been invented...

We headed out of town and southeast along the coastal road, burning out of Pisa and racing into the sun.

I wrapped my arms around Sebastian's waist and thought what a difference a day can make. Yesterday, I'd been unhappy and abandoned. Today ... well, it was the start of the rest of my life.

~

The campsite I'd found was just an hour from Pisa, outside the village of Polveroni. The Mediterranean stretched before us and the sun heated the sea gently. Better still, from Sebastian's perspective, long breakers rolled in, providing perfectly rideable waves of between three and four feet.

His eyes lit up at the surf barreling up the beach, and just when I thought the day couldn't get any better, we saw a shop with boards to rent.

"Game on!" he said to himself.

We parked the mean machine and Sebastian practically sprinted inside, talking animatedly with the owner. He returned a few minutes later with a battered longboard, a huge beach towel, and a pair of garish board shorts.

"Hey, Sarge! You're in danger of doing color!" I teased him.

He smirked at me. "Yeah, well, it was all they had. Either that or I'd have to do it in the nude. What do you think, Caro, naked surfing?"

"It could catch on, or you could get arrested. But I'm telling you, Sebastian, if you do get arrested and I don't get laid tonight, I'm going to be mighty pissed at you."

He laughed delightedly.

"Now you're talking. By the way, the guy in the shop said that he rents out rooms. He said it's pretty basic—just a big, old bed and a small bathroom. But I thought it would be kind of cool to be able to hear the sea tonight. Is that okay?"

"Very okay."

He grinned at me, but his smile slipped away as he gazed in horror at the sensible, navy-blue one-piece that I was holding in my hands. It was the swimsuit that I usually wore to the public pool.

"Wait," said Sebastian, "*that's* what you're going to wear?"

"Yes, why?"

I stared at him, utterly baffled.

"Stay here."

He strode off back toward the beach shop. He returned a few minutes later with a tiny bit of string and a few triangles of material and handed it to me.

"Here. Wear this."

I held out the skimpy bikini. It left absolutely nothing to the imagination. It was barely big enough to cover my nipples, let alone anything else.

"I can't wear that, Sebastian, there's nothing to it! I'm forty, not twenty!"

"You'll look amazing, Caro. I want every guy on the beach to know how hot my woman is."

"I may as well go topless!"

His eyes heated, and a licentious expression appeared on his face. "Yeah, baby."

I shook my head at him. "You're crazy."

"Crazy in love," he said, scooping me into a kiss that made my bones rattle.

"Fine, I'll wear it," I said, breathlessly.

He gave me a dark look that said I damn well would.

Sebastian held up the beach towel to cover my modesty while I changed into the tiny bikini. Although 'modesty' and 'tiny bikini' in the same sentence didn't really seem to be a good fit. Like the bikini. Whichever way I tugged it, more flesh than seemed acceptable was exposed.

"I can't wait to take that off you," he whispered in my ear.

"Sex or surfing, Sebastian?"

"Sex," he said, at once.

I laughed, even as my body overheated.

"Well, you'll have to take a rain check—we haven't reserved that room for the night yet. And I've warned you what will happen if you get arrested."

He smirked at me.

"You owe me a lot of rain checks, Caro. I'm going to enjoy cashing them in."

He didn't bother using the towel when he changed into his board shorts—he just dropped his pants and briefs right out there in the open.

"Sebastian!" I muttered, glancing around to see if anyone was watching.

He'd already pulled on the garish board shorts by the time my eyes flickered back to him. He laughed at my surprised expression.

"Years of practice changing out of my wetsuit in windswept parking lots along Sunset Cliffs, Caro," he said. "I'll show you how quick I can get out of my clothes now if you like?"

"Go. Surf."

"Here—look after these for me."

He pulled off his dog tags and placed them around my neck, where the small metal tags nestled between my breasts. He stood back for a moment.

"Those look hot on you, Caro. Really fucking hot."

He scooped me up in a ridiculous Hollywood kiss, dipping me so low, my hair was touching the sand, then he put me back on my feet. I was still off balance as he ran down to the water.

I loved to watch him surf, it brought back many good memories of our time in San Diego. There had been too few from that turbulent summer, but being on the beach with Sebastian, watching him in the waves, those had been happy times. He was so graceful out there, charging down the glassy, green surfaces, diving through the foam.

I'd taken my camera with me, so I zoomed in and snapped some photographs of Sebastian surfing. I had a pretty decent lens, and I got some really good close-ups of him in action.

Hmm, photographs of Sebastian in action, now there was a thought to warm a cold winter night.

I lay back on our beach towel, relaxed and filled with a quiet happiness. Once again my life had swung across the pendulum from bitterness and despair to an overwhelming sense of love and being loved. And this time I would allow myself to believe in it.

The warmth of the sun was pleasant, adding to my sense of peaceful well-being. It wasn't really hot, maybe a balmy 68°F or 69°F. Enough to be relaxing: not enough to worry about getting burned.

Suddenly I realized someone was standing over me.

"*Buon giorno!*"

An attractive man about my own age was smiling down at me.

"*Ciao?*" I replied.

I sat up, wondering what he wanted.

"It's a beautiful day, isn't it?" he said, in Italian.

"Yes," I agreed, rather puzzled.

"It looks like you're enjoying the sun."

Oh crap! He was hitting on me. Was he hitting on me?

"Um, yes. It's very pleasant."

"Are you here on vacation?"

"Yes, we are," I replied with the faintest emphasis on the plural.

"Ah," he said, looking around him for my absent companion.

"My boyfriend is surfing," I explained, with a small smile.

"Then he will be having some good rides," replied my new friend, who then winked at me and ambled away.

I could see Sebastian jogging up the beach to join me.

"What did he want?" he asked, looking none too pleased.

"Don't blame me, Sergeant," I said, raising one eyebrow, "You're the one who bought this itsy bitsy teeny weeny bikini for me. Anyway, I told him my boyfriend was surfing, so you don't need to worry."

Sebastian scowled.

Oh boy, talk about double standards.

"Did you have fun?" I asked, trying not to laugh at him.

"Yeah," he agreed, looking in the direction where my 'friend' had vanished, "not bad. Had some good rides."

"I know, I was watching." I pointed to the camera, "I got some great shots, too."

"Really?" he sounded delighted, and turned his full attention to me. "I've never seen any pictures of me surfing."

My heart gave a quick, unhappy flop. My poor boy had never had parents who cared that he was good at something.

He sat down on the towel next to me, his skin glistening with drops of seawater. Trying not to get distracted, I showed him the shots I'd caught, and he raised his eyebrows.

"Wow! You're a really good photographer, Caro."

"I have excellent subject material," I said, then snapped a close-up of his exquisite face and chest.

"What's that for?" he asked, blinking in surprise.

"Just so I know you're real," I told him. "I think you're a figment of my overwrought imagination, and you might disappear when I wake up. But now," I said, waving the camera at him, "I have proof."

He grinned and shook his head, as if I was a little crazy. Which I was. Like he'd said: crazy in love.

He pushed me down onto the beach towel with his damp body, and kissed me in a way that told me how he felt. I stroked my hand over his wet hair and smiled up at him.

"You're so cute when you're wet."

"So are you," he said, with a leer.

We ate lunch on the beach, panini from the shop and some fresh fruit sold by a bored teenage boy, who was slouched under a sunshade.

Sebastian continued to flirt with me, tease me, and toy with my bikini straps, which I found ridiculously adorable. It was all I could do to stop myself from leaping on him there and then. But we were both enjoying just touching each other, playing and spending time together, without having to worry about what anyone else thought, said or did.

In the afternoon, he fell asleep in the sun and I lay watching him for nearly an hour, almost unable to believe my luck—he was really mine, and that I was his.

We spent the rest of the day on the beach. Sebastian even persuaded me to go for a surf with him, although I thought the water was really too cold to be pleasurable.

"Come on, Caro, I've wanted to try this for a long time. Let's take the board out and catch a wave together. I'll do the paddling and I can stare at your gorgeous ass while I'm doing it."

Which was an offer I couldn't refuse.

I lay on the board first, and Sebastian jumped on behind me. He couldn't resist giving my ass a quick bite.

We paddled out to just behind where the waves were breaking, then as the water started to rise, Sebastian turned the board around and we began to speed down the front of the wave.

"Get ready to pop up!" he yelled, above the crashing surf. "Go!"

I scrambled to my feet and felt the board wobble slightly, then Sebastian was behind me, one hand steadying my hip as we raced down the face of the wave.

It was the most extraordinary feeling, riding that wave together. In some ways it was a metaphor for the life we were starting out on. Who knew when we'd fall off? But by trusting each other and moving as one, the ride would be longer.

Eventually, Sebastian conceded that I really was cold, and we belly-boarded back into the beach.

"Your nipples are hard," he said, pointing out the obvious.

"Well, what a shocker," I said. "I've never seen them like that before."

"Is that right? I'll see what I can do about it later."

"Promises, promises," I sighed.

His eyes widened and his nostrils flared with the challenge.

"Bed, woman. Now."

"Don't you want to find somewhere to have dinner first?"

He shook his head. The Master Sergeant wanted sex, not food. I really, really wasn't going to argue.

We paid for the room behind the beach shop, but were interrupted en route to our sexcapades by the owner, who was desperate to talk to Sebastian about surf spots in California. I left them mulling over whether San Diego or Monterey had the better breaks, even though I could feel Sebastian's eyes following me across the beach.

I collected our overnight bag from the bike and carried it into the small room.

It was like being in a log cabin: wooden walls, wooden floors, wooden furniture. But Sebastian was right—the bed was huge. I tested it out gingerly. Nope, no creaking springs to distract us tonight.

While I was waiting for him, I checked my emails. I was surprised to see that there was one from Nicole.

> *To: Lee Venzi*
> *From: Nicole Olsen*
> *Re: WTF*
> *Venzi! WTF are you doing in Italy? How come I had to hear about it secondhand from Jenna? Don't you think it's time you had mindless sex with an Italian stallion? Call me for tips. Have fun. Nx*

That was so like Nicole. If only she knew. I decided I'd send her a photo of Sebastian to cheer up her gray, New York morning.

I picked the one of him sitting back on the beach towel, his beautiful face and divine chest in full view. I wasn't going to send her the one where his board shorts showed the ammo he was packing: Nicole would probably implode.

> *To: Nicole Olsen*
> *From: Lee Venzi*
> *Re: Re: WTF*
> *Thinking about your advice. Traveling through Italy with an old friend. Thought you'd like this eye-candy to brighten your day. Lx*

I was still smiling to myself about Nicole's message and my reply, when Sebastian strolled in.

"What's so funny?"

"Oh, I just had an email from my friend Nicole in NYC. She wants me to have mindless sex with an Italian stallion."

Sebastian didn't look amused. "Why is she saying stuff like that to you?"

"Oh, don't be such a prude, Sebastian! It's just a joke. She's always nagging me to find a man."

"What about me?" he asked, sounding ridiculously hurt.

I rolled my eyes. "I haven't told anyone about you. I like having you to myself. But I will, if you want me to."

"I want to know your friends, Caro. Although I'll fucking tell *Nicole* that she can keep her comments about 'Italian stallions' to herself."

Uh-oh, the Master Sergeant was riled.

Now *that* was going to be an interesting meeting—Sebastian and Nicole were both fiery. I wasn't going to place bets on who'd win that encounter.

Suddenly my phone started ringing. I stared at it in amazement, as if it had suddenly grown wings. Why on earth was Nicole calling me?

"Nicole, hi! Wow, it's great to hear from you. How are you?

"Don't give me that, Venzi. Where did you get that smokin' hot picture? Have you turned into one of those women who ogles younger men?"

"Like you, you mean?"

Nicole snorted. *"Exactly! Since when did you start taking photos of hot guys? And who's this 'old friend' that you're suddenly traveling around Italy with?"*

"Nicole, I sent you a picture of him. His name is Sebastian."

Sebastian glanced over at me, a smile on his face.

"Come on, Lee. Why won't you tell me who you're traveling around with?"

"No, seriously, Nicole. That's a photo of my friend."

"The Stud Muffin is your 'old friend'?" she yelled down the phone. "You're bullshitting me, Lee!"

I laughed. "I promise you, Nicole."

"Have you been holding out on me? Where did you meet him?"

Her words poured out in a torrent.

"I'll tell you some other time," I said, shaking my head, as Sebastian gazed at me quizzically.

"No! Tell me now!" she shrieked.

"I can't. Later."

"Why not now?"

"Because he's standing right here, Nicole."

Sebastian raised his eyebrows.

"Bullshit! I don't believe you."

"It's true."

"Put him on the phone."

"What?"

"I think you've been without sex too long, Venzi. You're hallucinating."

I handed the phone to Sebastian. "She wants to talk to you."

He took the phone, looking amused. "Hi, Nicole. This is Sebastian."

I saw him listening intently, a slight frown on his face. I wondered what on earth Nicole could be saying to him.

"You don't want me to use her?" he said, glancing toward me. "Well, Nicole, I was planning on taking her to bed and using her in ways that aren't even mentioned in the Kama Sutra, but now you've told me, I think I should go take a cold shower instead."

I snatched the phone back, glaring at him. Sebastian just smirked at me.

"Sorry about that, Nic!"

There was a long silence at the other end.

"Nic?"

"Fuck me!" she said, huskily. "Don't be sorry, Lee. That is the hottest thing I've heard in years. He sounds like a sex machine! Look, I think you should write a sex manual with this guy, but you'll have to take photographs ... lots of photographs."

I laughed. "I'll get back to you on that, Nic."

At which point, restive and impatient, Sebastian started untying the straps of my bikini. I tried to shoo his hands away, but it was awkward, what with trying to hold onto my phone and continue the conversation. I gasped as he tossed my bikini top onto the floor and massaged my nipples with his fingers.

"Oh my God, Lee! Are you guys doing it right now? Can you put it on speaker on?"

"I'll have to call you back, Nic," I said, breathlessly.

I cut the call while she was still yelling, and launched myself at Sebastian.

My phone clattered to the floor, and one part of my brain was already assessing what damage that might have caused, but the greater part of my brain, by far, already had Sebastian stripped and ready for action. My fumbling fingers had to play catch up but luckily my tackle had knocked him backward onto the bed.

I straddled him and pinned his wrists back with my hands, my mouth crushing his, my breasts forcing themselves into his chest.

He could easily have overpowered me, being about fifty times stronger than I was, but he seemed content to let me have my wicked way with him. I had some serious catching up to do, and he had rain checks that needed cashing.

Our tongues were gliding together, our teeth clashing, and I could feel Sebastian getting aroused beneath me.

He sat up suddenly, cradling his arms around my waist, as mine flew up in surprise. He kissed my neck, running his hot tongue over my throat.

"You taste like the sea," he murmured, "and your skin smells like sunshine."

He ran his fingers up my back, and let them tangle in my hair, pulling my face down to his.

"I want to be inside you, Caro."

I smiled against his lips, and then rolled off him, scooting down to the bottom of the bed.

"Raise that glorious ass," I said, tugging on the hem of his board shorts.

He grinned at me and lifted his hips from the bed. I pulled off the shorts, threw them behind me, then sat back to enjoy the view.

His legs were long and tan and muscled like a runner, his thighs and hips pale, and his rich, pubic hair was light brown. My eyes wandered up his body, taking in his erection that hovered above his tight, toned stomach, where his skin turned to gold again. He propped himself up on his elbows and smiled at me, his head on one side, as if he was asking what I found so fascinating.

"You're beautiful, Sebastian. I love to look at you. I love to see you like this, when it's just the two of us. Why does it feel so right?"

He shook his head slowly.

"Maybe it was just meant to be. I mean, shit, could we have had any more challenges thrown at us?"

I could think of one big challenge that we still had to face, but I refused to let that spoil the here and now.

"We've certainly had our share," I sighed.

He sat up and held my cheek with his hand.

"Don't be sad, Caro. We've got our second chance ... or maybe we're on our third ... I kinda lost count already."

"That is very true." I laughed, lightly. "Now you seem to have a very desirable hard-on there, so should we have some fun with that?"

"I'm all yours."

I grinned and jumped off the bed. "Are the condoms in your toiletry bag?"

"Yeah, baby."

I rooted through the overnight bag until I found what I was looking for.

"Sebastian, there's only one condom left in here," I said, shaking the now empty box at him.

"Shit! You're kidding! Fuck, how did I ... ah, crap. Give me that fucker—I'm going to make the most of it."

"Oh no, Hunter," I smiled, waving the foil packet at him, "this one is all mine."

His eyes heated instantly and his cock twitched.

"Feeling a little needy, baby?" I said, continuing to tease him, as I walked around the bed.

"Fuck, Caro!"

He lunged for me but I danced away.

"Dear me, someone is impatient."

"Yeah, very!" he said, sounding both amused and slightly annoyed.

I stood at the end of the bed.

"Would you like me to take these off?" I asked, tugging gently on the delicate laces of my bikini bottoms.

He nodded silently.

"Or maybe you'd like to take them off me?"

He swallowed and nodded again.

I climbed up from the foot of the bed and crawled all the way up him, the foil packet held in my teeth. I hovered above him and he reached down to untie first one, then the second ribbon, and the small strip of material fluttered to the floor.

I took the condom packet out of my mouth while his right hand drifted up my thighs and his index finger slid inside, slowly massaging me. My eyes were locked on his: watching him, watching me, watching him.

Then he pushed another finger inside me, moving faster, and my breath began to come in short gasps.

"Come on, baby," he said, his voice tight.

My body responded and I tried to push his hand away, not being able to take any more.

"No, baby," he said softly, "you can take more."

"I can't! I can't!" I begged him, but he wouldn't stop, and the most intense, demanding, draining orgasm arched my spine and made my body shudder, the tremors coursing through me like the aftershocks of an earthquake.

Because my legs were apart, still kneeling across him, it seemed to go on and on and on.

I collapsed onto his chest, and I felt his fingers stroke my back, tracing my spine through my skin.

Gently, he rolled me onto my back, and kissed me across my neck and chest, sucking and tugging on my nipples with his teeth. My over-sensitized body responded quickly. It was as if the lightest touch sent a charge of electricity racing through me.

He pushed up my knees and before my brain had caught up, I felt him plunge inside me.

"Sebastian, no! Don't!"

"Come on, baby, you feel so good."

He rolled his hips, and sensation flooded through me.

"No!"

I pushed hard on his chest and, reluctantly, he pulled out, his sea-green eyes accusing.

"What are you doing, Sebastian?" I gasped, staring at him in shock.

"I just want to make love to you, Caro."

"I know ... but, you're not wearing a condom."

I opened my hand, begging him to look at the foil packet that I was holding, still unopened.

"We don't need that, Caro."

Did I hear him right?

"What? Are you crazy, Sebastian? I could get pregnant!"

He stared down at me.

"Would that be so bad?"

"You *want* me to get pregnant?" I stammered.

He sighed and closed his eyes, rolling onto his side.

"I want to have a life with you, Caro, for the rest of my life. Look—kids—whatever. If it happens, then great, if it doesn't, that's fine, too. Just as long as we're together. This time, forever."

I flung my arm over my eyes, shutting out the vision of his beautiful face, trying to regain some order among the craziness.

He pulled my arm away from my eyes, forcing me to look at him.

"Caro?"

"Sebastian..." I stuttered, not sure where to start. "We were apart for ten years. I saw you again a week ago, we had sex, a couple of dates, more sex, we fought, we broke up ... and now you're saying you want to have children with me?"

He smiled and raised his eyebrows. "Yeah."

"Do you know how crazy that sounds?"

"That's our story, Caro. Crazy in love."

I didn't know whether to kiss him, hit him, or have him committed.

"I ... I don't know what to say."

He shrugged. "You don't have to say anything, Caro. You don't have to *do* anything. Like I said: if it happens or not ... whatever ... we'll deal."

"And what ... you'll give up being a Marine to look after the kids?"

His mouth dropped open, then he grinned at me. "Kids? As in, plural? Sure, why not?"

"You ... you'd do that?"

By now I was gaping at him.

"Caro, I'll do whatever it takes to be with you. I've been in the Marines for nearly ten years now and I've had tours in Iraq and Afghan, been stationed in Germany, Paris and Geneva. I didn't care because I didn't have anywhere to go home to. But with you, we'll have a home, and I won't want to be away from you."

I struggled to sit up, still feeling tremulous from my very recent orgasm. Or it might have been the complete head-spin Sebastian had just thrown at me.

"I ... I..."

He smirked at me. "I thought you were supposed to be the one who was good with words, Caro."

"Usually," I choked out.

He stroked my stomach suggestively, letting his hand drift lower.

"So, what do you think? Should we just keep going?"

"I ... no ... look, just give me some time to think about this. We've got this lonely, little condom, so let's use it and talk again later. Okay?"

He sighed and looked resigned, but I could tell he was disappointed. Then he glanced down at his dick, which had lost some of its delicious hardness.

"Feeling a little flat here, baby. You wanna pump me up?"

His mood swings left me reeling, but I couldn't help smiling at the hopeful expression on his face.

"Yes, I think I can do something about that. Lie back."

He grinned up at me. "What are you going to do?"

"Absolutely nothing."

"What?" he said, frowning.

"I'm not going to touch you, Sebastian, and you're not going to touch me. Yet. I'm going to show you how good I am with words."

"I have no idea what you're talking about baby, but it's making me feel horny."

I smiled. "That's the point, Sebastian. I'm going to make you so hard, I'm going to get you so wound up, I'm going to turn you on so much, that all I'll have to do is touch you with one finger to make you come."

"Fuck!" he breathed, his eyes wide.

I lay down next to him so we were close, but not touching.

"Close your eyes," I breathed.

He gave me one, long, hot, lingering look, and then did as I asked.

"I want you to see it all in your mind, Sebastian. Imagine everything I'm saying: see it, hear it, taste it, feel it, breathe it in. Understand?"

He swallowed and nodded.

"You're lying on the bed and it's very quiet. It's night time, but there's a full moon, and the shadows on the floor are almost blue. You hear the door open, but your eyes stay closed. You hear my footsteps across the wooden floor, you know it's me because you recognize the soft sound of my footfalls. I'm standing right next to you, looking down at your naked body. You can hear the rustle of my clothes as I slowly start to take them off. You can hear the zipper of my dress. I must be wearing silk, because the material whispers as it falls from my body. Then you feel the mattress moving under you and my weight presses down on your body. My naked breasts are brushing against your skin, it's cool and my nipples are hard when you take them in your mouth."

He groaned softly and I saw that his cock was almost completely erect again.

"I move up your body, hovering over you. I moan slightly and you know it's because I'm touching myself, turning myself on for you. My fingers are inside me, circling slowly, and when I pull them out, I place them on your lips and you suck them hard. You can taste me and you can smell the muskiness of my scent. You long to touch me, but then I take your fingers in my mouth, sucking them one by one. You imagine what my mouth would feel like around your cock: my lips, my teeth, my tongue swirling around. You can imagine what it would feel like when you move into my mouth and your tip touches the back of my throat."

I could see that his cock really was hard and ready for action.

Not yet, Sebastian.

"My hair brushes the skin on your chest as I arch away from you, and your skin is so sensitized you can feel every strand, every wave, every individual hair. I take your hand and move your fingers against my clitoris. I'm wet, very wet, and you know it won't be long before your hot, hard cock is stroking inside me. I run my fingers around you, gripping you, squeezing you, and you know that I want you—every inch of you—inside me. You're at the entrance of my sex, and you sink into me: slowly at first, then getting faster and harder, going deeper and deeper. Your control is unraveling because you can feel that hot, soft, sweet flesh all around you. My body starts to buck under yours and you know that I'm close. You can feel ripples of pleasure pulsing through me and you're wondering how long you can hold on before you come. You're trying so hard to hold it back but then I clench around you, squeezing you, milking everything you have. And I'm begging you to give it to me again. I'm begging you to take me from behind, so you pull out, even though you're aching to come, your balls hot and heavy, and then you're looking at my ass, knowing that I want you so badly, waiting just for you."

By now Sebastian's breathing was becoming rapid and his hands were hovering over his body as if he was desperate to touch me or to touch himself. My own words were making me moist and needful, but I carried on.

"You plunge into me and it feels so deep this way, it's never felt this good before. You're so hard, your cock is aching for release but you want to enjoy every moment of it, so you hold back, hold back, hold back. But it's hard, so hard, because I'm coming again and you desperately want to come with me, but you want me to have every second, every ounce of pleasure, so you hold back, hold back. And then I'm coming hard, like you've never felt before, and it's so hot and wet and sweet—you spill into me, on and on and on."

And with those words, I grasped his cock, hard, and Sebastian came in my hand immediately. I stroked him a few more times, watching the creamy fluid spill onto his stomach, his chest muscles heaving with the effort of breathing, his eyes screwed shut.

I kissed him softly on the lips and lay back next to him, snuggling into his shoulder.

Eventually he opened his eyes and looked down at himself in amazement.

"Fuck, Caro!" he croaked. "How ... how..."

"So, you're the one who's speechless now?" I said, smugly.

I watched him for a while, as he tried to pull all his shattered pieces together. I reached over to my toiletry bag and grabbed a Kleenex to clean him up.

He watched me with vacant eyes as I stood up to throw the tissue away, then I sat back on the bed and smiled wickedly at him.

"Enjoy my bedtime story?"

"Fuck, yes! I still can't believe you did that to me, Caro," he said.

"Well, Sebastian, now you have something to think about when we're apart, or when you're doing a tour. Now you can imagine me talking to you."

"Are you fucking kidding me? With twenty other horny Marines sharing the same grot?" He groaned. "Oh, God! I won't be able to get rid of that image now."

I laughed, "That's kind of the point, Sebastian."

He shook his head, slowly.

"Fuck, Caro! You are so fucking amazing. Did I ever tell you that?"

"You may have mentioned it once or twice, but feel free to repeat yourself."

He still looked baffled: it was so cute.

I slapped his chest. "Come on, let's go shower. I'm hungry. For food."

I jumped off the bed and headed for the shower. I'd already shampooed and conditioned my hair, soaped myself clean and dried off with a towel, before the Marine managed to stagger into the bathroom.

I thought these guys were supposed to be in good shape?

Nicole would be so disappointed.

CHAPTER NINE

The shower revived Sebastian enough that I felt almost safe letting him take us on the bike.

"You okay?" I said. "You seem a little discombobulated."

"Fuck, yes, and I don't even know what that means," he said, nodding his head. "Fuck, Caro, I can't get over that. I mean, you barely touched me. It was just ... hot."

I smiled. "Ah, the power of words."

"There's going to be payback," he promised, with a devilish smile.

"Sebastian, if I wasn't so damn hungry, I'd be dragging you back to the bedroom now and tying you down until you made a dishonest woman of me."

He stared at me with admiration and not a little surprise.

"Jeez, you've gotten so ... bossy. I like it."

I laughed delightedly. "Oh, Sarge, I think you've been taking orders from the wrong people—but I'm going to help you with that."

"Can't wait," he said, shaking his head in disbelief.

Then he pulled me into a hug and buried his face in my neck, tickling my skin with his warm breath.

"I have missed you so much."

"I've missed you, too, *tesoro*."

We stood there quietly, his arms around me, each of us unwilling to break the spell.

Eventually, he rubbed my back and kissed my hair lightly. "Let's go eat."

Just three miles down the road was the pretty Marina di Cecina. Our friend at the beach shop had recommended that we eat at one of the restaurants on the waterfront. It probably belonged to an uncle or cousin, but it looked nice and had sensational views over the Mediterranean.

"What the hell is that?" said Sebastian, pointing at the menu. "*Cipolline agrodolci alla Cinque Terre*. Is that onions?"

"Yes, sweet and sour onions: it's a local delicacy. You want to try them?"

"Normally I'd say yes, but I'm really craving ... steak," he said, apologetically.

I rolled my eyes. "You're so American! You want fries with that?"

"Yeah, now you mention it. Anyway, I have to keep my strength up. This woman I've met is milking me dry. She can't keep her hands off me."

"What a slut."

He smirked at me. "Well, she hasn't been that slutty, but I'd really like to see her in slutty stockings and garter straps—no panties."

"Hmm, well I'm sure we can arrange it at some point, but I have to admit, Sebastian, I don't actually own anything like that."

He looked surprised. "Not at all? I thought all women..."

He stopped mid sentence, looking embarrassed, and wishing he could bite back the words.

"Maybe all your previous women, Sebastian," I replied, rather cuttingly, "but no, not me, I don't."

Wisely, he buried his eyes in the menu.

"Sebastian, apart from you, I last had a date nearly three years ago. And there's not a lot of need for slinky underwear on assignment to military bases—well, not for me, anyway. Maybe you know differently?" and I raised my eyebrows at him.

"Why don't you date, Caro?" he asked, looking up, his voice puzzled. "I mean, you're fucking gorgeous, anyone can see that, and you're clever and funny. Any man would have to be blind not to want you."

And I realized he meant it. Would I ever get used to hearing him say things like that to me? I hoped not.

"I've just ... not been that interested. No one's really caught my eye."

He shook his head in amazement.

"Oh, wait, Major Parsons asked me out: Mike. He was pretty cute," I said, casually glancing at Sebastian.

"That fucking bastard!" he snarled, sounding really angry.

"Sebastian, I said no. And actually, he was really sweet about it. He wasn't pushy or anything."

I was regretting making Sebastian jealous, but damn, it made me feel wanted. And I really wasn't used to that.

I decided to change the subject before his temper spoiled our meal.

"What were you thinking, that first day, when we saw each other at the press training? You looked really mad."

His gaze became distant, remembering the day, only one week ago.

"Just so fucking shocked. I saw the name 'Lee Venzi' on the training list. I recognized it because I'd read some of your articles..."

"Really?"

"Yeah, sure. I check out all the journos who go on these gigs. I want to know what kind of shit ... sorry, what kind of writing they do. I thought yours was good."

I shot him a look.

"No, really. I'm not just saying that. I kind of assumed you were ex-forces because of the way you understood the military. And we were all expecting you'd be a guy. Obviously somebody screwed up on the background checks. But as far as your online presence, you're definitely a man."

I smiled serenely at him. "That's the general idea. I've had quite a few assignments given to me because people assume I'm a man, jobs they wouldn't give to a woman."

Sebastian frowned at me. "Yeah, but there could be a good reason for it, too. I mean, some of the places you go are dangerous and..."

I caught his hand and placed my fingers over his lips.

"Shh, *tesoro*. They're a lot less dangerous than where you go, and we're not having this conversation."

He scowled and started to argue.

"No, I mean it. This is my work. Please drop it."

He didn't look happy about it, but he didn't argue further either, instead he gave me a look that said the discussion wasn't over, merely postponed.

"You were going to tell me what you thought when you first saw me," I reminded him.

"Shock. At first I thought you'd done it deliberately somehow. And then I saw the look on your face, like you didn't know what to say to me either, and I realized it was just as weird for you as it was for me."

"And then?"

"I just kept thinking how mad I was at you, blaming you for all the shit. I kept trying to hold on to all that anger, but you just looked so ... you looked just the same. And I kept thinking, maybe I got it wrong. And then I remembered that you hadn't come looking for me and ... it was so fucking confusing, Caro."

He stared out at the water washing over the beach.

"And then you tried to talk to me and I just freaked. I couldn't ... not in front of all those people, not with all the things I wanted to ... I found a bar and just started drinking ... getting up the courage to go see you. I really screwed that up, didn't I?"

"Completely," I said, nodding my head.

He looked apologetic and stared at his hands.

"It doesn't matter now, Sebastian," I said, quietly.

He shook off the memory, but I could tell it still bothered him.

"What did you think, when you saw me?" he said.

"You mean after the oh-my-God moment? I thought you looked bitter: your eyes looked so cold and hard. Gorgeous, of course, but you looked like you'd really changed. I was ... intimidated. And then Liz told me you'd got this reputation ... as something of a ladykiller..."

Sebastian scowled.

"Well, you did ask."

"Yeah, well ... what else did you think?"

"She said you were brilliant, too, if that makes you feel any better."

"Not much."

I sighed. "I just thought I'd try and talk to you by yourself, but you kept avoiding me. So, I assumed you didn't want anything to do with me. I was ... hurt, but I guess I accepted it. Can we talk about something else? This is making me feel blue."

"Sure, baby," he said, smiling softly. "How about we plan the rest of the trip?"

I smiled back. "Yes, please."

He reached over to his jacket, which was hanging from the back of his chair, and pulled out the map.

"Well, it's up to you, Caro. We could keep going down the coast road to Salerno, look up your dad's old village. Or take it slower, go see some of Tuscany. Siena is supposed to be amazing and there's this old hilltop town, Montepulciano that looks really cool. Or go right down to the bottom—check out Sicily."

"What do you want to do, Sebastian? I don't mind having another day on the beach if you want to do some more surfing—it's your vacation, too."

"Nah, that's okay—it's going to be flat tomorrow—I already checked."

I rolled my eyes. "Of course. Silly me."

"It's about 200 miles to your dad's village. We could be there this time tomorrow. If you want."

I thought about it for a moment. I was probably investing too much in what would inevitably be a big disappointment.

"No, let's take it easy. I'd like to see some more of Tuscany. I've heard of Montepulciano: they have good wine. And honey."

He smiled at me, amused. "How come you know all this food stuff?"

I stared back as if, for once, *he* was missing the blindingly obvious. "I'm Italian, Sebastian."

He laughed out loud, and swept my hand off the table to kiss my fingers.

The waiter arrived with our order, interrupting our moment, although he smiled apologetically.

The food, including Sebastian's enormous *Bistecca Alla Fiorentina* steak with fries, was good, and we were quiet for several minutes as we ate.

I toyed with my question for some time.

"What is it?" said Sebastian, at last, laying down his knife and fork.

"What do you mean?"

"You have that look on your face—like you want to ask me something. You can ask me anything, Caro."

I was amazed—people didn't usually read me that well. But then again, Sebastian knew me better than anyone. How strange.

"Well, there was something ... did you mean what you said about quitting the Marines?"

"Sure. I mean, I re-upped two years ago, so I'd have to do another two before I punch out..."

Disappointment flooded through me. *Two more years.*

"And Afghanistan soon."

He looked at me thoughtfully.

"They're short of interpreters, especially non-locals, and military intelligence..."

He stopped abruptly, realizing he'd said too much.

"Sebastian, whatever you tell me, that's between us. I would *never* use it in my work."

"I know that, baby, but there are some things I can't tell you ... and some things that it's better you don't know."

I wasn't happy that there were secrets between us, but I understood.

"They're not going to be pleased that you're dating a journalist."

He glanced away, briefly, then smiled at me. "Nope. Don't think so, although they couldn't stop me..."

"So ... I guess it would be better to keep this between us, just for now?"

He nodded, then leaned back in his chair.

"Would *you* give it up, Caro? Working in war zones, traveling all over the world?"

I'd been waiting for him to ask me that question, but I still didn't know how I was going to answer it. The truth was I didn't want to give it up. I'd worked hard to achieve the position I'd reached—and I enjoyed it. Yes, my work took me into dangerous areas, but it was rare that I was on the frontline, not like Sebastian. Oh, yes, my hypocrisy knew no bounds.

So, what was the compromise? He gave up everything and I gave up nothing? But if I did give up my work, how long would it be before I felt resentful and tied down. *And* he wanted us to have kids. Whatever he said about 'seeing what happened', I knew that was high on his list of priorities.

"I wouldn't want to give it up completely, Sebastian, that's the truth. But I could agree to a maximum amount of time I spent away in a year, maybe."

He nodded slowly and sighed. "Okay, I guess."

He stood up and stretched, gazing around the restaurant.

"Where are you going?"

"Restroom. I'm hoping they have machines that sell rubbers."

I smiled. "We still have one left."

"Yeah, but that's not nearly enough for what I have in mind ... unless you want to do what we talked about earlier?"

I could hear the hope in his voice, but I shook my head.

"That's another discussion for another time, Sebastian." He pouted, and I couldn't help smiling. "When you've finished this next tour, we'll talk about it then, I promise."

He returned a few minutes later, scowling.

"Fucking useless!" he fumed. "They didn't have any in the restrooms and I checked with the waiter—all the nearby supermarkets and pharmacies are closed on Sunday evenings."

"Oh, dear," I said, smiling. "Well, never mind. We'll just have to get creative."

"Yeah, okay," he said sulkily.

I raised my eyebrows at him. "I hope you're not getting bored with me already!"

He rolled his eyes. "You're like a freakin' drug to me, Caro. I can't get enough of you. And I really like wake-up sex."

I couldn't help laughing out loud. "We'll figure something out. Don't sweat it, Hunter."

Sebastian was still in a bad mood when we left the restaurant. Okay, it wasn't the ideal situation for two apparently sex-starved adults who were behaving like rampant teenagers, but I thought we'd already proved that we could be creative—and I had one or two things in mind. Besides, I'd brought the rest of the bottle of wine from the restaurant, so we could always have a quiet evening with a glass of vino and watch the stars appear.

Sebastian, however, was a lot less relaxed, accelerating hard out of the parking lot in a shower of gravel, tires squealing.

I gripped him tightly around his waist, hoping that he'd slow down, but instead he went faster, taking the turns on the coast road at such a speed that our knees were ridiculously close to the ground. I closed my eyes and hung on, until he slowed abruptly. I soon saw the reason. Two Italian police officers were waving their table tennis-shaped batons at us.

Crap.

We'd been caught speeding.

Sebastian pulled over to the side of the road and swung one, long leg over as he climbed off. Watching as he removed his helmet, I decided to follow him. He was so hotheaded, I could imagine him mouthing off at them and spending a night in a cozy, Italian jail.

"French?" asked the first policeman, looking at the license plates on Sebastian's motorcycle.

The officer looked like Groucho Marx, which was rather distracting. The second one was younger and stared at us through his Aviator shades, even though it was dusk.

"No, American," replied Sebastian.

The policemen looked surprised.

"Is this motorcycle yours, *signor*?"

"Yes."

"You have papers for it?"

"Yes, in my wallet."

Sebastian started to reach into his jacket, and the younger officer immediately went for his gun.

I gasped and Sebastian swore. The next second, they were forcing him to kneel on the ground and put his hands behind his head. I could see the older man reaching for handcuffs.

"No, please!" I called out. "He was just trying to show you his papers."

"*Signora*, he was driving at 120km an hour, the speed limit here is 90km an hour."

"Please, let him show you. I'll get his wallet!"

I moved slowly so they could see exactly what I was doing. I reached into Sebastian's inside jacket pocket and carefully lifted out his wallet.

"What am I looking for?" I whispered, urgently.

"The *Certificat d'immatriculation*—the papers in gray. Caro, I..."

"Just don't speak, Sebastian," I hissed at him. "Let me handle this."

Silently, I handed over the document, although it was clear neither of the officers could read French.

"Are you authorized to ride this motorcycle, *signora*?" said the older, gentler officer.

"No, but..."

"Then we'll arrange to have it removed," he said, kindly.

"Please don't arrest him!" I begged. "He's only on leave for two more weeks, then he's going back to Afghanistan."

The two men looked at each other. I was hoping that the military/police solidarity that existed back home also held true in Europe. I pulled Sebastian's ID card out of his wallet, the one that identified him as a US Marine, and showed it to them.

"We only have two weeks," I repeated, not needing to fake my desperation.

"My son-in-law is serving out there," said the older officer, shaking his head. "Very well, we will let you go, but this one time only. Obey the speed limits."

They let Sebastian stand, and handed back his papers.

"Thank you so much," I said, feeling slightly tearful at our reprieve.

"Make him obey the speed limits, *signora*," said the older officer, wagging his finger at me.

"I will. Thank you!"

"I will pray for you both," he said, simply.

We watched as they wandered back to their car, chatting amiably to each other.

"You were great, Caro," said Sebastian, grinning.

I slapped him hard on the arm. "No more speeding!"

"I don't know ... I have my own Caro-shaped 'get out of jail free' card."

"Yes, well, do that again, and you might be finding out what Italian jails are like."

"You wouldn't let that happen to me, baby."

"Don't bet on it, Sarge! I have enough gray hairs without you giving me anymore."

He pulled me in for a hug.

"Nope, can't see any," he said, kissing my hair.

I pushed him away, crossly.

"Another two weeks with you and I'll have to color my grays," I said, grumpily.

He laughed.

"It's not funny!"

"God, you're beautiful, Caro!"

I climbed back on the bike, irritated to see that Sebastian was still grinning, but at least he drove to the campsite at a more moderate pace.

When we arrived back, Sebastian parked the bike while I stomped off to our room, feeling very irritated with him. If he was this reckless in Italy ... no, I really didn't need to start thinking like that.

I hunted around for a corkscrew to dig out the damn cork that the waiter had managed to ram back in. I was just contemplating smashing off the neck and sieving the wine through a clean sock to remove any broken glass, believing that desperate times called for desperate measures, when Sebastian sauntered into the room.

"I can't open the fucking wine!" I snarled at him.

He looked taken aback.

Yeah, well, he wasn't the only one who knew how to swear.

"What's the matter, Caro?"

"I just told you!" I yelled, "I can't open the wine!"

Quietly, he took the bottle from my hand, produced a Swiss Army knife from his pants pocket, and proceeded to dig the cork out using a small blade.

"I think some of the cork fell in," he said, placing the bottle on the table.

"Thank you," I muttered, rather sullenly.

"Caro..."

"What, Sebastian? You could have been arrested back there? That was so stupid and reckless!"

He stared at me in amazement. "Nothing happened..."

"It could have!" I shouted at him. "And if you take chances like that out in..."

But I couldn't finish the sentence. Angry and frustrated, I was furious when I felt tears spring to my eyes. I scrubbed them away with my fists, while Sebastian watched me in silence.

"Hey, come here," he said, softly. "It's okay."

He pulled my stiff body into an embrace, but I stood rigidly, fighting back tears, willing anger not fear to win out.

"Caro, tonight was just dumb, I admit that, okay. I'm just enjoying being ... free, here and now, with you. Don't cry."

"I'm not crying!" I yelled. "I'm mad at you!"

"Yeah, got the message, baby."

Eventually, I pushed him away, grabbing the wine bottle as I walked past the table, and took a good slug. Then I threw myself on the bed, piled the pillows behind me and tipped another large quantity of wine into my mouth, rubbing the back of my hand across my face to catch the drips.

"Are you going to share that?" he asked, at last.

"No. You drink too much."

"You're just going to sit there and finish the whole bottle by yourself?"

"Yes."

"You don't like drinking."

"I do tonight."

"It'll make you sick."

"I'm being reckless. You do it all the time."

"Caro," he said tiredly, rubbing his forehead, "come on, that's enough."

He pulled the bottle out of my hands and put it on his side of the bed.

"Give me my goddamn wine, Sebastian."

"No," he said, evenly, sitting next to me.

I tried to reach over him to get it, but he blocked me.

I wanted to scream with frustration, even though I knew I was behaving childishly.

"Fine."

I slammed out of the room and walked down to the beach without a coat. It was cooler now that it was night. Oh well, I'd wanted to see the stars.

I sat down on the sand and moodily wrapped my arms around my knees. A light breeze was blowing off the sea, and moonlight glimmered on the water. The surf had almost completely dropped away. Sebastian was right:,it would be as flat as glass tomorrow.

I buried my boots into the still-warm sand and listened to the tide lapping against the shoreline, as regular as breathing.

I was irritated with myself for my tantrum, but I was more than annoyed with Sebastian for nearly getting himself arrested—and for not appearing to think anything of it. But at the heart of it was my fear that his recklessness would lead him to doing something really stupid when he was *out there*. I didn't even want to think about where he was going—where we were going.

It wasn't long before I heard his quiet footsteps in the sand. I pulled my arms around my knees more tightly as Sebastian sat down next to me, gently placing his old, leather jacket around my shoulders.

"Want some wine?" he asked. "It tastes great straight from the bottle."

I leaned against his shoulder, and he wrapped his arm around me.

"Sebastian, promise me you won't be reckless. I couldn't stand it if anything happened to you now."

"Caro, I'm never reckless when I'm working. Well, maybe some of the off-duty stuff, but not when I'm working, I promise. I'd never have gotten promoted if I was a complete fuck-up. Don't worry about me. Besides, I have a reason to come home now, okay?"

"I will worry."

"And I'll worry about you, too. You still have a chance to go home where I know you'll be safe, Caro. Please?"

I sat up stiffly.

"Don't even think about screwing up my papers again, Hunter!"

"Whoa! Slow down!"

He held out his hands defensively.

"I promised I wouldn't, Caro, even though I really fucking want to." He paused. "So, have you finished stomping all over me with your boots?"

I sighed. "For now, unless you ask me to, nicely."

He laughed gently. "I'll bear that in mind. Can I kiss you, or am I risking serious injury?"

I pushed him back onto the sand and made myself comfortable lying across his chest.

Under the moonlight his skin was pale and silvery, every hint of tan bleached away. I traced his profile with my finger, and then tilted his face toward me, kissing him lightly on the lips.

"This brings back memories," I said, feeling soothed.

He smiled up at me. "Yeah! Sex on the beach was one of those things that everyone at school used to brag about, and then I got to do it with you. That first time, that was one of the best nights of my life."

"The first time we ever spent a whole night together."

"You want to relive good times, Caro?"

"Can't."

"Why not?"

"I left our one and only condom in the room."

He sighed and closed his eyes.

"Besides," I continued, "I kind of have a thing for beds these days. Call me old-fashioned."

"Yeah, I guess," he said, wistfully. "I really liked having sex in your car though. That was hot."

"Oh my God, yes! Although I'd have to say that sex in that closet at the country club was pretty amazing, too. No, wait, the hotel in Little Italy. That room looked like a wild animal had rampaged through it by the time you'd finished!"

"Wild animal, huh?" he said, looking pleased with himself. "Yeah, well, I think I can improve on that now, baby."

"Oh, you do, do you? Because I have to tell you, Sebastian, you never ran out of condoms when you were 17."

"Ouch! Low blow, Ms. Venzi."

I laughed. "True, though."

"Yeah, well, I'll fix that tomorrow and then you won't be having *any* sleep, woman."

"Heard it all before, Sergeant, but it ain't happened yet."

I lay back down on his chest, and drew pictures on his t-shirt with my finger.

"So, who was your first woman, after me, I mean?"

I felt his arms tense.

"Why do you want to know that?"

"Just curious."

He sighed. "I don't really want to go there, Caro. It was ... a bad time for me."

"Okay, I'm sorry. You don't have to answer."

We lay there in silence for some minutes.

"Will you tell Ches that we're ... back together?"

"Of course I will, Caro. Ches is my brother," he said simply.

"He'll be surprised."

"Fuck, yes!"

"Do you think he'll be okay about it? I mean, I'm sure my name would have been dirt with him."

"Ches isn't like that. He was pretty shocked by everything that went down that day at your place, but he knew that what we had was real. He'll be pleased."

"When are you going to tell him?"

"I hadn't really thought about it. When are you going to tell your friends about me?"

"Are you kidding?" I laughed. "After your little stunt with Nicole it'll be hot news in NYC by now. Your photograph will be on screensavers everywhere."

"Yeah?"

"Oh, don't be all coy with me, Hunter. You know you're cute."

He grinned up at me. "Just as long as you think so."

"I think you're devilishly handsome, with the emphasis on 'devil'."

"Yeah, well as it happens, Ms. Venzi, I think you've got some devil inside you, too."

"Oh, I'd really like to have some devil inside me right now, Sebastian."

He sat up, pulling me with him.

"Let's go," he said.

It wasn't a request.

I stood up and brushed some of the sand from my pants, while Sebastian retrieved the bottle of wine that he'd stashed in the dunes.

We strolled back to our room, and every now and then, Sebastian would pull my hand to his lips and kiss my fingers gently.

But once we were in the room it was a different story. It was as if someone had flicked a switch in his body: gone was sweet, gentle Sebastian, in his place was a man on a mission who knew what he wanted, and he wanted it now.

No sooner had we closed the door than he pushed me up against it and started kissing me hard, one hand molding my breasts, the other pushing down inside my jeans.

"Where's that fucking condom?" he muttered.

"Bedside table," I gasped.

He strode over and snatched up the condom, and had already ripped the foil off before I'd taken three steps.

"Sebastian, the bed?"

"No, here."

He unzipped his pants and expertly rolled the condom over his erection with one hand. Then he yanked down my zipper and lifted me up by my hips.

"Wrap your legs around me," he said, the tension evident in his voice.

"How?" I gasped, pointing at my jeans, still trapped around my knees.

He swore and yanked them further down, but found they were caught by my boots. Instead of waiting the 30 seconds it would take for me to kick them off, he stepped over the denim and ignored the trailing material.

He rammed into me and I cried out. His face was buried in my neck, his breath coming in loud gasps as his body worked faster and faster. I held onto his shoulders while he pounded me into the door. It was so raw and urgent, so completely unexpected, I thought I could see stars.

And then his phone rang.

"Oh, fuck!"

"What? Don't stop, Sebastian!"

He carried me over to the bed, still joined together, and pulled his phone out of his jacket pocket.

"Sebastian," I whimpered.

"Just a minute, baby, I have to take this call. It's my CO's ringtone."

What?!

"Hunter, sir."

Then there was a long pause and I shifted uncomfortably, still clinging on, and Sebastian frowned at me.

Fuck you, Hunter! You're answering the phone during rampant sex, and you're frowning at me?

He raised one eyebrow, smirked, then started moving again in a way that should not be permitted while carrying on a phone conversation.

Thrust.

"Yes, sir."

Thrust.

"No, Italy, sir."

Thrust, thrust, thrust.

I gasped and bit back a moan.

Thrust, thrust, hip roll, thrust.

"Um ... I've just been out for a run."

Thrust, thrust.

"Yes, sir."

Hip roll, thrust, thrust.

"Yes, sir."

Pound, pound, pound, thrust, thrust, thrust.

"I'll be there."

Then he threw the phone in the corner, dropped me onto the bed, angling his hips in a way that made me gasp, and I threw my head back. He fastened his mouth over my nipple so I could feel his teeth through my bra and t-shirt.

I came loudly and he followed with two quick moves.

"Sebastian?" I gasped, astonished by what he'd just done.

He pulled out and looked down at me, grinning wickedly. "Did you get what you wanted, baby?"

"Excuse me?"

"You said you wanted some devil inside you. I aim to please."

I slapped his arm and tried to wriggle away from him, but his body was still pinning me down.

"Sebastian, you just fucked me while you were talking to your CO!"

"What, you think men can't multitask?"

I stared up at him in astonishment.

"I can't believe you did that!"

He laughed. "Felt good! Don't tell me you didn't enjoy that because either it was you moaning, baby, or my CO had a stomachache."

"I ... you ... that ... unbelievable!"

He lay down next to me, pulling me onto his chest.

"I haven't even taken my boots off," I muttered, to no one in particular.

"Me either," he said, with a grin.

He sat up and peeled off the condom, tossing it in the garbage can. Then I heard the sound of him zipping up his pants.

I was still trying to decide whether I was mad at him, or too well fucked to care that he'd taken a phone call during sex with me.

He wandered off into the bathroom, and I heard the shower running while I was still prone on the bed.

He strolled back in, looking completely relaxed and at ease. I felt him pick up my left foot and he started to undo the laces. He tossed the boot over his shoulder where it landed with a thump, then peeled off my sock, and sucked my toes one by one.

"Sebastian," I whimpered, "you're supposed to do foreplay *before* sex."

He grinned but didn't reply, simply copying his movements with my right foot. Then he reached up to tug off my jeans and panties. It didn't take much effort as they were already hanging off me. I was now naked from the waist down.

"Very nice," he said, planting a soft kiss on my belly button.

He pulled me up and hauled my t-shirt over my head, then reached around to unhook my bra.

"Mmm," he said, tasting both my nipples, his eyes glinting with mischief.

I slapped him away.

"Don't start what you can't finish, Sebastian."

"Who says I can't finish? You were the one who said we should be creative. I'm just following orders, ma'am."

He unbuckled his heavy biker boots and kicked them into the corner, tugged off his socks and dropped his jeans and briefs to the floor in one quick movement.

Then he tugged his t-shirt from the back of his neck and pulled it over his head, scooped me up and carried me into the bathroom with military efficiency.

The shower was deliciously hot: so was Sebastian.

He lathered up the soap, and carefully washed every inch of my skin, stopping only to kiss me softly.

"You want some more, Caro," he asked, smiling down at me, and suggestively massaging between my thighs.

"I'd love to say yes, but really I just want to go and sleep. Rough sex during phone calls always does that to me."

"Always?"

"Always."

"Hmm," he said, frowning.

"By the way, why was your CO calling? What did he want at this time of night?"

Sebastian sighed and looked away.

"He wanted to know where I was."

"I gathered that. Because?"

"I'm sorry, Caro, I'm going to have to be back in Geneva in four days. And then back to Afghanistan."

"Four days?"

Oh no.

"I'm so sorry, baby."

"Well, we'll just have to make the most of the four days then."

"I'll make it up to you, I promise, Caro."

"Sebastian, don't worry. Every day with you is a bonus. And we've got the rest of our lives to see Italy."

"Promise?"

"I promise."

I pulled him into my arms and we stood together in the tiny shower, letting the hot water flow over us, trying to reassure each other that it would be okay.

Eventually the water began to cool and I turned off the faucet.

"Come here, let me dry you, *tesoro*."

Sebastian stood with his arms outstretched, as if waiting for an embrace that didn't come. Instead, I used the large, fluffy towel to dry his back and shoulders, chest, stomach, arms and legs, slowly, carefully, methodically, soaking up each droplet of moisture.

"There you are—all done."

He handed me a fresh towel to wrap around myself, then carefully rubbed my hair with a small hand towel.

"You shouldn't sleep with damp hair," he scolded me.

His words made me smile.

"Sebastian, I've done a lot of foolish things—reckless, you might say—since I met you: sleeping with damp hair doesn't figure particularly high on that list."

He scowled.

He looked so cute when he did that.

I kissed him on the tip of his nose.

"Race you to the bedroom!"

I ran from the bathroom before he could move a muscle, and launched myself onto the bed.

"You're so slow, Hunter," I laughed at him. "You're really out of shape. Maybe you should go for a run, like you told your CO."

"Tomorrow, Caro, I'm getting a fucking sack-load of condoms, and I'm going to make you regret every word you've just said."

I smirked at him. "Like I said, Sebastian, promises, promises. I keep hearing about these fuckathons, but nothing ever happens."

His eyes flared with the challenge, and I knew for sure that I'd live to regret my taunts. I was looking forward to it.

I yawned loudly, and he looked amused.

He lay down beside me, his body warm and still slightly damp from the shower, pulling the sheets over us. I snuggled into him, and he wrapped his arms around me so I was curled up on his chest, our legs entwined.

"God, Caro. You make it all worthwhile," he said, kissing my hair. "Thank God for you."

"I love you, *tesoro*," I whispered.

CHAPTER TEN

Waking up in the morning, the first thing I saw was Sebastian's beautiful blue-green eyes gazing down at me.

"Hey," he said, smiling.

"*Ciao, bello!* How long have you been awake?"

"Not long. Just enough time to remind me that I'm a lucky bastard."

I smiled and stretched, feeling his warm body against mine.

"I could get used to this, Sebastian, waking up next to you."

As soon as I said the words, I felt a breath of sadness. Our time was limited.

I forced a smile, certain that the last thing Sebastian needed to see before he shipped out was a miserable, moping face.

"So, what's the new plan, Sarge? Do you want to see some more of Tuscany, or should we go further north?"

He looked bemused. "What about Salerno?"

"It's too much driving, Sebastian. We don't have a lot of time and you..."

"Hell, no! I want to see where your dad came from as much as you do. Fuck the driving, Caro! We're going to Salerno. If you get your beautiful ass out of bed, we can be there in maybe five hours."

I felt the pull of Salerno and the warm south. I'd tried to be selfless but Sebastian had once again weakened my resolve, as in so many things.

"Anyway," he continued, "we're out of condoms, and much as I'm enjoying being creative, I really just want to fuck you into next week."

"Such sweet words, Sebastian. How did you get to be such a smooth talker?"

He grinned at me. "I don't know, baby, but it works every time."

"Every time, huh? But you know, I have to say, last night wasn't particularly creative—we weren't even naked."

He laughed happily.

"Not creative? Hell, Caro, I managed to keep a conversation going with Cardozo, I thought that was pretty fucking creative."

"Is that the name of your CO?"

"Yeah, he's an okay guy."

"He must have his hands full dealing with you." I paused. "What's his wife like?"

Sebastian grinned wickedly. "Blonde, attractive ... about forty. Why, are you jealous?"

"Of course," I said, evenly.

He kissed me softly on my lips, his eyes gentle with love. "You've got nothing to worry about, baby."

Love, lust, passion—all swirled through me, his touch blinding me with desire. I kissed him back, pushing my tongue between his parted lips as our bodies began to move together. At my hip, I felt his cock twitch. I wanted him badly. It was, as he'd said: total addiction.

"Caro," he groaned, quietly, as I ran my hands over his thighs.

"Shh, *tesoro*."

Ten minutes later, we were both lying on our backs, panting. There was a lot to be said for a quick burst of hand-to-mouth creativity before breakfast.

I was filled with a warm, satisfied glow, as Sebastian lazily stroked my thigh.

"You ready to get up, baby?"

I sighed, happily. "Mmm, if I have to. But to tell you the truth, I'd be quite happy staying here all day, if someone brought us food. And condoms."

Sebastian kissed me quickly on my chest, then kicked the sheets back, the cooler air making me flinch.

"Hey!" I complained.

"Up," he said, as he stood over me.

Then he leaned down and fastened his teeth over my nipple, tugging gently.

"You cheat," I grumbled, staggering the short distance from the bed to the shower.

He swatted my ass, which I felt was unnecessary: he'd already made his point.

The water wasn't hot, which didn't encourage us to linger, and I stood in the bedroom, shivering slightly as I dressed.

"It doesn't take you long to get ready, does it, Caro. You never even bother to put on makeup."

Sebastian was sitting on the bed, smiling at me as he buckled up his boots.

I was slightly taken aback by his remark. Did that mean that he wanted me to wear makeup—that he thought I should?

"I do sometimes," I replied, trying not to sound defensive, "if I'm going out somewhere dressy. But not usually, no. Why?"

He shrugged. "Nothing. Just saying. It drives me crazy when women spend hours getting ready to go out."

I felt relieved—and annoyed at myself for feeling relieved. I was a modern woman who didn't need a man's approval on how I dressed. Except, maybe ... yes, damn it! I wanted Sebastian's approval on how I dressed. I craved the way he looked at me, like he'd never seen anything so precious. Maybe I ought to make a little more effort. Just for the next few days: give him the best memories I could, before we were parted.

I vowed to buy some lipstick and mascara in the next pharmacy or supermarket we found.

"You remember that time we went clothes shopping in San Diego?" he asked, pulling me out of my self-flagellating thoughts. "You had to buy a new dress?"

"Oh, sure, I remember that! The sales assistant was flirting with you?"

He looked surprised. "She was?"

I rolled my eyes. "Don't you remember, she was asking you if you were a pilot from Miramar?"

Sebastian shook his head, amused and puzzled at the same time.

"Well, I'm not surprised," I said, smiling to myself, "in those days you never used to notice other women flirting with you: you were such an innocent. Not like now."

"Hell, you shouldn't complain, Caro! You were the one I lost my innocence to —a hot, older woman."

I slapped his arm. "You know what I mean."

His look of amusement faded and he caught my hand, pulling me down, until I was sitting across his knee.

"Caro, you're all I want. You don't have to worry about other women. Yeah, so I fucked around a lot, but you know what? It was just a game—I was using them, they were using me. It gets pretty old after a while." He paused to tuck my hair behind my ear and kiss my throat. "But I might have to hunt down those old boyfriends of yours and beat them to a pulp."

I laughed. "Double standards, Sebastian?"

"Nope, just two sets of rules ... but I was thinking about the cute, black dress you bought. You looked so fucking hot in that."

"I've still got it somewhere, although I haven't worn it in years."

"We should do that, Caro, go out somewhere upscale."

I sighed. "I used to fantasize about seeing you in a tux."

"Really?"

"Sebastian, I spent far too many hours fantasizing about you in a variety of, um, situations. And just recently, it's become my new hobby."

He laughed, delightedly. "I've never worn a tux."

"Never? Not even at your high school prom?"

"I didn't go. I hadn't met you again, and I'd split up with Brenda. Ches didn't have a date either—he swiped some of Mitch's beer, I scored some weed—and we got trashed on the beach instead. It was a pretty good night—I think. I don't remember that much about it. We didn't need any women," he said, looking at me with a sly expression. "But that was before I met you again."

"Hmm, very virtuous of you. But didn't you wear a tux for Ches and Amy's wedding?"

"Nah, Amy kind of got off on the whole military thing, even though she didn't want Ches enlisting, so she asked me and Mitch to come in our Dress Blues. I don't know, I think she thought it would look cool in the wedding pictures."

He rolled his eyes.

"She turned into a complete nightmare-bitch-from-hell over the whole wedding thing. Ches was freaking out, thinking he was about to marry some crazy person. She even tried to ban him from having a bachelor party," he said, indignantly.

"Gee, I wonder why ... maybe she didn't trust *you*," I said, sarcasm dripping from my voice.

He grinned at me, wickedly.

"Yeah, well, she was probably right about that..."

"I don't want to know, Sebastian!"

He kissed me again. "So what do you think?"

"About what?"

"Going somewhere upscale? I'd love to see you like that again."

"Well, okay. Let's do that when you get back from this tour. Then we can really celebrate."

"Let's do it *now*," he said, decisively. "There must be some place in Salerno you can get women's stuff."

"Stuff?!"

"Yeah, silky dress, stockings, high heels ... stuff. And then I could undress you—slowly."

His eyes heated at the thought, and my heart skipped a beat.

"Okay, I'll do it if you do."

He laughed. "Sure, if I can find somewhere that will rent me a tux, why not? It'll make a change from being in uniform."

Then he kissed me quickly, scooped me off his lap and set me back on the floor.

"We'd better get going. Got me a date planned with a really hot woman."

Instead of traveling along the pretty coast road, Sebastian headed inland for the Autostrada del Sole, the highway that ran from Milan to Naples. It was terrifyingly busy, with huge trucks roaring too close to us, but the route was designed to get us to Salerno in the least amount of time. I clung on and gritted my teeth.

We stopped briefly just outside of Rome, at a café on the highway where they produced fresh pasta to restaurant standards, then carried on south, past Naples and on to our final destination.

Sebastian finally pulled up at the curb when we ran out of road. Behind us, the small town of Salerno clung to the cliffs, the buildings square and white with terracotta roofs, and glistening below them, the Mediterranean was azure in the afternoon sunshine.

He pulled off his helmet and stretched out his back before climbing off. I felt as if the bike was still in motion and my ass had been molded into the shape of the saddle.

Sebastian grinned at me, then helped me take off my helmet. It was as if I'd been underwater and I could finally hear properly again.

"You all right, baby?"

"I'm fine," I lied. "How are you?"

"Yeah, good. Look, I think it might be easier to find a *pensione* or hotel in Salerno than in your dad's village. We're only a couple of miles away so we could easily shoot on over there in the morning. What do you think?"

"Anything that doesn't involve getting back on your bike sounds good, Sebastian," I grimaced. "My ass is numb already."

He pulled me into a hug, and rubbed his hands over the portion in question.

"Better, baby?"

"Mmm, much."

He kissed me lightly. "Come on then, let's walk for a while. We'll find a room —and a pharmacy."

"Good to see you've got your priorities in order, Sebastian."

"Trained by the Marines, baby, what can I say?"

We strolled through the sunlit streets, listening to the rumble of local traffic, which seemed to consist of crazy drivers in beaten up cars, and teenagers on scooters buzzing around. Everywhere, people chatted, gossiped, talked, yelled and waved their hands in the air, animated conversations surrounding us. It reminded me of Papa when he got excited, and I could imagine him as a child running down the hill from the village, and climbing back in the evening, dusty, tired and happy.

Sebastian slung his arm around my shoulders with casual possession, and I let my fingers creep around his waist.

It was too warm to wear the leather biker jackets for long, so we found a small pavement café and gratefully sat, relaxing in the sun.

"I could really use a beer," said Sebastian.

I wasn't sure if he was just commenting or asking my permission. Either way, I had something else in mind.

"This is the home of *limoncello*, Sebastian, the real thing—made with Sorrento lemons. I think we should try some."

"Yeah!" he said, enthusiastically. "You used to make those amazing ones when I was a kid." He frowned, and I knew what he was thinking—he didn't like to be reminded of our age difference either.

I shrugged. "Sure, but these are alcoholic." I glanced at him sideways and smiled. "We could order them with a pitcher of water, too."

"Sounds good," he said, raising an eyebrow.

The young waiter slouched over, seemingly unconcerned as to whether or not he would serve us. But when I spoke to him in Italian, he seemed to cheer up slightly, his demeanor a fraction less surly.

"And would you know of anywhere we could rent a room for a couple of nights—nothing too expensive?" I asked, with a smile.

"My uncle might," he acknowledged, surprising me with a friendly grin. "I'll go and ask him."

When I glanced over at Sebastian, he was scowling at me.

"You didn't have to flirt with him, Caro," he spat out.

I stared at him, utterly astonished.

"Excuse me? Flirt with him? I was being friendly, that's all."

"Well, it didn't look like that from here," he said, obviously angry.

I shook my head in amazement. "Rule number three, Sebastian, of my conditions for coming on this road trip with you: no displays of adolescent jealousy. Remember?"

He leaned back in his chair and folded his arms.

Oh, great—sulky Sebastian. I should have added that to my list.

Our waiter returned with the *limoncellos*, water, and an older man with jet black hair and dark olive skin.

"My nephew tells me you're looking for a room. For how long?"

"Just a couple of nights. Somewhere in town—nothing too upscale—although somewhere with a bath would be great. We've been on our motorcycle all day."

"I have just the thing," he said, happily. "My mother-in-law's sister's neighbor rents rooms. Her villa overlooks the sea—very pretty rooms. Only €50 a night. I could call her for you, if you like?"

"Thanks," said Sebastian, deciding to take charge. "We'll take a look."

The waiter's uncle—Aberto—soon returned, smiling.

"You're in luck, *signore e signora*. She has a room available. I've written the address down for you."

"Thank you," I said, "that's very kind of you."

He nodded and turned to leave.

"Aberto, can I ask you something else? My father was from Capezzano Inferiore. He left many years ago, but I was wondering, do you know anyone with the surname of 'Venzi'?"

I held my breath as he scratched his head.

"No, I'm sorry, *signora*, I don't know that name. I could look in the phone book for you?"

"Thank you. That would be so helpful."

Sebastian held my hand while we waited for Aberto to return.

"Ah, I'm sorry, *signora*," he said, "there's no one with that surname in the town —some in the province, but none within 70km."

I breathed out slowly, feeling everything deflate inside me. How ridiculous. I'd allowed my hopes to get blown out of proportion.

"Thank you for looking, Aberto."

He nodded, and walked away.

"Sorry, baby," murmured Sebastian. "I know you had gotten your hopes up."

"I was just being stupid. I just wanted ... I just hoped I'd find some family."

He kissed my hand gently.

"Hey, I get that. I know what it's like."

"I never even asked you, Sebastian, but do you have grandparents? You never mentioned any."

He shrugged. "No, not really. Mom's parents died when I was a kid, Dad never spoke to his. Big surprise. I don't even know where they live."

"And you've never wanted to find out?"

"I thought about it once. Anyway, I'm not sure I'd want to find anyone who was related to that bastard. Besides, they never showed any interest in me ... it made me wonder if the bastard was really my dad. I dunno..." he shrugged. "Ches and his kids, Mitch and Shirley—they're my family."

"And Amy," I said, teasing him gently.

He groaned. "Yeah, and she's thrilled about that."

"Well, she'll be much happier when we show her the new, improved Sebastian Hunter. I could tell her that I've tamed you."

He gave me a knowing look. "You're treading on dangerous ground there, Venzi."

I sat back and smiled at him. "You're so masterful when you talk like that, Sebastian."

He leaned forward and stared at me. "Yeah, well, if we can find a fucking pharmacy, you'll find out just how 'masterful' I can be."

"Looking forward to it."

We sipped our *limoncellos* as we watched the world go by: yachts and fishing boats in the harbor, scooters, bikes and cars, people of all ages, strolling, chatting, enjoying the afternoon sunshine.

"You know what we should do, Caro?" said Sebastian, stretching his arms above his head. "We should drive up to Amalfi. The coast road has some gnarly mean bends—see what the bike can really do. There should be some great views, too."

I swallowed hastily. I could just imagine Sebastian tearing up the mountainside and carving his way around another terrifying set of hairpin turns.

"That sounds fun," I said, trying to restrain the quaver in my voice.

I didn't fool him at all, and Sebastian laughed out loud. "That's my girl!"

After we'd paid Aberto, we wandered through the town, on the lookout for Via Roma, which turned out to be a wide avenue running alongside the harbor.

To Sebastian's delight, we also found a pharmacy, where he purchased two boxes of 12 condoms, much to my embarrassment and the amusement of the elderly woman serving him. I think she may have given me a sympathetic glance, too.

I felt a little lightheaded when I did the math: 24 condoms, three nights.

But I also found cheap mascara and a dark cherry lipstick.

"Looking forward to tasting that lipstick on you later," whispered Sebastian.

"Looking forward to tasting you later," I whispered back, which earned me a very hot look.

Signora Carello's villa was a small but pretty, whitewashed building overlooking the sea, as promised.

I'd expected another well-built motherly type, but the Signora was a bone-thin racehorse of a woman, perhaps 70 years of age, with swept-up black hair and immaculate taste in clothes.

"Ah, the young travelers Aberto mentioned. Welcome to my home. Please, come in. Let me show you the room."

She led us up a flight of shallow steps that looked like they could have been carved out of marble, or some other polished, creamy stone—and opened the door into a beautiful, dreamlike room.

A large, white bed dominated, with fronds of net curtains hanging down, and a wardrobe that was Oriental style, made from a wicker material. The balcony doors were open, and the curtains drifted on the breeze, brushing across a small mosaic table with two matching chairs.

"Oh, this is just lovely!"

"Thank you, *signora*," she said, obviously pleased by my reaction.

"Actually, it's *signorina*," I said, not wishing to mislead this charming woman.

"I'm working on that," said Sebastian, challengingly, and I saw Signora Carello try to hide a smile.

"The *bagno* is on the right," she said, gesturing elegantly toward a white door.

The bathroom was plain and white, but, joy of joys, it had a gigantic enamel tub in the center of the room, as well as a small shower in the corner.

I clapped my hands together and grinned at Sebastian.

"We have a motorcycle," he said, smiling at my obvious happiness. "Do you have somewhere I could park it overnight?"

"Oh, I used to enjoy riding on a motorcycle in my day!" she said. "Oh, yes, young man ... I was quite fast in my youth."

And Sebastian blushed. He actually blushed. I hadn't seen him do that in ten years. I was almost jealous of Signora Carello.

She smiled pleasantly at him and when she looked at me, she winked. I grinned back. Oh, I liked this woman.

"I'll go and get the bike," he muttered.

"Sebastian, would you mind if I stay here and take a bath?"

"No, that's fine, Caro," he said, suddenly brightening up. "I'll see you later."

Hmm, what was on that tricky Hunter mind now?

I shrugged and left him to walk back down the stairs, chatting animatedly to the *signora*.

I was delighted to see that two enormous, fluffy, white towels had been laid out for our use. I started running the water immediately and peeled off my sticky clothes, enjoying the cool stone of the bathroom floor beneath my bare feet.

I ran the water as hot as I could stand it, then climbed in, luxuriating in the sensation. I wished Sebastian was there to share the moment—and to scrub my back—but it was rather wonderful to stretch out, too.

I lathered my hair, using shampoo that smelled like lemons, from the small pot that the *signora* left out for us, and then wallowed for a good half an hour. By which time, the water had cooled, but Sebastian still hadn't returned. I let the water drain away and wrapped myself in the huge towel and boldly sat out on the balcony, enjoying the late afternoon sun.

I heard the mean machine before I saw it. I watched Sebastian drive along the street and stop at the villa's entrance, before cutting the engine and pushing it around to the yard at the back. I wondered what on earth he'd been doing, he'd been gone ages.

I heard him running up the stairs and I called out to him.

"You missed a great bath. I've been sitting here enjoying the view—naked, except for a towel."

He walked up behind me and kissed my damp hair.

"I was beginning to think you'd gotten lost."

"Had some business to take care of, baby."

I twisted around to look at him. He was grinning like a Cheshire cat.

"Come on, Hunter, spill. What business?"

Sebastian grinned and bit his lip, but I knew he was dying to tell me. It took about three seconds before he caved.

"Signora Carello told me somewhere I can rent a tux, so it's game on for tomorrow night. We're going upscale, baby."

"Really?" I said, excitedly. "Where?"

He grinned down at me. "Can't tell you. Not even if you torture me."

"Are you sure about that? Because I think it can be arranged, Sebastian."

"I was hoping you'd say that."

He picked me up out of the chair and carried me into the bedroom. I fastened my arms around his neck and kissed him hungrily.

"Ugh, you're all sweaty!" I complained.

"Yeah? Any objections if I get you all sweaty, too?"

"None whatsoever."

And those were almost the last words we spoke for the next two hours, although I may have moaned his name several times. We got through three condoms and had seven orgasms between us.

I was a wreck, and I had no one but myself to blame. All my teasing and taunts had quite an effect on the Master Sergeant. It was time to pay or play: I did both.

"Oh my God, I can't move!" I gasped.

"Fuck!" said Sebastian, who was somewhat less loquacious than usual.

I lay there panting for several more minutes. I felt the bed move, but I was too exhausted to open my eyes.

"I know you're looking at me, Sebastian," I grumbled, "but whatever you have in mind you can just forget it. I admit it all: you're an animal in bed, and I will never, ever question your virility again."

He laughed softly.

"You can question it as often as you like, baby, because that just means I have to prove it to you."

He dragged the sheet over us, and pulled me into his arms, where I flopped unattractively.

"Do you want to go find something to eat?" he said.

"Go? As in, leave the room? No, no. Bad, bad idea. Call takeout."

"I don't think they deliver to naked people in hotel rooms, Caro."

I groaned.

"Come on, baby, time to get up."

"I can't," I whined.

He left me lying in bed while he showered, I was nearly asleep by the time he returned. I heard him moving around the room, dressing and pulling on a pair of sneakers instead of his biker boots.

He sat on the bed next to me, and I realized he was holding my pink t-shirt in his hands.

"Not your color, Sebastian," I mumbled.

"No, baby. I want you to wear it."

"Why?"

"You look cute in pink."

Oh!

"And I got you something while I was out."

I sat up, ignoring several aching muscles.

"You got me something?"

I could hear the excitement in his voice, and he handed me a shopping bag from a woman's clothing store.

"You bought me clothes?"

"Just look in the goddam bag, Caro!"

I reached in and my hands fastened around a small piece of folded cloth: black with a design of tiny, pink flowers embroidered along one edge. It was a skirt, a miniskirt, a *very short* miniskirt.

I was astounded. Was this how he saw me? Barely-there bikinis and micro-miniskirts? These were the clothes a twenty-year old would wear, they weren't right for me. Maybe it was just wishful thinking on his part.

"Don't you like it?" he asked, sounding hurt.

"Sebastian, I ... it's very pretty, but..."

"But what?"

"It's not really me. I'm more a jeans and t-shirt sort of person these days. Besides, I don't have any shoes—I've only got my walking boots."

He smiled, and pulled another bag out from under the bed.

Inside was a pair of soft, black leather ballerina flats. And in my size.

"Do you like them?" he asked anxiously.

I slipped them on my bare feet and held them out for him to look at.

"So, you'll wear the skirt?" he said hopefully.

It seemed a small thing to do to make him happy.

"Yes, *tesoro*, I'll wear the skirt."

I carried my new outfit into the bathroom and stared at myself in the mirror. I was horribly afraid I'd look like mutton dressed as lamb. Did all women with younger men feel like that? Like they had to dress to match the age of their boyfriend?

The skirt was so short, I could hardly bring myself to look at it, and I certainly wouldn't be able to bend over in it with any degree of modesty.

I brushed my hair out and applied some of my newly purchased mascara and lipstick. I felt awkward and uncomfortable, a fraud, like I was trying to be something I wasn't.

But Sebastian's appraisal was very different from mine.

"Wow! I mean ... wow! You look awesome, Caro. Really fucking sexy!"

He ran his hand up my bare thigh and cupped my behind.

"Mmm, this skirt is great: it's making me horny."

"Thank you for my gifts," I said. "But right now, I need food more than I need your body, Sebastian."

He smiled, kissed my neck, then walked over to the door to hold it open for me.

"After you, baby."

The evening air was still warm, although I suspected it would feel chilly later. I'd brought a sweater with me to wear, although there wasn't much I could do to keep my legs warm, and I was wishing I hadn't gone along with Sebastian's whim. It didn't help matters that two men walking in the opposite direction whistled at me and called out endearments—rather crude ones.

Sebastian scowled and started to turn, as if he was going to go after them.

"Oh no, eyes front, Hunter. You bought this skirt, and now you're suffering the consequences: suck it up."

He frowned, but let me lead him out of the danger zone.

When we found a pizzeria that we liked the look of I couldn't help noticing that Sebastian made sure I was seated so that my legs were hidden by the tablecloth. Talk about double standards, it was almost comical. And time for a new topic of conversation.

"What do you want to do tomorrow, Sebastian? Apart from spring your surprise on me?"

He grinned, his good humor instantly restored.

"I thought we could walk up to Capezzano Inferiore, take a look around. Even if there aren't any Venzis there, it would be kinda cool to see where your dad grew up, wouldn't it?"

He was so sweet. A complete pain in the ass, but really sweet.

Our pizzas arrived, pepperoni for Sebastian, *quattro formaggi* for me, and he also ordered a light beer. Then he surprised me.

"Tell me about your place in Long Beach, Caro."

I didn't know why it surprised me: maybe because it didn't seem to be part of 'us', maybe I'd been unconsciously avoiding it.

"Oh! Sure, okay. Well, it's small, a bungalow in an area called the West End. It was built about ninety years ago, and it was pretty beaten up when I bought it. I restored the porch at the front so I can sit out and watch the ocean, and in the winter the windows are covered in salt from the wind coming off the Atlantic. I have some really great neighbors, and they look after the place while I'm away. My friends like to come out from Manhattan on the weekends. You spoke to Nicole, she works in merchant banking; and then there's Jenna, who's a bitch-on-wheels attorney, but actually she's really lovely; and Alice, she's a Professor of literature at NYU. I met her when I was going to school there..."

I stopped suddenly.

"What's wrong, Sebastian?"

He'd stopped eating, and was staring at me with dark, angry eyes.

"How am I going to fit in with your life there, Caro? All your friends have these amazing careers ... and I'll just be a jobless grunt with a high school diploma."

"Sebastian, no!"

"You know what they'll think: Muscles Are Required Intelligence Not Essential."

"Hey! No one will think that, and you know what? I don't give a shit anyway. Sebastian, haven't we had to listen to enough crap in the past to care less what anyone else thinks now? Isn't that what you've been telling me?"

He shifted in his seat, but didn't answer.

"Sebastian, do you love me?"

He looked up instantly.

"You know I do, Caro. *Sempre*."

"Then whatever happens, we'll deal. I vaguely remember someone saying that to me. Oh, wait, that was you a couple of days ago. Sebastian, the only thing my friends will care about is that I'm happy."

I took his hand in mine.

"What about your plans to be a personal fitness trainer? And, jeez, Sebastian, we'll be in New York, you could do something amazing with your language skills. Don't go and get all shy on me now, Hunter!"

He took a deep breath, forcing himself to relax.

"Yeah, okay. Sorry. I just kinda freaked for a moment there."

"I know and I understand. It's weird for me, too, and we haven't been doing this for very long. I guess you could say we're out of practice with the whole dating thing. I feel very un-me sitting here in this shockingly short miniskirt, but I tried it, for you."

"Shockingly short?" he said, his grin returning.

I took his hand under the table and let him run his fingers up my thigh.

"Yeah," he agreed, "shockingly short."

"Okay, Columbus, you've discovered enough for one evening," I said, slapping his hand away as it began to travel even higher.

He pouted at me, and I laughed out loud.

"Come, *tesoro*, take me home."

~

When we returned to our beautiful room, and our beautiful, large bed, Sebastian made sweet, slow love to me. Maybe it was the romantic setting, or the way we were gradually getting to know each other again and defeat our fears one by one, but the way he touched me seemed to have a new depth and intensity. I was dreading the moment, just a few days away, when we'd have to say goodbye. Again.

We woke with yet another day of bright sunshine spilling in through the open windows.

"*Ciao, bella*," he said, copying the words I'd said to him the day before.

"*Ciao*," I said, smiling back at him.

I stretched, and several muscles grumbled at me. I'd thought I was in pretty good shape, but I'd been worked over by a US Marine, for several hours. There was definitely something to be said for a having the services of a personal trainer.

Sebastian's morning wood poked me in the side and his hand drifted over my hip.

Uh-oh, round two. Or three. Were we up to four? What the hell—seconds out.

Signora Carello served us breakfast on a small, private terrace to one side of her villa. She had a tiny garden filled with bougainvillea that was just coming into its full glory.

We invited her to have her coffee with us, and she happily accepted our invitation.

"So, you are hoping to find family in Capezzano Inferiore?"

"Well, that would be the icing on the cake, but really, I just want to see the village where my father came from. If I find family, well..."

She smiled sympathetically and patted my hand.

"Perhaps you will find family in a different way," she said, glancing at Sebastian, who grinned back at her.

There were several ways I could interpret her remark, I chose to ignore all of them. Although, it wasn't easy with Sebastian sitting opposite, smirking at me.

We wandered through Salerno, stopping to admire the neat yachts lined up in the harbor.

"I should take you sailing some time," said Sebastian, staring out at the deep, blue waters of the Mediterranean. "If we had more time, I'd rent us a boat and teach you how to sail."

"I already know," I said, smiling at him. "Although I haven't been out on a sailboat for years."

"Really?" he said, intrigued. "I didn't know you could sail."

"Ah, you don't know all my talents yet, Hunter."

He smiled. "I'm looking forward to finding out. But when did you learn?"

Damn, I should have kept my mouth shut—we were definitely sailing into dangerous waters.

"David taught me," I said.

Sebastian's face clouded over at once. "The asshole?"

It was his favorite name for my ex-husband.

"The very one."

His good humor evaporated and I sighed. I could have predicted that response—I *should* have predicted that response.

"It was a long time ago, Sebastian. And we agreed we couldn't change the past, so stop looking so mad, or I'll have to kiss you indecently in public."

His expression changed to one of surprise, then darkened perceptibly to lust.

"Nope, still pissed off, Caro. You'll have to kiss me. I don't know if it'll work, but you could try."

His eyes were challenging.

"Are you sure, Sebastian?" I said, in my most sultry voice. "Because I don't want to get you all hot and bothered."

"I'll risk it," he said, arrogantly.

I turned to face him, standing so close that our bodies almost touched. And then in full public view, I ran my hand over his ass, up beneath his t-shirt, and dragged my nails down his back. With my other hand I pulled his head down toward me and kissed him hard. And I might have also rubbed him over his zipper, causing him to take a sharp intake of breath.

"Fuck, Caro," he whispered. "Let's go back to our room right now."

I laughed. "No, Sebastian. That was just my distraction technique, which, by the way, I didn't learn in the Marines."

He groaned and had to adjust his pants.

"Should we go to Capezzano Inferiore now?" I asked innocently.

He gave me a look that said payback would be a bitch.

It was a steep walk to my father's village, but the view more than made up for it. Salerno glittered jewel-like below, the Mediterranean a polished glass of an implausible cerulean blue. In the crystal-sharp air, we could see a landmass on the horizon that I guessed must be Anacapri.

The village itself was quiet and dusty: a few cars passed us, all heading downhill. There was a fountain in the center that coughed and spurted arthritically, and a skinny dog idly scratched itself. All the life seemed to have been bled out of it, draining down the hill to the more confident town of Salerno. For the first time, I truly understood why my father might have wanted to leave, why America, with all its garish, New World charms, advertised by a thousand color movies, had been such a draw. And, perhaps, why my blonde, blue-eyed mother had seemed like a dream worth chasing.

It was making me sad, and it felt like a mistake to have come here.

"We don't have to stay, Caro," said Sebastian, squeezing my fingers.

I sighed. "It's okay. I don't know what I was expecting: Papa always said it was a one-horse town where the horse had died. I guess he was right."

"Look, that guy over there is just opening up his café—let's go get a drink, okay?"

The café owner was surprised but delighted to have some business. I imagined he didn't get many customers.

Sebastian ordered a beer and I opted for an espresso. Maybe a shot of caffeine would help to lift my mood.

The beer was served in a frosted glass, and my espresso arrived in a miniature coffee pot with raw cane sugar and a glass of water.

"Excuse me, sir," said Sebastian, politely. "But my girlfriend's father came from this village. We were wondering if you might have known him: his surname was Venzi."

The man scratched his head. "That name seems familiar, but I'm not sure. Let me ask my wife—she's lived here her whole life."

My heart began to beat more rapidly, and I sat up anxiously in my seat.

"Don't get your hopes up, Caro," Sebastian said, gently.

"No, I'm not," I lied, unable to beat back the sudden expectation that had flared.

A moment later, the owner's wife appeared.

"*Buon giorno*. You are asking after the Venzi family? How can I help you?"

"I was just wondering ... my father, Marco Venzi, he was born here. Did you know him?"

"Goodness! Marco Venzi! That's a name I haven't heard in a very long time. He was the boy who left to live in America. Your father, you say? Yes, I knew him."

She knew him. She really knew him. I felt tears welling up in my eyes.

"It's so exciting to meet someone who remembers Papa," I choked out, gazing at the woman's warm and sympathetic face.

"Yes, we were at school together: he was a few years older than me, and always in trouble. He had the devil in him, that one."

"His daughter is just the same," said Sebastian, with a quiet smile.

The woman laughed. "And how is dear Marco? Did he make his fortune in America like he said? He was crazy for your American movies. Said he was going to be a big star, like Valentino."

"Mr. Venzi died some years ago," answered Sebastian, knowing I was finding it hard to speak.

"Ah, I see," she said. "Forgive me, young woman, my condolences. Your father was always so full of spirit. Too big for this little town."

"Do you know if he had any relatives here?" said Sebastian.

"Well, there was his mother, but she died a long time ago. Marco had a sister who was much older than him, I remember. But she married and moved away, to Naples, I think. I'm sorry, I don't remember the name of the man she married, so that's all I can tell you."

She nodded, and moved back inside the shadowy café.

Sebastian held my hand, stroking his thumb over the back of my knuckles.

"We could try and find her," he said, gently. "She might have had kids—you could have cousins you don't know about."

"Yes, I might. I probably do."

I closed my eyes, remembering the happiness my father found in everything to do with America: the music, the movies, the TV shows, the cars—especially the cars. A large, pale blue Cadillac had been his pride and joy. The damn thing drove like a bus. I used to get seasick just from sitting in the back seat.

But that was in the past, it was all in the past, and I was planning a future.

"It doesn't matter, Sebastian," I said, slowly. "Signora Carello was right: even if there are cousins, they're not my family—not really. I have my friends and I have you. You're my family now."

He bowed his head and held my hand to his lips. Then he stood up, taking me by surprise.

And in that dusty little square, in that nondescript, one-horse town where the fountain coughed and spluttered and the cars passed by without a second glance, he sank to one knee.

"Carolina Maria Venzi: I love you, and I want to spend my life with you. Will you marry me?"

CHAPTER ELEVEN

I STARED DOWN IN AMAZEMENT AS SEBASTIAN KNELT BEFORE ME, HIS beautiful face torn with anxiety.

I could think of a thousand reasons why marrying him was sheer lunacy, and only one reason why it wasn't.

I took a deep breath, willing all my doubts and fears away.

"I love you, too, Sebastian. And the answer is yes."

He let out a shout of delight and leapt to his feet, pulling me into his arms, and holding me tightly as if he'd never let me go. I laid my head on his chest, listening to the pounding of his heart through his thin t-shirt.

"I'll do everything to make you happy, I promise, Caro," he whispered. "Everything, baby. You are my life."

"And you are mine, *tesoro*. We'll find a way—we always do."

He sat back down on the hard, wooden seat and pulled me onto his lap, nuzzling my neck.

"Oh, fuck!" he said, angrily.

"What? What's the matter?" I asked nervously.

Had he changed his mind already?

"I forgot to give you the fucking ring," he snarled. "Fuck it! I wanted this to be so smooth. Jeez, I said it enough times in my head."

"You did? You practiced this?"

I loved that he'd practiced.

He smiled, slightly abashed. "Yeah, once or twice. Maybe a few times more ... maybe a lot of times more... Ah, fuck it, Caro. See if the damn thing fits."

I couldn't help laughing out loud from sheer happiness—plus, he was so damn funny.

"You're in danger of sweeping me off my feet again, Sebastian. How can I resist such sweet words: I'll treasure your proposal forever, 'See if the damn thing fits'."

He grinned at me, then pulled a small ring box out of his back pocket, opened it, and laid it on the table.

Nestled in the dark blue satin was a small but breathtaking blue-white diamond solitaire, simply mounted on a gold band.

I gasped, as the diamond blazed in the sun, scattering tiny rainbows across the table.

"Sebastian, it's beautiful! Where on earth did you get it ... and *when?*"

"Try it on."

He lifted the ring out of the box and slid it onto the third finger of my left hand.

"Perfect."

"Yes, it is. Thank you, *tesoro*."

I twisted around and kissed him softly, leaning down to enjoy the feel of his lips on mine.

Sebastian looked as if he'd just climbed Mount Everest or defeated the Mongol hordes single-handedly.

"So, *fiancé*," I said, "what should we do now?"

My new name took him by surprise.

"Wow, *fiancé*, huh? I didn't think it could sound so cool."

"I disagree, Sebastian. I think it sounds *hot*. Maybe we can agree to disagree, or just accept that it's an all-temperature sort of title."

He laughed loudly, the sound filled with a ridiculous and infectious joy that I couldn't help sharing.

"Well, *fiancée*, I thought we could check out those gnarly bends on the Amalfi coast. What do you think?"

"I think you're crazy, probably certifiable, and I'm horribly afraid it's contagious."

He grinned at me and stood up, tucking my hand under his arm, as we floated back down to Salerno.

The sun was blazing in the sky, the air warm, and the feeling that filled me, indescribable. I felt both calm and fizzing with joy, happy and anxious, loved and terrifyingly in love. I was falling off a cliff, one I'd thrown myself from willingly, hoping I'd fly. Crazy in love.

When we reached the villa, Signora Carello was standing in her garden, watering the bougainvillea.

"Did you have any luck finding your family, my dear?" she asked kindly.

"Yes, I did," I said, gazing stupidly at Sebastian.

Sigora Carello gasped as she saw my ring flashing in the sunshine.

"Oh, felicitations, *congratulazioni per il vostro fidanzamento*, my children! I'm so happy for you."

And she kissed us each three times, while Sebastian grinned away as if nothing could ever dim his happiness.

"And now for your surprise?" she said, patting Sebastian on his arm.

He winked and nodded.

I actually felt jealous that I wasn't in on the secret, but I couldn't help smiling anyway.

"Some lunch before you go? I was going to fix myself *insalata tricolore*—you're welcome to join me."

We sat in the *signora*'s pretty garden, enjoying the tranquility that came from within.

"So, when will you marry?" she asked, with keen interest.

We answered simultaneously.

"I don't know," I said.

"As soon as possible," said Sebastian.

The *signora* laughed.

"Oh, you two have some talking to do, I can see that. Never mind, my dears, you'll work it out. Have you decided where you'll live?"

"Caro has a place near New York," said Sebastian, "but I could be stationed anywhere."

"You're in the army?"

"No, ma'am, US Marines."

Signora Carello nodded slowly, a frown of concern crinkling her eyes.

"He has to do two more years," I said, staring at my plate, and trying to keep the tremor out of my voice. "And he's being sent out to Afghanistan. On Thursday."

"Ah," she said, and shook her head sadly.

"Hey, it'll be fine," said Sebastian, emphasizing the final word. "Besides, I might see you out there."

Signora Carello looked confused.

"Caro is a reporter—a foreign correspondent," said Sebastian. "But I wish she..."

He stopped mid-sentence.

"Well," said the *signora*, forcefully, "you young people don't choose the easy path, but it is your own path. I wish you both well. Please come back and have your honeymoon here."

"Honeymoon!" said Sebastian, looking as if he'd just won the lottery. "Hell, I'd forgotten about that! Yeah, we should definitely have a honeymoon, Caro. With room service—so we don't have to get out of bed."

I felt hugely embarrassed he'd said that in front of the *signora*, but she just laughed and he winked at her.

When Signora Carello took the plates back into the villa, I elbowed Sebastian in the ribs.

"Don't say things like that in front of her—she'll be embarrassed!"

Sebastian laughed. "You're the only one who's embarrassed, Caro, which is pretty fucking funny. Signora Carello used to be 'fast', remember? Anyway, I didn't say anything that wasn't true."

And then I recalled that the *signora* had already cleaned our room that morning, I cringed, thinking about the large number of condoms that we'd deposited in the garbage can. Oh, God, how embarrassing was that? Sebastian's inappropriate comment paled to nothing when faced with more tangible evidence of how we'd spent our time.

We collected our leather jackets from the tidy room, and Sebastian changed into his heavy boots before we headed off for the 'surprise'. He looked so sexy bending over to fasten the buckles. What was it about jeans, boots and leather jackets? I wondered what it would be like riding through upstate New York on Sebastian's mean machine. Now *that* would be fun.

I was puzzled when the *signora* cornered us by the front door and kissed us again, whispering something to Sebastian, and patting his arm.

I had the distinct impression that they'd planned something together: no doubt the Hunter charm and the Italian love of intrigue had been cooking up something.

The Amalfi coastline was like a huge James Bond set. Dizzying, narrow roads arced up the mountain, with the cliffs falling away into the sea, many hundreds of feet below.

I clung onto Sebastian, as he took the turns with terrifying speed. I could tell he was enjoying himself, but I had my eyes closed and grit my teeth so hard, I was afraid I would grind them into chalk dust or make them come flying out of my mouth like so many peanuts.

At the top of the path, above the small town of Pontone, Sebastian pulled off the road next to a lemon grove, and cut the engine.

"It's a great view, baby. You want to get your camera out?"

I opened my eyes and pulled off my helmet. He was right—it was stunning. And, with my blood pressure returning to normal, I felt able to capture the astonishing landscape in the lens. I snapped a few of Sebastian, too, looking all bad-boy next to his motorcycle.

I climbed a little higher to get some more views of the sea, when I slithered back down the mountainside, I was surprised to see that Sebastian was digging around for something in one of the bike's saddlebags.

"Don't you want to ride on a little further?" I asked, puzzled.

"Nope, we're staying here. Picnic," he grinned at me, holding a miniature bottle of champagne in one hand, and two crystal flutes in the other. "Borrowed from Signora Carello," he said, answering my unspoken question.

"I think the *signora* has a soft spot for you, Sebastian."

"Must be my animal magnetism, baby."

I rolled my eyes at him.

"Hey, don't knock it—it works on you."

"That is true, Sarge."

He led us to a patch of dry, springy grass and opened the champagne, where the cork flew off like a rocket, making us both duck.

"Huh, guess it got shook up on the road."

Yeah, and it wasn't the only thing that got shook up, I thought, uncharitably.

He poured the champagne, half-filling the glasses with froth and bubbles.

"Here's to us, Caro," he said, softly and seriously. "Today, tomorrow, forever. Promise?"

"Yes, *tesoro*. Forever, I promise."

We sat, high above the Mediterranean, as if at the top of the world, sipping our champagne and speaking quietly, promises and words of love. Then we lay in each other's arms, feeling the warm sun on our faces.

"I love my surprise, Sebastian," I said, contentedly.

He chuckled quietly. "This is only part of it, Caro. There's more."

"More?"

"Much more."

"Such as?"

"You'll see."

Feeling a little lightheaded from both the ride and the champagne, I mounted the motorcycle once more, and we headed back down toward the sea. This time, I screwed up my courage and managed to open one eye as Sebastian raced down the hill, taking the curves with what, to me, seemed like reckless speed.

We arrived in the village Conca dei Marini without incident and, to my surprise, Sebastian pulled up in the forecourt of Il Saraceno, a hotel so grand, I was sure it must be frequented by the great and good, the wealthy and the beautiful. Sebastian fit right in—especially on that last one. I looked dusty and travel-stained, as if I'd just crossed the Sahara on the back of a smelly camel.

Il Saraceno clung to the cliffs, a series of fortress-like arches that mimicked the ancient Moorish architecture of Spanish Grenada. The views down to the sea were in danger of bringing on an attack of vertigo.

"Here?" I asked uncertainly, aware that my hair resembled a squashed bird's nest.

"Here," he said, with a smile.

I was surprised when he unpacked the bike's saddlebags, and handed the keys of his machine to a man at the reception desk. I couldn't imagine him letting anyone else park it, I supposed the valet would simply wheel it around to the parking area.

The receptionist smiled, and handed an envelope to Sebastian, along with a room key.

"We're staying here? But we left all our things at Signora Carello's?"

"Actually, we haven't. I asked the *signora* to pack us up while we were out this morning. She was cool about it. Besides this is kind of her idea. Well, she helped me pick out somewhere special."

"But a place like this must cost a small fortune, Sebastian!"

"I can afford it, baby. This is my first night as an engaged man—and I want to enjoy it. Hey, don't worry. The only thing I've spent my pay on in the last ten years is booze and bikes. I'm good for it."

Which wasn't the point, but he was in such high spirits, I didn't have the heart to argue with him.

But the surprise didn't end there. At the door to our room, Sebastian swept me up into his arms and insisted on carrying me over the threshold, his wonderfully romantic gesture leaving me breathless.

The bed was huge, almost seven feet wide. I'd never seen anything like it—but I quickly formed plans for how we could use it. I barely noticed the opulence of the rest of the room, the chandelier and long curtains trailing across our own private balcony. The bathroom alone was an essay in magnificence: an enormous whirlpool bathtub, plus a vast hydro-massage shower. Both were fashioned from marble, and could probably have accommodated an entire soccer team. I couldn't wait to try them out with my very own United States Marine.

Sebastian pulled open the wardrobe doors and didn't seem at all surprised to see two suit carriers hanging up inside.

"This one is for you, baby."

Staring at him in amazement, a smile creeping over my face, I unzipped the carrier that he handed me, to reveal a stunning, floor-length evening gown, in midnight blue.

"Sebastian, it's beautiful! What have you done?"

He grinned at me. "And I have a tux—like you wanted. Except mine is just rented. You get to keep the dress."

I laid my beautiful gown on the bed, and wrapped my arms around his neck.

"How did you get to be so perfect, Sebastian, because I could have sworn you were a giant pain in the ass."

He laughed. "Next time I piss you off, I'm going to remind you that you said that, baby. Which will probably be in about five minutes."

"Probably," I agreed, with a smile.

"Come on, let's shower, and then I want to see you in that dress."

"Why, Sergeant! You want to put me *into* clothes?"

"You have another idea?" he murmured into my neck.

"Oh, yes, most definitely, and it involves getting you naked on that bed, having my wicked, wicked way with you *before* we take a shower."

His smile grew even bigger.

"So, let me get this straight, Caro, that's *two* lots of wicked?"

"The thing is, Sebastian," I said, stroking his cheek and watching his expression of amusement turn to lust, "if you're going to make an honest woman of me, I want to get in as much sinning as possible first."

I pushed him back on the bed, just in case he wasn't on the same page as me, and ripped his t-shirt over his head, loving that moment when his eyes heated with desire. I knelt across him, then ran my tongue from his waist to his throat, making a delicious diversion where I tugged his nipples with my teeth.

Yes, two could play at that game.

I gripped his wrists with my hands and held them over his head, trapping him. Then I leaned down to kiss him, tracing his soft lips with my tongue and letting his warm breath wash over me.

"Mmm, you taste so good, Sebastian, I won't want anything else to eat tonight."

He laughed lightly, and gently pulled his hands free, before running them down my back.

"Yeah? Well, I'm starving, so unless you want me to eat downstairs alone, baby, you'll have to put up with a three-course meal. And I guarantee you'll need your energy later."

I pouted at him. "Sure you don't want the starter now?"

He didn't answer with words, but moved his hands around to my waistband, tugging my t-shirt free, and pulling it over my head. It landed somewhere on the floor, while he unfastened my bra one-handed.

There had been a time when bras had presented him with something of a challenge—not any more.

"Mmm, I like this position," he said, sitting up and nuzzling my nipples, then sucking hard. I moaned and arched my back, pushing my breasts into his willing hands.

He fished a condom out of his jeans pocket and handed it to me.

"Take your pants off, baby."

"I will if you will," I replied, teasingly. "Race you!"

I bounced off him and quickly unlaced my boots, dropping my jeans and panties to the floor in record time.

"Ah, hell," muttered Sebastian as he struggled to unbuckle his boots.

"You're a slouch, Hunter," I jeered at him. "Just look at what you're missing."

I gave a quick twirl, which didn't help his concentration.

"Fuck!" he hissed, hopping around the bed, one boot on, one boot off.

"Maybe you should have been a fireman instead of a Marine, then you'd be used to undressing quickly."

There was a loud thud as his second boot landed on the floor, a moment later his pants and briefs hit the deck, too.

Damn, he looked so fine standing there, all tall and erect, all hot and devilish. I definitely wanted some of that.

"Lie on the bed," I ordered.

"Yes, ma'am."

I decided to have a quick taste, feeling his hips arch upwards so he filled my mouth. Okay, maybe not so quick: he tasted salty, his skin silky and delicious.

I held the condom in my hand as I continued to enjoy feeling his arousal between my lips, in my mouth, under my writhing tongue. I ran my fingernails up and down his chest as I continued to stroke him with my mouth. I was beginning to resent the intrusion of our little rubber friends, and wondered what would be the best time to start taking the birth control pills: perhaps a month before he got home on his next leave? That would be a good surprise for him. A welcome home present for both of us.

"Baby, I'm going to come if you keep doing that," he growled, his voice strained.

Oh, I'd completely lost track of what I was doing. Hmm, better not admit to that.

I released him and sat back, watching the rapid rise and fall of his chest as he tried to pull himself together. Before he got the chance, I rolled the condom down, and positioned myself over him, sinking down slowly. Very slowly.

He moaned softly and I leaned down to kiss him. At the same time, he flexed his hips upwards, filling and massaging me at just the right place, causing sensation to spill through me.

"Fuck, Caro! I can't control myself with you!"

He started pumping his hips, bouncing me up as I slammed down to meet him.

He came quickly and used his fingers to make sure that I followed him.

I slumped down on his chest.

"Sorry, baby," he said, breathlessly.

"You have nothing to be sorry about," I gasped, impressed I'd managed to string a whole sentence together.

He smiled and stroked my back. "Ready for the main course?"

"You've got to be kidding me, Hunter? I'm still..." and my body clenched around him.

"Oh, wow," he said, his eyes wide, "I really felt that."

"Good," I said, rather grumpily. "So did I."

He laughed, and lifted me off him as he sat up.

"I'm going to go shower."

With bleary eyes, I watched him saunter into the palatial bathroom, snapping off the condom as he went.

I glanced down at my hand and caught sight of the unfamiliar ring on my finger. I still wasn't certain how that had happened. But it felt good. It felt right. Although explaining it to my friends would be interesting. I shook my head: hell, explaining to myself would be pretty damn interesting, too.

I heard the bathroom door open again, and Sebastian strolled out drying himself. Or rather, the way he looked, the way he looked at me—that was explanation enough for our impetuous engagement, certainly as far as I was concerned.

"What?" he asked, smiling.

"Just wondering how the hell I ended up engaged to such a hot Marine. It's been quite a week, Sarge."

He frowned. "You're not having second thoughts, are you, Caro?"

I shook my head. "No, Sebastian, I'm not. But you have to admit, it's all been pretty fast."

"It's been ten years, Caro," he said, seriously. "I've waited long enough."

His response floored me: he had a way of just cutting through all my bullshit.

"I love you so much, *tesoro*," I said.

His eyes softened. "Love you, too, Caro. Now get your ass in that shower, before I throw you in there."

"Fine, fine," I grumbled. "I'm going."

He waited until he was sure I really was moving.

"I'll meet you in the restaurant, Caro."

"You're not going to wait for me here?"

"Nope. I want to see you coming down that staircase, and have all the other bastards wanting you, but knowing I'll be the one taking you to bed later." He saw the expression on my face. "Humor me: it's a guy thing."

I shook my head. Honestly!

When I climbed out of the shower, the room was empty, except for my beautiful dress which Sebastian had laid across the bed. I didn't want to think how he'd gotten so good at choosing women's clothing.

I hunted through the drawers until I found a hair dryer. Luckily, I had some hairpins in my bag, and, after a couple of false starts, I managed to sweep my hair up into a reasonably elegant chignon.

I realized then that Sebastian had laid another set of bags on the bed. What the hell had he done now? Inside the first was the most exquisite set of silvery-gray silk bra and panties, all chic and obviously designer—they must have cost a fortune. I'd never owned anything so glamorous in my life. In the second bag was a pair of high-heeled satin pumps in the same midnight blue as the dress. In my size. Of course. I dreaded to think how big a hole this had put in Sebastian's savings. Things were going to be a lot tighter when we were married.

Married.

I hadn't had time to think about what that meant. I'd been married for 11 years from the age of 19, and they had been difficult and unhappy years. I'd promised myself I'd never marry again, and I'd had absolutely no intention of getting involved with a man in the armed forces. Nope, never, no way. And yet here I was: promising myself to Sebastian forever. It helped that he wasn't planning on staying in the Marines, because there was no way I'd want to live on a military base ever again, despite my fascination with reporting from, and writing about them.

There were so many things Sebastian and I had to work out. We'd both been single for so long that blending our lives together wasn't going to be easy.

I'd promised Sebastian we'd find a way. He deserved to be loved for everything he was. And for whatever crazy reason he had, he loved me, too.

I shimmied into the tiny silver panties, enjoying the whisper of the sheer material over my damp skin. The bra hugged my breasts and felt incredibly sensual. It made me feel sexy—and Sebastian had chosen them. And I realized that's how he saw me, as someone desirable, someone he desired. Well, tonight I was going to do my best to live up to that.

I applied some mascara, cursing when I managed to deposit a gluey lump on my cheek. I had better luck with the lipstick. By some miracle, I'd managed to buy one that went on creamily and didn't bleed. For the second night running, a stranger's face stared back at me in the mirror.

But the dress ... oh, the dress was something else. It was a floor-length, flowing gown, cut low at the back, and plunging dangerously at the front, and with a thigh-high slit that only revealed itself when I walked. And yet it was so cleverly constructed, that I felt safe. Well, I wasn't afraid that anything would be revealed by mistake. I was fairly sure I wouldn't be safe from Sebastian later. I was looking forward to that. I hoped he didn't tear anything when he took it off me, because that would be a crying shame.

Before I left the room, I put the packet of condoms on the table next to my side of the bed—they'd need to be where we could find them in a hurry.

Now, if I could just get down the main staircase without breaking my neck in those perilously high heels...

I took a deep breath and left the safety of our room.

At the top of the stairs, I glanced down. My breath stuttered in my throat. I thought I'd slipped through a crack in time because in front of me, my fun-loving surfer boy, my rough, tough, sexy Marine, had transformed into a nineteenth century gentleman.

He was dressed in black: the pants legs edged in a narrow, satin stripe, an elegant, fitted tuxedo-jacket rested on his broad shoulders, over a fine cotton piqué shirt. A black bowtie accentuated his beauty still further.

And the woman he was talking to, looked like she was stripping him with her eyes, before dragging him to her room.

I eyed up the competition. She was perhaps two or three years younger than me, expensively dressed in a vivid purple halter top about the size of a handkerchief, with long, sexy harem pants. There was no doubt she had the figure to carry off such an outrageous outfit, although if I was inclined to be critical, I'd say that her boobs had the volume, shape and rubbery bounce of beach balls, her teeth were whitened to a degree that could cause snow blindness, and she had fake talons that could remove an eyeball at a hundred paces. But only if I was being critical.

And she was flirting with my fiancé.

I was about to be seriously pissed off when she laid a predatory hand on his arm, in an apparently friendly gesture.

I saw Sebastian turn slightly, so she was forced to drop her hand. I felt like cheering. He wasn't interested in her.

Then he glanced up at the stairs and his eyes widened as he saw me, before his face broke out in a huge grin.

The Orangeade woman turned to see what he was staring at, and if looks could kill, I'd have shriveled on the spot. But I didn't shrivel. I gave her a small, oh-so-magnanimous smile, before I carefully made my way down the stairs.

Sebastian strode across to meet me and took my hand, lifting it to his lips.

"You look beautiful, Caro."

"Thank you, kind sir."

He held out his arm. "May I escort you in to dinner, ma'am?"

"Why, yes you may."

Sebastian glowed with happiness, although the glint in his eyes was still wicked. I'm sure, that evening, that I reflected his joy, felt it wash over me, I basked in it and bathed in it. At that moment, at that time, there was nowhere in the world I'd rather be.

The dining room was exquisite, a small piece of perfection, with the Mediterranean at its feet. The chairs were swathed in linen that matched the tablecloths, and the starched napkins had been folded into shapes like a bishop's miter.

Sebastian led me to a table in a small alcove, where the arched windows looked down onto the sunset over the sea. A waiter rushed forward to pull out my chair, but Sebastian waved him away, carefully seating me himself, before brushing his lips over my bare shoulder in a soft, lingering kiss.

"I can't wait to get you out of that dress," he whispered in my ear, as he ran a long, cool finger from my earlobe down to the base of my neck.

Then he sat across the table from me and smiled smugly.

"Every man in this room wants you, Caro. I'm so fucking proud, I can't stop smiling."

"Hmm, well I think you may be a little biased, I thought I was going to need a crowbar to pry that woman off you. Is it just me, or had she overdone the fake tan, because I haven't seen that shade of orange outside of a drag review."

He raised his eyebrows. "My girl's got grit: I like it."

"I felt like swinging her around by her hair extensions. Maybe some of your Marine training is rubbing off on me."

"That comes after the main course," he said, confidently.

"Thank you for today, Sebastian," I said, serious for once. "It's been perfect. Thank you."

He smiled at me across the table.

"It's been a long time coming, Caro, but it was worth the wait."

I could see in his eyes that he meant what he said.

"Where did you get this beautiful ring?" I murmured, admiring the way it glinted on my finger. "Because I didn't see any shops in Salerno that..."

"I didn't buy it in Salerno," he said, interrupting me.

My mouth popped open in surprise. "Then where?"

"Geneva," he said, grinning at me, completely unabashed. "You know I was supposed to be at that fucking dull hostile environment briefing—which they'd given me as part of my 'rehabilitation' after Paris..." he raised an eyebrow, "but after I saw you ... I couldn't face going back. I was wandering around trying to get my head straight, and I saw it in a jeweler's shop."

I was dumbfounded.

"But ... you still hated me then!"

He shook his head vehemently. "I never hated you, Caro, although I tried, I really fucking tried. But I just couldn't do it."

He sighed and rubbed his hands over his hair.

"That ring has been burning a hole in my pocket ever since. I was just waiting for the right time to give it to you."

I blinked back tears: tonight was not a night for crying, although I was certain that would happen in the lonely days to come.

"You've always been so sure," I whispered, "I don't understand why."

"I told you, Caro," he said, softly. "It's only ever been you."

I stretched out my hand, admiring the ring as it sparkled under the light of the chandelier. "Thank you for giving it to me."

He caught my fingers and kissed the ring. "Thank you for wearing it."

The wine waiter arrived with an expensive-looking bottle and opened it with an understated flourish.

Sebastian held his glass and watched the bubbles effervesce. Then he looked up, staring into my eyes.

"Thank God for you, Caro," he said, his voice low and aching with sincerity.

"And you, Sebastian, *semper fidelis*."

As the hours passed, the tension that had been so briefly and beautifully absent from our relationship began to creep back. Once again, our summer was slipping away, and we could count it in minutes and seconds.

Tomorrow, the dream would be over—but, for now, tonight was still ours. I had to remember that.

We dined on *antipasti di frutti di mare*, a *primo* of ravioli with pumpkin and almonds with sage, and as *secondo*, a melt-in-your-mouth *ragú di pecora*, as the sun set, sinking into the sea beneath us. It was a perfect and poignant end to a magical few days.

We walked back up the grand staircase, hand in hand, and my gentleman escorted me to our room. I was waiting for him to revert to my sensuous and very physical lover, but there was one more surprise to come.

He led me out onto the balcony, where two glasses of Galliano liqueur blazed in the light of a single candle. And next to that, in a crystal vase, was a perfect pink rose.

In silence, he handed me the drink and took the second for himself. His gaze was heated, and his eyes never left mine.

The golden liquid burned as it trickled down my throat, but the burn was not as fierce as the way my *fiancé* looked at me.

He finished his drink and placed the glass back on the table, then took mine. With a look that made my body tingle and dried my throat, he held out his hand and led me toward the bed.

In silence, he cupped my face with his hands and kissed me until I was breathless and dizzy.

Then he turned me around, and rested his hands on my waist, gently unzipping my dress, stroking my bare flesh as the material shivered to the floor. I stepped away from it, and regarded him intently as his gaze flowed up and down my body.

My turn.

I moved toward him, and slid his jacket over his shoulders, tossing it onto the chair. I loosened one end of his bowtie and undid the top button of his shirt while he gazed down into my eyes.

He kissed my neck, his warm lips sending ripples of desire through me, then he dipped down, scooping me into his arms, and carried me to the bed.

I lay, looking up at him as he undid his cufflinks, then slowly he unfastened each button on his shirt, never taking his eyes from mine.

He shrugged the shirt off and my gentleman became a soldier again, his dog tags glinting in the candlelight, his tattoo a dark bruise on his golden skin.

He bent down to untie his shoes and peel off his socks, then he stood up, watching me silently, with wonder on his face.

I sat up and hooked my finger into the waistband of his pants, and pulled him toward me. I held his eyes as I slid the button free and lowered the zipper.

He pushed the material over his hips and threw the black pants onto the chair with his jacket.

As he stood in front of me, I could see the defined muscles of his stomach, diaphragm and chest moving with each breath.

I let my fingers drift over his bare skin and felt a shiver run through him, his breath caught in his throat, and his eyes fluttered closed.

I pushed his briefs down his long legs and he stepped free.

The way he looked at me took my breath away. Desire, need, love and lust: the emotions chased each other across his beautiful face, the candlelight throwing shadows that emphasized the perfect symmetry of his cheekbones.

I sat up, wrapping my arms around his waist, and placed soft kisses across his chest and stomach, before dipping down to plant a gentle kiss on the tip of his erection. He breathed in deeply and closed his eyes.

I kissed him again, then reached over to find a condom, tore the packet open and slowly rolled it down his length. He sat next to me on the bed and carefully pulled out my hairpins, one by one, until my hair fell down my back and shoulders. Then he tangled his long fingers in my hair, and tipped my head back to kiss my throat.

His hands traveled across my body, and I felt him unhook my bra, sliding the straps over my shoulders, before leaning down to kiss my breasts. I stroked his short, soft hair as he continued to run his tongue over and around my nipples, teasing them into rigid points.

I lay back on the bed, my arms stretched above my head, and he hovered over me, his erection probing softly at the entrance to my sex, before he kissed his way down my chest and belly, running his tongue along the edge of my silk panties and rubbing his chin over my mound.

He hooked his fingers under the delicate material and threw the panties somewhere behind him.

He kissed me softly and sweetly, then nuzzled his way back up my body.

I lifted my knees, ready for him, running my hands over his strong forearms and biceps, tracing his tattoo with one finger.

His dog tags jingled softly as they fell onto my chest, and Sebastian's body loomed over me, his eyes locked on mine.

He pushed inside me slowly and I groaned loudly, feeling his body filling me. I lifted my hips, taking that extra length, and I heard his breath exhale sharply.

He gazed into my eyes, his hands stroking my face, as his hips moved and flexed rhythmically. My body trembled in response and he lowered his face to kiss me deeply, his tongue twining with mine.

He pulled back slightly, nuzzling my throat, and rolling his hips so every part of me felt him inside. I clenched around him and I heard a responding growl deep in his throat.

A quiet moan escaped me and his body recognized the sound, moving one degree faster. I lifted my hips again and I heard the breath hiss through his teeth. I cried out, on the edge of all sensation, then he buried his head in my neck and started thrusting rapidly until he reached his climax, and his body went rigid.

For a moment, his full, crushing weight pinned me to the bed, then, with a soft sigh, he pulled out of me and rolled onto his back, one hand resting across my stomach.

No words had been spoken, there was nothing that needed to be said.

For the rest of that night, we slept, woke briefly, made love and slept again, until dawn turned the sky gold and purple, with flames of orange reflected in the sea. We had spoken quietly, describing our love, and expressing our need for each other with our bodies.

We slept late, and Sebastian insisted on ordering a decadent breakfast of a dozen fresh fruits, a range of olive breads and light pastries, freshly squeezed orange juice with Sorrento lemons, and a large pot of coffee.

We sat on the balcony in our bathrobes to enjoy the feast, but our carefree happiness had slipped away with the night. Today, we had to return to Geneva. And this time tomorrow, Sebastian would be headed out to one of the most dangerous countries on earth. I would follow when I could.

I sighed, staring out at the sea, and Sebastian held my hand, lifting it to his lips at intervals.

"As much as I hate to say it, *tesoro*, but I think we should get going. We've got a hell of a long drive ahead of us, or rather you have, and you didn't have much sleep last night."

He smiled at the memory. "Yeah, but it was worth it. Anyway, don't worry, Caro, we're not taking the bike, we're flying back from Naples. Our flight is at 4PM, we've plenty of time."

"Flying? But what about your bike?"

"Sold it, baby. I can't take it with me, and they won't send me back to Geneva after this tour."

I was astonished. "When did you organize all this?"

"When we were in Salerno, I didn't think you'd mind."

"I don't, it's your bike, but I wish you'd told me—it would have been one less thing to worry about."

He smiled at me. "Sorry, baby. I guess I'm just used to doing stuff on my own."

I frowned. "Yes. Me, too. I suppose we'll just have to practice the whole sharing and communicating thing. I promise that I'll write to you every day, *tesoro*."

"Really?" he said, looking both pleased and surprised. "That would be cool. I never get mail. Well, Shirley always sends me a birthday card, but that's about it. Ches is shit at staying in touch. So am I."

"Well, I will expect an effort from you, Sebastian. Will you be able to email me?"

He pulled a face. "Maybe, I'm not sure. For a few days, but then ... I'll be out of range. Caro, don't worry if you don't hear from me regularly." He paused, watching my expression. "The places they send me, I can be away from the main Base for days, sometimes weeks, in shithole little villages, trying to persuade the locals to work with us. Nonmilitary comms is limited. Your letters will catch up with me—eventually, but emails—probably not that often."

"I understand," I said, a chill creeping across my heart. "But in an emergency, what's the procedure for contacting you?"

I could see he was toying with an answer.

"I'll give you a number you can call but only in a real, fucking emergency, Caro. I'm not supposed to give it out."

"Okay," I said softly, then steeled my nerve to ask my next question. "If ... if anything happens that I need to know about, how will anyone know to contact me?"

He leaned back in his chair and closed his eyes. "Same as you, Caro. We have to do a call-list—the Emergency Contact Form—of who to notify. I've been wondering how, I mean, I can't put you down as 'Lee Venzi' or even 'Caro Venzi' because they'll recognize the name, they'll start in asking questions, and you could be in deep shit."

"What about Carolina Hunter?" I suggested, looking across at him. "They'll just assume I'm a cousin or something, in fact, why don't you do that? Put me down as a relative."

I could tell by the look on his face that he'd been hoping I'd make that suggestion.

He smiled. "Yeah, that would work."

I hated having to talk about these things, but it was important, very important.

"Hey, baby, nothing's going to happen to me. I can take care of myself. I'm more worried about you. Reporters get ... hurt all the time."

"I know, Sebastian, but I'll be embedded with a Marine unit from Leatherneck, safest place to be. I heard US Marines are tough, and I know for a fact they're hot. In fact the word 'embedded' has me thinking all sorts of interesting things."

I could tell he didn't know whether to smile or scowl.

"You stay away from those bootnecks, Caro. They're a bunch of horny bastards."

"I've noticed! But really, don't worry about *that*. I've learned to say 'no' in even more languages than you."

He took my hand, fiddling with my ring.

"Well, at least they'll know you're taken when they see this."

I didn't answer. He'd be hurt if he knew I wasn't planning on wearing it. I couldn't tell him that it would draw too much attention. I could either cover it up with a band-aid, or wear it around my neck on a chain—my own, unique dog tag.

"How long do you think you'll be in Afghan?" he asked, still running his finger over the diamond.

"Assuming my papers arrive," I said, giving him a look which he wisely ignored, "maybe a month, six weeks. Certainly no more. I'll have a couple of days in Kabul, maybe in Kandahar, too—meeting some of your top brass. Then I'm hoping I'll be able to hitch a ride out to Leatherneck. I'll just have to see how it goes. Maybe I'll see you out there?"

He frowned. "I want you home, safe, Caro."

"Likewise, Sebastian."

We stared at each other, aware we'd reached an impasse.

He shook his head and changed the subject.

"Do you want to take a swim?" he asked suddenly. "I'll be God knows how many miles from the nearest pool out there, and hundreds of fucking miles from the ocean."

"Sure," I said, relieved at the new topic. "And I get to see you in those ridiculously loud board shorts again."

"And you'll wear the bikini?"

"Only if you promise not to punch anyone who looks at me."

"Can't promise that, baby," he said, with a smirk.

~

The time passed too quickly, and it seemed just moments later that we were sitting in the back of a taxi taking us to the airport at Naples, a short drive away.

It felt strange to be traveling in a car again and, much as Sebastian's driving had scared the living daylights out of me, I missed the mean machine—it had been so sexy feeling his hard body through the leather jacket, my thighs clamped around him. I wondered if he'd get his other bike shipped over from Ches's garage. I hoped so. I wanted him to feel that his home was in Long Beach, not a bunch of boxes in San Diego.

I decided to broach the subject.

"Sebastian, when do you think you'll tell Ches about us?"

He turned to look at me, a slight frown on his face.

"I don't know. Why?"

"Well, I just thought I could have all your belongings sent over from the west coast, but it's going to make it tricky to organize if Ches doesn't know about me."

He blinked at me in surprise.

"And there are some beautiful places in upstate New York that we could ride out to on your other bike ... if you want."

A happy smile spread over his face. "You'd do that?"

I was confused by his question. "Of course. Why wouldn't I? You'll need your things when you come home."

I couldn't understand Sebastian's surprise, he was shaking his head and smiling at me.

"Okay. I'll email him tonight," he said with a grin. "He'll be pretty fucking surprised."

I laughed darkly. "Yes, that probably about sums it up—to say the least."

He pulled my face toward his, and kissed me hungrily, ignoring the fact that our driver had a grandstand view in the mirror.

~

The airport was a small, modern, glass and steel structure with a single runway.

We were separated by security, and I watched anxiously from a distance as Sebastian was questioned and patted down. It wasn't until he was able to persuade them to look at his US Marine ID card, that they finally let him go.

He smiled as he walked over to me. "Guess I have a criminal face or something."

"I could have told you that," I laughed. "I'm just glad they didn't have one of the female security guards or you'd never have gotten away."

He rolled his eyes.

The flight was short, less than two hours and we were back in Geneva, carless, bikeless and sunless.

The city was much cooler than the southern Mediterranean, but I felt colder inside, too. Our time together could now be counted in hours.

We took a taxi to Sebastian's attic-like room, and I hovered by the door as he threw back the shutters, letting the thin, gray, northern light of dusk into the room.

He saw the stricken expression on my face.

"We can check into a hotel, Caro."

"No, this is fine. It's not the room..."

"Don't say it, Caro," he said, softly. "Please, baby. I can't bear it when you look at me like that."

"Sorry," I whispered. I made an effort to pull myself together, for his sake. "So, single bed, huh? That's going to be cozy. We'll have to improvise."

He smiled at me gratefully.

"I just gotta pack up my shit, baby, then we'll go find somewhere to eat, okay?"

"Sure, go ahead. I'll write up my notes and check my messages."

Predictably, I had long emails from both Jenna and Alice begging me to tell them if it was true that: a) I'd met a man, b) I'd actually had sex with him, and c) could it possibly be the hottie in the photograph. Nicole's email was much shorter and so explicit in her demand for information, that I angled my laptop screen away from Sebastian, in case he happened to glance over.

There was also an email from my editor saying that my credentials were on their way and I had a flight booked to Kabul 12 hours after Sebastian. I decided not to tell him, knowing it would give him something else to worry about—or possibly try to delay again, no matter what he said to the contrary. Although I did wonder if he'd perhaps put a word in for me after all, to expedite my papers.

It didn't take Sebastian long to pack, he owned so little. He wouldn't need his civvy clothes or the majority of his books, which were boxed up to be sent back to the U.S., everything else went in his duffel bag.

"You can stay here if you like," he offered, rather apologetically. "It's paid up till the end of the month. The owner is Madame Dubois. Just leave the key with her when you go: she's cool."

"Thank you, I'll do that."

He smiled, glad to be able to do something for me.

"Any interesting emails?"

"All my girlfriends are drooling over your photograph," I said, skating over the news that my editor had been in touch. "They can't quite believe you're real. Neither can I sometimes."

He smirked and pulled me into a hug. "I could prove it to you now if you like," he said, pushing himself lightly into my body.

I didn't answer, but ran my hands across the front of his jeans and squeezed, not very gently. His eyebrows shot up, making me laugh.

"Sex instead of food, Caro?"

"Yes," I said, kissing his neck, "I don't know what's come over me—you must be a bad influence."

He responded with enthusiasm, and I'd gotten as far as stripping off his t-shirt when his damn phone rang. I recognized the ringtone—it was one I wasn't likely to forget—Sebastian's CO. I'd have to have words with that man.

I raised my hands in defeat, and Sebastian scowled as he answered.

"Hunter. Yes, sir. Back in Geneva."

He listened intently for almost two minutes without speaking. I was squirming with curiosity, desperate to know what his CO was telling him, certain it was to do with where he was being sent.

He ended the call with a curt, "Yes, sir," then he looked at me. "Pick up 05:00."

I wrapped my arms around his neck and clung to him.

We stood together, unmoving, needing that closeness for as long as we could.

Eventually, Sebastian kissed my hair.

"Let's go get some food," he said, quietly.

I nodded without speaking.

We stepped out into the evening, and I shivered in the chilly air. Sebastian held my hand and we walked slowly, the mountains behind us silent sentinels of our unspoken misery.

He led me to a small, intimate bistro, where the owner nodded at him familiarly, seemingly surprised to see him with company.

"I come here most days," he said, shrugging slightly.

I'd noticed that his room didn't have anywhere to cook. In fact, he didn't have so much as a kettle. My love lived simply.

I tried to lighten the mood, wanting him to remember our last night together for something other than the crushing pain I felt.

"Hmm, seems to me you need some cooking lessons, Sebastian. When you come home—to Long Beach—we'll have to have some fun with food."

His eyes glinted with mischief.

"Yeah, that would be great! Remember that chocolate sauce you bought that time? That was amazing—and I don't even like chocolate that much. Although it tasted damn fine on you."

"Don't use language like that with me, Sebastian. Chocolate is not something I joke about."

He grinned. "Okay, I get it. How do you feel about peanut butter?"

I wrinkled my nose. "I'll buy some for you: crunchy or smooth?"

"Crunchy," he replied, making the word sound incredibly dirty.

I smiled, happy to see him planning for our future, wishing it could be sooner, wishing things were different.

We didn't linger in the bistro. Even though it wasn't busy, we didn't want to spend our precious hours with anyone else.

Sebastian's room was barely warmer than outside when we climbed that narrow staircase for the last time, and I shivered.

"Cold, baby?"

"A little. Can we turn the heat on?"

He smiled at me. "No heating."

I stared at him in amazement. "None? Not even a space heater?"

He shook his head, amused. "Don't worry, Caro—I'll warm you up."

Oh well, who needed space heaters when hot Sebastian Hunter was an option?

I brushed my teeth in the chilly bathroom, and leapt into the narrow bed, still wearing my t-shirt and panties.

Sebastian was far hardier, strolling into the bedroom naked.

I feasted my eyes, trying to fix the image in my mind, and had to restrain myself from whipping out my camera for a more permanent memento. I reminded myself that I had many photographs to treasure from the last few days: pictures and memories, good memories.

He slipped in next to me, wrapping his body around mine.

"You know, Sebastian, while I really enjoyed the floor show, you'll have to wear more clothes at home."

He frowned. "Why?"

"Because," I smiled, "I live in a bungalow—and I have elderly neighbors. *We* have elderly neighbors, and I don't want you giving them a heart attack."

"Okay, boss," he smirked.

On the other hand, it would be a shame to miss out on that every night. Hell, I could buy thicker drapes.

He pulled me against his body and kissed me slowly, deeply and seriously. And then we made love, again and again, unwilling to waste a single second where our bodies were not intimately connected.

Sebastian moved inside me slowly, filling me inch by inch, rolling his hips, so I could feel him in every part of my core. Then he rolled onto his back, pulling me with him. He laid his hands flat on my belly as I arched up over him.

I placed my hands over his.

"Can you feel yourself inside me?"

"Yes," he said, with a smile, "I can."

We both remembered that I'd said those words to him the very first time we'd made love, when his eyes had been as wide with innocence, as they were now, with experience.

Too soon the night was over.

It was still dark when the alarm summoned him. Sebastian had left it as late as possible, needing every last minute with me, just as I needed him. I insisted on getting up and showering with him, sliding my hands over his body for one last time.

Then I watched him dress, and my lover became the soldier, pulling on his desert khaki utility uniform. It was the first time I'd seen him in the clothing he'd wear in combat. I wanted to scream and cry and cling to him and beg him not to go. I did none of those things. I pulled him to me, kissed him again and again, told him how much I loved him, again and again.

"*Tesoro*, go with my love, but take this with you. It's just silly, but I've always carried it with me when I leave home—but now I have your ring to wear."

I handed him a tiny pebble of polished quartz.

"I found it the first time I went to Long Beach."

He closed his eyes and kissed my hair.

"I've never had something to come back to before, Caro. Don't worry about me—just take care of yourself."

He kissed the little pebble and slipped it into his pocket.

"I love you, *tesoro*. Stay safe for me."

A car horn sounded in the street below us.

"Time to go, baby. Love you."

I watched from the window as he tossed his duffel bag into the car that waited for him. For a second he stared up at me, smiled, and then he was gone.

CHAPTER TWELVE

I WATCHED AS HIS CAR DISAPPEARED INTO THE DAWN, AND THE EMPTINESS I felt inside spilled out around me. I lay in Sebastian's bed, drinking in the scent of sheets that still smelled of him, stretching my hands into the cold void where he had slept, and cried myself into an exhausted stupor.

He had gone: when and where we would meet again was out of our hands. I hoped desperately, of course, that I would see him in Afghanistan, but beyond that, a long six months apart seemed more likely. I tried to tell myself that we'd weathered ten years. What was another few months?

With the sun rising higher in the cool, gray sky, I forced my eyes to open and stare around the empty room. My throat hurt from crying, and the skin on my face felt stiff from salty tears. Tough. Get on with it. Do your job and do it well.

Despite my mental ass-kicking, Sebastian's small shaving mirror offered a view of red, puffy eyes, lined with dark rings. I was glad he couldn't see how ghastly I looked. I wondered where he was now. Probably on his way to some military airfield in Germany, before being cooped up in an uncomfortable C5 troop transporter airplane with perhaps as many as 200 other soldiers, for six or seven hours.

Sebastian's possessions were piled into two boxes, ready for shipping stateside. I opened one, and placed inside the beautiful evening dress and matching shoes, silvery-gray underwear, and miniskirt that he'd bought for me. The leather ballerina flats I left out to take with me.

I laid out the rest of my clothes and equipment on the bed, checking and re-packing it for departure. I had kept hidden my own set of body armor from Sebastian. We'd both colluded in the illusion that our work was nothing to worry about, nothing to fear—a walk in the park. Hiding evidence of the lie had made it easier.

I'd acquired the body armor after my first visit to Sudan, when I discovered that the standard issue didn't fit someone who wasn't a six foot three, two-hundred pound soldier. After two weeks of wearing ill-fitting equipment day and night, I had backache that felt terminal, abs that would have thrilled a bodybuilder, and no boobs to speak of. My custom fit equipment was slightly smaller, but only a little less heavy. It was blue, to distinguish me from the military, although that was a double-edged sword: I wouldn't be shot as a soldier or a spy, but sometimes journalists and nonmilitary personnel were targeted as the more valuable kill. Even insurgents knew the value of PR.

The rest of my things were, perhaps, a little eccentric, but based on experience of several previous assignments to hostile environments. When working within US military zones, I always included Copenhagen Black tobacco as a gift for the soldiers who'd be assigned to babysit me. I'd learned that many of the men, especially those from the south, appreciated that little piece of home. I also carried garlic tablets, as one of the best means of avoiding insect and mosquito bites, and several packs of gum to counter the remedy. I had a pair of flip-flops, which were useful for crunching across floors where cockroaches had the run of the place in the night, a large sarong that could double as a towel, lightweight sheet, sleeping bag or mosquito net, and a knee-length man's shirt that I wore in Muslim countries, to provide some modesty over skimpy t-shirts. I'd tried wearing a burka but found I couldn't run in one, and somehow, it seemed more disrespectful to the local customs than simply showing that I understood their culture by covering up. I always carried a black headscarf: useful across the spectrum, from Catholic churches in Portugal, to bazaars in Baghdad.

Dry shampoo was a luxury as far as my male colleagues were concerned, but for me, it made the difference between feeling revoltingly and disgustingly dirty when there was no chance to shower for several days, and just a little less grubby. And thank heaven for whoever had invented baby-wipes. One other essential nonessential was a humble bottle of *tamari* soy sauce. People laughed at me when I produced my small bottle, but by the time they'd had MREs ration packs, three times a day for two weeks, the flavor my soy sauce could add, made me the most popular person around. Mango chutney was also a favorite.

I also carried lavender oil, earplugs, an eye-mask, and a thin, inflatable mattress given to me by a US Army captain whom I kissed when I realized how comfortable it was. Which wasn't something I'd be telling Sebastian about. His jealous streak was only ever a heartbeat away, and I had to remember that. I didn't like to see that side of him, but damn, it made me feel wanted.

I tried to keep my mind on the job—thinking about him would have me in tears again.

I checked my first aid supplies: dehydration tablets were important, but one of the most useful things for a woman, was a Mooncup, for those awkward times when sanitary napkins and tampons were impossible to find. I usually carried condoms with me, too. I'd never needed to use them, but I'd given them out to colleagues on a fairly regular basis. I'd been planning to buy some in Geneva while I was waiting for my permits to come through, but I'd met Sebastian first. Funny the way things worked out.

I also kept photocopies of my passport and Press ID badge, and would print out a dozen copies of my new credentials when I arrived at the airport. I kept JPEGs of important documents, which I emailed to a secret account that only I could access.

There was one more important job to do.

I booted up my laptop and emailed all the photographs of Sebastian to the same private account, then deleted everything from my camera, memory stick, laptop and phone. I couldn't risk anyone seeing them and identifying him as a US Marine. I was sorely tempted to keep one photo to look at, but it wasn't worth the risk, for either of us.

The tears began again as, one-by-one, those photographs that recorded our all too few days of happiness were wiped from my camera's memory. I knew Sebastian didn't have a photograph of me either. All he had was my stupid little pebble. Suddenly that seemed terribly important and I was glad I'd given it to him.

I stared at my beautiful engagement ring, then pulled it off my finger, placing it on a thin, gold chain around my neck, where I could imagine it was near to my heart.

I followed Sebastian's instructions for having his belongings shipped home, and then returned his door-key to a confused, elderly woman who answered the bell at his landlady's apartment.

I smiled and explained that *Monsieur* Hunter had left. She kept asking me if he'd gone back to America and, in the end, it seemed the easiest explanation to give her. I don't know who she thought I was, but she shook my hand and kissed me on both cheeks.

My taxi dropped me at the airport ninety minutes before my flight. From Geneva, I'd fly to Frankfurt and then pick up a charter to Kabul with a Turkish airline. There were a few commercial flights to Afghanistan, and I expected that I'd either be seated with NATO servicemen and women, or private contractors, engineers, doctors and builders, who were trying to help put the poor, broken country together again, plus a few Afghans, bravely returning home.

By the time we touched down to land in Afghanistan, I'd been traveling for nearly 18 hours. I'd slept a little on the plane overnight, but I was exhausted, although keyed up and excited as well.

My first sight of Kabul showed a sprawling, thriving city, squatting at the bottom of the Koh Daman Mountains of the Hindu Kush. Many of the ugly, boxy homes that had begun to creep up into the foothills were made from the same dusty yellow as the soil itself.

It was a city of contrasts where ancient palaces stood next to a few modest skyscrapers, small mud houses snuggled next to gaudy compounds, narrow alleys led out to wide, modern roads thronged with vehicles of every brand, age, and stage of decay, and modern opulence walked side by side with biblical poverty.

Men with Rolex watches had their Mercedes washed by children who had no shoes. International aid had flooded the desperately poor country with money, but the distribution left much to be desired, and it was whispered that billions of aid dollars had flowed out of the country into private numbered accounts in Swiss banks.

The streets were full of people going about their business: women in blue headscarves, men in a mixture of traditional robes and western clothing. Cars coughed fumes into the hot, dry air, and motorcycles with carpets for seats roared around, ignored by the donkeys pulling carts, and herds of goats that seemed to roam freely. The ever-present sound of people talking, arguing and selling their wares poured from rows of dimly-lit doorways.

But everywhere were signs of war: bomb-blasted buildings, walls with bullet holes, and ugly, burned out patches where cars had been used as weapons, exploding to shower hot fragments of metal over anyone who had been too close.

The bulletproof car that collected me from the heavily guarded airport now dropped me in a secure parking compound at the Mustafa Hotel. I was escorted inside by a burly Marine sergeant who answered to the name of Benson. I didn't know if that was his first name or last, but his comfortable bulk made me feel safer.

The hotel was a favorite with correspondents, as was the owner, a regular Mr. Fix-it. And, even better, I'd heard from Liz before I'd left Geneva: she was still in Kabul, waiting on a ride out to Camp Bastion to report on how British troops were training the Afghan National Army, with a view to a complete handover by 2014. There were few who didn't think 'the sooner the better', but it was hard to see how the country would ever be ready to rule itself. Perhaps democracy didn't suit a land where decisions were traditionally made at a tribal level. But I was there to report, not have an opinion or look for solutions—thank God.

Liz had sent me a message saying that she'd happily share her twin-bed room at the Mustafa Hotel, which was perfect. There was safety in numbers, especially for women traveling alone. She'd also ensured that the room was not on the ground floor (too unsafe, for obvious reasons), and no higher than the third floor, as the fire escapes in Kabul were notorious for their shoddy construction.

I checked in, and was then escorted to my room by a cheerful boy in dirty white robes whose only English seemed to consist of 'Hello', 'yes' and 'jolly good'. I suspected Liz had taught him the latter phrase.

The room was eye-wateringly colorful, decorated in a discordant array of oranges, yellows and reds. But it was comfortable and reasonably clean. Better still, it had its own bathroom. A luxury I'd be doing without once I was at Leatherneck.

I was grateful to drop the heavy bags and read the note that Liz had left. She informed me that we'd been invited to a dinner party being held by the UN for local military, Press, and important Afghan government officials. It was taking place at the Intercontinental Hotel—and I had 40 minutes to get my 'arse' over there.

So much for having a rest.

The shower sputtered intermittently, but it was nearly hot, and washed away most of the yellow dust that seemed to coat every part of me.

Formal functions in some Muslim countries could be a cultural minefield. Since this dinner was including women, it wasn't going to be truly orthodox, so I wasn't too worried about what to wear. I had my tried and trusted black cocktail dress, and planned to match it with the black ballerina flats that Sebastian bought for me. My ring was on the necklace hidden beneath my dress, but I could feel it, and that was important.

The dress had long sleeves, a high neckline, and a knee-length skirt. It passed in more conservative circles, and Liz had thoughtfully informed me that there would be a number of Muslim guests tonight. And although they were likely to be of the more liberal persuasion as women would be present, I didn't want to risk giving offense. I had my plain, black headscarf in my purse to cover all eventualities.

It was lucky I was dark haired and dark eyed, because once I'd donned my headscarf, I attracted little interest. If I'd been blonde haired and blue eyed, it would have been a very different story. As soon as my sweet Sergeant Benson escorted me to the Intercontinental, I went to the restroom to take off my headscarf and brush out my hair.

My attention was caught by a stunning woman in a jade-green, designer gown, with plunging neckline and exposed back. She would have been perfect for a glitzy LA premiere, but here she was jaw-dropping—and not in a good way.

I suspected she was with the UN—certainly no journalist would be so ridiculously overexposed and underprepared, and I was surprised that no one had warned her to dress more appropriately. In the spirit of sisterhood, I decided to give her a heads-up.

"Excuse me, hi. My name is Lee Venzi, I'm with the Press. Forgive me, your dress is really beautiful, but it might give you some problems here tonight: for Muslims, green is Mohammed's favorite color—they might find your choice, as a Western woman, disrespectful. And a more ... conservative style usually goes down better."

"Oh, I never bother with formalities like that," she sneered, rolling her eyes up and down my simple, black dress with obvious contempt.

I was left speechless by her arrogant attitude. I seriously considered jamming her head under the faucet to see if her heavy mascara really was waterproof.

She left me standing, and turned to her friend who was applying an indecent amount of lipstick, although at least her dress was more respectful and less revealing.

"You're dressed to impress, Natalie," said the second woman, in a heavy, German accent. She gave her friend's designer gown the same visual appraisal as my own, but with less honesty. "I wonder if I can guess who you have your eye on —seeing as you mentioned you'd bumped into him again."

The woman named Natalie smiled coolly.

"What can I say, Hanna? He's a five-star fuck: stamina and expertise, with fabulous packaging. Paris was memorable. I'm planning on having another night to remember. Who'd have thought Kabul could be so entertaining."

I followed the two women out of the restroom, shaking my head.

"What a bitch!" I muttered to myself.

"You don't know how right you are," said a familiar voice.

I whirled around, beyond thrilled.

He looked dashing and so handsome in his Dress Blues, my heart leapt with joy, reveling in the fact that he was here, that I was here—that we were together so much sooner than either of us could have hoped.

"Sebastian! What are you doing here? I thought they were sending you to Kandahar?"

"Change of plan," he said, his eyes dancing with happiness. "I've had a two-day stopover and I'd heard the Press would be here tonight, so I wangled an invite. I wasn't sure when you were arriving." He grinned at me wickedly. "But now that you're here, I'm planning on seducing you behind the potted palms."

"Or somewhere a little more private, I hope," I breathed out.

His eyes flared with excitement. "Yes, ma'am."

"By the way, do you know her?" I asked, jerking my head in the general direction of the rude woman.

He smirked. "Her name is Natalie Arnaud. French. She's a PA for some guy at the UN; she likes people to think she's important."

"And you know her because...?"

He didn't answer, looking away.

"One of your Parisian conquests."

'He's a five-star fuck.' Oh no.

"It was just a warm body, Caro," he said, correctly reading the expression on my face.

"I understand that," *sort of*, "but she's going to get herself into trouble. She's only dressing like that to impress you, Sebastian, so you'd better speak to her."

I felt proud of myself for taking the moral high ground. Sebastian scowled at me, clearly unhappy with the mission I'd just given him.

"Suck it up, Hunter," I smirked at him. "You could say that you created this situation, so you have to deal with it. And then find somewhere private for us."

He shook his head in irritation at my insistence he deal with the woman, but smiled and threw me a cocky salute.

"Yes, boss."

Then his smile faded and his eyes darkened in a way that made me long to run my hands over his strong body, and push my tongue between his soft, sensual lips.

I knew he was on the same page, because he glanced around, took my hand and tugged me down the corridor. We were clearly in the staff area of the hotel, because we passed several cramped rooms full of desks and crammed with filing cabinets.

But when Sebastian found an empty office that was larger than a closet, he pushed me inside, slammed me against the door, and kissed me roughly, the buttons of his uniform pressing painfully into my breasts.

His hand was under my dress, dragging the skirt up to my waist, his fingers circling the edge of my panties, and then he ran one long finger under the material and inside me, making me cry out.

"Fuck, you're wet," he hissed.

I moaned in reply.

"I am so fucking hard right now," he growled into my ear. "Here and now: yes or no, Caro?"

"Yes!"

He unzipped his fly quickly, rolling a condom over his erection, while I shimmied out of my panties.

"Bend over the desk," he ordered, as he gripped my hips.

"Sebastian, the door!"

"Fuck," he snarled, spinning around and wedging a chair against the handle.

I leaned over the desk, completely aroused by the unexpected and illicit nature of the moment.

He hauled my dress up over my ass, forced my feet apart with his, and plunged inside me. I heard his breath hiss out through his teeth. He pulled out slowly, then pushed back in, making me feel every inch of him.

He angled his body and rolled his hips, making me clutch hold of the edge of the desk. My insides quivered in response, and I could hear his soft grunts as he continued to thrust deeply.

I pushed my hips backward to meet him and he groaned loudly, picking up the pace and pounding into me frantically, almost desperate in his desire and need.

I couldn't take any more—I thought my legs were going to buckle when I came—but he didn't stop, pounding on and on and on, in a way that would leave bruises across my hip bones from the wooden desk.

I felt his body shudder and empty into me, and his chest rested on my back for a brief moment before he pulled out. I sank to my knees, and collapsed onto the floor. He lay down next to me, his breath hot on my neck. I twisted around to gaze into his eyes, softly brushing the tips of my fingers over his face.

I didn't need to ask why he'd fucked me like that, with such desperation: it was an adrenaline rush—the heightened sense of awareness that came from being in a war zone and close to death. It was an intense need to prove that you were still alive, to reaffirm life.

"Fuck, that wasn't enough, Caro. I want you again."

"We can't, Sebastian," I panted. "As it is, we'll be missed if we don't hurry."

He frowned unhappily and tugged my limp hand to his lips, sucking my fingers, one by one.

"I need you, Caro. Let me come to your room tonight, please, baby."

"You can't, I'm sharing with Liz."

"Get rid of her!" he whispered, persuasively into my ear.

Suddenly someone rattled the door handle, and I could hear men's voices outside.

"Fuck it," he hissed, tucking himself in quickly.

"My panties," I said, feeling panicky.

Sebastian grinned at me, and searched around until he found them hanging disconsolately from a handle on the desk drawer like the flag of a defeated army.

"I think these are yours, ma'am."

"Thank you," I said, hurriedly pulling them on and straightening my skirt.

The door handle rattled again, and I held my breath, but the voices receded into the distance, arguing with each other.

Sebastian helped me up, and listened intently at the door. He hesitated, glancing back at me, then opened it cautiously.

"You're good to go," he said, quietly, his eyes searching the corridor in both directions.

I raised an eyebrow. "You're not so bad yourself, Sarge."

He grinned wickedly. "Later?"

But then we heard more voices coming toward us, I smiled once, and hurried away.

He let me go first, and I made my way into the reception area, where people who'd been invited to the dinner were circulating.

I was concentrating on calming my breathing when I heard someone say my name.

"Hello, Caroline."

I recognized that voice. And only one person called me 'Caroline'.

A cold shiver ran down my spine, and I turned slowly.

My ex-husband stood in front of me, a stiff smile on his face. He looked handsome, in a silver fox sort of way.

"Hello, David," I said warily, as feelings of dislike and distrust swept over me.

"I heard you were here tonight: the famous war correspondent 'Lee Venzi', as you're known now."

I listened out for the sarcasm in his words, but I wasn't certain I could hear any. How odd.

"I see you've been promoted, Captain Wilson," I replied, keeping my voice neutral. "Congratulations, David."

He looked pleased and surprised. "Thank you."

Meeting one's ex-husband was never going to be a Kodak moment, but this was perhaps more than usually awkward, bearing in mind my cheeks were still flushed from screwing Sebastian in an office about 40 yards away.

But David's next comment took me by complete surprise.

"I've enjoyed reading your articles, Caroline. They show great insight."

He gestured around him to indicate all things military. Compliments from David were rare. Very rare.

"Thank you very much," I said, as my eyebrows rose up to my hairline. "I'm ... flattered."

I thought David was going to say something else, but what he saw over my shoulder made him lose his composure, and a familiar expression of haughty disdain transformed his features.

"I see you're still with him," he said, coldly.

I knew immediately who he was talking about, of course.

"I must say I'm surprised, Caroline."

I felt the heat of Sebastian's furious glare as he came storming over.

Military protocol demanded that he salute a superior officer, even one from another service, and David was Navy, not the Marine Corps. Instead, Sebastian shoved his hands in his pockets with deliberate insolence.

David frowned, but just when I was sure he would insist on his dues, he simply ignored Sebastian and looked back at me.

"Good to see you, Caroline. You look lovely tonight. I hope you enjoy the evening."

And he strolled away, greeting a few people as he moved through the room.

"What the fuck were you doing talking to that asshole?" snarled Sebastian.

"What are *you* doing making it so damned obvious that you care?" I shot back angrily.

"Why aren't you wearing your ring?" he asked, sounding hurt.

I guess he'd been too busy fucking me over a desk to notice before.

"I am wearing it—just not where anyone can see it. But right now I am so furious with you: all you've done is make it absolutely necessary for me to go to my ex-husband and beg him not to tell anyone about us. Have you any idea how that makes me feel, Sebastian? Do you? Because he's the last person I'd want to ask a favor from."

"I'll handle him," said Sebastian, arrogantly. "I'll..."

"You'll do nothing," I hissed. "Absolutely nothing, do you hear me? Now leave me alone. You've already attracted enough attention tonight."

I walked away, leaving him standing, his expression wounded, angry and defiant.

I forced myself to smile politely as I moved through the crowd, but inside I was fuming: Sebastian wasn't particularly risking his own career, but he was damn well risking mine—again. Who the hell did he think he was?

I made myself concentrate. I was here to meet the unit commander that I'd be embedded with, a Captain Ryan Grant. In all likelihood he'd resent having a journalist assigned to him. As far as he'd be concerned, having some hack looking over his shoulder when he was trying to do his job was nothing more than an irritating, additional worry. I just hoped he'd behave with polite tolerance rather than make my position more difficult. At least I knew that someone senior to him had made the decision to give me access, which meant I shouldn't have a problem with open hostility. I hoped.

I'd been informed that I'd be seated next to him at dinner. I could wait until then for introductions.

First, thanks to Sebastian's ridiculous territorial display, I had to go and grovel to David. I hated the fact that he'd handed David the power to ruin my career with a few, quiet words in the right ear.

My former husband was standing talking to an Army Major when I walked up.

"Hello, again," I said, blandly.

He blinked, looking surprised, then politely introduced me. I was taken aback when he used my professional name: that was decent of him.

We chatted casually for a few minutes, before the Major was claimed by a colleague and moved away.

"David," I said, taking a deep breath, "I won't insult your intelligence. I'm here to ask you not to reveal what you know about me and Master Sergeant Hunter."

He raised his eyebrows.

"It was certainly a surprise, Caroline, but no, of course I wouldn't dream of saying anything that could hurt your career."

I was shocked he was being so magnanimous. I'd expected that he'd take the chance to belittle me. He'd been an expert at it while we were married.

"Thank you, David. That's very good of you."

"I would suggest, however," he said, calmly, "that you advise him to act with more circumspection."

"Yes. I've already mentioned it," I said, a little bitterly.

He gave a thin smile.

"He seems just as hotheaded as ever."

Yes, you could say that.

"You were taking a great risk, continuing your relationship," he couldn't help adding. "But despite what you may think of me, Caroline, I have never wished you ill."

I met his eyes, but saw only sincere concern.

"Thank you for that," I said, with more warmth than I thought I'd ever feel for him. "I will try to minimize any more ... risk."

He cocked his head to one side and looked at me quizzically.

"I meant it was a risk to continue seeing each other when he was ...well, younger."

I stared at him, finally realizing what he was alluding to.

"David, that's not it. I haven't seen Sebastian for ten years. We met again by accident, eleven days ago in Geneva."

He looked dumbstruck. "But I thought ... the way he behaved just now ... well, I see I was mistaken."

At which point an announcement was made in English, French and Pashto to call us in to dinner.

"I do wish you well, Caroline," he said, briskly. "And I meant what I said: you look lovely tonight."

He smiled briefly, and then offered his arm to escort me in to dinner.

I accepted, baffled by his pleasantness and consideration.

He helped me into my seat, then with a half-smile, disappeared toward his place at another table.

CHAPTER THIRTEEN

I SAT AT ONE OF THE LONG BANQUETING TABLES IN A STATE OF MILD SHOCK. I had never known David to be so considerate, especially when it was anything concerning me. During our 11 years of marriage, he'd been a domineering bully and ... no, 'domineering bully' said it all. Since the divorce, I'd had nothing to do with him, I certainly hadn't known he'd be in Afghanistan. Maybe he was working at the hospital at Bagram Air Base north of Kabul.

My attention was diverted when I noticed that the woman in green had swooped into the room and was eyeing the place cards. I had a strong suspicion that if I kept watching her, I'd see her swapping them around. Well, that was Sebastian's lookout, I doubted he'd have too many problems with her—I was pretty certain he'd had plenty of practice dealing with overly friendly women. I tried to brush the thought away—I had other, more important issues to concentrate on tonight.

"Excuse me, ma'am, I think you might be in the wrong seat."

I looked up to see a man in the Dress Blues of a US Marine Corps captain gazing down at me. He was perhaps a few years younger than me with a strong face, and clear, gray eyes.

"Captain Grant?"

"That's right, ma'am," he said, looking puzzled. "And you are?"

"Lee Venzi. I'll be embedded with you for the next month. It's good to meet you."

He looked bemused. "*You're* Lee Venzi?"

"Let me guess," I said, with a polite smile, "you were expecting a man. I get that a lot."

He gaped, looked thoroughly pissed off, then settled for a cool disinterest.

"It's a pleasure to meet you, ma'am."

We shook hands as he eyed me cautiously.

Don't worry: I won't bite—you're not my type.

"Please don't be concerned, Captain Grant. This is not my first time being embedded with US troops, and I don't expect any level of comfort beyond that of the average private. I will try to impact on your command as little as possible. I would suggest we meet soon to discuss protocols for the next month. I'm not here to do a hatchet job, Captain."

"Then you'll let me read what you write before it's filed?"

"That's one of the protocols we can discuss, but no, my editor is the only person who sees my work prior to publication."

It was important to explain up front how I worked. I didn't particularly want to do that over the dinner table, but as he'd asked, I'd give him the courtesy of a clear and concise answer.

A reluctant smile crept across his face.

"Something to discuss, ma'am."

"Certainly there will be many things to discuss, Captain," I said, politely. "I have agreed to the rules of being embedded with your unit, but beyond that, my authorial independence will not be something we discuss."

He raised his eyebrows but wisely didn't pursue the point.

From the corner of my eye, I saw Sebastian enter the room and move toward a group of Afghan men dressed in the traditional *salwar kameez*, worn with the oval *qaraqul* hats. He exchanged some pleasantries, then went to search for his place card. He looked puzzled because it wasn't in the general area that he'd expected. When he saw the Green Bitch, comprehension washed over him and he looked pissed.

I couldn't help feeling a mean little frisson of self-righteousness.

Your problem, Hunter.

He seated himself politely next to the French woman, who looked like she wanted to perform a lap dance before the antipasti.

At first, he seemed to shrug off her advances, but then I saw her lay a discreet hand on his thigh, and my blood boiled.

"Lee! Are you stalking me, woman?"

Liz's dulcet tones turned heads and I couldn't help smiling, more than a little grateful for her timely interruption of my silent fuming.

She was wearing an ankle-length dress in navy blue, so voluminous, that she looked like a ship in full sail.

"Hi, Liz. Thanks for the room-share. Let me introduce you to Captain Ryan Grant; Captain, Elizabeth Ashton—she's a correspondent for *The Times* of London."

They shook hands, each weighing up the other.

"Have you seen that miserable bastard Hunter is here?" Liz said to me, as soon as the brief pleasantries were over. "Up to his old tricks with the French floozie."

I winced, and saw Captain Grant frown.

"Yes, there are a few familiar faces, Liz. Stroud and Van Marten are here."

"Really? I must go and chew on their earflaps for a minute, Lee. I'll see you later. Captain," and she hurried off.

"A colleague of yours, ma'am?"

"Yes, and a friend."

I could see that Captain Grant was beginning to be grateful that it was me and not Liz who was going to be embedded with him. But then his eyes flickered back to Sebastian, who was staring coldly at his dinner companion. When she laid a proprietary hand on his arm and leaned across to touch one of his medals, Captain Grant's eyes narrowed.

"Excuse me, ma'am," he muttered.

He stood up abruptly and walked toward them. Sebastian rose to his feet and saluted sharply. It was clear the Captain was asking about the seating arrangements, and Sebastian was trying to point out he'd just followed the place card's instructions.

I watched as Captain Grant took him to one side and seemed to be giving him a dressing down. Sebastian stood to attention, and I could see that he was gazing about three inches above the Captain's left shoulder.

After that, Sebastian left the room, leaving the disappointed woman by herself, and Captain Grant returned to my side.

"Is there a problem, Captain?" I asked, casually.

"No, ma'am, just my interpreter, he'd been seated at the wrong table."

"*Your* interpreter," I said, feeling a shiver travel down my spine.

"Yes, newly assigned to my command."

Oh crap.

"I gather you know him, ma'am?" he said, looking at me astutely.

"We've met," I said, maintaining a casual smile. "Master Sergeant Hunter was the languages expert when I had my hostile environment briefing in Geneva. He lectured on useful phrases in Pashto, Dari and Arabic if I remember correctly."

Captain Grant nodded, accepting my words at face value, and we talked about the forthcoming deployment to Leatherneck and beyond.

I didn't see Sebastian again during the meal, and the Green Bitch had an empty space next to her for the entire time. I also noted that someone must have spoken to her, because she now wore a black pashmina that covered up her cleavage and shoulders for the rest of the evening.

It was fascinating to see who had been invited to the dinner and who had not. There were a number of UN officials that I recognized, as well as British, German, and American officers. Among the Afghan men—and there were no women—I sensed there was something more going on than a simple meet and greet. I kept track of the comings and goings, who was talking to whom. There was definitely excitement in the air.

The evening ended without any more tangible developments occurring. Captain Grant nodded politely and said he'd send a driver to my hotel at 5AM the following morning. We'd be loading up and heading out to Camp Leatherneck, 350 miles away along the notorious Kabul–Kandahar Highway.

Two decades of war and neglect had left the road connecting Afghanistan's two main cities in disrepair. The US had funded the rebuilding of three-quarters of the road, with Japan chipping in another chunk of money. It was currently in slightly better repair, but it had become a favorite target of the Taliban—and not a journey to be undertaken lightly, even by the mighty US armed forces. Certainly not by a woman-journalist from Long Beach.

I waited in the lobby for Liz, and when she finally emerged, she was fizzing with excitement. She eyed our driver, the same bulky Sergeant Benson who'd dropped me off at the start of the evening, before allowing him to escort us to our car. She grabbed my elbow and began whispering at top speed.

"I picked up some very interesting snippets, Lee. Something is definitely in the air."

"Yes, I thought so, too. Azimi was talking to Chalabi, and you don't often see Sunnis and Shiites being that friendly."

Liz raised her eyebrows. "Interesting! Well, I'd say, looking at the bigwigs there tonight, it's a US op. Could be going down from Leatherneck, Lee. Keep your ear to the ground for me, will you?"

"You think I'd hand you a scoop?" I asked, teasing her.

"No, of course not, but I'm sure you won't leave your old mucker out in the cold, either."

"I'll take it under advisement."

"Huh, bloody colonials," she snorted.

I laughed. To Liz, half the population of the world were 'colonials'.

We drove quickly through the busy streets, people hurrying home before the night-time curfew.

Back at the hotel, Liz tried to persuade me to have a drink with her in the bar. She'd heard that someone had gotten hold of alcohol from the local market. Apparently the blanket ban wasn't taken too seriously by some of the locals despite the Sharia law, although punishment for those who bought, sold or consumed the evil brew could be a fine, imprisonment, or even 60 lashes with a whip.

"Come down with me, Lee, it should be a laugh. After I get out of this god-awful frock," she said, tugging on the hem of her blue tent.

"No, thanks, Liz. I'm going to take a hot bath. Since it'll be my last for a month, I want to enjoy soaking in an actual tub."

Liz had just changed out of her dress and into her usual Berghaus hiking pants and long-sleeved shirt, when there was a soft tap at the door.

We were immediately on the alert: it was a golden rule never to let anyone know which room you were staying in. If you needed to meet a contact, you met them in the lobby. Journalists were deemed to be easy targets—and our bodyguard was long gone.

"Who knows you're here?" Liz hissed at me.

"My embed liaison and my editor. You?"

"Same. Stay away from the door and get ready to phone for help."

I picked up my cell, checking that I had Sergeant Benson on speed dial. I nodded at her, my finger poised over the button, and she called out aggressively,

"Yes?"

"Ma'am, I'm looking for Lee Venzi?"

I recognized Sebastian's voice at once, relief, lust and irritation each took their turn as I moved toward the door.

"What are you doing?" Liz whispered, grabbing my arm.

"It's okay, I know who it is."

She relaxed a fraction, but still hung onto my arm.

"Is this a romantic assignation, Lee?" she said, with surprise and some annoyance.

"Kind of," I muttered, "although I didn't know he'd come here tonight. It wasn't planned. I'm sorry, Liz."

"This really isn't like you," she said, frowning.

"I know," I said, apologetically.

I pulled open the door, and Sebastian quickly stepped into the room.

Liz's face was a picture.

"Sebastian, you've met my friend Liz Ashton."

"Yes," he said, stiffly.

"Sergeant Hunter," replied Liz, glaring at him with obvious dislike.

I rubbed my forehead.

"I'm sorry about this, Liz, but can you give us some time alone?"

She snorted and shook her head, muttering something that sounded like, "bloody fool".

I presumed she meant me, although her words fit Sebastian just as well. I had a few choice words of my own to say to Master Sergeant Hunter.

"Two hours, Lee," she said, glancing at her watch with zero subtlety. "I'll be downstairs in the bar if you need me."

She threw a final, accusing look at Sebastian and left.

I was still deciding what to say to him as I shut and locked the door, but before I could speak, he tugged me into his arms and kissed me.

His tongue was in my mouth and his hands pressing into my flesh, chasing all thoughts but one from my overheated brain.

When he finally let go, I was breathless and aroused—which was probably his plan—but I wasn't letting his outrageous behavior go unchallenged either.

"What the hell are you doing, Sebastian?"

He shrugged and grinned at me. "I thought I'd kiss you before you yelled at me. Guess it didn't work."

"You think this is a joke?" I asked, my voice rising with frustrated disbelief. "First David, now Liz. Why don't you just skywrite it?"

"What did the asshole say to you?"

I sighed. "He's not going to tell anyone—he was really nice about it."

Sebastian scowled.

"Liz won't say anything to anyone either—I'll just have to listen to her chewing me out later. But I'd have much rather she didn't know just now—she's my *work* colleague. You've got to stop taking these risks, Sebastian. For my sake, if you won't do it for yourself."

He grimaced. "I'm sorry, Caro. I just go a little crazy around you."

Not good enough.

"Well, you have to get it under control. Now please, please tell me your assignment to Ryan Grant is temporary."

He stared at me. "Fuck! I was wondering why they'd seated you next to him. Are you embedded with him? Shit!"

"Exactly my thoughts. He can't know, or it'll really screw things up for both of us—well, mainly for me. Sebastian, you're going to have to act like you did in Geneva, as if you still dislike me—or at the very least, ignore me. Can you do that?"

"Fuck, Caro," he sighed. "Yes, I can do it. But I'll hate every fucking minute."

"At least if we're in the same Camp, I'll know what you're doing and that you're safe."

He gave me a small smile.

"Same goes for you. Yeah, there is that. And we might get a chance to hook up?"

I shook my head, even as the image took shape.

"No, too dangerous. You can't risk it and I *definitely* can't risk it. Grant isn't an idiot."

"No, he seems on the ball."

"On the plus side, Grant already thinks you dislike me."

Sebastian frowned. "Because...?"

"Liz—she mentioned that we'd met in Geneva, and at that stage, she still thought you were an ass. Well, that hasn't changed, but just a different sort of ass now."

He gave me a crooked smile.

"An ass?"

"Big time."

He leaned against the door and crossed his arms, his head cocked to one side, a damn sexy smile on his face.

"What happened with your friend Natalie?" I asked, not prepared to let him off the hook just yet.

His smile vanished. "She's no fucking friend. She wouldn't take no for an answer, and then Grant kicked me out because of her."

"What did he say to you?"

Sebastian shifted uncomfortably.

"Oh, well, never mind—I can guess. She didn't look pleased either—I think she was planning to have you for dessert. Was it you who told her to cover up?"

"Yeah, not that it made any difference."

"She must have listened to someone. At least you tried. And you are *very* trying, Master Sergeant Hunter. Part of me wants to slap some sense into you..."

"And the other part?" he murmured, wetting his lips with his tongue.

"Well," I said, running a finger down the red braid that edged his uniform jacket, "I was wondering what we could do for the next..." I checked my wristwatch, "...115 minutes?"

I thought Sebastian would leap on me but he closed his eyes, as if he was in pain.

"What's the matter, *tesoro*?"

"I really fucking hate this, Caro. We're always running in different directions, we're always running out of time. I just want to wake up with you in my arms every day."

Oh, he could say the most romantic things at the time when I most needed to hear them.

"I know, Sebastian, and I feel the same. But it won't be like that forever—we will be together. We just have to be patient." I stroked his cheek, "And for now, we have 113 minutes left."

His eyes snapped open.

"Fuck!"

Suddenly we were all fumbling, hurried hands, panting into each other's mouths, as Sebastian tried to tear off his uniform and undress me at the same time. I was naked and ready long before him, so I lent a helping hand, which didn't seem to help much.

"Damn it, Caro," he groaned, as I pressed myself against him, feeling the thick material against my heated skin.

He backed me toward my bed, his erection rigid against my thigh. I fell backward and then burst into laughter.

"What?"

"The whole pants around the ankles thing—it's not a great look."

He grinned ruefully as he toed off his shiny shoes.

"Guess I'd better lose the socks, too."

"Definitely."

When every item of clothing had been stripped off, he stood next to the bed and gazed down at me. I didn't feel like laughing now.

"You like what you see, Caro?" he asked, with a low, rough voice.

I nodded, my mouth suddenly dry.

"After tonight, well, we don't know when ... so I want you to remember me like this ... when you look at me—see me like this, wanting you."

And he stroked himself, his eyes half closing as he breathed in deeply.

"And when I look at you, this is what I'll be thinking about: close your eyes."

Reluctantly, I let my eyelids flutter down.

The mattress moved beneath me, and I felt Sebastian's warm hands on my ankles. Slowly, he moved my legs apart, then he kissed his way up to my thigh, and my breath caught in my throat.

He didn't stop, and I didn't want him to stop. I wanted him loving me forever.

Sometime later, we lay in each other's arms, peaceful and blissfully sated.

Suddenly, an enormous explosion erupted outside, rattling the windows of the hotel. Sebastian grabbed me and pulled me onto the floor by the side of the bed, away from the window. He waited for ten seconds, then cautiously rose to his feet, standing to one side of the window to peer out.

"Probably a car bomb—about half a mile away."

I was still shivering on the floor.

"It's okay, Caro. We're okay."

I'm sure we were both thinking the same thing: we were okay, but somewhere out there in the night, people had lost their lives, even now lying on the ground, bleeding into the dust. I wondered if Liz would be off to the site, to report on what had happened. Sometimes it felt important to be on the frontline, telling people back home what was happening in this far away war, but sometimes if felt like we were no better than war pornographers, capturing the misery of other people on film or in photographs, asking them at their most desperate moment to give us a sound bite to file and send home. Job done.

It was a fine line to tread, and not one we always got right. But I still thought that what we did was ultimately worthwhile—I had to.

I stood up hesitantly, naked and feeling exposed.

Usually when I was on assignment in a dangerous location, I wore clothes day and night. You never knew when you might have to evacuate your hotel room in a hurry, when the time it took to put on pants and a t-shirt was going to be the difference between life and death.

But with Sebastian, I broke all the rules.

"Caro, are you okay, baby?"

"Yes, I guess so. Just knowing that out there ... you'll be facing that soon."

He strode over to me.

"Christ, I know that, Caro, and it kills me to know that you'll be out there, too. Please, baby, please, go home while you still can. I'm fucking begging you, Caro!"

He held me tight against his chest, and I could feel his heart hammering as he buried his head in my hair.

"Please, baby. I need to know you're safe. If anything happened to you now..."

My arms crept around his neck, and I pulled his face down to kiss him softly.

"I have a job to do, Sebastian, you know that. So do you, and I will worry about you every day. I pray to God that you'll come home to me. Please, *tesoro*, promise you'll look after yourself—no unnecessary risks?"

He sighed. "I promise, Caro."

"Then come back to bed with me," I said, tugging his hand.

Time was slipping away too fast.

He lay on his back and I snuggled into his arms, one hand on his waist, and my head resting just above his heart, listening to its firm, even rhythm.

I didn't want our last night together to be filled with such sadness.

My fingers drifted over his muscular chest, across his ribs and down to his flat stomach. I pushed the sheet down, exposing his hair and the tip of something even more desirable and arousing.

"Sebastian, if that's what I have to imagine every time you look at me, I'm not going to get any work done."

He smiled and kissed my hand.

"Let's go back to Signora Carello's place for our honeymoon, Caro. We could fuck for days without getting out of bed."

I could tell that he was trying to lighten the mood, too, I was happy to play along with the fantasy.

"What, you think she could just push food under the door so you can keep your strength up, because I have to say, Sebastian, you were getting a little out of breath just now. I really thought the US Marines had higher standards of fitness: I might have to write about that in my next article. Of course, the research is incomplete—I've only documented one Marine's fitness levels in detail..."

"And it's going to stay that way," he said, firmly.

I laughed. "Feeling threatened? Me alone with all those horny Marines, I'm quoting, of course."

"Not funny," he grumbled.

"Okay, I won't tease you. Yes, we could go back to Signora Carello's, but there are lots of other places I'd like to see in Italy. Florence, the open air opera in Rome—I'd love to do that. But you know, I really like the idea of taking your old motorcycle and seeing upstate New York. What do *you* want to do?"

"Other than have a lot of sex?"

"My God! That's exactly the same answer you gave me ten years ago when you were a horny teenager!"

"So? I'm consistent. I thought women liked that in men?"

He had a point.

Lazily, he ran one hand between my breasts, toying with the chain that held my engagement ring.

"You have the most fantastic breasts, Caro. I can't stand those fake ones, they just feel so..."

He realized what he'd said, or nearly said, and stopped abruptly.

"Hmm, I was thinking, Sarge, maybe you should be one of those men who are strong and silent. You know, nice to look at, not so good at the talking."

He playfully bit my shoulder and twisted around, pushing me into the mattress.

"Is that right?"

"Yes. Hearing you talk about your *conquests* when I'm in a state of post-coital bliss isn't going to earn you round two."

"Huh, so I can't *earn* round two—does that mean I can pay for it instead?"

I slapped his ass, hard. "You couldn't afford me."

"You sure about that, baby? What's your price?"

"What have you got to offer, Sebastian?"

He used his hips to pin me down, his chest hovering over mine. "An orgasm?"

"That's just *quid pro quo*."

"Fuck, I love it when you talk dirty. What about two orgasms?"

"Two? Beginning to sound interesting, but do you think you're up to the job?"

One thing about Sebastian: he was always up for a challenge. Up and up.

Over an hour later, we were collapsed on the bathroom floor, flushed and breathless.

"I'd forgotten you had a thing for bathrooms," I gasped.

He kissed the back of my neck. "I like the mirrors."

"You know, that's a little kinky, Sebastian."

"You think? I'd like to get kinky with you, Caro," he said, tugging on my earlobe with his teeth and running his fingers over my hipbone.

The thought was intriguing.

"What did you have in mind?"

I felt him shrug. "You could tie me up again: that was hot."

"Hmm, well, I could talk to one of the MPs at Leatherneck—maybe I'll see if I can borrow a pair of handcuffs, Sebastian."

He didn't answer, so I nudged him in the ribs.

"Yeah, if you like, Caro."

"If *I* like? What do *you* like?"

He hesitated. "There's some stuff we could try."

"Such as?"

There was a soft tap at the door and I heard Liz's voice.

"Oh, hell. You'd better get dressed, Sebastian, unless a three-way with Liz was one of your fantasies?"

He shuddered. "Fuck, Caro! I'm going to have that image in my head now."

I grinned at him. "Better get your pants on then, Sarge."

I pulled on a baggy t-shirt and some pajama bottoms, checked Sebastian was halfway decent, and opened the door.

"Lee, I ... oh, is he still here?"

"He's just leaving, Liz."

Sebastian was sitting on my bed, tying his shoelaces when Liz marched into the room.

"There's a curfew on, Hunter," she said, crossing her arms across her substantial chest.

"Thanks," he said, shortly.

"You must have heard the car bomb: three dead, multiple injured. Bastards packed the bomb with nails."

"So evil," I murmured.

Liz nodded silently, and Sebastian pressed his lips together without speaking.

He stood up, pulled on his jacket and fastened the buckle on his white web belt.

He ignored Liz's chilly gaze and pulled me into a tight hug, leaning his forehead against mine.

"Remember what I said, Sebastian."

"I'll try, baby. And you remember what *I* said, what I'm thinking about when I look at you."

He rested his lips gently on mine.

"Never take my ring off, Caro," he whispered.

"*Ti amo tanto*, Sebastian."

He smiled softly. "*Sempre e per sempre*."

He glanced briefly at Liz, and then quietly left.

Liz closed the door behind him, and looked at me sternly.

"Bloody hell, Lee. You've fallen for him, haven't you? The priapic bastard has lured you into his lair to be one of his foreign territories. How can you be so damn stupid?"

Her words stung, but, to be fair, I could see exactly how it looked from her point of view.

I had two choices: I could say nothing, and leave her with the view that I'd been naïve and duped by a man who was a Casanova in a US Marine uniform, a total player, or I could tell her the truth.

"It's not like that, Liz," I said, rubbing my eyes tiredly.

"Don't give me that bullshit, Lee, you're lucky I'm the only one who knows what's going on. Otherwise, you'd be on the first plane home, and Hunter ... well, I don't know what they'd do to him. Not that he'd care, but it would be your career down the drain. Is that what you want?"

"No, of course not," I snapped.

"Then would you please tell me what the hell is going on, because I've never known you to behave like this—and it's not like you haven't had offers. Why him, Lee? Of all people—he's shagged half the female staff at the UN. Is that what you wanted—just a young stud? What if he tells someone? Bragging about his Kabul conquest?"

She was really building up a head of steam. I had to head her off.

"We're going to get married, Liz, as soon as his tour is over."

Silence.

I waited.

More silence.

"Have you lost your mind, Lee!" she bellowed suddenly, making me jump. "Is this some kind of hormonal surge or midlife crisis? You've let him shag you a few times and you're imagining he'll marry you? You barely know him!"

"I know him better than anyone, Liz. I've known him since he was eight years old."

She gaped at me.

"I think you'd better tell me the whole bloody story, Lee, because otherwise I'll have to assume that one of us is barking mad, and right now my money is on you."

I sighed. I'd never told anyone the full story before—not even my closest friends: guilt, sadness, and a wish to move on with my life had kept me silent.

"Fine. Make yourself comfortable, Liz." I took a deep breath, trying to marshal my thoughts.

"I met my husband, David, when I was 17, and we married a month after my 19th birthday. He was in the Navy, so we moved around. We had six months in San Diego after we'd been married about a year-and-a-half. Sebastian was the son of David's CO. He was a sweet, lonely child—his parents were just monstrous—and we became friends. That's all, I swear it. He used to come by after school and we'd talk about books and listen to opera. Then David was posted to Lejeune and that was that. But nine years later, we were back in San Diego again. Sebastian ... found me. He was nearly 18 and God, Liz, he was gorgeous even then. At first, I just thought of him as the kid I used to know, but it soon became obvious that he ... had other feelings for me."

Liz was watching me intently, a deep frown of concentration on her face.

"And ... one thing led to another. I'd been unhappy in my marriage for a long time. And Sebastian was just so loving. He was sweet and funny—fun to be with. And he encouraged me with my writing: if it hadn't been for him, I don't think I'd ever have become a journalist. Well, his parents found out ... and because he wasn't quite 18, it was a felony in California. His parents said they wouldn't prosecute me if I left quietly and didn't come back. The statute of limitations was three years: they threatened me, saying that if we tried to stay in touch, they'd have me arrested. Even if I didn't do jail time, I'd have had a criminal record. So I stayed away."

I paused, trying to scrub away the desolate feelings that thinking about those events always wrought in me.

"But Sebastian waited for me. When he was 21 we tried to find each other, but it never happened. I won't go into the details, but he realized eventually that I wasn't coming for him ... and that's when all the drinking and womanizing started. I hadn't seen him for 10 years when we met in Geneva again. He still loves me, Liz. He says he's always loved me—and I love him: desperately. We're engaged and we're going to be married. But no one can know while I'm still out here. No one."

She looked at me steadily and shook her head slowly, a worried expression etched on her face, her eyes kind and concerned.

"Bloody hell! That's quite a story." She shook her head. "You and the beautiful Sergeant Hunter. I hope you know what you're doing, Lee, I really do."

She stood up and paced to the window, then turned to look at me.

"I'll say one thing: if Shakespeare had known you, he wouldn't have had to steal all his plot lines, because that's one hell of a yarn. I hope you're right about him, because the man you're describing is not the one I've seen in action. Take tonight, for example, that French tart was all over him."

"I know," I said, with a small smile. "One of his Parisian conquests. I asked him to tell her to dress more appropriately. It was his fault she was dressed like that. Of course, that was after Sebastian and I had sex in one of the hotel's offices. Over a desk."

She stared at me, then laughed out loud.

"You are extraordinary, Lee, you really are! I thought I knew you. I mean, I knew you were tough on the quiet, but you must have balls of iron—or tits like Exocet missiles. Fine, if that's what you want. Far be it for me to tell you you're making a giant, Hoover dam-size mistake."

She paused.

"Is he as good as they say?"

My jaw dropped and I gaped at her, far, far beyond embarrassed that she'd asked me that question.

"I'll take that as a 'yes'," she said with a wry smile.

I winked, but didn't reply.

CHAPTER FOURTEEN

THE JOURNEY TO LEATHERNECK WAS HELL.

What would have been a six- or seven-hour journey back home, turned into 15 hours of baking sun, choking dust and gut-churning fear.

The fear was sporadic, triggered every time I saw turbaned men with AK-47 rifles. I was traveling in a heavily armored car that looked more like a tank than anything else, and I was told it had been designed to withstand roadside bombs, but every time I saw the Afghan forces at checkpoints, a chill went through me. Green-on-blue attacks were escalating to the point where each International Security Assistance Force unit had appointed at least one soldier as a 'guardian angel' to act as a lookout—to keep an eye on our Afghan allies.

It had been both unnerving and arousing to see Sebastian armed with his M16 for the first time. He looked so damn hard and kick-ass. I wanted to go and run my teeth down his exposed neck, and then expose a lot more of his body. What the hell was happening to me? I couldn't stop thinking about sex.

I blamed Sebastian.

The convoy I traveled in was well-armed, but I would be relieved to get off this exposed stretch of road, pockmarked with bomb craters, and with blackened carcasses of burnt-out cars strewn at the side.

It was comforting to know that somewhere in the back of the line of trucks and armored vehicles, Liz was traveling with British forces on their way to Bastion. We'd agreed to try and meet up but, as ever, nothing was guaranteed.

Our destination, 50 miles west of Kandahar, housed 28,000 British troops, several thousand Afghan National Army soldiers at Camp Shorabak, and 20,000 US Marines. Altogether, the three sections must have covered nearly

4,000 acres. Leatherneck, by itself, was bigger than many small towns, supported by four gyms, a vast dining area that could serve 4,000 people at a time, three chapels and, best of all as far as many of the troops were concerned, calling centers where they could phone and email their families back home.

The housing arrangements were restrictive, so the two- or three-thousand female soldiers and contractors were kept segregated, not that there was much privacy for anyone, should a romance develop. A fact which didn't go unnoticed by me. In any case, most of the female staff didn't go outside the wire, unless they were needed on a special assignment to speak to Afghan women.

When we finally crawled into Leatherneck, I was allocated a bunk in a tiny room shared by Private First Class Mary Sullivan from Beckville, Texas, a small town, some 150 miles east of Dallas—or so she told me. She was 24 and duly impressed that I worked as a journalist. She was one of a team of 15 women who worked in the motor pool, repairing damaged vehicles—and she was truly envious when she learned that I'd be traveling into the countryside and beyond the wire fence.

She chattered away about her hometown as I unpacked, shrugging off the sadistic body armor, then she showed me the way to the female shower area. A hot shower: what bliss.

It was less blissful when she insisted on continuing to chat while I washed myself. Despite being surrounded by people 24/7, I got the impression she was lonely. And she called me 'ma'am', which made me feel old.

"Do you have a boyfriend, ma'am? I couldn't help noticing you were wearing a ring on that chain around your neck."

"Yes, I do. You?"

"Nah, and it's not so easy to hook up with people here. I only enlisted because I thought I'd meet loads of cute guys, and get a free college education. So, what does your boyfriend do? Is he a reporter, too?"

"No, he's not. I have friends who are reporters—one of them is over at Bastion right now."

"Uh-huh. Where's your boyfriend at?"

She really was tenacious: maybe they taught that in the Marines. Either that or the forces attracted tenacious people.

"I don't really like to talk about him, Mary. It just makes me sad that we're not together."

By this time I was drying myself off, and I could see her eyes widen with interest at my words.

"Oh, my God! You must really love him!"

So not going there.

"You know, I'm surprised, Mary, a nice girl like you—haven't you seen anyone that you think is cute?"

She twisted her dog tags around her fingers, as she thought about my question.

"Yeah, there's this one guy..."

"And?"

"Nothing."

"Why? If you like him, go talk to him. I don't know—offer to change his oil."

She giggled.

"You think I should?"

I shrugged. "It's up to you, but all I can tell you for sure is that life is short. And wouldn't you rather know once and for all if he liked you or not? If he does, great, if he doesn't, it's his loss and you can stop worrying about him."

After that piece of advice, which I was so much better at giving than taking, PFC Sullivan escorted me to the briefing room where I was due to meet Grant and the rest of his officers.

But the first person I saw was Sebastian, looking hot, dusty and pissed. Clearly he hadn't had the luxury of time for a shower and a friendly chat about his love life.

His eyes lit up as he saw me and he started to smile. When he remembered we were trying to be discreet, he dropped his eyes back to the map he was studying.

Luckily, Captain Grant had been focused on the map spread out beneath his hands, so he hadn't noticed Sebastian's slip.

I caught the tail end of Grant's monologue.

"If a guy sticks his head around the corner he could very easily have a gun. If you can't see his hands, he could have something, a hand grenade, say. Pulling a trigger is easy—we need to bring him in. It's not about that one person, it's about the team. I'll need you to go in first and..."

He became aware of my presence and ground to a halt, looking irritated.

"I can come back," I offered, calmly.

"No, that's fine, Ms. Venzi. We're done here."

He nodded to Sebastian, who saluted and left the Nissan hut-type room, throwing me a quick smile as he passed.

"We'll be moving out in the morning, Ms. Venzi," continued Captain Grant. "It's going to get a lot less comfortable—and a lot more dangerous. We'll be heading out to a remote location further north in Helmand. We'll have BGAN satcomms, but I can't guarantee you'll always be able to get your stories out."

"I understand, Captain."

He sighed, and I suspected he'd been hoping I'd change my mind.

We ate our long-delayed evening meal with Lieutenant Crawley, the executive officer, four second lieutenants, and Sebastian. How very cozy.

Sebastian spent most of the meal staring at his food, or gazing into the distance. I could tell that he was irritating the hell out of Grant, who was burdened with the lion's share of trying to make polite conversation with me, although Crawley made a good stab of asking me about my work. My poor *fiancé* was trying hard to ignore me: he wasn't very good at it, and it just made me love him a little bit more.

I was well chaperoned, and I knew that there was absolutely zero chance of 'hooking up' as Sebastian had eloquently put it and, to tell the truth, I was so tired, I was almost on my knees.

The men stood up as I left our table in the dining area, Sebastian looking at me longingly.

"Sleep well, gentlemen," I said quietly.

As they sat down again, at least six of them relieved by my absence, I saw Sebastian glance over and smile again. I ran my finger along the chain around my neck and smiled back. It was enough.

Back at my bunk, PFC Sullivan was waiting for me, practically dancing on the spot with unrestrained energy. I felt every single one of my forty years as I eyed her exuberance wearily.

"I did it! I totally did it! I asked him out and he said 'yes'!"

We swapped a high five, and she then proceeded to tell me all about Frank, a mechanic in the motor pool. Halfway through her description of his 'fine ass', I fell asleep. I had my own memories of a fine ass to dream about.

"Hey, Lee! Wake up!"

"Huh, what?"

Mary was shaking me awake, her little face puckered up with concern.

"Captain Grant is after your ass!"

My ass?

"What? Why?" I stared at my watch. I stared at it again, utterly horrified, and willing the hands to rewind at least an hour.

"I'm sorry," whimpered Mary, "I thought you were awake, you *said* you were awake an hour ago. He's really kinda mad at you."

"Oh, crap!"

She giggled. "At least he can't give you cleaning duty."

"Want to bet?" I muttered, hastily pulling on my boots.

Mary helped me carry my gear out to the waiting vehicle, and a very sullen and irritated Captain Grant was waiting for me impatiently.

"I'm so sorry," I mumbled, "I overslept. It won't happen again."

He couldn't even bring himself to reply. I didn't blame him. He was responsible for 160 men, and one stupid woman reporter, who was fucking things up on day two of a one month embed. I'd be pissed, as well.

I pulled my body armor over my aching body, swept my hair into a rough ponytail, and slapped on my helmet.

Grant scowled, and did the one thing he could to show his displeasure: he seated me next to Sebastian. I climbed in creakily, annoyed at myself for being so unprofessional, but as soon as I saw Sebastian grinning in my direction, I realized that the gods were on my side for once, and I couldn't help smiling to myself.

"Good morning, Ms. Venzi," he purred. "I trust you slept well?"

"Too well, thank you, Sergeant Hunter," I politely replied, and saw him smirk at my response.

He looked fresh and delicious. I probably looked like old ham next to him, but I didn't care. Which was something of a revelation—it didn't matter what I wore, or how much sleep I'd had or not had, he always looked at me as if his world began and ended with me. How could I not be affected by that? By the certainty of his love?

As we headed north into the dusty, barren landscape, bumping along a broken road, heading up into the foothills, the heat was already building and I was starting to sweat. We'd all be soaked and stinking by the time we stopped for the night—and I already knew that there wouldn't be any showers.

I squinted into the harsh light, staring at the stark surroundings. Our road followed the side of a riverbed, and for a hundred yards in each direction, a strip of green vegetation broke up the bleakness of the lunar landscape.

Scattered in the scrubby fields, we saw several fortified farms with high walls, built from a mixture of mud and straw so they blended into the very dirt they were made from. Some were gathered into loose hamlets for company and protection, but most seemed to be abandoned. The only signs of life were a few skinny goats. If the owners were around, they were hiding from us.

I was still staring out of the window, when I felt Sebastian's hand drifting up to rest casually on my thigh. I shifted my daypack slightly, so that his hand was hidden, and slowly lowered mine, allowing our fingers to entwine on my leg.

In the middle of that blighted country, bumping along a dirt road in 90-degree heat, I felt a moment of peace.

~

Our destination was the town of Now Zad, grim was too kind a word. It might have been prosperous once, with evidence of a market area, but now it looked like it had been blasted by the desert.

Broken shops hung open to the elements, shutters drooping loosely. Only one person seemed to exist in this ghost town—an elderly man selling a few potatoes and eggs from a rug outside an empty building. He waved as we went past and called out something to us. Maybe that was a hopeful sign.

I glanced at Sebastian.

"What did he say?"

I saw Grant's head incline toward us, also waiting for the answer.

"Nothing I'd like to repeat, ma'am," he said, running his thumb over the back of my hand.

I nudged my knee against his and held back a grin. Playing footsie with Sebastian and having Grant sitting in front of me, gave me an almost irrepressible urge to laugh. Among other things.

My light heartedness disappeared when I saw the place that was to be our home for the next month.

Our compound had been a police station at some point in its life, but used many times over by ISAF soldiers from both British and US forces. It was basic, to say the least. There was no fresh water, no electricity, and the men were to sleep in the old cells, up to a dozen per room. I was given a space the size of a closet: I could just about stretch out there—it certainly wouldn't have done for anyone taller than me. I felt lucky to have a room to myself and that level of privacy. No one else did—not even Captain Grant.

I kept out of the Captain's way while he was organizing the camp. Instead, I tapped out notes on my laptop and blew up my oh-so-comfortable mattress.

PFC Sullivan had given me enough material for my first article, and the dreary town of Now Zad would supply plenty more. Being stationed here was a very different prospect from the relative comfort and safety of Leatherneck. I couldn't believe that our flimsy-looking mud walls would do much to protect us from an attack where rocket propelled grenades were used.

After a long while of being ignored, I started to feel hungry—particularly since I'd missed breakfast, and lunch had been a strange, flatbread sandwich on the road. No one had come near me, and I suspected I'd been conveniently forgotten. But now I saw men lining up near the area which I presumed had been designated as the kitchen. I joined the end of the line and looked hopeful.

The Marines all seemed so young. Most were in their early twenties, several were only nineteen. I remembered that Sebastian had been even younger than that when he'd first been sent to Iraq, and Fido hadn't made it to twenty.

They were all sweetly shy around me, calling me 'ma'am', of course, and insisting I go to the front of the line. We were having MREs (meal ready-to-eat) ration packs. I was told the food was chicken and noodles; the noodles I recognized, the anemic-looking meat I was less sure about.

I squatted down with the group nearest to me, and brought out my trusty bottle of soy sauce. It wasn't long before it was doing the rounds—even among the boys who'd never heard of soy sauce, let alone the *tamari* variety.

I asked each of them where they came from and what had made them enlist. For some, the Marine Corps was a chance to have a real family for the first time in their lives, for others it was a means to an end: learning a trade, or a college education, several said they wanted to serve their country, motivated by the events of 9/11. And for a few, I guessed, it was the difference between a slippery slope into a life of crime, and a chance to contribute something useful and make something of their lives.

I saw Sebastian once. He was standing at the compound's entrance, next to one of the sangar observation posts, talking to a group of locals. He looked tired, and I wondered if he'd had a chance to eat.

"I don't know how he talks that Greek shit," said Larry, a friendly kid from Pittsburgh, who was nodding at Sebastian.

"It's not Greek, fool!" snorted Ben, a native of Kansas City. "It's Arabic, isn't that right, ma'am?"

"Whatever, man: it's all Greek to me," said Larry, with a wide grin.

"It'll either be Dari or Pashto," I said, gently amused when Ben looked crushed by my correction. "I'm sure he'll teach you a few words if you're interested."

He shrugged, noncommittal. I understood: Sebastian was an unknown quantity—one of them, yet not one of them.

Gradually, the men became more relaxed in my presence, and the laughter and joking attracted more people to our corner of the compound. Laughter that petered out the moment Captain Grant wandered over to see what was going on.

I think he was mildly surprised to find I wasn't being a pain in the ass for a change, because he was almost civil to me, my early indiscretion forgotten, or at least forgiven.

Eventually, I decided to call it a day, and despite being implored to stay and shoot the breeze, I headed to my closet.

The bathrooms were basic, and I was dreading becoming familiar with them. But at least I wouldn't have the incredibly gross job of burning the waste every day. I wondered if it would be reserved for a punishment duty.

I brushed my teeth and rinsed with a mouthful of tepid water from my canteen, swiped some of the dust off my face with baby-wipes, kicked off my boots and laid my body armor where I could reach it in a hurry. I knew I was probably a little ripe from a day of constant sweating, but I was too tired to care, and it wasn't as if I could slip on my yoga pants after soaking in a hot tub.

Instead, I listened to the sounds of the camp around me: men going to their sleeping quarters, others going on watch. I realized what was missing—there was no birdsong. Nothing, not a single sound of any animal at all. The thought disturbed me, waking me more thoroughly than the alarm I had slept through this morning.

And then I heard a soft footfall outside my door.

"Caro?" he whispered.

I pushed open the door, and saw Sebastian crouching in the dim light. He wound himself through the narrow opening and wrapped his arms around me, holding me tightly.

"It's like a dream having you here," he murmured. "I keep thinking I'm going to wake up and find I've imagined you."

I clutched him tightly. "My dreams aren't usually this good."

"Mine are," he whispered, softly. "Or they used to be. When you first left, I dreamed about you all the time."

"What was I doing?" I said, stroking his cheek.

He leaned into my hand, breathing deeply. "Mostly, we were just by the ocean, walking on the beach."

"Mostly?"

He grinned. "Sometimes we did other stuff."

"Stuff? I'm not sure I know what you mean by 'stuff'," and I rubbed the front of his pants suggestively, hoping he'd feel the need to elucidate.

"Caro!" he groaned. "Fuck, I just came to make sure you were okay in here. I have to get back to the comms room."

"Right away? You can't take a few minutes?"

He kissed me hungrily. "I really can't, baby. Grant's waiting for me."

"You're such a tease," I said, slapping his ass. "You come in here, raising my expectations..."

"That's not the only thing that was raised," he said, dryly.

I smirked at him. "Well, I'd have been happy to meet those expectations, but apparently you have to go be a soldier."

"Actually, I have to go be an interpreter ... I could try and come back later, Caro."

"Sebastian, seriously—do what you need to do. You know where I am, and I trust you to know whether or not it's safe to take that risk. It worries me that I'm a distraction here for you. The most important thing is that you focus on your job. We have the rest of our lives after that."

He kissed me again, then rested his forehead against mine.

"I'm a lucky bastard—thank God for you, Caro."

"I'll see you at breakfast, Sarge," I said, running my hand over his hair.

"One other thing," he said, looking at me seriously, "there's been some radio chatter and the Taliban definitely know we're here. I don't think they'll do anything tonight—they're not in position, from what I can work out, but if you hear someone yell 'incoming', get your body armor on, keep your head down, and stay in here away from the windows. Whatever happens, Caro, stay in here. Everyone out there knows what they're doing: we don't need your help. You know what I'm saying, baby?"

I hugged him tightly. "I promise. I don't want you thinking about me when you have more important things to concentrate on."

He smiled briefly. "There isn't anything more important than you."

Then he kissed me gently, pressing his soft lips against mine. A moment later, and he was gone.

I settled back on my mattress, enjoying the relative coolness of the night air. I hoped Sebastian would be able to come back later, but I wasn't counting on it. Just knowing he was nearby was soothing.

The alarm on my wristwatch awoke me shortly before dawn. I sat up abruptly, my heart hammering in my chest. I could see a dark shadow curled up in the corner of my room. It moved and stretched.

"Sebastian!" I whispered. "What are you doing?"

"Hey, baby," he mumbled, sleepily.

"How long have you been there? Why didn't you wake me up?"

"Couple of hours, I think. I didn't want to wake you—you looked so peaceful."

I crawled up the mattress and wrapped my arms around his neck. I could feel the stubble on his cheek.

"You didn't even take your boots off," I said, burying my face in his neck.

He chuckled quietly. "Didn't seem much of a point." He kissed my hair and climbed to his feet. "Gotta go, baby."

"Already?" I said, disappointed.

He smiled. "Yeah, need to get a wash and shave before dawn patrol."

"You're lucky," I said, with a wry smile. "I'm relying on baby-wipes while I'm here. You'll get to know me in a whole new way, Sebastian."

He laughed quietly. "Looking forward to it, baby. See you later."

I quickly completed my morning ablutions (two baby-wipes over my face and under my arms, and a tiny squeeze of toothpaste to brush my teeth). I was touched, more than touched, that Sebastian had slept at the foot of my mattress, making sure I was okay, when he would have been better off crashing on his own bedroll for a few meager hours. Somehow that told me far more about the way he felt than if he'd woken me up for a rousing bout of illicit sex. I wouldn't have minded that either, and I'd been disappointed that he'd had to go so quickly. I knew he was trying damn hard to keep our relationship a secret. God love him for trying.

Which reminded me, he'd gone outside to wash and shave. I grabbed my camera and headed out.

The sun was just beginning to appear behind the mountains, weaving pink and purple clouds around the summits, when, like a gift from heaven, I saw a row of Marines, naked above the waist, who were washing outside in the cool air. Nicole would have gone crazy: all that taut, toned male flesh on display. It was a damn fine sight, but I was on the lookout for one sexy, muscular back that I'd gotten to know very well in the last two weeks.

I hid behind my camera, and snapped images of compound life. Yeah, right.

Finally, I had a photograph of Sebastian that I could keep legitimately while I was working.

Then one of the older Marines spotted me.

"You gonna blow up a nice big print of me, lady?"

And then the catcalls started. Marines of all shapes and sizes started flexing their biceps and even rubbing their nipples in my general direction.

I couldn't help laughing, more at the furious scowl on Sebastian's face than anything else.

"Gentlemen," I said, "it's too early in the day for all that. I haven't even had my breakfast MRE yet."

The good-natured teasing continued as I made my way across the compound to the line for chow. Hmm, more noodles and meat in dinky little plastic packs. No wonder this food was also known as 'Meals Rejected by the Enemy' or even 'Man Ready to Eat'. I was really hoping we'd have a helicopter drop of some fresh fruit and A-rations at some point over the next three-and-a-half weeks. Otherwise, my bottle of soy sauce wasn't going to last long.

Captain Grant stuck his head out, searching for the source of gratuitous good humor. When he saw me, he looked surprised and nodded politely. I nodded back, but couldn't help grinning at him.

He smiled cautiously, then bobbed back inside.

Ten minutes later, I joined the officers and gunnery sergeants for the morning's briefing. Sebastian was there, too, freshly-shaven and looking grumpy.

"This morning we'll have four patrols moving out. Crawley, I want you and your team with me heading northeast along the river bed wadi. Romero, northwest by the edge of town. Jankowski, your men take the old market area with Holden flanking you at 100 yards.

"Hunter, you're in charge of the terps—brief them before we go. The population here are Sunnis. Are any of your men Shiite?"

"Two, sir," said Sebastian. "I've told them to stay behind today."

"Does that leave us short?" said Grant, frowning.

"No, sir, but one of the teams will have to use Angaar: his English is so-so."

"Then send one of the others with him."

"They don't get along, sir. Could cause problems."

"Then damn well make sure it doesn't, Hunter!" snapped the Captain.

Sebastian didn't argue the point further, but I could tell he was slightly pissed.

As the meeting broke up, I ventured to put my hand in the air. Part of me hoped I'd be with Sebastian's patrol, part of me hoped I wasn't, because I knew I'd be a distraction for him.

"Which team would you like me with, Captain Grant?"

He looked up, clearly irritated.

Well, fuck him! He wasn't the only one doing a job here.

"Perhaps 'like' was too strong a word, Captain," I suggested, coolly.

I saw Sebastian's lips quirk up in a small smile, before he quickly stifled it. He wasn't the only one—I saw two of the other officers grin openly.

"You'd better come with me, Ms. Venzi," the Captain muttered, somewhat unwillingly. "And you, Hunter."

"I feel like Fox Mulder," I murmured loud enough for Grant to hear, but not loud enough that he'd feel the need to reply. "The Marines' 'most unwanted'."

The Captain's forehead creased in a frown, but I thought I detected a hint of humor in his eyes, too.

The dawn patrols left the compound on foot. Today's mission was to scout the area and get a hands-on idea of the terrain. The two patrols checking the old marketplace probably had the most dangerous job—although there weren't really any safe ones. But those old bazaar buildings provided places where IEDs could be planted, or gunmen could hide.

By comparison, my stroll up the river wadi would be easy. Or perhaps 'easier' was a better way of describing it, because the heat was already building uncomfortably, and nothing would be easy today.

I'd been positioned in the middle of the patrol for safety. Sebastian was up front with the Captain when we saw our first locals.

Four small boys, aged about eight or nine, were sitting in a patch of dirt when they saw us. They stood up in a hurry, looking scared, but Sebastian called out to them, and they stared at him in surprise. He said something else and I saw the biggest boy, who seemed to be acting as the leader, shake his head. Then the boy pointed up into the foothills.

I snapped a quick picture while no one was looking.

"He says there are Taliban up in the hills, sir," Sebastian said to Grant, quietly. "They moved into position during the night. He doesn't think they'll come out in daytime. Not sure I'd take that as an ironclad guarantee, but it could mean they'll hit us at dusk, or first thing in the morning."

I saw him glance at me.

"Anything else?" said the Captain.

Sebastian sighed. "He said his father has promised to get him a rifle like mine when he's ten."

I couldn't help wondering how long this war would go on, when children were being used to carry it forward.

Then one of the boys spotted me and gaped, openly pointing me out to his friends. They rattled off a question and Sebastian grinned.

"They want to know if Ms. Venzi is your wife, sir, or if you just brought her to do the cooking."

I'll get you for that, Hunter!

Some of the troops laughed, but Grant looked slightly flustered.

"Tell them she does the cooking," he said.

Sebastian gave them the answer and the boys nodded wisely. Then he handed each of them a hard candy, and we moved on, watching as they waved goodbye.

From a distance, I snapped another photo of them waving, then hurried to catch up with Grant.

"Would you like to explain that to me, Captain Grant," I asked mildly, while secretly giving him the evil eye.

"I don't want word getting out that we have a journalist with us," he said, shortly.

He had a point, and, despite the heat, I felt a shiver go down my spine. As I fell back to my place in the middle of the patrol, I glanced over to see Sebastian looking at me, a serious and worried expression on his face.

We moved slowly next to the dried riverbed when one of the Marines on point yelled out, "Incoming!"

I looked up to see a bright flash in the sky and heard an intensely loud roaring overhead. I half-dived, half-fell into the wadi, following the Marines who'd hit the deck the second their colleague had shouted.

The rocket propelled grenade shook the ground as it exploded, and the percussion from the hot air deafened me. Even though I was terrified, I could tell that the noise wasn't dangerously near to us.

"RPG, sir!" shouted the gunnery sergeant. "Bastards missed by 300 yards. Up in the foothills, sir. They'll have us in range any second."

He was right: we were in their sights and pinned down. The wadi gave us good protection but we couldn't move either.

Sebastian crouched down next to me.

"You okay?"

"I'm fine, don't worry about me. I won't move. Promise."

He gave an anxious look, then made his way back to Captain Grant.

Two men moved forward with a small mortar and fired off a couple of rounds. The rush of sound was distinctly comforting.

"Hewitt," shouted the Captain, "call in air support. I want the shit bombed out of those fuckers. Give them the coordinates—now!"

I managed to turn around in the confined area and took photographs of the Marine on the radio calling air-support, and of the two Marines firing the occasional mortar round.

Two more RPGs came in, each landing a little closer, although not close enough to concern the men around me. I thought I was having an out-of-body experience: everyone seemed so calm, including me, although another, quieter, rational part, was scared witless.

Luckily, I had something else to focus on. Despite the heat and despite the fact I'd sweated enough to leave salt marks on my clothes, I was dying to pee.

Maybe it was just fear after all, but I didn't know how much longer I could hang on.

Another fifteen minutes passed and the pressure on my bladder was becoming intolerable. I was seriously considering just peeing my pants right there. It was so hot, my clothes would dry quickly, the sting of humiliation would, however, last considerably longer.

I felt better when I noticed several of the Marines discreetly peeing into the wadi. God, it was so much easier for men. I should have worn a long skirt like the local women, then I could have just squatted down in the dirt and no one would have been any the wiser.

At that moment, I heard the sound of a jet streaking past overhead.

"Harrier," muttered the bored-looking Marine who was kneeling down next to me.

There was an explosion so loud, it sounded as if a whole mountain had been blown up. A second explosion followed shortly afterward. I pressed my face into the dirt at the bottom of the wadi and tried to remember to breathe. I counted to a hundred before I dared to look up again. A thick cloud of dust and smoke hung over the foothills, lazily drifting down into the yellow valley.

I sat up to take a quick photo. I even remembered to take off the lens cap, which I thought was pretty damned impressive under the circumstances—and I still wanted to pee.

Then I noticed that several of the men were grinning at me.

"Was that your first time under fire, ma'am?"

"First time it was that damn close," I said, with a thin smile. "I almost peed my pants."

They laughed easily. "Well, you looked pretty cool, ma'am. We should make you an honorary Marine."

"I'm sure Captain Grant would be delighted with that suggestion," I muttered, and winked at them conspiratorially.

I looked across to see Sebastian smiling at me. I pressed my hand over my heart, and smiled back.

After waiting to see if there would be any further RPG attacks, we slowly made our way back along the dried up riverbed.

By now, my bathroom needs had intensified and I practically sprinted the last hundred yards to what passed for restrooms in the compound. 'Sprinted' might have been an exaggeration: I was wearing nearly 22 pounds of body armor, 'staggered' was probably more accurate.

But the relief could not be exaggerated. I floated out, oblivious to the catcalls and helpfully unhelpful comments from the Marines who were watching me with wide grins on their faces.

All I needed now was a hot shower, a good book, and a hot man. I'd come very near to an up-close-and-personal encounter with the Taliban: some life-affirming sex would be very welcome. I couldn't see Sebastian among the sea of desert utility uniforms, but I hoped he'd find me later.

I dragged my sorry carcass to my room, dumped the body armor gratefully, then took my laptop and solar charger outside, and sat in the shade, writing my notes.

I could see a small flurry of activity going on at one side, with Marines hoisting up bits of rope and old jerry cans. My body was too weary to wonder what they were doing, and my brain was too stunned to care. But then I noticed that Sebastian seemed to be organizing the work party. After another ten minutes, he strolled over casually and squatted down next to me.

"How you doing, baby?" he said, in a low voice.

"Pretty damn good, Sarge," I replied, "considering I nearly got my ass shot off today."

He chuckled quietly. "You are so fucking amazing, Caro."

"You're not so bad yourself, Sebastian."

We both noticed the speculative gazes we were garnering at the same time. He stood up abruptly. "We've fixed you up a makeshift shower."

"Excuse me?" I said, certain that I'd misheard.

"The guys wanted to do something for you—they think you're a ballsy woman. So they've made you a shower. You've got about two-and-a-half minutes of lukewarm water. How's that sound?"

"What? How?"

I gaped at him and he smiled back.

"I just left some cartons of water out in the sun during the day. They got pretty warm: all we had to do was hoist them up and make a shower head. You're good to go. Except you won't be able to take off your clothes, but it's better than nothing, I guess."

"God, I love you!" I murmured. "But I think I love them, too!"

He snorted, but thankfully looked amused as I waved at the shower-building team.

"I'll be right back!"

I hurried to my room and grabbed a small sachet of shampoo. I hadn't thought I'd need it, but I was so happy that I'd included it after all.

The shower felt wonderful: washing the salt and dust out of my hair felt even better. I even managed to make a stab at washing my clothes while I was wearing them, before the water ran out. Then I sat out in the afternoon sunshine and let my clothes dry on my body, while I chatted to some of the guys, listening to their stories.

Captain Grant came out to check on me and I even managed to get a smile from him. I hoped the truce would hold—provided I managed not to oversleep again, of course.

Another box of MREs, four hard candies, and a really bad coffee later, I crawled into bed. If Sebastian came into my room in the night, he'd have to poke me awake with a sharp stick. My shoulders ached from wearing the heavy body armor all day. I couldn't imagine how the guys must feel: their armor was even heavier, plus they had to carry their packs, ammunition and an eight pound rifle.

Their entire equipment and packs probably weighed more than I did.

And with that thought, I was asleep.

CHAPTER FIFTEEN

IT WAS DARK WHEN I WOKE UP, I REALIZED I WASN'T ALONE.

"Hey, baby," he whispered. "I didn't mean to wake you—I just wanted to see you."

He was sitting at the bottom of my mattress again. I peered into the dark, his outline faint against the darker shadow of the wall.

I rubbed my gritty eyes and reached out for him. "You're too far away," I grumbled, holding up my arms toward him.

He uncoiled himself from the floor, and tried to stretch out next to me, but his boots hit the door.

"Fuck," he muttered, "they've given you a damn hutch to sleep in."

"At least it's private, Sebastian," I said, running my finger across his stubbly chin.

He smiled. "Yeah, that's something."

He leaned over me, taking his weight on his arms, and kissed me, softly. I think he just had a simple goodnight kiss in mind, I certainly didn't.

I wrapped my arms around his neck and locked our faces together. Needing more, I pushed my tongue between his lips, and explored his mouth hungrily. He tasted of salt and mint gum. Desire bloomed inside me and I ran my hands down his back, resting them on his fine ass, feeling the rough material beneath my fingers, and squeezed hard.

"Are you sure, Caro?" he breathed.

"Yes," I whispered back. "Here and now."

He groaned softly, and I felt the weight of his body press down onto my chest.

"But you're going to have to get naked," I added.

He sighed and pushed back from me.

"It's going to take some explaining if the Taliban attack and I run out of your room with my ass hanging out," he replied.

It was a fair point, and he was only trying to protect my honor and act professionally, just as I'd asked. And yet … I weighed up the pros and cons, realized he was right, and decided to strip him anyway.

We'd come under enemy fire today, and faced it together. I realized how lucky I was: surviving had made me damned horny, and I craved a bout of rough, life-affirming sex with my gorgeous *fiancé*. I felt, quite literally, that life was too short not to grasp something so good with both hands.

This man, lying in my arms, had told me over and over again that he loved me—that he'd always loved me. And, despite everything that fate had thrown in our path—time, distance, and age difference—we were in love. The why and how didn't seem to matter anymore: finally, finally I'd accepted that this was real and that it wasn't going to go away—that Sebastian wasn't going to go away. I'd accepted that he was beautiful and sexy and younger than me, and that women with far better bodies and far fewer years would want him, too. And I'd accepted that he wasn't perfect, and had a string of conquests on at least three continents, and I'd accepted that life was going to continue to throw new hurdles in our path—and I didn't damn well care.

It wasn't perfect. So what? Life isn't perfect—life is what happens while you're waiting for your moment in the sun and if you miss it, waiting instead for the perfect illusion that Hollywood sells, then more fool you. I'd spent half my life waiting for the right moment. I was done with waiting.

"Time to get naked, Sarge," I ordered.

"Make me," he shot back.

Oh, willingly.

"Okay, what can I trade you to take your shirt off?"

His eyebrows shot up.

"Trade?"

"Yes. I want you to take your shirt off, but it seems like I'll have to give you something in return. If I agree to your terms, you lose the shirt. If I don't agree, you get to keep it on."

"For real?"

"Yes, Sebastian," I said, pleased with my invention, but also intrigued to see what he'd come up with.

"A shirt for a shirt, Caro."

Okay, so he was starting out easy. But I was wearing fewer clothes than he was.

I undid my shirt and watched his eyes widen as he took a deep breath, his gaze drawn to my breasts. His jacket and t-shirt hit the floor and we were both naked from the waist up.

"So far so good. I want you to take off your boots and socks."

He thought for a moment.

"Okay, but I want you to touch your breasts, Caro, touch yourself until your nipples are hard."

I ran my hands lightly over myself, toying with my nipples while I stared into his eyes.

"Fuck!" he said, wetting his lips with his tongue.

"Boots," I said, my voice sharp with need.

It took a minute for him to unlace his boots and tug his feet out of them, then peel off his socks. His coordination wasn't helped by the fact that I continued to massage my breasts, turning myself on with my hands and his dark gaze.

"I want you to take off your pants, Sebastian."

"And you have to lose those pajama bottoms, Caro,"

I slipped them off quickly, adding them to the pile of clothes in the corner.

Sebastian matched me, unzipping his pants and tossing them away. My eyes were drawn to the very noticeable bulge in his briefs. But I needed to get them off him first—and I didn't have any clothes left to trade.

"I want you naked, Sebastian," I whispered.

"I want you to touch yourself between your legs, Caro. I want to see you come."

I pulled a face.

"What?" he said, looking confused.

"Sebastian, I can do that any night of the week. Frankly I was hoping you'd do it for me."

He grinned. "Yeah, but it'll be a real fucking turn on for me."

"All right then, but you, too."

"Me, too, what?"

"Lose the briefs, get handy, and make yourself come."

He hesitated for a moment. "Ah, what the hell."

He lay on his back and lifted his butt, so he could slide his briefs over his hips. His erection leapt free immediately.

Then he pulled himself into a sitting position, leaning against the wall facing me, and started stroking himself. I knelt up, spreading my knees wide and began to rub my clitoris slowly.

I felt utterly aroused watching him touch himself so intimately, staring into his eyes as his breath began to come faster, as I listened to myself moan softly. He wrapped his right hand firmly around himself, and started gripping harder, and I copied him, matching him stroke for stroke, my back arching as my insides began to tremble and my body begged for release.

"Oh, fuck this," he snarled. He launched himself forward, forcing me onto my back, and slammed into me, pumping hard.

I smacked his shoulder and pushed him off. "Condom!"

"Fuck! Fuck! Fuck!"

He pulled out of me hurriedly, grabbed his pants and dragged them toward him, fumbling in the pocket for a foil packet. He swore again as he dropped it and had to search for another.

"I'm sheathed up," he hissed, at last.

"From behind: make it rough."

I heard his breath catch, but he didn't need to be asked twice. I rolled onto my hands and knees and felt him grip my hips. He rammed into me so hard, I had to stifle my cry with one hand. I collapsed onto my forearms as he let himself go, hammering into my body, using me for sex, just like I'd told him to. It was rough and raw and just what I wanted—what I needed.

I pushed my ass back against him, and felt his balls slap against my skin as he plunged into me again and again.

He leaned over and reached down to palm my left breast, squeezing the nipple hard enough to make me cry out. Then he let go and moved his hand lower, his fingers circling me and reaching far enough back, so that I knew he was touching his shaft at the same time, feeling himself move in and out of me.

I brought my hand up to meet his, and we twined our fingers together, quite literally feeling our connection.

My body gave way as I came, and Sebastian hooked his arm around my waist to hold me up, until his own climax had him collapsing onto my thin mattress.

I was gasping for breath, on the verge of passing out, and Sebastian was breathing hard. I could feel the sweat on my chest and back.

Sebastian pulled out of me, a movement that made me wince. I'd asked for rough sex and I'd got it. Oh, boy had I got it.

I felt his breath on my neck and his hand rested on my hip.

"Are you okay?" he breathed, softly.

"Yes," I gasped. "Apart from the fact tomorrow I'll be walking like I just rode a camel across the Gobi desert. You?"

"Yeah, I think I ripped my foreskin—what's left of it," he muttered.

"Really?" I turned around to face him. "Are you okay?"

He smiled and stroked my cheek. "Kidding, Caro. That was fucking awesome. You were like some wild woman."

"You were pretty wild yourself. But you're right—I don't know what got into me—other than you, of course. Do you want to go again?"

"Christ, Caro! Are you trying to kill me?"

"Hmm, death by orgasm. What do you think? A handful by morning?"

"If you want, Caro, but you know what I'd really like to do now?"

"Thrill me."

He pulled me into his arms and looked at me seriously. "I want to make love to you, Caro. I freakin' loved that, but it was just sex. Can we take it slow, baby? Take our time? I want to touch every part of your body."

He kissed me gently and ran his hands across my shoulders and down to my waist, expressing with his hands what he'd told me in so many words.

His movements were tender and loving and gentle. There were so many different sides to this complex man. It was an education learning all his facets, and learning how trust was growing between us.

At last he fell asleep, his body curled around mine, his head resting on my chest.

As the night drifted past, and morning was just a breath away, I was reluctant to wake him. He'd missed a lot of sleep to take care of me the last two nights, and he needed to be alert. I waited until the very last possible second to wake him.

"Time to get up, Sebastian," I said reluctantly, running my hands over the silky skin of his back.

He blinked and tried to stretch, but ended up kicking the door again.

"Very stealthy, Sarge," I remarked, watching him sit up and search for his briefs.

He grinned back at me. "Yeah, trained in stealth, camouflage and concealment, baby."

"You were certainly concealed in me last night—several times, I seem to remember."

"Did ya lose count, baby?" he smirked.

I didn't bother to answer that one, instead, I had another question. "By the way, how come you're managing to get in here without anyone noticing you're not where you're supposed to be?"

He frowned. "It's not that hard—I'm kind of separate from everyone. I'm on attachment so none of them know me. I'm in charge of the other interpreters, but they're all Afghan, so I'm not part of that either. It was different when I was still with my unit, but this way no one knows when or where I'm on duty. Except Grant, and he has more to worry about than where I sleep. Works out pretty well, huh, Caro?"

I realized that his job must be lonely on occasions, and spending time with me meant he wasn't bonding with other members of the unit.

The military machine worked at its best when everyone knew their job and did it: lives depended on that. But when it came down to it, I couldn't help thinking that men fought for their friends, for the guys in their unit, rather than for their country. That came into it, sure, but in this kind of guerrilla warfare, your life usually depended on the other guy you broke bread with. They were your family.

I looked up and saw that Sebastian was gazing at me, his head on one side, as if he was trying to read what was going on in my mind.

I smiled at him, hiding my concern.

"Time to move your ass, Sebastian. I'll see you later?"

He kissed me quickly, and then darted out through the door. Half a minute later I saw him strolling casually across the compound, greeting some of the other men who were either waking up or coming off watch.

I yawned and stretched, and took a moment to freshen myself up with some more baby-wipes, before heading out to join the line for chow.

The day's new gossip was that fresh rations would be dropped in by helicopter in the next couple of days. Other than the butt-clenching fear of being under fire, it was as exciting as things got.

I realized that if there was going to be a food drop, then there might well be mail, too. I decided I'd keep my promise to Sebastian and write him a letter.

Thankfully, the day passed far less eventfully than the previous one. I wasn't sent out with Sebastian, but accompanied Lieutenant Crawley and a cheerful Afghan interpreter called Gawhar, who told me his name meant 'jewel'. He was fascinated by the fact that I wasn't married and didn't have children. He kept asking who was 'in charge' of me. He couldn't comprehend my answer of 'no one'. I wouldn't like to imagine how puzzled he'd be if he ever met a woman officer with men under her command. I hoped my presence gave him another point of view, at the very least.

Gawhar thought women should be educated "up to the age of 11", so that they could be more useful in childrearing. At one time, women in Afghanistan had been able to go to college, but now anyone attempting to educate girls was living very dangerously. Gawhar's attitude was relatively liberal, compared to many.

I sighed. This poor country had a long way to go.

Our patrol was the first one back at the compound. Grant had confirmed that a food drop would be happening soon, so each Marine could have a one-minute shower with what was left from the water ration. Soon, there was an awful lot of naked flesh on display. I was glad I had a pair of sunglasses behind which to hide my blushes—or maybe it was my interest that I was hiding. I'd never used to pay much attention to that sort of thing, even though I lived by a beach. Huh, I blamed Sebastian.

I headed back to my room and started typing up notes and polishing a couple of articles that were almost ready to go. I was pleased with the photographs, too. The ones from the previous day were particularly dramatic, although looking at them brought back some of the knee-trembling terror that I'd felt.

After an hour of typing, I flipped shut the laptop lid, and sat outside to write an old-fashioned pen-and-paper letter to Sebastian. I was determined that if mail did arrive soon, he'd have a letter to open. I spent my time being creative: he said he wanted to get kinky with me, so I roughed out some ideas, to see if any of them were on his 'to do' list. It was a shame our time and space was so limited right now. I wanted to show him what a formerly-sexually-frustrated forty-year-old with a good vocabulary could imagine.

Sebastian's patrol was the last to return to the compound. Even from a distance, I could see that his face was strained. He glanced over to where I was sitting, and shook his head imperceptibly.

A few minutes later he emerged from Grant's makeshift office, and strode over to me.

"Captain Grant would like to see you, ma'am," he said, formally.

I followed him across the compound, feeling anxious as he pressed his lips together in a hard line.

Grant's office seemed gloomy after the punishing sunlight, he waved me to the only other chair in the room and Sebastian stood silently behind me.

"Ms. Venzi, your presence is causing some interest among the local population. Master Sergeant Hunter heard some talk while on patrol that concerned him."

I glanced up at Sebastian who remained resolutely mute.

"And what does this talk say?" I prompted.

"At the moment it's vague, but the news of having a woman with us will spread quickly now. We have a new cook and a new medic arriving in six days, so the heli will be putting down briefly. If you become a person of interest, as I think you will, you'll be at risk and you'll be putting my men at risk, too. I want you on that flight, Ms. Venzi."

I felt like he'd punched me, and all the air left my lungs. But I understood, as well. He was making a strategic decision. He hadn't tried to persuade or softball me, he just told it like it was.

"I see. Well, thank you for being so candid and explaining the situation to me, Captain Grant. I'll ensure that I get as much work done as I can, and I'll be ready to leave when you advise."

The Captain looked relieved. Perhaps he'd expected me to argue, or throw a hissy fit. I may have been a stupid woman who overslept on her first day embedded with his unit, but I wasn't selfish enough to risk the lives of others. Especially not Sebastian's.

The worst part was that I'd be leaving him behind. I'd always known that day would come, I just thought we'd have a little longer first. He was right: we always seemed to be traveling in different directions.

I stood up, and Sebastian escorted me out of the Captain's office.

"Sorry, baby," he murmured.

"That's okay," I replied, quietly. "I don't want to cause more problems out here. Besides, I can get some stories from Leatherneck, so the paper won't be shortchanged."

"If anything happened to you..." he began.

I interrupted him quickly. "I told you, Sebastian, I'm not going to take risks. If you care about me, you won't either."

"*If* I care about you?" he said angrily.

"You know what I mean—and keep your voice down."

He scowled, and looked mutinous.

Great. Sulky Sebastian was back.

Reluctantly, he left me outside my room, and marched off to the other side of the compound where he threw angry glances at me until it was meal time.

I was just drowning my sorrows in some piss-weak coffee, when Lieutenant Crawley emerged from Grant's subterranean office.

"Supply chopper on its way," he announced, then picked out a platoon to retrieve the goodies.

A few minutes later, we all heard the distinctive thrum of the Black Hawk's twin engines chewing up the air around it, and small parachutes began raining down.

Once the swag had been collected and relocated to the compound, everyone gathered around the supplies: ammunition, water and—thank you God—fresh rations. There was also a bag of mail which I volunteered to sort, much to Captain Grant's obvious surprise.

There weren't as many letters as I'd expected. My two shadows, Ben and Larry, helped me, and explained that any parcels from home would be held back until there was room (or spare weight) on the next heli drop.

When they weren't looking, I casually slipped my letter to Sebastian into the pile. It didn't take long to finish sorting, and it was easy to tell which of the guys were family men—they had the most letters, some obviously addressed by their kids.

As he'd said, Sebastian didn't get many letters and that day, mine was the only one addressed to him.

The rest of the unit circled us like sharks, waiting for the moment they heard their name. I saw Sebastian's surprise when Larry called out 'Hunter'.

"You got mail, Sergeant," and he waved the thin envelope at Sebastian.

Of course, I hadn't written a return address, so that should have clued him in, but instead he just looked puzzled. I watched him as he scrolled down the first few lines of my scandalous letter. Then his eyes widened in shock, and a wicked grin crept across his face. He glanced up, and I winked at him.

He read through the whole letter, sitting in the dirt, leaning against the mud wall of the compound. Then he closed his eyes and let his head rock back: he was still smiling.

Yeah, think about those positions, Sarge.

One of the other men, a young guy named Ross from Minneapolis, scrunched up his letter in disgust and dropped it in the dirt.

"What's up man?" said Larry.

"Fucking 'dear John' letter," he said bitterly. "She said she didn't want to spoil my last few days of leave, so she thought she'd wait till I got out here to tell me she was seeing someone else. Bitch."

He got some sympathetic looks. A lot of the men had been there. It could be hard to hold onto relationships in the military.

The sun had sunk behind the mountains and the air was beginning to cool, when there was a sudden flurry of activity.

"Incoming!" came the yell from the sangar.

Suddenly, men were flying everywhere, running for their body armor and weapons. I sprinted for my room, but tripped over an abandoned jacket, and went sprawling in the dust.

The first RPG exploded about 200 yards outside the compound. The noise was horrendous, and the plume of dirt rocketed 90 feet into the air.

I covered my head with my hands, and pushed my face into the loose dirt on the ground. When the dusty shower had subsided, I crawled on my hands and knees into my room, and pulled on my body armor and helmet in double-quick time. Then I grabbed my camera and nervously pointed it out of the tiny window, taking snap after snap of the Marines as they took their positions. Then the *durg-durg* of the heavy machine guns started.

Another RPG exploded, closer this time, and I dropped to the floor, counted to ten, and peered out of my window. After a minute of what seemed like organized chaos, bellows and shouts, silence rippled outwards.

My heart was thundering in my chest, and I realized my hands were shaking. I began to wonder if a nice, safe job in a bank might be a good career move.

Sebastian's head suddenly appeared around my door, and I nearly yelled out in fright.

"You okay, baby?"

"Yes, fine. Don't worry about me," I replied, rather breathlessly.

He nodded, and disappeared.

The Taliban had a new tactic: sleep deprivation. Intermittently throughout the night, they'd fire an RPG randomly toward us. None of them came close enough to cause concern, but it was successful at stopping us resting, not that sleeping in body armor was possible anyway—at least not until complete exhaustion had set in.

Sebastian didn't have another chance to come near me again. I guessed he was in Grant's office to interpret the insurgents' radio chatter and thus help the gunners try to work out targets. At dawn, we were all gritty-eyed and pissed off as we stumbled into line for breakfast.

I don't know why, but an old Beatles song came into my head, and I started humming the opening bars of 'I'm So Tired'—the lines that said his mind is on the blink because he hasn't slept a wink. That was exactly how I felt.

The Marine behind me started singing the tune softy, and I turned around to smile at him and joined in. Then two more started with the harmony. Soon, about 20 burly Marines were singing out of tune and getting their groove on in the breakfast line. It wasn't much, but it was damn funny—and we really needed to laugh.

Captain Grant appeared from his office, unshaven and with dark rings around his eyes, accompanied by Crawley and Sebastian. When Grant saw the kids from 'Glee 'getting funky to the Beatles, his face split with a huge grin. I didn't even know the man had teeth. He gave me an ironic salute, and disappeared back into his den. Crawley laughed out loud, and Sebastian smiled at me proudly.

From that moment on, the men called me 'Yoko', and I laughed happily, seeing their pleasure in something so simple.

It was the last time I laughed for a very long time.

~

The patrols that day were kept short. Crawley and his team checked out the old marketplace, which seemed to have taken the brunt of most of the RPG activity, two others moved parallel to either side of the main road, Sebastian was gone the longest, disappearing into the foothills with Jankowski and a fast-moving foot patrol.

When they returned, long after everyone else had finished their evening meal, Sebastian looked hot, sweaty, and tired.

He smiled at me wearily, and went to debrief with Grant and Jankowski.

The kitchen reopened, handing out chili-flavored MREs to the dusty crew. Sebastian had just started eating, when Grant called him back into the office. He was in there nearly half-an-hour, and his abandoned food gone cold, when he suddenly re-emerged and headed my way, his face set and grim.

"What is it? What's happened?" I said, scared by the expression on his face.

"Grant wants to see you," he said, ignoring the curious gazes from the other men.

I stood up stiffly, and followed him into the office.

"Please take a seat, Ms. Venzi," said Grant, gently.

My heart rate accelerated. *What the hell was going on?*

"I'm afraid I have some bad news for you ... I told you yesterday that Master Sergeant Hunter picked up some threats to you, well, I'm afraid it's become much more direct. The Taliban have heard that you're with us—and they're viewing you as a prize kill."

I was vaguely aware that Sebastian was scowling at Grant, probably because the information had been so candid, but my brain was in free-fall. *They were targeting me?*

"They're aware of the value of publicity," he said tiredly, "and I'm afraid earlier today, they killed another journalist—a woman—and Hunter has just had confirmed radio chatter that you're a definite target. I'm calling in a heli to evacuate you back to Leatherneck as soon as possible. Ms. Venzi? Ms. Venzi?"

I looked up at him, stunned. "Who?"

"Excuse me?" he said, clearly puzzled.

"Who was the journalist they killed?"

He glanced over to Sebastian questioningly.

"Liz Ashton," said Sebastian, his eyes soft with pity.

No. No no no no no no no.

I dropped my head into my hands.

"I'm sorry," said Grant, uncomfortably. "Of course ... you knew her."

I nodded slowly. "She was my friend."

"I'm sorry," he said again, "but we can't risk our mission here and..."

He bit off what he was going to say, but it didn't matter. I'd guessed that there was some special reason his unit had been sent to Now Zad, and a reason why he didn't want me here in the first place. A remote part of my brain remembered Sebastian had hinted that he'd be traveling to remote villages, out of touch for days or even weeks.

But I was going home.

I looked up into Grant's face, recognizing that this wasn't the first time he'd had to break this sort of news.

"How did she die?"

Grant looked away, and it was Sebastian who answered. "Sniper. She died instantly."

I think Grant tried to say something else to me, but I didn't hear him. I walked out of his office, dry-eyed, my throat aching, vaguely aware that Sebastian had started to reach out for me as I walked past him.

I crossed the compound in a daze, ignoring everyone who spoke to me. I closed the door of my room behind me, and crouched down in the corner.

Not Liz. How could it be Liz? She was indestructible, larger than life. No, not larger than life. She was dead.

Put out the light, then put out the light.

Now her light was gone. One less stuttering candle in the darkness, one less person to tell the truth about this wretched war.

I refused to cry for her: not here, not in this godforsaken outpost.

Wrapping my hands around my knees tightly, I let my head fall forward, pressing my head down, as if to make as small a target as possible.

I don't know how long I hid in the corner, before I heard a soft tap at the door.

I didn't look up—I already knew it would be Sebastian. He shut the door behind him quietly, then sat down next to me and pulled me into his arms.

He didn't speak, just rocked me gently and kissed my hair.

After a while, I let my body relax against him, curling into his chest.

"I'm so sorry, Caro," he murmured. "I know she was your friend."

We sat in silence until night fell, and I took strength from his touch and his unspoken love.

Outside, we heard the sounds of men changing watch, and Sebastian sighed. "I'd better go, or Grant will wonder what the hell we're doing."

He shifted me off his lap and started to stand, but I grabbed hold of his hand.

"Don't go, Sebastian, please. It doesn't matter who knows now—I'm being sent home anyway. Let me spend my last few hours with you."

He sank down again. "I was hoping you'd say that," he admitted, his voice gentle.

We lay on the mattress, fully dressed, our arms and legs tangled together.

"I'm not very good at gardening," I said, thoughtfully.

"What's that, baby?"

"I can't grow things. Plants seem to wither when they see me. Can you grow things?"

I felt him shrug, confused by my question.

"I don't know, Caro. I've never tried."

"I'd like to plant something," I mumbled, "see it live and grow."

He tightened his grip, and stroked my hair.

"Does your place in Long Beach have a backyard?" he asked, gently.

"Yes. It could be pretty. Remember Signora Carello's bougainvillea? Maybe we could grow something like that."

He kissed my hair. "Baby, I can't even spell bougain ... whatever it is." He sighed. "But I guess I could try. Was that the purple stuff?"

I nodded.

"Okay, baby. We can grow purple stuff."

"And pink?"

"Sure, baby, with yellow fucking stripes if you want."

"Okay."

CHAPTER SIXTEEN

I DIDN'T SLEEP THAT NIGHT. I THOUGHT AT ONE POINT SEBASTIAN MIGHT have slept, but as I gazed up at his face, I could see that his eyes were open.

When we couldn't put it off any longer, I packed my equipment, and rolled up my deflated mattress, while Sebastian watched in silence.

"I'll miss having you here," he said, at last. "But I'm glad you're getting the fuck out of this shithole."

I wrapped my arms around his waist and leaned into his chest.

"Just come home safe, Sebastian. No heroics, please."

"The only thing you've got to worry about is when I self-combust, especially if you're going to send me more letters like that one you wrote me yesterday."

I tugged on his uniform. "I mean it. Stay safe."

He sighed and nuzzled his face into my hair. "I'll do my best, baby. Promise." Then he lifted up my chin with one, long finger and kissed me softly.

"Fuck, I'm going to miss you, Caro."

"I love you, *tesoro*. So much."

He held my face between his hands and gazed into my eyes. "*Sei tutto per me*."

Our moment was over, and it was time to go.

Sebastian carried my bag out to the compound, ignoring the open stares of the other men. Captain Grant and Lieutenant Crawley shook hands with me, the latter offering his condolences.

Several of the men I'd been closest to came over and gave me awkward, one-armed hugs.

As soon as we heard the helicopter, eight Marines with M-16s escorted me to the pickup spot, 200 yards outside the compound.

The dust spewed into my eyes, churned up by the rotor blades that didn't stop. Coughing, with my eyes watering, I was yanked inside and had a headset thrust into my hands. We took off immediately, not wishing to offer too easy a target to the unfriendly faces that were sure to be watching from the foothills.

I squinted out of the window, rubbing grit from my eyes, trying to pick out Sebastian from among the small dots of men standing in the compound, but with all of them wearing desert utility uniforms, I couldn't tell which one was him.

My teeth rattled from the helicopter's vibration, and I had to grab onto my seat buckle to stop being thrown around as we banked sharply.

"Excuse me, Miss Venzi." A voice with an English accent reverberated through my earphones. "I'm Flight Lieutenant Reeves, and I'll be escorting you to Bastion."

Oh. I thought I'd be going back to Leatherneck. I guessed it was just a case of who could give me a ride at short notice. In any case—the American and British sections were only a few miles apart.

Camp Bastion, the British base in Helmand, was even larger than Leatherneck. It felt strange to be surrounded by English accents, and I kept expecting Liz's voice to bellow in my ear.

I wasn't sure what they were going to do with me—I assumed they'd transport me over to Leatherneck and let the US decide how to ship me out.

But I was wrong about that. I was bundled into a Land Rover and, instead, escorted to the Field Hospital.

I was greeted by a stocky man in the uniform of the Royal Army Medical Corps.

"Miss Venzi, I'm Major Gibson. I understand you're here to claim the body of Elizabeth Ashton."

I swallowed, my throat suddenly dry, and stared at him.

"No, I..."

He frowned. "I understand you were her next of kin?"

"She was my friend," I said quietly.

"I'm sorry," he said, shortly. "I understand this must be difficult for you. But her employers have given me her death-in-service contact list, and she's named you as next of kin. She was quite specific about that."

"I didn't know," I whispered. "But I don't mind. What did she ... what did she want to happen if...?"

"Her body will be repatriated to the UK. I understand she's requested a cremation and a service at St. Bride's church, Fleet Street."

That made sense. I remembered her telling me that the church's rebuilding after the Second World War had been paid for by journalists—it was their special place. I liked that.

"What do I need to do?"

"There's some paperwork," he said, kindly, "and her personal effects. Her newspaper is arranging for everything else."

I nodded slowly. "Can I see her?"

He looked me in the eye. "I'm sorry, Miss Venzi, that won't be possible."

I could guess the reason.

I signed the forms he gave me, and was given a box with Liz's name on it. Her camera was on top, with her laptop and notebooks at the bottom.

I pulled out her Nikon D4—six-thousand dollars worth of camera. Liz was—had been—serious about her work, she'd always had the best equipment.

"You can take anything you want, Miss Venzi," said the Major.

"Thank you. Did she leave any letters?"

He shook his head. "Not that I know of. She probably filed something with her paper before she flew out."

"Okay, thank you."

We were interrupted by a young woman in scrubs.

"I'm sorry, Major, but we've got three Cat-A wounded coming in."

He stood up, quickly. "I have to go. I'm sorry, Miss Venzi. Your escort will be out front—you're booked on the next flight to Kabul."

He left abruptly. I didn't mind. He couldn't help Liz. Not anymore.

I sat for some minutes, staring at her box. Then I took her camera, stuffed it into my daypack, and headed out.

For the next two hours I sat in a hangar at Camp Bastion, waiting for my flight back to Kabul. I emailed my editor to explain that I needed a flight to the US, and sent the seven features that I'd already written with the photographs from the RPG attacks, as well as life at Leatherneck and from the compound. In other words, I did what Liz would have expected of me: I did my job. I would not let my paper be shortchanged—and I still had a lot to say.

Then, with my laptop balanced on my knee, I wrote Liz's obituary. I wrote about her love of life, her compassion, her curiosity, her fine journalistic sense, her decency and belief in the value of all human life. I remembered her tall stories, her hip-flask—always full of the best Scottish whisky, her sympathy, her stoicism and, most of all, her humanity.

As I wrote, I wondered what would have been said about me, had I died. Would anyone have mentioned Sebastian? Other than Liz, who knew of our affair, our crazy love? Marc knew a little, and Nicole had an inkling, but other than that, would he even have been a footnote?

My insistence on secrecy seemed ridiculous now. Certainly, I wouldn't have been allowed out to Now Zad had our engagement been known, but I could have been sent to another of the US military's remote outposts.

And then I wondered about the two thousand US troops killed in Afghanistan. Who wrote their obituaries? Were their stories carried in small-town papers across the country? Or the 500 British troops, 158 from Canada, 88 from France, 56 from Germany, Italy, Denmark, Australia, Poland, Turkey, Latvia, Finland, Jordan—even Lithuania.

And 37 journalists: now, 38. So many deaths, so much loss.

I took Sebastian's ring off the chain around my neck, and slipped it back onto the third finger of my left hand, where, God willing, it would stay forever.

Back in Kabul, I checked into the Mustafa Hotel again. The manager was surprised to see me, but welcomed me and gave me my old room back.

I wished he hadn't. He'd meant to be kind, but staring at the twin bed where Liz had slept—and snored through half the night—I just felt sad.

I worked all night writing a rough draft, then polishing the remainder of the features that I owed the newspaper. All the time I wondered what Sebastian was doing. I hoped he'd finally get some sleep without me being there to distract him.

I sen an email to let him know I was back in Kabul and awaiting a flight home. I didn't know when he'd see it, but it was still important that I sent it. I also hand wrote a letter, telling him how much I loved him and missed him, and then spoke about all the things we could do when he was home with me in Long Beach. It seemed a long way away.

I was ready to pack up and try to sleep when I received an email from my editor. He was doing his best, but warned me it could be three or four days before he managed to get a flight. And he wanted to speak to me.

Just as I was about to call him, the signal on my cell disappeared again. I trudged down to reception to call him from the hotel's landline, which was only slightly more reliable.

When I finally got through, I gave him more information about Liz's death—the things I hadn't been able to put in her obituary. Sounding shocked, he promised he'd get me out as soon as possible.

After that, I didn't feel like sleeping, so, instead, I spent the day wandering the echoing halls of the Afghanistan National Museum. Seventy percent of the artifacts had disappeared during looting over the past three decades, but the museum was slowly coming back to life. I took the opportunity to interview several of the enthusiastic, but poorly-paid, curators. They were hopeful that the long, cultural history had a future in their country.

I hoped they were right, and I was glad that someone felt optimistic about Afghanistan's future.

Wearily, I returned to my hotel room and wrote another letter to Sebastian. This time I told him about the surf spots at Long Beach, up to the Hamptons and as far as Montauk.

I tried hard to make my letter upbeat and cheerful, but it was difficult when I knew I wouldn't see him for at least another five months.

When I'd finished, I kicked off my boots and lay down.

I hadn't eaten and I wasn't hungry. At least I was tired: I curled up under the sheets, in the unbelievable comfort of the narrow bed, and wished that Sebastian's warm body was next to me, with his breath on my neck, and his arms around my waist.

A loud knock on the door woke me from a light sleep. I sat up in bed, my heart pounding. I squinted at my wristwatch: 2.45AM.

"Who is it?" I asked loudly and clearly.

"Phone call."

It was a voice I didn't recognize.

"Who's calling me?"

"Phone call."

I couldn't tell if it was simply that the person outside my door didn't speak English, or whether I was in danger. I didn't like it at all, and my anxiety levels shot up to Defcon 1.

Without speaking again, I slipped on my boots, and picked up my evac-grab bag, with my finger one button away from dialing the emergency contact number on my cell.

I looked through the peephole in my door but couldn't see anyone; I listened carefully but couldn't hear anything. I was well aware that someone could easily be waiting for me out of my sightline.

I took a deep breath and yanked the door open: the corridor was empty. Which meant the phone call could very well be genuine and not a ruse. I hurried down the stairs, avoiding the elevator, and made my way to the reception area.

A young man in a heavily embroidered vest over a loose, white shirt was sitting at the desk, half asleep. As I approached, he jerked awake.

"Venzi?"

"Ao," I replied. *Yes.*

"Phone call," he said, pointing at the telephone on his desk.

I picked it up tentatively.

"*As-salaamu' alaykum*. This is Lee Venzi."

"Caroline. At last! It's David."

"David?" What the hell was my ex-husband doing calling me in the middle of the night? Was he drunk? "What's wrong? How did you find me, David? Are you all right?"

"Caroline, listen, I don't have much time. I'm at the field hospital at Camp Bastion. It's Hunter."

"Sebastian?"

Oh no, please God, no.

"I'm sorry: he was brought in five hours ago. I've been trying to find you."

I felt sick and cold, and my knees gave way. I slumped into a chair, clattering the legs against the front desk and making the young man jump.

"What's happened? David, please tell me!"

His voice crackled at the end of the line.

"They're still trying to establish the facts, but off the record, it was another green-on-blue attack: sniper and a suicide bomber, they think. Caroline, you can't report any of this."

"I don't care about that, damn it! How's Sebastian? Is he ... is he hurt? Badly? How badly?"

He hesitated long enough for my world to end.

"Yes, it's pretty bad." He paused briefly, then snapped into doctor mode. *"He has a gunshot injury that has induced a pneumothorax—a collapsed lung. We're not too worried about that as the exit wound is clear and the bullet passed through cleanly, although there may be some nerve damage to his left arm resulting in limited fine motor skills..."*

All the breath left my body.

"But he has a Category A..." he paused again, before continuing slowly. "He has a severe injury to his right thigh with multiple debrided shrapnel wounds. They're taking him into surgery now—they'll decide then if the leg is viable. If not, it will be a trans-femoral amputation..." he paused again, "an above-the-knee amputation."

There was a long silence and all the light in my world poured into a deep, dark hole.

"I'm sorry, Caroline ... I thought you'd want to know."

I held my hand over my mouth, as if I could press back the fear that was threatening to choke me.

"Can I see him?"

He sighed. "At the moment the answer is no. You're not ... look, I'll try and get you access, Caroline, but you'd have to get yourself here and I don't know how easy that will be. I'll see what I can find out ... but it's a long shot. I can't promise anything."

"I see."

Breathe. Breathe.

"Thank you, David. Will you let me know ... if the situation changes."

"Yes, of course. I..."

Whatever he wanted to say died as he tried to speak, and the words remained unspoken.

"I'll be in touch," he said, quietly. "Goodbye, Caroline."

The phone line went dead and I stared at the receiver.

Oh, God, no.

No. NO! They were not going to stop me seeing Sebastian. I didn't care if I'd have to fight the whole damn US Army. My love needed me, and no force of hell on earth could stop me being with him.

And that thought galvanized me into action: now was not the time to go to pieces. I whipped out my phone and scrolled through to find the emergency satcomms number that Sebastian had given me. Emergencies only he'd said—this sure as hell qualified.

The man at reception looked like he wanted to say something about my liberal use of the hotel's telephone, but my ferocious expression stopped him.

I dialed quickly, and it was answered on the second ring.

"Grant."

Oh!

"Captain Grant, this is Lee Venzi. I need a favor: I'm in Kabul but I have to get back to Leatherneck. Can you help me get papers, transport, anything?"

"Miss Venzi?" He sounded surprised and annoyed. "How did you get this number? Look, now isn't a good time."

"I'm sorry, but it's urgent, Captain."

For only the second time since I'd known him, he swore.

"I've just lost three of my men, and a further two are Cat A wounded, and..."

I screamed at him.

"I know that!"

"How the hell do you know that?" he barked back.

"It doesn't matter—I just do."

"The fuck it doesn't! If someone is leaking our movements and..."

I took a deep breath: losing it now was not helping.

"No!" I managed to say, in a more measured tone. "No, it wasn't anything like that: I have a medic friend at Bastion's field hospital, I got the information from him."

"I didn't take you for a ghoul, Lee," he said grimly.

"Fuck you, Grant!" I snarled. "I have a *friend* who is just being operated on and I don't know if he's going to get through alive so just fucking get me there!"

There was a short pause.

"You're talking about Hunter, aren't you?"

"Yes," I said, trying not to let my throat close up.

"Okay, Miss Venzi," he said, in a more even tone. "I'll see if I can pull some strings to get you there. But don't call this number—and don't ask me again."

"I won't," I barked into the phone.

"Where are you staying?"

I gave him the hotel's address and hung up.

I thought he'd try to help me, but he had other men to worry about—other casualties. I chewed on a nail, wondering who else I could call on.

Inspiration struck. There was one more number I could try: Ches Peters—Sebastian's best friend. A man whom I was pretty certain despised me.

I did the math to work out the time difference—it was about seven o'clock in the evening in San Diego. He had two young kids, so I hoped he'd be home.

The phone rang three times before it was answered.

A child's voice trilled down the line.

"Hello, Peters' residence. This is Ben Peters speaking."

"Hi, Ben. Can I talk to your daddy, please?"

"He's making popcorn," said the little boy.

"Could you get him for me? It's important."

There was an angry huff, a short pause where I could hear muffled voices, and then I heard Ches come on the line.

"Hello, who's this?"

"Ches, this is Lee ... this is Caroline Venzi ... I was Caroline Wilson and..."

"I know who you are. What do you want?"

His voice was cool, but full of unspoken contempt.

"I need your help. Well, Mitch's, I guess—I know he's still in the Marines. I'd have called him direct but I don't have his number."

I realized I was babbling. I needed to focus.

"Ches, I'm calling from Afghanistan. Sebastian has been hurt. Pretty badly..."

I had to hold the phone away from my face for a moment, stifling the choking sobs that bubbled up my throat.

"How bad?" Ches whispered.

"Bad. They're taking him into surgery now. They might ... they're talking about amputating his right leg."

I heard Ches's shocked curse.

"He's at the field hospital near Camp Leatherneck, but I'm stuck 300 miles away in Kabul, and without papers. I can't get to him. I know you think I'm a first class bitch and that I ruined his life, but I'm begging you, Ches, begging you..."

I had to pause to catch my breath, forcing the pointless tears away.

"Please," I choked out, "if there's anything you or Mitch can do to get me there. I'm pulling in every favor I can think of, using every contact. I'll do anything. If you know anyone, anyone at all ... please, Ches, please..."

"I'll do what I can, Caroline," he said in a stunned, quiet voice. "Give me the details."

I told him everything I knew, which wasn't much. But it was more than most people would have known in the same circumstances—and it was thanks to David.

I was sorely tempted to call my editor, but I suspected his immediate reaction would be to tell me to stay put until he got me on a flight home. He'd been shocked into silence when I'd told him the reason I was pulled out of Now Zad, and coming on top of what had happened to Liz, I didn't know how much help he'd be.

In fact I was pretty certain he'd try to block me getting back to Kandahar.

Desperate as I was to get to Sebastian, I had to think, I couldn't just charge in. It even crossed my mind to try and speak to Natalie Arnaud: she worked for the UN—she might have contacts. I decided I would wait until morning before I tried my riskier avenues. By then David or Grant might have made some wheels spin, and I was damn sure that Ches and Mitch would pull every string they could.

I went back to my room, and packed up everything, ready to leave at a moment's notice.

When there was nothing left to do, when every last bit of fight and determination had been used up, I lay on the bed clutching Sebastian's ring, and wept.

They say there are no atheists in foxholes. I say there are no atheists when you're begging God to keep alive the person you love.

~

At exactly 5.57AM I woke up and swore.

Damn it! Why hadn't I thought of this last night? *This* was why it was important not to go to pieces in an emergency.

I checked my phone and sent up a silent prayer, thanking the saints of telecommunications.

"Sergeant Benson, this is Lee Venzi—you were my bodyguard last week."

I could tell from his fuzzy voice that he'd been asleep when I rang.

"Miss Venzi?"

"I'm sorry I woke you up, and I'm sorry it's so early, but I need your help. I'm in Kabul..."

"Kabul?"

"Yes, I'm back at the Mustafa Hotel. I got evac-ed from Leatherneck and, well ... it's a long story. Look, I've just found that my ... *fiancé* has been injured and I *have* to get back out there. Can you help me?"

He sounded wide awake now.

"I'm real sorry to hear that, Miss Venzi, but you'll have to go through the usual channels. Have your newspaper contact the Corps' Division of Public Affairs and..."

"I don't have time for that! Listen to me! He's hurt really badly—I don't know if he'll ... I *have* to get there. Please, Sergeant ... he's one of your own—he's a United States Marine."

There was a silence at the end of the line. Then he said, "Give me three hours."

Sergeant Benson was as good as his word.

I called Ches to let him know I was on the move, and promised to get in touch as soon as I had any further news.

A hundred-and-fifty minutes later, I was on my way back to Lashkar Gah. Sergeant Benson had moved heaven and earth to get me where I needed to be. I would never forget his kindness.

To say David was surprised to see me would be a vast understatement. But he didn't waste any time asking me stupid questions either.

As soon as he saw me, he said, "He's still alive, Caroline."

"Thank God."

Those brief words flooded through me, and some of the weight on my chest that had made it hurt to breathe, eased just a little.

He led me through a complex of tents and portable huts, and into what looked like the ICU department of a modern, urban hospital.

"He's in here."

The room was small and brightly lit. Sebastian lay on a hospital bed with a number of tubes and monitors attached to him. His left arm was elevated and he was breathing on a ventilator, his chest rising and falling in time with the machine. It was the only sign he was alive: he was so still and pale.

Below his waist, he was covered with a thin blanket which rose in a mound over the cage that protected his right leg.

Thank God—they'd saved his leg.

A man in desert utilities was standing over Sebastian. At first I thought he was a doctor, but then I heard what he was saying, the rhythmical cadence of words repeated too many times.

"O Father of mercies and God of all comfort, our only help in time of need..."

I recognized the prayer for the sick.

"We humbly beseech thee to behold, visit and relieve thy sick servant Sebastian Hunter, for whom our prayers are desired. Look upon him with the eyes of thy mercy, comfort him with a sense of thy goodness, preserve him from the temptations of the enemy, and give him patience under his affliction. In thy good time, restore him to health, and enable him to lead the residue of his life in thy fear, and to thy glory, and grant that finally Sebastian may dwell with thee in life everlasting, through Jesus Christ our Lord. Amen."

"Amen," I echoed, softly.

The man turned around, and I wasn't surprised to see that he was wearing the white collar of a priest.

I crossed myself.

"Thank you, Padre."

"Is he a friend of yours?"

I nodded. "He's my *fiancé*," I said, quietly.

I couldn't see David's face, but I heard his sudden intake of breath behind me.

The priest patted my arm.

"God hears all prayers, my child. And your young man is very strong."

He gave me a small smile, nodded at David, and left the room.

"You're marrying him?" asked David, his voice oddly strained. "You didn't say that when I saw you before in Kabul. You said you'd only just met again."

I looked up sharply. "I wasn't lying, David. This is ... very new."

"I'm sorry..." he began. Then he cleared his throat and started again.

"They've managed to save the leg for now, but there's still some doubt about whether it's viable. The next few days will be critical. There was dirt in the shrapnel and he's contracted acinetobacter baumannii—it's a common infection out here. We're treating it with antibiotics but..." he sighed. "And he's been put into a medically-induced coma: we were worried about brain swelling as he received a shockwave from the bomb. Well, that's quite typical with these sorts of injuries."

I nodded, unable to speak.

"I'm sorry, Caroline," he said again. "Well, if you need anything..."

Hesitantly, David rested his hand on my shoulder, then turned and left me alone with my grief.

I picked up Sebastian's hand and held it in my own. The fingers felt cold, so I held them to my mouth and blew on them softly, trying to heat them with my breath, just as he had done, only three weeks before in Chamonix.

Dear God—that seemed a lifetime ago. He'd been so alive, so vibrant, so full of hope, and now...

I held his hand to my cheek and closed my eyes.

"Come back to me, Sebastian. Please, *tesoro*, you have to fight. You've always been so strong, don't give up now, don't give up on us. I need you. Come back to me. Please, come back to me."

The ventilator rose and fell, his chest rose and fell, but Sebastian's eyes remained closed.

I talked to him all day: telling him about the bungalow, and the way the ocean trembled with light in the summer sun; how the sky seemed to reach long fingers down to the waves in a storm, spray mingling with rain.

I told him about Alice's kindness and humor, about Jenna's fieriness, and the way Nicole was always trying to set me up on dates—but that I didn't need her to do that anymore. And I told him what Ches had said to me on the telephone.

"He told me to kick your butt right out of this hospital bed, Sebastian. You promised him you'd go surfing in California after this tour, a fact that you completely forgot to mention to me, I might add. Do you want to have our honeymoon in California, *tesoro*? Because I don't care where we have it.

Anywhere you like, my love. Sebastian, can you hear me? I love you so much—we have our whole lives ahead of us. I'll go anywhere, do anything to be with you. Just please wake up, *tesoro*."

A medic came past and checked the machine's readouts, before methodically pushing some more meds into the IV bag that was suspended next to the bed.

"You a friend of his, ma'am?"

"Yes, I am."

"Perhaps you can help me then? We found a letter on him when he was brought in, but the name isn't anyone on his emergency contact list. We just held onto it, kinda hoping we could find someone to give it to. Do you know a 'Carolina Hunter' ma'am? We figured it was some relative of his, but so far we can't trace her."

I gasped slightly, then nodded. "Yes, I know her. I'll make sure she gets it."

"Thank you, ma'am."

He reached into a locker next to Sebastian's bed and pulled out a muddy envelope.

When he handed it to me, I realized it wasn't covered in dirt, but blood—Sebastian's blood. The medic shrugged his apology, and walked away to check on his next patient.

My hands shook as I tore open the envelope.

There was a single sheet of lined paper with a ragged edge inside, probably torn from a notebook. One side contained a short message in Sebastian's careful handwriting.

> *Caro, my love,*
>
> *Just writing these words makes me happier than I can remember being for a very long time—ten years, in fact.*
>
> *I'm not one for words—I leave that to you—my beautiful, talented Caro. But we've had the news we were waiting for and soon we'll be heading out. I hope you never read this letter, but if you do, it means I've gone on to the next big adventure.*
>
> *Knowing that you are in the world and wearing my ring, makes me the happiest man alive, and the last few weeks have been the best and happiest of my whole life.*
>
> *Be happy, Caro, because that's what you deserve.*
>
> *I love you, I have always loved you, and wherever I go after this world, I will always love you. Sempre e per sempre.*
>
> *Sebastian*

I clutched his letter to my chest, trying to find a way to fill the aching void. I couldn't understand why my heart was still beating.

I gave up trying to be strong. I lay my head next to his hand, and my tears soaked into the crisp, white sheet.

My love was slipping away from me, and there was nothing I could do.

The night passed and I sat staring at Sebastian's face, memorizing every line and angle: the softness of his cheeks, now covered with a fine, light brown stubble, the full, sensual lips, distorted by the breathing tube that had been placed into his throat, the strong, straight nose, the wide forehead, the beautiful symmetry of his cheekbones. But his lovely eyes, the windows to his sweet soul, were hidden.

I whispered my secrets to him, all my desires and fears, hoping that in some way he knew that I was with him. I ran my fingers along the back of his hand and up his forearm, tracing the faint veins, knowing that they were still pumping blood through his body, and that the fight wasn't over.

David returned at some point, although whether it was day or night by then, I couldn't tell.

"Caroline, perhaps you should try and get some sleep. I've arranged for you to have a cot-bed in the doctors' lounge. Well, it's not much of a lounge, more of a shed really."

"Thank you, David. That's very kind of you. Maybe later."

He looked at me thoughtfully.

"He's holding on, Caroline. He's strong, but ... they're trying to decide whether to medivac him to Germany. It just depends on ... whether he's stable enough to make the journey."

I stared up at him.

"Why are you being so nice to me, David? I always thought you must hate me after ... everything that happened."

He looked surprised, then rubbed a hand tiredly across his cheeks.

"I tried to hate you. I thought I did, for a while, but I couldn't really. I knew it was my fault."

I blinked with surprise, amazed by his words.

"Why did you think that? I was the one who ... had the affair."

His eyes closed briefly and when he opened them again, he seemed to have made a decision.

"You were so full of life, Caroline, and I loved you so much. I tried so hard to hold onto you, but the harder I tried to hold on, the more you slipped away from me. I ended up crushing you. I was so terrified you'd see through me ... I did everything I could to stifle you. I knew it was wrong, but I couldn't stop myself. I will regret that to my dying day."

Then he gestured toward Sebastian. "He brought you back to life."

I hung my head, humbled by his admission and his apology, remembering all his cruelty and bullying. And remembering, too, his new kindness in my hour of need.

"I'm so sorry, David. For everything that happened between us. For what I did to you. I never meant to hurt you. But ... I fell in love."

"I know," he said, softly. "I just wish it had been with me."

He smiled sadly, and walked away.

The days and nights began to blur together. If it hadn't been for David, bringing me food or insisting that I slept, I don't know how I would have coped.

I called Ches each day, but there wasn't much I could tell him. I heard the hope in his voice every time I called, and every time I could only repeat the same words, "There's no change."

The chaplain visited us daily, and told me not to give up hope. Sometimes he prayed with me, sometimes he brought me a sandwich. Both were equally welcome.

I'd been there four or five days, the colorless hours merging together, when David told me that Sebastian was stable enough to be moved. Some news, at last.

"We're going to bring him out of the coma, then he'll be sent to the Landstuhl Regional Medical Center in Germany. From there, on to Bethesda in Maryland or Walter Reed in DC. I'm not sure which."

"Will I be able to go with him?"

He sighed. "Normally, I'd say that was highly unlikely. But, off the record, Caroline, if you can use your Press connections, then maybe."

"Thank you," I said, quietly, touching his hand.

He smiled briefly.

That was all the encouragement I needed. I was on the phone to my editor within 20 minutes and I refused to take no for an answer. I promised as many articles as he wanted, exclusive interviews and photographs of life in a military medical center. In the end, he agreed to help. I don't know how many strings he pulled in Washington, but he promised me he'd get me on the same flight as Sebastian.

When I returned to Sebastian's room, I couldn't work out what was different —and then I realized it was too quiet. The ventilator had stopped working. I panicked, looking around wildly for help, but then ... I saw that Sebastian's eyes were open, and he was looking at me.

He spoke, and his voice was so soft and hoarse that I could barely hear him.

"I *knew* you wouldn't give up on us," he said.

~

We were flown out that evening, and arrived at the medical center in Germany at dawn. The critical cases were taken off first—those with brain injuries and missing limbs. We waited on the chilly tarmac for 15 minutes before the rest of us were loaded onto a fleet of blue buses.

We were met by the Head of the Critical Care Team, and the army chaplain.

"You're here at the US army hospital. We're going to take good care of you. We're praying for you. You're here at the US army hospital. We're going to take good care of you. We're praying for you."

Over and over again, the tired-looking chaplain repeated the words, as stretcher after stretcher passed him, the syllables blurring and becoming meaningless.

Sebastian held my hand tightly but didn't speak.

We were there for just two nights while Sebastian was 'processed'.

The harried but sympathetic staff gave me a small, cell-like room in the women's quarters. Day and night the injured arrived: there wasn't time to learn the names of the soldiers with so many identical injuries who streamed through the hospital, some from Iraq, most from Afghanistan. They were treated and moved on. Treated and moved on. An endless flow of mutilated flesh and tortured minds.

Sebastian had the option to go back to San Diego or to an East Coast facility. We decided it would be easier if we were near home—my home—our home, and we flew out to Walter Reed in Maryland on a Thursday at the start of May.

The journey from Germany was long and painful for Sebastian, he didn't complain once, even though I could tell he was in agony, his body covered in an unhealthy sheen of sweat. But he didn't speak to me either, and that scared me.

There were many who were far worse off. One young man I spoke quietly with during those dreary hours was named Lance. He'd lost both legs and one arm. He told me that he was 'glad' it had happened to him, because he wouldn't have wanted it to happen to any of his buddies in his platoon.

He was 22.

~

Our arrival back on US soil was without fanfare. I traveled with Sebastian the whole time and saw him settled into a unit, before I found myself accommodation nearby in a cheap motel. There were other wives and family members staying there and we became close, sharing our hopes and dreams—or rather, forging new dreams that were far more limited in their scope than formerly.

Liz's memorial service came and went. I sent a letter to her editor, asking him to read it out for me, and I asked him to recite the poem 'High Flight' by Pilot Officer Gillespie Magee. I knew it had always been a favorite of Liz's.

Oh! I have slipped the surly bonds of earth

And danced the skies on laughter-silvered wings,
Sunward I've climbed, and joined the tumbling mirth
Of sun-split clouds—and done a hundred things
You have not dreamed of—wheeled and soared and swung
High in the sunlit silence. Hov'ring there
I've chased the shouting wind along, and flung
My eager craft through footless halls of air.
Up, up the long delirious, burning blue,
I've topped the windswept heights with easy grace
Where never lark, or even eagle flew –
And, while with silent lifting mind I've trod
The high untrespassed sanctity of space,
Put out my hand and touched the face of God.

Alone in my motel room, I said a prayer for her, too.

For nine weeks, I waited and watched with anxious eyes as Sebastian slowly began to heal.

He was given intensive physiotherapy to help him use his left arm and to walk again. He became breathless and tired quickly, but, in the face of so many with worse injuries, he hid his true feelings. I think I was the only one who could see the simmering anger beneath the surface.

To other soldiers and to the staff, he seemed cheerful and worked hard at whatever exercises he was given. But to me, he was closed and distant. He'd always been so honest and open with me, I felt lost and alone—more truly lonely in his company than when I was by myself.

It soon became obvious that the extent of his injuries would render him unfit for duty. One of the prerequisites of being a Marine was the ability to run without a limp. The doctors thought it extremely unlikely that Sebastian would ever be able to walk without using a crutches, let alone run. A medical discharge was the most likely scenario.

The military was generous to those wounded in combat, and although Sebastian wouldn't qualify for a medical pension, not having served his 20 years, he was told he could still expect to receive between a third and half of his current salary. He would be a disabled veteran.

Those words sent him into a fury. He ranted at me for nearly half an hour.

"I won't take it," he growled.

"What? Why not?"

"I just won't," he said, with finality.

"Sebastian, you deserve that—after everything you've been through..."

"I'm not fucking taking it, Caro. I'm 27. I don't fucking want disability pay!"

"Okay, *tesoro*. That's your choice."

I think the fact that I wouldn't fight with him just made it worse. He had vast reserves of pent-up anger, and I was the nearest target—and probably the only one he felt he could take it out on.

The military also offered him the chance to take college courses through the GI Bill, but he wouldn't discuss that either. The list of unmentionable topics became longer each day.

The tense silence between us was exhausting. At a loss, I thought it might help if I gave him some space and let him come to terms with everything that had happened without my constant presence—and without what he seemed to feel was my constant interference.

I decided we needed a break from each other and I wanted to go and check on my house, too. Alice had been going over there regularly, but I longed to be in my own home. I really thought it might help our tenuous relationship if I just visited Sebastian on the weekends. It was also getting expensive staying in the motel, although I didn't mention that to him.

We were resting on a bench in the grounds after Sebastian had managed to walk almost 200 yards, leaning heavily on a crutch. It was hard for me to see him struggle when he had always been so strong and vigorous, but how much harder it was for him, I could only imagine.

"You did well today, Sebastian."

He grunted an answer, and I couldn't tell if he was agreeing with me or not.

I sighed, then took a deep breath.

"I've been thinking I should go back to Long Beach. Just to make sure everything is okay at home. I want to try and start working a little more..."

My words died away as he looked at me with something like loathing.

"You're leaving me."

It was a statement, not a question.

"No, *tesoro!* Why would you say that? No, never!"

"Don't fucking lie to me, Caro," he shouted. "You've made it pretty fucking obvious you don't want to be here. Well, fine. Just fucking go."

And he turned away from me.

I tried to speak, but I choked on the sounds.

"Please, Sebastian," I said, touching his arm. "That's not what I'm saying. I just wanted to ... try and get some ... some normalcy. I'd visit on weekends."

He shrugged me off.

"Don't fucking drag it out, Caro," he said, bitterly. "I'm not completely fucking dumb."

I stood suddenly, and the movement made him look up.

"Damn you, Sebastian!" I yelled. "I'm not leaving you! You'll never get rid of me, so you can just stop trying. Right now."

He looked away again.

"Whatever," he said.

That was a bad, bad day. I wondered how much further we had to fall—and I dreaded finding out. But I also realized that although Sebastian sniped and snarled at me day after day, he needed me to be with him. I decided to stay in Maryland: Alice would be able to continue looking after the bungalow.

We'd manage—somehow.

Seven days later, the Physical Evaluation Board Liaison Officer, a friendly but efficient woman whom I knew as Joan, told Sebastian that the PEB would, 'authorize his disability separation, with disability benefits, as he had been found unfit and his condition was incompatible with continued military service'.

Sebastian was no longer a US Marine.

CHAPTER SEVENTEEN

THE DAY SEBASTIAN CAME HOME SHOULD HAVE BEEN THE HAPPIEST OF OUR lives, but my love was broken in body and spirit.

I arranged for a taxi to pick us up from the airport. Nicole and Jenna had both offered to drive us, but I thought it would be better for him to have a quiet return. Sebastian was in no shape to meet my friends, no matter how well-meaning.

Alice had been to the bungalow to clean and air it, and had also promised to stock up the fridge.

I'd arranged for a wheelchair to take Sebastian from the plane to the airport's entrance, but he refused to even consider it.

"I'm not fucking using it, Caro, so just drop it," he snapped at me.

I quietly acquiesced, and watched his slow and painful struggle through the terminal building, using the crutch to support his right leg, which still couldn't bear his weight.

The taxi driver chatted away during the journey back to Long Beach, and I tried to keep up a desultory conversation while Sebastian stared out of the window.

I thought I detected a slight change in him when he saw the ocean, today a sharp, slate-blue under the August sunshine, but then he closed up and the shutters on his emotions came crashing down again.

When we arrived at my bungalow, the driver collected our bags from the trunk and deposited them on the porch. I stood back while Sebastian struggled from the car, desperate to help him, but knowing he'd hate it and resent the interference.

"Dude, what happened to your leg?" the driver suddenly asked him.

"Bomb."

"Say what?"

"Bomb: got blown up."

"Cool!"

I thought Sebastian would smile or roll his eyes or give some indication of the callousness of the driver's comment, but he didn't. The light had gone out of his eyes and I didn't know what it would take to rekindle it.

We'd find a way. We'd always find a way.

But it was hard.

Sebastian was exhausted and in pain. He made his way to my couch and lowered himself carefully, biting back the groan that rose to his lips.

"Do you want to lie down, *tesoro*?"

I badly wanted him to make a joke, to say something about me wanting to get him into bed as soon as possible, but he didn't. He just shook his head.

"I'll stay here for a while."

"Okay." I hesitated. "Well, I'll put your bags in the spare room for now. We can go through them later."

He didn't answer.

I shoved his duffel bag and backpack under the bed. I decided I'd unpack these when he was asleep. He didn't need to see his uniforms now. I didn't even know if he'd want to keep them.

When I walked back into the living room, he was staring into space.

"Are you hungry? Would you like some pasta?"

He shook his head. "No."

I bit back my words, which would have insisted that he eat something.

He'd lost weight, a lot of weight, his face gaunt, and his beauty, which had always seemed so tangible, had become ethereal.

"Maybe later," I said, softly.

He didn't answer.

I felt odd and ill at ease being home after such an extended absence and Sebastian's silent, volcanic presence intimidated me.

"This wasn't what I'd planned," he said.

"It's not what either of us had in mind, but we'll deal, won't we?"

"I thought I'd be carrying you over the fucking threshold," he said, his face twisted with disgust.

"That doesn't matter, Sebastian. We..."

"Yes, it does fucking matter, Caro!" he shouted, making me jump. "It really fucking matters! Christ, can't you understand something as fucking simple as that?"

I blanched, his anger cutting me to the core.

"I'm sorry, Sebastian, I just..."

"Just what, Caro?"

"Nothing," I muttered, walking into the kitchen, and holding onto the sink.

I will not cry. I will not cry.

I needed something to do with my hands to stop them from shaking. I hunted through the fridge, trying to think of something he might like to eat. In the end I kept it simple—a cheese sandwich with lettuce and tomato. It wasn't really the sort of thing I enjoyed eating, but I hoped if I had the same food, it might tempt him.

I took two plates into the living room and set one down next to him. He didn't even look at the food, just continued staring into space, as if his outburst had never happened.

I tried not to panic: he'd been through a lot. How trivial that sounded—he'd nearly died and he was a long way from recovering—even the doctors still failed to agree on how full that recovery would be.

I couldn't stand the silence. Eventually, I turned on the TV, something I rarely did when I was by myself. I had to change channel several times before I found something that didn't have news programs or anything to do with Afghanistan. We ended up watching something about meerkats in Africa: very educational—neither of us heard more than half a dozen words, and Sebastian didn't touch his food.

"Do you have any beer?"

"Oh, no, sorry," I stuttered. "I could open some wine?"

He nodded. "Yeah, that'll do."

I opened a bottle Chianti and watched him drink three glasses, one after the other. He would have finished the bottle if I hadn't taken it into the kitchen.

"Caro, what are you doing with the fucking wine?"

No. I wasn't having this. He wasn't going to drown his sorrows in a bottle.

"You haven't eaten anything, and you have to take your pain killers, Sebastian. So, no, the wine stays in the kitchen."

He exploded. Swearing at me, shouting and yelling. Who the fuck did I think I was? Who was I to tell him how to live his life? And on and on.

I hoped that when he'd finished, he'd have gotten some of the poison out of him, but he soon reverted to the cold silence that hurt the most.

By 9PM, his face was gray with tiredness.

"Should I show you where the bedroom is?"

"It's a fucking bungalow, Caro," he said, "how fucking difficult do you think it's going to be? I'm not a fucking moron, even if I am a cripple."

"Sebastian..."

But he didn't want to listen. He pulled himself off the couch, gasping as pain lanced through him, and he clenched his teeth.

After a false start, where he crashed into the spare room, he found his way to the bedroom. I gave him a few minutes, then followed. He was lying on his good side, facing away from my side of the bed.

I brushed my teeth and slipped in next to him, carefully curling my body into his and enjoying the moment when my arm rested across his waist, feeling his bare skin again after nearly three months.

He shifted minutely.

"Don't," he said.

I pulled my hand back as if stung.

He didn't want me to touch him? He didn't want me to touch him.

I'd learned during my first marriage that it is possible to cry without making a sound, I didn't think Sebastian would take me back to those years. And that was more painful than anything. I lay next to him as the tears slipped silently down my cheeks.

Over the next few days, things became worse. He had no interest in anything; I had to nag to get him to shower or change his clothes, and he refused point blank to shave, so his beautiful face was covered in a light-brown stubble that was unfamiliar and unwelcome.

He ate little, preferring instead to work his way through my small collection of wine, and cut off any attempt of mine to stop him.

He barely spoke to me. His usual responses included shouting and yelling, or just ignoring me. He didn't read, he didn't watch TV, he didn't do anything except drink.

My friends wanted to come and visit. Tentatively, I suggested it to him, thinking he might be persuaded into making an effort for them, if not for me.

"Yeah, they want to come see the fucking war cripple," he sneered, "make them feel good, like fucking charity. What's the matter with you, Caro? Do I look like I'm ready to see anyone?"

"Sebastian, they're my friends. They want to meet you, and they want to see me. You don't have to put on a performance for them." *Even though that was exactly what I'd hoped.*

He shrugged, and said that if they came, he'd stay in the bedroom.

I decided to ask them to postpone their visit.

Before I'd returned from Afghanistan, I'd telephoned each of them, explaining everything about Sebastian: how we'd met, why we'd been forced apart. It had been deeply uncomfortable, and I was afraid of their censure. Instead, they'd been supportive, although I could tell that they were hurt that I'd never been completely candid with them before. I hoped they understood my reasons. I hadn't told them we were engaged, although I wasn't sure why.

I took my phone and walked down to the beach alone.

"Nic, it's Lee."

"Hey, honey! What time do you want us tomorrow?"

"Look, it's not good timing. Sebastian is ... struggling. He's not ready to meet anyone."

She could hear the tremor in my voice.

"Fuck that, Lee! I want to see *you*. This isn't something you have to do by yourself."

"I know that, Nic, but now just isn't good. Maybe in a few weeks."

There was a short silence.

"How bad is it, Lee?"

"Bad," I said. "Really bad."

And then I started crying, and couldn't stop.

Nicole listened to me sobbing into the phone for several minutes. When I finally began to calm down, she spoke to me firmly.

"Lee, you need professional help on this, Sebastian needs professional help. Can't the VA hospital do something? I mean, the military has programs to help with exactly this problem."

I shook my head wearily, wishing she was there to throw a comforting arm around me.

"He refuses to talk to anyone, Nic. He barely talks to me. I don't know what to do—he says he's had enough of hospitals and never wants to see another doctor. I get that, and I feel the same in some ways, but I'm at the end of my rope here. And he's drinking, he hardly eats. He doesn't touch me, and won't let me touch him. I don't know what to do."

She hesitated for a moment.

"Are you sure you want to do this at all, Lee?"

I took a sharp intake of breath.

Out of everything I thought she'd say, that had been furthest from my thoughts. And I had considered that I might not be what he needed, but I'd always assumed that he'd be the one to walk away.

"I can't abandon him now, Nic. He needs me, more than ever."

"I'm sure he does, but unless he accepts your help, you can't do anything. He has to want to get better."

I knew she was right, I just wasn't sure what to do about it.

By then the nightmares had started, too. Or rather, I hadn't realized how bad they had become, but now we were sharing a bed, it became clear to me how traumatic they really were. Sebastian would have intense dreams and wake up screaming. Once, I thought he was going to attack me, his flashback was so vivid. He held back at the last second, his eyes wild and black with terror. I think it was seeing my fear that stopped him from ... from hurting me.

He started checking that the windows and doors were locked two or three times a night before we went to bed, and he became paranoid about people coming to the house, whether it was the mailman or one of our neighbors dropping a leaflet through the door.

He refused to leave the house, but hated me going out, too. We became virtual recluses. I tried to carry on working, but there was only so much I could do from home, and I began to resent his attempts to control me.

One day, he yelled at me because there was no alcohol in the house and I'd refused to buy any more.

I yelled back.

"If you want a fucking drink, then get your fucking ass off that couch and go get it yourself, Sebastian!"

I marched out of the bungalow, my blood boiling.

I felt horribly guilty the moment I slammed the door behind me, but I wasn't backing down. We'd reached an impasse: something had to change.

When I'd calmed enough to go home, a place that was no longer a refuge, Sebastian had gone to bed. He didn't even acknowledge me as I climbed in beside him. Our bed had become another battleground.

And he wouldn't touch me: he barely looked at me, shunned any embrace, and we didn't make love. We were strangers to each other, but sharing a bed.

In the morning, I wearily dragged myself awake, both of us having slept badly. He'd had another terrifying nightmare, screaming out in fear. I longed to hold him, but he wouldn't even look at me. When I touched him, he flinched.

I didn't know how much longer we could go on like this. And he still refused to speak to any doctors.

"What the fuck do they know about it, Caro?"

"A lot: you're not the first Marine who's been injured."

"Former Marine, former fucking Marine, Caro. I'm nothing now. Maybe you can try and fucking remember that."

His words cracked my heart.

He'd been my lover, he'd been a Marine, and now he was neither. The past was another country and the future was ... well, he couldn't see that he had a future. We lived from each slow hour to the next.

And he felt guilty—so guilty for having been the one who had survived. No one would tell me exactly what had happened but from what I'd pieced together, and from what David had told me during that first phone call, someone on the inside, an ally, had started shooting and then detonated a bomb. Three other Marines had died and two more were injured, although not as badly as Sebastian. Surviving wasn't about skill, it was about luck.

During those long, dark days, two things kept me going. The first was his letter, the one he'd written before his last mission. The paper had become soft and fragile with the number of times I'd read it. I looked at it often when I was alone for a few seconds, even though I'd long memorized the words.

The second was a small thing, ridiculous really, but it signified a lot to me, and I think to Sebastian, too.

I'd been sorting through a pile of dirty clothes: one of those joyless, thankless jobs that we all have to do, but never get finished because they're never-ending.

I was making sure buttons were done up, and shirts were turned inside out before I threw them into the washer, tedious but necessary, when I picked up Sebastian's jeans. As usual, he'd tossed them into the hamper unbuttoned and unzipped. I thought I'd better check the pockets, too ... and that's when I found it.

I felt a hard lump in the hip pocket. I pushed my hand inside and pulled out a small, white pebble. It was the little piece of quartz that I'd found on the beach, that silly sentimental gift that I'd given to Sebastian the day he'd flown out to Afghanistan. And he'd kept it. More than that, he kept it with him even now.

My throat started to ache with tears but I refused to let myself cry, because they would have been hopeful tears. If Sebastian cared enough to keep that little pebble, surely it meant he still cared for me? That he was still capable of caring for me?

A loud crash brought me running to the living room.

Sebastian was thrashing around on the floor, swearing up and down, cursing like it was going out of fashion, and surrounded by books.

"What happened?" I asked breathlessly.

"I fucking fell! What does it look like?" he snarled.

I guessed that he'd lost his balance and tried to hold onto the bookshelf, but pulled the whole thing down instead.

I bent down to help him up.

"Leave me alone! I'm not a complete fucking cripple."

I bit my lip and watched as he struggled to his feet. His frustration at what he perceived as his helplessness boiled over several times a day. I had to remind myself that he wasn't mad at me, but sometimes it was hard. It hurt to see him fight so hard: fight his own body as it continued to heal, fight me, fight everyone.

He was sinking deeper into depression each day, and I didn't know how to help him.

He even refused to talk about getting married or anything that involved planning for our future.

"I'm not going to let you marry a useless, fucking cripple," he roared, when I'd been foolish enough to press the subject. "If I can't even walk down the fucking aisle without a fucking crutch..."

I bit back my angry retort that there wouldn't be an aisle at City Hall, and left him alone to stew in his own black anger.

My own hopes and dreams drifted further away.

In silence, I bent down and started picking up the books that had tumbled down around him—the ones out of his reach. He watched me sullenly for a moment, then reached out to collect the volumes nearest to him. As he picked up my copy of 'Lolita' by its cover, an envelope fell out, fluttering to the ground. I knew at once what it was and leaned over to pick it up. Sebastian was faster.

"What's this?" he asked, his voice puzzled. "It has my name on it."

He looked up at me. "The date on it ... that's the day we first..."

"Yes, I know," I said, quietly.

The small envelope did indeed have Sebastian's name scrawled across one corner in my untidy handwriting. The date was ten years ago: the day I'd found him alone in the park, bruised and bloodied after yet another fight with his father. The bastard had hit him several times and then hacked off chunks of Sebastian's long, surfer hair. I'd taken him to my house, patched him up, and shaved the rest of his hair into an elegant buzz cut, trying to mask the evidence of his father's assault. It was also the night we'd first made love.

"What's in it, Caro?" he asked, fingering the small, paper package.

It was the only time he'd shown a spark of interest in anything in weeks.

I shrugged. "Open it."

He propped himself up against the couch then heaved himself up so he was leaning against the cushions. He fumbled, trying to open the sealed envelope, the motor skills of his left hand still limited.

He was probably expecting to find some sort of letter inside, but he was wrong.

A lock of long, blond hair fell out.

I saw the shock of recognition on his face.

"This is mine: my hair. You kept it—all these years?"

"Yes, *tesoro*. It was all I had of you."

He closed his eyes, holding the lock in his hand.

"Caro, I don't understand. Why do you love me?"

"Just because ... because the sky is blue and the sea is green."

And then he started to cry. He fisted his hands over his eyes and sobbed into my arms. And, at last, I could hold him. I wrapped my arms around him and held him tightly, willing the darkness away, trying to heal him with my body, with my touch.

"I love you, Sebastian, please don't push me away. I love you."

"Oh God, Caro. I just don't know what I'm doing any more, I'm so fucked up —I feel like I can't fucking breathe. Don't give up on me, Caro. Please don't give up on me. I need you, baby. I love you so much. I'm so sorry."

I could forgive anything now that he'd let me touch him.

I held him for an hour, just stroking his hair, as he rested his head in my lap, my fingers running over his rough beard. I realized he'd taken one small step toward me, toward living again—I needed him to take another.

"It's time to go out now, Sebastian," I said, softly.

He closed his eyes and swallowed.

"I don't know if I can do that, Caro."

"You don't have to do this by yourself, Sebastian. We go together. Come on, *tesoro*. Together."

I could tell he was nervous, so we took it slowly. I gave him my Yankees baseball cap, which he pulled down over his eyes, and he wore his old biker jacket, which hung loosely from his shoulders, emphasizing how thin he'd become.

I took his hand, and, with Sebastian leaning heavily on his walking cane, we made our way slowly along West Beech Street. Sebastian kept looking over his shoulder, checking the windows of buildings along the road, and I knew he was unconsciously looking for snipers. I didn't hurry him, we went at his pace, but the feeling that flowed through me from being with him outdoors at last was almost overwhelming.

"There's a café over there, Sebastian. Why don't we go have a coffee?"

"I don't know, Caro ... sitting outside? I wouldn't feel ... safe."

"Sebastian, you know rationally that there's nothing to worry about. Let's just try it for a couple of minutes: if you really can't handle it, we'll leave."

He twitched unhappily, but didn't argue.

The waiter came toward us and Sebastian flinched away from him.

"I'll have an espresso. Sebastian?"

His eyes were wide with fear, constantly flicking nervously about him.

"And a Bud Light," I answered for him.

The waiter wandered away, he was used to crazy among his customers.

I couldn't say that Sebastian truly relaxed, but he sipped his beer and began to look a fraction less anxious.

He seemed happier once we were moving again. I could tell he was tired, but I wanted him to see the ocean up close, and not just from the windows of our small home.

The boardwalk was busy, full of people strolling in the sunshine. A teenager on a skateboard swept past and my poor, wounded man trembled with terror at the sudden noise.

"It's okay, *tesoro*. You'll be okay."

"Fuck, Caro," he said, his face white with fear.

We carried on walking, Sebastian clinging onto my hand and trying to control his rapid breathing.

It hurt badly to see him so scared when he'd always been so strong, but I knew the only way to help him was to force him to face his fears. We'd face them together.

When we reached the end of the Boardwalk, we found an empty bench and sat looking at the ocean. He breathed in deeply, and I saw that it calmed him.

The waves tumbled across the sand and the repeated, rhythmical motion soothed us both. A couple of kids were playing on body boards, shouting out happily. Sebastian leaned forward to watch them, his face alight with interest. The ocean had always been his place of refuge, somewhere his parents couldn't touch him, and the beach had always had a special significance for us. I became determined that we'd walk here every day, because I believed it would help Sebastian to get stronger. And it would bring us together.

"The ocean always reminds me of you, *tesoro*. It's the same color as your eyes today."

He looked at me in surprise, then lifted my hand to his lips, kissing it gently.

"Caro."

He breathed my name softly, like a prayer.

As we sat in the sunshine, a light breeze ruffling my hair, I felt life flowing back into his body. He closed his eyes, relaxing in the summer warmth, his face held up toward the light like a young plant that had been kept in the dark.

"Thank you for this, Caro," he whispered.

I leaned against him and he wrapped his good arm around my shoulder, pulling me in.

"Ready to go home, *tesoro*?"

He nodded, and we stood up to walk back to our home.

I led us back by a different route to the bungalow, and we strolled past a café that I'd not seen before. It must have opened while we were living as hermits. Three men with black hair, olive skin and dark eyes, seemed to be arguing loudly. I wanted to take the long way around in case they reminded him of Afghanistan, but something about them intrigued Sebastian. He looked up, and I could tell he was listening to what they were saying. I realized they must be speaking a language he recognized, which could mean they were Afghans.

I was really worried, wondering what to do for the best. I glanced around, seeing if there were any taxis nearby. And then I was astonished to see a small smile lift Sebastian's lips.

My heart soared. I hadn't seen him smile like that since he'd come home.

As we walked past, Sebastian threw in a comment. The men stared at him in amazement. One called out something else and Sebastian replied. Suddenly all the men started shouting at once. They came toward him, and I was worried it might be too much, but soon they were deep in conversation and I could tell they were asking him questions. Then Sebastian grinned at them. It was like seeing the sun after a month of rain, and I dared to feel hope.

They talked a little longer and then Sebastian introduced me. The men greeted me respectfully but with little interest, and eventually, after several more minutes where I didn't understand a single word, but stood happily as Sebastian stroked my hand, watching him chat away, he said goodbye and we carried on walking.

"What on earth were you talking about for so long?"

"Baseball," he said.

I stared at him doubtfully.

"You're kidding me?"

He smiled again, "Universal language, Caro."

And just like that, the world began to turn again.

The first change was that Sebastian started doing the exercises that the therapist had given him: exercises to help build up dexterity in the fingers of his left hand, and leg stretches to help the damaged muscles of his right thigh, and he even used the exercise bike that I'd ordered for him—although he'd shouted at me the day it had been delivered. He also began doing sit-ups and push-ups with a vengeance.

The second change came a week after meeting the Afghan men. It was evening, and I was standing in the kitchen, cooking pasta *arrabiata* for our supper, when Sebastian poked his head around the door, a quizzical expression on his face.

I stared at him for a moment before I realized what was different.

"You've shaved!"

"Well, you didn't like the beard, did you?"

"That's putting it mildly, Sebastian."

He looked so beautiful, my heart gave another, small, hopeful lurch.

The third, and most startling change, was that he slipped his hands around my waist and nuzzled my neck. I was so shocked, I froze. His smile fell away and he let go of me.

"No, *tesoro*, no!" and I pulled his arms back around my waist, laying my head on his chest. I couldn't help the tears spilling down my cheeks, soaking into his t-shirt.

"I'm so sorry, baby," he said, stroking my hair.

"Oh, God, I've missed you, Sebastian."

"I know, baby," he said, gently, "but I'm here now."

It felt so good to have his arms around me after months of his numb coldness and distance.

I lifted my head to look at him, and he wiped my tears away with his thumbs.

"I'm sorry I made you cry, baby," he said, softly. "I never meant to hurt you. I know that I did."

I locked my arms around his neck and pulled his head down, kissing his lips, gently at first, and then with increasing hunger and need.

He hesitated for a fraction of a second, then his lips parted and I felt his tongue sweep into my mouth, and sudden, hot, unexpected arousal flooded through me.

I moaned into his mouth, the intensity of my desire taking me by surprise. Sebastian gasped and stepped back half a pace, gazing down at me.

Inside, I was begging him not to reject me again, but I felt strongly that the next step needed to come from him.

"I want to make love to you, Caro."

His voice was so quiet I could hardly hear him.

"You do?" I breathed.

"God, yes, baby. Only if you want to."

I stared at his face, and found the love in his eyes that seemed to have been hidden for so long.

"I've waited and waited to hear you say that, *tesoro*."

I turned off the gas stove, abandoning the pasta.

He held my hand, gazing into my eyes as we walked into the bedroom.

CHAPTER EIGHTEEN

THE LAST TIME WE'D MADE LOVE IT HAD BEEN IN A SMALL, STINKING MUD-built room, in a former police compound in Now Zad, now it was very different.

He stood hesitantly next to the bed, and it reminded me so much of our very first time together. He'd been broken then, too.

I pulled the curtains, but the sun was still high in the sky and the room was filled with a soft, muted light.

I walked back over to him and reached up to stroke his face. He leaned into my hand and his eyes closed.

"I don't know if I can..."

"Shh, *tesoro*. I just want to feel your skin next to mine. Anything else, well, that's a bonus."

I kissed him slowly and tenderly, remembering, relearning, starting again. He returned my kisses, carefully to begin with, and I felt the first small flames of passion heat his blood. He swept my hair off my neck and ran his tongue up to my jaw. His hands massaged my waist, kneading my flesh. Then his right hand crept up my body and I felt his touch hover over my bra strap, before his left hand slowly descended to cup my behind.

It felt so good to have his hands on me again and, despite what I'd said to him, I was desperate for him to know me as a man could know a woman, but I also knew I couldn't rush this.

I pushed my hands up under his t-shirt and stroked his warm, silky skin. Carefully, I traced my finger across the small, round scar, where the bullet that punctured his lung had exited his body. I needed him to know that it didn't make any difference to me, that I loved him regardless.

He tensed slightly, so I moved my hand away, instead letting my fingers drift down his spine, stroking his back and shoulders.

He continued to kiss me, his touch slowly becoming more assured. He weaved his fingers into my hair, tightening his grip.

I could taste his desire and need, but I could feel his anxiety, too. It had been so long since we'd touched each other that there was an additional pressure and weight of expectation.

Gently, I reached for his t-shirt, feeling his slight resistance before he let me pull it over his head.

I could see his ribs plainly, but his muscle tone was beginning to recover. Plenty of love and home-cooking: that's what he needed. And time—a whole lifetime of love.

I wondered, briefly, where he'd put his dog tags, they'd disappeared shortly after he'd come home. I hoped he hadn't done anything hasty, like destroying them or throwing them away, because I knew he'd regret that one day.

I reached for his belt, cinched in two more holes because of his weight loss, but he caught my hands and shook his head.

"I don't think I'm ready for this, Caro. What if...?"

My frustration was ready to boil over, but then I was struck with sudden inspiration.

"Want me to show you how I reminded myself of you when you were in the hospital?" I said, looking directly into his eyes.

He nodded, his pupils dilating in a way that filled me with confidence, because it showed that he still desired me.

"I will, if you take off your pants."

"Caro..."

"That's the deal, Sebastian. Non-negotiable."

He hesitated for a moment, then unbuckled his belt and dropped his jeans to the floor. He angled his right leg away from me, and I knew it was because he was trying to hide the ugly scar that ran the length of his thigh. But it didn't hide the slight bulge in his briefs—it wasn't a full erection by any means, but it was a start.

"Sit in the chair, make yourself comfortable—I could be some time."

I was rewarded with a slight smile.

"First, I'd draw the curtains," I said, pointing toward the windows like a flight attendant. "Then, I'd pull back the duvet and arrange the pillows."

As I spoke, I flicked back the sheets and piled up the pillows near the headboard.

"Then I'd put on a little mood music..."

I pointed the remote control at my CD player, and the sounds of *Martha's Harbour* swirled softly from the speakers.

> *You are an ocean wave, my love*
> *Crashing at my bow...*

"I'd kick off my sneakers, because, well, I'm really not a Manolo sort of girl ... that's high heels to you, Hunter."

He rolled his eyes. "I lived in Paris for six months, Caro. I have heard of Manolo Blahnik."

"Yes, well, he's from Spain, so there's no need to look so superior, Sebastian."

Secretly, I was thrilled he was playing along and had relaxed enough to be able to tease me.

"Besides," I went on, "I can't walk in high-heels unless I have you to hang onto ... but I'm not averse to wearing them in the bedroom."

His breath caught in his throat, and his hands gripped the edge of his chair. I tried not to stare at his briefs, but that was the area I really wanted to affect. I hoped our banter would help him to relax, because I longed to feel his body—next to mine, inside mine.

I kept the smile plastered on my face and tried to sound natural and cheerful—maybe even a little bit sensual, if I could remember how.

"So, after I've kicked off my sneakers, I'd peel off my socks, because leaving them on just isn't sexy, and if you ever do that, Hunter, I'll be justified in filing for divorce—after we're married, of course, which *you* keep putting off."

He frowned slightly, so I decided to concentrate on the mission in hand, so to speak.

"I'd imagine your fingers teasing me around my waistband," I said, mimicking my words. "And then I'd think about you unzipping my jeans and standing back while I shimmy out of them."

His eyes followed my pants, as I slid them down my legs to the floor.

"And I'd pull off my t-shirt because I'd be feeling hot, just thinking about you touching me."

My t-shirt followed my jeans, making a small pile.

"And then I'd touch my breasts like this, Sebastian," I said, squeezing my breasts together and throwing my head back, "like you asked me to once before, and I'd imagine you running your hands over me and unhooking my bra, and you'd torment my nipples with your hands and your hot, sweet mouth, your tongue moving around and around me like this."

I glanced at him, and saw that his eyes were transfixed by my breasts and—yes! There was a significant bulge in his briefs—my plan was working.

I unhooked my bra, dropped it to the floor, and then turned my back on him.

"And I'd have to climb onto the bed, just like this, Sebastian," I said, provocatively wiggling my ass at him, as I slunk up toward the pillows.

Then I knelt up and turned around to face him. "And I'd think about how you'd toy with the lace on my panties, just like this, and how your fingers would tease me, sliding inside me, finding me all hot and wet and wanting."

I rubbed myself inside my panties, and closed my eyes as sensation began to pulse through me, making me moan softly.

"And I'd think what it was like to feel your mouth on me, and your tongue inside me, tantalizing and torturing me, bringing on an orgasm with a flick of your tongue."

"Fuck!" I heard him hiss.

"And I'd lie back on the bed and imagine your long, hard cock, sliding inside me, thrusting fast—really fast—and bringing on another orgasm, just like this."

I lay back on the bed and shimmied out of my panties, then propped myself up on the pillows, pulled my knees up slightly and opened my legs.

I gazed up at him from beneath my eyelashes as I continued to touch myself. I saw him lick his lips and shift on the chair.

"And I'd wish you were with me, Sebastian, because although I have a damn good imagination, I'd rather have the real thing any day."

I closed my eyes for a moment, then looked up to meet his.

"I'm so wet for you, Sebastian. Do you want to touch me?"

He swallowed and I saw some of his anxiety return, so I closed my eyes and rubbed myself harder.

Then I heard the floorboards creak as he stood up, and felt the mattress shift as he climbed onto the bed. He hesitated for a second, and then I felt him nudge my hand out of the way, as he circled his fingers around, then pushed two inside me.

I groaned loudly when he fastened his mouth over my breast and started to tease the nipple out, sucking hard. I ran my hands over his shoulders and felt a slight tremor ripple through him. He moved over to my other breast, swirling his tongue around and over me, pulling lightly with his teeth, filling me with need.

Then his kisses trailed down my body, and I held my breath as I felt his tongue sliding inside me.

I called out his name, and he pushed my legs further apart, really working me, and I orgasmed loudly, watching as he moved up to kiss my thigh.

"Much, much better than my imagination, Sebastian!" I gasped.

He chuckled quietly.

I brushed my hands over his briefs, unable to help myself.

"Oh, you're so hard, *tesoro* ... I want you inside me."

"Where are the fucking condoms, Caro," he said, in a tight voice.

"Don't need them: I've been taking the pill. Just you, Sebastian, now."

I pushed his briefs over his hips, and fastened both hands over his erection and guided him inside me.

He groaned, a long, drawn-out sigh of pleasure.

It felt so good, stretching and filling, deep inside me. I clenched around him.

"Fuck, Caro!" he gasped.

"Don't try and control it," I begged him, "Just love me. Love me, Sebastian."

He flexed his hips and began to thrust into me.

It felt so intense, we were so intimately connected, joined together, man and woman, moving as one body, one soul, one purpose.

He cried out and shuddered, pouring himself inside me, filling me with his love and trust, bringing us together again.

When he'd finished, he rested between my thighs, his face buried in my neck, his breath still coming in gasps. I stroked his back and told him I loved him.

Eventually he pulled out and curled up next to me: I could feel his cheeks were wet with tears.

"Are you okay?" I asked quietly.

He nodded without speaking, and then he opened his eyes and smiled at me.

"Very okay, Caro. I'm very okay."

And we held each other without the need to speak again.

After that, the dam holding back our intimacy had been breached, and Sebastian's mind started to heal as well as his body.

There was something I had to ask him, and I didn't know if it was going to be a good idea or not.

We were slumped together on the sofa, drinking herbal tea just before going to bed. I didn't really enjoy the thin, bitter liquid, but caffeine made Sebastian jumpy.

"Sebastian, can I ask you something?"

"Sure, baby," he said, running his hand down my arm, and twining his fingers with mine.

"Well, I was wondering ... what are your nightmares about?"

I felt him tense immediately, and regretted my question.

"It's hard to talk about, Caro," he said, his voice low and quiet.

"It's okay—you don't have to tell me."

"I just don't want you to have that shit in your head."

"Sebastian, you wake up screaming every night—it doesn't have to be me, but I think you need to tell someone."

"I'm not seeing a fucking shrink," he said testily.

I didn't reply.

We sat silently, staring out of the windows, watching the horizon growing paler as the sun sank behind the sea.

And then he began to speak.

"I can't tell you everything, Caro, because it's classified, and you can't report any of this."

"Of course not!"

I was hurt that he'd even think that.

"Sorry, baby, I had to say it." He sighed. "We were in Now Zad in the first place to make contact with someone—a local guy—who was going to get us to one of the Taliban leaders—so we could take him out. That's why they wanted me there, because they were worried about using local interpreters for a sensitive op. It was supposed to be a small patrol, just the 14 of us, with Jankowski in charge. At the last minute, Grant was told we had to take these two guys from the Afghan National Army with us. He wasn't happy, but he was overruled. We headed out into the mountains for what we thought would be three or four days, but we didn't get that far. When we arrived at the village for the meet, we knew right away that something was wrong—it was just too damn quiet. There was nobody in the fields, no one sitting outside their houses. We were all on edge.

"I went ahead with the ANA guys and they were calling out for the man we were supposed to meet. Then this guy came out from behind one of the buildings and he was talking really fast, and he looked fucking terrified. I realized he was quoting from the Koran and I knew then he'd been turned into a human fucking bomb. I yelled at everyone to get back, but then I felt like I'd been punched in the shoulder and I realized I'd been shot. One of the ANA guys had tried to take me out, then shot his colleague and turned his rifle on the rest of the squad. The firefight started, and I could hear Jankowski yelling at the contact to get down. Mark and Jez came running over to help me—and that's when the bomb was detonated."

Sebastian swallowed and closed his eyes.

"The Afghan contact was just pink mist: Jankowski, Mark and Jez were caught in the blast. If Jez hadn't been so close to me, I'd have been killed, too, but he took it for me."

Sebastian's voice dropped to a whisper.

"I had pieces of Jez all over me. That's what I dream about."

His hands were shaking and his breathing had become shallow.

"I understand, I do, *tesoro*," I murmured, gently stroking his cheek. "When I was in Iraq ... it was the sound of the helicopters, they were bringing in wounded and I saw ... I saw. But I don't have that nightmare anymore, Sebastian, because my worst nightmare is losing you."

I held him tightly, because that was all I could do.

~

Two days later, just as he was finishing his exercises, a sheen of sweat making his body glisten in a way that made my mouth water, I decided it was time to take a further step into the world.

"How do you feel about another challenge, Sebastian?"

He glanced over at me and smiled. "Sounds interesting. Does this one involve leaving the bedroom?"

I grinned at him. "Yes, it does, but now you've got me thinking other things, Hunter, and my once pristine thoughts are getting a little dirty."

"How dirty?" he said, his eyes heating under my gaze.

I stood with my hands on my hips and looked him in the eye.

"*Very* dirty."

He groaned. "Why didn't you say that *before* I did that damn workout, Caro?"

I laughed. "Rain check until tonight, Hunter. It's a beautiful day, we should be outside."

He nodded his agreement, then lifted my hand to his lips, brushing soft, sweet kisses over the tip of each finger.

"Yeah, okay. I need to see Atash anyway. He's got some problem with immigration that he wants me to look into."

Atash was the name of one of the Afghan men from the café and, against the odds, he and Sebastian had become friends. Atash's family had been forced to leave their village near Lashkar Gah in Helmand province and were lost and alone in a new country. Being useful to them brought Sebastian back to life, day by day. And day by day, it brought him back to me.

I wasn't sure if Sebastian and Atash had bonded over baseball, or simply because Sebastian was probably the only other person in all of Long Beach who spoke his language. But most days they found an excuse to meet up. And once Sebastian had started helping Atash and his family with their legal status, they spent even more time together.

Atash was shy about coming to our home so, mostly, Sebastian walked over to see him. I was glad he had a reason to leave the bungalow, and one that was completely separate from our life together. He needed it, and I think he knew that.

"So, if you're not talking about sex, Caro," he prompted me, "what's this challenge that you're on about?"

"I want you to meet my friends. I miss them, and they really want to meet you."

His gaze dropped to the floor.

"Okay, I guess it's time."

He didn't look thrilled by the idea, but he didn't object either.

I spoke to Nicole first.

"He's doing much better now, and I'd like you to meet him. We want to invite you over this weekend."

"Oh, he's finally going to let you see the light of day, is he, Lee?"

I was taken aback.

"That's ... harsh. He's been ill, Nic."

I could sense her indignant and judgmental silence on the other end of the line.

"Okay," she said, rather reluctantly. "Yes, of course I'll be there. Do you want me to talk to Jenna and Alice?"

"No, that's fine," I said, trying to keep my tone neutral and the hurt I felt out of my voice. "I should make the calls. Come for lunch?"

As Saturday approached, I threw myself into a frenzy of cooking. I'd dragged Sebastian all over Long Beach to find the ingredients I wanted. He was beginning to look much more like himself. Although he was still very slender, he was beginning to pile the muscle weight back on. His hair was longer than I was used to seeing it, turning into a crazy, blond mop.

"Thought I'd grow it for a while," he said, casually.

"Fine by me," I grinned, tugging a lock in my hand.

Day by day, he was looking more like the surfer boy I'd fallen in love with. He still had bad days and some very bad nights, and he was still in a considerable amount of pain from the shrapnel wounds in his thigh. But on good days he was able to walk without a cane, although he still had a significant limp.

"I spoke to Ches while you were out," he said casually.

"You did?"

I was pleased that he'd finally gotten around to talking to his friend—but nervous about what had been said: particularly about me.

"And?"

"He said he and Amy would fly out for our wedding."

I caught my breath and stared at him.

"If you still want to marry me, Caro?"

The small stone of grief that I'd been carrying in my heart melted away.

"Of course I do, Sebastian. I ... I thought you'd changed your mind."

He shook his head slowly, his eyes full of love.

"Never that, Caro, but I didn't want to marry you if ... if I couldn't be a man ... with you. And I promised myself I wouldn't be using a fucking cane when I walked down the aisle."

"They don't have aisles in City Hall," I said, somewhere between a laugh and a sob.

He gathered me into his arms and rocked me slowly, repeatedly kissing my hair.

"So what else did Ches say?" I mumbled into his chest.

I was pleased that I'd managed to get the words out without sounding too pathetically shaky.

"He said that he'd decided if he still hadn't heard from me by Labor Day, he was going to come out here and kick my ass himself."

"Good idea," I agreed with a murmur, "he should do that anyway. Did he say anything about me?"

Sebastian smiled.

"I guess he was surprised—and pleased, I think—that you hadn't kicked me out. He's cool, Caro, don't worry about him."

"And Amy?"

"Oh, she just wants to kick my ass, period."

I smiled. "I think I'll get along with her."

"That's what I'm afraid of," muttered Sebastian.

He was only half joking.

He held my face gently and looked into my eyes.

"Just promise me you won't turn into one of those bat-shit crazy women about the whole wedding thing, Caro."

"Such sweet nothings you whisper," I teased him. "Don't worry, Sebastian, that's not my style." I slapped his chest. "I don't care if I get married in jeans."

"Jeans?" he said, raising his eyebrows.

"Well, my favorite jeans," I replied, with a challenging stare.

"Okay, jeans. Cool."

~

Sebastian was nervous about meeting my friends, understandably, perhaps. I tried to reassure him, but he felt they'd be judging him: he was undoubtedly right.

He looked delicious in a white t-shirt and blue jeans, and, with his bare feet jammed into a pair of flip-flops, he looked like he'd just strolled off the beach. Except for the fact that when he walked, he still had a pronounced limp.

I heard Nicole's car pull up and I leaned out of the window, waving excitedly. I pretended not to hear Sebastian murmur, "Incoming."

I ran out of the door, and Alice leapt on me first, hugging me tightly.

"Oh my God! It's so good to see you, Lee!"

"You've lost weight, beotch!" yelled Nicole, grappling me around the waist, and smearing a lipstick kiss onto my cheek.

"I've brought chocolate and champagne," sang Jenna, flinging her arms around me.

And then Nicole shrieked.

"Omigod! Omigod! Is that what I think it is?"

She grabbed my left hand and stared at my engagement ring. There were loud gasps and shocked looks from Alice and Jenna.

I nodded.

"You guys are all invited to a wedding in the fall," I said quietly.

At that, there were loud shrieks and cries of congratulations, plus a few tears. They all hugged me again but I was growing uncomfortable, aware that Sebastian would be watching, and waiting for us to come in.

"When did this happen?" asked Alice, grabbing my hand again to look at the ring.

"That's a nice piece of rock, Venzi," murmured Nicole. "But are you sure about this? I mean right now, the way everything is..."

"I'll tell you all about it later. Just be ... cool, okay?"

"Well, come on," said Nicole, rather tersely, "let's meet the paragon."

"Nic!" I said, my voice warning.

She held up her hands. "I'll be good."

Which didn't fill me with hope.

Sebastian was standing in the middle of the living room when my friends walked inside. I could tell he was nervous, but to anyone who didn't know him, he would have merely appeared arrogant.

I introduced everyone, and Nicole couldn't help herself, running her eyes up and down Sebastian's body: it was practically a Pavlovian response with her when she saw a cute guy. Jenna and Alice had taken sneaky peeks, too, they were just more subtle about it.

The girls settled themselves around the room, and then an uncomfortable silence descended, with everyone's eyes fixed on me. I could tell Sebastian was feeling overwhelmed at having so many people in our small home, so I smiled at him, took his hand, and led him back to his favorite chair.

I could see the pitying faces of my friends as they watched Sebastian limp painfully across the room. I wished they wouldn't—Sebastian loathed being pitied—but their reaction was understandable.

I perched on the arm of his chair, and he rested his hand on my knee. It was as if he needed physical contact with me to get him through what he clearly saw as an ordeal.

"Well, you know what I've been doing," I said, calmly. "I want to know what all of you've been up to."

Gradually the conversation began to flow. Sebastian was silent at first, but slowly Alice began to draw him out, asking about his plans to go back to school.

"I was going to study Italian and English Lit," he admitted, "but that kinda got interrupted." He glanced at me and I squeezed his hand. "But I don't know now."

"Lee says you speak several Arab languages, too."

"Plus Italian and French," I added.

Sebastian looked slightly embarrassed. "Well, yeah, I can speak Arabic, but I don't read it well."

"Could that be something for you?" she asked.

He shrugged. "I thought maybe I'd look into some paralegal studies. I've kinda been helping out a neighbor who's got immigration problems."

"You didn't tell me about that idea, Sebastian?" I said, delighted that he was planning ahead.

"I haven't decided anything yet, Caro, I'm still thinking about it."

"Well, there's plenty of time—you don't have to decide now."

"No, I can just continue sponging off you," he said, quietly.

He was still refusing to touch his disability pay checks, and the money was collecting dust in his bank account.

The conversation died away, my friends staring everywhere but at us.

"Sebastian, no," I whispered, really upset.

"It's what all your friends are thinking, Caro," he said, heatedly. "I can see it in their eyes."

"Don't assume you know what I'm thinking," snapped Jenna.

"I agree," said Nicole, evenly. "Because I was actually thinking that nearly dying in the service of your country earns you the right to time off—and if my friend is having as many orgasms as she says she is, you must be doing something right."

Sebastian looked startled, then amused.

"Is that what she said?" he murmured, glancing over to me, before fixing his gaze on Nicole.

"I'm paraphrasing, of course," replied Nicole, meeting his eyes.

Sebastian shrugged. "She taught me everything I know."

Jenna chuckled, and Alice laughed out loud.

"Don't mind me," I said, my face glowing beet red.

"Later, baby," said Sebastian, taking my hand and grazing my knuckles with a kiss.

There was a knock at the door, which was a welcome interruption to my public embarrassment.

"I'll get it," said Sebastian, pulling himself out of the chair.

Nicole's eyes followed him across the room, then she turned to smile at me and winked.

"You and I will be having words," I hissed at her.

"Just telling him the way it is, Lee. He didn't seem to mind. I don't know, is he the kind of guy who keeps score, because I dated a musician once who used to make a note of my orgasms in his diary, not that he could even tell which ones were faked."

"I've never faked one," I batted back at her.

"God, I hate you!" she said.

I was half-listening for Sebastian's voice at the front door. When he switched from English, I guessed who our new visitor must be.

Nervously, Atash made his way into the room, smiling at my friends, while they turned to stare, giving brief, puzzled smiles back.

"Hi, Atash," I said, and quickly introduced them to him.

He smiled again and nodded politely, but looked uncomfortable.

"We'll be next door," Sebastian said to me.

Then he steered Atash into the kitchen, where I heard him filling the kettle to make the horribly sweet tea that was traditional in Afghanistan, while they chatted away.

"What language is that, Lee?" said Alice. "Is that Arabic?"

"No, that's Dari. Sebastian says it's related to Persian not Arabic. He speaks Pashto, too," I added, proudly.

They looked suitably surprised, and I was pleased that Sebastian had had a chance to impress them with something other than his looks—or his hot temper. I knew that had been bothering him.

"With those language skills, I'm surprised Military Intelligence didn't snap him up," continued Alice.

I didn't answer, but couldn't meet her eyes.

"Oh," she said, knowingly, and swapped a significant look with the others.

And then I heard Sebastian's laughter coming from the kitchen—a long, loud, joyous laugh. I thought my heart would stop.

"Lee, are you okay?" said Jenna anxiously. "You look..."

"Sebastian's laughing." I could hear the tremor in my own voice.

"Oh, honey," said Alice, giving my arm a squeeze.

"You're doing okay, Venzi," said Nicole, formerly Sebastian's harshest critic. "I think you're both doing okay."

Atash left soon after, hurrying out of the door, smiling shyly.

"What was all that about?" I said, thrilled to see that Sebastian was grinning broadly.

"Atash wanted to know if I needed some hashish," he said, casually.

Jenna and Alice looked slightly shocked, and Nicole frowned.

"Excuse me?" I said, sharply. "I hope you said no."

Sebastian shrugged. "He said it's good for pain."

I noticed Sebastian hadn't answered me directly, and he *so* wasn't getting away with an excuse like that—but it was a conversation to have in private.

"And what else?" I asked, eyeing him curiously. "What aren't you telling me, Hunter?"

Sebastian's grin became wider.

"He was wondering why I'm making the tea when I have four wives to do it."

My mouth dropped open, and Nicole snorted with laughter.

"Well, I hope you put him straight! Sebastian?"

He grinned wickedly.

God, I'd missed that smile.

"I'll put him straight, Caro. Eventually."

Jenna started to laugh and then Nicole joined in. Soon we were all laughing our asses off. Damn, it felt good.

"You and I will have words later, Hunter," I said, in a threatening voice.

"Looking forward to it, baby," he said, still grinning at me.

After Atash's visit, we moved outside to sit in my yard, enjoying the nice weather. I'd dug out an old sundress to wear, and had the pleasure of watching Sebastian's eyes drift up and down my legs. I hitched my skirt slightly higher and raised an eyebrow at him, as his eyes followed my movement and he ran the tip of his tongue over his lips.

"Oh, just stop it, you two," Nicole groaned. "I haven't been laid in months and you're wafting all this sexual tension around. It's so unfair."

Alice laughed at her. "Lee got lucky—and it isn't like she hasn't put in more than her fair share of waiting over the years," she pointed out. "Besides, I've decided to give up on men: I'm going down the B.O.B. route."

I could see Sebastian was puzzled.

"Battery-operated boyfriend," I whispered in his ear.

He smirked at me and sat back to listen. I could see he was intrigued, watching me with my friends, seeing a different side to me.

Alice nodded.

"No offense, Sebastian, but men just take up too much energy. Or maybe it's just the men I meet. I can't tell you how many times I've been to dinner parties and listened to them droning on about football, or fishing, or how damn important they are at work. One even gave me a blow-by-blow description of building a model airplane. I mean, come on!"

Jenna agreed.

"Although maybe it's just men our age. We should do what Lee has done and find ourselves some younger guys."

"I'd definitely recommend it," I said, winking at Sebastian, whose eyes were flicking between Alice and Jenna so quickly, he looked as if he was watching a table tennis match.

He grinned at me, while Alice continued.

"Well, I'm a little out of practice now, I admit it, but food has some serious advantages over sex."

I laughed out loud, and Nicole told her she was talking bullshit.

"I'm serious!" she said, ticking off the points on her fingers. "Eating: you can do it every day, at least three times a day, with snacks in between; you can do it with as many people as you want, of any gender, and you don't have to worry about their sexual orientation; there are more good recipes and restaurants than hot, available men around—and believe me, I've done some research on this; I'm not going to get pregnant or STDs by eating ice cream; and, best of all, even if you gorge yourself with different people every time, no one calls you a slut."

"You're just a food slut!" yelled Jenna.

"We should ask Sebastian's opinion," said Nicole. "Where do you stand on the whole food versus sex thing?"

"Nic," I said, knowing she was deliberately baiting him.

But Sebastian didn't need my help.

"Caro's a great cook," he said, smiling at me. Then he whispered in my ear so no one else could hear him, "but I think you feed me well because you know I'll need my energy later."

"Ugh!" shouted Jenna. "I *know* you just said something really hot," she accused Sebastian. "It's so mean of him, Lee! Come on, you could at least tell us what he said."

I shook my head. "Need to know basis, Jenna, and you don't need to know."

Sebastian grinned, not looking the least embarrassed. I was relieved: sometimes my friends could be a real handful.

After a couple of hours, I could tell he was getting tired. He was moving awkwardly, and I knew that sitting so long was hurting him.

"Why don't you go take a nap, *tesoro*," I said, quietly. "We'll just be chatting out here for a while. You've more than done your part."

"You don't mind?"

"Of course not. Just take care of yourself and rest."

He smiled. "Okay, but wake me up before they go?"

"You really want some more?" I said, pretending to be shocked.

"They're okay," he said, smiling. "They really care about you, Caro. That's all that matters."

He made his apologies and left us alone outside. I knew their evaluation of him would be offered up any second.

Nicole weighed in first.

"Well, he's even hotter in the flesh, Lee, hot-tempered, too."

"Both are equally true," I agreed.

"You guys look good together," said Jenna, thoughtfully. "I must admit I had my doubts, but it's obvious he adores you. Hell, that's as good a start as any."

Alice nodded. "He needs to find a new direction, Lee. He's not the kind of man who can just sit around."

"I know, but it's still new. I'm not going to rush him. I'm just enjoying having him home and seeing him getting stronger."

"So when do you think you'll be getting married?" asked Alice

"No, don't encourage her!" whined Nicole. "This is baaaad. Where are we going to go to ogle hot surfer guys?"

"You can still come here," I said, laughing.

"What? And ogle your hot husband? That's just plain weird!"

"That's not what I meant at all, and you know it, Nicole! Look, you guys are my friends—you'll always be welcome here."

Nicole rubbed her hands together. "Well, I'm going to enjoy making you shop, Lee—get you out of your damn jeans for a change, although I see you've made an effort today."

I smiled at her. "Nope, no shopping."

"What?"

"I'm not turning into one of those Bridezillas: it'll just be you three and Sebastian's friends from San Diego. My friend Marc said he'd try and fly in, depending on the date. We're going to see if we can get October 2nd—it'll be Sebastian's 28th birthday."

"Oh, God! Twenty-eight," sighed Alice. "That sounds so young! Oh well, at least he won't be able to forget your anniversary."

The girls were just getting ready to leave, and I was wondering whether or not to let Sebastian carry on sleeping, when he screamed loudly again and again, a chilling, heart-rending sound.

Alice jumped and Nicole swore, but I was already on my feet and running.

Sebastian was thrashing around, his face contorted, his body covered in sweat. I shook him awake urgently.

"It's okay, it's okay, I'm here."

He clung to me, his breath shuddering in his chest.

"It's all right, Sebastian, it's going to be all right, *tesoro*."

"Fuck, Caro," he gasped. "I keep seeing..."

"I know, baby, I know."

He covered his eyes with trembling hands. "I can't go out there, Caro. I can't see *them* like this."

"You don't have to. Stay here, I'll see them off. Two minutes, *tesoro*."

In the yard, my friends were sitting staring at the backdoor as I came out.

"Jesus, Lee! What the hell was that?" Nicole asked for them all.

"He was blown up, Nic—three people died in front of him, men he worked with. He gets nightmares."

"Are you sure you know what you're taking on?" Jenna asked quietly.

I shrugged. "I love him."

I could see the concern in their eyes and Alice offered to stay, but I needed to be alone with Sebastian.

They said goodbye, and I promised that I'd be in touch.

When I went back to our room, the bed was empty and I could hear the shower running. Sebastian was leaning against the tiles, his hands outstretched, and the water pouring down over his head.

I pulled off my clothes, and walked into the shower behind him. He turned, and wrapped his arms around me, and we stood together, letting his fear wash away.

The next day Sebastian was in a foul mood. He was embarrassed that my friends had seen, or rather heard him, at his most vulnerable, and he blamed me. When I'd had enough of his sulking, I went for a long walk on the beach, and took my time sipping an espresso at a café on the boardwalk.

After a couple of hours to myself, I felt ready to go home and face whatever emotional grenades he'd be tossing at me today.

I think he must have been watching out of the window, because when I walked in, he was waiting by the door.

"I'm sorry, baby," he said, pulling me in for a hug and kissing my hair. "I know I'm being a dumb-ass."

"That's one of the words I had in mind."

He smiled. "Yeah, I bet. Hey, I have something to show you."

He took my hand and tugged me into the living room.

"What's that?"

A beautiful, red cedar Spanish guitar was lying on the coffee table.

"Your friend Nicole dropped by."

"Really?"

"Yeah, apparently you told her I wanted to learn guitar. She said she didn't need this, so she's given it to me. We talked for quite a long time—seeing as I'd pissed you off and you weren't here..."

He arched an eyebrow.

I decided to ignore that comment.

"Nicole isn't quite the ball-breaker you thought she was?"

"I didn't say that ... but she was ... okay."

"Praise indeed."

"Yeah," he said, with a smile. Then he paused. "Baby, when did I tell you I wanted to play guitar?"

"A long time ago," I said, softly. "Ten years ago."

He stared down at me, his eyes filled with love.

"You take my breath away, Caro."

He pulled me into a tight hug and I stood there drinking him in. He kissed my hair, nuzzling me softly.

"Oh, hey. You got mail."

He let go of me and reached over to pass me an envelope that had been tossed onto the table.

"On a Sunday?"

"Yeah, it went to Mrs. Levenson's house by mistake, she just came back from her grandson's today and she brought it over."

I turned the envelope over, looking at the sender's address.

"It's from England."

I frowned. I didn't know anyone in England—not any more.

I tore open the thick, parchment-type envelope and read the typewritten letter. As I took in the meaning, I couldn't help gasping with surprise.

Sebastian looked concerned. "What is it, baby?"

I slumped down onto the couch, and handed him the letter without speaking.

"Lawyers?"

He sat down next to me and read through the pages.

When he'd finished, he set the letter down and wrapped his good arm around me, pulling me against his chest.

"I didn't know," I whispered. "She never said anything. I knew Liz didn't have any family, but I never thought..."

"It's a lot of money, baby. What are you going to do with it?"

I shook my head. I was still trying to process the information.

The letter was from Dougal and Bright, Liz's lawyers. She'd named me in her Will and had left me everything—her entire estate. She hadn't owned much, but her small apartment in north London was worth over $550,000.

"Why did she leave it to me? We were friends, but ... I don't understand."

"What don't you understand, Caro? She loved you. Why do you always have a hard time realizing that, baby?"

I shrugged.

"This is good news," he said, stroking my hair. "Out of all of this shit, it's something good."

"I know. It's just ... so unexpected."

He hesitated before he spoke again. "It'll pay off your mortgage. You wouldn't have to work overseas ... if you didn't want to..."

I knew what he was trying to say, but I couldn't make a decision like that here and now.

"Anyway, it's *our* money," I said quietly.

Sebastian shook his head angrily.

"I'm not going to take your fucking money, Caro!"

I placed my hand over his mouth, cutting off his stormy words.

"I mean it, Sebastian. Either we're in this together, or we're not. If you won't accept it, then I won't accept it. I'll give it to the Journalism Without Borders charity before I let this money come between us. You said yourself we deserved some good luck."

He ran his hand through his hair in frustration.

"She didn't even like me, Caro. There's no way she'd want me to have anything to do with your inheritance. Hell, as far as she was concerned, I was just fucking you for something to do and..."

"You're wrong. She knew all about us."

His rant ground to a halt, he looked stunned.

"She did?"

"Of course. I told her everything—and I told her we were going to get married."

Sebastian leaned back and stared at me. "You told her? Everything?"

"Yes, *tesoro*."

He scratched his eyebrow thoughtfully. "What did she say?"

I gave him a small smile. "She wanted to know if you were as good in bed as she'd heard."

I thought he was going to choke, but then I saw a wicked gleam in his eye. "And what did you say?"

I gave him a prim look. "Nothing, of course ... although..."

"Although what?"

"I may have winked at her."

He smirked at me.

"Sebastian," I said, my voice serious, "if it hadn't been for me, you would have gone to college, gotten your degree..."

I waved away his denial.

"We both know that's true. Well, here we are—I can pay off the mortgage, you can use the GI bill, go to college, get your degree, if that's what you want."

He shifted uncomfortably. "It doesn't feel right, Caro. Let me think about it."

He was so frustrating, I wanted to hit him. Or kiss him. Probably both.

And, as we were on a roll, I decided to tackle one more task that we'd both been putting off.

I took a deep breath.

"Sebastian," I said, gently, "it's time you decided what you want to do with your uniforms—and your medals."

His sudden, sharp intake of breath showed how hard he found this, but he nodded slowly, staring at the floor. Then he squared his shoulders and met my steady gaze.

"Okay. Let's do it."

We stood up and I took him by the hand, leading him into the spare room. He leaned against the door frame, his arms folded tightly across his chest. I gave him a quick, encouraging smile, then pulled out his duffel bag and backpack from under the bed.

His Dress Blues and khaki Service Uniform were crumpled and rather sad when I dragged them out. There was no sign of his desert utility uniform, I didn't want to think about the reason why—I assumed the doctors would have had to cut him out of it when...

He stared at the clothes coldly, keeping all his emotions tightly contained.

"Get rid of them, Caro. I don't want to see them again."

"And the medals?"

His Service Uniform was festooned with an array of colorful ribbons and medals. I ran through them in my mind, as I touched them one by one: his Afghanistan Campaign Medal, Marine Commendation Medal, Meritorious Service Medal, Navy and Marine Corps Overseas Service Ribbon, National Defense Service Medal, Defense Meritorious Service Medal, and a Navy and Marine Corps Medal. And, still in its presentation box at the bottom of his backpack, his Purple Heart, for being wounded in action.

As Sebastian watched, I opened the box, stroking the ridges of silky ribbon, and ran my finger over the embossed words, 'For military merit'.

"Do what you want with them," he said, his face creasing with pain. "I don't want to see them. Ever."

I took another deep breath.

"You don't want to save them to ... maybe ... show our children ... if..."

He looked up suddenly, a smile hovering around his lips. "You ... you'd try?"

"Yes, Sebastian ... *we* will try."

He let out a shout of pure happiness and scooped me up, twirling me around.

"Let's start trying right now," he breathed out onto my skin.

"I'm still on the Pill!" I laughed.

"Doesn't matter," he murmured into my neck. "I want to practice."

I kissed him hard, as he walked me backward into our bedroom.

As Sebastian had once said, if children happened, we'd welcome them, if not, well, that was okay, too.

We had our whole lives ahead of us.

EPILOGUE

When a woman reaches forty, she is no longer young, but not yet old. My friends had offered this piece of wisdom on my birthday seven months ago.

And yet, it seemed that my life was starting again, or, perhaps I should say, entering a new phase.

Surrounded by love, my beautiful 28 year old husband stood at my side, and in front of our friends, we were joined together by the sacred vows of marriage.

Marc, between assignments, had flown in from France and we'd had an evening drinking to Liz's memory, recalling her humor and craziness, her warmth and strength—crying just a little. And the day before, Ches and his family had arrived from San Diego. His children had peered at me shyly until they spotted Sebastian, and then they'd tried to throw themselves at him, their mother gently restraining them, afraid they'd hurt him. He waved away her concerns and let them climb all over him. It was a wonderful thing to see and my spirits soared, full of hope for the future.

Mitch and Shirley had arrived from South Carolina, and Shirley wept copiously, apologizing over and over. I finally realized that she was apologizing for not having received my letter seven years earlier. We cried together and hugged each other, and agreed to leave the past in the past. Even Donna had flown up for our special day, although Johan had been too ill to travel. Donna had written to us with their congratulations as soon as Shirley had given them the good news. It was strange to see her after all those years, but having her there—smiling with maternal pride—somehow everything had come full circle.

Nicole, Jenna and Alice were there to support me: Nicole determinedly arguing until the last second that I should go on at least one shopping spree to find a bridal outfit, and me stating with equal determination that it would never happen.

My friends' initial wariness of Sebastian had long since worn off, and they treated him something like a younger brother, much to his irritation and my amusement.

Sebastian stood by my side in front of the deputy clerk at City Hall and promised to love me every day for the rest of his life. I cried tears of joy, and said I would never again let anything separate us.

The day was cold and clear, and the crystal sun shone on our small party as we celebrated the life that Sebastian and I were, at last, going to have.

Despite the difficulties we had been through, despite the difficulties we had yet to face, I had never been happier in my whole life, full of hope and gazing through tears at the man I loved. We were beginning again, or, perhaps, adding a new chapter to our story.

The bride wore jeans.

THE END

And that is Seb and Caro's story—what a ride it's been. These characters mean so much to me, and I just haven't been able to say goodbye to them completely.

I wrote 'Semper Fi' which is the retelling of this book, 'The Education of Caroline', but this time from Sebastian's POV. Proceeds from Semper Fi book are donated to the UK bomb disposal charity Felix Fund.

You'll also be able to read 12 bonus chapters which cover parts of the missing years, as well as the next ten years of their life from the end of this story.

I told you I loved them!

Oh, and ***three bonus epilogues*** *in this book—click here*

AUTHOR'S NOTE

Sebastian's battle with PTSD was a difficult part of the story to write, and I tried to make this as accurate as possible to do justice those who live with it on a daily basis.

While I was researching the subject, and talking to friends who have been in the military, I was inspired by a number of websites whose organizations seek to help those men and women who are or were serving military personnel.

If you're interested in finding out more, please go to:

www.woundedwarriorproject.org

www.woundedwarriors.ca

www.soldieron.org.au

www.helpforheroes.org.uk

www.felixfund.org.uk

Thank you.

JHB

BONUS EPILOGUE 1

Christmas at Long Beach

Three months later

Sebastian

"For fuck's sake, Caro! How many people have you invited?"

I'm staring at a fucking Himalaya of food covering our coffee table, our kitchen table, and across every surface in the kitchen.

She's slumped on our couch, looking so fucking sexy, hair all mussed up.

She glares at me, but I can see the amusement in her eyes, too.

"Huh! We both know you'll eat at least half of this, Hunter." *Which is true.* "You know that I've only invited the girls, Atash and his family." *Which is also true.* "I feel like I've been standing in the kitchen all day—my feet are killing me."

I have married a fucking wonderful cook. Hell, she's just a fucking wonderful woman, period.

"Want me to rub your feet, baby?"

"Oh, please, Sebastian."

"Scoot over."

I sit on the couch and pull off her sneakers and socks. She moans softly as I massage her feet—fuck, that sound turns me on. And she has beautiful feet: kinda reminds me of some of those fucking boring statues she dragged me to see when we were in Italy.

She closes her eyes, then says, sleepily, "That's not my foot, Sebastian."

"I know, baby. What can I say, if a job's worth doing..."

I lie on the couch and press myself into her. I can't help it: I get hard just looking at her, but touching her. Yeah ... definitely her fault.

"Ugh, you're all sweaty, Sebastian!"

True. I've been out for a run. Well, more of a slow, fucking limping jog along the boardwalk. I hate being so fucking feeble, but it's getting better. The doc says I'll always have a limp—well, what the fuck does he know?

It's already dark outside, but the boardwalk is buzzing, everyone drinking, having a good time, celebrating Christmas Eve.

I'm beginning to feel part of it, like this really is my home. But the truth is, home could be anywhere, as long as I'm with Caro. I am one lucky bastard. Even with a bullet hole through my damn shoulder and a chunk of muscle missing from my right thigh.

She pushes me off.

"Hold that thought, Hunter. I'm going for a shower."

She slides out from underneath me and heads for the bathroom. I wait until I can hear the water running and then I follow. Although I may have just taken a slight strategic detour to taste some of that amazing fucking food along the way.

I peel off my sweatshirt and t-shirt in one go and somewhere between the living room and the bathroom, I kick off my sneakers and socks. I know she'll be mad at me for that later, as I leave a trail of clothes through the house, but I fucking love it when she chews me out: the way her dark eyes flash, and her nostrils give that little flare. My sweatpants and briefs make it as far as the bathroom door before I lose them. She keeps reminding me we have elderly neighbors and thin curtains. Whatever.

I slide into the shower behind her and she gives a little gasp.

Her hair is all lathered up so I run my hands through it, massaging her scalp, and she gives a groan of pleasure. Yep, definitely feeling that in my dick.

Then I take the shower gel and wash her all over, sliding my hands over her gorgeous, soft skin, over her fantastic ass, and, my favorite, her beautiful breasts.

I bend down to kiss her and the water from the shower pours over us both, but I don't need the warmth of the water—I'm fucking on fire just touching her.

I'd like to crouch down to taste her delicious, wet pussy, but the truth is it's fucking agony stretching out my thigh muscles like that. The thought pisses me off. Whatever. There's other stuff I want to do. *A lot* of other stuff.

"Sebastian, I'm slipping!"

I pick her up around her waist and carry her out into the bathroom, sitting her on the edge of the tub.

Yeah, kneeling—that'll work!

I fall to the floor in front of her and spread her knees out wide. She gasps as I go down on her and that sound alone is enough to make me come. *Hold it in, Hunter, you fucking lightweight.*

I work her some with my tongue and some with my finger, but then she comes suddenly and unexpectedly. *Jeez, that was quick.*

"Fuck, Caro! You okay, baby?"

I look up at her and I love that hot, abandoned look. Her hair is hanging down her back, almost to her waist, and those beautiful breasts are rising and falling rapidly with her *very* fast breathing.

She nods but doesn't seem capable of speaking, and that makes me smile. I pull her up and half-carry her to the bedroom.

She sprawls out on her back and then holds up her arms and wiggles her fingers at me. That means she wants me to lie down with her. I fucking love that we have this unspoken language between us. I've done a lot of shit with a lot of women, but I've never had this level of intimacy with any of them. Only Caro. It's only ever been Caro.

I lie down and kiss her throat, feeling her hot, sweet skin next to mine, as she stretches out like a cat, arching her back and smiling.

"You want to go from behind, Sebastian?" she says, looking up at me, with that wicked gleam in her eye that really fucking turns me on.

"No, baby, I want to *come* from behind."

She slaps my chest but rolls onto her front, and lifts her ass in the air.

"Come and get it, big boy!"

I can't help laughing out loud.

"What movies have you been watching, Caro? *Come and get it, big boy?*"

She smiles over her shoulder at me.

"I made that one up. Original, huh?"

"Yeah, baby. It turns me on."

She smirks.

"Sebastian, according to you, you get turned on when I ask you to do the dishes!"

"I know, baby, I think it's the hot water and foam—gets me thinking stuff."

"I've noticed," she says, drily. "Now am I going to have to wave my ass in the air forever, or are you going to do something about it?"

I'm too much of a fucking gentleman to keep her waiting any longer.

"You want it hard or soft, baby?"

"Both."

Yeah, I can do that.

I slide myself into her gently, feeling that fucking amazing slight resistance that turns into hot, sweet flesh closing all around me.

"Fuck, Caro!"

She pushes back into me.

Fuck, if she does that again, there ain't gonna be much chance of 'soft'.

I slide all the way out, then push into her again, rolling my hips so I can feel her all around me, massaging her inside.

I manage one more slow action before I feel her quiver again and that tips me over the fucking edge. I grip her hips and start pounding into her, the headboard is banging so hard, I think it's going to go through the fucking wall.

Again, I'm surprised when she comes really quickly: normally we have better timing than that. Not that I care, because feeling her clenching around me just brings me on faster. Fuck, that woman can milk me!

I wonder, briefly, if it's possible to run out of cum. *Yeah, well, not so far.*

She clenches around me again and I spill into her, pressing her body into the mattress. I pull out carefully and roll onto my back, breathing hard.

Fuck, that felt good!

I didn't know Christmas Eve could be so much fun—it never has been before, although some of the Christmases I spent with Ches, or Shirley and Mitch were pretty good. Nothing like this, though, obviously.

And I fucking love the fact that we've given up condoms. No matter what anyone says, the sensation just isn't the same. And as for being spontaneous, forget that. I mean, have you ever tried to have shower sex when you're using condoms? Yeah, well, see what I mean?

But more than that, I love that Caro has given up taking the Pill. It's like there are no barriers between us. I know she's worried about being an older mom, but she'll be so fucking amazing at it. Hell, she's so fucking patient with me, and I know I've given her a really shitty time since I got back from Afghan. But things feel like they're really on track now.

And she's promised she'll give up the war reporting stuff. I know I should feel guilty about that, but I just can't. I'm relieved that she's not going to put herself in danger like that anymore. And after what happened to Liz Ashton, I'd fucking burn Caro's passport and chain her to the bed before I let her get anywhere near an airplane.

But she's had another offer, one I'm much happier about. She wrote a piece about us biking through Italy. I didn't even know she'd done it, but one day she came in with this travel magazine and a photograph of me next to my Kawasaki ZZ-R1400 somewhere above Amalfi. That was a great bike. Might have to get another of those.

Turns out the travel mag people have offered her a couple of features, including some motorcycle rides in the US. I'm *definitely* up for that. But they're talking about Spain, too. Oh yeah, I'll carry her bags on that job. Yes, ma'am!

I'm still not sure what I want to do, but sorting out Atash's immigration shit has been really interesting. Caro thinks I could make a good attorney but I'm not sure I'd have the patience for that. I'd have to do a degree then a Master's degree. And even if I could take all that studying, which would be enough dry words to choke a camel, I'd probably end up mouthing off to the judge and getting thrown in jail for contempt of court or some shit. I've had some work doing interpreting, but until I get my reading of Arabic and Persian up to speed, it'll remain limited. Guess I'm just kinda looking around.

But one thing that does interest me is doing fitness training with people who have disabilities. I've worked with some great therapists who helped me get my shit together—and some fucking useless ones who shouldn't be let near a real live human being. I'd always thought I might do something along the lines of a personal trainer—I can't imagine being stuck in some rabbit hutch of an office all day—but this kind of appeals. At least I'd know what the fuck I'm talking about.

Alice got me a pass to use the NYU cardio room and weight room. One day, there was this British woman doing one of those motivational talks. I was going to skip it but I heard her say that she'd broken her back paragliding and the doctors told her she probably wouldn't walk again. So she told them all to shove it, ignored all medical advice and, three months later, took her first steps. Now she runs those ultra long-distance marathons*.

I'm not interested in that, but I really like the idea that the doctors didn't know everything. They've told me I'll always have a limp and I'll never get my full fitness back. Well, fuck that. They don't know *me*. Caro told me she doesn't care if I have a limp, so long as I haven't got a limp dick. No way, baby! No chance of that with her. Fuck! She's so sexy and she really doesn't know it.

Shit! I can't keep my mind off sex for two fucking minutes.

Focus, Hunter!

I also heard that the Wounded Warriors Project takes vets on surfing vacations. Although I'm not sure about getting involved with anything military again ... being on the outside now. But I'll find out about that—maybe I could teach or something. Not that I've been back on a board since ... but next year, definitely. We'll both go. That would be cool.

It's been weird getting used to doing stuff together. I don't mean all the relationship stuff, because I fucking love that. But all the day-to-day stuff that I never thought about: joint bank accounts, for one. I really love that we have a checking account that says 'Mr. and Mrs. Hunter' but I hate using it because most of the money is hers. Well, given to her by Liz Ashton. I have quite a lot of savings from the Marines because I only ever spent my money on drinking and fucking around, oh, and a couple of motorcycles, but it's not like I ever had a home to pay for before, so it's a chunk of cash.

I talked to Ches about it and he kinda put things in perspective for me. He said I should stop thinking about *my* money and *her* money and try and think about it as *our* money. I get what he's saying, but it's not easy. Caro says we'll get used to it, and she's not really wrong about this shit. I guess I'm the one who's fucked in the head about it.

It was fucking amazing seeing Ches and the kids when Caro and I got married. I really love those little bugs: they're so fucking honest and open—you know, not afraid to love. I don't ever remember being like that when I was a kid, but when you've had assholes for parents, you learn that if you're going to cry, you do it alone in your room. I think I stopped crying when I was about six. The only person who can make me cry now is Caro. I think she knows that, but it's not something we talk about.

She hasn't mentioned the kids thing since she stopped taking the Pill and I'm not going to push it. I meant what I said: if it happens that would be fucking awesome, but if it doesn't, our lives are really rich already. I just don't want her to miss out on anything because of me.

"Hey, where did you go just now, Sebastian?" she says, her eyes all soft and full of love.

The way she looks at me just cracks my heart wide open. It's like I've answered all her questions, just by being alive—I can't get enough of that look.

"Been right here, baby. Just thinking how cute you're going to look in your Christmas stockings."

She twines her hand through mine.

"Sebastian, you do realize that it's *a stocking* as in noun: singular—and that you're supposed to hang it up by the chimney for Santa to fill *if* you've been a good boy—which, of course, you haven't."

"Yeah, well, I think we should start a new tradition. Caro in stockings for Christmas. Hey, that alliterates, too."

"Gosh, you do know some big words, Sebastian," she says, laughing.

"You taught me everything I know, baby," and I fasten my teeth around her nipple and tug gently.

She gasps. "Although I never had to teach you that move, did I?"

"Mmm," I say, in agreement, "guess I'm a natural."

I tug slightly harder and my right hand moves down to her thighs.

"Again?" she says, in amazement.

"Yeah, it's Christmas, baby, and I want my presents early."

~

Waking up next to Caro is my favorite fucking thing in the world. I mean, yeah, I fucking love being buried inside her and I love seeing her face when she comes, but the absolute best thing is that moment when I watch her wake up. She's soft and sweet when she's asleep and then her eyelids blink open and there's that wicked gleam in the depths of her dark brown eyes. She stretches out and I feel her arms and legs and body brushing my skin. And I know she's all mine—forever.

And I really fucking love wake-up sex. Since she told me that trick about her orgasm being more intense if she hasn't been to the bathroom, I always try and get a quickie in before breakfast. It's a great way to start the day. She comes like a fucking train—yeah.

"Merry Christmas, Sebastian," she says softly.

God, I love hearing those words. This is the best fucking Christmas ever—and it's still only 7AM.

"Merry Christmas, Caro. I love you so much, baby."

She leans over to kiss me, sighing into my mouth. And Christmas Day starts really, really well.

Two hours later, she starts to get up.

"Uh-uh, baby. I'm going to make you breakfast in bed."

She smiles, that lovely sexy, sleepy smile.

"You can't cook, Sebastian, despite my best efforts to teach you."

Wow, that hurts. I'm a really good cook: I can make coffee and ... espresso.

"You want coffee in bed, baby?"

She laughs and nods.

My real reason for getting up is to go fetch her present. I found a really cool hiding place at the back of the closet in the spare bedroom. It's high up and, being such a shrimp, she'd need to stand on a chair to find it. I'm pretty fucking pleased with myself.

And I remember to make the coffee. Yeah, she's got me tamed—and I fucking love it.

I carry the coffee in two mugs, with the parcel under my left arm. The coffee is in danger of slopping over the sides because I've overfilled *again*, but also because my fucking leg is so damn useless first thing in the morning and my limp is a lot worse. Caro never says anything, but she knows it bothers me.

I put the coffee down and toss her the gift.

"For me?"

"Yeah, kind of."

She raises her eyebrows and then pulls on the ribbon holding it together. A riot of colorful silk spills out onto the bed. She gazes up, a slow smile spreading across her face.

"Colors, Hunter?"

She's teasing me: my entire wardrobe consists of white, gray, black, and blue jeans. Oh, and a pair of crazily-bright boardshorts that I bought in Italy.

She holds up one of the pieces of flimsy silk and lace.

"Yes, ma'am. A different color for every day of the week."

"What color would you like me to wear today?"

"Red: it's Christmas."

She laughs. "Ok, I'll wear the red. Are we saving black for Saturday nights?"

Fuck! That sounds hot.

"Whatever you like, baby."

She knows I'm lying and she smirks at me.

"Your present is under the bed, Sebastian."

What? I go to all that trouble to hide her gift properly, and mine is under the fucking bed?

She laughs at my expression.

"I learned being sneaky from this hot Marine I used to know..."

She stops mid-sentence.

"It's okay, baby," I say, quietly.

Her hands are on her mouth. "I didn't mean it like that, Sebastian."

And her eyes fill with tears.

"I know, baby. Don't cry, Caro. It's okay. I'm not ... it's okay."

Fuck. Will I ever get used to this? Being a 'former' Marine? Sometimes it just hits me like a fucking sledgehammer.

"Where's that damn present that you've hidden so stealthily?"

She smiles, wiping a tear away, and I feel so fucking bad that I made her cry —on Christmas.

I hang off the bed and look underneath.

That is a fucking big present!

I pull it out and even though I know exactly what it is—because she couldn't exactly hide it—she's gift-wrapped it in Christmas paper.

"I hope you like it," she says, nervously.

"Baby, I love it already."

She's bought me a surfboard. It's a thruster in style, pointed at the nose, but I can see that it's slightly longer and wider than someone of my height and weight would usually have. The extra width and length will give it more buoyancy—it's going to make it easier for me to surf on, because my balance is still fucked.

But when I unwrap it...

"Do you like it?" she says, chewing on her lip.

The design is clean and simple: a single blue-green stripe trimming the edge, and across the middle are the words, *Semper Fidelis*.

"Baby, I love it."

And I do. I really do.

She looks relieved.

I kiss her, showing her without words how much she means to me.

She kisses me back, weaving her magic around me, and the world disappears.

When she pulls away from me, I'm hard again, and I try to tug her back, but she laughs and shakes her head.

"Our guests will be here in 45 minutes and neither of us are showered, let alone dressed. And unless you want Nic, Alice and Jenna to see you in your shorts—which I suspect they'd be thrilled at, by the way—I think you should put some pants on.

Ah, crap. The three witches.

Okay, they're not that bad, but they can be really fucking patronizing. Sometimes I just feel like a piece of meat, the way they look at me when they think I'm not watching. I mean, fuck! They're my *wife's* friends. That's so fucking uncool.

Caro just laughs and reminds me I'm the one who married an older woman with older friends, so I should just suck it up.

The other day we were in a store buying groceries and were lining up to pay.

Caro realized she'd forgotten some weird cheese she wanted, so she went off to find it. Then this woman in a pant-suit who was standing behind us in the line starts chatting to me. I'd like to believe she was just being friendly, but then she reached over and laid her hand on my chest in this flirty little move. I mean, she'd just seen me with *my wife*, for fuck's sake! What is with these women? Caro thought it was pretty damn funny.

I haven't told Caro the real reason it pisses me off, because it would upset her, but they're exactly the kind of women I used to hit on when I was single—tough, career women who told themselves they'd never fall for me—older women who reminded me of Caro.

I push the thought away because this is our first Christmas together and I don't want to spoil it.

Caro won't let me shower with her: she knows me too well. So I make the bed while she's in the bathroom and tidy up the kitchen where I spilt the coffee when I was making it. She never says anything when I clear up, but I know she loves it, because she gets this look on her face like she can't believe I do stuff around the house. She just doesn't get that I want to take care of her in whatever way I can. Because I fucking love her.

When I go back into the bedroom, she's just slipping her cute, black cocktail dress over the red, silk underwear I bought her.

Fuck! I was too late.

"Rain check, Hunter," she says, in a firm voice.

Ah hell. I'll just have to walk around with a boner all day, knowing she's wearing that fucking sexy bra and panties under her dress.

I take a shower—a cold one.

I'm just pulling on a t-shirt when a car pulls up outside. I open the front door for Caro's friends, and she runs out and takes the lion share of the hugging and kissing, thank fuck. I'm relieved when I see Atash's family walking up the street.

"*As-salaamu' alaykum!*"

They come in, looking a little nervous, but soon everyone is sitting on cushions on the floor—because we don't have enough chairs—and chatting away. Atash and his brother Kambiz are the only ones in their family who speak any English but it all works out pretty well.

And, I'm not going to tell Caro, but Kambiz knows where to get the best hash. I don't do it very often, but sometimes I just need to chill.

Caro's food is fucking amazing, which is a real ice-breaker. She's made Italian dishes: some weird salted cod thing, baked pasta, capon, fish salad and a whole bunch of stuff I can't even pronounce, let alone recognize.

Kambiz's eyes are popping out of his head when he sees the Afghan food that she's made, as well: *Qabli Pulao* of rice, raisins and carrot with lamb, *mantu* dumplings with minced beef and onions, spicy vegetables, and two *chalow* rice dishes.

Atash just smiles because he's had Caro's cooking before.

I feel so fucking proud of her. She did most of it herself: okay, well, all of it. I tried to help but she nearly fucking lynched me when I managed to let the rice burn dry ... um ... the first lot of rice. I'll do my part later—all the fucking washing up. Thank fuck she insisted on getting paper plates to eat off.

And during the day, I have a revelation. I fucking love Christmas!

It was a nightmare when I was a kid: lots of drunken arguments, and most of the time I'd try and hide in my room. It was better when Ches and his folks moved to San Diego because they'd invite me over and I'd spend as much time as I could with them. Yeah, those were pretty good. Got to surf on Christmas Day a few times, although Shirley tore a strip off Mitch if he brought us back late for the food.

I've had four Christmas's overseas: one in Iraq with my unit, which was kind of okay, although a lot of the guys were going on about missing their families, and I never had anyone to miss; one in Afghanistan, where we got the fuck shelled out of us on Christmas Day, which kind of put a damper on things; and one where it was just the chaplain going on about some shit or other. Last Christmas I was in Switzerland and I spent it screwing some rich German woman in a fucking amazing hotel in Klosters. Something else I haven't mentioned to Caro. Did some snowboarding, too.

Caro knows I've done this shit, but she never asks and she never uses it as a weapon when we're fighting, which is pretty fucking cool of her.

I could have flown back to spend Christmas with Ches last year, but since I'd fucked Amy's friend *and* her friend's friend, she's been kinda pissed at me. Not that I cared about that, but I didn't want to screw things up for Ches, so I stayed away.

Amy was kind of okay with me when Caro and I married. It really helped that they got along so well. I think Amy was in a state of shock that I was 'settling down' as she put it (several times, for fuck's sake).

But I wasn't surprised that she got along with Caro: everyone loves Caro. She's just so positive, energetic, kind, generous, and no one is capable of hating her for it, she's so beautiful but she's even lovelier on the inside. She doesn't see it—but everyone else does. And she's so fucking sexy.

This Christmas was perfect, so full of fun and love and laughter. I am a lucky bastard. I don't know what I've done to deserve such ... such happiness.

I have one more gift for her, but I'll wait until everyone has gone home.

Finally, *finally*, we get the place to ourselves. Caro made everyone take food home with them so at least we don't have to wrap up a load of leftovers. Atash's family were really pleased with that. Probably enough to last them a few days.

"I'm just glad to see it gone," says Caro, groaning. "I can't eat another thing. Never, *never* show me another mince pie."

"You did amazing, Caro. Now sit down and let me do the dishes."

Of course, she doesn't.

"Don't be silly, Sebastian. I can tell your leg is hurting you. Just let me take care of it all."

"Damn it, woman!" I half yell at her. "Aren't you ever going to take a fucking order?"

"Sure," she says, laughing at me, "when you tell me to get my ass in your bed."

I groan. How the hell am I going to be able to concentrate on anything else now?

We clear up together and when we're done, we collapse onto the couch and she snuggles up on my chest.

"Today was fun," she sighs. "It felt ... right."

"I know what you mean, baby."

"Let's go to bed, Sebastian. I'm beat."

"Yeah, okay, baby ... I have another gift for you first."

"Does it involve getting naked in a variety of new and interesting positions?"

Fuck! She's a mind-reader!

"Well, yeah, that, too, but ... um ... there's something else. I don't know ... you might think it's lame."

She sits up and looks at me.

"Sebastian, I'd never think *anything* you gave me was lame. *Not ever*."

"Yeah, well ... you might when you've heard it."

"Heard it?"

"I ... um ... I ... I wrote a song for you, Caro."

She looks stunned.

"For me?"

I've been trying to learn guitar. It's really fucking hard—my left hand won't do shit since I got shot in the shoulder, but it turns out that most songs only have about four chords anyway. I don't think I'll ever play a diminished seventh. Fuck it.

And I stand up to go get the guitar before I lose my nerve.

I've been practicing while Caro has been out. Sometimes it sounds okay, sometimes it sounds like crap.

I walk back into the living room, but I can't meet her eyes.

I position my fingers over the strings and take a deep breath. *Fuck. My mouth has gone dry.*

Here goes.

Just when I'd seen it all
Just when I'd heard it all
And the road got weary
I heard you call.

BONUS EPILOGUE 1

I thought I knew it all
I thought I called the shots
No colors in my life
So far to fall.

Filled with sunshine
That's in your smile
Always loving
I'll walk that extra mile.

No place to call my home
No woman of my own
But then you rescued me
And your love is the key.

Filled with sunshine
That's in your smile
Always loving
We'll go that extra mile.

The last note dies away and I still can't look up.

The silence hangs in the air.

She stands up and takes the guitar from me, and lays it carefully on the table. Then she sits on my knee and my arms automatically curl around her waist.

"You made me cry," she says, softly.

"Oh no, baby. Was it that bad?"

"Idiot!" she sniffs, between her tears. "It was beautiful. Oh, Sebastian, it was just wonderful. I love it. And I love you. So much, *tesoro*."

Relief floods through me and all the tension drains away. *She loved it.*

I stand up with her still in my arms.

"Good, let's go to bed."

She snuggles into my chest, and lets me carry her into the bedroom.

I'm *really* looking forward to unwrapping my next present and seeing her in all that fucking sexy red underwear.

I put her down on the bed and yank my t-shirt over my head.

Oh, crap! I think I heard the seam rip again.

"Wait!" she says, loudly.

I stare at her, puzzled.

"I have another present for you yet, Sebastian."

"I know, baby, and I'm looking forward to unwrapping it."

She rolls her eyes.

"A *different* present."

"You got me something else?"

I can't help smiling.

Fuck. I love getting presents—I've never had that many before. I kinda get why people like Christmas now.

She opens the drawer of her bedside cabinet and pulls out a small envelope, and hands it to me.

"What is it?"

"Sebastian, the whole point is that you open it," she says, with a smile twitching at her lips.

I toss the pillows behind me and sit propped up against the headboard.

I tear open the envelope and pull out a small photograph. I have no fucking idea what I'm looking at. It's a weird black and white, swirly picture. For all I know it could be a Klingon vessel attacking the Starship Enterprise.

One.

Two.

Three.

"Oh fuck!"

Four.

Five.

Six.

"Caro?"

Seven.

Eight.

"Is this?"

Nine.

Ten.

"Yes," she says. "We're going to have a baby—you'll be a father. Merry Christmas, Sebastian."

My wife is the only person in the whole fucking world who can make me cry. And tonight, for the first time in my miserable fucking existence, I cry tears of joy.

BONUS EPILOGUE 2

Three Years Later

Caroline

Marco really is a beautiful little boy. I know every mother says that or at least thinks it about their own child, but in Marco's case it's true. Just last week, I was approached by a woman who said she was a scout from a modeling agency, and that she was sure she could find plenty of work for him: catalogues, magazines, even TV commercials.

She was pretty pushy, and couldn't believe that I wasn't interested in making money out of my two-year-old son. I took her card out of politeness, but I really wanted to tell her to shove it where the sun don't necessarily shine.

My language skills have plummeted since my marriage to a certain potty-mouthed former-Marine named Sebastian Hunter. Two and three-quarter years of marriage haven't managed to curtail the habits picked up from his ten years in the United States Marine Corps. He swears like a drunken sailor on shore leave—and he doesn't even notice he's doing it.

But I think the fact that Marco is starting to talk and understand whole sentences, might have a more salutary effect than all of my nagging. But I'm not holding my breath: if Marco drops the f-bomb at Kindergarten, I'm blaming his father.

My eyes must have glazed over because the model agency woman was staring at me like I was simple. But then she spotted something behind me, and I saw her suck in her stomach and stick out her boobs.

I could almost predict what she'd seen. Right on cue, I heard Marco's happy whoop as Sebastian scooped him into his arms.

"Papa! Papa!"

Hearing my son using those words was a bittersweet experience. Now I was a mother, I missed my own dear father so much more. We named our son after him.

"Hey, little man!"

And I turned around as Sebastian plastered a loud, squishy kiss on the top of Marco's head, causing him to laugh and squeal.

"I can see where your son gets his looks," said the agency woman, her gaze ravaging Sebastian's body.

I couldn't blame her for looking. I'd long suspected that half of the mothers in the park came here at this hour to enjoy the scenery: and I wasn't talking about the wonderful view across the beach toward the ocean. I was talking about 6'2" of solid muscle, sculpted abs, broad firm pecs, an ass you could bounce a quarter off (which I knew for a fact, having spent an enjoyable pre-baby afternoon doing exactly that), all topped by a face so beautiful that I was used to people stopping to do a double-take. I'm biased, of course, but it was no exaggeration that men and women were drawn to Sebastian's ridiculous good looks.

But the best thing, the absolute best thing, was that he was always smiling. Happiness radiated from him. And because there was a time when it seemed like he'd never be happy again, each smile was a small miracle, a special gift, and I treasured every one of them.

The agency woman was still eye-fucking my husband.

"Have you ever done any modeling?" she purred, one hand raised as if she wanted to stroke his stomach. "Because I was just telling the nanny—clients would pay a lot of money to use photographs of you and your son in an advertising campaign." She laughed lightly. "Obviously the apple didn't fall too far from the tree."

The nanny? Good to know that my son's looks had absolutely nothing to do with me. Although, to be fair, he did look far more like Sebastian than me. Except for his eyes. Marco had my eyes: brown. Well, I called them brown, Sebastian called them hot chocolate, which always made me laugh. His own eyes were a remarkable shade of blue-green that seemed to change like the color of the ocean.

Sebastian shot me an amused glance as he balanced Marco on his hip, transferring his weight to his good leg.

Even though he'd worked hard to retain a high level of fitness, his injuries from Afghanistan still bothered him, more so when he was tired, or when the weather was particularly cold.

But today it was hot and sunny, and all he was wearing was a small pair of running shorts, his chest and shoulders glowing with sweat. Delicious.

"Yeah, I do modeling," he said, looking straight at the agency woman as she started to drool. "But only in private ... for my wife. Hey, baby."

Then he leaned down to kiss me, and the agency woman looked as if she had been wading through dog poop in her $600 Louboutins.

"Oh. You're the mother."

I raised my eyebrows at her but she didn't even have the courtesy to blush. She shoved another business card at Sebastian and threw the words, "Call me!" over her shoulder.

"You gonna bitch-slap her, Caro?" he asked, nuzzling my ear, "'cause you really look like you want to right now."

"Not at all," I said, primly. "I'm modeling good behavior for our son."

He smirked at me. "I love it when you're good, baby, but I love it even more when you're bad."

After that encounter, it was nap time. Marco slept soundly while I was thoroughly fucked by 190 pounds of prime manhood.

Sebastian called it 'practice'. What he meant was that we were hoping to conceive baby number two. He didn't say it, but I knew that he hoped Marco wasn't going to be an only child. Sebastian had grown up alone and he didn't want that for his son. Thank goodness he'd met Ches and the Peters' family when he was 13. It was the only time he'd known what a real home was like—until now.

But unlike my impossible-to-wear-out 30-year-old husband, I was 43—having a toddler running around who was learning how to get into everything, was exhausting enough. We'd been trying for another baby for the last year. I was beginning to think it would never happen.

It wouldn't be so bad if it didn't, but still, I hoped.

Every month I'd be disappointed when my period started. Even this morning, my heart pounding like a subway train in rush hour, I'd peed on a little plastic stick. I was two days late, and I had my fingers crossed, my eyes crossed, although not my legs crossed—obviously.

Not Pregnant.

The words on that little piece of white plastic haunted me. I wanted to cry but then a little golden-haired bundle of cuteness tugged on my leg.

"Beach, mommy!"

I'm instantly smiling.

I was supposed to be working on an article for one of the nationals about wounded service men and women learning to surf. But the sun was shining, and my walking, talking, loving son wanted to go to the beach. I shut down my laptop, and was a willing accomplice to his desire to sit on sun-warmed sand and paddle in the ocean.

Besides, my deadline was still several days away. And over the past three years since Sebastian and I had met again, I'd learned not to take these precious moments for granted. Work could wait, even work I greatly enjoyed.

I picked up my beach bag that was waiting by the front door, ready for action. It was a sort of mommy's version of my journalist's grab bag for emergency evac. But instead of passport, solar-powered phone charger, first aid supplies, dried food, water, flashlight, and pocket knife, I now carried baby wipes, mints, sun screen, cell phone, swim diapers, pail and shovel, a towel, some water and a snack, wallet and three baseball caps. Today we'd only need two because Sebastian was in the city working at the gym, although only for the morning. He didn't usually work on a Sunday, but he was doing it as a favor for one of his clients.

Over the last two years, he'd really started to build his business as a personal fitness trainer, specializing in people who'd suffered traumatic injury, including loss of limbs. Not all of his clients were ex-military. One 19-year-old he worked with had lost a leg in a motorcycle accident, and another was born without the lower portion of his left arm.

Sebastian had lost 17% of the muscle from his right thigh, and was left with femoral nerve dysfunction, which could be very painful at times. He'd also been shot in his shoulder and had diminished motor skills in his left hand. You'd hardly know it to look at him, although when he wore his running shorts, the ugly scar covering the upper portion of his right leg was hard to miss.

He'd been very self-conscious of it at one time, but now it didn't bother him when people openly stared. I was more likely to be annoyed by their curiosity than he was.

A couple of months ago he'd starting volunteering as one of the instructors for the Wave Warriors Surf Camp at Virginia Beach. So every other weekend throughout the summer, we were making the seven hour drive south and joining in with the other ex-services families. I'd gotten to know some really amazing people, some of whom were the focus of my article.

And Marco loved it. He was turning into a little surf rat, taking after his father in so many ways. They even shared the same crazy mop of blond hair, although Sebastian was threatening to shave his off again, saying it was getting too long. I'd begged him to keep it, but I wasn't sure how much longer I'd win that battle.

As far as the surfing went, the long-term plan was for Sebastian to start a similar surf camp for veterans nearer to home.

But right now, we were waiting on even more exciting news. His work with disabled people had been noticed, and the gym manager had put Sebastian's name forward to be a personal trainer at Rio in 2016 for the US Paralympics team. Essentially, he'd be helping athletes to use the on-site equipment, although it was a job that was more about kudos than pay. He'd been learning Portuguese via an interactive online program in the hope that this would help his application, even though it wasn't a requirement. He was picking it up easily, which was very annoying, as my own language skills were severely limited, but damn, I was proud of him, too.

If he got the job, I was planning to join him for at least one of the three weeks he'd be there. At first, I'd been reluctant to agree to go, not wanting to be a distraction while he was focusing on something so important. But then he said he'd been away from me long enough during the ten years we were apart—a comment that filled me with guilt, almost as much as it made me swoon. We were undecided on whether Marco would come with us. If not, Ches and Amy had offered to take him. But Sebastian wanted his son with him, and I suspected he'd get his way. I found it hard to say no to him, a fact which he exploited shamelessly at times.

Once a year, we made a point of traveling out to San Diego to spend time with Sebastian's best friend, Ches, and his family. Not only that, but Ches's parents now lived on the west coast and I thought it was good for Marco to have a chance to experience what it was like to have grandparents. Sebastian was estranged from both his mother and father, and I hadn't heard a word from my mom in 13 years. We'd never got along, and my divorce from David gave her the excuse she'd wanted to cut me out of her life. I knew she was still alive, but that was all.

I didn't want Marco to miss out on anything, and Ches's parents, Shirley and Mitch, treated him as part of their family, and Sebastian had always been a second son to them. I wanted to make sure we kept as much connection as was possible even though we lived 3,000 miles apart.

I loved living at Long Beach. It was near enough to urban life, but also had a real small town community vibe about it. And very importantly as far as Sebastian was concerned, it had a good-size surf, with waves coming off the Atlantic that provided long, workable rides.

While Marco and I were strolling toward the beach, I texted my girlfriends to see if they wanted to come and join us. They enjoyed driving out from the city, leaving behind the frantic bustle to have some quality beach time. They also enjoyed ogling the local surfers as they dove through the blue-gray waves, their perfectly toned bodies rippling in the summer sun. Let's just say they enjoyed the window-dressing.

Things were changing in my group of friends. Nicole had started dating some high-powered Swiss banker, so they only saw each other every couple of weeks. It wouldn't have suited everyone, but it seemed to work for them. Jenna was still happily single, but Alice had recently become engaged to a fellow professor at NYU, an archeologist who was currently away on a field trip in Peru.

It was rare that the four of us got together these days, so it was almost like old times, except for the fact that Marco was making sandcastles next to us.

Sebastian joined us an hour later, thankful to be back from the madness that was NYC. He scooped up Marco to go for a swim, which meant having Marco's chubby arms fastened around Sebastian's neck as he swam up and down.

"It's almost indecent how hot your husband is," sighed Nicole. "And seeing him with Marco, I swear my ovaries start doing salsa moves."

I laughed. "Thinking of joining the club, Nic?"

"God, no! I'll leave motherhood to you, Lee. You're a natural—you make everyone else look bad."

I snorted. "Hardly. It's an uphill struggle sometimes, and I'm not getting any younger."

Alice looked at me sympathetically. "Still feeling broody?"

I sighed. "I don't know. Yes, no, maybe. Sometimes I think ... well, if it's meant to be, it will happen."

Jenna patted my arm. "Whatever happens, Lee, you've got Sebastian behind you. That man completely adores you."

"Yes," agreed Nicole. "Actually, it's rather nauseating."

We all laughed, and the subject was dropped.

~

The following Monday, Sebastian texted me to say he'd be late home. His Afghan friend, Atash, had asked him to drop by after work.

Atash was a near neighbor. He and his family were refugees from Lashkar Gah in the south of Afghanistan, one of the few Shi'a Muslims in Helmand Province, a largely Sunni area.

Some people thought it strange that Sebastian was friends with Afghans, when it was people from that nation who'd caused his life-changing injury and killed two of his colleagues in front of him. But Sebastian never blamed individuals, his hatred was saved for the politicians who'd let it happen.

But I'd been waiting for hours, watching the lasagna I made slowly desiccating in the oven, and Marco had to go to bed without Daddy's goodnight kiss. He was very grumpy about that, and I thought it might be tantrum time. I had to promise that Daddy would sneak in and kiss him when he came home. Marco was satisfied with that. Just about.

When I finally heard the front door open and close again quietly, it was nearly 11PM.

"Hey, baby," Sebastian said, tiredly.

He slumped down next to me on the couch, his limp more pronounced than usual, and I curled up into his side.

"Is everything okay?"

He sighed heavily.

"Yeah, I guess. I've been with Atash and his family for the last four, God, five hours."

He rubbed his forehead, and I started to pull away, meaning to go to the kitchen and get him something to eat.

"Later," he said, tightening his arms around me. "There's something I need to talk to you about."

"Okay," I said, cautiously.

His serious tone was making me nervous, but then Sebastian's smile quirked up one side of his beautiful lips.

"It's nothing bad," he said. "Not really."

"So what's up?"

He leaned back and closed his eyes, settling me onto his chest. As I felt the steady rise and fall of his warm body, I began to relax again.

"Atash has a cousin—some sort of second cousin 37 times removed," he began.

I had to smile. Working out Atash's family relations was an impossible task.

"He's arrived in the US and landed on Atash. They're kind of cramped there already ... and he has this kid with him ... another distant cousin or something, I don't think he even knows how they're related. Anyway, her parents were killed during an IED explosion in the market at Now Zad. Caro, she doesn't have anyone really, and she's only three. Her name is Sofia."

"Sebastian, what are you trying to tell me?"

He opened his eyes and gazed down at me.

"We have room here," he said, softly.

"What? You didn't! You didn't make any promises, did you?" I said, pulling away from him.

"Not exactly..." he muttered.

"Then exactly what, Hunter?" I snapped.

"I just thought ... well, it would be good for Marco to have a big sister, wouldn't it? I mean, I know that you could still ... but she needs a home *now*, Caro. You should see her: she's so cute, with all this long, brown hair and big brown eyes. She kinda reminds me of you."

His smile was wistful and I felt my heart miss a beat.

"So ... what does that mean? What do you think is going to happen? That'd she'll come and live with us for a while? What happens when Marco becomes attached to her and then she just leaves? There are laws in this country, Sebastian. You can't just go around taking children from their families!"

"I know that, Caro," he said calmly as my voice began to rise. "We could ... help ... maybe ... adopt her? She needs someone, baby. Sure, she's got Atash's family, but they're busting at the seams there, and she needs something secure. Fuck knows what she's been through already. She lost her parents ... she saw them die."

My heart went out to that lost little girl, but I had to be practical here, because God knows Sebastian wasn't going to be.

"Do you even know if they've entered the country legally? And Child Services need to be informed so..."

"Fuck that! I have no idea and I don't care. Rules aren't for us, baby. They never were—not when it really matters, not when the law is shit and makes no fucking sense."

His words stung me. I wanted to cry out and yell and say, *No! There are consequences. Look what happened last time—we lost 10 years!* But I didn't. I couldn't.

"She needs us *now*," he stressed, gripping my shoulders. "Baby, you've got so much love to give. You're an awesome mom. You're amazing with Marco, so fucking patient. We can do this, Caro. We can give her the home she needs."

"Does she even understand English?"

"No, but that won't be a problem. She's Pashtun—I can talk to her."

"There are rules! We'd have to apply to be her adoptive parents and that could take a couple of years and..."

His eyes sparkled. "So that's a yes?"

"It's a maybe," I said tentatively, feeling angry at being bulldozed and guilty about being the sensible one. "This isn't something we can go into without really thinking it through."

"So we'll go see her tomorrow," he said, pulling me into another hug.

"I said *maybe!*"

But I knew I was losing the battle. The truth was, I didn't want to win it, but I *had* to be sensible. Taking on another woman's child—I didn't know if I could do it.

That night, Sebastian made slow, sweet love to me, whispering hot, dirty, passionate words in my ear, worshipping me with his body. At times like this, it felt like life had a greater meaning than the two of us, than our small family. It was hard to explain, and I wasn't sure I wanted to try and see how the magic worked.

Sebastian fell asleep quickly that night, but I lay awake for hours, thinking, wondering. I tried hard to keep the practical problems in front of me: lack of space in our little bungalow for one, adoption procedures for another. Maybe I was too old to be approved as an adoptive mother. I just didn't know. And there was a good chance that Child Services would think Sofia would be better off with another Afghan family, people who shared her culture and religion. But if we did go ahead, it would undoubtedly help that Sebastian spoke Pashto, but still ... were we the right family for her? And how would Marco react? The only child, suddenly presented with a ready-made sister?

My eyes widened as I realized that I'd already thought of Sofia as his sister.

I watched Sebastian sleeping for a long time.

Moving as quietly as I could, I rolled out of bed.

"Where're you going?" he murmured, sleepily.

Darn Marine! He slept like a cat.

"Bathroom," I whispered.

He grunted something inaudible and rolled onto his side.

Instead, I headed for my laptop, stopping briefly to look in on Marco.

He looked like a tiny angel, a cherub, his face flushed from sleep, one arm flung over his head. My heart skittered, and I closed the door quietly, then decided to leave it slightly ajar.

I flipped up the laptop's lid, and switched it on.

I was journalist and I needed facts: they were my bread and butter.

The bottom line was that in order to even have a child see a doctor it would need to be under our insurance or else pay out of pocket. If we wanted to add Sofia to our insurance, we would need a birth certificate or court documents. The same held true for going to school. We would need to have proof of custody or guardianship or a birth certificate in order to register her. So technically, Sofia could live with us for months, but not long term. We would need to make arrangements to adopt her and start the process immediately.

I batted the idea back and forwards for hours, unsure what to do, finally crawling back to bed and falling asleep a couple of hours before dawn.

I was woken too early by some small person yanking on my arm, wanting pancakes and a glass of milk.

Sebastian sat up yawning, and exhausted as I was, I couldn't help but appreciate the beauty of his hard body, tousled hair, face sleep-softened.

"Let mommy rest, buddy. She's real tired."

He pulled on his running shorts and a t-shirt, discreetly tucking his morning wood away, before taking Marco by the hand, their voices disappearing in a quiet murmur.

Of course, I couldn't get back to sleep, and in the end I got up and showered, my body still half asleep, my mind whirring.

When I staggered into the kitchen, Sebastian was halfway through burning a batch of pancakes. Okay, they weren't completely burned, but perhaps just a little darker than I would have made them. His cooking skills had only improved slightly. Very slightly.

I took over while he poured milk into a sippy cup for Marco, and made us coffee. I felt his warm hands circle my waist as I stacked the pancakes.

"So, any thoughts?"

"Lots of them, and all confused."

"Oh, okay."

There was a world of disappointment in those two words.

"But I think we should go and see her—see Sofia—as a family."

"Really?"

I turned to face him and his eyes were lit up with surprise and pleasure.

"Really? You'll go see her?"

"Yes, but it's just to say hello. Nothing more."

I said the words, but inside it felt like that once we'd seen her, there'd be no going back.

Marco picked up on Sebastian's excitement, and went running around the kitchen yelling and shrieking at a piercing level. He laughed even louder when Sebastian pretended to chase him, and I left them playing hide and seek with the kitchen furniture.

Dear God! If Sofia did join our family, I was in danger of having two toddlers, and one grown-up kid who was more work than the rest of them combined. I couldn't help smiling at the thought.

A sister for Marco. *Our daughter*.

I gave myself a good talking to for jumping the gun, but the nervous excitement was bubbling up inside me, too, as we reached Atash's house.

Two men I didn't recognize were sitting on the steps, but they seemed to know Sebastian, calling out a greeting. He replied, "*As-salaamu' alaykum*," and I smiled and nodded as we walked inside.

As usual, organized chaos flowed through the small house. Children ran screaming happily, and the babble of voices filled every room. Sebastian hadn't been joking when he said the house was splitting at the seams. Atash's house had become an informal community center for the local Afghan population. A good number of them seemed to use it as a staging post to start their journey to other family members spread across the country.

Atash came to greet us, offering the ubiquitous sweet tea. We both accepted, even though I couldn't stand the stuff, my teeth aching just from looking at it. Sebastian tolerated it better, but had perfected the practice of making one small cup last as long as his visit entailed.

Marco ran out into the tiny backyard, completely at home, mingling happily with the other children, uncaring that they spoke a different language. Maybe when you're a child, that's the only language you need.

Sebastian nudged me.

"That's her. The one sitting by the fence."

A small girl in a dowdy brown shalwar kameez was pushing her hands in the sandy soil and making a dusty pile in front of her. Her hair was long and loose and her feet were bare, a pair of tattered flip-flops lying next to her. Even though she was a year older than Marco, she didn't appear much bigger.

She glanced up suddenly, and her huge brown eyes made me catch my breath. She looked so lost and alone, such an adult expression of suffering on her small face.

I could help myself. I went over and sat next to her, kicking off my sandals and making my own mud pie next to hers. She watched me seriously, then continued to make her pile grow, her hands and nails filthy, like mine.

"Sofia," I said quietly, not looking at her. "That's a pretty name."

There was the tiniest pause, when she heard her own name.

I talked quietly, chattering about nothing in particular, until Marco came and plopped himself in my lap.

Sofia's eyes widened, and after a moment's thought, she reached out to touch his gold-colored hair.

Marco squirmed and blinked with one eye scrunched up. Without warning, he launched himself at her, squashing her mud pie completely flat then laughing like a small hyena.

And that was it. They were up and running around the garden together, squawking and chattering, each with their own childish babble.

Sebastian came and sat down in the dirt next to me.

"What do you think?"

I shook my head slowly. "I think I'm in a lot of trouble."

He put his arm around my shoulder and pulled me in for a hug.

"Guess we'll be in trouble together then."

"Guess we will."

Of course, it wasn't as simple as that, no matter how much we might have wished it. For one thing, Child Services were horrified by the informal way everything had happened, and threatened to take Sofia away. But by then, she'd been living with us for six weeks and had settled incredibly well. And yes, I admit it, we'd deliberately dragged our feet informing them.

They continued to be quite threatening for a while, but I played the journalism card, and then the refugee card on Sofia's behalf. Sebastian threw in the vet card as well as the work he'd done in the local refugee community, and in the end, they had to admit that they didn't have any better alternatives to offer her. A fact that we already knew.

Her formal adoption would take much longer, but to us that was merely a thin strip of red-tape.

Marco loved his new ready-made sister and she seemed happy, as well, although there were times when she was too quiet and we wondered what heavy thoughts and memories troubled her.

She had night terrors sometimes, but that was something we understood, having lived through Sebastian's PTSD as well as my own grim, clouded souvenirs of war.

We'd decided that it was important for Sofia to know as much about her own culture as possible, so we spent even more time with Atash and his extensive family. Not only that, but Sebastian spoke to her in Pashto, so she wouldn't lose her language. I spoke to her in English, and she seemed to grasp that distinction very easily.

Soon, she was chattering away in both languages. Marco took it all in his stride, but surprised us one day by calling Sebastian 'baba'—the Pashto version of 'daddy'. It seemed likely that we'd have two bi-lingual children on our hands.

Sofia had been with us for three months and I couldn't have been happier, but then something else happened that sent my well ordered world spinning on a different axis. Again.

And I blamed Sebastian.

That man had always been trouble. God, I loved that about him. One of the many things.

Marco and Sofia were safely corralled, playing in the backyard. Sebastian was in the living room doing sit-ups, a sight that very nearly distracted me from what I had to say.

I sat down on the edge of the couch, more than a little anxious.

He grinned at me as he caught me checking out his abs. Alright, I was counting them—and possibly imaging running my tongue over them.

He winked and did another ten crunches before I finally got up the nerve to speak.

"Sebastian, we need to talk about your ... about your disability money."

He stopped immediately and scowled.

The money he'd been given for his injuries had been gathering dust in a bank account, untouched for three years.

"For fuck's sake, Caro! You know I don't want anything to do with that shit. It feels ... I just can't."

"I know, but we're going to need it. Now we have Sofia."

He sighed.

"They're just kids, Caro. They can share a room for a few years."

"Yes, but I think we'll need somewhere bigger than the bungalow before that."

"You need an office, baby. I know. Maybe I could build something in the yard and..."

"No, Sebastian. We'll need another bedroom."

His eyebrows drew together in a frown. "Why? What did you do?"

I took his hands in mine and smiled at him. "It's more what *you* did." Nope, the penny wasn't dropping. He continued to look at me blankly, I was going to have to spell it out. "I'm pregnant."

His eyes widened. "Holy fuck!"

"Quite. And if I remember correctly, that's what I said at the time."

He gave a happy shout of laughter and picked me up in his arms, whirling me around. Then he put me down as carefully as if he were handling glass.

"Fuck me, you're amazing!"

"You're pretty amazing yourself, Sebastian. You're so great with Marco and Sofia. You think you can handle another one?" I laughed a little anxiously. "Three kids under the age of five."

"Yeah, that's really something."

He shook his head disbelievingly. "Everything's changing so fast."

My heart clenched painfully.

"Too fast?"

"Fuck, no! It's just more ... more than I ever dared dream of. You, Marco, and then Sofia. Now this. It's so fucking amazing, it scares me. I feel like I don't deserve to be such a lucky bastard."

That was so typical of him, and I was going to spend the rest of my life proving that he deserved every good thing that happened to him—to us.

"You're everything I ever wanted, Sebastian. Thank you for giving me this wonderful life."

His eyes became glassy, and his arms tightened around me.

"I love you, Caro."

"And I love you, Sebastian. *Sempre e per sempre*."

It was time to begin the next chapter in our lives.

BONUS EPILOGUE 3

Tenth Wedding Anniversary

Sebastian

"Hey, hot mama!"

I take a moment to appreciate the beautiful woman who's my baby mama. Well, the kids are not so much babies now. Marco is nine-going-on-nineteen, if the way he notices girls is anything to go by—little dude has all the moves. Our baby girl, Shirley, is nearly six, named for the woman I think of as my mom. And Sofia, our adopted daughter is 11 and such a beautiful soul. She loves being a big sister and shows it in everything she does—the way she looks after her brother and sister, the way she talks to them and tells them stories. Cutest fucking thing ever. Sometimes it's hard to believe that her life started in the stark mountain ranges of Afghanistan. I talk to her in her own language every day so she has some connection with her homeland, but in all other ways, she's an American girl, just starting junior high. And I will personally FUBAR any teenage boy who lays eyeballs on either of my daughters. EVER.

I look at my family and wonder how I got to be such a lucky mofo. It's not all been smooth sailing, not by a long shot, but life is good right now, we're good.

Caro had her 50th birthday a few months back. I know it bothers her, although she doesn't say much, but I caught her coloring her grays in the bathroom with a home dye kit.

"Grays show up more when you've got dark hair, Sebastian," she snapped at me when I asked her why she was doing it, although her eyes were glassy with unshed tears when she said it.

"Baby, I don't care. If you want to color your hair pink, green and purple, then go ahead. You'll always be beautiful to me."

"It's alright for you," she snorted, torn between tears and laughter. "You're blond—no one will ever notice."

And although she didn't say it, sometimes the fact that I'm 13 years younger still bothers her.

Things had gotten a little tense between us for a while, and it was for the dumbest of reasons.

Since I was medically discharged from the Marines, I work as a personal trainer at an upscale Manhattan gym four days a week. That sounds fucked up, but when I was discharged, the docs thought I'd never walk well again, and the bullet that went through my shoulder left me with poor motor skills in that arm. But I've worked really hard to get as much function back as possible. I'm fitter than most guys in their thirties.

So now I work with people like me—I mean guys who've been injured. I even had to go back to school to learn all the biology shit to be a personal trainer, but it was worth it in the end. When I first started out, I used my USMC connections to cut a deal with a gym owner, Connor Gibson, a guy who has a chain of gyms across the East Coast. He wanted to do something for ex-servicemen and women, so I persuaded him to let me do rehabilitation work with guys who'd lost limbs in Iraq and Afghan. When he saw that it was good marketing, good for business, and highly fucking motivating for the able-bodied in his gym, he made it a core concept for the whole chain. But part of the deal was that he wanted me working more on the marketing side, as a kind of poster-boy for people recovering from injuries. What-the-fuck-ever if it helped my guys.

I definitely had injuries: as well as being shot, I'd lost 17% of muscle mass from my right thigh after getting caught in a suicide bombing in Afghan.

But then Gibsy had the bright idea of putting me on the front of a fucking calendar that he sold for the charity Wounded Warriors. That was bad enough, but it got worse. Because that's when I was approached by a model agency to do underwear modeling for them. I'm not kidding! How fucking embarrassing is that? A bunch of strangers staring at my junk! But the killer in the contract was that they'd fundraise on behalf of Wounded Warriors—a deal that would net hundreds of thousands of dollars for the charity. How could I say no to that? And Caro talked me into it, as well.

So seven or eight times a year, I'm flown off to some beach or photo studio, and paid crazy amounts of money to strut around in skivvies. Too fucking funny. Except that I started getting stopped in the street by strange women, or even groped in public.

At first Caro thought it was kind of amusing, but the way these women treated her wasn't. Yeah, it caused some tension for a while. I said I'd stop the dumb modeling, but she pointed out how much money the charity would lose, and the publicity meant that Gibsy gave extra free memberships to rehab guys to use his facilities. I guess you could say I was locked into it.

I'd just gotten back from a shoot in Florida and surprised Caro and the kids by turning up three hours earlier than they'd expected.

Caro is sitting on the deck in the backyard reading a book. She jumps when I whisper in her ear.

"Hey, hot mama."

"Sebastian!" she manages to breathe out, before I give her the long, hot kiss that I've been imagining for days.

Then Marco looks up from where he's been kicking a soccer ball and a huge smile spreads across his face.

I never had that as a kid. The only emotions my dad invoked in me were fear and hatred. My kids would never know what that was like. Never.

"Dad!" yells Marco. "It's Dad!"

Shirley runs out of the house, shrieking at an ear-splitting volume, and she and Marco start using me like a jungle gym. Then Sofia joins in and it becomes a group hug-a-thon, and we crumple onto the deck while they climb all over me. I fuckin' love it.

"Hey, can we have a BBQ tonight?" yells Marco.

"Sure, bud—at Atash's place. Me and my girl are having a date night."

Marco kicks at a dandelion growing in the cracked paving, sending the seeds floating into the air.

"That means you're going to have sex," he grimaces. "That's gross."

What the fuck? I mouth to Caro.

She shrugs, as if to say, *You're his dad—you fix it.*

"Don't disrespect your mom," I say to Marco seriously. "I've missed her and we just want to spend some time together."

"I think it's romantic," giggles Sofia, and I can't help rolling my eyes.

Fuck knows what books she's reading these days. I leave that shit up to Caro.

"Sorry, Mom," Marco mutters when I give him another hard stare.

"Did ya miss me, too, Daddy?" asks Shirley.

"Yeah, I missed all my babies!" I say pulling her into a hug.

But she wriggles away looking annoyed. "I'm *not* a baby anymore, Daddy!"

"Aw, you'll always be my baby," I laugh.

Sofia takes Shirley's hand and herds Marco toward the door.

"Come on, we're going to Uncle Atash."

"I'll pick you guys up at twenty-hundred hours!" I call after them, and laugh as Marco salutes.

Kid wants to be a Marine and is forever asking Caro about my medals and where I served. He knows I don't like talking about it, so he asks her. She's gently trying to dissuade him from enlisting and figures that she might be successful with another nine years of persuading him to go to college instead, but I'm not so sure. He reminds me a lot of me at that age—stubborn and single-minded, just a lot happier.

Besides, the only thing I ever really wanted was Caro.

They wave goodbye and I stare at my wife. "Bed, woman. Now."

She sucks her teeth and looks down. "Can we talk first?"

That doesn't sound good. I sit next to her and hold her hand. "Sure, baby, what's up?"

She's silent, just staring down at our joined hands until she lets go and rakes her fingers through her hair.

"I feel like we're drifting apart," she says, and the words threaten to shatter me. She hasn't finished talking and I'm trying not to freak out. "You have the gym and your modeling work. The kids are in school now. I'm bored with covering local events for community news-sites. And you and I..."

My heart clenches. *What the fuck is she trying to say?*

"Well, frankly, Sebastian, the only time we see each other is in bed and we're..."

"Fucking like it's the end of the world?"

She laughs suddenly and I feel my shoulders relax for the first time since she told me she wanted 'to talk'.

"Something like that," she smiles, shaking her head. "I just meant we don't have much time to talk about 'us'."

"What's worrying you, baby?" I pick up her left hand and start playing with her wedding rings. "This isn't like you."

Her lips twist in a wry smile that fades quickly.

"I suppose it's a lot of things, Sebastian. You're this super-hot model and doing all these photo shoots..."

"Which you know I'd stop quicker than ass on ice..."

"I know, but you're jetting off to exotic locations with all these young models..."

"You think I give a fuck about them? Seriously?"

She looks down.

"No, not really."

"Then what? Because you know that you're the only woman I've ever looked at. For fuck's sake, Caro! You think I'm screwing around on you?"

My heart is starting to race. How did we get here? How did we get to be one of *those* couples?

She sits up straighter. "No, I don't think that. I didn't mean it to come out like that. You've never given me a moment's concern in that direction. It's just that..."

"Then what is it, baby?"

"I feel old."

There's a beat as I stare at her in surprise. My reply is as dumb as it sounds. "No, you're not."

She gives a small smile. "I feel it sometimes. You're so fit and..."

"Caro, when the winter storms roll in, I'm the one limping around like a fucking retiree!"

She rests her hand on my right thigh, over the ugly scars that there're always so fucking anxious to show in photo shoots.

"I know, *tesoro*. But..." she huffs out in frustration. "My periods have stopped."

She looks up and stares at me.

"You're pregnant?!"

"No!" Her voice cuts across my happy thoughts.

Now I'm just freakin' confused. "Um, okay?"

Her lips thin slightly and she crosses her arms. Not sure how I'm pissing her off...

"It's menopause, Sebastian," she explains, her voice brittle. "It's a big deal. A very big deal. I can't ... I'm not..."

Now I'm getting it. Okay, so not always the sharpest pencil in the box when it comes to this shit, but I know what to do.

I pull her into my arms.

"Caro, I get that this, um, change of life, is a big deal, I do. But I love you, baby, and nothing else matters."

"I just feel so *old* compared to you. You're a model, for God's sake. I feel old and frumpy and I'm just so *bored*."

She pulls away from me and I'm wary now. I swallow several times.

"Bored with me?"

Her head whips around so fast, her hair fans out around her.

"No, *tesoro!* God, no! Never that! But I need to be challenged—and not just athletically in the bedroom."

I can't help a small smirk at that comment, but I reel it back in because her eyes are flashing with annoyance.

"So what sort of challenge do you want?"

"Well, there was that assignment in Syria that came up and..."

"No! No fucking way! We talked about that!"

"Actually, we didn't talk about that, Sebastian. You lost your temper and stormed out of the house."

True.

"Caro, it's fucking dangerous out there. No more war zones. No more places you have to wear body armor. Don't tell me we didn't discuss *that*, because we fucking did. You're not going."

"Stop telling me what to do!"

"Stop being so fucking selfish!"

She gasps and her eyes glitter dangerously, but I'm not backing down.

"I mean it, Caro. We've got three kids. What the fuck do you think would happen to us if something happened to you? I couldn't..."

I can't finish the sentence, so we sit there glaring at each other. Caro takes a deep breath and I can tell that she's trying to talk calmly.

"All I was going to say is that since I turned down the Syria assignment, I've felt ... adrift. I need a good story to get my teeth into." She pauses. "And I had an offer this morning."

"Not a war zone."

She rolls her eyes. "No, not a war zone."

"Okay, then."

"Okay, what?"

"You've gotten a new assignment. It's not a warzone. How long will you be away for?"

I hate this bit. I hate her going away, but she hates it when I leave, as well. And this is a partnership.

She smiles slightly. "Well, it would be about a month ... or two..."

That's a lot longer than I was expecting, but I can see the excitement inside her. I'll miss her like fuck, but we'll deal. Somehow.

"Fuck, Caro, two months ... that's a long time," I say quietly. "But if it's what you need..."

My words trail off. I'm already imagining what it will be like to be without her for so long. Fucking grim.

She runs her warm hands down my arm. "Don't you want to know what the assignment is?"

"Sure, baby," I say, trying to smile.

"I'll be sailing to Hawaii from San Diego. They want me to write an article about the challenges ... for a family."

I look up, wanting confirmation for what I've heard. "A family? What?"

"It's a series of articles about alternative ways of family life. You know, families who go backpacking around the world, families who live in eco communities and grow their own food. Well, the editor is following a family at the start of their sailing-around-the-world trip. I've been asked to go and report on it ... and then I suggested to the editor that we all go for the first month, so I get a real flavor of what it's like. All of us."

Her words run together rapidly and I'm not sure who she's trying to persuade —me or herself.

"It would be an amazing learning opportunity for the kids: geography, sailing, navigation, cooking in a galley, fishing ... I don't know! Lots of things. It would be good for us, as well, Sebastian, to spend time together."

She's pretty much convinced me, and I can see how amazing it would be to do something like that. But one thing worries me.

"It sounds great, Caro, but I don't know ... Sofia has only just started at her new school and she really likes it. It could fuck things up if we take her out for a couple of months now."

Caro smiles at me. "You're such a good father, Sebastian. So responsible."

I know she's teasing me, because I used to be kind of wild, but this shit is important.

"I'll have to ask permission to take the children out of school for so long, but if the school goes for it, do you have any other objections?"

"No, baby. Not even one."

Caro smiles at me in a way that has my dick hardening immediately. That's something that's never changed—no other woman has ever gotten me so hot so quickly. And she knows it.

"We'd be away for your birthday and our tenth wedding anniversary," she says, as if I could forget that.

"Baby, all that matters is you being happy."

"So, you think I should take the assignment?" she asks.

I roll my eyes. "Caro, you made up your mind before I walked through the door."

She thinks about this. "No, I hadn't made up my mind, but I'd have been disappointed if you thought it was a bad idea. So, I'll tell the editor yes?"

"Yeah, baby."

She kisses my lips softly. "I love you, *tesoro*." Then she runs her hand over my straining zipper. "Now, I think you need to be thanked properly."

I scoop her up and carry her into the bedroom. I know *exactly* how she can thank me.

~

We start making plans the next day. Gibsy is pissed until I throw him a bone and promise I'll do some shots for his fuckin' calendar while I'm in Hawaii. Then he starts getting excited about doing a shoot at the Marine Corps Base in Kaneohe Bay. He doesn't care that I'll get the piss ripped out of me. Whatever. It raises money.

One of the best parts of the plan is that we'll be able to spend some time with my brother Ches in San Diego. We try to meet up twice a year but it's not always possible with family commitments as well as work.

Caro is glowing. It hurts somewhere deep inside my chest because I can see now the difference in her. I'd stopped noticing—hadn't realized she wasn't happy—and that is un-fucking-forgivable. I won't let shit like this happen again.

Marco is ecstatic that he'll be getting time off school, until Caro points out that he'll lose his place in Little League. I take him to one side and promise that we'll do a load of surfing and all his friends will be jealous as shit.

Then I have to get him to promise that he won't tell his mom I said 'shit'. Little dude worked me for five bucks.

The schools aren't very happy with us, but Caro talked the Principals into it somehow. I was left behind for that discussion. She says the male teachers get defensive around me, and the female teachers are too busy checking me out to make sensible decisions. Yeah, whatever.

We have to pack light because there won't be a lot of room on the boat. Shirley is in tears when Caro tells her that she can only take one Barbie doll with her. I promise that I'll buy her a Hawaii Barbie when we get there. I've no idea if there is such a thing, so Caro might have to figure out how to make a grass skirt and a lei for a doll. And then I start wondering how Caro would look in just a grass skirt and a lei, but because the kids are eating their supper, I have to shake that thought and take a cold shower instead.

It's a long flight to San Diego. All the kids have done it before, but it doesn't mean it gets any easier. Thank fuck for laptops and DVDs. We're taking one with us on the boat, but that's strictly for Caro's use. No one is allowed to touch her laptop—that would be like another Marine touching your M16. That shit is just wrong.

Ches is waiting for us at the airport with his Suburban.

I'm shocked by how fat he's become. It's been nine months since I've seen him and if he wasn't a guy, I'd swear the fat fucker was pregnant. Caro elbows me in the ribs, which means I must have been staring. But come on! I grew up with this guy—he was as fit as me. I mean yeah, I know that he has an office job and I work in a gym, but that's no excuse. I'm going to have words with my best friend.

His wife Amy meets us at the front door and even manages to hug me without pulling a face. She's never been a fan of mine, and she has her reasons. Well, two friends who won't talk to her because of me. But that was a long time ago now. Women sure have long memories—or maybe the sex was just that good. What? I'm a guy—that's how we think.

Caro goes with Amy to get the kids situated, and I go with Ches to get take-out.

I can't hold it back any longer.

"What's with the beer gut, man?"

"Fuck you, Seb! You spend all your day at the gym. It's hard to find time to work-out. You don't know what it's like."

"I'm calling bullshit on that. I see plenty of guys who have families and office jobs. What's really going on?"

He looks at me sideways then glances back to the road.

"You wouldn't understand."

That pisses me off.

"I see guys every day with their legs blown off. Yeah, they have great prosthetics, but the best equipment in the world isn't as good as a real leg, and you're not using yours. It's just frustrating, man!"

Ches blows out a breath. "Just life, I guess. Kids are growing up. I'm in the same freakin' job I was ten years ago, jeez, Seb, the same place where we bussed tables when we were 17. I just feel like life is passing me by. And look at you and Caro, doing all this crazy stuff. Amy has her friends, her job, her book club—she doesn't need me. I just..."

His words trail off.

"I think you're wrong," I say seriously. "But maybe you need to think about what you want for you. Spend some time at the beach, go surfing. We always used to go there to figure things out." He nods slowly. "And I'll draw you up an exercise schedule, something to get you fine and fuckable, my friend."

He gives me the finger and we both laugh.

We eat pizza and I can't help smiling as Ches tries to force down some salad instead of a fourth slice. It's a start.

I get the kids bathed and into bed, and then collapse onto the sofa with Caro curled up next to me.

Ches and Amy are filling the dishwasher, so I take the opportunity to slide my hands under Caro's shirt, running my hands across her ribs and brushing the underside of her breasts.

"Sebastian," she chides in a breathy voice before kissing the hell out of me.

Amy interrupts us. I knew she hated me.

"OMG, you guys! Don't you ever stop? You're like a couple of horny teenagers!"

Caro looks embarrassed, but I just grin at Amy and raise my eyebrows. I always did know how to piss her off.

We spend three days with Ches and Amy before we head to the Harbor Yacht Club to find our host family and the boat we'll be sailing on.

The Falcon looks like something out of a pirate movie with two tall masts and a web of rigging, the sails stored for now.

It's a beautiful, sleek boat, and I know from the research we did that she's 74 feet and can sleep 12 people. I did a lot of sailing when I was a Marine, but never in anything this upscale. I can't wait to be on board. The kids are just as excited, and Caro's eyes are shining with happiness.

Our host family come out to meet us. We've skyped with Ken and Ellen so we know what to expect. But all the same, I make sure that Ken keeps his eyes off of Caro. He seems cool, but you never know.

But his enthusiasm is contagious. And soon we're clambering all over the yacht, admiring when Ken tells us about it ... her.

"She was originally built in Genoa in 1948," says Ken.

I can't help turning to grin at Caro. We had some good times there before we were married. She smirks at me and I have to look away before there's an uprising below decks. Yeah, totally getting into a nautical mood.

Ken is oblivious, but Ellen is smiling at me and Caro. I like her already.

"*Falcon* was completely restored and rebuilt in the nineties," Ken continues, "and converted to a twin screw gaff rigged schooner with six cabins—all with AC."

The polished oak and mahogany gleams in the sunshine.

"Fuck me, she's a beauty," I say, still grinning at Caro.

She shakes her head at my language, but smiles back.

Caro

My man has a serious potty-mouth—the habit of ten years in the Marines that he never could break, although I'm not sure how hard he's tried.

He's so excited about this trip. I think it'll be good for both of us. There was something about turning 50 that really got to me. I can't even find the words to explain, but I suppose it's the feeling that I'm truly in middle-age and the signs are obvious, not just the grays in my hair. Whereas Sebastian, he seems to get even more handsome with age, something I didn't think was possible.

He has women falling all over him, but he barely notices, or if he does notice, he doesn't do anything about it. I've never had to worry about him like that.

My beautiful boy.

I watch as his muscles ripple under his silky skin—the blue of the sky, the green of the sea in his expressive eyes, the sun forever fixed in his golden hair. The kindness and goodness that matches his beauty on the outside.

He turns to smile at me, his eyes asking why I'm staring at him so intently. The answer? Because I know I'm loved. My skin will wrinkle and my hair will go gray, my body will bend with age—and I will be loved. In this life and in the next. I will be loved. Whatever the world throws at us, wherever the next adventure leads, I will be loved.

Sempre e per sempre.

THE END

Don't forget to check out the additional bonus chapters on my website

BONUS CHAPTER 1

The First Time

I was bored out of my brain, idly wondering if Ches had any weed left from the weekend. Studying was so fucking boring. Yeah, I knew I needed to get good grades and that my AP courses were important, but I'd much rather have been at the beach—or with Caroline.

Caroline.

God, seeing her again—it was like a dream.

When dad casually mentioned that the Wilsons were moving back to San Diego, I thought I was going to freak out. So many times, *so many times*, I'd thought about her over the years: wondering what she was doing, where she was living. Remembering all the stuff we'd talked about when I was a kid. She used to just talk to me, I mean really *talk* to me. And she was beautiful, so goddamn beautiful. At least, she was in my memory. I'd never had a picture of her, and I hadn't seen her in nine years.

I was going crazy wanting to ask dad more questions: when would she (they) be coming back? Where would she (they) live?

Most of all I wondered: would she remember me?

I'd had a thing for brunettes ever since, which was kind of funny because Brenda, my ex-girlfriend, was a blonde. I'd dated a couple of times in high school, but Brenda and I had gone out for nearly nine months. I'd sort of thought I was in love with her, until Ches told me that she'd been screwing Jack fucking Sullivan. Turned out I wasn't as much in love with her as I'd thought. Turned out I didn't give a shit when we broke up. Not really, but still fucking humiliating.

Afterwards, I hadn't had much interest in dating anyone else.

And then I heard Caroline was coming back. I really wanted to see her, to find out if she lived up to my memory of her. I didn't think that would be possible; I mean, she must have changed. It had been nine years: she must have changed, right? For all I knew, she was fat and had kids. Even so, I'd been desperate to think of a way to see her, and find out once and for all. She probably didn't even remember me: I was just some kid that she'd taken pity on.

And then I'd seen her at the beach, and she'd taken my breath away. She was so beautiful. She had the same long, brown hair that looked almost auburn in the sun; and her eyes were almost hazel and her skin was all glowing and tan, looking fucking hot.

She was so beautiful laying there in that bikini; I got hard just looking at her, and my eyes damn near dropped out of my head and rolled down the beach. It really made me pissed to think that the other guys were probably thinking the same thing. I'd had to hold my surfboard in front of me, so she couldn't tell how I was feeling. How fucking embarrassing was that?

When she sat up and I could see her breasts, I nearly came on the spot. Ugh, God!

At first, she hadn't recognized me. I was shocked by how much that hurt; but then I told her who I was and she smiled at me. Her smile fucking knocked me out.

"So, that's *your* Mrs. Wilson, huh?" said Ches, leering at me as he jogged my elbow. "She's freakin' hot."

"Heh heh! I bet Seb's wishing she was a cougar," said Fido. "I wouldn't say no."

I slapped him upside the head, and he kept his mouth shut after that, but Ches kept throwing me these cheesy looks.

I couldn't concentrate on anything but the way she looked at me. It was a miracle I didn't drown when I went back out to surf.

Then at the party, later. She talked to me again ... she looked so beautiful, and she was so sweet and funny. The way she talked to me, it sounded like she really cared, like she was really interested in *me*.

And then my fucking father had to turn up and humiliate me in front of her. I really wanted to fucking kill him.

But thanks to Mrs. Vorstadt's barbecue, I knew that Caro would be at home the next morning. I could offer again to help her finish her unpacking—and get to talk to her alone.

I set the alarm to wake up early, but not so early that I'd bump into her bastard husband as he left for work. Mom would be asleep till lunchtime, so I didn't have to worry about her.

Walking over to Caroline's was one of the scariest fucking things I'd ever done. I didn't know what I'd say to her. Well, offer to help with her moving-in stuff, obviously. It was fucking irritating to be so nervous. I'd been fine when I'd talked to her last night. Maybe that was because I didn't know she was going to be there—I hadn't had time to turn into a fucking pussy.

I took a deep breath and knocked on her door.

Her expression was faintly irritated when she answered. *Fuck! That didn't look good.*

I shoved my hands in my pockets to stop them shaking, and stuck on a fake smile.

"Hi, Mrs. Wilson."

"Oh, hello! It's nice to see you again, Sebastian. What can I do for you?"

"You said you had to unpack crates; I thought I could help." *And I wanted to see you alone.*

She didn't look very happy and my nerve began to falter, wither, and fucking die a humiliating death.

"That's very sweet of you, Sebastian, but I don't think your parents would be happy if they knew you were here instead of studying."

"I'm taking a break," I lied.

"I'm sure they won't object to Sebastian helping a neighbor."

Fuck! Mrs. Vorstadt. Damn. I'd thought Caroline would be alone.

"That's very thoughtful of you, Sebastian," she continued, in a tone that sounded like she knew *exactly* why I was standing on the doorstep.

"Well, I could certainly use some help." Caroline sounded flustered, but she hadn't said 'no' either.

"Great! I'll go get started."

I practically ran to her garage, hoping Mrs. Vorstadt wouldn't put two and two together.

I faintly heard Caroline mutter "thank you", but I didn't want to hear what else they might say about me, so I started hauling stuff out of crates like my life depended on it.

When Mrs. Vorstadt drove away, Caroline walked into the garage, shaking her head.

"You really don't have to do this, you know."

"I want to help."

It wasn't a lie exactly: I did want to help her. But more than anything, I just wanted to talk to her, spend time with her.

I pulled out a box full of paperbacks.

"Where do you want this?"

"Oh, could you take that into the living room? There's a cabinet with a bookshelf—they can be tucked away in there."

I carried it inside and unpacked her books. Most of them were by authors I'd never heard of. I tried to memorize some of the titles so I could read them, then talk to her about them.

Yeah, I know, but being near this woman was driving me fucking insane.

For one thing, I could smell the shampoo that she'd used, and for another, she was wearing this cute little sundress, and when she stood in the doorway to the garage, I could see right through it. I was going to spend the whole morning as hard as fucking rock. I just hoped she wouldn't notice.

Adjusting myself carefully, I wandered back out to the garage. She was struggling with a huge box, and I had to brush past her to take it out of her hands. I nearly came in my jeans when she backed her fucking amazing ass into me.

"Oh, sorry!" she laughed. "I'm so clumsy!"

"Nah, it was my fault. Where do you want this?"

That box had to go in her bedroom. Jeez, I really wanted to see *that* room, but when I got there, *his* fucking dress uniform was lying on the bed, reminding me that she was married.

I hated everything about her husband. He was an arrogant fucker and he treated her like shit.

I trudged down the stairs and back out to the garage. Then she looked up and smiled, and I remembered why I was here.

"So, how's school? Not too long until you graduate now."

"Nope, I can't wait."

"Do you have plans for the summer?"

"Yeah. Surf. A lot."

She laughed. "Of course! Your endless summer. Anything else, or is that a 24-hour a day surf?"

"Yeah, something like that! Nah, I'll have to get a job. The less time I'm at home, the better."

She frowned, then nodded. "Well, that sounds like a plan. Maybe you could get a job in a surf shop?"

God, she was great. She totally understood me.

We chatted easily for hours, and I couldn't remember why I'd been nervous to come over here.

"Oh crap! It's nearly lunchtime," she said, staring at her watch.

She looked kind of annoyed, and I wondered if she was late for something.

"Did you have to be somewhere?"

"No, no, I'm worried about you. Your parents ... your studying."

Fuck that.

"No sweat."

"Look, I'm not going to be responsible for you flunking out. I'll fix you some lunch, and then you must go study. Deal?"

Food and Caroline. I was one happy fucker.

"Okay, deal!"

She showed me where I could wash up and when I walked into the kitchen, she was reaching up to get some glasses. I realized how darn little she was. Just so fucking perfect. Just the right size for me to ... *And*, I was hard again. Little fucker wouldn't stay down.

I reached up to get the glasses for her.

"I'll get those for you."

I don't think she'd realized I was there, because she jumped when she heard my voice. But having her so near to me, it was like her whole body was a magnet pulling me in. I stood there like a scary fucking moron with those damn glasses in my hand, just staring at her.

She took them from me without comment. But two seconds later she was leaning into the fridge, her perfect ass waving at me. It took every ounce of control not to leap on her. And then she started talking about lemon pressé. She could have offered me bong water and I'd have drank it without noticing.

"Yeah, I'll try that, please, Mrs. Wilson."

"Sebastian, you can call me Caroline. Mrs. Wilson is so formal ... and it makes me feel ancient."

Well, shit!

"Okay, Caroline."

I couldn't help grinning like a loon. *Caroline*. I loved the way it sounded when I said her name out loud.

"Now, I can make you a chicken salad sub or ... tricolored salad."

Oh, yeah. Time to impress.

"*Insalata tricolore, per favore*."

She looked so fucking surprised, I nearly laughed out loud.

"I've been learning Italian. A correspondence course. My high school only offered Spanish." For you. Caroline.

"Really? *Molto bene!*"

"And I've been listening to opera, too. I like Verdi."

I was lying—it sounded like cats fighting.

"The fallen woman."

What the fuck? What did she mean? What was she trying to say to me?

"Excuse me?"

"*La Traviata*: I presume that's what you mean when you say you like Verdi. Or maybe *Aïda*? *Rigoletto*?"

Oh.

"Yeah, all of those."

"I thought teenage boys only listened to heavy rock music."

Shit. She knew I was being a pretentious fucker.

"I'm glad you like opera," she said, softly. "My father loved it."

Yeah, I remembered him. I was so fucking jealous that she had a great dad like that.

"I remember you and him singing opera in your kitchen."

"Really, you remember that?"

"I remember everything." *Everything about you, Caroline.*

"That was a great visit when Papa came to stay."

"Yeah, he was fun. We blew up a lot of things."

"Yes, David wasn't very happy about it."

That fucker. Change of fucking subject coming right up.

"How is your dad?"

"He passed away two years ago."

Oh shit.

"I'm sorry. I didn't know."

Fucking moron! You've made her cry! Shit, I'm sorry, Caroline!

I could have kicked myself, because then the shutters came down, and she became all formal again.

"Thank you for your help this morning, Sebastian. It was really very thoughtful of you, but I'm going to have to insist that you go and do some studying as soon as we've eaten. I don't want to get you into any more trouble."

Yeah, I deserved that. She wanted me the fuck out, and I couldn't blame her. *Fucking idiot.*

She made me a really amazing meal. I hadn't had anything to eat since the barbecue, and I was so hungry, my stomach was yelling at me to get the food in as quickly as possible without stopping. Everything she made was wonderful. I could have kissed her. *And I really fucking wanted to.*

I don't want to come off like a dick, but at school I could have any girl I wanted. Not that there was any way I was going to be a player like my old man. And I'd never been a mute fucking moron who could hardly string two words together before. But now...

She offered to drive me home and I couldn't help thinking it was just so she could get rid of me, which really fucking hurt. Then I realized we were nearly outside my house, so I made her stop the car.

"Can you drop me here?"

"But we're not at your place yet?" she said, sounding confused.

"There'll be fewer questions this way." *Ain't that the truth.*

She pulled over and waited for me to get out. I had to find some way to see her again—to let her know that I wanted to spend time with her. So what did Mr. Fucking Genius come up with?

"Will I see you again?" *Yeah, right.*

She looked puzzled.

"I expect so. Everyone bumps into everyone on the Base. Now, promise me you'll study this afternoon."

Oh God! So not what I meant! But I couldn't think of anything else to say.

"Okay, Caroline. See you later."

"Bye, Sebastian."

I climbed out of the car and watched her drive away.

I walked home slowly. Mom was still in bed. No fucking change there.

The next day, I was still no nearer to deciding how to get to see Caroline, without coming off like a crazy stalker guy.

Irritated at the direction my thoughts had taken, I stared down at my text book. Just a few more months and I could get out of this shithole and never come back. Except that ... Caroline was here now.

The main house phone rang, interrupting my thoughts.

Sighing, I picked up the receiver.

"Hunter residence. May I help you?"

Nobody responded. Probably a telemarketer. God, I hated that. What a fucking tedious job.

"Hello?"

And then I heard her soft voice.

"Hi, Sebastian ... it's Caroline."

I couldn't help taking a sudden, sharp breath.

"Caroline, hi! How are you?"

"Good, thanks. I was expecting to reach your mother..."

No! Talk to me! "I had a free period — and I'm graduating on Thursday anyway." *Idiot! Don't remind her you're still in high school!*

"Oh, well, as luck would have it ... I wondered if you could help me with an article I'm writing?"

"Sure, anything!" *Oh, God, I'll do anything for you.*

Her voice sounded firmer now.

"Well, when we were talking at the barbecue the other day, you mentioned that your friend's dad surfed—I think you said his name was Ches? Well, I wondered if you could give me his number; I'd like to speak to him."

What? Fuck, no! She liked Ches?

"You want to speak to Ches?" The words nearly choked me.

"Well," she said, hurriedly, "I really wanted to talk to Ches's dad. I'm writing an article about personnel from the Base who go surfing. I thought it would make a great piece for 'City Beat'."

"Oh, right." I was ridiculously relieved. I hoped that she couldn't tell. "Sure, I can get you that. We were going to hang out at the beach this afternoon. There's a swell coming in that looks awesome. Mitch was going to ride with us. You want to come, too?"

Please say yes. Please say yes!

"Mitch?"

"That's Ches's dad. He's a Staff Sergeant."

"Well, that would be great."

I could have got down on my knees and thanked God.

"What time were you going to go?"

"About 3:45. We could pick you up?"

"Um ... are you going to Point Loma again?"

I wondered why she wanted to go there.

"Maybe ... we were going to sort of drive around until we found the best break." That's what we usually did. *Please come with me!*

She hesitated long enough for my heart to stop.

"In that case, yes, I'd love a ride," she said. "Are you sure it'll be okay with Mitch and your friends?"

"Sure!"

Damn. No points for being cool.

She gave this cute little laugh. Hell, if I'd heard the desperation I knew was leaking through my voice, I'd have laughed, too.

"Well, okay," she agreed at last, "but I'd feel happier if I could talk to Mitch first."

"No, it'll be fine. Really."

I don't want to give you Ches's number! Talk to me. ME.

"I really think I should," she said, gently.

Fuck. I couldn't say no to her. Reluctantly, I gave in, reeling off Ches's number.

"So I'll see you after school—um 3:45. I'll pick you up. Um, Mitch'll pick you up. Um, 3:45 PM. Okay?"

Stop babbling, moron!

Eventually, she hung up. I could feel the heat in my cheeks, a direct result of my mutant rambling. I must have sounded like a complete idiot. I really had to get my fucking act together before I saw her later, or I was going to have another bad case of word vomit.

I stood up, then realized my dick was rock hard. Huh, interesting. I headed for the shower and whacked off. Twice.

I mean, I knew it was dumb, having a shower before I went surfing, but I just wanted to look good for her, like I'd made an effort. Hell, I even took a couple of minutes to shave. I didn't usually shave more than once or twice a week, but this was a special occasion.

It was a freakin' long five hours of school, before Mitch swung by to pick me up.

"Hey, Seb. You ready man?"

I nodded and tried to smile normally, as he stared at me.

"You okay?" he said, frowning slightly.

Ches's dad was cool. I wished I had a dad like him, not the sack of shit I was saddled with. But sometimes, I didn't want Mitch to see everything; the man was too observant.

"Yeah, I'm fine," I lied.

He didn't look convinced, but he didn't push it either.

I climbed into the back of the van, crashing down next to Fido, and Ches nudged my shoulder.

"'Sup, man? You look kinda sick, like you're jonesin' for a hit or something. You're acting like a fucking lunatic."

I blew out a long breath of air, and tried to calm the fuck down.

Ches threw me another look and Fido just looked stoned. I mean, he wasn't—Mitch wouldn't put up with that shit—it was just the way Fido looked.

A few minutes later we stopped and I held my breath, thinking we'd arrived at Caroline's place. But it was Mitch's buddy, Bill, who climbed into the front of the van. He was such an asshole; I could never figure out why he and Mitch were friends. He was always ragging on me, just because my dad was an officer. It was pretty fucking irritating.

Then Mitch spoke, and I couldn't help thinking it was as much for Bill's benefit as anyone else's.

"Listen, guys, Mrs. Wilson is going to be joining us this afternoon, so I want the language kept clean. She's a lady and an officer's wife, so cut the crap. You hearin' me back there?"

"Yes, sir!" called out Ches, laughing.

Fido mumbled something, and then Bill, the asshole, said, "I hear she's hot. Too good for that fucker, Wilson."

I felt my hands clench into fists.

"Cool it, Bill," said Mitch calmly, but his voice also said he wouldn't take any shit either.

When we got to Caroline's, I couldn't help acting like a fucking preschooler, leaping out of the van and helping carry her stuff.

"Hi, Caroline!"

"Hello, Sebastian. Could you help me with this? I brought some sandwiches for you and your friends."

"Wow, thanks!"

She'd made a load of sandwiches. *God I loved her!*

The thought stopped me in my tracks. *Wait, what?* Sweaty palms—check. Accelerated heart rate—check. Insane fucking jealousy when any other man looked at her—check. Aching fucking rock hard boner—check. Was that love? I pushed the thought away.

I realized she was waiting for me to introduce her.

"Um, this is Mitch, um, Staff Sergeant Peters."

"Mrs. Wilson, pleased to meet you."

I winced when he used her married name.

"Oh, call me Caroline, please," she said with a smile. "You're doing me the favor. I really appreciate you letting me tag along on your surf safari."

"No problem, Caroline. It'll make these beach bums mind their manners. Right, boys! This is my son, Chester; and those two yahoos in the back are his friends Seb and Fido; and this here is Bill Fenenko."

"Hey, Caroline," said Bill.

As he helped her climb into the van, I saw that he was checking her out, his eyes glued to her ass. I wanted to reach over the seats and punch his windpipe through his spine.

Instead, I threw myself into the back of the van, and clutched my knees to my chest, trying to control my breathing.

"What's your damage, man?" whispered Ches.

I shook my head, too angry to speak.

I could hear that Caroline was speaking and I strained my ears, trying to hear her over the noise of the van's engine. She was asking about the rash vests piled up on the front seat.

"They're to stop the wetsuits rubbing around the neck and under the arms when you're paddling out," explained Mitch. "We won't need them, the water at this time of year is around 63 degrees."

She shivered and laughed to herself, then turned around, snapping a quick photo of us sitting in the back of the van. I couldn't help smiling at her; I didn't notice until too late that Ches and Fido were making faces and flipping the bird.

Then she passed the food around and damn, it was good. It wasn't store-bought either, she'd made those sandwiches with her own hands. I couldn't help imagining what else she could do with her hands.

Which wasn't such a great idea, trying to eat a sandwich, with a hard-on pressing against my jeans. Again. This woman was going to be the death of me. What a way to go.

Mitch drove across Coronado Bridge, and then stopped a couple of times so we could check out the surf running along Silver Strand.

"See, Caroline, we're looking for a steady swell and offshore breeze to hold up the waves; the best conditions for producing long, workable rides. If the wind is onshore, it's just froth and white water—no good for surfing."

In the end, Mitch pulled up at the side of the road near Cays Park, and we piled out of the back.

Mitch's commentary had given me an idea. It was obvious that Caroline didn't know anything about surfing, and she wanted to write an article about it. I could help with that—in fact I planned to. As soon as everyone was in the water, I was going to catch a ride in, and talk to her by myself.

The thought made my heart thud in my chest, and I was amazed to see that my hands were shaking slightly. *What the fuck was that?*

"Just forget I'm here," said Caroline.

Like that was even possible.

"I'll just watch and soak up the vibe."

"Yes, ma'am," said Bill, and the ass wipe started undressing in front of her.

Fuck that!

I tore off my own t-shirt and hoped that Caroline was looking my way. *Shit!* I wished I had more chest hair. Okay, I didn't want to look like a fucking Neanderthal like Bill, but, you know, just a *little* more would have been cool.

Mitch handed me his thruster.

"I think I'll take my longboard out today, Seb. You have this one."

"Thanks, Mitch," I muttered.

My psycho dad had trashed my Quiksilver board, saying I'd been spending too much time at the beach. What the fuck did he know? I did my studying; I was keeping up my grades. What more did the bastard want?

But Mitch understood.

Caroline took some more photographs, and I thought I was going to break my fucking jaw trying to smile, while Bill showed off, fucking smirking at her the whole time.

We headed out into the surf, and I felt the shock as the first wave of cold water hit my chest. I dove through it, and paddled for the lineup.

I caught a couple of waves just so no one would get weird on me, and then headed back to the beach. Back to Caroline.

She was sitting on the sand, writing in her notebook and sometimes taking photographs. Her arms and legs were bare in her fucking adorable sundress.

When she looked up at me and smiled, I thought I was going to pass out. Aaand, cue hard-on.

"You finished already?"

"I thought it might help if I explained some more for your article," I mumbled, gripping the board in front of me for dear life, saving me from total fucking humiliation.

"That would be great. It all looks kind of the same to me."

God, she was so cute. I couldn't help laughing.

"Not really. See, Mitch is using a longboard with a rounded nose. He can work the smaller waves with that, and do some hippie shit like hang ten. Ches is riding a shortboard, so he can slash across the wave, catch some air and do the more radical stuff."

When she smiled again, I nearly forgot my own name.

"What sort of board do you have—have you borrowed?"

"This is a shortboard, a thruster..."

Jeez, just saying the word 'thruster' made me hard. Okay, harder, for fuck's sake.

"Er ... it's the same as Ches' and Fido's. See how fast they're going there? You can't do that on a longboard."

She took a load of notes, and it felt really good that I was helping her.

"How many guys on the Base surf?" she asked.

"Quite a few. Once you have your board, the ocean is free. You can be an individual out here—you know, different from military stuff."

She nodded, and I think she understood what I was saying: out there, you can be whoever you want to be.

"So there are no rules for surfing?"

"Well, there are some rules: you don't drop in and steal someone's wave. That's bad etiquette. The guy who takes off first, that's his wave."

"And the second?"

"You go help anyone in trouble."

She smiled.

"Sebastian, don't let me keep you from your friends; I'm quite happy to sit here and watch."

No! Let me sit here with you!

I knew that any moment, she was going to get up and walk away. I had to tell her how I felt. I *had* to let her know how much she meant to me. After all these years, she'd come back. I felt like she'd come back *to me*.

"I can surf anytime; I'd rather be here with you."

My voice came out like a croak, and I could have cheerfully ripped my tongue out. She stared down at her notepad.

But her reply cut my fucking heart out.

"I wish you wouldn't say things like that, Sebastian. I'm a married woman. It makes me ... uncomfortable."

Shit! Shit! Shit!

"I really like you, Caroline."

I got up every fucking ounce of courage I had, and touched her arm. Her skin was silky and warm from the sun—she felt amazing.

She stood up suddenly, making me blink, then walked away down the beach. I thought I was going to be sick.

What the fuck was I thinking? Shit, no. No! *Stupid, stupid, stupid.* I shouldn't have said that. She'd think I was some sick, crazy stalker. Or worse, she'd think I was a dumb kid.

Shit! Shit! Shit!

And then I saw her talking to Mitch, and a wave of jealousy and anger surged through me. I really wanted to hit something. Badly.

Mitch called a timeout and said we were heading back. I felt like I was going to hurl, and I couldn't look at her, because I didn't want to see disgust or pity on her face.

I didn't even remember getting changed, and the next thing I knew, I was sitting in the back of the van with Ches and Fido.

"Hey, man, you weren't in long today," said Ches. "What's up with that? You've been fucking nuts wanting to get out here." He flicked his eyes towards Caroline. "Guess you're distracted."

"Fuck off, Ches," I snarled.

He smiled, knowing he'd scored a hit.

"Look man," he said, quietly, "I know you—and I know what you're thinking. Yeah, she's hot, and really nice, too, but she's *married.* Just wise the fuck up."

Then I heard Caroline ask Mitch to read her article when she'd finished writing it; to make sure the surf facts were right.

Mitch laughed.

"I don't do words, Caroline, not reading and writing words. You should ask one of the boys—that's more their thing."

"Sebastian will do it," said Ches, throwing a look at me.

Fido snickered, and I seriously considered pummeling his dumb ass into dust.

"Okay with you, Seb?" asked Mitch.

"Sure," I said, quietly. "Whenever you like, Caroline."

She didn't look very happy about it, but she didn't argue.

We dropped her off and I watched her run into the house, like she was eager to be home. *She was married.* I didn't stand a chance, and the realization made my chest throb like my ribs were going to break. *What the fuck was wrong with me?*

When we pulled up at my house, Mitch looked worried.

"Seb, your old man's car is here. You want me to walk in with you, have a word?"

I shook my head. I knew why he was offering, but I just wanted to get the fuck out of there.

"No, thanks," I said. "It's cool."

It really wasn't.

I couldn't bear the pitying way they were all looking at me. I hauled my ass out of the van and pounded on the side, telling them they were good to go.

But as I walked into the house, I knew I'd made a mistake going home. I could hear my parents arguing as soon as I opened the door, and from the sound of it, they were both drunk.

I closed the door as quietly as I could, but they heard me as I tried to make it up the stairs.

"Where have you been, you little shit?" snarled my dad.

I stared back at him, folding my arms across my chest.

"Well?"

"Out," I said, holding his gaze.

I just didn't see what was coming next.

His right hook caught me on the cheek, sending me flying backwards against the wall. I hit my head so hard, I saw stars.

"Answer me, you little shit!" he shouted.

"I did my work this morning!" I yelled at him, blinking hard to try and clear my head.

"You're a useless fucking waste of a life. Look at you! You look like a fucking hippie! People must be pissing their pants laughing at me when they see you. You're a fucking beach bum, useless fucking..."

He hit me again. This time I knew he'd split my lip, even while the pain was still cutting through me. Before I could get up off of the floor, I saw a flash of metal. I thought he was really going to kill me this time, but instead he hauled me up by my hair. But it wasn't a knife; he had a pair of scissors. I was still dizzy from his blows and could only struggle feebly as he hacked off several long chunks of my hair. He staggered as I fought against him, and I managed to punch him in the gut—a really good, solid punch. Fucker.

He went down hard. I jumped over him and slammed out of the front door, running as fast as I could, adrenaline pumping through me.

By the time I reached the park, my lungs were burning and my legs were giving out. I slumped down onto the first bench I found and sat there, shaking, as the adrenaline left my body.

Now what the fuck was I going to do?

I'd never hit the bastard before, although I'd wanted to. I couldn't go back there, he'd crucify me. Maybe I could go to Ches's? I knew Mitch and Shirley would take me in, but I also knew the bastard would come and drag me back. I didn't want to involve my friends in this shit.

I really didn't understand that part—the part where my dad would drag my ass back home. You'd have thought he'd be glad to see the back of me. Instead, it was some sort of family honor that I stayed. No matter how fucked up we were, he painted this picture of a happy family.

Ches's family knew the truth. Others might guess, but nobody ever said anything. Real closed ranks. There was a saying in the military: snitches get stitches and wind up in ditches. That was pretty damn close to the truth.

I stared down at my hands. They were still shaking.

What the fuck was I going to do now?

I jumped when somebody spoke my name.

"Sebastian?"

It was Caroline. Her hand hovered over her mouth when she saw me. I knew she was looking at my bruises and split lip. I probably looked like shit. I couldn't face her. It was too hard to see her standing there, so shocked and upset.

"Oh, my God! Are you alright? What happened?"

I didn't know how to answer that. What could I say? *My father is a sadistic bastard. I love you.*

I felt her soft hand on my face and jerked away. I didn't want her to see me like this.

"Don't look at me."

"Did your father do this to you?"

I nodded slowly.

"Sebastian, let me see. I want to make sure you're not hurt too badly."

"I'm okay," I mumbled. "I've been hurt worse than this."

Which was true—but hitting him back had stirred up a load more shit than I knew how to deal with.

She touched my face, the tips of her fingers so gentle.

"Don't cry, Sebastian. It'll be okay."

Had I been crying? I hadn't realized.

She stood in front of me, forcing me to look at her.

"Come back to the house. I'll fix you up and drive you home. Okay?"

It took a moment for her words to sink in. I didn't know how she could help me, and I really didn't want her driving me home, but it was soothing to hear her voice. So I followed her, my body and brain numb.

She kept talking in a low, quiet voice, as if she was trying to calm a wounded animal. I wanted to smile, but it caught behind my lips and my mouth refused to move.

When we got to her house, it was dark. I was glad her husband wasn't there. I couldn't face one of dad's good ole buddies right now.

She opened the door, switching on lights as she drifted through the house, her footsteps as soft as dreams. When I saw she'd taken me into her kitchen, I managed to pull myself together enough to sit in the chair she pointed me towards.

A loud noise made me jump, and my head jerked up.

"Oh, sorry!" she said softly, picking cubes of ice out of a tray. She passed me a hand towel full of ice to hold to my cheek. It felt good. She was taking care of me. No one had ever really done that for me before. I liked it. A lot.

Before I realized what she was doing, she pulled the hood of my sweatshirt down and gasped. At first, I couldn't figure out why. Then I remembered my dad shearing off chunks of my hair. From her reaction, it must look pretty bad. Not that I cared anymore. Not about that.

I closed my eyes.

"Your father?" she whispered.

I looked up for a second, meeting her beautiful, sad eyes. I nodded, and looked away.

"Because of the surfing?" she said, softly.

I nodded again.

"Because of me?"

There was a terrible sadness in her voice, and my eyes blinked open. She thought it was her fault? How could she think that? I had to try and explain.

"No, it would have happened anyway. I'd already planned to go out with Ches and Mitch today. It's not your fault..."

She took a deep breath, and I looked away again.

"Do you want me to fix it for you?"

Fix it? What? My life? How could anyone fix that fucked up mess?

"Do you want me to turn it into a buzz cut?"

Oh. She was talking about my hair. What a fucking joke.

"Okay."

She gestured for me to follow her, and led me upstairs, into her bathroom. She pushed out a chair for me to sit on, but it was facing the mirror. I didn't want to see the mess the bastard had made of my face, and I couldn't bear to see the pity in her eyes anymore.

"I don't want to look at myself," I said, angling the chair away so I couldn't see my reflection in the mirror.

As if from a great distance, I heard the buzzing of a shaver, and felt her gentle strokes, as she passed it over my head. I watched, apathetic, as clumps of hair fell to the floor.

When she stopped, her voice was hoarse.

"All done."

Was she sad? Sad for me?

"It'll be okay," she said, quietly.

If anyone can make it right, you can, Caroline.

I looked up, her eyes meeting mine. "Will it?"

"Yes. When you leave home. You won't have to see him again—either of them."

I nodded slowly. It didn't seem possible.

"Would you like me to get the ice?" she asked quietly.

I shook my head.

"Let me look."

Gently, she lifted my chin.

It felt so good to have her touch my face, I couldn't help myself. I laid my hand over hers, feeling the shock of her skin beneath mine, the sensation as strong as if powered by an electric charge.

"Don't," she said, her voice pleading with me.

But I couldn't stop. I *had* to speak to her; I *had* to make her understand how I felt about her. The way she'd looked after me—it made me feel so much. She *had* to know; I *had* to tell her. I knew it wouldn't make any difference, that there was no way on earth she could want a fuck-up like me, but I *had* to say the words.

I stood up, still holding her hand.

"I love you, Caroline."

She gasped, and I closed my eyes, waiting for her rejection.

But it didn't come.

Amazed, surprised, dumbfounded, I felt her hand on my cheek, then brushing over the fine bristles of my hair and around to the back of my neck, pulling my head towards her.

I couldn't believe what was happening. *She wanted me? Me?*

BONUS CHAPTER 1

It was the moment that I'd been dreaming about since she came back. I kissed her, thrilled and disbelieving that she was responding to me.

I felt her tongue on my lip and I opened my mouth gratefully, feeling an intense wave of pleasure as her tongue stroked mine.

I couldn't believe this beautiful, amazing, wonderful, kind woman was kissing me, responding to me, telling me that she felt the same. That she wanted me, despite everything.

My soul soared, and happiness like I'd never known surged through me.

She gripped my neck with one hand, and slid her fingers down my throat, to my chest.

Oh, God, that felt amazing. I wanted her. I really fucking wanted her.

My hands hovered over her waist, and when she didn't stop me, I locked them around her, pulling her small body in tight against mine.

Feeling her soft and warm against me nearly sent me over the edge. I groaned into her mouth and couldn't help pushing my hips against her.

Suddenly she stepped away, and my arms fell to my sides. *Shit, no!* I didn't understand. Had I got it wrong?

But then I realized she was tugging on the hem of my sweatshirt. She pulled it over my head and my body felt like it was on fire. I was desperate to touch her, to feel her soft skin against mine, but I could sense she was conflicted.

I begged her silently: *love me, Caro. Love me, please.*

She ran her fingers underneath my t-shirt, and I shivered at her touch. Then she ripped it off and brushed her hands over my chest. If I'd died then, I'd have thought all my dreams had come true.

When I felt her fingers on the zipper of my jeans, stroking my hard cock, I nearly came in my pants. I gasped, and my eyes flew open.

She pulled me towards her and continued stroking me. I moaned loudly, and she sighed into my chest.

I didn't even know my hands were moving, until they were resting on her waist again. But when she kissed me, I didn't hold back. This was my one chance, my only chance.

I tightened my grip around her, and moaned loudly when she slid her hand into the front of my jeans.

Holy shit! That felt good—her hand around me.

"Undo my zipper," she said.

It took a moment for me to understand what she was telling me; my brain had left the building. She turned around and I pulled down the zipper of her dress, my hands shaking, this time from desire, from pure, physical need. *I needed her. I fucking needed her. I wanted her—I wanted it all.*

The dress fluttered to the floor and she turned around to look at me. My eyes slid from her face, to her breasts, and suddenly I was finding it hard to breathe.

I stepped towards her again, my hands moving from her hips to her waist; I really wanted to run my hands over her whole body, to touch her breasts, taste her soft, beautiful skin.

"Yes. Touch me," she whispered, as if she could read my mind.

I swallowed as heat coursed through me, then, slowly, carefully, she lifted my right hand to her breast, moving my fingers in a slow circle. She shivered beneath my touch, and the sensation of flesh on flesh scorched me.

I curled my free hand behind her, slowly drifting upwards, then pressed the palm flat against her spine. I kissed her again, bewitched by the way her tongue tasted, the way it moved against mine.

"Kick off your shoes. I want to undress you."

I toed off my sneakers and took a deep breath when she undid the button on my pants. I stared down at her, stunned, as she unzipped my jeans and pushed the denim to the floor.

She stood up slowly, then started to stroke my cock.

It was almost too much. Complete fucking overload.

I felt my entire body shudder, and I had to squeeze my eyes shut, trying to find some way to cope with the sensations flooding through me.

I'd thought about sex *a lot* over the last four or five years, wondering what is was like with a woman, wondering who and when and where, thinking about all the things I could do, that my body was programmed to do. Ches and I had been through my dad's entire porn collection. But nothing compared to this. My brain was flooded, my body on fire. I could barely see straight, let alone think; it was all movement, touch and sensation—and I was lost.

Her hands left me, and my eyes snapped open. She was undoing her bra, and my breath caught in my throat. She was so fucking beautiful. At that moment, I wanted to give her the sun and the stars; I wanted to give her myself, body and soul.

Take me, Caro, I'm yours.

She held out her hand towards me, and then I knew she wanted the same. I couldn't help myself. I was like a fucking barbarian, touching her everywhere, tasting her skin, feeling her heat.

Her hand wrapped around my cock again, and I cried out.

It was too much. Too much. I came in her hand, pulsing streams of cum down her thigh.

Fuck, no! Oh God! Oh God, no! NO!

I couldn't bear it. I couldn't fucking bear it. I didn't want her of all people, looking at me with such pity in her eyes.

I turned away and felt my knees buckle.

"I'm sorry! I'm sorry! I'm sorry!"

Stupid. Useless. Pathetic. Miserable fucking...

I hid my face in my hands, unable to look at her. I thought she'd tell me to get the fuck out. But she didn't. I waited for her to say the words. They never came.

"No, don't. It doesn't matter. It's okay."

I could hear her talking to me, but I could barely understand what she was saying. She kept stroking my back, whispering to me.

"Sebastian, it's okay. Sebastian. Look at me."

But I couldn't.

"I'm sorry," I muttered again.

Then she grabbed hold of my hand, tugging gently.

"Come on. Come."

She tugged on my hand again, but I couldn't work out what she wanted me to do. I followed her, filled with confusion, humiliated and miserable.

She pulled me into the bedroom, gently pushing me onto the bed.

"Lie down."

I lay back, watching her carefully as she walked around the bed, laying down next to me. She pulled up the sheets and I felt her gentle fingers on my cheek. Her kisses fluttered across my face and lips, then down my throat.

I could feel her silky hair drifting across my chest, and I felt a sort of peace that surprised me, filled me and freed me.

She wasn't rejecting me. She was giving me another chance. Because she was beautiful and kind and she knew I needed her.

I ran my hand down her arm and she smiled. Cautiously, I lifted my hand to her breast and circled the nipple with my thumb, watching fascinated as it formed into a hard little bud that I was longing to taste.

She gasped, and I dropped my hand away.

"No, don't stop."

She wanted me to touch her.

She continued kissing me across my chest and down to my stomach, and I knew I was getting hard again. Of course I was hard. She was so amazing. Her touch, the way her body felt, the way her body felt beneath my fingers.

She placed a gentle kiss on the tip of my cock, and a long, drawn-out sigh of pleasure escaped me. She smiled, and twined her fingers through mine, moving them down to her thighs.

"You can touch me," she said, quietly.

She was letting me touch her pussy. She *wanted* me to touch her pussy. Fuck, she was so wet! My fingers glided in and out, circling her clit with my thumb.

"Yes, that's right," she groaned. "Like that."

Hearing her turned on like that, wanting *me* was fucking intense.

"Slowly: yes, in and out."

I stretched to kiss her throat, watching her whole body flush, responding to my fingers inside her.

She touched my cock again, then sat up suddenly. I stopped, staring at her in panic.

Had I done something wrong? Was she upset with me?

When she kissed me roughly, I groaned into her mouth. She pushed her body onto my hand, and I moved my fingers quickly. Suddenly, I felt her body pulsing around my fingers.

It was the most intense, amazing experience, feeling her come around my hand.

She lay back, quiet, her eyes closed.

"Are you okay?" I asked, begging her to say that she was.

She hesitated, and I felt my heart shudder.

"Yes," she whispered, at last. "Very okay. Very, very okay."

I did that. I made her feel that. I felt like I should get a fucking medal.

Then she opened her eyes and gazed up at me, a slight smile on her face.

"Now your turn," she said.

What? Oh, fucking yes!

When she knelt across me, I groaned in anticipation. She grabbed my cock and as she positioned herself above me, I felt myself slide inside her. So warm, so wet, so tight.

Holy shit! Fuck! That felt good. That felt fucking amazing. I never wanted to leave this place. It felt right; it felt like home.

This was my woman, and we were making love. *Fuck, I loved her so much.*

She sat up and leaned back, placing my hands against the base of her belly.

"Can you feel yourself inside me?"

"Yes," I whispered. "I can."

Fuck! I didn't even know that was possible, but I could. I could feel a thick bulge inside her—I could feel me *inside her.*

I must have looked like a fucking idiot, staring at her with my mouth open, but the heat in her eyes made me feel like a man.

She leaned forward again, her hands resting on my chest, moving her hips up and down in a steady rhythm. I pushed my head back into the pillow, unable to prevent my body from thrusting into hers, pushing myself deep inside her.

And suddenly I couldn't stop. I started moving faster, feeling another orgasm build, a tightening in my balls, flickers of fire running up my spine.

My eyes blinked open and widened as I stared at her face, her beautiful face, riding me, her expression wild and free, her head thrown back. When her eyes locked on mine, I came hard, my body shuddering inside her.

Un-fucking-believable!

She collapsed onto my chest and we lay there for several minutes. When she slid off me, I felt the loss of her immediately. I wanted nothing more than to be inside her again, feeling her body around me, feeling the intensity of her passion.

BONUS CHAPTER 1

God, she was so beautiful. I leaned up on my elbow so I could see her properly.

She opened one eye and looked at me, her expression soft and warm.

"Hi," she said, a smile twitching at the corner of her lips. "You okay?"

I nodded, unable to find the words. "That was ... that was..."

"Yes, it was," she said, still smiling.

I couldn't explain what I was feeling. So many emotions were surging through me. I'd waited longer than most guys I knew to *do it*, and I was suddenly really glad I had; glad that I'd done it with her. It had been the most amazing experience of my life. I felt alive, like she'd taught me to breathe.

She stroked my cheek, and I leaned into her hand with a sigh. I kissed her palm and said the words that were rushing through me.

"I love you, Caroline. I always have. My whole life."

I meant every fucking word.

She smiled and laughed gently. I knew she wasn't laughing at me. She looked happy.

"That's a very long time," she said, raising one eyebrow. "You're only 18—your whole life isn't that much, really."

I smiled. "It feels like it sometimes. Anyway, I'm not 18 for another four months; I'll let you know then."

Her expression changed immediately.

"What?" she gasped. "You ... you're *only seventeen?*"

I nodded, not sure why she was so upset.

"For God's sake, Sebastian! *Seventeen?*"

My mouth went dry. "What's the matter?"

She refused to look at me, throwing an arm over her eyes.

I started to feel desperate. *Why wouldn't she look at me?*

"Please, Caroline. You're scaring me."

She moved her arm and glared at me, her expression almost hateful. I felt my heart jolt with the shock. With pain.

When she finally spoke, she spat the words at me.

"The matter, Sebastian, is that you're a minor. What we've just done ... what *I've* just done ... it's against the law. It's a felony, for God's sake!"

Oh. Was that all?

"But I love you."

Simple. See how easy it is?

But she didn't look happy.

"Sebastian, it's *statutory rape!* Do you know what that means? I could go to prison. If anyone found out..."

Fuck, no! That can't be right!

"I won't tell anyone. I love..."

"Don't say it! Do *not* say it!" she yelled the words, and it was just as if she'd hit me. I couldn't understand what was wrong. I wasn't going to tell anyone—tonight had been the best night of my whole life. I didn't want her to feel bad about it, just because I was a few weeks shy of my eighteenth birthday. Nobody cared about that shit. Half the kids in my school were fucking each other. You couldn't go to a football game without tripping over couples screwing behind the bleachers.

Suddenly, she sat up and ran to the bathroom, kneeling over the toilet as if she was going to be sick. I leapt off the bed, standing behind her, afraid to see her reaction.

If you'd just let me hold you!

"Caroline, please."

But she held out her hand like a traffic cop. She didn't want me. *She didn't want me!*

"Please!" I knew my voice was begging, begging her. "Oh, God, please, Caroline!"

I tried to hold her, but she pushed past me.

"No!" she shouted.

She collapsed onto the bed, her whole body shuddering.

"What have I done? What have I done?"

She repeated the words over and over, then hid her head in her hands.

Slowly, I sat down next to her, trying to find the words to explain how I felt; trying to find some way to show her that it was okay.

"I'm not sorry," I whispered. "That was the best experience of my whole life. I love you; I can't help it."

I felt relieved when she let me pull her against my chest, wrapping my arms around her, stroking her arms and kissing her hair.

But then she sat up and pushed me away. Again.

"I apologize, Sebastian. It isn't your fault. Please forgive my ... behavior." Her voice was so cold, a shiver of terror ran through me. "I think you'd better leave now."

Oh God, no! NO!

"Please. Don't send me away."

But she didn't reply. She didn't reply because she didn't want me.

The world crashed around me and I thought I was going to pass out. My heart was hammering in my chest, and my vision was blurred. Was I crying? I touched my face, amazed to find that my cheeks were wet.

Her body was turned away from me, stiff and unyielding.

Moving as if in a dream, I walked into the bathroom and dressed slowly. By the time I'd pulled on my sweatshirt, she'd already gone. The bedroom was empty, and only the rumpled sheets showed that my world had just imploded.

I made it down the stairs without breaking, but when I saw her, standing in the kitchen, her face softened and she started to cry.

"Oh, Sebastian!"

Half a heartbeat later, she was in my arms, her cheek against my chest, and she let me stroke her hair.

Oh, God, just let me hold you, Caro. Please don't send me away.

"Don't be sad, Caroline, I love you. It'll be okay."

She started laughing, her hiccupping giggles mixing in with gasps and cries. She stared up at me, so beautiful, and I wiped away her tears with my thumbs, heartbroken that I'd made her feel like this.

I had to show her how I felt; I had to let her know that it was going to be okay—that *we'd* be okay. I opened my mouth to speak, but it was too late.

We heard the car at the same time.

"David!"

That fucker.

I could hear the panic in her voice.

"You have to go! Quickly! Out through the backyard. Go!"

I turned to run to the door, then skidded to a halt. "When will I see you again?"

"I don't know! Go! Go!"

I was desperate.

"Promise I'll see you again! Promise me!"

"Okay, I promise!" she said, staring horrified at the front door.

I pulled her to me, kissing her fiercely. *My woman.* And then I ran.

I'd only gotten as far as the fence at the bottom of her yard, when I stopped. *This was wrong*, so wrong. What if she needed me? What if he'd come home because he knew? What if he hurt her? I *had* to stay.

I stood in the shadows, staring up at the light in her window.

My body was tense, my hands welded into fists at my side. I couldn't leave her with *him*. I loved her, she loved me. We were supposed to be together. *This was wrong.*

"Caroline," I whispered. "I love you."

I'd find a way for us to be together. No one would stop us.

BONUS CHAPTER 2

Long Time Living

"He's a mess, Mom."

"I know."

"Yeah, but I'm really worried about him."

She gave me a look—the one that said, *What aren't you telling me?*

"Ches?"

It was breaking the code: the brother code, as well as the military code that said, *Snitches get stitches and wind up in ditches.*

I took a deep breath.

"He had another bruise today. He wouldn't say anything, but I'm pretty sure his dad..."

Her lips thinned with anger.

"...and he was sent home from work again. If he shows up with another bust lip or black eye, he'll lose his job. Miss Perez said she can't have him looking all banged up like that in front of the members."

I didn't tell Mom that the only reason Seb still had a job at all was because he was popular with the country club's cougars. Not that he ever did anything with them even though he had plenty of chances—he was only interested in one cougar, and she was history.

I'd taken up quite a few of the offers I'd gotten, but I kept it on the down low because despite everything I thought about Seb's Mrs. Wilson, he missed her—and she'd been his first.

I was really surprised when he told me that, because I'd always assumed that he and Brenda had got it on. He said they hadn't, and I believed it. What I didn't tell him was that Brenda was singing a different tune—pretty loudly, too.

Sebastian is like my brother and I'd helped get him the summer job at La Jolla country club where I already had part-time work. It had been good. Hell, it had been great. But then the whole cluster fuck with Caroline Wilson had happened.

I couldn't believe my best friend had been so dumb as to get involved with a married woman. Not just involved, but fucking deaf, dumb and blind in love with her. And even though she was like 30, which is practically ancient, I had to admit she was hot—a total babe, if I'm honest.

Seb said that they loved each other. At first, skeptical had been my middle name but it seemed like it was true. She'd left her husband for my friend, and lost everything in her old life. The last words that she said to him before they sent her away was that she loved him.

Well, that's what he told me she'd said. She was speaking Italian at the time so I guess it was like a private message from her to him. But there was no doubting what I saw in his eyes. The mindbender was she was in love with him, too.

But, like I said, she was 30 and even now Seb was still six weeks away from his 18th birthday. Seb's asshole dad threatened to have Caroline arrested if she didn't leave quietly. Not only that, but she has the Statute of Limitations hanging over her for the next three years. If they contact each other, Donald will try and have her sent to prison, or at the very least, get her name put on a sex offender registry.

And Seb is falling apart. He'd been in pieces since she'd gone. He kept saying that she was the only good thing that he had in his life. If it wasn't for the fact that he was holding onto the hope that they could be together again in three years, I think he might have done something even more dumb.

It scared me to see how desperate he was.

But when I thought about it, it wasn't that surprising either. Seb had a shitty mom and a bastard of a father. There were no grandparents, as far as I knew, and my own mom and dad had been more parents to him than his own.

Mom was still watching me, and I realized that I'd left her hanging.

"Can Seb come and stay with us? I mean, it's only like six weeks—maybe a couple of months—and then he'll be joining the Marines and he'll be away from here."

"I don't know," she said, slowly. "I'd love to say yes, but I can't see Donald and Estelle going for it."

"Mom, they freakin' hate him! His dad is whaling on him, his mom yells at him all the time or is drunk off her ass! He's miserable—it just sucks. He's damn near *my brother*!"

She sighed heavily.

"Has he said that Donald hits him?"

"No, but it's pretty fu... freakin' obvious."

She shook her head and muttered something under breath that I couldn't catch.

"I'll speak to your father."

That's all I could do for now.

"Okay, thanks, Mom. I gotta go—Seb and I got the late shift so I won't be home till after midnight."

She pulled me into a tight hug, which took me by surprise. She didn't usually go around hugging people that much, even me.

When I got to Seb's place, I leaned on the horn. We were cutting it close and he should have been outside waiting for me.

I saw the front door open and Seb walked out. Limped might have been a better word, and he'd got his hood pulled up.

"Ah shit, man! Not again!"

He didn't speak as he pulled himself onto the front seat, but I could see that his cheek was bruised and he had a black eye.

I shook my head. "No way Perez will let you work looking like that."

"The other guy looks worse," he said, an ironic smile twisting his mouth.

I put the van in drive and headed out to La Jolla. Seb didn't speak the whole way, just stared out of the window, but I don't think he was looking at the passing scenery.

I parked around the back of the country club and jumped out. Seb was moving slowly, holding his ribs.

His luck was so shitty that I really shouldn't have been surprised when Miss Perez walked out at the exact moment we were heading in.

She did a double take when she saw Seb.

"What happened to you *this* time, Mr. Hunter?" she snapped. "Another surfing accident? Tripped over paving stone on the sidewalk? I don't think so. It's quite clear to me that you've been fighting. Well, I can't have you upset the members by them seeing you like that. You've had one warning already and..."

"He wasn't fighting!" I said, quickly. "Ask his fucking father how he got those bruises!"

"Ches, no!"

Seb looked furious as he clipped out the words, but Miss Perez was shocked.

"Commander Hunter ... your father did this to you?"

"It was an accident," said Seb, refusing to meet her worried gaze, instead staring over her left shoulder.

"Just tell her, man!"

"Stay out of it, Ches."

She sighed. "I'm sorry, Sebastian, very sorry, but I can't let you work looking that. I need someone here I can rely on. This is third time I've had to send you home. I'm making it official—I'm letting you go."

I couldn't believe what I was hearing, but Seb just nodded curtly and turned on his heel.

I glared at her. "You can't fire him like that!"

"Watch your tone, Mr. Peters," she said, her voice a warning. "I can't get the Club involved in this—Sebastian needs to tell the police if there's a problem at home."

"You know he won't," I said, bitterly.

"Take him home," she said, "but if you want to keep your job, be back here by 4PM."

Then she walked away.

Seb was already halfway down the long driveway when I caught up with him.

"Get in, I'm giving you a ride."

He shrugged, but didn't speak. I didn't know what else to do, so I drove him home. To my home.

Dad's car was there and Mom was standing out front on her way to the grocery store.

"Chester why are you home so ... oh, Sebastian! Oh sweetheart!"

She bustled him into the kitchen and got an ice pack from the freezer.

"Here, this will help with the swelling."

He took it wordlessly and pressed it against his cheek, wincing slightly.

Then Dad walked in from the backyard and took in the scene with a single glance. When he looked at me, he nodded once.

"Seb, buddy, you need to stay here for a few days," he said.

Seb shook his head. "Can't. Dad says we have to ... keep up appearances."

"You leave Commander Hunter to me." My father's voice allowed no argument. "Ches, give me a hand, son."

Outside, Dad grabbed a hold of my shoulder. "We'll get this figured out, I promise. Seb can stay here as long as he likes. I'm going to the Hunters' place now. You might want to clear some space in that pigsty you call a room." He gave me a thin smile. "I'll bring back as much of Seb's things as I can."

"Thanks, Dad."

He nodded, but didn't reply.

I watched as he drove off in the van, his face tight with anger. I wondered what he was going to do. No, that's not right. I knew *what* he was going to do; I just wondered *how* he was going to do it.

Mom was talking to Seb quietly in the kitchen, so I headed up the stairs to my room. Dad was so damn military: what he called a 'pigsty' was a pair of old jeans and two pairs of boardshorts that I hadn't put away. And some t-shirts, and a bunch of CDs, old copies of *Surfer* magazine, a few used coffee mugs. It wasn't *that* untidy. I mean, there wasn't any green moldy food...

I cleared some space in my closet and shoved the magazines and CDs under my bed.

Then I pulled out a cot and put a sheet on it and a couple of blankets. Seb had slept on it a load of times; he'd been overnighting here since we'd met as freshmen at high school. Seemed like a million years ago right now.

A few minutes later, I heard Seb coming up the stairs. His face still looked puffy and the bruise around his eye was coming out, but he seemed calmer now, less jittery.

"You wanna talk?"

He shook his head. "Mind if I crash out here? I didn't sleep much last night."

"Sure. I've gotta get back to work. Look, I'll talk to Perez. Maybe I can..."

"Nah, that's okay. I was sick of working there anyway. It's not the same since Caro..."

His words trailed off.

"What are you going to do?"

He shrugged painfully. "There's a help wanted sign posted at Stone's Reef Surf Shack. I'll drop by there later."

He stretched out across the bed and closed his eyes, so I left him to sleep off whatever demons were haunting him.

Mom gave me a ride back to the Club, saying she'd text me when Dad was back.

I was on lifeguard duty by the outdoor pool when I groaned to see who had just arrived. This day wasn't getting any better.

"Hi Ches!" Brenda said in an irritating sing-song voice. "Is Seb around?"

She stood there smiling, her hand on her hip, with no fucking clue of the carnage she'd created in my friend's life.

"Nope," I said, then added quietly, "and if he was, he wouldn't want to talk to you."

Her face showed a range of emotions: surprise, guilt, pleasure, anger, annoyance.

"What's that supposed to mean?"

"It means," I said, lowering my voice still further, "that he wouldn't want to talk to a trouble-making bitch like you."

Her superior smile faltered for a moment, then her lips curled into a sneer.

"Caroline fucking Wilson deserved everything she got."

My temper snapped.

"You're a bitch, Brenda. I don't know when or how that happened, but you're a fucking, cold bitch."

And I walked to the other side of the pool, just to get away from her.

She scowled, but didn't try to follow me.

It was nearly 1AM by the time I got home. I was physically tired but my brain was wide awake. It didn't look like anyone else was sleeping either, because the lights were still on in the house.

Mom was curled up on the couch with a blanket over her legs, and Dad was watching a ballgame.

"How come everyone's still up? Where's Seb?"

"Sit down, Chester. We just need to lay down a few ground rules now Seb is going to be living here."

Dad didn't usually call me by my full name so I pinned back my ears and listened.

"I went to see Donald Hunter. He's agreed to allow Seb to stay here until he turns 18 and enlists. I've brought most of his things, so there's no need for him to go back there. But this stays in the family, okay? I don't walk you telling this to anyone."

"Yeah, yeah, I get it, Dad. No breaking the military code—even for a douche like Donald Hunter."

"It's not that, son." I watched as Dad scrubbed his hands over his buzz cut. "I had to make some serious threats against him—against a senior officer—do you understand what that means?"

"Your father could get in a lot of trouble," Mom said, resting her hand on my arm. "And it's better for Sebastian if he can just put this whole, horrible business behind him."

I didn't know if she meant Seb's father beating him or his affair with Mrs. Wilson. Probably both."

"Yeah, okay, but what does Seb say?"

"Not much. He's happy to stay here for now."

"So, the douche is still making him enlist? No college?"

Mom sighed. "That's still the deal."

It really sucked ass. For the last two years Seb and I had planned what we were going to do when we went to UCSD together. We were going to room together, take the same Liberal Arts classes, hang out, surf. Now that was all gone.

"And there are some other rules," said Dad. "No drinking in the house. I don't mind you guys having the occasional beer, but stay off the liquor. In fact, don't let Seb drink too much anywhere. He doesn't need to end up like his mom."

That hit home. Seb's mom was a whoring lush.

"Yeah, got it. Anything else?"

"No smoking weed. I find you've been doing that again, I'll be taking the keys to the van. Got it."

"Sir, yes, sir," I muttered under my breath.

"Excuse me?" he snapped.

"Yeah, I got it, Dad. I'm not a kid."

But the truth was I kind of felt like one, especially when I thought about Seb's problems. He'd left home at 17, and would be enlisting soon. No drunken college nights for him, no all-nighters cramming for a test. He'd do his basic training, then he'd be shipped off to wherever the Marines wanted him. Smart money said Iraq.

He'd fallen in love, got his heart stomped on, and the shit beaten out of him by his own father.

Compared to that, being told not to touch Dad's whisky and stay off the weed ... I had no problems. None.

When I went up to my room, Seb was lying on the cot again, but I could see that he'd stowed some clothes and a few books. Funny enough, the place looked tidier, even though it had more stuff in it.

"Hey, man. 'Sup?"

"You cool with this, Ches? I'll only be in your hair for a few months ... just till I leave for basic training."

"Sure, of course it's cool. You're my brother, man." I laughed uneasily. "*Mi casa, su casa*."

He sat up, staring out at the night sky.

"I can't believe she's gone. I keep thinking she'll find a way to get in touch. Write me or something. But it's been two weeks now."

"You know she can't, buddy."

He sighed and looked down at his hands.

"I know, but I can't help hoping that she will. Fuck, I know that makes me sound like a pathetic pussy but ... I miss her."

He scrubbed at his eyes and I didn't know what to do.

So like a complete dumbass, I said something to make it worse. "I saw Brenda today. She was looking for you."

His eyes narrowed dangerously. "That whore better stay out of my way. Fuckin' bitch. This is all her fault," and he punched his pillow hard.

I cleared my throat a couple of times. "Any luck with the job hunt?"

He blew out a long breath, then nodded. "Yeah, starting at Stone's Reef in the morning." He flashed a small smile. "In about five hours."

"Seriously? Why so early?"

"Gonna be a good swell—they want to be open for breakfast."

I don't know if he slept that night, because every time I woke up, I could see that his eyes were open.

After that, we got into a rhythm. We worked when we had to, surfed when we could, and didn't talk about Caroline Wilson or what had gone down. But it was there, simmering under the surface. And Seb was just plain miserable. He never wanted to hang out with the guys anymore, and I felt he only just tolerated my company sometimes. He preferred to be by himself, and when we surfed, he was always the furthest away from us. Fido was pretty cut up about that.

But my best friend was hurting and I didn't know how to help.

One thing that definitely *wouldn't* help was Brenda fuckin' Wiseman.

BONUS CHAPTER 2

Even after I'd told her that Seb didn't work at the country club anymore, she kept coming around and bothering me, trying to find out where he was working now.

Girl wouldn't take no for an answer.

I was just taking my break when she turned up *again*.

"Ches, can't you at least give him a message from me? I really need to see him."

I sighed heavily. "He doesn't want to see you, Brenda. He doesn't want to talk to you, and you know what, he doesn't even want to *think* about you. You fucking cheated on him with Jack Sullivan, and then you shit all over his new relationship. Believe me when I say you're better off *not* hearing what he thinks about you."

Her eyes watered, and I held back a frustrated curse. I hated it when girls cried. It was like the ultimate weapon against a guy.

"Does he hate me that much?"

"Pretty much, yeah," I said, not caring to sugarcoat it.

"That ... that woman, Mrs. Wilson. He was *really* into her? But she was, like, *old?*"

I couldn't help rolling my eyes. "Yeah, he was *into* her. He loved her." *And still does.*

Brenda looked shocked. "He told you that? He told you that he loved her?"

"For fuck's sake, yes!"

"Well, she couldn't have loved him back, because I heard she just drove away and left him."

I grabbed her arm and pulled her around to the side of the pool where there were fewer people who could overhear us.

"Jesus, are you so freakin' dumb? Caroline—Mrs. Wilson—was forced to leave because Seb is underage. It was either that or get arrested."

Brenda's eyes widened and her mouth popped open in a silent O. Then she pulled herself together.

"Well, she was way too old for him anyway."

It was all I could do to keep from slapping her.

"I had no idea you were such a selfish bitch, Bren. If you hadn't screwed around on Seb, none of this would have happened."

I wasn't sure how true that was because there was no doubt how deep Seb was in with Caroline Wilson—and always had been.

I walked away from Brenda, but as I looked back, the breeze caught the summer dress she was wearing, and it wrapped tightly around her body. At first I thought she'd put on weight, but the blood drained from my face as I realized that her belly wasn't just fat—she was pregnant.

She saw the look on my face and paled.

I marched toward her, and she took a step back, as if looking for somewhere to hide.

"You're pregnant."

It wasn't a question.

She nodded slowly.

"Are you saying that it's Seb's? Is that why you've been stalking him?"

She bit her lip and looked down.

This time I did grab her arm and gave her a small shake.

"Tell the fuckin' truth for once. Did Seb knock you up?"

She yanked her arm free.

"No!" she shouted. "I wish it was him, but it wasn't. I wish..." her words broke off and this time she really was crying.

"Ah shit," I said, quietly.

I led her out to the staff parking lot and she sat in my van, crying and ruining her makeup. What a fucked up story.

Jack Sullivan had given her some skunk—much stronger weed than she was used to. They'd had sex, even though she was still going out with Seb at the time. When she woke up in the morning and realized she wasn't a virgin anymore, she was afraid to tell him what she'd done. So she broke up with him instead.

To try and make herself feel better, she'd gone from party to party, getting high, getting drunk, sleeping with guys, including several more times with Jack. She'd gotten pregnant at the exact same time that Caroline Wilson came back into Seb's life.

In Brenda's fucked up mind, that meant that Caroline was her competition, so she'd gone out of her way to get rid of her.

"I know Seb won't ... be interested in me now," she cried. "But I just hoped ... I thought if he slept with me one time..."

"You'd tell him the kid was his. And Caroline being around messed up your plan to get Seb to sleep with you. That is fuckin' low, Brenda."

"I know, but I was desperate," she gasped out between sniffing and hiccupping.

Chicks don't cry as pretty in real life as in the movies.

"What do you think is going to happen between you if you do see Seb again?"

She looked down.

"I don't know. Nothing, I guess. But it would be nice to have the chance to see ... if there's anything still between us. We were ... we were good together."

"He moved on," I said.

She sighed.

"Yeah, I get that. Although I still don't understand what was so great about *her*."

I couldn't face getting into *that* conversation again.

"Look, I'll tell him you need to talk to him, but after that it's up to him."

"Thanks, Ches. I owe you."

"No, Brenda. You owe, Seb. Big time."

Boy, I really wasn't looking forward to telling Seb about any of this. I waited till we were in the van on the way home from a late night stealth mission. I'd parked on the beach and left the van's lights on, so we'd have something to aim for, as we caught wave after wave in the ink-black ocean.

It had been good, almost like old times, but Seb could sense the tension in my body.

"You look like you've got a stick up your ass, so why don't you tell me what's bothering you," he said, eyeing me steadily.

"Uh yeah, so ... I saw Brenda today."

"Again?"

"Yeah, she still wants to talk to you."

"Un-fuckin'-believable." He paused. "You told her no, right?"

"Well...

He rolled his eyes. "Since when did you get to be on her cheer team? You hated the bitch even before I did."

"I just think you should hear what she's got to say. She knows she screwed up and she knows you're not going to take her back."

"Then why bother?"

"Just talk to her, man. It's important."

"Ah fuck it. Okay, tell her to meet me at the surf shack after work. No, wait. I don't want her knowing where I work. Tell her the park. She can have five minutes."

He looked pissed about it, but at least he agreed.

It was two days later that he had his talk with Brenda. He came home looking upset.

"So, how'd it go?"

He shook his head.

"Fuck, I can't believe it, man. She's fuckin' *pregnant*."

"Yeah, I know. It was kind of obvious when I saw her up close."

"She told her parents yesterday. They're freaking out. She said they asked her what *I'm* going to do about it."

"Seriously?"

"Yeah, she hadn't even told them we'd broken up, even though it was like five months ago."

"But she's put them straight now?"

He shook his head, looking irritated.

"Not exactly. She wouldn't tell them who the father is. I'm not even sure *she* knows. She thinks it's Jack Sullivan, but she's not sure."

"Shit."

"Yeah, but because she's not saying, her parents won't believe that it's *not* me. She had to stop them going over to see my old man."

He shook his head in disbelief.

"That's why she's been trying to talk to me."

"What are you going to do?"

He gave me a look.

"What the fuck am I supposed to do? It's not my kid. If it was ... if it was mine, I'd look after them, or something. No kid should come into the world unwanted. I should fuckin' know. But I'm not gonna fall on my sword for her either. She fucked up when she told my mom about Caro. I can't forgive her for that."

"I can't believe you never slept with Brenda. I always thought you guys were doin' it like bunnies."

He shrugged. "We were going to. It was supposed to be this big deal." He side-eyed me. "Because we were both virgins. We did some other stuff, but we never fucked."

I slapped him on the shoulder. "Well, you've ticked that box now, bro."

Instead of a fist-bump, he scowled at me.

"It wasn't like that with Caro."

My eyebrows shot upward.

"You're telling me you didn't sleep with her? Because, dude, I saw your back and she had some serious claws."

His cheeks reddened. "I meant it wasn't fucking. Well, yeah, it was. But it was more than that. When I was with her ... it was like the whole world went away and it was just us." He shook his head. "I can't explain it."

"Have you heard anything from her? From Caro?"

"Nah, man, and it's driving me crazy, not knowing where she is or what she's doing. Not knowing if she's safe..."

"Maybe she went back to her mom's."

He studied the rug on the floor that was rough with sand we'd trekked in from the beach.

"I don't think so. They weren't close—not since her dad died."

"So where do you think she's gone?"

"I don't know. I don't fuckin' know."

He looked at me hopelessly.

"What are you going to do?"

His gaze dropped to the floor again.

"I'm going to wait for her."

"That's three years, man. That's a long time."

He shrugged, and a ghost of a smile made its way onto his face.

"Life is a long time living, but without Caro it would just be a long time dying. I love her. So I'll wait for her. And I know that somewhere on this rat infested planet, she's waiting for me, too."

I hoped he was right. But it was damn hard trying to believe it.

BONUS CHAPTER 3

Twenty-one

"Yeah, this is the place."

Ches pointed towards a low-rise, khaki-colored building with a sign announcing 'Porter's Pub'. It was a typical student dive: happy hour and cheap beer. Sounded good.

To be honest, I didn't really care where we went. I was just happy to have a couple of quiet drinks with my best friend.

Inside, it was a dark, narrow room set out with wooden tables and chairs, and a stage at one end.

Ches started to lead the way towards a table near the back, but before we got there, someone called his name.

"Ches! My man! What're you doin' here, dude?"

The speaker was obviously a college kid: long, greasy hair, looking like he'd just stepped out of a Red Hot Chili Peppers video.

"Hey, Vince. How's it going?"

"I'm long, loose and full of juice, my friend."

I tried not to roll my eyes, I really did.

I was feeling pretty fucking tense and on edge, excited really, but so not in the mood to party with Ches's college buddies. It looked like I didn't have a choice. Whatever.

Other than the ass-hat, there were four other guys that Ches introduced, and a girl whose name I didn't catch. I noticed her running her eyes up and down my body, and it made me uncomfortable.

"This is Seb, a friend from high school."

They nodded and muttered, eyeing my military haircut, and the girl smiled.

"I thought you said you were busy tonight, Ches, man?" said Vince.

"Well, yeah. We were just going to go out and have a couple of drinks now that Seb's back in town."

"Did you go away to school?" asked the girl. Her name might have been Stacey.

I didn't get a chance to be evasive, because Ches answered for me.

"Nope. Seb enlisted. He's a Marine—just got back from Iraq. A gen-u-ine hero, right, man?"

That shit was just fucking embarrassing—but typical of Ches.

"Wow, really?" said Del.

"Yep," said Ches, "and looking damn skinny. Man, didn't they feed you out there?"

"You try wearing ninety pounds of equipment in 110 degrees, you fat fucker," I muttered.

Ches laughed and patted his stomach, which was slightly larger than last time I'd seen him.

"Man is a large animal. Besides, wait till you try Amy's cooking."

Amy. This was Ches's new girlfriend, and, according to him, the love of his life. I hadn't met her yet, but if she made my friend happy, that was good enough for me. And he was—happy, I mean. Happiness rolled off him in waves. Not that I was jealous. Okay, that was a lie. I was jealous as fuck, but still really pleased for him. I knew what it was like to be in love—except right now, it was fucking painful. For me, anyway.

I'd earned a few days' leave, and had managed to be in San Diego this week. I was waiting for Caro. I'd been waiting for her for three long years.

The guys around the table eyed me like I was a fucking Martian. I could see what they were thinking: too dumb to go to college. It didn't bother me, I just didn't want to spend the evening talking about being a Marine. I was having a night off.

I mumbled something and stood up to get the beers, pulling my wallet out of my back pocket.

"Nah, man, your money's no good tonight," said Ches, pushing me down into my seat.

"Huh?" said Vince, looking annoyed.

"It's my buddy's birthday," announced Ches loudly, as I stifled a groan. "Twenty-one and legal at last."

A chorus of 'congratulations' and 'happy birthday' rolled around the table. I cocked an eyebrow at Ches, and he shrugged, a wide smile across his face. He signaled to the waitress and ordered beer for everyone. Then he pointed to me:

"It's his birthday, so don't let him pay for any drinks tonight, okay?"

The waitress winked at me.

"He's so cute, I wouldn't make him pay for anything anyway."

"Whoa! You're in there, man," said Vince, as the waitress sashayed back to the bar.

Stupid fucker. I scowled at him and he leaned back in his seat, looking surprised. I hadn't so much as looked at another woman in the three years I'd waited for Caro—I wasn't going to blow it now.

Ches threw me a warning glance. I nodded once and looked away. I'd gotten the message.

Yeah, yeah, it wasn't Vince's fault I was so on edge. But listening to a bunch of college kids talking about midterms and professors wasn't really doing it for me. Technically, they were all older than me, but they just seemed really young. Ches was the only one who knew what it had been like for me since I enlisted. His dad was a Staff Sergeant, so he understood. The rest of them were civvies. And that created a distance. Besides, they were Ches's friends, not mine.

But because they were Ches's friends, I knew I just had to chill the fuck out.

"Hey, Seb," Ches nudged me. "Look I hadn't really planned on everyone being here tonight; I know you just wanted a quiet drink. But since they are here, would it be cool with you if I texted Amy to join us?"

"Sure, why not? It'd be good to meet your girl, man."

Ches grinned. "You're going to love her. You've never met anyone like her..." His words trailed off. "Sorry, man. I know you're hoping Caroline's gonna turn up, but come on..." He looked at me seriously. "Even if she was in town, she's not going to know which bar you're at, is she?"

I ran my hands over my hair in frustration. "I know she'll be here; I just know it. I mean, fuck, I've left my cell number for her at your mom and dad's old place, her old place and at the civvy entrance to the Base. She's gonna go to one of them, isn't she?"

Ches didn't answer. Instead, he became very interested in staring at a hole in the toe of his sneaker.

"Sure, Seb," he said, quietly.

He was my best friend, and he was a lousy fucking liar.

Picking up my beer, I chugged half the bottle.

"How's it feel drinking legally?" said Stacey, jogging my elbow.

"Pretty much like any other time," I snapped.

"Well, excuse me!" she snorted.

I was being an asshole.

"Sorry," I said, grimacing at her. "I'm just..."

I didn't know what to say to her.

She smiled. "Apology accepted. I guess this isn't what you really wanted, is it? You know, a big crowd of strangers. We must seem pretty immature to you."

I looked at her in surprise.

"Yeah, my big brother is in the Old Guard out at Fort Myer."

I nodded slowly. "It's just a bit ... weird. I only flew in this morning. I'm still..."

She touched my arm. "It's okay, I get it. You don't have to explain."

I smiled with relief, and she blinked a couple of times.

"Thanks. Stacey, right?"

"So you were paying attention!"

I grinned at her. "Must have been. Who knew?"

She clinked her beer against mine. "Here's to paying attention."

After my fifth beer, I started to loosen up a bit. Even so, I couldn't help checking my cellphone for the fortieth fucking time.

"You waiting for someone ... your girlfriend ... or...?" asked Stacey.

"Yes. No. Kind of. I don't know."

She raised her eyebrows.

Truthfully, I was waiting. I knew Ches thought I was crazy. I mean, I hadn't heard from her for three years but there was a reason for that: a really good fucking reason. And I knew, I just fucking *knew* that she'd be looking for me. She'd promised me—we'd promised each other.

It really bothered me that I didn't even know her surname. I mean, I knew her married name, but I'd assumed she'd have changed it. And I was such a fucking idiot, I'd never thought to ask her what her maiden name was at the time.

I'd tried to find her but got nowhere: turns out you need to know someone's name if you want to find them. Yeah, right. But I knew she'd be able to find me back in San Diego. That's why I'd cashed in every favor I could to make sure I was here for my 21st birthday. I'd left messages at all the places that had meant something to us: she had to find one of them. All I could do was wait. Yeah. That's all. It was fucking killing me.

Ches understood. He'd been there, and he'd been the one who picked up the pieces after Caro had left. I was a fucking wreck, but his mom and dad helped. I even lived with them for a few months until I enlisted. They were my real family.

I couldn't be bothered to explain everything to Stacey. But I was a Marine, and trained in evasive tactics.

"Do you want to dance?"

She looked surprised.

"Sure! I'd love to. I didn't know Marines danced."

I smiled at her and winked. "This one does."

Stacey was a pretty good dancer and followed my lead easily. I kind of enjoyed having a girl in my arms again, even though it wasn't *the* girl I was waiting for. Her hands crept around my neck and I pulled her into my chest. It occurred to me later that she probably wanted me to kiss her. Like *that* was going to happen.

She must have sensed my mood, because she started talking instead.

"Wow, you can really dance, Seb! Where'd you learn those moves?"

I laughed. "Ches's mom and dad."

"You're kidding me!"

"Nope: Base salsa champions back in the day."

"I've never seen Ches dance," she said, eyeing him speculatively.

"Yeah, well, I think that talent skipped a generation."

Stacey laughed. "I'll tell him you said that."

I smiled back. "He already knows."

We'd danced for a couple of songs when I saw two girls join the table: one was a girl with light brown hair who threw herself into Ches's lap. He kissed her like he needed her air to breathe, and I guessed this must be Amy.

Stacey turned to see what had caught my attention, then grinned up at me.

"Looks like Amy's here."

"You know her?"

"Sure! She's my roommate. Let's go say 'hi' before their lips get permanently locked together."

"I think it's too late for that," I muttered, but she just laughed.

"Hey, Ames!" she called.

Reluctantly, Amy pulled her mouth off of Ches and leaned back. I saw him shifting uncomfortably and couldn't help smiling. Dude must have had a helluva boner after that make-out session.

"Hey, Stacey," said Amy, slightly breathless, then turned to me. "You must be Seb. I've heard sooo much about you: it's really good to meet you."

"You, too," I said grinning, as we shook hands. "Although you look too smart to be going out with this asshole."

Ches tried to punch me on the arm, but I ducked away and Amy laughed.

"Oh, happy birthday, by the way."

"Thanks," I mumbled, not really wanting to be reminded.

A look of sympathy crossed her face and I realized that Ches must have told her everything. It made me slightly uncomfortable but that's what couples did, right? Shared their secrets. At least she hadn't said anything to Stacey, and I appreciated that. Seemed like Ches's girl was cool. I was glad about that. Ches was family: he was my brother.

"By the way, man," said Ches. "Mom sent you a birthday card. It's back at my place. Remind me to give it to you later."

"Really?" I couldn't help smiling. Shirley, Ches's mom, always did stuff like that. "Tell her I said thanks."

"Tell her yourself, you lazy bastard. You do know how to use email, right?"

I gave him the finger and he laughed at me.

I didn't get much of a chance to talk to either Ches or Amy after that, because they spent the rest of the evening making out. It was kind of strange for me, seeing my friend like that, and remembering that Caro and I had never been able to behave like that in public. I really resented that we'd hardly had any time to just be us. I wished again that she was here. Now that there was nothing stopping us, I missed her even more. I knew it was dumb to expect her to walk into the bar, but I couldn't help looking anyway. Every time I saw a woman with long, brown hair, my stomach flipped over—but it was never her.

I checked my phone again: no messages.

I'd just decided to wallow in misery and get shitfaced, when Ches announced that the party was moving to his place. I groaned, inwardly. I'd really hoped we could just go back and chill.

No chance of that now.

We trailed back to the house that Ches shared with a couple of guys from his Business and Economics classes. Gareth had already got the party started with a couple of kegs, three crates of beer, and a baggie of weed that he was using to roll joints. I looked longingly at the joint that was being passed around, but I knew I couldn't risk it. I only had another four day's leave and I'd be tested as soon as I got back. I didn't know for sure how long that shit stayed in your blood.

"Sorry, man," said Ches, following my gaze.

"No worries, I'll just stick to beer and my good friend, Jack," I said, showing him the bottle of Jack Daniel's that I'd brought with me in my duffel bag.

He smiled, and then looked nervously over his shoulder, shuffling from foot to foot.

"'Sup man?"

"Ah, shit, Seb. I wasn't planning on seeing Amy tonight, what with it being your birthday an' all, but now that she's here..."

Yeah, I got what he was saying.

"Nah, it's cool. Go make your girl happy. I'll be fine. Just tell me you'll still be up for a surf tomorrow morning."

"Deal, my friend."

He grinned at me, then grabbed Amy's hand and pulled her up the stairs.

Well, fuck. I checked my phone pointlessly. No messages. This was turning out to be a real bastard of a birthday.

"Hey," said Stacey, walking towards me with a couple of beers, "looks like we've both been abandoned. D'you wanna go sit outside? It's not so smoky out there."

I shrugged. I didn't really have a choice. I was supposed to be sleeping on the couch, but right now it was occupied by a bunch of strangers smoking weed. Fucking great.

We sat down under a large mulberry tree and leaned against its broad trunk. I passed her my bottle of Jack and she took a large gulp and followed it up with a beer chaser. I smiled when she coughed slightly.

"You okay?"

"Sure, it just went down the wrong way," she lied.

"If you say so," I agreed.

She was quiet for a moment.

"Seb, can I ask you something?"

I nodded silently, wondering what she was going to say.

"This girl you might or might not be waiting for—is she your girlfriend?"

Oh, right. Pretty damn obvious question now that I thought about it.

I sighed. "She was. I'm ... hoping she will be again. I don't know. We haven't spoken for a while—I just thought she'd be here tonight."

She looked at me, her expression serious. "Bad break up?"

I snorted, almost amused by her question. Almost.

"Yeah, you could say that—pretty fuckin' bad."

"I'm sorry," she whispered.

I didn't know what to say to that, so I didn't say anything.

We sat there talking quietly, drinking the Jack. She told me about her brother who'd done two tours in Iraq, and she told me about her classes and how much she liked living in San Diego. She told me about Amy, too, and it was all good stuff. It made me feel a bit less like shit, even though she was a stranger and my best bud had abandoned me on my birthday to get it on with his girl.

Yeah, I know: I was a whiny pussy.

Fuck, Caro—where are you? The question pulsed through my brain.

By 3AM, I was feeling kind of out of it, and Stacey's head had dropped onto my shoulder. The party was winding down so I decided to make it official. I cleared everyone the fuck out of the house, and thanked my lucky stars I'd brought my bedroll with me.

I swept a load of empty beer cans off of the couch onto the floor and kicked them out of the way. I laid out one of my blankets and went back outside to find Stacey. She was passed out under the tree, so I picked her up and carried her inside, placing her carefully on the couch. She was kind of cute and had long, brown hair, a bit like Caro.

I pulled the blanket over her, then left her to sleep it off. It was cooler outside, but it smelled a helluva lot better than Ches's living room, so I spread my bedroll out under the tree and stared up at the night sky, wondering if my girl was looking at the same sprinkling of stars.

I woke up about four hours later feeling like some bastard had stuffed my head with broken glass. Yup, it was officially no longer my birthday and I was as hung over as fuck.

The first thing I did was to check my phone: no messages. What a freakin' joke. I felt like throwing the useless piece of shit into the ocean. Instead, I shoved it in my jeans pocket and stumbled into the bathroom to take a long and much needed piss.

When I wandered back into the living room, Stacey hadn't moved. There were a couple of other bodies lying around the room, and it smelled like ass. My stomach coiled and rolled so I headed for the kitchen and drank some water. A lot of water.

There was only one thing that cured a hangover like this. I dragged myself up the stairs and banged on Ches's door.

I heard a grunt and a shuffling sound, then Ches's voice.

"What the fuck?"

"Come on, man. We're going surfing. Get your sorry ass down the stairs now!"

"Are you fucking kidding me, Hunter?"

"No, you miserable fucker! You owe me."

He moaned and bitched some more, but I banged on the door again and heard Amy cursing under her breath. That got Ches's ass moving. Yeah, I liked that girl.

My old surfboard and wetsuit lived permanently in Ches's van, but my board shorts were boxed up with a load of shit in a storage unit. Didn't matter—I'd do without.

Ches stumbled down the stairs, his hair sticking out at all angles. One advantage of a buzz cut—there's not enough hair to get that bed-head look.

"You look like crap," I said cheerfully, feeling slightly superior—probably because I'd had time to drink some water.

He gave me the finger and muttered something that sounded like, "fuckin' jarhead".

"Come on, man. I'll buy you breakfast later. You and Amy."

He pulled a face. "Sure, if she's still talking to me. Or you."

"Hey! What did I do?" I asked, innocently.

"Disturbed her beauty sleep," he shot back. "She's an animal if she doesn't get eight hours—and not in a good way."

Ches drove us out to La Jolla. I felt a bit guilty when I saw him yawning his ass off; it also occurred to me that he was probably still over the blood-alcohol limit. But once we were paddling out to the lineup, the cold water revived us both, and he was over his sulk.

"Oh man, I haven't done this for a while," he said.

"Seriously? We used to surf every damn day."

"Yeah, but I've got school, I work at the country club, and I've got Amy. Just don't get the time anymore. But I'm glad you pulled me out here, brother."

I grinned at him. "This wave's got my name on it."

A wall of green started lifting up behind me. I stroked through the water, and as soon as I felt the board begin to tip forwards, I leapt to my feet and rode that mother almost to the beach, carving along the surface and ripping through the wave.

For the first time in a long time, I felt like I could be me again; not a Marine, not Lance Corporal Hunter. Just me.

After about an hour, Ches called timeout and we caught a wave back into the beach.

"Man, that felt good. Now you owe me breakfast!"

"You want to go back and get Amy?"

"Nah, she hardly ever eats breakfast. It's a girl thing."

We dried off using worn out beach towels, and changed into our clothes by the side of the road, not caring if we were seen.

I checked my phone again. Still no messages. Ches glanced over at me.

"Anything?"

I shook my head and stared out of the window, trying to beat back the fear that was beginning to chew at me. *Caro, where are you?*

"You know, Seb..." Ches began quietly.

"Don't," I snapped at him. "She'll be here. I know it."

I heard him sigh out a deep breath, but he didn't speak again.

In silence, Ches drove us to a Burger King and we loaded up on the sausage, egg and cheese biscuit meal. And drank coffee. A lot of coffee.

By the time we got back to his house, Amy was up and dressed, and whipping the remaining party goers into shape. She had two of the guys collecting cans and bottles, and another one emptying ashtrays. Stacey was in the kitchen washing glasses, looking tired but not too hung over.

"Hey! Where'd you guys go?" she called out. "You've missed all the cleaning!"

"Surfing," I said, smiling my ass off. "Anyway, I'm using the it's-my-birthday so I have a get-out-of-cleaning-free card," I replied. "But I don't think Ches has an excuse—he'd love to help."

Ches punched me on the shoulder.

"And now he's broken my arm, so I can't do anything," I said, pretending to wince.

"Fucker," he muttered, under his breath. Amy flung him a look and I winked at him.

Yeah, pussy whipped!

Then we heard a knock at the front door. I was the only one not doing something, so I offered to get it.

I wasn't expecting the person standing in front of me.

"What the fuck do you want?" I snarled, my good mood vanishing like a virgin on prom night.

An amused face smiled back at me.

"Just wanted to see my son and heir on his birthday," he sneered the words.

"Yeah? Well you're about a day late, *Dad*."

The bastard ignored my comment.

"Did that whore of yours show up?"

All coherent thought rushed out of my brain and I swung a punch. Ches pulled me back just in time.

"Seb, no! That's what he wants. Your dad's an officer: it'll be non-judicial punishment if you hit him. Walk away, man. Walk away."

I really, really wanted to hit the bastard, to hurt him the way he'd hurt me over and over again. But I wasn't going to let him ruin my career the way he'd ruined my life. I started to turn away, but then something in me wanted an answer.

"Why do you hate me so much, Dad?"

The words came out quietly, but I knew he'd heard them. He looked surprised, then his expression darkened.

"Because you're a fucking pansy—a useless waste of space. You made your mother miserable and you've been nothing but a fucking deadweight around my neck from the moment you were born. You've been a disappointment from day one. Son."

Yeah, about what I'd thought he'd say.

"Good," I said. "Because a compliment from you would fuckin' choke me."

I turned my back and slammed the door in the fucker's face.

I was breathing heavily, and I could feel cold sweat on my face. Then I realized the house was too quiet. Everyone was staring at me, pity and shock on their faces. I didn't need that. I needed *her*. I needed Caro.

I scowled at my audience, then picked up my leather jacket and headed towards the door.

"Seb, man..."

"Leave it, Ches."

I pushed past him roughly and slammed through the kitchen into the backyard.

My motorcycle was leaning next to the side of the house, covered by a waterproof tarp. I tore it off, listened to the roar of the engine as I started it up, then peeled out of there, going nowhere too fast.

For a few minutes, I opened up the throttle and let the speed and rush of adrenaline cleanse me of all the furious thoughts that seeing my father had allowed to flood through me. I still couldn't understand why he showed up today, why he hated me so badly. But did hate need a reason? I hated the bastard right back—except I had plenty of reasons for the way I felt.

After a while, I slowed the bike and made an illegal U-turn, before heading towards the military base where I used to live.

I pulled up outside a nondescript town house that I'd visited a few days ago, and cut the engine. I knew there wasn't any point coming here again, but I couldn't help myself.

I knocked on the door and eventually a man in sweats staggered to the door.

"You again! Look, I told you a couple a days ago, kid. No letters, no messages, and no brown-haired broads. Now leave me the fuck alone."

He slammed the door before I could say a word.

My Caro used to live in that house. It was the place where she'd helped me and healed me and made love to me. But there was nothing left of her there now. Just memories.

The ache in my chest pulsed, and I couldn't help rubbing the spot, just above where my dog tags rested on my chest.

I made two more stops: at the house where Ches's mom and dad had lived before they were transferred to Germany, and the Vorstadts' place—people who'd been Caro's friends. It was the same story: no they hadn't seen her; no they hadn't heard from her; no, there were no letters or messages for me.

I felt like driving the damn motorcycle off of the nearest cliff.

Caro, where are you?

Eventually, I returned to Ches's place. Where else could I go? I had three more days before I had to report to Camp Lejeune in North Carolina for the language training my CO had signed me up for.

Most of the people had cleared out—just Ches and Amy were still there. She disappeared discreetly as I slammed through the door.

Ches didn't say anything, he just handed me a beer and sat next to me on the couch.

I spent the next two days in a drunken haze. It helped. A little. I even stopped looking at my phone. There were never any messages, so what was the point? Useless piece of junk.

On my last evening before shipping out to North Carolina, Ches persuaded me to leave the house to meet some of his buddies for a drink. I think he was just bored of being with a miserable bastard who'd refused to shift himself off of the couch for the last 48 hours. Amy had wisely chosen to leave me alone and let Ches deal with my sorry ass. I was just about sober enough to walk to the cab he had come pick us up.

The bar was crowded and noisy. It was just what I needed. If the music was loud enough, maybe it could pound out the thoughts scorching my brain.

Ches steered me to a table and I slumped into a chair. His friends stared at me warily, none of them dumb enough to speak to me. I was pretty certain every fiber of my body was yelling at everyone to stay the fuck away from me.

The waitress arrived with a bottle of whiskey and seven shot glasses. Yeah, she was eye-fucking me big time, but she was a blonde, and I *so* wasn't interested.

Ches poured the drinks and spoke quietly.

"Look, I'm really sorry, man. You know, about Caro..."

Pain lanced through the numbness, punching a bigger hole into my chest. My lungs felt as if they'd shrivel from the burn of hearing her name.

"Ches," I snarled. "Don't ever mention that bitch's name to me again."

He nodded slowly. "Done."

I didn't understand. I *couldn't* understand. I was so certain Caro would have been here, with me. She was a fucking journalist—how hard could it be for her to find me? Obviously it wasn't. The only answer was that she didn't want me. And I was such a fucking fool.

Suddenly, I felt angry. Three years I'd waited for her. *Three fucking years.*

I threw another shot of whiskey down my throat. When I opened my eyes, I nearly had a heart attack—a woman with long, brown hair was staring at me. For a split second, I thought it was Caro. Of course, it wasn't—just a nice-looking, older chick. Her eyes were blue, not brown. Her eyes were the wrong color.

She smiled at me and raised her eyebrows as if she was asking me a question.

Whatever.

The answer was 'yes'.

I pushed myself to my feet and walked over to her.

"Hi," I managed to slur out.

"Hi yourself, handsome."

"Can I buy you a drink?"

"Sure, honey, if you're old enough."

I stared back at her. "I'm old enough for a lot of things."

"Hmm, that sounds interesting."

She patted the vacant barstool next to her and when I sat down, she laid a possessive hand on my thigh. Even through the denim, I could feel the warmth of her touch.

We talked for about half an hour, I have no idea what about. I do remember the moment when she leaned over to kiss me, 'accidentally' brushing her hand over my junk.

I pulled her onto my lap and kissed her hard, feeling the vibrations through her body as she moaned into my mouth. She tasted of nicotine and beer, which made me feel slightly sick, on top of all the alcohol I'd drunk.

"You wanna come outside, soldier?" she said, her voice husky with lust.

I nodded, and followed her as she pulled me through the crowded bar, dragging me into an alley at the side.

Before my brain could catch up with what she was doing, she forced my body against the wall and started tugging at my belt.

"You'd better not be too drunk to get it up, soldier," she said, her hands rough on my body.

You don't need to worry about that, baby.

"Holy shit!" she gasped, as she tugged down the zipper of my jeans.

We fucked in the alley.

Until that moment, the only woman I'd ever been with had been Caro. I thought *this* would burn away the memories. I thought *this* would make me feel something other than pain. But I couldn't lie to myself. I wanted Caro, just her. I didn't want *this*.

But it wasn't Caro. It wasn't ever going to be Caro.

BONUS CHAPTER 4

The Best Man

The C-5 Galaxy was a noisy bastard of a plane but listening to *Elephunk* and *Meteora* on my iPod, I could tune out most of it. God, I loved my iPod—best invention ever.

I was flying Space-A*, courtesy of being a Marine, so at least I was able to avoid commercial airports. And it was cheaper. We were flying into Edwards Air Force Base and from there I was hoping to hitch a ride to San Diego or, failing that, take the bus.

After a long and uncomfortable flight, I was more than ready to fucking walk the rest of the way, but that was a hundred or more miles. So my luck was definitely in when a CLR* captain said he was heading for Miramar and could give me a ride most of the way.

I didn't feel much like talking and luckily he wasn't a chatty Cathy. Plus, it was kind of a policy not to say anymore than 'Yes, sir' and 'No, sir' to an officer. Most of the time I stared out of the window of his Escalade, thinking about the weirdness of the next few days.

As we traveled further south, I began to recognize the names of places that we passed. I was heading home, I guess you could say. Not that it was much of a home. Ever. From San Clemente onwards, I could name every cove, harbor, and surf break. I could tell you which waves were gnarly, which suited a goofy foot, which had reefs, and which broke straight onto sand. A lot of good memories—especially with Ches. I pushed away the not so good ones, and I definitely wasn't going to think about *her*.

"You visiting family, son?"

The captain's words interrupted my thoughts.

"Yes, sir. My brother's getting married—and I'm best man."

Which wasn't a lie. I considered Ches my brother, not just my buddy. And with my bastard father and bitch of a mother, Ches and his parents were the only real family I had.

The captain chuckled as he glanced over, amused by the obvious chagrin in my voice.

"Got your speech worked out?"

"Not so much."

Yeah, that was a bit of a sore point. I wasn't really looking forward to the whole public speaking thing.

I saw him shake his head. Well, he was in logistics so he probably planned every day down to the last shit. Whatever.

"When's the wedding?"

"Four days."

"You've got some time then, Corporal. Where are you stationed?"

"I've been at Camp Le Jeune, sir."

"Been there long?"

"Just a week. Been doing a debrief after a tour in the sandbox, um, in Baghdad."

"Uh huh. And now?"

Jeez, were all officers such nosy bastards? Probably.

"I just got my permanent change of station, so I'll be at Pendleton after this leave."

"Well, that's good. Nearer to your family."

"Yes, sir."

There was no reason to think I'd bump into my father, but I really fucking hoped I wouldn't. Hitting an officer is a non-judicial punishment—that could mean anything from a reduction in rank to a court-martial. Either way, I didn't want to give the bastard the satisfaction.

As we approached Torrey Hills, the captain slowed his car.

"I wish I could take you downtown, son, but I'm on a schedule."

"That's fine, sir. Thank you taking me this far."

He pulled over just past the I-5 off-ramp and popped the trunk so I could retrieve my duffel bag, bed roll and garment bag.

"Good luck, Corporal. I'm stationed over at Del Mar so we might run into each other."

"Yes, sir. Thank you, sir."

He accepted my salute and drove off, the tires sending plumes of dust into the light breeze and settling onto my utility uniform. For a few seconds, I enjoyed the feeling of peace and freedom. The Iraqi desert had been fucking hot and North Carolina was humid—I was glad to be away from both. I dug out my cell phone and texted Ches to come get me. I was a bit earlier than I'd expected, but I was still kind of pissed when he replied that he was hung up at work and he was sending Amy instead. His *fiancée*.

I mean, she was okay. I liked her well enough but I'd been looking forward to catching up with Ches.

After about 20 minutes, I saw a beat up Toyota pull over and Amy waved out of the window. She didn't look happy to see me.

"Get in."

Yeah, and hi to you, too.

I slung my luggage on the rear seat and climbed in next to her.

"Hi Amy, congrat..."

"Where's your dress uniform? Tell me you didn't forget it, because everything would just be ruined and I've planned everything, just like *everything* and..."

To my horror I realized she was starting to cry.

"Um, no, Amy. It's all good. The dress blues are in my garment bag."

"Oh!" she sniffed, making an effort to control herself. "Okay, then. Look, I really don't think going down to Tijuana is such a great idea."

Wow, she could shift gears quickly. Now she was complaining about the plans for Ches's bachelor party? Give me a fucking break.

"Once you're over the border," she snapped, "*anything* could happen. I don't see why you need to go all that way just to have a few drinks."

"It's only 20 miles from your house, Amy," I said, trying to reassure her.

"Oh, that is just typical of you! It's in Mexico, Seb! Who knows what could happen? If you do anything, *anything* to fuck up my wedding, I'll feed your balls to the coyotes."

I couldn't help wincing, more at the crazed look in her eye than at what she was actually saying. I hoped Ches knew what the hell he was doing, because right now she was a bitch on wheels. If I hadn't met Amy before, I'd seriously doubt that my friend was in his right mind wanting to marry her.

I decided that saying nothing was the best answer. She reminded me of a drill sergeant I'd had in basic training, and I wondered what would happen if I yelled, "Sir, no, sir!" Hell, she'd probably run my ass out of town.

And that would be after she gave the coyotes their next meal.

We arrived at the small cottage she and Ches had recently rented. It was about a twenty minute drive from the ocean and Ches's job at the country club. It was a neat, suburban street, similar to the house I'd grown up in, just a bit smaller and shabbier. Appearances had been everything at the Hunter residence when I was growing up. Outward appearances had to be maintained at all costs. The memory made me want to puke.

I climbed out, glad that the wheels had finally stopped turning. I'd been traveling 16 hours with a four hour lay-over at Altus AFB, Oklahoma. My body felt numb.

"I don't see why he needs a bachelor party anyway," Amy muttered to herself.

"What's wrong with having a few beers and throwing some steaks on the grill at home?"

She shot me an accusing look even though I'd had nothing to do with planning Ches's party. After all, I'd been out of the country for the last nine months. I didn't think that was going to score me any points with Amy. I kept my mouth zipped.

"You'll have to sleep on the couch," she snarled. "I've made up the guest room for Shirley and Mitch, and I don't want it messed up."

I shrugged. It didn't bother me where I slept. It was bound to be better than a tent with 19 other sweaty guys, where the daytime temperature was 110 degrees.

"When are they flying in?"

"Friday lunchtime. I *told* them they should have gotten an earlier flight..."

She looked like she was on the verge of tears again. I reached out a hand tentatively and patted her arm; the same gesture I'd use on a sad dog. Just sayin'. For a moment, she seemed to relax and I thought she'd be okay, but then I blew it by speaking.

"It'll be fine, Amy. I'm sure..."

"Oh, you're *sure*, are you? Well, that's just peachy, isn't it? If *you* say it's *fine*, what on earth could possibly go wrong?"

I stepped back, waiting for her head to start revolving.

Thank fuck Ches arrived when he did.

He took one look at Amy bristling with fury, while I withered under her steely glare. They should send her against Saddam Hussein.

Ches rolled his eyes, giving her a swift kiss on the cheek before he held out his hand then pulled me into a bear hug.

"Damn, it's good to see you, man," he said, a huge smile lighting up his face. "How the hell are you?"

Amy stomped into the house without a word, and Ches sighed.

"It's nothing personal—she's been like that all week. Make that all month. I'll be glad when this wedding shit is over."

I looked at him cautiously. "Do you still want to go through with it?"

He gave a small smile. "Yeah, sure. She's not usually like this. She's turned into a complete Bridezilla over the whole thing. She used to laugh at this kind of crap, but she's totally lost her sense of humor. She'll be fine." Then he muttered under his breath, "I hope."

I slapped him on the back.

"Well, I'll just have to make sure your bachelor party is memorable, my friend, so when she's got your balls nailed to a chair, you'll remember what it was like to have a life."

"Fuck off," he said, laughing.

"So, anyone I know going to TJ with us?"

"Um, Vince, Del, Gareth—you met them last year. The other guy is Amy's brother, Tyler. You don't know him. He's okay."

Ches didn't sound very enthusiastic but I guessed he'd been bludgeoned into inviting his soon to be brother-in-law.

"How we getting down there? Are we taking your van?"

"Naw, man. That bastard only does 15 to the gallon. Gareth's rented a minivan so we'll be able to bring all our boards and shit, too."

The plan was to drive down to TJ, have dinner, go to a club, drink until we passed out, and sleep on the beach. Then we could wake up and spend the day surfing, before driving back. Simple.

Ches had only graduated a few months before and money was tight. Besides, we both loved the beach and I was pleased we weren't heading for Vegas. I'd had enough of fucking deserts after two tours of Iraq in three years. I didn't want to think that after 20 weeks at Camp Pendleton, the next stop would be Afghanistan. I'd worry about that next year.

"Sounds good, bro."

His smile dropped away when we both heard Amy yelling from the house.

"Beer?" he said, rubbing his forehead tiredly.

I nodded, slung my duffle bag over my shoulder and followed him inside.

"Oh my God, Chester!" shrieked Amy. "You drank all the milk! We don't have any milk! And now we have Seb staying..."

She burst into tears, and Ches pulled her towards him as she sobbed into his shirt.

Embarrassed and feeling like a third wheel, I quietly went out the back and sat down on a plastic lounger that had seen better days.

I pulled my patrol cap down over my eyes, and was nearly asleep when I heard the distinctive pop of a beer cap hitting the deck, soon followed by a second.

"Sorry about that," said Ches, sitting down next to me. "She's ... a little tense."

"Look, if it's awkward me being here, I can find a hotel. It's not a problem."

Ches shook his head. "No way, man. It's okay. She'll be fine. Anyway, I'm just glad you could get leave. I wasn't sure you were going to make it when they changed your dates."

"Yeah, sorry about that. But I wasn't going to miss your wedding—I pulled in some favors." I shook my head. "I can't believe you're getting married."

I'd known him since I was 13, and he'd been my best friend for all that time. He knew all the shit I'd been through—and I knew he'd back me, no matter what.

Ches smiled. "Tell me about it. It's a real head spin sometimes. But I want it all with her—marriage, kids—I want *forever*, you know."

I looked down at my hands, twisting the Corona around, feeling the cool glass under my fingers. Yeah, I knew what he meant. I'd wanted all that once—and I'd thought *she* wanted the same. Turned out I was wrong.

"So," he said, after a long pause. "You seeing anyone?"

"I've been in the fucking desert surrounded by hairy-assed guys for the last nine months. What do you think?"

"No women at all?"

"A couple of hook-ups—women from the motor-pool. Nothing serious."

He slapped my shoulder.

"The Best Man always gets laid at weddings. It's like a law or something."

I grinned back at him, but thought I'd better change the subject when I heard Amy stamping towards us.

"I've ordered pizza," she snapped.

Ches caught her around the waist and pulled her onto his lap.

"Thanks, babe," he said into her neck.

Her body held tense for a second, then relaxed.

"I know. I'm behaving like a crazy person," she said. "Sorry. Sorry, Seb."

I waved my beer at her. "No blood, no foul."

"God, I'm a horrible hostess. I didn't even ask how you are."

I couldn't help smiling at her. She'd done a complete one-eighty from the bitch who gave me a ride 40 minutes ago.

"Glad to be stateside, and that's the truth."

She nodded, thoughtfully.

"Do you still like being a Marine? Even after..."

We all knew she was talking about Fido. Poor bastard got blown up nearly three years ago. Didn't make it to 19. IED. Bastards.

"Yeah, it's okay. I mean, I can do it and I like doing the interpreting. I get to talk to ordinary Iraqi people." I shrugged. "It feels like it makes a difference. Sometimes."

It was hard to explain what I meant by that and the conversation was making me uncomfortable. I was on leave for my best friend's wedding—I didn't want to talk about work. I changed the subject quickly.

"So what do you have planned for your bachelorette party?"

She gave a small smile.

"Stacey's organized it. We're going to have cocktails here while we get ready; downtown for dinner; and then a club." She raised an eyebrow at Ches. "There could be strippers."

"Just don't let any of those oily bastards touch you, babe," snorted Ches.

"Oh, I'll be the one stuffing dollar bills in their posing pouches."

I couldn't help laughing, as much at the revolted expression on Ches's face as anything else. I was happy he was happy, that he'd found his One. My mood soured as I tried not to think of *her*.

Christ, just get over it already! She'd taught me how to fuck—I should be grateful. I hadn't had any complaints since I'd started seeing other women. Yeah, I'd kind of been making up for lost time.

Ches nuzzled Amy's neck. "I'll pose in a pouch for you any time, baby."

"Oh, Jesus! Too much information, buddy."

Ches laughed.

"If it's okay with you guys, I'll take a shower and change into civvies."

Ches waved me away, too busy with his girl to answer.

It felt good to wash off the dust and grit, and I took my time enjoying the hot water and privacy. One thing being a Marine had taught me was to find a private place inside my head. You had to learn how to do that when you were with a bunch of jarhead grunts 24/7.

I pulled on a plain t-shirt and jeans, and headed down, hoping to hell that the make-out fest was done. Otherwise it was going to be a long, damn evening.

I was relieved to see that the happy couple had disentangled themselves, and Ches was setting out placemats and paper napkins.

"I thought we were having pizza?"

"We are," he said, shaking his head in exasperation, "but Amy wants to do things nice."

"And there's nothing wrong with that!" I heard her yelling from the backyard.

I smirked at Ches, and mouthed the words, "Pussy whipped!"

He sighed, but I could tell he really loved it.

The pizza arrived, and Ches pulled out some more beer to serve with the meal.

"Oh, hey, man, so I saw Brenda last week. She asked after you."

"Yeah? How's she doing? How's Kimberley?"

"She's good. I can't believe the kid is four now. I told her you'd be stationed at Pendleton."

I threw Ches a look, and he raised his hands in apology.

I didn't mind hearing about my ex-girlfriend, even though she'd royally fucked up the one important relationship I'd ever had in my life. She'd been pregnant and scared, so she'd made some bad decisions. But she'd apologized a shitload and we were okay. Even so, I didn't want Ches making like I wanted to get back with her.

"Nah, she's cool man. She's started seeing some guy that works at a used-car dealership. She seems pretty into him."

Well, *that* was a relief. I didn't want her to think I'd be up for dating or any of that shit. Friends—I could do that.

"Yeah? Maybe I'll call her."

"And Stacey was asking about you, too," added Amy.

I must have looked blank because she said, "You met her last year at your twenty-first ... light brown hair in a cute bob, bangs ... you know? She's one of my bridesmaids."

"Oh, sure. I remember. You have a brother out at Fort Myer, right?"

Amy smiled brightly. "Yes, that's her."

Ches threw me a warning look, and I took the hint: Stacey was off limits.

After dinner we headed out to the garage so I could check on my bike. She started on the second try which was pretty good considering she hadn't been ridden in nearly a year. Ches had kept her running, but he hadn't taken her out. Like I said—pussy whipped.

Ches climbed on behind me, and we rode out toward the ocean.

I stopped when we reached one of our favorite surf spots. The setting sun had turned the water blood-red, and the wind had dropped, so the only sound was the breakers rolling across the shore.

"Had some good times here, huh?" said Ches.

I nodded. It was true. We'd come here with Fido the night of our senior prom, when Ches didn't have a date and I'd broken up with Brenda. We'd gotten wasted on Mitch's beer and some weed that I'd scored. But this beach—it was also somewhere that I'd taken *her*.

"Hey, Seb," said Ches, wiggling his eyebrows at me oblivious of the direction my thoughts had taken, "want to relive some of those good times?"

And he held out a baggie and blunt wrappers. Then he frowned.

"Can you? It's cool if you'd rather not..."

"Nah, it's not a problem."

Drug testing was mandatory in the Corps but I was confident that by the time I arrived at Pendleton, there'd be nothing but a higher tolerance for alcohol in my system after this vacation.

We found ourselves a comfortable dune out of sight from the road, and sank down to the cooling sand.

"You do this often?" I asked, raising one eyebrow. "I kinda thought Amy would have your balls in a vise for something like this."

He twitched a smile.

"Yeah, she'd like to think so. But, I don't do it that often anymore—responsible citizen and all that."

"Damn pillar of the community," I laughed.

"God help that community," he mumbled.

I watched him roll the joint, glad I was here to spend these last few days of bachelorhood with him.

"You really love her, don't you?"

A grin crept over his face.

"Yeah. You noticed, huh? She's amazing."

He smiled to himself, and took a long hit before passing it to me.

"Kind of obvious, my friend. I'll miss you, buddy."

"Jeez, Seb! It's a wedding, not my funeral!"

"Yeah, keep telling yourself that."

His face was suddenly serious.

"I want it all with her, man. House, mortgage, kids—all of it." He looked at me sideways. "I thought you'd understand that—you of all people."

I closed my eyes and sucked in the smoke, letting it sting the back of my throat and drawing it into my lungs before blowing it away.

Yeah, I'd wanted all that. Once. But I wasn't going to let that happen now. I'd wised up—and I wasn't going to give any woman the chance to shatter me into dust. Not again.

"Besides," said Ches, "Amy's got great tits." He sighed. "God, I love burying my face in her tits."

"Yeah? Well just don't let her get on top, man," I couldn't help saying.

"Why the fuck not?"

"You'll suffocate."

Ches looked pissed, and then couldn't help a quiet chuckle.

"That's my future wife you're talking about, Hunter. And by the way, a message from the future Mrs. Peters—she says no hitting on the bridesmaids. Got it?"

"Yeah, whatever."

I took another drag and passed the joint back. We'd been doing this shit since I was 15 and Ches was 16. It was easy to score down by the pier—pretty much whatever you wanted. Mostly, we'd stuck to weed. It was easier to get hold of than liquor at that age.

"Got any plans for your birthday?" said Ches.

"Yeah, forget the fuck about it," I said, with a scowl.

My 22nd birthday was five weeks away. Last year had been so shit, that my only plan this year was to dive into a bottle of whisky and stay there until I passed out.

"Fair enough," he said, evenly. "We'll be back from the honeymoon in plenty of time—we should head out, have a few drinks."

I grunted something non-committal and he was wise enough to leave it.

We finished the joint in silence, then rode back to the house.

***

"Goddamn it, get your ass in the van, Peters!"

Gareth was yelling at Ches while the groom said goodbye to Amy—*again.*

I sat in the back of the minivan, my sunglasses pulled down over my eyes. You got used to waiting around in the military—it was kind of, *Hurry up and wait!* So although it didn't bother me, Gareth was getting really wound up.

Eventually, Ches unglued his lips from Amy, and with Gareth behind the steering wheel still looking pissed, we headed south on the I-5 to Tijuana. We'd barely left Ches's street before he was texting Amy. I remembered what that was like—treasuring every moment, every message.

Jeez, I really had to get my head out of my ass! This was my brother's bachelor party and I was thinking like a moody emo-bitch.

We crossed into Mexico soon after. I thought I was going to get some shit when the border guards examined my ID, muttering about me being a Marine. We'd all learned some Spanish at school, but it was the vibe and the way they were looking at me that freaked me out. They thought we were a bunch of rich, white Americanos coming for the cheap drinks and cheap chicks—which was true. Except for the being rich bit. I probably had more money than the rest of the guys as Ches, Gareth, Del and Vince had only just graduated and were all paying off their student loans. I wasn't sure about Tyler as he was a few years older, so he probably worked. I hadn't had much to spend my pay on in the desert. Maybe it was time to upgrade the motorcycle.

But at least there were a load of US military passing through at the same time —Marines and Navy. Guess I looked different, what with hanging with guys who actually had hair.

Eventually, the border guards waved us through without shooting us or arresting us, but we'd wasted an hour of valuable surfing and drinking time.

Tyler kept giving me this dirty look, like I was personally responsible for the delay. What a dick.

The Tijuana Sloughs had been pumping as we'd driven past, so once we were on the Mexican side, we found ourselves a patch of road and just pulled over.

"Ah, you gotta be kidding!" whined Tyler. "This motherfucker breaks onto rock reef. I don't want to get my face mashed three days before my sister's wedding!"

Ches frowned, but I could see Tyler's thinking had gotten to him. I decided to keep out of it, despite the draw of the pumping five foot barrels.

Del stretched and yawned. "Let's go get a coffee first and then find somewhere more mellow."

So we piled back in the minivan and headed south for another 20 minutes. I remembered that Baja Malibu had a rep as a good beach break—bit gnarly for beginners, but it was spitting top to bottom barrels. Too good to miss.

"Hey, Gareth, if you pull off here we can park next to Tecate Jack's. Then we have surf and beer."

He nodded and exited from the toll road, then parked on the dead-end street on the north side of the Baja Malibu housing development.

The tide was falling, which made the rides even better. I was stoked. It had been a long time since I'd surfed. I could sense Ches's excitement, too. He'd even put his cell phone away. Thank fuck for that.

We piled out of the minivan and I couldn't help noticing that Tyler looked like he was shitting himself but trying to hide it. I guessed he wasn't that great of a surfer.

"I'm going to get caffeined up," said Del, strolling in the direction of Tecate Jack's. "I'll catch up with y'all later."

"Yeah, me, too," muttered Tyler, and no one seemed sorry to see him go.

Gareth and Vince started suiting up while I was still mesmerized by the awesome surf.

"You okay, bro?" asked Ches, a puzzled look on his face.

"Yeah, sure. Just... thinking, you know."

He nodded but didn't speak. He didn't need to.

He slapped me on the back, and that snapped me the fuck out of it. I pulled off my t-shirt and caught Ches staring at my new tat. I forgot about it most of the time. Most guys that served had something. Mine was done just before I shipped out to Iraq.

"*Semper Fi*, huh?"

I shrugged. "Yeah, guess it seemed like a good idea at the time." I'd had the Corp's logo inked onto my shoulder. I'd almost had 'Infidel' in Arabic, but luckily I hadn't been drunk enough to go for that. "Whatever, man. Let's surf!"

The ocean was colder than a witch's tit, the swell coming in from Alaska by the feel of it. But it was epic: me and Ches, just like old times. Until the asshat dropped in on me, grinning like a loon as I got trashed by a wave breaking on my head. I thought I'd snapped the leash the way that it was tugging on my ankle. When I broke the surface, the bastard was laughing at me.

"You're out of practice, dude!" he crowed.

I decided I owed him for that—and I was going to get him so wasted, he'd wish he was going home in a body bag. Game on.

We surfed for a couple more hours and Del and Tyler joined us for a while. I was right about Tyler—the guy was seriously out of his depth. Even though he acted like a dick, I didn't think it would be cool if the bride's brother didn't make it back from TJ. I don't think he knew it, but Ches and I were tag-teaming him, just to make sure when we called time-out, he'd still be breathing.

But after I'd heard him complain about only being able to take a basic cold shower on the beach, I was ready to toss him back in the ocean. Ches just rolled his eyes, and the other guys ignored him.

Once we dressed and spiffed up for the rest of the day and night, we drove back toward TJ and left the van by the beach, taking a cab the couple of miles back to town. La Revolucion Boulevard was the main strip where all the bars were lined up, ready for inspection. As soon as we got out of the cab, I saw a bunch of Marines and Navy guys who were already wasted, and about one minute from beating the shit out of each other. Ches spotted them at the same time, and we took a long walk around them, not wanting to get caught up in a turf war when there were plenty of other bars to check out.

As we looked for somewhere to eat, there were all these little kids, like six or seven selling gum. I mean, where the fuck were their parents? If they were my kids, I wouldn't be letting them hang around the streets like that.

We decided not to waste time and money on a sit down meal, but loaded up at one of the taco stands that seemed to be on every corner. Ches insisted we all get some crappy TJ t-shirts as souvenirs, for fuck's sake, and Tyler was taking photographs like a fucking tourist. I couldn't help wondering if his camera phone would still be in his pants pocket by the end of the night. We zoned in on a bar called Papas and Beer. Jeez, what a fucking meat market for the young and willing. Tyler looked like he was about to blow his wad just by looking. When we scooted into a booth, I made sure I wasn't sitting near him. Even though it was still early evening, there were people dry humping everywhere you looked.

Ches looked kind of uncomfortable, but I had the feeling it was going to be hard to get the other guys to go somewhere else.

"Hi! My name is Dina and I'll be your server this evening."

Vince and Del make no secret of eye-fucking our waitress. I couldn't blame them—she was *hot*. She had this really pretty, auburn hair that was kind of curly. I know some girls paid a lot of money to get their hair permed that way, but hers looked natural. But, hey, no one was looking at her hair when her jeans shorts were cut so high, I could see the curve of her ass cheeks. And long, long legs. Nice.

"What do you guys need?"

"I need you to sit on my face," said Tyler.

I'd really had enough of his shit. "Shut the fuck up, you douche!" I snapped. "Sorry about that, ma'am. He woke up an asshole and then got uglier."

I shook my head in apology while Dina gave Tyler the stink-eye.

"Feel free to piss in his beer," I said, not entirely joking.

Dina turned to me and grinned. "Well, I might just think about that! What would the rest of you like?"

"We'll take a pitcher of beer, a bottle of tequila and six glasses, pretty lady," said Vince.

As she walked away, the sway of her hips was really fucking fascinating. Every single one of us had our eyeballs glued to her butt-cheeks. Including Ches. There was no doubt about it: Dina was one hot mama.

Ches caught my eye and grinned. "Whatever you're thinking, man, just don't miss our morning surf or your ass is grass."

"You're joking!" laughed Tyler. "She's gotta be like 35!"

"Seb digs older chicks," said Ches, with a shrug.

I frowned as I looked at him, and he had the grace to look a little abashed. "Sorry, man," he muttered.

Luckily Tyler didn't make anything of it, or I'd have been tempted to rearrange his face.

When Dina returned with the drinks, she leaned down so her chest was almost in my face and I had to sit back in the booth or get two black eyes.

"I get off at two, honey. Stick around."

Not going anywhere, baby.

Only Ches heard what she said to me, but he didn't comment. He pulled out his wallet to pay for the drinks, but I stopped him.

"No way, man! It's your bachelor party—your money's no good."

"Aw! Is he getting married?" said Dina, with a sweet smile.

"Yup," said Ches, proudly. "To the prettiest girl in San Diego."

Now, I loved Ches, I really did, but calling Amy 'the prettiest girl in SD' was stretching things. She had great tits, true enough, but not even Ray Charles would have called her 'pretty'. It was living proof that love is blind.

"Who's the best man?" said Dina.

"My buddy, Seb," said Ches, throwing his arm around my shoulders. "I've known this fucker for nine years."

Dina smiled again, winked, and walked away.

Ches raised his eyebrows. "Don't forget to love with a glove, man," he smirked.

I saluted him in the usual way, "Go fuck yourself."

We started knocking back the liquor and talking trash to all the tourist girls who were there—most of them down from San Diego. A lot of college girls came because the drinking age is 18 here, and they weren't going to get carded.

Vince and Tyler were kind of assholes, yelling out, "Damn, look at that ass!" or "Hey baby, where you goin'?"

I told them that if they did that again when the girls were with any military guys, they were going to end up in a good ole beat-down. Dumbasses didn't listen.

We were on about our fifth or sixth round of drinks when the show started. It was pretty tame—nothing I hadn't seen before. Strippers, pole-dancing, tassels, fake tan, and fake boobs. Traditional for a bachelor party, you know. Half way through, I wandered up to the stage to order a lap dance for Ches.

"You want a *private* dance, honey?" asked a woman with long black hair and a really cute Mexican accent.

"Um, yeah, for my friend, please, ma'am."

"Not for you, baby?" she said, running a long fingernail down my t-shirt, and resting her hand on my belt buckle.

I caught her hand before it drifted any further.

"Thanks, but some other time. Just for my buddy. It's his bachelor party."

"Pity," she said. "Which one's the guy?"

I pointed out Ches, who was doing shots so fast, his hand was practically a blur. Man, he was going to be wasted in the morning. Served the fucker right after dropping in on me. Then I remembered I'd promised Amy to look after him—and she scared the shit out of me. So I decided to have a word with our server.

She saw me looking for her. Dina. Right.

"Hey, honey! You're eager!"

"Well, yeah!" I said, honestly. "But, um, could you water down the drinks at our table? I don't really give a shit about the rest of those a-holes, but I don't want the groom dyin' on me."

She smiled and pinched my ass. "You got it, handsome."

Ches had his lap dance, and Tyler had his face slapped by the dancer. Served the bastard right. The guy really was a dick. I hoped Amy had a different set of genes than her brother, otherwise Ches was in big trouble.

An hour later, I lined the guys up outside, ready to pack them into a taxi. I told Del that I'd meet them back at the beach in the morning. He was the only one who wasn't falling over drunk. I had my own appointment to keep.

But then Tyler-half-a-brain, started yelling out to some girl.

"Hey, gorgeous! You wanna give me your number? I'll show you a good time, not like that no-brain gorilla you're with."

Holy shit, the guy had a death wish. He'd just picked on a mean looking jarhead, with the swagger that spoke of a skinful of liquor.

"What you say, you fuckin' pussy?" the gorilla slurred.

"Nothing, man," I said quickly. "The asshole is trashed. He apologizes to your girl."

"No, I don't!" laughed Tyler.

That was when the gorilla threw a punch. I managed to block most of it, but Tyler still ended face down on the sidewalk.

Then the other Marines piled in. Ah shit, I wasn't going to see Ches get all beat up. I waded in, pulled the big fucker off of Tyler and got a few punches in before his fist caught me in the ribs. Fuck, that hurt.

Luckily, Dina had been keeping an eye out for me. I saw her empty out a pitcher of beer into the mass of bodies. That cooled it down long enough for me to push the rest of them into a taxi and get them the fuck out of there.

Dina was waiting for me, a smile on her face.

"Wow, thanks for that, ma'am ... um ... Dina. You're pretty spry."

"I'm a lot of things, honey," she said, with a huge smile. Then she whispered in my ear. "I do yoga—I'm very bendy."

Holy fuck!

She linked her arm through mine to walk along the street.

"What's your name, honey? I can't keep calling you that..."

"Sebastian."

"That's a nice name. Unusual—suits you. Well, Sebastian, I thought I'd take you home and rock your world! Do you think you can keep up with me?"

"Sounds good to me, ma'am, I mean, Dina."

And it did. It sounded really fucking good. I loved Ches, but all this wedding shit was making me a little crazy. I wanted to be able to forget everything. It was easy to fall headlong into a bottle, but Dina's idea was turning me on big time. I loved it when a woman talked dirty—especially if she could do it in Italian. I'd have to remember to ask her later. Yeah, Spanish would work, too.

"So what else are you guys doing in TJ, other than getting trashed?"

"Surfing, hanging out, you know. Maybe some swimming, body surfing."

She laughed, then pulled me into a darkened doorway.

"Baby, the only body surfing you'll be doing is on me. Right here. Right now."

Shiiit!

My back thudded against the door, and Dina was digging her nails in, as if she was trying to crawl up my body. Fuck, it hurt, but it was *hot*.

"You want to be bad with me, Sebastian? Because I sure as hell want to feel your hard dick in my ... *fuck me!*"

Yeah, that was the general plan. Wait, *what?*

Dina had grabbed a hold of my junk, and sue me, but I was hard as hell.

"You got a stick of dynamite in there, honey, 'cause that's sure as hell gonna blow my brains!"

She wrestled her door key out of her purse while I attacked her neck and bare shoulders with kisses.

We fell into the stairwell, and it was so damn dark, we were literally groping around. I had no problem with that, until she accidentally kneed me in the balls, and I crashed against the wall, cursing like a squid (sailor, in civvy-speak).

Dina laughed her ass off while I was writhing around on the ground.

"Sorry, honey. Please God tell me you can still use that equipment."

I groaned out something that might have been a yes, I still wasn't sure. In fact the only thing I *was* sure about was that I'd deflated faster than a Fourth of July balloon.

When she finally finished laughing, she took pity on me and put some lights on to lead me inside. I staggered to my feet, and went after her. I could hear music, and I guessed she'd put on a CD. She was singing along and dancing to the song—it was kinda sweet. But the next thing I saw were her denim shorts, abandoned on the floor. I followed the trail of clothes through her apartment, until I stepped out of a glass door and into the yard.

Hot tub! Oh fucking yes!

Dina was leaning back, smiling up at me, while bubbles swirled and frothed around her. Her gorgeous tits were floating. I mean, seriously—floating!

"Join me," she said, waving an arm, and I wasn't sure if it was an order or a request. I didn't care. And if her backyard was overlooked by a dozen different windows, well hell—I hope they enjoyed the show.

I yanked off my t-shirt, pretty certain a few seams had just ripped, then kicked off my boots and socks.

I saw she was staring at my tattoo.

"Hmm, Marine, huh? I like!"

Damn, that tat was worth its weight in pussy.

"Yes, ma'am," I said, watching her face. "We stole the eagle from the Air Force, the anchor from the Navy, and the rope from the Army. On the seventh day when God rested, we overran the perimeter and stole the globe—we've been running the show ever since. We live like soldiers, talk like sailors, and slap the hell out of both of them at the same time. Fighter by day, lover by night, drunkard by choice, and a United States Marine by an act of God."

She laughed long and loud.

"God, you're so young and cocky. I fuckin' love that!"

Oo-rah!

I dropped my pants and briefs, watching Dina's eyes as she followed their descent. I could swear the woman was spitting sparks. And I was hard again. This time, I hoped she'd keep her knees to herself.

The water was hot, and felt fucking fantastic as I sank down into it. It was also good to soak off some of the salt that had been sticking to me ever since surfing earlier.

"How long can you hold your breath, Marine?" she said.

"Um, a couple of minutes? I don't really know."

She smiled this slow, sexy smile. "I can hold mine for three and a half minutes."

"Okaaay?"

And then she went down on me, right there in the hot tub. Woman sucked like a fucking hoover. Jesus, I wasn't going to need three and a half minutes if she carried on like that.

I had to stop myself from grabbing her hair and ramming her head down my cock, but I was still a bit nervous of her—woman had teeth, and I didn't think she'd be afraid to use them.

About a minute into the show, I felt my balls tighten in a way that had nothing to do with her left hand squeezing them.

I tapped her on the shoulder, being polite and all.

"Um, Dina, shit! Um, I'm gonna ... fuck! I'm gonna..."

She pulled away immediately, and finished me off with a twist of her hand, that wasn't particularly gentle.

I came all over her tits, and she just sat there smiling at me.

"Sorry, honey. I'm the fluffer—I don't swallow that shit. It's a pity my roommate Stephanie isn't here. She *loves* to swallow."

I *may* have passed out while she was speaking, because when I opened my eyes, she was straddling my legs and biting the hell out of my neck. *Shit,* her teeth were sharp—I was really glad they weren't near my dick anymore.

It took me about a minute to get hard again. What can I say? I was 21 and had been in a fucking desert for nine months. I knew I shoulda used a condom, but how the hell was I supposed to do that in a hot tub?

She rode the hell out of me, yelling and saying all this dirty shit. It was such a fucking turn on. She didn't care who saw her or what they heard. She was just wild—and I loved it.

Just as we were getting pruney from the hot water, she grabbed me and dragged me into her lair. She called it a bedroom, but I wasn't so sure.

She wanted to tie me up, but I was still remembering how she'd manhandled me earlier.

"Why don't you let me tie *you* up?" I suggested as an alternative.

She glanced at the clock next to her bed.

"Okay. My roomie will be back soon, so if you get too weird, she'll use the blender on your balls. Fair enough?"

I swallowed. *What was it with women threatening my equipment?*

"Um, yeah. Fair enough."

This time I did use a condom, and after I'd tied her hands to the headboard, I turned her over and took her from behind. I was actually kinda lusting after her ass, but it seemed rude when we didn't know each other that well. Maybe, if I was still here in a few hours.

Anyway, we were rocking that big old bed when fuck me if her roommate didn't just walk right in on us. She didn't even look surprised.

She strode in and slapped my ass while I was fucking her roommate. *Yeah, what?* Shit, I came so hard, I saw stars.

"Oh, hey," said Dina, breathlessly. "Sebastian, this is Stephanie—Steph. Do you mind if she joins us?"

By that point, I was pretty sure I was hallucinating.

The new woman had black hair and brown eyes, and was holding a can of Bud Light. She shed her clothes before I could answer, and my eyes wandered over some really insane tats on her back and leg.

Round three. Or was it four? I'd lost count.

"Hmm, let's take it to the next level," said Stephanie. "Whaddya say, bitch?"

I wasn't sure if she was talking to me or Dina, but neither of them seemed to care what I thought. My dick was just happy to join the party.

By the next morning, I was like the walking dead, and my cock had had more of a workout than when I was 15 and jerking off morning, noon and night. I had bite marks all over my chest, and probably my ass, too, from what I could remember. One of them—maybe both—had scratched the shit out of me, and I looked like I'd been wrestling with a wildcat, which was about right.

I'm not sure how I walked out of there without my knees buckling. Dina gave me this huge, happy grin as I pulled on my pants, and I wondered if she was going to give me a certificate or something.

She pointed one of her claws at my chest, and I swear my dick whimpered.

"You are a credit to the Corps, Sebastian," she said.

Stephanie leaned up on one elbow and blew me a kiss, before heading back down under the sheets to ... hell, by that point, I was so tired, I didn't even care what she was doing. I just gave a half-hearted wave and trudged out of the door.

Oo-rah.

When I got back to the minivan, I saw that all bodies were present and accounted for, stretched out on the cold sand, muffled in their sleeping bags. I almost envied them. I had muscle strain in places I didn't know could be strained. Dina had been right about the body surfing—all I wanted to do was lie my aching body the fuck down and die a happy man.

I crawled into the minivan, and passed out on the back seat.

It felt about five fucking minutes later when some bastard was crashing around, waking me up.

"Hey, bro!" said Ches. "You look like shit. Rough night?" He dragged my t-shirt away from my neck. "Jeez, man! That must have been some chick!"

"Yeah, and her friend," I said, yawning my head off.

"Outstanding!" he yelled.

"Gimme a break," I muttered, laying down again.

"Oh, hell, no!" laughed Ches. "We're going surfing! Get your ass into gear and move it, Marine!"

"Fuck off!"

The bastard pushed me hard, and I fell off of the seat and crashed onto the floor. *Fuck!* As if my body wasn't already damaged enough.

Ches jumped from the minivan, laughing his ass off.

By that time, everyone was awake and my chance of sleeping off the damage was non-existent.

We surfed some more, ate tortillas at Tecate Jack's and then hung out on the beach. I fell asleep in the sun, and had maybe a couple of hours' shuteye, before Ches nudged me with his foot and said we were heading out.

His folks were flying in that evening and he wanted to be back.

Gareth dropped us off first and about a second later Ches's mom, Shirley, was hugging the crap out of both of us.

"My boys!" she said with a huge smile. "You're still in one piece!"

Amy looked pretty happy, too, and I saw her copping a feel of Ches's ass when she thought no one was looking. Mitch strode out and we shook hands before he punched my shoulder and gave me a guy hug.

Mitch had been stationed at Camp Panzer Kaserne in Germany for the last year, so we compared notes and talked shit about the Corps, and then moved onto more general stuff. Amy was a lot calmer with them around, and I wasn't the only one who was grateful for that.

Or so I thought.

I went out to the kitchen to get a glass of water, and Amy followed me.

"You promised me that you'd look after Ches!" she hissed.

I was taken aback. What the hell was she on about?

"What? I did look after him! He's fine. Nothing happened."

She folded her arm across her chest, which was a pretty fucking amazing achievement, given the size of it.

"You left him!" she snapped. "You went off with some woman. He *told* me. Look at you! You're covered in hickeys—it's disgusting."

She was really beginning to piss me off.

"Hey! I made sure his drinks were watered down, and I got him into a taxi. Nothing happened to him! So what's your freakin' problem?"

I wanted to tell her that it was her dickwad of a brother who'd almost gotten us into a fight.

"Just keep your pathetic hands off of my bridesmaids. They're my *friends*, Seb, if you even know what that means. I'm not kidding! I..."

Luckily, Shirley came into the kitchen, and Amy left immediately, her face still twisted with anger.

"Everything okay out here?"

I shrugged and drank my water.

When she didn't leave, I should have known something was on her mind.

"Are you bringing a date to the wedding?" she asked, too casually.

"Why would I want to do that when you're going to be there?" I replied, trying to go for casual.

She laughed. "I'll save you a dance. Maybe one of Amy's friends...?"

I knocked that idea back PDQ. "Nah, Best Man duties is enough for me, Shirley."

She looked at me, her face serious. "Look, I know the last few years since Caro ... the last few years have been hard..."

Fuck. I really didn't want to hear that name—not now.

"Shirley, I'm good. It's fine. You don't have to worry about me."

"Of course I worry about you, Sebastian, the same as I worry about Ches. Just ... just don't give up on the idea of meeting someone. You've got to stop pushing people away. And I'm not talking about your hook ups." She waved a hand. "Don't worry, Ches hasn't told me ... much ... but I hate seeing you being so ... hard when I know that's not you." She looked me in the eye. "She did love you, you know. Caroline—she did love you."

I closed my eyes and turned away.

"Yeah, but not enough."

And I'd *really* had enough of that conversation. Shirley kissed my cheek and left me alone.

I wasn't sure what to make of what she'd just said. I mean, I'd moved on, right? I was seeing other women. Yeah, casual stuff but so what?

I tried to shake off what she'd said, but it left me with an uneasy feeling.

None of us were in the mood for staying up late, so we had an early night. I tried to get comfortable on the couch, but couldn't sleep. I ended up dragging my bedroll into the backyard and falling asleep under the cold stars.

A loud scream woke me, and I automatically reached for my M16 before I remembered where I was. I realized the sound was more happy squeals than screams, and decided that the bridesmaids must have arrived.

That was our cue for getting our shit and driving out to the country club for breakfast. Shirley took pity on me, and made me a cup of coffee before Ches, Mitch and I were kicked out.

We had a quick breakfast at the club, and then checked into our rooms. Ches was beginning to look nervous, and he asked me three times to show that I'd kept the rings safe. On the fourth time, I told him that if he asked me again I was going to swallow them, and then he'd have to wait for me to shit them out. That kept him quiet—for about five minutes.

I ordered a bottle of tequila from room service, and we did a couple of shots just to help him calm the fuck down. Then he headed back to his room to get dressed.

I set my phone to wake me in 45 minutes and managed to cat-nap before showering, shaving off the stubble, and changing into my Dress Blues.

Even though Amy hadn't wanted Ches to enlist, she had a thing about me and Mitch wearing our uniforms. Whatever. I didn't get to wear the Blues that much, and it saved renting a tux.

I realized I'd better make a start on writing my speech, but then Mitch came in and we did some more shots, while he was rambling on about when Ches was a kid.

I really envied what they had. My bastard of a father had never given a shit about me, and there was no way he'd be reminiscing on my wedding day—assuming I was dumb enough ever to get married. I was kidding myself—no chick would be dumb enough to have me. I was damaged goods, and I knew it.

Their ceremony went off well. Amy looked cute, and the dress managed to corral her tits somewhat. I saw her friend Stacey checking me out, but reminded myself that she was off limits. Shirley cried and even Mitch wiped a tear away. I didn't swallow the rings, and I didn't drop them either. Job done.

And Ches was a married man. *Well, fuck me.*

The meal was pretty nice but I couldn't enjoy it, because, firstly, I was sitting with Amy's parents and Tyler on one side, who was slowly getting wasted; and secondly, I knew that my speech was coming up, and I'd written zero, zip, nada, zilch. But then the emcee announced the Best Man, and it was time for me to do my thing. *Don't fuck up! Don't fuck up!*

"Um, hi, everyone. So, this is when I have to do the Best Man's speech thing. That's cool."

Which was a fucking lie—I was sweating bullets, especially wearing my Dress Blues.

"But Ches already knows I'm the best man—isn't that right, brother?"

I know he wanted to tell me to fuck off, but he couldn't with his new in-laws sitting there. It was pretty funny.

"I've known Ches since he was 14, this skinny little kid, but he had a pair of Tom Boyle Vans—not that I'm still hung up on it or anything."

I saw a couple of Ches's guy friends nodding in the audience, but everyone else just looked confused.

"He was the new kid at school and I was the runty Navy brat who was a year younger, but we bonded over his wheels, and have been friends ever since.

"And then I met Shirley and Mitch. Man, I was jealous! They were the coolest parents, and in case you didn't know, Base Salsa champions—four years running. Shirley, you shake your bootie like no one else!"

"Hey!" shouted Ches. "That's my mom you're talking about, you perv!"

"Pity you didn't inherit any of her dance skills, dude. You have two left feet!"

I could see Amy nodding in silent agreement, and snickers amongst Ches's college friends.

"Yeah, well me and Ches, and later on our buddy Fido, too, we did a whole load of shi... um ... stuff, hanging out at the pier in the summer, surfing our asses off. We had a lot of firsts together—junior prom—that hell on earth. No one, *no one* should force a 16 year old guy into a suit, let alone a tux—that's just evil. So we blew off our senior prom and got wasted on some good wee ... on, um, Mitch's beer—thanks for that Mitch, by the way."

"You can pay me back later," he yelled.

"Not gonna happen, Mitch. And just so's you know, it was Ches who drank your Jack Daniel's on Christmas that year."

"I can't believe you ratted me out!" whined Ches.

"Don't get me started, man! Yeah, so we did that a lot, senior year, pretty certain that we'd spend our lives on the beach, me, Ches, Fido. But no one has a choice about growing up. I know Ches wouldn't want to forget the third wheel of our wonky train, even though he isn't here to be with you today, brother."

The sudden silence was profound.

"So please join me in a toast to Fido, and the others who didn't make it home: To absent friends."

Everyone drank the toast with me, and I knew I'd killed the buzz. I had to get it back.

"Yeah, and there was another time Ches was so hungover, he threw up in his book bag and then forgot about it. Until the next day—when we had Biology. Man, that stunk so bad! Shirley and Mitch weren't too happy when Ches had his ass handed to him by Principal Hernandez two days before graduation. Ches, when it comes to whisky, man, just say no!

"Well, after that we spent our senior prom night on the beach like I said, dissing girls and saying how it was way cooler to just hang—guys only. And then Amy came along and rocked his world. Man, you should have seen the sappy look in his eye when he talked about her. I was about ready to puke—no offense!"

Her eyes snapped as she stared at me, and I really wished Ches hadn't told her about my TJ hook-up.

"But then I met her, and saw how cool she was, and how she kept his ass in line. And how much she loved him. And how much he loved her ... the kind of love that you know is going to make it no matter what shit life throws at you..."

I took a deep breath, not wanting to sound like a fucking pussy.

"Amy, not only are you marrying a great guy and my best friend—my brother—but you're joining an awesome family, and I know how happy they are to have you as a part of it."

I really meant that. I was almost jealous that she got to be part of their family, but I knew Mitch and Shirley considered me another son, pretty much.

"So, please raise your glasses to toast a beautiful bride and a damn fine groom: To Amy and Ches."

I sat down, relieved that I'd managed to speak in an almost coherent way, without swearing. Much.

Shirley nudged by arm.

"That was a really nice speech, Seb. I'm glad I wore waterproof mascara," and she leaned over to kiss my cheek.

"Me, too," said Mitch, raising his eyebrows and puckering his lips.

Shirley slapped his arm and laughed.

It felt really good being back with my family, my real family, even if I couldn't help feeling that everything had changed now that Ches was married.

I watched him take Amy's hand and lead her onto the floor for the first dance. They'd picked Van Morrison's *Brown-eyed Girl*, and I really wished they'd chosen any fucking song but that one. It brought back too many memories of another brown-eyed girl.

After a minute Shirley and Mitch took to the floor. Damn they could move. It was a real pity Ches hadn't inherited the rhythm gene—Amy looked like she was dancing with a lame bullock. Sad fucker.

I headed for the bar, and duties done, I had a couple of tequila shots lined up.

The short bridesmaid kept eyeing me up, so I got my focus on the bottle in front of me, until Shirley came over to bust my chops. I knew I was in trouble when she used my full name.

"Sebastian! What are you doing drinking here by yourself?"

"Just chillin', Shirley."

"You're supposed to dance with the bridesmaids—it's traditional."

"No way! Amy chewed my ass out for thirty minutes, telling me to stay the fu... hell away from her friends. I like having my testicles attached to my body."

She snorted, and I didn't know if she was annoyed by my language or amused. I'd had just enough tequila that I didn't care. Almost.

"She told you not to sleep with them, Seb, not that you couldn't dance with them!"

"Yeah, well..."

"Oh for goodness sake! Dance with me instead!" She grabbed my sleeve, and hauled me off to the dance floor and we stayed for a couple of numbers before she palmed me off on Stacey. Which was probably her plan in the first place.

"I think you guys have met?" Shirley said, smirking at me as she spoke.

"Hi, Mrs. Peters. Yes, we've met a couple of times," said Stacey. "But I've never seen you in uniform before, Seb."

"He looks very handsome, doesn't he?" said Shirley, her voice fond.

"He sure does," said Stacey, trying not to laugh.

"Jeez, Shirley! I'm standing right here!"

"Well, shape up, Marine! This lovely young lady is without a dance partner."

She pushed us together and strolled off. As much as she could in five inch heels.

"Sorry about that," I mumbled. "You don't have to dance if you don't want to."

"Oh, I don't mind," she said quickly.

"Yeah, but I'd like to survive this wedding in one piece, and Amy gave me strict instructions not to ... um..."

"Not to what?"

Fuck!

"Ah, hell! She told me not to hit on you, okay?"

Stacey blushed. "She said that?"

"Um, yeah. Sorry."

"Well, I'm sure I can risk your charms for one dance."

I raised my eyebrows at her sassy tone. "Sure about that?"

"Quite sure," she said, her voice challenging.

"Well, okay, then."

I held her hand, and walked her toward the dance area.

I remembered that I'd danced with her once before, on my 21st birthday, before it had all gone to shit. It felt ... good. I mean, she seemed like a nice girl, and I was going to be at Pendleton for the next five months. Maybe we could take it a bit further. Maybe I could finally forget the woman who'd ripped my heart out.

Maybe.

I pulled her in closer and Stacey smiled up at me.

CLR—Combat Logistics Regiment

Space-A—Space Available; military members can travel on military planes between bases if there is room available on that particular flight.

BONUS CHAPTER 5

Geneva

You learn a lot in the military. Well, I thought, being an adult, it would be a good career move to have somebody inspect me every day to make sure I put my pants on the right way, and had my shoes on the correct feet.

I did get to be a real Marine while I was out in Iraq. I was still with my Unit then, still with my buddies. And I spent most of the Afghan tour in mudbrick villages trying to persuade the tribal elders to side with the allies. Maybe it helped to make a difference. Now I'm stuck in the armpit of Europe on a chickenshit assignment all because my last CO in Paris was a dickless dumb-ass.

So I fucked his wife.

Funny enough that's a big no-no in the military—the kind of thing that can get you a court martial followed by a dishonorable discharge. Like I give a shit. I think it's something to do with having to trust your life with the guy who's got your back—so fucking his wife kind of puts a downer on things. And usually I don't go near married women—not any more. But they both deserved it. Long story, short: the no-ball pen-pusher didn't want anyone to know his wife was screwed by a noncom, so he had me assigned to a PR det in Geneva instead.

There are worse places. There are worse countries. I've seen a few of them. But there comes a point when you're so fucking bored that you bore yourself thinking about how bored you are. I'd reached that point two months ago.

I'd even thought about getting the hell out and doing something else with my life, although I had no clue what. But I'd re-upped two years ago, so I had another two to go. The only glimmer of light was that they needed US interpreters in Afghan. I'd put my name out there, so who knows.

This was my tenth year in the Marines. It had been an interesting life up until

Paris, two years ago. I'd found that I was good at languages—which was a big fucking shock to actually be good at anything—and had been promoted through the ranks. I'd been proud of being a Sergeant and had even thought about trying to get my degree so I could progress further. And then Paris had happened. For the last two years I'd been kicking my heels in one miserable office job after another, although I'd made Master Sergeant—just to get me out of their hair, I think. But now I'd got a new CO, so there was a chance I'd get moved. This guy was in that oxymoron of Military Intelligence. I'd met him briefly when he was out here for a few days. Nice wife. Blonde. Not my type.

At least I had some leave coming up.

My buddy, Ches, had asked me to come stateside and see the family. I was tempted, but since an incident with his wife's best friend and *her* best friend, let's just say I wasn't as welcome as I might have been. Whatever.

I was toying with the idea of taking off on my motorcycle and seeing some of Italy. I'd never been, although it was somewhere I'd wanted to see, ever since I was a kid. And the border was just a few miles away. What the hell. I had nothing better to do. Well, I did have one offer that I was considering. I'd spent last Christmas in the ski resort Klosters, with Benita from Düsseldorf. I had an open invitation to visit. I don't normally do reruns, but did I mention I was bored? And I hadn't been laid since Christmas—it was nearly fucking Easter.

Except for Dorota from Poland, who had some business at the UN. She was only in town for one night. Classy chick. Nice ass.

I realized I'd spent 20 minutes just staring out over the rooftops of Geneva towards the lake. It was peaceful.

I liked my apartment. It was pretty basic but nobody came here. It was owned by an old lady, Madame Dubois. She was always trying to introduce me to her granddaughters but apart from that, she didn't bother me.

Today's lesson in sheer fucking tedium was an ear-achingly dull hostile environment briefing—my fifth this month. It was part of my 'rehabilitation' after Paris. I don't know how it was supposed to rehabilitate me. I mean, what part of sending me to Switzerland was supposed to teach me to keep my cock in my pocket when it came to the CO's wife? My new boss was 3,000 miles away. With his wife. I'd need fucking super strength sperm to cause any trouble from this distance.

This month I was with a British team: Major Mike Parsons and a Lieutenant Tom waste-of-fucking-air Crawley. I'd learned some new words since I'd met Crawley: 'wanker' was one; 'tosser' was the other. Both suited him. Parsons was okay except for the fact that he hated me. Probably because I always turned up late. I think he knew why I'd gotten this assignment, so he never gave me much shit about it. I think if he'd been my CO, he'd have handed me my ass, and I wouldn't have blamed him. But we were only allies: civility was an optional extra.

As I pulled on the jacket of my khaki service uniform, my attention was caught by the half-empty bottle of Jack Daniel's that was still next to my bed. Yeah, a quick hit of that might actually get my ass moving and make the morning's mind-numbing monotony more bearable.

Might.

I was thirty minutes late, which was pretty good for me.

Crawley was droning on about some tedious shit that even had the journos present yawning their heads off.

Parsons didn't look happy when he saw me. Guy had a broomstick up his ass like the rest of the Brits when it came to punctuality. Yeah, well, it was probably an army thing. I was a Marine.

"Thank you, Tom. We'll take a short break now, ladies and gentleman, and meet back here at 1100 hours. Refreshments will be served in Les Nations lounge. And we're very glad to have our colonial colleague Chief Hunter to join us. I'm sure his insight will be invaluable."

Wow, wounded by sarcasm at close range. The Brits sure fight dirty. Next it'll be harsh language.

But my timing was pretty good—coffee break already.

I hightailed it out of the hotel, knowing that if I stayed I'd be asked a shitload of dumb questions. I've had some journos come onto me, acting like they're my best friend in the hope that I'll dish the dirt. They must think I'm a fucking moron if they expect me to trust them after five minutes. Besides, I usually prefer to get kissed before I get screwed.

It was all I could do to drag my weary ass back in that seminar room and hope that my brain didn't completely atrophy before the afternoon patisseries. The Swiss French made awesome cakes.

"Just a quick roll-call before we go on," said Major Parsons, "now everyone is here..."

Yeah, yeah I can take a hint. Jeez, he'd be hurting my feelings in a minute.

"Elizabeth Ashton?"

"Present and almost correct."

"Telek Burczyk?"

"Tutaj."

"Henri Ducat?"

"Oui."

"Ricardo Esteban?"

"Si."

"Heinrich Keller?"

"Jawohl."

"Marc Lebuin?"

"Je suis présent."

"Lee Venzi?"

A woman at the back raised her hand but didn't speak. I glanced over.

BONUS CHAPTER 5

What the fuck? No fucking way!

"You're Lee Venzi?"

I must have spoken out loud because I realized everyone was staring at me. I rearranged my face back to boredom. Inside I was anything but. My heart was beating so fucking hard I thought it would break out of my chest.

It took every ounce of self-control that I'd learned over the last 10 years to keep standing and not completely lose it and run out of the room. My mouth was dry and I felt a cold sweat break out all over my body. Adrenaline was burning through me and I couldn't tell if it was fight or flight. I wanted to run. I was frozen to the spot. I wanted to hit something. My hands were shaking so badly, I shoved them in my pockets and tried to concentrate on getting air into my lungs.

How could it be her? After all these years? How could she *be here?*

I thought I was having an out-of-my-fucking-mind—out-of-body experience. I fought to breathe normally, all the while thinking I was having a fucking heart attack.

My body was shaking so hard I thought it must be fucking obvious. This was worse than a goddamn RPG attack by the fucking Taliban in Afghan.

How? What was she doing here? Was it some sort of set up? Did she know I'd be here? No, not possible. She looked so fucking shocked. Shit, she hadn't changed. She looked exactly the same as the day she walked out on me.

Fuck! Fuck! Fuck! Breathe, you dumb fuck, breathe.

I stared out of the window, but it wasn't Geneva I was seeing—it was Point Loma beach in San Diego. I was 17 and she was so fucking beautiful, wearing that yellow bikini, her skin all golden from the sun.

I blinked, trying to clear the image, but it was as if the whole summer we were together was nailed to my brain and playing relentlessly like a horror film where you know someone's going to get the guts ripped out of them. Yeah, that was me. I was the one who got ripped to pieces. And as for her? She got to walk away and start a new life.

Bitch.

Why the hell did she have to come back and haunt me now? The ghost of fucks past.

How was I going to get through the next day and a half? I was sweating just thinking about being in the same room as her. I needed to get out. I could go off sick. Jeez, the way my body was responding, nobody would doubt that I was completely fucked.

Crawley continued his mindless lecture. It was an almost pleasantly dull rumble in the background. Mentally, I was ten years and 6,000 miles away.

God, she'd been so beautiful—the most beautiful woman I'd ever seen. And, if I was honest, no one else had come close since. Well, fuck. She'd fooled me. I thought I was something special. Really got that fucking wrong. At least I knew that she hadn't gone back to the asshole she'd been married to at the time.

I risked a quick look.

So fucking beautiful. I turned away—it hurt to look at her. But I couldn't help noticing she was slumped in her seat and her cheeks were flushed. I'd have given my left nut to know what she was thinking.

Crawley droned on.

"Because most attacks occur on reaching home, always ensure that you can drive straight into your garage or compound, and secure the door or gate behind you."

I could hear the British woman whispering something that made the other journos laugh. Crawled-up-his-ass Crawley didn't like that.

"This is serious, madam. What I tell you today may save your life."

The British woman inflated immediately. Fuck, her tits were enormous—and not in a good way.

"Listen, sunshine, you may think you're something special with a weapon of mass destruction dangling between your legs, but let me tell *you* a thing or two: I've been to the frontline of every war since Uganda in 1979, before you were bloody well born." She started ticking them off on her fingers. "Angola, Croatia, Rwanda, Bosnia, Iraq, Kuwait, Afghanistan ... bloody hell, places you've never even heard of. And this woman," she pointed her chin at Caro, "has been in more hot spots than you've had hot dates."

Of course. *Lee Venzi.* She'd changed her name, which was why I hadn't recognized it when Parsons gave me the list of attendees. I'd read some of the articles and assumed this Venzi character was a guy—probably ex-military. But Caro had been around military bases for ten years while she'd been married to Admiral Asswipe. She knew military.

I wasn't happy to hear that she'd reported from dangerous places, but what the fuck was I expecting? This pack of journos was all heading for Afghan. I glanced over again and couldn't help smiling, but turned away the minute she looked towards me. I couldn't give her a way in or she'd fuck me over again.

Shit. Was I really that weak?

Parsons stepped in to retrieve the situation, and Crawley was allowed to carry on with his boring crap.

I tried to keep my eyes off of her, but every time they were magnetically drawn back.

Focus, you pathetic fucker! Translate the fucking National Anthem into Pashto, if you have to! Don't look at her.

By lunchtime, I was fucked. The second Parsons called timeout I was out of the blocks like a goddamn 100 meter sprinter.

I didn't know what the fuck I was doing: I just knew I couldn't go back to that damn hotel and see her and not touch her. I was a fucking lunatic. I *hated* that woman. She destroyed my life and hadn't even looked back when she walked out on me, leaving me behind with no clue of how to find her.

And the worst of it was I'd believed that she'd loved me. Some fucking fairytale. But I'd believed her, and I'd waited for her. I wouldn't let anyone say a word against her for three long years. I thought she'd find me when I was 21. But she never came. I never heard from her again. And she was a journalist—how fucking hard would it have been for her?

I stormed down the street, ignoring pedestrians who jumped out of my way for fear of being mown down.

I found myself crossing the Rhone and heading for my favorite bar. Appropriately enough it was called L'Antidote. I really fucking hoped it would live up to its name tonight. It was long and thin, with almost no daylight. It was as close as the Swiss came to a dive, but it would do.

I headed inside and saw Yannis the bartender. He nodded at me and poured a whiskey without me even having to ask. I tipped it straight down.

"*Suffit de laisser*."

He raised his eyebrows but pushed the bottle towards me.

After my third shot, I started to pull myself together, disgusted by being such a fucking pussy and running out.

Fuck, I used to be *good* at my job. You know, actually *cared* about it. Paris changed all that. My CO had hated me from day one. He tried to bully me and constantly belittled me. Then I found out he was a buddy of my old man. Figured. Bastard even had my promotion blocked. I'd fucking *earned* that promotion. So I decided if he wanted to screw around with me, I'd screw around with him—or rather, his wife. That was easy. Getting caught was harder because he was so fucking unobservant. She was definitely the brains in that marriage.

But he got the message eventually. Found his wife with her mouth wrapped around my dick. That was a good day. By that point, I didn't give a shit what happened to me. But it brought me here.

To her.

I took another shot, wondering how I'd make it through the next 30 hours. Well, it was only 2PM—and I knew how the next 12 hours would be spent: just me and a close relative of my good friend Jack Daniel.

By 6PM I was well on my way to being completely wasted. I only knew it was later because the bar started filling up with office workers. They must have sensed I wasn't in a friendly mood because they all gave me a wide berth.

I wondered what *she* was doing. She'd looked pretty cozy with that French journalist, Lebuin. Fucker was practically drooling over her, all smiles and Gallic fucking charm. It made me want to punch his guts out through his backbone.

I tried to think of something else, but every time I came back to the look of shock on her face when she saw me. Not pleasure—shock.

I emptied another shot down my throat, enjoying the increasing numbness that it gave me.

"May I sit?"

I looked up slowly. For a second I thought it was *her*—the long, chestnut colored hair was so familiar. I remembered that hair sweeping over my chest as we made love in the sand dunes. But this woman's eyes were blue.

I tried to clear my head, gave up, then waved at the seat vaguely.

"*Merci.*"

I grasped the bottle of whiskey as if I was afraid she'd steal it.

"You like to drink alone, perhaps?"

I shrugged, and she turned to Yannis to order herself a glass of white wine.

Yeah, buy your own drinks, baby. I'm not interested.

I looked at her again. She was attractive, dressed in a sharp skirt suit, high heels, with long legs. For a moment I could imagine those legs wrapped around my waist.

She saw the direction of my gaze and smiled.

"Or perhaps you prefer some company? I'm Gabriella."

She held out her hand and after a second's hesitation, I shook it.

"Sebastian."

"American?"

"Yes, ma'am."

"No, no. That makes me feel old. Please, you must call me Gabbi." She paused. "So, why is a handsome young soldier drinking alone? It is either money or women. I do not think it is money."

Her tone annoyed me, and I turned to glare at her.

"And why is an attractive woman talking to strange men in bars? It's either business or pleasure. I don't think it's business."

"*Touché!*" she said laughing lightly, then ran her hand over my thigh. "I am French, not Swiss. It is always pleasure with us—even in Geneva."

She leaned forward and I caught the smell of her perfume. It was strong and musky—nothing like Caro. My stomach churned and I stood up suddenly, taking her by surprise.

"You're right, *mademoiselle*. It is a woman. It's always a woman—the same fucking woman."

She rested her hand lightly on my arm. "Perhaps I can make you forget her?"

I laughed harshly. "Yeah, good luck with that. I've been trying for ten fucking years."

I pushed past her, seeing the look of disappointment painted on her face. When I hit the fresh air outside, I nearly staggered.

Fuck, I was more wasted than I'd realized.

I could have hailed a cab, but I didn't live far, so I wandered home, occasionally cannoning off lampposts that seemed to leap into my path. Goddamn if I wasn't seeing double.

I don't remember getting up the stairs or falling asleep fully dressed.

BONUS CHAPTER 5

The alarm scared the fuck out of me when it went off at 5:30AM. I set it early so I could go for a run before whatever drudgery the US Marine Corps was doling out. But this morning there was no chance of that. I just about made it to the bathroom before I threw up.

I splashed some water on my face, which made absolutely no fucking difference and then drank straight from the tap.

I crawled back into bed for another two hours.

When I woke up for the second time, there'd been no miraculous cure—I was still hung-over as fuck, and the room stank of whiskey.

Revolted, I pulled off my rank uniform and stood under the tepid shower for as long as I could stand it.

After I'd shaved, and managed not to cut my own damn throat, I glared at my service uniform. It looked like I'd slept in it. Which I had, strangely enough. I had a clean khaki shirt, but there was no way I'd have time to get the pants and jacket dry-cleaned.

Sighing, I pulled on a pair of jeans and a t-shirt and went to beg use of the ironing board and iron from Madame Dubois: desperate times called for desperate measures.

She took one look at my pathetic condition and took pity on me.

"*Les hommes ne peuvent pas repasser!*" she insisted.

I wasn't going to argue if she was going to offer to iron my uniform for me. When she'd finished I kissed her on the cheek to thank her.

"*Vous êtes un garçon effronté,*" she sniffed and waved me off.

Yeah, *gran-mère* was hot for me.

The second day of the training began much like the first—I was late, and Parsons was pissed. I'd eaten a roll of mints before I walked in, but I was pretty certain he could smell whiskey on my breath.

I tried to keep my gaze off of *her*, but it was an impossible task. After the first hour, I wanted to tear out my eyeballs and use them in a pinball machine.

The first lecture was on how to spot a minefield. I'd heard it all before. Didn't mean it wasn't useful, but it wasn't new material either.

Next up was my language section, which meant an hour with Caro's eyes focused on me. I didn't know why I didn't combust on the spot. Except she seemed embarrassed to look at me. How fucking ironic.

I went through my usual spiel for the Afghan tour: how to introduce yourself (differently for men and women), how to give your job title, the agency you worked for, and nationality. And I always threw in a useful passage from the Koran for emergencies.

This shit could save lives, so it really fucking pissed me off that Caro wasn't paying attention. Shit, she could end up smeared all over a Kabul street if she didn't take it in.

"Perhaps Ms. Venzi can answer that question," I said, nearly choking on my tongue as it wrapped itself around her name.

"Excuse me? Um, what was the question?" she stammered.

Fuck, I couldn't look at her—it was too much. I was only fucking human.

Shit! Shit! Shit! What could I tell her that she might actually remember, that might actually be useful?

Inspiration struck.

"A typical answer to a question an Afghan can't answer would be for him to say, 'because the sky is blue and the sea is green'," I said by rote, risking another glance at her.

She looked annoyed and my heart punched against my ribs.

I had to get out. I *needed* to get out.

I don't remember anything about the last 45 minutes of the seminar. As soon as Parsons cleared his throat, signaling the end, I was out of there.

And then she spoke to me.

"May I have a word, please, Chief Hunter?"

I almost skidded to a halt, afraid to turn and look at her, afraid of what it was going to make me feel to look in her eyes again.

"I'm rather busy, Ms. Venzi," I coughed out.

"Too busy to say 'hello'?" she snapped.

God, she was so beautiful.

And then I realized I hadn't answered her.

"Yes, I'm too busy for that," and I ran.

Fucking pussy! Candy-ass chickenshit fucking pussy!

I couldn't go back but I couldn't kid myself anymore either. I wanted her. Badly. And maybe, if I had her one more time, I could stop thinking about her. Maybe if I fucked her hard, I could exorcise her ghost once and for all.

On impulse I stopped and bought some condoms from a small *pharmacie*. I had a semi just thinking about using them with her.

Jesus, just seeing her and I was suddenly 17 again.

And how the hell was I going to make that fucking fantasy happen? I'd barely spoken to her for the last two days.

I needed to get her alone. I couldn't do it—whatever 'it' was—with an audience. I needed to talk to her.

I wandered through Geneva, trying to work out what I was going to say to her; how I'd get to fuck her. We used to have this amazing chemistry. We'd just look at each other and get turned on. I wondered if it was still there.

My steps slowed as my thoughts grew heavier, remembering everything that had passed between us, the plans we'd made. We'd talked about it all: living together, marriage, kids. I'd wanted it all with her—and I thought she'd wanted it with me.

I realized I'd stopped walking altogether and was standing outside a jewelers.

One of those small, unassuming, family-run places that you could still find in that part of Geneva.

My eyes were drawn to a display and I found myself staring at the rings. One of them caught my attention—a smallish but pretty single diamond mount on a gold band. The breath left my body as I imagined how that would look on her small hand, with those delicate fingers that used to touch...

This was seriously fucked up. I need to walk away, fast. But I couldn't. I walked inside and was soon talking to the sales assistant, an elderly man who looked like a gnome. And then he was showing me the ring and placing it in a dark blue satin ring box, and I was handing over my credit card for €2000.

Back in the fresh air, I knew I'd lost my goddamn mind, but somehow I couldn't care.

Eventually, I went home and took another shower, then changed into civvies. I was going to go straight to her hotel, but I wimped out.

I went back to L'Antidote and started drinking.

There were so many things I wanted to say to her—and I had no fucking clue how to start. I had another drink, trying to calm the fuck down. Then another. And another.

When I'd finally got up the courage to talk to her, I headed towards the Place des Nations. Her hotel was nearby. For some reason, my body seemed disconnected from my feet. It took for fucking ever to get my ass going in the right direction. Weird.

Finally, I was there—standing in front of her door—knowing that she was just a few feet away from me.

I knocked three times.

There was a pause, followed by a scuffling sound, then her voice.

"Who is it?"

"Let me in, Caro."

There was another pause—longer this time.

"What do you want, Sebastian?" she called through the door.

"Let me in. I need to talk to you."

This wasn't going how I'd planned. She needed to open the door for me to talk to her properly.

I banged on the door again.

"Caro!"

Slowly, the door opened. All she was wearing was a thin, silky robe.

My cock leapt to attention as my eyes drank her in.

"Caro."

Christ it felt good to say her name.

"What do you want, Sebastian?"

No, not like this. I needed to be in the same room as her. I pushed my way past her. *Fuck, she smelled good.* I was inside the room, but I wanted to be inside *her*.

"What are you doing?" she asked sharply.

She was so feisty. God, I loved that about her.

"Catching up with old friends," I said, smiling at her.

"How did you find me?"

Seriously? Didn't she know what I did?

"Military intelligence," I said, tapping the side of my head.

I thought that was funny as fuck.

While she closed the door, I took off my jacket and threw it onto the chair. There was nowhere else to sit, so I sat on the bed and hoped she'd take the hint.

"Come and sit with me, Caro."

But she stayed standing, her arms folded across her chest.

Beautiful.

"Why are you here, Sebastian? You had your chance to talk to me earlier today, but you preferred to ignore me."

Did I?

"You still have a great ass, Caro."

"Okay, I think you'd better go now. Whatever you have to say to me can wait until you're sober."

She had a great everything.

She walked towards me and my heart started pounding in my chest again. *Christ, it hurt so fucking much. How could it hurt so much and I wasn't dying?* Or maybe I was. I didn't know anymore. Because when she came towards me, it was just her and me again. Just us. No one else. She wove her magic and the world went away.

I buried my head in her body, kissing her, relishing the feel of her flesh against my lips. It had been so long. *So long.*

I tried to tell her that I loved her, that I'd always loved her. I don't know if she could understand what I was saying. I just knew that her arms were around me and we were together again.

I don't remember much about what happened then, but I fell asleep with her at my side.

***

The next morning I woke up to the sound of an alarm ringing in my ear—it was fucking annoying. Then I realized I wasn't in my room—and I wasn't alone.

What the fuck?

I opened my eyes and looked up.

"Caro?"

I wasn't sure if I was awake or still dreaming.

"You're awake then," she said, sharply.

Oh. Awake. Right.

And yet again: *what the fuck?*

I vaguely remembered coming to her hotel and wanting to fuck her. Did we do it? I had no memory. Some fucking irony. I'd planned to get rid of that ghost once and for all—and I couldn't even remember doing it.

"Did we...?"

"No, we most definitely did not. You woke me up in the middle of the night by banging on my door, and then passed out on my bed."

Shit. She sounded pissed.

"Oh, right."

I leaned up on one arm and looked down at the clothes I was still wearing. Huh, maybe we hadn't then. I really fucking wanted to.

"Sorry about that. We can make up for it now if you like?"

Yeah, that could have come out better. Fucking word vomit.

"Astonishing as this may seem, Sebastian," she said in a voice that could have frozen helium, "your charming offer doesn't thrill me."

Fucking bitch was always on my case. Hell, *she'd* invited *me* into her room. I think.

"Whatever."

I started to get up and realized I was lacking footwear.

"Where are my boots?"

"Under the chair," she said, pointing. "Along with your jacket."

Ah hell, morning wood, just to add to the overall sense of joy. I don't suppose she'd let me... nah, no point thinking about it.

Then she said, "Why did you come here last night, Sebastian?"

The look on her face was so sad, my heart started to crash in my chest. Her eyes were hurt and confused, and all the words I wanted to say to her just dried on my tongue.

Christ, just let me get the fuck out of here. If she says one more word, just one, I'll be down on my fucking knees begging her to take me back.

I shrugged. "I don't remember."

I had to see her just once more, to memorize her face before I left.

"See you around, Caro."

When I closed her door behind me, shutting out the image of her, I couldn't lie to myself anymore. I wanted her badly. I still needed her.

And she hated my fucking guts.

~

Les hommes ne peuvent pas repasser = men can't iron

Tu est un garçon effronté = you're a cheeky boy

This story from Sebastian's point of view is continued in the full-length novel Semper Fi

BONUS CHAPTER 6

Sebastian's Christmas Eve Dinner

"Fuck! FUCK! Shit! SHIT! SHIT! OUCH! Fucking hell!"

"Oh, boy! Wait until I tell Mom what you said!"

My ten year-old son, Marco, is staring at me with his hands folded across his chest and an enormous shit-eating grin on his face.

He was supposed to be anywhere but here, and I throw him an irritated look, waving my hands through the air, trying to clear the smoke. Marco opens the backdoor as I walk around the kitchen opening all the windows and then staring at the heap of burned ash that I've just tossed into the sink.

The defeated, shrunken carcass of what was once roast pork is still smoking slightly.

"Goddamn it all to Hell!"

"Forty dollars!" yells Marco from the backyard.

Why didn't anyone tell me that cooking was this hard? Caro always makes it look easy. Turns out it's not as simple as it seems.

All I wanted to do was treat my wife to a homemade dinner on Christmas Eve. It was a good idea at the time, but now I'm thinking that I should have just gotten us a table at her favorite Italian restaurant. Yeah, okay, I did try that, but when you call the day before for a reservation on one of the busiest days of the year, it would take an act of God for there to be a table available.

Signor Aconi was heartbroken—he loves Caro almost as much as I do.

Marco walks back into the kitchen, pretending to choke on the non-existent smoke. He peers at the pork as if it's a science experiment gone wrong. Which it kinda is.

"Mom won't eat that. Your cooking really sucks, Dad."

I sigh, staring at the charred mass.

I can strip an M-16 in under a minute, taking it down to the skinny (barrel, mag, trigger and butt), and reassemble faster. I can run a mile in six minutes, which isn't bad considering my right leg has lost seventeen per cent of the muscle mass, courtesy of a suicide-bomber in Afghanistan. I'm fluent in Pashto, Dari, Arabic, and I can get by in French and Italian, maybe even Spanish. I'm good at a lot of shit that's pretty damn useless living in Long Island, New York. But can I make a roast dinner for my wife? No, I fucking can't.

And that pisses me off.

It looks like I'm going to be that guy ... the poor pathetic sap who has to order takeout for Christmas Eve dinner. I don't know if Caro will laugh or cry. Obviously, I'm hoping for the former. I'd rather she laughed her ass off at me—anything rather than see tears in her beautiful brown eyes. I don't want to disappoint her. I love her beyond anything in this world or the next. She gave me back my life when I was just a shell of a person. I've always loved her.

But that doesn't solve my problem: *I can't fucking cook.*

Luckily, my troops can.

"Where are your sisters?" I ask, trying to act casual.

Marco's eyes narrow.

"You said that *you* were cooking for Mom, and that you didn't need a bunch of kids getting underfoot."

Shit! I did say that.

"Well, I think it would be fun if we all helped, don't you? Go find your sisters."

"You owe forty dollars," he says, sticking out his lower lip.

"No freakin' way! It can't possibly be that much!"

"I was counting, Dad. And you said..."

"Don't repeat it!" I yell, running my hands over my head in frustration. "Fine, go get the jar."

He grins, his blue eyes shining up at me. Kid's getting tall. Caro says he's going to be just like me. Let's hope he has his mom's brains instead.

"Forty dollars!" he says, holding out the glass jar that's labelled *Daddy's Swear Jar*. It's already got close to $300 in it. I really try not to swear around my babies, but ten years of having a potty-mouth in the Marines is a habit that's hard to break.

I take out my wallet and stuff $40 in the jar, sighing heavily. Marco screws on the lid tightly and puts it back on the counter.

"I'll get Sofia," he says, running up the stairs yelling her name.

Sofia is our adopted daughter. She was born in a tiny, nameless village in the mountains of Afghanistan, but now she's a beautiful American girl, nearly 13 years-old. I speak her parents' language with her every day, and it helps keep me fluent, as well as connecting her with her heritage.

She's so like Caro—long, dark hair and big soulful eyes. All the women in my life are beautiful: Caro, Sofia and Shirley, the baby of the family at six years old—six going on sixteen.

Sofia is smiling when she walks in the kitchen.

"Smells kind of smoky, Dad."

"I know," I sigh. "Any ideas?"

"Mommy loves pizza," Shirley says encouragingly, as she scoots down the stairs and runs up to me for a hug.

"I know someone who loves pizza, but I don't think it's Mommy," I point out, keeping my face serious.

"Everyone loves pizza," says Shirley, pouting just a little now.

She's fucking adorable, and the spitting image of her mother.

"Mom's favorite is Fettucine Alfredo," Sofia says knowingly.

I frown, not convinced.

"Yeah? Which one's that?"

"Pasta with cheese sauce, Dad!" shouts Marco from the back garden. "Everyone knows that."

"Okay, shopping trip, troops."

"We gotta get candy for Mommy!" Shirley reminds me. "And flowers!"

What would I do without my kids? They're fucking awesome.

Sixty minutes later, I've survived the supermarket, and Sofia is showing me how to make the sauce for the pasta.

"So there's no meat in it?" I ask, disappointed.

"It's *Alfredo*, Dad!"

Like that's supposed to mean something to me?

Sofia drills it into me how long I have to cook the fettucine for, then takes the kids off to their Uncle Atash for the evening.

By the time Caro walks in the door an hour later, looking beat from her last-minute Christmas shopping trip, everything is perfect.

Candles lit. *Check.*

Table set with silverware. *Check.*

White tulips in a vase. *Check.*

Candy wrapped in pink fucking paper. *Check*

Most beautiful fucking woman in the world walking into my arms. *Check* and *check.*

Her eyes light up as she sees the table, the exhaustion fading away.

"Sebastian! This is amazing! Did you do this all by yourself?"

"Sure did, baby. Do you like it?"

"I love it! It smells great. Sofia is becoming quite a little chef."

Busted.

"Yep. I totally made this by myself, but I let the kids help."

She smiles, her eyes crinkling as she wraps her arms around my neck, kissing my lips softly.

I want more. I always want more with her. And for a moment, the world floats away as the love of my life is pressed against my body, a promise and a longing in the way her fingers stroke under my t-shirt, skin to skin.

"I love you, Sebastian," she breathes against my neck. "*Sempre e per sempre*."

And I have to swallow the lump in my throat, because I have no idea how I got to be so fucking lucky.

"Love you, too, Caro. Always have, always will. Merry Christmas, baby."

BONUS CHAPTER 7

Dear Sebastian

The kids had all gone to Atash's for the afternoon, so me and Caro were having some quality grown-up time—in bed.

I rolled onto my back panting, thinking that there was no workout in the whole world that beat making love with my girl.

"Oh my God! I'm exhausted," she mumbled, her arm flopping like a wet fish as it slapped down on my chest.

"Told you that Pilates class was a waste of time," I said. "You don't need that when you have me."

"I don't even have to open my eyes to know that you're looking very smug right now," Caro huffed.

"You know it, baby."

I rolled onto my hip and stroked my hand down between her breasts, feeling my dick twitch as I enjoyed the heavy fullness and hard nipples.

"Don't even think about it," she groaned. "I'm done."

I laughed lightly. I could always go again when it came to Caro, but I settled for kissing her and sucking her tits gently. They were still in great shape, despite breastfeeding two of our babies.

She sighed, a soft smile on her face as I pulled her into my arms.

"Did you ever think we'd get here?" she asked.

"Yeah."

She paused. "That's it? Just 'yeah'?"

"It was always you for me. I knew we'd get here one day."

She shook her head.

"You were always so sure, despite everything. If you could write a letter to your seventeen-year-old self, what would you say?"

I snorted.

"What kind of question is that?"

She looked up at me and smiled.

"Just pretend for a moment that you do introspection, Hunter. Go on, what would you say to him? What would you write?"

Caro loved these fuckin' stupid questions. Maybe it was the journalist in her.

"Jeez, I don't know! 'Dear Loser ... keep your muzzle dry and never fuck without a condom ... unless it's Caro, in which case...'"

Caro pinched my waist and tried to tickle me.

"I'm being serious, Sebastian! What would you say to him?"

"I'd say, 'Kiss her till she stops talking'."

So I did.

But later on that evening when the kids were bathed and tucked in bed, Caro was writing on her laptop, and I was fixing a ding in Marco's surfboard, I thought again about what she'd said. What advice would I give to my seventeen year-old self? What could I say that would help me through the dark days, the ten long years when Caro wasn't in my life? I'd held faith for three years, right up to my 21st birthday before I'd given up and realized that she wasn't coming for me, that she hadn't waited like she'd promised.

I'd forgiven her for that years ago, and tried to forgive myself for the bitterness I'd felt. Is there anything I could have said that would have made it better?

I imagined writing a letter, putting into words something that might have made it easier. Something that I might have believed...

Hey kid,

I know it's tough and you've got a shitty mountain to climb, but it won't always be like this. I know what it's like to love a woman hard, and the punch in the gut when you realize that she's not in your life anymore.

It's fuckin' grim, and no one will ever be able to tell you otherwise.

Just follow your instincts. Remember that she was the biggest part of your life, and that she made you the man you are, the man you'll be. That's not something to regret. The love you shared was real, and that's a fuck-ton more than most suckers ever get.

So you're feeling sorry for yourself? Big boo-hoo. You'll get over it.

Be the best fuckin' Marine that you can be: keep your muzzle dry, your reactions fast, your brain cool, and your memories warm.

'Cause you know what, kid? I have a feeling that Lady Luck ain't the bitch that you think she is.

Hang loose,
Your buddy, Seb

Yeah, that's what I'd tell my younger self. Because despite everything, I am the luckiest mofo that ever lived.

REVIEWS

Reviews are love! Honestly, they are! But it also helps other people to make an informed decision before buying my book.

So I'd really appreciate if you took a few seconds to do that.

Thank you!

MORE BOOKS BY JHB

Series Titles

**The Education Series*

An epic love story spanning the years, through war zones and more...

*The Education of Sebastian (Education series #1)

*The Education of Caroline (Education series #2)

*The Education of Sebastian & Caroline (combined edition, books 1 & 2)

Semper Fi: The Education of Caroline (Education series #3)

**The Traveling Series*

All the fun of the fair ... and two worlds collide

*The Traveling Man (Traveling series #1)

*The Traveling Woman (Traveling series #2)

*Roustabout (Traveling series #3)

*Carnival (Traveling series #4)

*Gypsy (Traveling series #5)

The Justin Trainer Series

The bodyguard and the billionaire

Guarding the Billionaire (Justin Trainer series #1)

Saving the Billionaire (Justin Trainer series #2)

* *The EOD Series*

Blood, bombs and heartbreak

*Tick Tock (EOD series #1)

* Bombshell (EOD series #2)

**The Rhythm Series*
Blood, sweat, tears and dance
*Slave to the Rhythm (Rhythm series #1)
*Luka (Rhythm series #2)

Standalone Titles
Contemporary Romance
The Lilac Cadillac
Battle Scars
One Careful Owner
*Lifers
At Your Beck & Call
The New Samurai
Exposure

New Adult
*Dangerous to Know & Love
Dazzled
Summer of Seventeen

Paranormal
*The Dark Detective: Venator (Book #1)
*The Dark Detective: Paukúnnum (Book #2)

Novellas
Playing in the Rain
*Behind the Walls

Anthologies of Short Stories
*The Year Book Volume 1
*The Year Book Volume 2
*The Year Book Volume 3

Audio Books
One Careful Owner
(*narrated by Seth Clayton*)

On the Stage
Later, After: Playscript
Trailer

With Alana Albertson
Father Figure

* These titles are published in languages other than English.
Please check Jane's website for details—and receive **a free short story every month** when you sign up for her newsletter :)

QR code for Jane's website

ROMANCE WITH STUART REARDON

My love co-author with these titles

Two book series - contemporary romance

*Undefeated

*Model Boyfriend

Three book series - romcom

*Gym Or Chocolate?

*The World According to Vince

*The Baby Game

Standalone

Survivor Love Island *(romcom)*

*Touch My Soul *(novella)*

WRITING AS BERRICK FORD

Police Thrillers, UK

Dead Water
Dead Man's Dive
Dead Reckoning
Dead Shore

www.berrickford.com

Printed in Dunstable, United Kingdom

64966670R00399